SOLIHULL S.F.C
LIBRARY

8 - DEC 2000

KU-209-438

RECEIVED 0 9 NOV 2000

36857
F/KIN

T

CHECKED   JUN 2008

THE DEAD ZONE

•

CUJO

STEPHEN KING
OMNIBUS

THE DEAD ZONE

•

CUJO

RECEIVED 0 9 NOV 2000

36857

F/KIN

LITTLE, BROWN AND COMPANY

A *Little, Brown* Book

This first edition published in Great Britain in 1999 by
Little, Brown and Company.

Copyright © Stephen King 1999
The Dead Zone copyright © Stephen King 1979
Cujo copyright © Stephen King 1981

The moral right of the author has been asserted.

*All characters in this publication and any resemblance to real
persons, living or dead, is purely coincidental.*

All rights reserved.
No part of this publication may be reproduced, stored
in a retrieval system, or transmitted, in any form or by
any means, without prior permission in writing of the
publisher, nor be otherwise circulated in any form of
binding or cover than that in which it is published
and without similar condition including this condition
being imposed on the subsequent purchaser.

A CIP catalogue for this book is available from the
British Library.

ISBN 0 316 85369 0

Printed and bound in Great Britain.

Little, Brown and Company (UK)
Brettenham House
Lancaster Place
London WC2E 7EN

THE DEAD ZONE

PROLOGUE

1 ·

By the time he graduated from college, John Smith had forgotten all about the bad fall he took on the ice that January day in 1953. In fact, he would have been hard put to remember it by the time he graduated from grammar school. And his mother and father never knew about it at all.

They were skating on a cleared patch of Runaround Pond in Durham. The bigger boys were playing hockey with old taped sticks and using a couple of potato baskets for goals. The little kids were just farting around the way little kids have done since time immemorial – their ankles bowing comically in and out, their breath puffing in the frosty twenty-degree air. At one corner of the cleared ice two rubber tires burned sootily, and a few parents sat nearby, watching their children. The age of the snowmobile was still distant and winter fun still consisted of exercising your body rather than a gasoline engine.

Johnny had walked down from his house, just over the Pownal line, with his skates hung over his shoulder. At six, he was a pretty fair skater. Not good enough to join in the big kids' hockey games yet, but able to skate rings around most of the other first graders, who were always pinwheeling their arms for balance or sprawling on their butts.

Now he skated slowly around the outer edge of the clear patch, wishing he could go backward like Timmy Benedix, listening to the ice thud and crackle mysteriously under the snow cover farther out, also listening to the shouts of the hockey players, the rumble of a pulp truck crossing the bridge on its way to U.S. Gypsum in Lisbon Falls, the murmur of conversation from the adults. He was very glad to be alive on that cold, fair winter day. Nothing was wrong with him, nothing troubled his mind, he wanted nothing ... except to be able to skate backward, like Timmy Benedix.

He skated past the fire and saw that two or three of the grown-ups were passing around a bottle of booze.

'Gimme some of that!' he shouted to Chuck Spier, who was bundled up in a big lumberjack shirt and green flannel snowpants.

Chuck grinned at him. 'Get outta here, kid. I hear your mother callin you.'

Grinning, six-year-old Johnny Smith skated on. And on the road side of the skating area, he saw Timmy Benedix himself coming down the slope, with his father behind him.

'Timmy!' he shouted. 'Watch this!'

He turned around and began to skate clumsily backward. Without realizing it, he was skating into the area of the hockey game.

'Hey kid!' someone shouted. 'Get out the way!'

Johnny didn't hear. He was *doing* it! He was skating backward! He had caught the rhythm – all at once. It was in a kind of sway of the legs ...

He looked down, fascinated, to see what his legs were doing.

The big kids' hockey puck, old and scarred and gouged around the edges, buzzed past him, unseen. One of the big kids, not a very good skater, was chasing it with what was almost a blind, headlong plunge.

Chuck Spier saw it coming. He rose to his feet and shouted, '*Johnny! Watch out!*'

John raised his head – and the next moment the clumsy skater, all one hundred and sixty pounds of him, crashed into little John Smith at full speed.

Johnny went flying, arms out. A bare moment later his head connected with the ice and he blacked out.

Blacked out ... black ice ... blacked out ... black ice ... black. Black.

They told him he had blacked out. All he was really sure of was that strange repeating thought and suddenly

2

looking up at a circle of faces – scared hockey players, worried adults, curious little kids. Timmy Benedix smirking. Chuck Spier was holding him.

Black ice. Black.

'What?' Chuck asked. 'Johnny . . . you okay? You took a hell of a knock.'

'Black,' Johnny said gutturally. 'Black ice. Don't jump it no more, Chuck.'

Chuck looked around, a little scared, then back at Johnny. He touched the large knot that was rising on the boy's forehead.

'I'm sorry,' the clumsy hockey player said. 'I never even saw him. Little kids are supposed to stay away from the hockey. It's the rules.' He looked around uncertainly for support.

'Johnny?' Chuck said. He didn't like the look of Johnny's eyes. They were dark and faraway, distant and cold. 'Are you okay?'

'Don't jump it no more,' Johnny said, unaware of what he was saying, thinking only of ice – black ice. 'The explosion. The acid.'

'Think we ought to take him to the doctor?' Chuck asked Bill Gendron. 'He don't know what he's sayin.'

'Give him a minute,' Bill advised.

They gave him a minute, and Johnny's head did clear. 'I'm okay,' he muttered. 'Lemme up.' Timmy Benedix was still smirking, damn him, Johnny decided he would show Timmy a thing or two. He would be skating rings around Timmy by the end of the week . . . backward *and* forward.

'You come on over and sit down by the fire for a while,' Chuck said. 'You took a hell of a knock.'

Johnny let them help him over to the fire. The smell of melting rubber was strong and pungent, making him feel a little sick to his stomach. He had a headache. He felt the lump over his left eye curiously. It felt as though it stuck out a mile.

'Can you remember who you are and everything?' Bill asked.

3

'Sure. Sure I can. I'm okay.'

'Who's your dad and mom?'

'Herb and Vera. Herb and Vera Smith.'

Bill and Chuck looked at each other and shrugged.

'I think he's okay,' Chuck said, and then, for the third time, 'but he sure took a hell of a knock, didn't he? Wow.'

'Kids,' Bill said, looking fondly out at his eight-year-old twin girls, skating hand in hand, and then back at Johnny. 'It probably would have killed a grown-up.'

'Not a Polack,' Chuck replied, and they both burst out laughing. The bottle of Bushmill's began making its rounds again.

Ten minutes later Johnny was back out on the ice, his headache already fading, the knotted bruise standing out on his forehead like a weird brand. By the time he went home for lunch, he had forgotten all about the fall, and blacking out, in the joy of having discovered how to skate backward.

'God's mercy!' Vera Smith said when she saw him. 'How did you get that?'

'Fell down,' he said, and began to slurp up Campbell's tomato soup.

'Are you all right, John?' she asked, touching it gently.

'Sure, Mom.' He was, too – except for the occasional bad dreams that came over the course of the next month or so . . . the bad dreams and a tendency to sometimes get very dozy at times of the day when he had never been dozy before. And that stopped happening at about the same time the bad dreams stopped happening.

He was all right.

In mid-February, Chuck Spier got up one morning and found that the battery of his old '48 De Soto was dead. He tried to jump it from his farm truck. As he attached the second clamp to the De Soto's battery, it exploded in his face, showering him with fragments and corrosive battery acid. He lost an eye. Vera said it was God's own mercy he hadn't lost them both. Johnny thought it was a terrible tragedy and went with his father to visit Chuck

4

in the Lewiston General Hospital a week after the accident. The sight of Big Chuck lying in that hospital bed, looking oddly wasted and small, had shaken Johnny badly – and that night he had dreamed it was *him* lying there.

From time to time in the years afterward, Johnny had hunches – he would know what the next record on the radio was going to be before the DJ played it, that sort of thing – but he never connected these with his accident on the ice. By then he had forgotten it.

And the hunches were never that startling, or even very frequent. It was not until the night of the county fair and the mask that anything very startling happened. Before the second accident.

Later, he thought of that often.

The thing with the Wheel of Fortune had happened *before* the second accident.

Like a warning from his own childhood.

2 ·

The traveling salesman crisscrossed Nebraska and Iowa tirelessly under the burning sun in that summer of 1955. He sat behind the wheel of a '53 Mercury sedan that already had better than seventy thousand miles on it. The Merc was developing a marked wheeze in the valves. He was a big man who still had the look of a cornfed midwestern boy on him; in that summer of 1955, only four months after his Omaha house-painting business had gone broke, Greg Stillson was only twenty-two years old.

The trunk and the back seat of the Mercury were filled with cartons, and the cartons were filled with books. Most of them were Bibles. They came in all shapes and sizes. There was your basic item, The American Truth-Way Bible, illustrated with sixteen color plates, bound with airplane glue, for $1.69 and sure to hold together for at least ten months; then for the poorer pocketbook there was The American TruthWay New Testament for sixty-five cents, with no color plates but with the words of Our Lord Jesus printed in red; and for the big spender

5

there was The American TruthWay Deluxe Word of God for $19.95, bound in imitation white leather, the owner's name to be stenciled in gold leaf on the front cover, twenty-four color plates, and a section in the middle to note down births, marriages, and burials. And the Deluxe Word of God might remain in one piece for as long as two years. There was also a carton of paperbacks entitled *America the TruthWay: The Communist-Jewish Conspiracy Against Our United States.*

Greg did better with this paperback, printed on cheap pulp stock, than with all the Bibles put together. It told all about how the Rothschilds and the Roosevelts and the Greenblatts were taking over the U.S. economy and the U.S. government. There were graphs showing how the Jews related directly to the Communist-Marxist-Leninist-Trotskyite axis, and from there to the Antichrist Itself.

The days of McCarthyism were not long over in Washington; in the Midwest Joe McCarthy's star had not yet set, and Margaret Chase Smith of Maine was known as 'that bitch' for her famous Declaration of Conscience. In addition to the stuff about Communism, Greg Stillson's rural farm constituency seemed to have a morbid interest in the idea that the Jews were running the world.

Now Greg turned into the dusty driveway of a farmhouse some twenty miles west of Ames, Iowa. It had a deserted, shut-up look to it – the shades down and the barn doors closed – but you could never tell until you tried. That motto had served Greg Stillson well in the two years or so since he and his mother had moved up to Omaha from Oklahoma. The house-painting business had been no great shakes, but he had needed to get the taste of Jesus out of his mouth for a little while, you should pardon the small blasphemy. But now he had come back home – not on the pulpit or revival side this time, though, and it was something of a relief to be out of the miracle business at last.

He opened the car door and as he stepped out into the dust of the driveway a big mean farm dog advanced out of the barn, its ears laid back. It volleyed barks. 'Hello,

6

pooch,' Greg said in his low, pleasant, but carrying voice – at twenty-two it was already the voice of a trained spellbinder.

The pooch didn't respond to the friendliness in his voice. It kept coming, big and mean, intent on an early lunch of traveling salesman. Greg sat back down in the car, closed the door, and honked the horn twice. Sweat rolled down his face and turned his white linen suit darker gray in circular patches under his arms and in a branching tree-shape up his back. He honked again, but there was no response. The clodhoppers had loaded themselves into their International Harvester or their Studebaker and gone into town.

Greg smiled.

Instead of shifting into reverse and backing out of the driveway, he reached behind him and produced a Flit gun – only this one was loaded with ammonia instead of Flit.

Pulling back the plunger, Greg stepped out of the car again, smiling easily. The dog, which had settled down on its haunches, immediately got up again and began to advance on him, growling.

Greg kept smiling. 'That's right, poochie,' he said in that pleasant, carrying voice. 'You just come on. Come on and get it.' He hated these ugly farm dogs that ran their half-acre of dooryard like arrogant little Caesars, they told you something about their masters as well.

'Fucking bunch of clodhoppers,' he said under his breath. He was still smiling. 'Come on, doggie.'

The dog came. It tensed its haunches down to spring at him. In the barn a cow mooed, and the wind rustled tenderly through the corn. As it leaped, Greg's smile turned to a hard and bitter grimace. He depressed the Flit plunger and sprayed a stinging cloud of ammonia droplets directly into the dog's eyes and nose.

Its angry barking turned immediately to short, agonized yips, and then, as the bite of ammonia really settled in, to howls of pain. It turned tail at once, a watchdog no longer but only a vanquished cur.

7

Greg Stillson's face had darkened. His eyes had drawn down to ugly slits. He stepped forward rapidly and administered a whistling kick to the dog's haunches with one of his Stride-King airtip shoes. The dog gave a high, wailing sound, and, driven by its pain and fear, it sealed its own doom by turning around to give battle to the author of its misery rather than running for the barn.

With a snarl, it struck out blindly, snagged the right cuff of Greg's white linen pants, and tore it.

'You sonofabitch!' he cried out in startled anger, and kicked the dog again, this time hard enough to send it rolling in the dust. He advanced on the dog once more, kicked it again, still yelling. Now the dog, eyes watering, nose in fiery agony, one rib broken and another badly sprung, realized its danger from this madman, but it was too late.

Greg Stillson chased it across the dusty farmyard, panting and shouting, sweat rolling down his cheeks, and kicked the dog until it was screaming and barely able to drag itself along through the dust. It was bleeding in half a dozen places. It was dying.

'Shouldn't have bit me,' Greg whispered. 'You hear? You hear me? You shouldn't have bit me, you dipshit dog. No one gets in my way. You hear? No one.' He delivered another kick with one blood-spattered airtip, but the dog could do no more than make a low choking sound. Not much satisfaction in that. Greg's head ached. It was the sun. Chasing the dog around in the hot sun. Be lucky not to pass out.

He closed his eyes for a moment, breathing rapidly, the sweat rolling down his face like tears and nestling in his crewcut like gems, the broken dog dying at his feet. Colored specks of light, pulsing in rhythm with his heartbeat, floated across the darkness behind his lids.

His head ached.

Sometimes he wondered if he was going crazy. Like now. He had meant to give the dog a burst from the ammonia Flit gun, drive it back into the barn so he could leave his business card in the crack of the screen door.

8

Come back some other time and make a sale. Now look. Look at this mess. Couldn't very well leave his card now, could he?

He opened his eyes. The dog lay at his feet, panting rapidly, drizzling blood from its snout. As Greg Stillson looked down, it licked his shoe humbly, as if to acknowledge that it had been bested, and then it went back to the business of dying.

'Shouldn't have torn my pants,' he said to it. 'Pants cost me five bucks, you shitpoke dog.'

He had to get out of here. Wouldn't do him any good if Clem Kadiddlehopper and his wife and their six kids came back from town now in their Studebaker and saw Fido dying out here with the bad old salesman standing over him. He'd lose his job. The American TruthWay Company didn't hire salesmen who killed dogs that belonged to Christians.

Giggling nervously, Greg went back to the Mercury, got in, and backed rapidly out of the driveway. He turned east on the dirt road that ran straight as a string through the corn, and was soon cruising along at sixty-five leaving a dust plume two miles long behind him.

He most assuredly didn't want to lose the job. Not yet. He was making good money – in addition to the wrinkles the American TruthWay Company knew about, Greg had added a few of his own that they didn't know about. He was making it now. Besides, traveling around, he got to meet a lot of people . . . a lot of girls. It was a good life, except –

Except he wasn't content.

He drove on, his head throbbing. No, he just wasn't content. He felt that he was meant for bigger things than driving around the Midwest and selling Bibles and doctoring the commission forms in order to make an extra two bucks a day. He felt that he was meant for . . . for . . .

For greatness.

Yes, that was it, that was surely it. A few weeks ago he had taken some girl up in the hayloft, her folks had been in Davenport selling a truckload of chickens, she had

9

started off by asking if he would like a glass of lemonade and one thing had just led to another and after he'd had her she said it was almost like getting diddled by a preacher and he had slapped her, he didn't know why. He had slapped her and then left.

Well, no.

Actually, he had slapped her three or four times. Until she had cried and screamed for someone to come and help her and then he had stopped and somehow – he had had to use every ounce of the charm God had given him – he had made it up with her. His head had been aching then, too, the pulsing specks of brightness shooting and caroming across his field of vision, and he tried to tell himself it was the heat, the explosive heat in the hayloft, but it wasn't just the heat that made his head ache. It was the same thing he had felt in the dooryard when the dog tore his pants, something dark and crazy.

'I'm not crazy,' he said aloud in the car. He unrolled the window swiftly, letting in summer heat and the smell of dust and corn and manure. He turned on the radio loud and caught a Patti Page song. His headache went back a little bit.

It was all a matter of keeping yourself under control and – and keeping your record clean. If you did those things, they couldn't touch you. And he was getting better at both of those things. He no longer had the dreams about his father so often, the dreams where his father was standing above him with his hard hat cocked back on his head, bellowing: *'You're no good, runt! You're no fucking good!'*

He didn't have the dreams so much because they just weren't true. He wasn't a runt anymore. Okay, he had been sick a lot as a kid, not much size, but he had gotten his growth, he was taking care of his mother –

And his father was dead. His father couldn't see. He couldn't make his father eat his words because he had died in an oil-derrick blowout and he was dead and once, just once, Greg would like to dig him up and scream into his mouldering face *You were wrong, dad, you were*

10

wrong about me! and then give him a good kick the way –

The way he had kicked the dog.

The headache was back, lowering.

'I'm not crazy,' he said again below the sound of the music. His mother had told him often he was meant for something big, something great, and Greg believed it. It was just a matter of getting things – like slapping the girl or kicking the dog – under control and keeping his record clean.

Whatever his greatness was, he would know it when it came to him. Of that he felt quite sure.

He thought of the dog again, and this time the thought brought a bare crescent of a smile, without humor or compassion.

His greatness was on the way. It might still be years ahead – he was young, sure, nothing wrong with being young as long as you understood you couldn't have everything all at once. As long as you believed it would come eventually. He did believe that.

And God and Sonny Jesus help anyone that got in his way.

Greg Stillson cocked a sunburned elbow out the window and began to whistle along with the radio. He stepped on the go-pedal, walked that old Mercury up to seventy, and rolled down the straight Iowa farm road toward whatever future there might be.

PART ONE

The Wheel of Fortune

CHAPTER ONE

1 ·

The two things Sarah remembered about that night later were his run of luck at the Wheel of Fortune and the mask. But as time passed, years of it, it was the mask she thought about – when she could bring herself to think about that horrible night at all.

He lived in an apartment house in Cleaves Mills. Sarah got there at quarter to eight, parking around the corner, and buzzing up to be let in. They were taking her car tonight because Johnny's was laid up at Tibbets' Garage in Hampden with a frozen wheel-bearing or something like that. Something expensive, Johnny had told her over the phone, and then he had laughed a typical Johnny Smith laugh. Sarah would have been in tears if it had been her car – her *pocketbook*.

Sarah went through the foyer to the stairs, past the bulletin board that hung there. It was dotted with file cards advertising motorbikes, stereo components, typing services, and appeals from people who needed rides to Kansas or California, people who were driving to Florida and needed riders to share the driving and help pay for the gas. But tonight the board was dominated by a large placard showing a clenched fist against an angry red background suggesting fire. The one word on the poster was STRIKE! It was late October of 1970.

Johnny had the front apartment on the second floor – the penthouse, he called it – where you could stand in your tux like Ramon Navarro, a big slug of Ripple wine in a balloon glass, and look down upon the vast, beating heart of Cleaves Mills; its hurrying after-show crowds, its bustling taxis, its neon signs. There are almost seven thousand stories in the naked city. This has been one of them.

Actually Cleaves Mills was mostly a main street with a

stop-and-go light at the intersection (it turned into a blinker after 6 p.m.), about two dozen stores, and a small moccasin factory. Like most of the towns surrounding Orono, where the University of Maine was, its real industry was supplying the things students consumed – beer, wine, gas, rock 'n' roll music, fast food, dope, groceries, housing, movies. The movie house was The Shade. It showed art films and '40's nostalgia flicks when school was in. In the summertime it reverted to Clint Eastwood spaghetti Westerns.

Johnny and Sarah were both out of school a year, and both were teaching at Cleaves Mills High, one of the few high schools in the area that had not consolidated into a three- or four-town district. University faculty and administration as well as university students used Cleaves as their bedroom, and the town had an enviable tax base. It also had a fine high school with a brand-new media wing. The townies might bitch about the university crowd with their smart talk and their Commie marches to end the war and their meddling in town politics, but they had never said no to the tax dollars that were paid annually on the gracious faculty homes and the apartment buildings in the area some students called Fudgey Acres and others called Sleaze Alley.

Sarah rapped on his door and Johnny's voice, oddly muffled, called, 'It's open, Sarah!'

Frowning a little, she pushed the door open. Johnny's apartment was in total darkness except for the fitful yellow glow of the blinker half a block up the street. The furniture was so many humped black shadows.

'Johnny . . . ?'

Wondering if a fuse had blown or something, she took a tentative step forward – and then the face appeared before her, floating in the darkness, a horrible face out of a nightmare. It glowed a spectral, rotting green. One eye was wide open, seeming to stare at her in wounded fear. The other was squeezed shut in a sinister leer. The left half of the face, the half with the open eye, appeared to be normal. But the right half was the face of a monster,

16

drawn and inhuman, the thick lips drawn back to reveal snaggle teeth that were also glowing.

Sarah uttered a strangled little shriek and took a stumble-step backward. Then the lights came on and it was just Johnny's apartment again instead of some black limbo, Nixon on the wall trying to sell used cars, the braided rug Johnny's mother had made on the floor, the wine bottles made into candle bases. The face stopped glowing and she saw it was a dime-store Halloween mask, nothing more. Johnny's blue eye was twinkling out of the open eyehole at her.

He stripped it off and stood smiling amiably at her, dressed in faded jeans and a brown sweater.

'Happy Halloween, Sarah,' he said.

Her heart was still racing. He had really frightened her. 'Very funny,' she said, and turned to go. She didn't like being scared like that.

He caught her in the doorway. 'Hey . . . I'm sorry.'

'Well you ought to be,' She looked at him coldly – or tried to. Her anger was already melting away. You just couldn't stay mad at Johnny, that was the thing. Whether she loved him or not – a thing she was still trying to puzzle out – it was impossible to be unhappy with him for very long, or to harbor a feeling of resentment. She wondered if anyone had ever succeeded in harboring a grudge against Johnny Smith, and the thought was so ridiculous she just had to smile.

'There, that's better. Man, I thought you were going to walk out on me.'

'I'm not a man.'

He cast his eyes upon her. 'So I've noticed.'

She was wearing a bulky fur coat – imitation raccoon or something vulgar like that – and his innocent lechery made her smile again. 'In this thing you couldn't tell.'

'Oh, yeah, I can tell,' he said. He put an arm around her and kissed her. At first she wasn't going to kiss back, but of course she did.

'I'm sorry I scared you,' he said, and rubbed her nose companionably with his own before letting her go. He

17

held up the mask. 'I thought you'd get a kick out of it. I'm gonna wear it in homeroom Friday.'

'Oh, Johnny, that won't be very good for discipline.'

'I'll muddle through somehow,' he said with a grin. And the hell of it was, he would.

She came to school every day wearing big, schoolmarm-ish glasses, her hair drawn back into bun so severe it seemed on the verge of a scream. She wore her skirts just above the knee in a season when most of the girls wore them just below the edges of their underpants (and my legs are better than any of theirs, Sarah thought resentfully). She maintained alphabetical seating charts which, by the law of averages, at least, should have kept the troublemakers away from each other, and she resolutely sent unruly pupils to the assistant principal, her reasoning being that he was getting an extra five hundred a year to act as ramrod and she wasn't. And still her days were a constant struggle with that freshman teacher demon, Discipline. More disturbing, she had begun to sense that there was a collective, unspoken jury – a kind of school consciousness, maybe – that went into deliberations over every new teacher, and that the verdict being returned on her was not so good.

Johnny, on the face of it, appeared to be the antithesis of everything a good teacher should be. He ambled from class to class in an agreeable sort of daze, often showing up tardy because he had stopped to chat with someone between bells. He let the kids sit where they wanted so that the same face was never in the same seat from day to day (and the class thuds invariably gravitated to the back of the room). Sarah would not have been able to learn their names that way until March, but Johnny seemed to have them down pat already.

He was a tall man who had a tendency to slouch, and the kids called him Frankenstein. Johnny seemed amused rather than outraged by this. And yet his classes were mostly quiet and well-behaved, there were few skippers (Sarah had a constant problem with kids cutting class), and that same jury seemed to be coming back in his favor.

He was the sort of teacher who, in another ten years, would have the school yearbook dedicated to him. She just wasn't. And sometimes wondering why drove her crazy.

'You want a beer before we go? Glass of wine? Anything?'

'No, but I hope you're going well-heeled,' she said, taking his arm and deciding not to be mad anymore. 'I always eat at least three hot dogs. Especially when it's the last county fair of the year.' They were going to Esty, twenty miles north of Cleave Mills, a town whose only dubious claim to fame was that it held ABSOLUTELY THE LAST AGRICULTURAL FAIR OF THE YEAR IN NEW ENGLAND. The fair would close Friday night, on Halloween.

'Considering Friday's payday, I'm doing good. I got eight bucks.'

'Oh ... my ... God,' Sarah said, rolling her eyes. 'I always knew if I kept myself pure I'd meet a sugar daddy someday.'

He smiled and nodded. 'Us pimps make b i i i g money, baby. Just let me get my coat and we're off.'

She looked after him with exasperated affection, and the voice that had been surfacing in her mind more and more often – in the shower, while she was reading a book or prepping a class or making her supper for one – came up again, like one of those thirty-second public-service spots on TV: *He's a very nice man and all that, easy to get along with, fun, he never made you cry. But is that love? I mean, is that all there is to it? Even when you learned to ride your two-wheeler, you had to fall off a few times and scrape both knees. Call it a rite of passage. And that was just a little thing.*

'Gonna use the bathroom,' he called to her.

'Uh-huh.' She smiled a little. Johnny was one of those people who invariably mentioned their nature calls – God knew why.

She went over to the window and looked out on Main Street. Kids were pulling into the parking lot next to

19

O'Mike's, the local pizza-and-beer hangout. She suddenly wished she were back with them, one of them, with this confusing stuff behind her – or still ahead of her. The university was safe. It was a kind of never-never land where everybody, even the teachers, could be a part of Peter Pan's band and never grow up. And there would always be a Nixon or an Agnew to play Captain Hook.

She had met Johnny when they started teaching in September, but she had known his face from the Ed courses they had shared. She had been pinned to a Delta Tau Delta, and none of the judgments that applied to Johnny had applied to Dan. He had been almost flawlessly handsome, witty in a sharp and restless way that always made her a trifle uncomfortable, a heavy drinker, a passionate lover. Sometimes when he drank he turned mean. She rememberd a night in Bangor's Brass Rail when that had happened. The man in the next booth had taken joking issue with something Dan had been saying about the UMO football team, and Dan had asked him if he would like to go home with his head on backward. The man had apologized, but Dan hadn't wanted an apology; he had wanted a fight. He began to make personal remarks about the woman with the other man. Sarah had put her hand on Dan's arm and asked him to stop. Dan had shaken her hand off and had looked at her with a queer flat light in his grayish eyes that made any other words she might have spoken dry up in her throat. Eventually, Dan and the other guy went outside and Dan beat him up. Dan had beaten him until the other man, who was in his late thirties and getting a belly, had screamed. Sarah had never heard a man scream before – she never wanted to hear it again. They had to leave quickly because the bartender saw how it was going and called the police. She would have gone home alone that night (*Oh? are you sure?* her mind asked nastily), but it was twelve miles back to the campus and the buses had stopped running at six and she was afraid to hitch.

Dan didn't talk on the way back. He had a scratch on one cheek. Just one scratch. When they got back to Hart

Hall, her dorm, she told him she didn't want to see him anymore. 'Any way you want it, babe,' he said with an indifference that had chilled her – and the second time he called after the Brass Rail incident she had gone out with him. Part of her had hated herself for that.

It had continued all that fall semester of her senior year. He had frightened and attracted her at the same time. He was her first real lover, and even now, two days shy of Halloween 1970, he had been her only real lover. She and Johnny had not been to bed.

Dan had been very good. He had used her, but he had been very good. He would not take any precautions and so she had been forced to go to the university infirmary, where she talked fumblingly about painful menstruation and got the pill. Sexually, Dan had dominated her all along. She did not have many orgasms with him, but his very roughness brought her some, and in the weeks before it had ended she had begun to feel a mature woman's greediness for good sex, a desire that was bewilderingly intermixed with other feelings: dislike for both Dan and herself, a feeling that no sex that depended so much on humiliation and domination could really be called 'good sex,' and self-contempt for her own inability to call a halt to a relationship that seemed based on destructive feelings.

It had ended swifty, early this year. He flunked out. 'Where will you be going?' she asked him timidly, sitting on his roomie's bed as he threw things into two suitcases. She had wanted to ask other, more personal questions. Will you be near here? Will you take a job? Take night classes? Is there a place for me in your plans? That question, above all others, she had not been able to ask. Because she wasn't prepared for any answer. The answer he gave to her one neutral question was shocking enough.

'Vietnam, I guess.'

'*What?*'

He reached onto a shelf, thumbed briefly through the papers there, and tossed her a letter. It was from the induction center in Bangor: an order to report for his physical exam.

'Can't you get out of it?'

'No. Maybe. I don't know.' He lit a cigarette. 'I don't think I even want to try.'

She had stared at him, shocked.

'I'm tired of this scene. College and get a job and find a little wifey. You've been applying for the little wifey spot, I guess. And don't think I haven't thought it over. It wouldn't work. You know it wouldn't, and so do I. We don't fit, Sarah.'

She had fled then, all her questions answered, and she never saw him again. She saw his roommate a few times. He got three letters from Dan between January and June. He was inducted and sent down south somewhere for basic training. And that was the last the roommate had heard. It was the last Sarah Bracknell heard, too.

At first she thought she was going to be okay. All those sad, torchy songs, the ones you always seem to hear on the car radio after midnight, they didn't apply to her. Or the clichés about the end of the affair or the crying jags. She didn't pick up a guy on the rebound or start doing the bars. Most evenings that spring she spent studying quietly in her dorm room. It was a relief. It wasn't messy.

It was only after she met Johnny – at a freshman mixer dance last month; they were both chaperoning, purely by luck of the draw – that she realized what a horror her last semester at school had been. It was the kind of thing you couldn't see when you were in it, it was too much a part of you. Two donkeys meet at a hitching rail in a western town. One of them is a town donkey with nothing on his back but a saddle. The other is a prospector's donkey, loaded down with packs, camping and cooking gear, and four fifty-pound sacks of ore. His back is bent into a concertina shape from the weight. The town donkey says, That's quite a load you got there. And the prospector's donkey says, What load?

In retrospect it was the emptiness that horrified her; it had been five months of Cheyne-Stokes respiration. Eight

22

months if you counted this summer, when she took a small apartment on Flagg Street in Veazie and did nothing but apply for teaching jobs and read paperback novels. She got up, ate breakfast, went out to class or to whatever job interviews she had scheduled, came home, ate, took a nap (the naps were sometimes four hours long), ate again, read until eleven-thirty or so, watched Cavett until she got sleepy, went to bed. She could not remember *thinking* during that period. Life was routine. Sometimes there was a vague sort of ache in her loins, an *unfulfilled ache*, she believed the lady novelists sometimes called it, and for this she would either take a cold shower or a douche. After a while the douches grew painful, and this gave her a bitter, absent sort of satisfaction.

During this period she would congratulate herself from time to time on how adult she was being about the whole thing. She hardly ever thought about Dan – Dan Who, ha-ha. Later she realized that for eight months she had thought of nothing or no one else. The whole country had gone through a spasm of shudders during those eight months, but she had hardly noticed. The marches, the cops in their crash helmets and gas masks, the mounting attacks on the press by Agnew, the Kent State shootings, the summer of violence as blacks and radical groups took to the streets – those things might have happened on some TV late show. Sarah was totally wrapped up in how wonderfully she had gotten over Dan, how well she was adjusting, and how relieved she was to find that everything was just fine. What load?

Then she had started at Cleaves Mills High, and that had been a personal upheaval, being on the other side of the desk after sixteen years as a professional student. Meeting Johnny Smith at that mixer (and with an absurd name like John Smith, could he be completely for real?). Coming out of herself enough to see the way he was looking at her, not lecherously, but with a good healthy appreciation for the way she looked in the light-gray knitted dress she had worn.

He had asked her to go to a movie – *Citizen Kane* was

23

playing at The Shade — and she said okay. They had a good time and she was thinking to herself, *No fireworks.* She had enjoyed his kiss goodnight and had thought, *He's sure no Errol Flynn.* He had kept her smiling with his line of patter, which was outrageous, and she had thought, *He wants to be Henry Youngman when he grows up.*

Later that evening, sitting in the bedroom of her apartment and watching Bette Davis play a bitchy career woman on the late movie, some of these thoughts had come back to her and she paused with her teeth sunk into an apple, rather shocked at her own unfairness.

And a voice that had been silent for the best part of a year — not so much the voice of conscience as that of perspective — spoke up abruptly. *What you mean is, he sure isn't Dan. Isn't that it?*

No! she assured herself, not just *rather* shocked now. *I don't think about Dan at all anymore. That ... was a long time ago.*

Diapers, the voice replied, *that was a long time ago. Dan left yesterday.*

She suddenly realized she was sitting in an apartment by herself late at night, eating an apple and watching a movie on TV that she cared nothing about, and doing it all because it was easier than thinking, thinking was so boring really, when all you had to think about was yourself and your lost love.

Very shocked now.

She had burst into tears.

She had gone out with Johnny the second and third time he asked, too, and that was also a revelation of exactly what she had become. She couldn't very well say that she had another date because it wasn't so. She was a smart, pretty girl, and she had been asked out a lot after the affair with Dan ended, but the only dates she had accepted were hamburger dates at the Den with Dan's roomie, and she realized now (her disgust tempered with rueful humor) that she had only gone on those completely innocuous dates in order to pump the poor guy about Dan. What load?

Most of her college girl friends had dropped over the horizon after graduation. Bettye Hackman was with the Peace Corps in Africa, to the utter dismay of her wealthy old-line-Bangor parents, and sometimes Sarah wondered what the Ugandans must make of Bettye with her white, impossible-to-tan skin and ash-blonde hair and cool, sorority good looks. Deenie Stubbs was at grad school in Houston. Rachel Jurgens had married her fella and was currently gestating somewhere in the wilds of western Massachusetts.

Slightly dazed, Sarah had been forced to the conclusion that Johnny Smith was the first new friend she had made in a long, long time – and she had been her senior high school class's Miss Popularity. She had acepted dates from a couple of other Cleaves teachers, just to keep things in perspective. One of them was Gene Sedecki, the new math man – but obviously a veteran bore. The other, George Rounds, had immediately tried to make her. She had slapped his face – and the next day he'd had the gall to wink at her as they passed in the hall.

But Johnny was fun, easy to be with. And he did attract her sexually – just how strongly she couldn't honestly say, at least not yet. A week ago, after the Friday they'd had off for the October teachers' convention in Waterville, he had invited her back to his apartment for a home-cooked spaghetti dinner. While the sauce simmered, he had dashed around the corner to get some wine and had come back with two bottles of Apple Zapple. Like announcing his bathroom calls, it was somehow Johnny's style.

After the meal they had watched TV and that had turned to necking and God knew what *that* might have turned into if a couple of his friends, instructors from the university, hadn't turned up with a faculty position paper on academic freedom. They wanted Johnny to look it over and see what he thought. He had done so, but with noticeably less good will than was usual with him. She had noticed that with a warm, secret delight, and the ache in her own loins – the *unfulfilled* ache – had also delighted her, and that night she hadn't killed it with a douche.

She turned away from the window and walked over to the sofa where Johnny had left the mask.

'Happy Halloween,' she snorted, and laughed a little.

'What?' Johnny called out.

'I said if you don't come pretty quick I'm going without you.'

'Be right out.'

'Swell!'

She ran a finger over the Jekyll-and-Hyde mask, kindly Dr. Jekyll the left half, ferocious, subhuman Hyde the right half. Where will we be by Thanksgiving? she wondered. Or by Christmas?

The thought sent a funny, excited little thrill shooting through her. She liked him. He was a perfectly ordinary, sweet man.

She looked down at the mask again, horrible Hyde growing out of Jekyll's face like a lumpy carcinoma. It had been treated with fluorescent paint so it would glow in the dark.

What's ordinary? Nothing, nobody. Not really. If he was so ordinary, how could he be planning to wear something like that into his homeroom and still be confident of keeping order? And how can the kids call him Frankenstein and still respect and like him? What's ordinary?

Johnny came out, brushing through the beaded curtain that divided the bedroom and bathroom off from the living room.

If he wants me to go to bed with him tonight, I think I'm going to say okay.

And it was a warm thought, like coming home.

'What are you grinning about?'

'Nothing,' she said, tossing the mask back to the sofa.

'No, really. Was it something good?'

'Johnny,' she said, putting a hand on his chest and standing on tiptoe to kiss him lightly, 'some things will never be told. Come on, let's go.'

They paused downstairs in the foyer while he buttoned his denim jacket, and she found her eyes drawn again to the STRIKE! poster with its clenched fist and flaming background.

'There'll be another student strike this year,' he said, following her eyes.

'The war?'

'That's only going to be part of it this time. Vietnam and the fight over ROTC and Kent State have activated more students than ever before. I doubt if there's ever been a time when there were so few grunts taking up space at the university.'

'What do you mean, grunts?'

'Kids just studying to make grades, with no interest in the system except that it provides them with a ten-thousand-dollar a year job when they get out. A grunt is a student who gives a shit about nothing except his sheepskin. That's over. Most of them are awake. There are going to be some big changes.'

'Is that important to you? Even though you're out?'

He drew himself up. 'Madam, I am an alumnus. Smith, class of '70. Fill the steins to dear old Maine.'

She smiled. 'Come on, let's go. I want a ride on the whip before they shut it down for the night.'

'Very good,' he said, taking her arm. 'I just happen to have your car parked around the corner.'

'And eight dollars. The evening fairly glitters before us.'

The night was overcast but not rainy, mild for late October. Overhead, a quarter moon was struggling to make it through the cloud cover. Johnny slipped an arm around her and she moved closer to him.

'You know, I think an awful lot of you, Sarah.' His tone was almost offhand, but only almost. Her heart slowed a little and then made speed for a dozen beats or so.

'Really?'

'I guess this Dan guy, he hurt you, didn't he?'

'I don't know what he did to me,' she said truthfully.

The yellow blinker, a block behind them now, made their shadows appear and disappear on the concrete in front of them.

Johnny appeared to think this over. 'I wouldn't want to do that,' he said finally.

'No, I know that. But Johnny . . . give it time.'

'Yeah,' he said. 'Time. We've got that, I guess.'

And that would come back to her, awake and even more strongly in her dreams, in tones of inexpressible bitterness and loss.

They went around the corner and Johnny opened the passenger door for her. He went around and got in behind the wheel. 'You cold?'

'No,' she said. 'It's a great night for it.'

'It is,' he agreed, and pulled away from the curb. Her thoughts went back to that ridiculous mask. Half Jekyll with Johnny's blue eye visible behind the widened-O eyesocket of the surprised doctor – *Say, that's some cocktail I invented last night, but I don't think they'll be able to move it in the bars* – and that side was all right because you could see a bit of Johnny inside. It was the Hyde part that had scared her silly, because that eye was closed down to a slit. It could have been anybody. Anybody at all. Dan, for instance.

But by the time they reached the Esty fairgrounds, where the naked bulbs of the midway twinkled in the darkness and the long spokes of the Ferris wheel neon revolved up and down, she had forgotten the mask. She was with her guy, and they were going to have a good time.

3 ·

They walked up the midway hand in hand, not talking much, and Sarah found herself reliving the county fairs of her youth. She had grown up in South Paris, a paper town in western Maine, and the big fair had been the one in Fryeburg. For Johnny, a Pownal boy, it probably would have been Topsham. But they were all the same, really, and they hadn't changed much over the years.

You parked your car in a dirt parking lot and paid your two bucks at the gate, and when you were barely inside the fairgrounds you could smell hot dogs, frying peppers and onions, bacon, cotton candy, sawdust, and sweet, aromatic horseshit. You heard the heavy, chain-driven rumble of the baby roller coaster, the one they called The Wild Mouse. You heard the popping of .22s in the shooting galleries, the tinny blare of the Bingo caller from the PA system strung around the big tent filled with long tables and folding chairs from the local mortuary. Rock 'n' roll music vied with the calliope for supremacy. You heard the steady cry of the barkers – two shots for two bits, win one of these stuffed doggies for your baby, hey-hey-over-here, pitch till you win. It didn't change. It turned you into a kid again, willing and eager to be suckered.

'Here!' she said, stopping him. 'The whip! The whip!'

'Of course,' Johnny said comfortingly. He passed the woman in the ticket cage a dollar bill, and she pushed back two red tickets and two dimes with barely a glance up from her *Photoplay*.

'What do you mean, "of course"? Why are you "of coursing" me in that tone of voice?'

He shrugged. His face was much too innocent.

'It wasn't what you said, John Smith. It was how you said it.'

The ride had stopped. Passengers were getting off and streaming past them, mostly teenagers in blue melton CPO shirts or open parkas. Johnny led her up the wooden ramp and surrendered their tickets to the whip's starter, who looked like the most bored sentient creature in the universe.

'Nothing,' he said as the starter settled them into one of the little round shells and snapped the safety bar into place. 'It's just that these cars are on little circular tracks, right?'

'Right.'

'And the little circular tracks are embedded on a large

29

circular dish that spins around and around, right?'

'Right.'

'Well, when this ride is going full steam, the little car we're sitting in whips around on its little circular track and sometimes develops up to seven g, which is only five less than the astronauts get when they lift off from Cape Kennedy. And I knew this kid ...' Johnny was leaning solemnly over her now.

'Oh, here comes one of your big lies,' Sarah said uneasily.

'When this kid was five he fell down the front steps and put a tiny hairline fracture in his spine at the top of his neck. Then – *ten years later* – he went on the whip at Topsham Fair ... and ...' He shrugged and then patted her hand sympathetically. 'But you'll probably be okay, Sarah.'

'Ohhh ... I want to get *offff* ...'

And the whip whirled them away, slamming the fair and the midway into a tilted blur of lights and faces, and she shrieked and laughed and began to pummel him.

'Hairline fracture!' she shouted at him. 'I'll give *you* a hairline fracture when we get off this, you liar!'

· 'Do you feel anything giving in your neck yet?' he inquired sweetly.

'Oh, you liar!'

They whirled around, faster and faster, and as they snapped past the ride starter for the – tenth? fifteenth? – time, he leaned over and kissed her, and the car whistled around on its track, pressing their lips together in something that was hot and exciting and skintight. Then the ride was slowing down, their car clacked around on its track more reluctantly, and finally came to a swaying, swinging stop.

They got out, and Sarah squeezed his neck. 'Hairline fracture, you ass!' she whispered.

A fat lady in blue slacks and penny loafers was passing them. Johnny spoke to her, jerking a thumb back toward Sarah. 'That girl is bothering me, ma'am. If you see a policeman would you tell him?'

'You young people think you're smart,' the fat lady said disdainfully. She waddled away toward the bingo tent, holding her purse more tightly under her arm. Sarah was giggling helplessly.

'You're impossible.'

'I'll come to a bad end,' Johnny agreed. 'My mother always said so.'

They walked up the midway side by side again, waiting for the world to stop making unstable motions before their eyes and under their feet.

'She's pretty religious, your mom, isn't she?' Sarah asked.

'She's as Baptist as you can get,' Johnny agreed. 'But she's okay. She keeps it under control. She can't resist passing me a few tracts when I'm at home, but that's her thing. Daddy and I put up with it. I used to try to get on her case about it – I'd ask her who the heck was in Nod for Cain to go live with if his dad and mom were the first people on earth, stuff like that – but I decided it was sort of mean and quit it. Two years ago I thought Eugene McCarthy could save the world, and at least the Baptists don't have Jesus running for president.'

'Your father's not religious?'

Johnny laughed. 'I don't know about that, but he's sure no Baptist.' After a moment's thought he added, 'Dad's a carpenter,' as if that explained it. She smiled.

'What would your mother think if she knew you were seeing a lapsed Catholic?'

'Ask me to bring you home,' Johnny said promptly, 'so she could slip you a few tracts.'

She stopped, still holding his hand. 'Would you like to bring me to your house?' she asked, looking at him closely.

Johnny's long, pleasant face became serious. 'Yeah,' he said. 'I'd like you to meet them . . . and vice-versa.'

'Why?'

'Don't you know why?' he asked her gently, and suddenly her throat closed and her head throbbed as if she might cry and she squeezed his hand tightly.

'Oh Johnny, I do like you.'

'I like you even more than that,' he said seriously.

'Take me on the Ferris wheel,' she demanded suddenly, smiling. No more talk like this until she had a chance to consider it, to think where it might be leading. 'I want to go up high where we can see everything.'

'Can I kiss you at the top?'

'Twice, if you're quick.'

He allowed her to lead him to the ticket booth, where he surrendered another dollar bill. As he paid he told her, 'When I was in high school, I know this kid who worked at the fair, and he said most of the guys who put these rides together are dead drunk and they leave off all sorts of . . .'

'Go to hell,' she said merrily, 'nobody lives forever.'

'But everybody tries, you ever notice that?' he said, following her into one of the swaying gondolas.

As a matter of fact he got to kiss her several times at the top, with the October wind ruffling their hair and the midway spread out below them like a glowing clockface in the dark.

4 ·

After the Ferris wheel they did the carousel, even though he told her quite honestly that he felt like a horse's ass. His legs were so long that he could have stood astride one of the plaster horses. She told him maliciously that she had known a girl in high school who had had a weak heart, except nobody *knew* she had a weak heart, and she she had gotten on the carousel with her boyfriend and . . .

'Someday you'll be sorry,' he told her with quiet sincerity. 'A relationship based on lies is no good, Sarah.'

She gave him a very moist raspberry.

After the carousel came the mirror maze, a very good mirror maze as a matter of fact, it made her think of the one in Bradbury's *Something Wicked This Way Comes*, where the little-old-lady schoolteacher almost got lost forever. She could see Johnny in another part of it, fumbling around, waving to her. Dozens of Johnnies, dozens of

Sarahs. They bypassed each other, flickered around non-Euclidian angles, and seemed to disappear. She made left turns, right turns, bumped her nose on panes of clear glass, and got giggling helplessly, partly in a nervous claustrophobic reaction. One of the mirrors turned her into a squat Tolkein dwarf. Another created the apotheosis of teenage gangliness with shins a quarter of a mile long.

At last they escaped and he got them a couple of fried hot dogs and a Dixie cup filled with greasy french fries that tasted the way french fries hardly ever do once you've gotten past your fifteenth year.

They passed a kooch joint. Three girls stood out front in sequined skirts and bras. They were shimmying to an old Jerry Lee Lewis tune while the barker hawked them through a microphone. 'Come on over baby,' Jerry Lee blared, his piano boogying frankly across the sawdust-sprinkled arcades. 'Come on over baby, baby got the bull by the horns ... we ain't fakin ... whole lotta shakin goin on ...'

'Club Playboy,' Johnny marveled, and laughed. 'There used to be a place like this down at Harrison Beach. The barker used to swear the girls could take the glasses right off your nose with their hands tied behind their backs.'

'It sounds like an interesting way to get a social disease,' Sarah said, and Johnny roared with laughter.

Behind them the barker's amplified voice grew hollow with distance, counterpointed by Jerry Lee's pumping piano, music like some mad, dented hot rod that was too tough to die, rumbling out of the dead and silent fifties like an omen. 'Come in, men, come on over, don't be shy because these girls sure aren't, not in the least little bit! It's all on the inside ... your education isn't complete until you've seen the Club Playboy show ...'

'Don't you want to go on back and finish your education?' she asked.

He smiled. 'I finshed my basic course work on that subject some time ago. I guess I can wait a while to get my Ph.D.'

She glanced at her watch. 'Hey, it's getting late, Johnny. And tomorrow's a school day.'

'Yeah. But at least it's Friday.'

She sighed, thinking of her fifth-period study hall and her seventh-period New Fiction class, both of them impossibly rowdy.

They had worked their way back to the main part of the midway. The crowd was thinning. The Tilt-A-Whirl had shut down for the evening. Two workmen with unfiltered cigarettes jutting from the corners of their mouths were covering the Wild Mouse with a tarpaulin. The man in the Pitch-Til-U-Win was turning off his lights.

'You doing anything Saturday?' he asked, suddenly diffident. 'I know it's short notice, but . . .'

'I have plans,' she said.

'Oh.'

And she couldn't bear his crestfallen expression, it was really too mean to tease him about that. 'I'm doing something with you.'

'You are? . . . Oh, you are. Say, that's good.' He grinned at her and she grinned back. The voice in her mind, which was sometimes as real to her as the voice of another human being, suddenly spoke up.

You're feeling good again, Sarah. Feeling happy. Isn't it fine?

'Yes, it is,' she said. She went up on tiptoe and kissed him quickly. She made herself go on before she could chicken out. 'It gets pretty lonely down there in Veazie sometimes, you know. Maybe I could . . . sort of spend the night with you.'

He looked at her with warm thoughtfulness, and with a speculation that made her tingle deep inside. 'Would that be what you want, Sarah?'

She nodded. 'Very much what I want.'

'All right,' he said, and put an arm around her.

'Are you sure?' Sarah asked a little shyly.

'I'm just afraid you'll change your mind.'

'I won't, Johnny.'

34

He hugged her tighter against him. 'Then it's my lucky night.'

They were passing the Wheel of Fortune as he said it, and Sarah would later remember that it was the only booth still open on that side of the midway for thirty yards in either direction. The man behind the counter had just finished sweeping the packed dirt inside for any spare dimes that might have fallen from the playing board during the night's action. Probably his last chore before closing up, she thought. Behind him was his large spoked wheel, outlined by tiny electric bulbs. He must have heard Johnny's remark, because he went into his pitch more or less automatically, his eyes still searching the dirt floor of his booth for the gleam of silver.

'Hey-hey-hey, if you feel lucky, mister, spin the Wheel of Fortune, turn dimes into dollars. It's all in the Wheel, try your luck, one thin dime sets this Wheel of Fortune in motion.'

Johnny swung back toward the sound of his voice.

'Johnny?'

'I feel lucky, just like the man said.' He smiled down at her. 'Unless you mind . . . ?'

'No, go ahead. Just don't take too long.'

He looked at her again in that frankly speculative way that made her feel a little weak, wondering how it would be with him. Her stomach did a slow roll-over that made her feel a bit nauseated with sudden sexual longing.

'No, not long.' He looked at the pitchman. The midway behind them was almost completely empty now, and as the overcast had melted off above them it had turned chilly. The three of them were puffing white vapor as they breathed.

'Try your luck, young man?'

'Yes.'

He had switched all his cash to his front pocket when they arrived at the fair, and now he pulled out the remains of his eight dollars. It came to a dollar eighty-five.

The playing board was a strip of yellow plastic with numbers and odds painted on it in squares. It looked a bit

35

like a roulette board, but Johnny saw immediately that the odds here would have turned a Las Vegas roulette player gray. A trip combination paid off at only two to one. There were two house numbers, zero and double zero. He pointed this out to the pitchman, who only shrugged.

'You want Vegas, go to Vegas. What can I say?'

But Johnny's good humor tonight was unshakable. Things had gotten off to a poor start with that mask, but it had been all upbeat from there. In fact, it was the best night he could remember in years, maybe the best night ever. He looked at Sarah. Her color was high, her eyes sparkling. 'What do you say, Sarah?'

She shook her head. 'It's Greek to me. What do you do?'

'Play a number. Or red/black. Or odd/even. Or a ten-number series. They all pay differently.' He gazed at the pitchman, who gazed back blandly. 'At least, they should.'

'Play black,' she said. 'It is sort of exciting, isn't it?'

'Black,' he said, and dropped his odd dime on the black square.

The pitchman stared at the single dime on his expanse of playboard and sighed. 'Heavy plunger.' He turned to the Wheel.

Johnny's hand wandered absently to his forehead and touched it. 'Wait,' he said abruptly. He pushed one of his quarters onto the square reading 11–20.

'That it?'

'Sure,' Johnny said.

The pitchman gave the Wheel a twist and it spun inside its circle of lights, red and black merging. Johnny absently rubbed at his forehead. The Wheel began to slow and now they could hear the metronome-like tick-tock of the small wooden clapper sliding past the pins that divided the numbers. It reached 8, 9, seemed about to stop on 10, and slipped into the 11 slot with a final click and came to rest.

'The lady loses, the gentleman wins,' the pitchman said.

'You won, Johnny?'

'Seems like it,' Johnny said as the pitchman added two quarters to his original one. Sarah gave a little squeal, barely noticing as the pitchman swept the dime away.

'Told you, my lucky night,' Johnny said.

'Twice is luck, once is just a fluke,' the pitchman remarked. 'Hey-hey-hey.'

'Go again, Johnny,' she said.

'All right. Just as it is for me.'

'Let it ride?'

'Yes.'

The pitchman spun the Wheel again, and as it slid around, Sarah murmured quietly to him, 'Aren't all these carnival wheels suppose to be fixed?'

'They used to be. Now the state inspects them and they just rely on their outrageous odds system.'

The Wheel had slowed to its final unwinding tick-tock. The pointer passed 10 and entered Johnny's trip, still slowing.

'Come on, come *on*!' Sarah cried. A couple of teenagers on their way out paused to watch.

The wooden clapper, moving very slowly now, passed 16 and 17, then came to a stop on 18.

'Gentleman wins again.' The pitchman added six more quarters to Johnny's pile.

'You're rich!' Sarah gloated, and kissed him on the cheek.

'You're streaking, fella,' the pitchman agreed enthusiastically. 'Nobody quits a hot stick. Hey-hey-hey.'

'Should I go again?' Johnny asked her.

'Why not?'

'Yeah, go ahead, man,' one of the teenagers said. A button on his jacket bore the face of Jimi Hendrix. 'That guy took me for four bucks tonight. I love to see him take a beatin.'

'You too then,' Johnny told Sarah. He gave her the odd quarter off his stack of nine. After a moment's hesitation she laid it down on 21. Single numbers paid off ten to one on a hit, the board announced.

'You're riding the middle trip, right, fella?'

37

Johnny looked down at the eight quarters stacked on the board, and then he began to rub his forehead again, as if he felt the beginnings of a headache. Suddenly he swept the quarters off the board and jingled them in his two cupped hands.

'No. Spin for the lady. I'll watch this one.'

She looked at him, puzzled. 'Johnny?'

He shrugged. 'Just a feeling.'

The pitchman rolled his eyes in a heaven-give-me-strength-to-bear-these fools gesture and set his Wheel going again. It spun, slowed, and stopped. On double zero. 'House numbah, house numbah,' the pitchman chanted, and Sarah's quarter disappeared into his apron.

'Is that fair, Johnny?' Sarah asked, hurt.

'Zero and double zero only pay the house,' he said.

'Then you were smart to take your money off the board.'

'I guess I was.'

'You want me to spin this Wheel or go for coffee?' the pitchman asked.

'Spin it,' Johnny said, and put his quarters down in two stacks of four on the third trip.

As the Wheel buzzed around in its cage of lights, Sarah asked Johnny, never taking her eyes from the spin, 'How much can a place like this take in on one night?'

The teenagers had been joined by a quartet of older people, two men and two women. A man with the build of a construction worker said, 'Anywheres from five to seven hundred dollars.'

The pitchman rolled his eyes again. 'Oh, man, I wish you was right,' he said.

'Hey, don't give me that poor mouth,' the man who looked like a construction worker said. 'I used to work this scam twenty years ago. Five to seven hundred a night, two grand on a Saturday, easy. And that's running a straight Wheel.'

Johnny kept his eyes on the Wheel, which was now spinning slowly enough to read the individual numbers as they flashed past. It flashed past o and oo, through the first trip, slowing, through the second trip, still slowing.

'Too much legs, man,' one of the teenagers said.

'Wait,' Johnny said, in a peculiar tone of voice. Sarah glanced at him, and his long, pleasant face looked oddly strained, his blue eyes darker than usual, for away, distant.

The pointer stopped on 30 and came to rest.

'Hot stick, hot stick,' the pitchman chanted resignedly as the little crowd behind Johnny and Sarah uttered a cheer. The man who looked like a construction worker clapped Johnny on the back hard enough to make him stagger a bit. The pitchman reached into the Roi-Tan box under the counter and dropped four singles beside Johnny's eight quarters.

'Enough?' Sarah asked.

'One more,' Johnny said. 'If I win, this guy paid for our fair and your gas. If I lose, we're out half a buck or so.'

'Hey-hey-hey,' the pitchman chanted. He was brightening up now, getting his rhythm back. 'Get it down where you want it down. Step right up, you other folks. This ain't no spectator sport. Round and round she's gonna go and where she's gonna stop ain't nobody knows.'

The man who looked like a construction worker and the two teenagers stepped up beside Johnny and Sarah. After a moment's consultation, the teenagers produced half a buck in change between them and dropped it on the middle trip. The man who looked like a construction worker, who introduced himself as Steve Bernhardt, put a dollar on the square marked EVEN.

'What about you, buddy?' the pitchman asked Johnny. 'You gonna play it as it lays?'

'Yes,' Johnny said.

'Oh man,' one of the teenagers said, 'that's tempting fate.'

'I guess,' Johnny said, and Sarah smiled at him.

Bernhardt gave Johnny a speculative glance and suddenly switched his dollar to his third trip. 'What the hell,' sighed the teenager who had told Johnny he was tempting fate. He switched the fifty cents he and his friend had come up with to the same trip.

'All the eggs in one basket,' the pitchman chanted. 'That how you want it?'

The players stood silent and affirmative. A couple of roustabouts had drifted over to watch, one of them with a lady friend; there was now quite a respectable little knot of people in front of the Wheel of Fortune concession in the darkening arcade. The pitchman gave the Wheel a mighty spin. Twelve pairs of eyes watched it revolve. Sarah found herself looking at Johnny again, thinking how strange his face was in this bold yet somehow furtive lighting. She thought of the mask again – Jekyll and Hyde, odd and even. Her stomach turned over again, making her feel a little weak. The Wheel slowed, began to tick. The teenagers began to shout at it, urging it onward.

'Little more, baby,' Steve Bernhardt cajoled it. 'Little more, honey.'

The Wheel ticked into the third trip and came to a stop on 24. A cheer went up from the crowd again.

'Johnny, you did it, you did it!' Sarah cried.

The pitchman whistled through his teeth in disgust and paid off. A dollar for the teenagers, two for Bernhardt, a ten and two ones for Johnny. He now had eighteen dollars in front of him on the board.

'Hot stick, hot stick, hey-hey-hey. One more, buddy? This Wheel's your friend tonight.'

Johnny looked at Sarah.

'Up to you, Johnny.' But she felt suddenly uneasy.

'Go on, man,' the teenager with the Jimi Hendrix button urged. 'I *love* to see this guy get a beatin.'

'Okay,' Johnny said, 'last time.'

'Get it down where you want it down.'

They all looked at Johnny, who stood thoughtful for a moment, rubbing his forehead. His usually good-humored face was still and serious and composed. He was looking

40

at the Wheel in its cage of lights and his fingers worked steadily at the smooth skin over his right eye.

'As is,' he said finally.

A little speculative murmur from the crowd.

'Oh, man, that is *really* tempting it.'

'He's hot,' Bernhardt said doubtfully. He glanced back at his wife, who shrugged to show her complete mystification. 'I'll tag along with you, long, tall, and ugly.'

The teenager with the button glanced at his friend, who shrugged and nodded. 'Okay,' he said, turning back to the pitchman. 'We'll stick, too.'

The Wheel spun. Behind them Sarah heard one of the roustabouts bet the other five dollars against the third trip coming up again. Her stomach did another forward roll but this time it didn't stop; it just went on somersaulting over and over and she became aware that she was getting sick. Cold sweat stood out on her face.

The Wheel began to slow in the first trip, and one of the teenagers flapped his hands in disgust. But he didn't move away. It ticked past 11, 12, 13. The pitchman looked happy at last. Tick-tock-tick, 14, 15, 16.

'It's going through,' Bernhardt said. There was awe in his voice. The pitchman looked at his Wheel as if he wished he could just reach out and stop it. It clicked past 20, 21, and settled to a stop in the slot marked 22.

There was another shout of triumph from the crowd, which had now grown almost to twenty. All the people left at the fair were gathered here, it seemed. Faintly, Sarah heard the roustabouts who had lost his bet grumble something about 'Shitass luck,' as he paid off. Her head thumped. Her legs felt suddenly, horribly unsteady, the muscles trembling and untrustworthy. She blinked her eyes rapidly several times and got only a nauseating instant of vertigo for her pains. The world seemed to tilt up at a skewed angle, as if they were still on the Whip, and then slowly settle back down.

I got a bad hot dog, she thought dismally. That's what you get for trying your luck at the county fair, Sarah.

41

'Hey-hey-hey,' the pitchman said without much enthusiasm, and paid off. Two dollars for the teenagers, four for Steve Bernhardt, and then a bundle for Johnny – three tens, a five, and a one. The pitchman was not overjoyed, but he was sanguine. If the tall, skinny man with the good-looking blonde tried the third trip again, the pitchman would almost surely gather back in everything he had paid out. It wasn't the skinny man's money until it was off the board. And if he walked? Well, he had cleared a thousand dollars on the Wheel just today, he could afford to pay out a little tonight. The word would get around that Sol Drummore's Wheel had been hit and tomorrow play would be heavier than ever. A winner was a good ad.

'Lay em down where you want em down,' he chanted. Several of the others had moved up to the board and were putting down dimes and quarters. But the pitchman looked only at his money player. 'What do you say, fella? Want to shoot the moon?'

Johnny looked down at Sarah. 'What do you ... hey, are you all right? You're white as a ghost.'

'My stomach,' she said, managing a smile. 'I think it was my hot dog. Can we go home?'

'Sure. You bet.' He was gathering the wad of crinkled bills up from the board when his eyes happened on the Wheel again. The warm concern for her that had been in them faded out. They seemed to darken again, become speculative in a cold way. *He's looking at that wheel the way a little boy would look at his own private ant colony,* Sarah thought.

'Just a minute,' he said.

'All right,' Sarah answered. But she felt light-headed now as well as sick to her stomach. And there were rumblings in her lower belly that she didn't like. Not the backdoor trots, Lord. Please.

She thought: *He can't be content until he's lost it all back.*

And then, with strange certainty: *But he's not going to lose.*

42

'What do you say, buddy?' the pitchman asked. 'On or off, in or out.'

'Shit or git,' one of the roustabouts said, and there was nervous laughter. Sarah's head swam.

Johnny suddenly shoved bills and quarters up to the corner of the board.

'What are you doing,' the pitchman asked, genuinely shocked.

'The whole wad on 19,' Johnny said.

Sarah wanted to moan and bit it back.

The crowd murmured.

'Don't push it,' Steve Bernhardt said in Johnny's ear. Johnny didn't answer. He was staring at the Wheel with something like indifference. His eyes seemed almost violet.

There was a sudden jingling sound that Sarah at first thought must be in her own ears. Then she saw that the others who had put money down were sweeping it back off the board again, leaving Johnny to make his play alone.

No! She found herself wanting to shout. *Not like that, not alone, it isn't fair . . .*

She bit down on her lips. She was afraid that she might throw up if she opened her mouth. Her stomach was very bad now. Johnny's pile of winnings sat alone under the naked lights. Fifty-four dollars, and the single-number pay-off was ten for one.

The pitchman wet his lips. 'Mister, the state says I'm not supposed to take any single number bets over two dollars.'

'Come on,' Bernhardt growled. 'You aren't supposed to take trip bets over ten and you just let the guy bet eighteen. What is it, your balls starting to sweat?'

'No, it's just . . .'

'Come on,' Johnny said abruptly. 'One way or the other. My girl's sick.'

The pitchman sized up the crowd. The crowd looked back at him with hostile eyes. It was bad. They didn't understand that the guy was just throwing his money

43

away and he was trying to restrain him. Fuck it. The crowd wasn't going to like it either way. Let the guy do his headstand and lose his money so he could shut down for the night.

'Well,' he said, 'as long as none of youse is state inspectors . . .' He turned to his Wheel. 'Round and round she's gonna go, and where she's gonna stop, ain't nobody knows.'

He spun, sending the numbers into an immediate blur. For a time that seemed much longer than it actually could have been, there was no sound but the whirring of the Wheel of Fortune, the night wind rippling a swatch of canvas somewhere, and the sick thump in Sarah's own head. In her mind she begged Johnny to put his arm around her but he only stood quietly with his hands on the playing board and his eyes on the Wheel, which seemed determined to spin forever.

At last it slowed enough for her to be able to read the numbers and she saw 19, the 1 and 9 painted bright red on a black background. Up and down, up and down. The Wheel's smooth whirr broke into a steady ticka-ticka-ticka that was very loud in the stillness.

Now the numbers marched past the pointer with slowing deliberation.

One of the roustabouts called out in wonder: 'By the Jesus, it's gonna be close, anyway!'

Johnny stood calmly, watching the Wheel, and now it seemed to her (although it might have been the sickness, which was now rolling through her belly in gripping, peristaltic waves) that his eyes were almost black. Jekyll and Hyde, she thought, and was suddenly, senselessly, afraid of him.

Ticka-ticka-ticka.

The Wheel clicked into second trip, passed 15 and 16, clicked over 17 and, after an instant's hesitation, 18 as well. With a final *tick!* the pointer dropped into the 19 slot. The crowd held its breath. The Wheel revolved slowly, bringing the pointer up against the small pin between 19 and 20. For a quarter of a second it seemed that the pin could not hold the pointer in the 19 slot; that the last of its dying velocity would carry it over to 20. Then the Wheel rebounded, its force spent, and came to rest.

For a moment there was no sound from the crowd. No sound at all.

Then one of the teenagers, soft and awed: 'Hey, man, you just won five hundred and forty dollars.'

Steve Bernhardt: 'I never seen a run like that. *Never.*'

Then the crowd cheered. Johnny was slapped on the back, pummeled. People brushed by Sarah to get at him, to touch him, and for the moment they were separated she felt miserable, raw panic. Strengthless, she was butted this way and that, her stomach rolling crazily. A dozen afterimages of the Wheel whirled blackly before her eyes.

A moment later Johnny was with her and she saw with weak gladness that it really *was* Johnny and not the composed, mannequinlike figure that had watched the Wheel on its last spin. He looked confused and concerned about her.

'Baby, I'm sorry,' he said, and she loved him for that.

'I'm okay,' she answered, not knowing if she was or not.

The pitchman cleared his throat. 'The Wheel's shut down,' he said. 'The Wheel's shut down.'

An accepting, ill-tempered rumble from the crowd.

The pitchman looked at Johnny. 'I'll have to give you a check, young gentleman. I don't keep that much cash in the booth.'

'Sure, anything,' Johnny said. 'Just make it quick. The lady here really is sick.'

'Sure, a check,' Steve Bernhardt said with infinite contempt. 'He'll give you a check that'll bounce as high as the WGAN Tall Tower and *he'll* be down in Florida for the winter.'

'My dear sir,' the pitchman began, 'I assure you . . .'

'Oh, go assure your mother, maybe she'll believe you,' Bernhardt said. He suddenly reached over the playing

45

board and groped beneath the counter.

'Hey!' The pitchman yelped. 'This is robbery!'

The crowd did not appear impressed with his claim.

'Please,' Sarah muttered. Her head was whirling.

'I don't care about the money,' Johnny said suddenly. 'Let us by, please. The lady's sick.'

'Oh, *man*,' the teenager with the Jimi Hendrix button said, but he and his buddy drew reluctantly aside.

'No, Johnny,' Sarah said, although she was only holding back from vomiting by an act of will now. 'Get your money.' Five hundred dollars was Johnny's salary for three weeks.

'Pay off, you cheap tinhorn!' Bernhardt roared. He brought up the Roi-Tan cigar box from under the counter, pushed it aside without even looking inside it, groped again, and this time came up with a steel lockbox painted industrial green. He slammed it down on the play-board. 'If there ain't five hundred and forty bucks in there, I'll eat my own shirt in front of all these people.' He dropped a hard, heavy hand on Johnny's shoulder. 'You just wait a minute, sonny. You're gonna have your payday or my name's not Steve Bernhardt.'

'Really, sir, I don't have that much . . .'

'You pay,' Steve Bernhardt said, leaning over him, 'or I'll see you shut down. I mean that. I'm sincere about it.'

The pitchman sighed and fished inside his shirt. He produced a key on a fine-link chain. The crowd sighed. Sarah could stay no longer. Her stomach felt bloated and suddenly as still as death. Everything was going to come up, everything, and at express-train speed. She stumbled away from Johnny's side and battered through the crowd.

'Honey, you all right?' a woman's voice asked her, and Sarah shook her head blindly.

'Sarah!' Johnny called.

You just can't hide . . . from Jekyll and Hyde, she thought incoherently. The fluorescent mask seemed to hang sickly before her eyes in the midway dark as she hurried past the merry-go-round. She struck a light pole

46

with her shoulder, staggered, grabbed it, and threw up. It seemed to come all the way from her heels, convulsing her stomach like a sick, slick fist. She let herself go with it as much as she could.

Smells like cotton candy, she thought, and with a groan she did it again, then again. Spots danced in front of her eyes. The last heave had brought up little more than mucus and air.

'Oh, my,' she said weakly, and clung to the light pole to keep from falling over. Somewhere behind her Johnny was calling her name, but she couldn't answer just yet, didn't want to. Her stomach was settling back down a little and for just a moment she wanted to stand here in the dark and congratulate herself on being alive, on having survived her night at the fair.

'Sarah? *Sarah!*'

She spat twice to clear her mouth a little.

'Over here, Johnny.'

He came around the carousel with its plaster horses frozen in mid-leap. She saw he was absently clutching a thick wad of greenbacks in one hand.

'Are you all right?'

'No, but better. I threw up.'

'Oh. Oh, Jesus. Let's go home.' He took her arm gently.

'You got your money.'

He glanced down at the wad of bills and then tucked it absently into his pants pocket. 'Yeah. Some of it or all of it, I don't know. That burly guy counted it out.'

Sarah took a handkerchief from her purse and began rubbing her mouth with it. Drink of water, she thought. I'd sell my soul for a drink of water.

'You ought to care,' she said. 'It's a lot of money.'

'Found money brings bad luck,' he said darkly. 'One of my mother's sayings. She has a million of em. And she's death on gambling.'

'Dyed-in-the-wool Baptist,' Sarah said, and then shuddered convulsively.

'You okay?' he asked, concerned.

'The chills,' she said. 'When we get in the car I want

47

the heater on full blast, and . . . oh, Lord, I'm going to do it again.'

She turned away from him and retched up spittle with a groaning sound. She staggered. He held her gently but firmly. 'Can you get back to the car?'

'Yes. I'm all right now.' But her head ached and her mouth tasted foul and the muscles of her back and belly all felt sprung out of joint, strained and achey.

They walked slowly down the midway together, scuffing through the sawdust, passing tents that had been closed up and snugged down for the night. A shadow glided up behind them and Johnny glanced around sharply, perhaps aware of how much money he had in his pocket.

It was one of the teenagers – about fifteen years old. He smiled shyly at them. 'I hope you feel better,' he said to Sarah. 'It's those hot dogs, I bet. You can get a bad one pretty easy.'

'Ag, don't talk about it,' Sarah said.

'You need a hand getting her to the car?' he asked Johnny.

'No, thanks. We're fine.'

'Okay. I gotta cut out anyway.' But he paused a moment longer, his shy smile widening into a grin. 'I *love* to see that guy take a beatin.'

He trotted off into the dark.

Sarah's small, white station wagon was the only car left in the dark parking lot; it crouched under a sodium light like a forlorn, forgotten pup. Johnny opened the passenger door for Sarah and she folded herself carefully in. He slipped in behind the wheel and started it up.

'It'll take a few minutes for the heater,' he said.

'Never mind. I'm hot now.'

He looked at her and saw the sweat breaking on her face. 'Maybe we ought to trundle you up to the emergency room at Eastern Maine Medical,' he said. 'If it's salmonella, it could be serious.'

'No, I'm okay. I just want to go home and go to sleep, I'm going to get up just long enough tomorrow morning

48

to call in sick at school and then go back to sleep again.'

'Don't even bother to get up that long. I'll call you in, Sarah.'

She looked at him gratefully. 'Would you?'

'Sure.'

They were headed back to the main highway now.

'I'm sorry I can't come back to your place with you,' Sarah said. 'Really and truly.'

'Not your fault.'

'Sure it is. I ate the bad hot dog. Unlucky Sarah.'

'I love you, Sarah,' Johnny said. So it was out, it couldn't be called back, it hung between them in the moving car waiting for someone to do something about it.

She did what she could. 'Thank you, Johnny.'

They drove on in a comfortable silence.

CHAPTER TWO

1 ·

It was nearly midnight when Johnny turned the wagon into her driveway. Sarah was dozing.

'Hey,' he said, cutting the motor and shaking her gently. 'We're here.'

'Oh ... okay.' She sat up and drew her coat more tightly about her.

'How do you feel?'

'Better. My stomach's sore and my back hurts, but better. Johnny, you take the car back to Cleaves with you.'

'No, I better not,' he said. 'Someone would see it parked in front of the apartment house all night. That kind of talk we don't need.'

'But I was going to come back with you ...'

Johnny smiled. 'And that would have made it worth the risk, even if we had to walk three blocks. Besides, I want you to have the car in case you change your mind about the emergency room.'

49

'I won't.'

'You might. Can I come in and call a cab?'

'You sure can.'

They went in and Sarah turned on the lights before being attacked by a fresh bout of the shivers.

'The phone's in the living room. I'm going to lie down and cover up with a quilt.'

The living room was small and functional, saved from a barracks flavor only by the splashy curtains – flowers in a psychedelic pattern and color – and a series of posters along one wall: Dylan at Forest Hills, Baez at Carnegie Hall, Jefferson Airplane at Berkeley, the Byrds in Cleveland.

Sarah lay down on the couch and pulled a quilt up to her chin. Johnny looked at her with real concern. Her face was paper-white except for the dark circles under her eyes. She looked about as sick as a person can get.

'Maybe I ought to spend the night here,' he said. 'Just in case something happens, like . . .'

'Like a hairline fracture at the top of my spine?' She looked at him with rueful humor.

'Well, you know. Whatever.'

The ominous rumbling in her nether regions decided her. She had fully intended to finish this night by sleeping with John Smith. It wasn't going to work out that way. But that didn't mean she had to end the evening with him in attendance while she threw up, dashed for the w.c., and chugged most of a bottle of Pepto-Bismol.

'I'll be okay,' she said. 'It was just a bad carnival hot dog, Johnny. You could have just as easily gotten it yourself. Give me a call during your free period tomorrow.'

'You sure?'

'Yes, I am.'

'Okay, kid.' He picked up the phone with no further argument and called his cab. She closed her eyes, lulled and comforted by the sound of his voice. One of the things she liked most about him was that he would always really try to do the right thing, the best thing, with no self-serving bullshit. That was good. She was too tired and feeling too low to play little social games.

'The deed's done,' he said, hanging up. 'They'll have a guy over in five minutes.'

'At least you've got cab fare,' she said, smiling.

'And I plan to tip handsomely,' he replied, doing a passable W. C. Fields.

He came over to the couch, sat beside her, held her hand.

'Johnny, how did you do it?'

'Hmmm?'

'The Wheel. How could you do that?'

'It was a streak, that's all,' he said, looking a little uncomfortable. 'Everybody has a streak once in a while. Like at the race track or playing blackjack or just matching dimes.'

'No,' she said.

'Huh?'

'I don't think everybody *does* have a streak once in a while. It was almost uncanny. It . . . scared me a little.'

'Did it?'

'Yes.'

Johnny sighed. 'Once in a while I get feelings, that's all. For as long as I can remember, since I was just a little kid. And I've always been good at finding things people have lost. Like that little Lisa Schumann at school. You know the girl I mean?'

'Little, sad, mousy Lisa?' She smiled. 'I know her. She's wandering in clouds of perplexity through my business grammar course.'

'She lost her class ring,' Johnny said, 'and came to me in tears about it. I asked her if she'd checked the back corners of the top shelf in her locker. Just a guess. But it was there.'

'And you've always been able to do that?'

He laughed and shook his head. 'Hardly ever.' The smile slipped a little. 'But it was strong tonight, Sarah. I had that Wheel . . .' He closed his fists softly and looked at them, now frowning. 'I had it right here. And it had the strangest goddam associations for me.'

51

'Like what?'

'Rubber,' he said slowly. 'Burning rubber. And cold. And ice. Black ice. Those things were in the back of my mind. God knows why. And a bad feeling. Like to beware.'

She looked at him closely, saying nothing, and his face slowly cleared.

'But it's gone now, whatever it was. Nothing probably.'

'It was five hundred dollars worth of good luck, anyway,' she said. Johnny laughed and nodded. He didn't talk anymore and she drowsed, glad to have him there. She came back to wakefulness when headlights from outside splashed across the wall. His cab.

'I'll call,' he said, and kissed her face gently. 'You sure you don't want me to hang around?'

Suddenly she did, but she shook her head.

'Call me,' she said.

'Period three,' he promised. He went to the door.

'Johnny?'

He turned back.

'I love you, Johnny,' she said, and his face lit up like a lamp.

He blew a kiss. 'Feel better,' he said, 'and we'll talk.'

She nodded, but it was four-and-a-half years before she talked to Johnny Smith again.

2 .

'Do you mind if I sit up front?' Johnny asked the cab driver.

'Nope. Just don't bump your knee on the meter. It's delicate.'

Johnny slid his long legs under the meter with some effort and slammed the door. The cabbie, a middle-aged man with a bald head and a paunch, dropped his flag and the cab cruised up Flagg Street.

'Where to?'

'Cleaves Mills,' Johnny said. 'Main Street. I'll show you where.'

'I got to ask you for fare-and-a-half,' the cabbie said. 'I don't like to, but I got to come back empty from there.'

Johnny's hand closed absently over the lump of bills in his pants pocket. He tried to remember if he had ever had so much money on him at one time before. Once. He had bought a two-year-old Chevy for twelve hundred dollars. On a whim, he had asked for cash at the savings bank, just to see what all that cash looked like. It hadn't been all that wonderful, but the surprise on the car dealer's face when Johnny pumped twelve one hundred dollar bills into his hand had been wonderful to behold. But this lump of money didn't make him feel good at all, just vaguely uncomfortable, and his mother's axiom recurred to him: *Found money brings bad luck.*

'Fare-and-a-half's okay,' he told the cabbie.

'Just as long's we understand each other,' the cabbie said more expansively. 'I got over so quick on account of I had a call at the Riverside and nobody there would own up when I got over there.'

'That so?' Johnny asked without much interest. Dark houses flashed by outside. He had won five hundred dollars, and nothing remotely like it had ever happened to him before. That phantom smell of rubber burning . . . the sense of partially reliving something that had happened to him when he was very small . . . and that feeling of bad luck coming to balance off the good was still with him.

'Yeah, these drunks call and then they change their minds,' the cabbie said. 'Damn drunks, I hate em. They call and decide what the hell, they'll have a few more beers. Or they drink up the fare while they're waitin and when I come in and yell "Who wants the cab?" they don't want to own up.'

'Yeah,' Johnny said. On their left the Penobscot River flowed by, dark and oily. Then Sarah getting sick and saying she loved him on top of everything else. Probably just caught her in a weak moment, but God! If she had meant it! He had been gone on her almost since the first date.

That was the luck of the evening, not beating that Wheel. But it was the Wheel his mind kept coming back to, worrying at it. In the dark he could still see it revolving, and in his ears he could hear the slowing ticka-ticka-ticka of the marker bumping over the pins like something heard in an uneasy dream. Found money brings bad luck.

The cabbie turned off onto Route 6, now well-launched into his own monologue.

'So I says, "Blow it outcha you-know-where." I mean, the kid is a smart-aleck, right? I don't have to take a load of horseshit like that from anyone, including my own boy. I been drivin this cab twenty-six years. I been held up six times. I been in fender-benders without number, although I never had a major crash, for which I thank Mary Mother of Jesus and Saint Christopher and God the Father Almighty, know what I mean? And every week, no matter how thin that week was, I put five bucks away for his college. Ever since he was nothin but a pip-squeak suckin a bottle. And what for? So he can come home one fine day and tell me the president of the United States is a pig. Hot damn! The kid probably thinks *I'm* a pig, although he knows if he ever said it I'd re-arrange his teeth for him. So that's today's young generation for you. So I says, "Blow it outcha-you-know-where." '

'Yeah,' Johnny said. Now woods were floating by. Carson's Bog was on the left. They were seven miles from Cleaves Mills, give or take. The meter kicked over another dime.

One thin dime, one tenth of a dollar. Hey-hey-hey.

'What's your game, might I ask?' the cabbie said.

'I teach high school in Cleaves.'

'Oh, yeah? So you know what I mean. What the hell's wrong with these kids, anyway?'

Well, they ate a bad hot dog called Vietnam and it gave them ptomaine. A guy named Lyndon Johnson sold it to them. So they went to this other guy, see, and they said, 'Jesus, mister, I'm sick as hell.' And this other guy, his name was Nixon, he said, 'I know how to fix that.

54

Have a few more hot dogs.' And that's what's wrong with the youth of America.

'I don't know,' Johnny said.

'You plan all your life and you do what you can,' the cabbie said, and now there was honest bewilderment in his voice, a bewilderment which would not last much longer because the cabbie was embarked upon the last minute of his life. And Johnny, who didn't know that, felt a real pity for the man, a sympathy for his inability to understand.

Come on over baby, whole lotta shakin goin on.

'You never want nothing but the best, and the kid comes home with hair down to his asshole and says the president of the United States is a pig. A pig! Sheeyit, I don't . . .'

'*Look out!*' Johnny yelled.

The cabbie had half-turned to face him, his pudgy American Legionnaire's face earnest and angry and miserable in the dashlights and in the sudden glow of oncoming headlights. Now he snapped forward again, but too late.

'*Jeeesus . . .*'

There were two cars, one on each side of the white line. They had been dragging, side by side, coming up over the hill, a Mustang and a Dodge Charger. Johnny could hear the revved-up whine of their engines. The Charger was boring straight down at them. It never tried to get out of the way and the cabbie froze at the wheel.

'*Jeeeeee . . .*'

Johnny was barely aware of the Mustang flashing by on their left. Then the cab and the Charger met head-on and Johnny felt himself getting lifted up and out. There was no pain, although he was marginally aware that his thighs had connected with the taximeter hard enough to rip it out of its frame.

There was the sound of smashing glass. A huge gout of flame stroked its way up into the night. Johnny's head collided with the cab's windshield and knocked it out. Reality began to go down a hole. Pain, faint and far

55

away, in his shoulders and arms as the rest of him followed his head through the jagged windshield. He was flying. Flying into the October night.

Dim flashing thought. *Am I dying? Is this going to kill me?*

Interior voice answering: *Yes, this is probably it.*

Flying. October stars flung across the night. Racketing boom of exploding gasoline. An orange glow. Then darkness.

His trip through the void ended with a hard thump and a splash. Cold wetness as he went into Carson's Bog, twenty-five feet from where the Charger and the cab, welded together, pushed a pyre of flame into the night sky.

Darkness.

Fading.

Until all that was left seemed to be a giant red-and-black wheel revolving in such emptiness as there may be between the stars, try your luck, first time fluky, second time lucky, hey-hey-hey. The wheel revolved up and down, red and black, the marker ticking past the pins, and he strained to see if it was going to come up double zero, house number, house spin, everybody loses but the house. He strained to see but the wheel was gone. There was only blackness and that universal emptiness, negatory, good buddy, el zilcho. Cold limbo.

Johnny Smith stayed there a long, long time.

CHAPTER THREE

1 ·

At some time a little past two A.M. on the morning of October 30, 1970, the telephone began to ring in the downstairs hall of a small house about a hundred and fifty miles south of Cleaves Mills.

Herb Smith sat up in bed, disoriented, dragged halfway across the threshold of sleep and left in its doorway, groggy and disoriented.

Vera's voice beside him, muffled by the pillow. 'Phone.'

'Yeah,' he said, and swung out of bed. He was a big, broad-shouldered man in his late forties, losing his hair, now dressed in blue pajama bottoms. He went out into the upstairs hall and turned on the light. Down below, the phone shrilled away.

He went down to what Vera liked to call 'the phone nook.' It consisted of the phone and a strange little desk-table that she had gotten with Green Stamps about three years ago. Herb had refused from the first to slide his two hundred and forty pound bulk into it. When he talked on the phone, he stood up. The drawer of the desk-table was full of *Upper Rooms, Reader's Digests,* and *Fate* magazines.

Herb reached for the phone, then let it ring again.

A phone call in the middle of the night usually meant one of three things: an old friend had gotten totally shitfaced and had decided you'd be glad to hear from him even at two in the morning; a wrong number; bad news.

Hoping for the middle choice, Herb lifted up the phone. 'Hello?'

A crisp male voice said: 'Is this the Herbert Smith residence?'

'Yes?'

'To whom am I speaking, please?'

'I'm Herb Smith. What ...'

'Will you hold for a moment?'

'Yes, but who ...'

Too late. There was a faint clunk in his ear, as if the party on the other end had dropped one of his shoes. He had been put *on hold.* Of the many things he disliked about the telephone — bad connections, kid pranksters who wanted to know if you had Prince Albert in a can, operators who sounded like computers, and smoothies who wanted you to buy magazine subscriptions — the thing he disliked the most was being *on hold.* It was one

57

of those insidious things that had crept into modern life almost unnoticed over the last ten years or so. Once upon a time the fellow on the other end would simply have said, 'Hold the phone, willya?' and set it down. At least in those days you were able to hear faraway conversations, a barking dog, a radio, a crying baby. Being *on hold* was a totally different proposition. The line was darkly, smoothly blank. You were nowhere. Why didn't they just say, 'Will you hold on while I bury you alive for a little while?'

He realized he was just a tiny bit scared.

'Herbert?'

He turned round, the phone to his ear. Vera was at the top of the stairs in her faded brown bathrobe, hair up in curlers, some sort of cream hardened to a castlike consistency on her cheeks and forehead.

'Who is it?'

'I don't know yet. They've got me on hold.'

'On hold? At quarter past two in the morning?'

'Yes.'

'It's not Johnny, is it? Nothing's happened to Johnny?'

'I don't know,' he said, struggling to keep his voice from rising. Somebody calls you at two in the morning, puts you on hold, you count your relatives and inventory their condition. You make lists of old aunts. You tot up the ailments of grandparents, if you still have them. You wonder if the ticker of one of your friends just stopped ticking. And you try not to think that you have one son you love very much, or about how these calls always seem to come at two in the morning, or how all of a sudden your calves are getting stiff and heavy with tension . . .

Vera had closed her eyes and had folded her hands in the middle of her thin bosom. Herb tried to control his irritation. Restrained himself from saying, 'Vera, the Bible makes the strong suggestion that you go and do that in your closet.' That would earn him Vera Smith's Sweet Smile for Unbelieving and Hellbound Husbands. At two o'clock in the morning, and *on hold* to boot, he

58

didn't think he could take that particular smile.

The phone clunked again and a different male voice, an older one, said, 'Hello, Mr. Smith?'

'Yes, who is this?'

'I'm sorry to have kept you waiting, sir. Sergeant Meggs of the state police, Orono branch.'

'Is it my boy? Something about my boy?'

Unaware, he sagged onto the seat of the phone nook. He felt weak all over.

Sergeant Meggs said, 'Do you have a son named John Smith, no middle initial?'

'Is he all right? Is he okay?'

Footsteps on the stairs. Vera stood beside him. For a moment she looked calm, and then she clawed for the phone like a tigress. 'What is it? What's happened to my Johnny?'

Herb yanked the handset away from her, splintering one of her fingernails. Staring at her hard he said, 'I am handling this.'

She stood looking at him, her mild, faded blue eyes wide above the hand clapped to her mouth.

'Mr. Smith, are you there?'

Words that seemed coated with novocaine fell from Herb's mouth. 'I have a son named John Smith, no middle initial, yes. He lives in Cleaves Mills. He's a teacher at the high school there.'

'He's been in a car accident, Mr. Smith. His condition is extremely grave. I'm very sorry to have to give you this news.' The voice of Meggs was cadenced, formal.

'Oh, my God,' Herb said. His thoughts were whirling. Once, in the army, a great, mean, blond-haired Southern boy named Childress had beaten the crap out of him behind an Atlanta bar. Herb had felt like this then, unmanned, all his thoughts knocked into a useless, smeary sprawl. 'Oh, my God,' he said again.

'He's dead?' Vera asked. 'He's dead? Johnny's *dead*?'

He covered the mouthpiece. 'No,' he said. 'Not dead.'

'Not dead! Not dead!' she cried, and fell on her knees in the phone nook with an audible thud. 'O God we most

SOLIHULL S.F.C
LIBRARY

59

heartily thank Thee and ask that You show Thy tender care and loving mercy to our son and shelter him with Your loving hand we ask it in the name of Thy only begotten Son Jesus and . . .'

'*Vera shut up!*'

For a moment all three of them were silent, as if considering the world and its not-so-amusing ways: Herb, his bulk squashed into the phone nook bench with his knees crushed up against the underside of the desk and a bouquet of plastic flowers in his face: Vera with her knees planted on the hallway furnace grille; the unseen Sergeant Meggs was in a strange auditory way witnessing this black comedy.

'Mr. Smith?'

'Yes. I . . . I apologize for the ruckus.'

'Quite understandable,' Meggs said.

'My boy . . . Johnny . . . was he driving his Volkswagen?'

'Deathtraps, deathtraps, those little beetles are deathtraps,' Vera babbled. Tears streamed down her face, sliding over the smooth hard surface of the nightpack like rain on chrome.

'He was in a Bangor & Orono Yellow Cab,' Meggs said. 'I'll give you the situation as I understand it now. There were three vehicles involved, two of them driven by kids from Cleaves Mills. They were dragging. They came up over what's known as Carson's Hill on Route 6, headed east. Your son was in the cab, headed west, toward Cleaves. The cab and the car on the wrong side of the road collided head-on. The cab driver was killed, and so was the boy driving the other car. Your son and a passenger in that other car are at Eastern Maine Med. I understand both of them are listed as critical.'

'Critical,' Herb said.

'Critical! Critical!' Vera moaned.

Oh, Christ, we sound like one of those weird off-off-Broadway shows, Herb thought. He felt embarrassed for Vera, and for Sergeant Meggs, who must surely be hearing Vera, like some nutty Greek chorus in the background. He wondered how many conversations like this

60

Sergeant Meggs had held in the course of his job. He decided he must have had a good many. Possibly he had already called the cab driver's wife and the dead boy's mother to pass the news. How had they reacted? And what did it matter? Wasn't it Vera's right to weep for her son? And why did a person have to think such crazy things at a time like this?

'Eastern Maine,' Herb said. He jotted it on a pad. The drawing on top of the pad showed a smiling telephone handset. The phone cord spelled out the words PHONE PAL. 'How is he hurt?'

'I beg your pardon, Mr. Smith?'

'Where did he get it? Head? Belly? What? Is he burned?'

Vera shrieked.

'*Vera can you please shut UP!*'

'You'd have to call the hospital for that information,' Meggs said carefully. 'I'm a couple of hours from having a complete report.'

'All right. All right.'

'Mr. Smith, I'm sorry to have to call you in the middle of the night with such bad news . . .'

'It's bad, all right,' he said. 'I've got to call the hospital, Sergeant Meggs. Good-bye.'

'Good night, Mr. Smith.'

Herb hung up and stared stupidly at the phone. Just like that it happens, he thought. How 'bout that. Johnny.

Vera uttered another shriek, and he saw with some alarm that she had grabbed her hair, rollers and all, and was pulling it. 'It's a judgment! A judgment on the way we live, on sin, on something! Herb, get down on your knees with me . . .'

'Vera, I have to call the hospital. I don't want to do it on my knees.'

'We'll pray for him . . . promise to do better . . . if you'd only come to church more often with me I know . . . maybe it's your cigars, drinking beer with those men after work . . . cursing . . . taking the name of the Lord God in vain . . . a judgment . . . it's a judgment . . .'

61

He put his hands on her face to stop its wild, uneasy whipping back and forth. The feel of the night cream was unpleasant, but he didn't take his hands away. He felt pity for her. For the last ten years his wife had been walking somewhere in a gray area between devotion to her Baptist faith and what he considered to be a mild religious mania. Five years after Johnny was born, the doctor had found a number of benign tumors in her uterus and vaginal canal. Their removal had made it impossible for her to have another baby. Five years later, more tumors had necessitated a radical hysterectomy. That was when it had really begun for her, a deep religious feeling strangely coupled with other beliefs. She avidly read pamphlets on Atlantis, spaceships from heaven, races of 'pure Christians' who might live in the bowels of the earth. She read *Fate* magazine almost as frequently as the Bible, often using one to illuminate the other.

'Vera,' he said.

'We'll do better,' she whispered, her eyes pleading with him. 'We'll do better and he'll live. You'll see. You'll . . .'

'Vera.'

She fell silent, looking at him.

'Let's call the hospital and see just how bad it really is,' he said gently.

'A-All right. Yes.'

'Can you sit on the stairs there and keep perfectly quiet?'

'I want to pray,' she said childishly. 'You can't stop me.'

'I don't want to. As long as you pray to yourself.'

'Yes. To myself. All right, Herb.'

She went to the stairs and sat down and pulled her robe primly around her. She folded her hands and her lips began to move. Herb called the hospital. Two hours later they were headed north on the nearly deserted Maine Turnpike. Herb was behind the wheel of their '66 Ford station wagon. Vera sat bolt upright in the passenger seat. Her Bible was on her lap.

62

The telephone woke Sarah at quarter of nine. She went
to answer it with half her mind still asleep in bed. Her
back hurt from the vomiting she had done the night before and the muscles in her stomach felt strained, but
otherwise she felt much better.

She picked up the phone, sure it would be Johnny.
'Hello?'

'Hi, Sarah.' It wasn't Johnny. It was Anne Strafford
from school. Anne was a year older than Sarah and in
her second year at Cleaves. She taught Spanish. She was
a bubbly, effervescent girl and Sarah liked her very much.
But this morning she sounded subdued.

'How are you, Annie? It's only temporary. Probably
Johnny told you. Carnival hot dogs, I guess . . .'

'Oh, my God, you don't know. You don't . . .' The
words were swallowed in odd, choked sounds. Sarah
listened to them, frowning. Her initial puzzlement turned
to deadly disquiet as she realized Anne was crying.

'Anne? What's wrong? It's not Johnny, is it? Not . . .'

'There was an accident,' Anne said. She was now sobbing openly. 'He was in a cab. There was a head-on collision. The driver of the other car was Brad Freneau, I
had him in Spanish II, he died, his girl friend died this
morning, Mary Thibault, she was in one of Johnny's
classes, I heard, it's horrible, just horri . . .'

'*Johnny!*' Sarah screamed into the phone. She was sick
to her stomach again. Her hands and feet were suddenly
as cold as four gravestones. '*What about Johnny?*'

'He's in critical condition, Sarah. Dave Pelsen called the
hospital this morning. He's not expected . . . well, it's
very bad.'

The world was going gray. Anne was still talking but
her voice was far and wee, as e.e. cummings had said
about the balloon man. Flocked images tumbling over
and over one another, none making sense. The carny
wheel. The mirror maze. Johnny's eyes, strangely violet,
almost black. His dear, homely face in the harsh, county
fair lighting, naked bulbs strung on electric wire.

'Not Johnny,' she said, far and wee, far and wee. 'You're mistaken. He was fine when he left here.'

And Anne's voice coming back like a fast serve, her voice so shocked and unbelieving, so affronted that such a thing should have happened to someone her own age, someone young and vital. 'They told Dave he'd never wake up even if he survived the operation. They have to operate because his head . . . his head was . . .'

Was she going to say *crushed*? That Johnny's head had been *crushed*?

Sarah fainted then, possibly to avoid that final irrevocable word, that final horror. The phone spilled out of her fingers and she sat down hard in a gray world and then slipped over and the phone swung back and forth in a decreasing arc, Anne Strafford's voice coming out of it: 'Sarah? . . . Sarah? . . . Sarah?'

3 ·

When Sarah got to Eastern Maine Medical, it was quarter past twelve. The nurse at the reception desk looked at her white, strained face, estimated her capacity for further truth, and told her that John Smith was still in OR. She added that Johnny's mother and father were in the waiting room.

'Thank you,' Sarah said. She turned right instead of left, wound up in a medical closet, and had to backtrack.

The waiting room was done in bright, solid colors that gashed her eyes. A few people sat around looking at tattered magazines or empty space. A gray-haired woman came in from the elevators, gave her visitor's pass to a friend, and sat down. The friend clicked away on high heels. The rest of them went on sitting, waiting their own chance to visit a father who had had gallstones removed, a mother who had discovered a small lump under one of her breasts a bare three days ago, a friend who had been struck in the chest with an invisible sledgehammer while jogging. The faces of the waiters were carefully made-up with composure. Worry was swept under the face like dirt under a rug. Sarah felt the unreality hovering again.

Somewhere a soft bell was ringing. Crepe-soled shoes squeaked. He had been fine when he left her place. Impossible to think he was in one of these brick towers, engaged in dying.

She knew Mr. and Mrs. Smith at once. She groped for their first names and could not immediately find them. They were sitting together near the back of the room, and unlike the others here, they hadn't yet had time to come to terms with what had happened in their lives.

Johnny's mom sat with her coat on the chair behind her and her Bible clutched in her hands. Her lips moved as she read, and Sarah remembered Johnny saying she was very religious – maybe too religious, somewhere in that great middle ground between holy rolling and snake-handling, she remembered him saying. Mr. Smith – *Herb*, it came to her, *his name is Herb* – had one of the magazines on his knees, but he wasn't looking at it. He was looking out the window, where New England fall burned its way toward November and winter beyond.

She went over to them. 'Mr. and Mrs. Smith?'

They looked up at her, their faces tensed for the dreaded blow. Mrs. Smith's hands tightened on her Bible, which was open to the Book of Job, until her knuckles were white. The young woman before them was not in nurse's or doctor's whites, but that made no difference to them at this point. They were waiting for the final blow.

'Yes, we're the Smiths,' Herb said quietly.

'I'm Sarah Bracknell. Johnny and I are good friends. Going together, I suppose you'd say. May I sit down?'

'Johnny's girl friend?' Mrs. Smith asked in a sharp, almost accusing tone. A few of the others looked around briefly and then back at their own tattered magazines.

'Yes,' she said. 'Johnny's girl.'

'He never wrote that he had a lady friend,' Mrs. Smith said in that same sharp tone. 'No, he never did at all.'

'Hush, Mother,' Herb said. 'Sit down, Miss ... Bracknell, wasn't it?'

'Sarah,' she said gratefully, and took a chair. 'I ...'

'No, he never did,' Mrs. Smith said sharply. 'My boy

65

loved God, but just lately he maybe fell away just a bit. The judgment of the Lord God is sudden, you know. That's what makes backsliding so dangerous. You know not the day nor the hour . . .'

'*Hush*,' Herb said. People were looking around again. He fixed his wife with a stern glance. She looked back defiantly for a moment, but his gaze didn't waver. Vera dropped her eyes. She had closed the Bible but her fingers fiddled restlessly along the pages, as if longing to get back to the colossal demolition derby of Job's life, enough bad luck to put her own and her son's in some sort of bitter perspective.

'I was with him last night,' Sarah said, and that made the woman look up again, accusingly. At that moment Sarah remembered the biblical connotation of being 'with' somebody and felt herself beginning to blush. It was as if the woman could read her thoughts.

'We went to the county fair . . .'

'Places of sin and evil,' Vera Smith said clearly.

'I'll tell you one last time to *hush*, Vera,' Herb said grimly, and clamped one of his hands over one of his wife's. 'I mean it, now. This seems like a nice girl here, and I won't have you digging at her. Understand?'

'Sinful places,' Vera repeated stubbornly.

'Will you hush?'

'Let me go. I want to read my Bible.'

He let her go. Sarah felt confused embarrassment. Vera opened her Bible and began to read again, lips moving.

'Vera is very upset,' Herb said. 'We're both upset. You are too, from the look of you.'

'Yes.'

'Did you and Johnny have a good time last night?' he asked. 'At your fair?'

'Yes,' she said, the lie and truth of that simple word all mixed up in her mind. 'Yes we did, until . . . well, I ate a bad hot dog or something. We had my car and Johnny drove me home to my place in Veazie. I was pretty sick to my stomach. He called a cab. He said he'd call me in sick at school today. And that's the last time I saw him.' The

66

tears started to come then and she didn't want to cry in front of them, particularly not in front of Vera Smith, but there was no way to stop it. She fumbled a Kleenex out of her purse and held it to her face.

'There, now,' Herb said, and put an arm around her. 'There, now.' She cried, and it seemed to her in some unclear way that he felt better for having someone to comfort; his wife had found her own dark brand of comfort in Job's story and it didn't include him.

A few people turned around to gawk; through the prisms of her tears they seemed like a crowd. She had a bitter knowledge of what they were thinking: *Better her than me, better all three of them than me or mine, guy must be dying, guy must have gotten his head crushed for her to cry like that. Only a matter of time before some doctor comes down and takes them into a private room to tell them that –*

Somehow she choked off the tears and got hold of herself. Mrs. Smith sat bolt upright, as if startled out of a nightmare, noticing neither Sarah's tears nor her husband's effort to comfort her. She read her Bible.

'Please,' Sarah said. 'How bad is it? Can we hope?'

Before Herb could answer, Vera spoke up. Her voice was a dry bolt of certified doom: 'There's hope in God, Missy.'

Sarah saw the apprehensive flicker in Herb's eyes and thought: *He thinks it's driven her crazy. And maybe it has.*

4 ·

A long afternoon stretching into evening.

Sometime after two P.M., when the schools began to let out, a number of Johnny's students began to come in, wearing fatigue coats and strange hats and washed-out jeans. Sarah didn't see many of the kids she thought of as the button-down crowd – upward-bound, college-oriented kids, clear of eye and brow. Most of the kids who bothered to come in were the freaks and long-hairs.

A few came over and asked Sarah in quiet tones what

she knew about Mr. Smith's condition. She could only shake her head and say she had heard nothing. But one of the girls, Dawn Edwards, who had a crush on Johnny, read the depth of Sarah's fear in her face. She burst into tears. A nurse came and asked her to leave.

'I'm sure she'll be all right,' Sarah said. She had a protective arm around Dawn's shoulders. 'Just give her a minute or two.'

'No, I don't want to stay,' Dawn said, and left in a hurry, knocking one of the hard plastic contour chairs over with a clatter. A few moments later Sarah saw the girl sitting out on the steps in the cold, late, October sunshine with her head on her knees.

Vera Smith read her Bible.

By five o'clock most of the students had left. Dawn had also left; Sarah had not seen her go. At seven P.M., a young man with DR. STRAWNS pinned askew to the lapel of his white coat came into the waiting room, glanced around, and walked toward them.

'Mr. and Mrs. Smith?' he asked.

Herb took a deep breath. 'Yes. We are.'

Vera shut her Bible with a snap.

'Would you come with me, please?'

That's it, Sarah thought. The walk down to the small private room, and then the news. Whatever the news is. She would wait, and when they came back, Herb Smith would tell her what she needed to know. He was a kind man.

'Have you news of my son?' Vera asked in that same clear, strong, and nearly hysterical voice.

'Yes.' Dr. Strawns glanced at Sarah. 'Are you family, ma'am?'

'No,' Sarah said. 'A friend.'

'A close friend,' Herb said. A warm, strong hand closed above her elbow, just as another had closed around Vera's upper arm. He helped them both to their feet. 'We'll all go together, if you don't mind.'

'Not at all.'

He led them past the elevator bank and down a hall-

68

way to an office with CONFERENCE ROOM on the door. He let them in and turned on the overhead fluorescent lights. The room was furnished with a long table and a dozen office chairs.

Dr. Strawns closed the door, lit a cigarette, and dropped the burned match into one of the ashtrays that marched up and down the table. 'This is difficult,' he said, as if to himself.

'Then you had best just say it out,' Vera said.

'Yes, perhaps I'd better.'

It was not her place to ask, but Sarah could not help it. 'Is he dead? Please don't say he's dead . . .'

'He's in a coma.' Strawns sat down and dragged deeply on his cigarette. 'Mr. Smith has sustained serious head injuries and an undetermined amount of brain damage. You may have heard the phrase "subdural hematoma" on one or the other of the doctor shows. Mr. Smith has suffered a very grave subdural hematoma, which is localized cranial bleeding. A long operation was necessary to relieve the pressure, and also to remove bone-splinters from his brain.'

Herb sat down heavily, his face doughy and stunned. Sarah noticed his blunt, scarred hands and remembered Johnny telling her his father was a carpenter.

'But God has spared him,' Vera said. 'I knew he would. I prayed for a sign. Praise God, Most High! All ye here below praise His name!'

'Vera,' Herb said with no force.

'In a coma,' Sarah repeated. She tried to fit the information into some sort of emotional frame and found it wouldn't go. That Johnny wasn't dead, that he had come through a serious and dangerous operation on his brain – those things should have renewed her hope. But they didn't. She didn't like that word *coma*. It had a sinister, stealthy sound. Wasn't it Latin for 'sleep of death'?

'What's ahead for him?' Herb asked.

'No one can really answer that now,' Strawns said. He began to play with his cigarette, tapping it nervously over the ashtray. Sarah had the feeling he was answering

Herb's question literally while completely avoiding the question Herb had really asked. 'He's on life support equipment, of course.'

'But you must know something about his chances,' Sarah said. 'You must know . . .' She gestured helplessly with her hands and let them drop to her sides.

'He may come out of it in forty-eight hours. Or a week. A month. He may never come out of it. And . . . there is a strong possibility that he may die. I must tell you frankly that's the most likely. His injuries . . . grave.'

'God wants him to live,' Vera said. 'I know it.'

Herb had put his face into his hands and was scrubbing it slowly.

Dr. Strawns looked at Vera uncomfortably. 'I only want you to be prepared for . . . any eventuality.'

'Would you rate his chances for coming out of it?' Herb asked.

Dr. Strawns hesitated, puffed nervously on his cigarette. 'No, I can't do that,' he said finally.

5 ·

The three of them waited another hour and then left. It was dark. A cold and gusty wind had come up and it whistled across the big parking lot. Sarah's long hair streamed out behind her. Later, when she got home, she would find a crisp yellow oak leaf caught in it. Overhead, the moon rode the sky, a cold sailor of the night.

Sarah pressed a scrap of paper into Herb's hand. Written on it was her address and phone number. 'Would you call me if you hear something? Anything at all?'

'Yes, of course.' He bent suddenly and kissed her cheek, and Sarah held his shoulder for a moment in the blowing dark.

'I'm very sorry if I was stiff with you earlier, dear,' Vera said, and her voice was surprisingly gentle. 'I was upset.'

'Of course you were,' Sarah said.

'I thought my boy might die. But I've prayed. I've spoken to God about it. As the song says, "Are we weak and heavy-laden? Cumbered with a load of care? We

70

must never be discouraged. Take it to the Lord in prayer." '

'Vera, we ought to go along,' Herb said. 'We ought to get some sleep and see how things look in the . . .'

'But now I've heard from my God,' Vera said, looking dreamily up at the moon. 'Johnny isn't going to die. It isn't in God's plan for Johnny to die. I listened and I heard that still, small voice speaking in my heart, and I am comforted.'

Herb opened the car door. 'Come on, Vera.'

She looked back at Sarah and smiled. In that smile Sarah suddenly saw Johnny's own easy, devil-may-care grin – but at the same time she thought it was the most ghastly smile she had ever seen in her life.

'God has put his mark on my Johnny,' Vera said, 'and I rejoice.'

'Good night, Mrs. Smith,' Sarah said through numb lips.

'Good night, Sarah,' Herb said. He got in and started the car. It pulled out of its space and moved across the parking lot to State Street, and Sarah realized she hadn't asked where they were staying. She guessed they might not know themselves yet.

She turned to go to her own car and paused, struck by the river that ran behind the hospital, the Penobscot. It flowed like dark silk, and the reflected moon was caught in its center. She looked up into the sky, standing alone in the parking lot now. She looked at the moon.

God has put his mark on my Johnny and I rejoice.

The moon hung above her like a tawdry carnival toy, a Wheel of Fortune in the sky with the odds all slugged in favor of the house, not to mention the house numbers – zero and double zero. House numbah, house numbah, y'all pay the house, hey-hey-hey.

The wind blew rattling leaves around her legs. She went to her car and sat behind the wheel. She felt suddenly sure she was going to lose him. Terror and loneliness woke in her. She began to shiver. At last she started her car and drove home.

There was a great outpouring of comfort and good wishes from the Cleaves Mill student body in the following week; Herb Smith told her later that Johnny received better than three hundred cards. Almost all of them contained a hesitant personal note saying they hoped Johnny would be well soon. Vera answered each of them with a thank-you note and a Bible verse.

Sarah's discipline problem in her classes disappeared. Her previous feeling that some returning jury of class consciousness was bringing in an unfavorable verdict changed to just the opposite. Gradually she realized that the kids were viewing her as a tragic heroine, Mr. Smith's lost love. This idea struck her in the teacher's room during her free period on the Wednesday following the accident, and she went off into sudden gales of laughter that turned into a crying jag. Before she was able to get herself under control she had frightened herself badly. Her nights were made restless with incessant dreams of Johnny – Johnny in the Halloween Jekyll-and-Hyde mask, Johnny standing at the Wheel of Fortune concession while some disembodied voice chanted, 'Man, I *love* to watch this guy get a beatin,' over and over. Johnny saying, 'It's all right now, Sarah, everything's *fine*,' and then coming into the room with his head gone above the eyebrows.

Herb and Vera Smith spent the week in the Bangor House, and Sarah saw them every afternoon at the hospital, waiting patiently for something to happen. Nothing did. Johnny lay in a room on the intensive care ward on the sixth floor, surrounded by life-support equipment, breathing with the help of a machine. Dr. Strawns had grown less hopeful. On the Friday following the accident, Herb called Sarah on the phone and told her he and Vera were going home.

'She doesn't want to,' he said, 'but I've gotten her to see reason. I think.'

'Is she all right?' Sarah asked.

There was a long pause, long enough to make Sarah

think she had overstepped the bounds. Then Herb said, 'I don't know. Or maybe I do and I just don't want to say right out that she isn't. She's always had strong ideas about religion and they got a lot stronger after her operation. Her hysterectomy. Now they've gotten worse again. She's been talking a lot about the end of the world. She's connected Johnny's accident with the Rapture, somehow. Just before Armageddon, God is supposed to take all the faithful up to heaven in their actual bodies.'

Sarah thought of a bumper sticker she had seen somewhere: IF THE RAPTURE'S TODAY, SOMEBODY GRAB MY STEERING WHEEL! 'Yes, I know the idea,' she said.

'Well,' Herb said uncomfortably, 'some of the groups she . . . she corresponds with . . . they believe that God is going to come for the faithful in flying saucers. Take them all up to heaven in flying saucers, that is. These . . . sects . . . have proved, at least to themselves, that heaven is somewhere out in the constellation of Orion. No, don't ask me how they proved it. Vera could tell you. It's . . . well, Sarah, it's all a little hard on me.'

'Of course it must be.'

Herb's voice strengthened. 'But she can still distinguish between what's real and what's not. She needs time to adjust. So I told her she could face whatever's coming at home as easily as here. I've . . .' He paused, sounding embarrassed, then cleared his throat and went on. 'I've got to get back to work. I've got jobs. I've signed contracts . . .'

'Sure, of course.' She paused. 'What about insurance? I mean, this must be costing a Denver mint . . .' It was her turn to feel embarrassed.

'I've talked with Mr. Pelsen, your assistant principal there at Cleaves Mills,' Herb said. 'Johnny had the standard Blue Cross, but not that new Major Medical. The Blue Cross will cover some of it, though. And Vera and I have our savings.'

Sarah's heart sank. *Vera and I have our savings.* How long would one passbook stand up to expenses of two hundred dollars a day or more? And for what purpose in the end? So Johnny could hang on like an insensible animal, pissing brainlessly down a tube while he bankrupted his dad and mom? So his condition could drive his mother mad with unrealized hope? She felt the tears start to slip down her cheeks and for the first time – but not the last – she found herself wishing Johnny would die and be at peace. Part of her revolted in horror at the thought, but it remained.

'I wish you all the best,' Sarah said.

'I know that, Sarah. We wish you the best. Will you write?'

'I sure will.'

'And come see us when you can. Pownal's not so far away.' He hesitated. 'Looks to me like Johnny had picked himself out the right girl. It was pretty serious, wasn't it?'

'Yes,' Sarah said. The tears were still coming and the past tense was not lost on her. 'It was.'

'Good-bye, honey.'

'Good-bye, Herb.'

She hung up the phone, held the buttons down for a second or two, and then called the hospital and asked about Johnny. There had been no change. She thanked the intensive care nurse and walked aimlessly back and forth through the apartment. She thought about God sending out a fleet of flying saucers to pick up the faithful and buzz them off to Orion. It made as much sense as anything else about a God crazy enough to scramble John Smith's brains and put him in a coma that was probably never going to end – except in an unexpected death.

There was a folder of freshman compositions to correct. She made herself a cup of tea and sat down to them. If there was any one moment when Sarah Bracknell picked up the reins of her post-Johnny life again, that was it.

CHAPTER FOUR

1 .

The killer was slick.

He sat on a bench in the town park near the band-stand, smoking a Marlboro and humming a song from the Beatles' white album – 'you don't know how lucky you are, boy, back in the, back in the, back in the USSR . . .'

He wasn't a killer yet, not really. But it had been on his mind a long time, killing had. It had been itching at him and itching at him. Not in a bad way, no. He felt quite optimistic about it. The time was right. He didn't have to worry about getting caught. He didn't have to worry about the clothespin. Because he was slick.

A little snow began to drift down from the sky. It was November 12, 1970, and a hundred and sixty miles north-east of this middle-sized western Maine town, John Smith's sleep went on and on.

The killer scanned the park – the town common, the tourists who came to Castle Rock and the Lakes Region liked to call it. But there were no tourists now. The common that was so green in the summer was now yellow, balding, and dead. It waited for winter to cover it decently. The wire-mesh backstop behind the Little League home plate stood in rusty overlapping diamonds, framed against the white sky. The bandstand needed a fresh coat of paint.

It was a depressing scene, but the killer was not depressed. He was almost manic with joy. His toes wanted to tap, his fingers wanted to snap. There would be no shying away this time.

He crushed his smoke under one boot heel and lit another immediately. He glanced at his watch. 3 : 02 P.M. He sat and smoked. Two boys passed through the park, tossing a football back and forth, but they didn't see the killer because the benches were down in a dip. He supposed it was a place where the nasty-fuckers came at night when the weather was warmer. He knew all about the nasty-fuckers and the things they did. His mother had told him, and he had *seen* them.

Thinking about his mother made his smile fade a little. He remembered a time when he had been seven, she had come into his room without knocking – she never knocked – and had caught him playing with his thing. She had just about gone crazy. He had tried to tell her it was nothing. Nothing bad. It had just stood up. He hadn't done anything to make it stand up, it did it all on its own. And he just sat there, boinging it back and forth. It wasn't even that much fun. It was sort of boring. But his mother had just about gone crazy.

Do you want to be one of those nasty-fuckers? she had screamed at him. He didn't even know what that word meant – not nasty, he knew that one, but the other one – although he had heard some of the bigger kids use it in the play-yard at the Castle Rock Elementary School. *Do you want to be one of those nasty-fuckers and get one of those diseases? Do you want to have pus running out of it? Do you want it to turn black? Do you want it to rot off? Huh? Huh? Huh?*

She began to shake him back and forth then, and he began to blubber with fear, even then she was a big woman, a dominant and overbearing ocean liner of a woman, and he was not the killer then, he was not slick then, he was a little boy blubbering with fear, and his thing had collapsed and was trying to shrivel back into his body.

She had made him wear a clothespin on it for two hours, so he would know how those diseases felt.

The pain was excruciating.

The little snow flurry had passed. He brushed the image of his mother out of his mind, something he could do effortlessly when he was feeling good, something he couldn't do at all when he was feeling depressed and low.

His thing was standing up now.

He glanced at his watch. 3:07. He dropped his cigarette half-smoked. Someone was coming.

He recognized her. It was Alma, Alma Frechette from the Coffee Pot across the street. Just coming off-shift. He knew Alma; he had dated her up once or twice, shown her a good time. Took her to Serenity Hill over in Naples. She was a good dancer. Nasty-fuckers often were. He was glad it was Alma coming.

She was by herself.

Back in the US, back in the US, back in the USSR –

'Alma!' he called, and waved. She started a little, looked around, and saw him. She smiled and walked over to the bench where he sat, saying hello and calling him by name. He stood up, smiling. He wasn't worried about anyone coming. He was untouchable. He was Superman.

'Why you wearing that?' she asked, looking at him.

'Slick, isn't it?' he said, smiling.

'Well, I wouldn't exactly ...'

'You want to see something?' he asked. 'On the bandstand. It's the goddamnest thing.'

'What is it?'

'Come and look.'

'All right.'

As simple as that. She went with him to the bandstand. If anyone had been coming, he still could have called it off. But no one came. No one passed. They had the common to themselves. The white sky brooded over them. Alma was a small girl with light blonde hair. Dyed blonde hair, he was quite sure. Sluts dyed their hair.

He led her up onto the enclosed bandstand. Their feet made hollow, dead echoes on the boards. An overturned music stand lay in one corner. There was an empty Four Roses bottle. This was a place where the nasty-fuckers came, all right.

'What?' she asked, sounding a little puzzled now. A little nervous.

77

The killer smiled joyously and pointed to the left of the music stand. 'There. See?'

She followed his finger. A used condom lay on the boards like a shriveled snakeskin.

Alma's face went tight and she turned to go so quickly that she almost got by the killer. 'That's not very funny...'

He grabbed her and threw her back. 'Where do you think you're going?'

Her eyes were suddenly watchful and frightened. 'Let me out of here. Or you'll be sorry. I don't have any time for sick jokes...'

'It's no joke,' he said. 'It's no joke, you nasty-fucker.' He was light-headed with the joy of naming her, naming her for what she was. The world whirled.

Alma broke left, heading for the low railing that surrounded the bandstand, meaning to leap over it. The killer caught the back of her cheap cloth coat at the collar and yanked her back again. The cloth ripped with a low purring sound and she opened her mouth to scream.

He slammed his hand over her mouth, mashing her lips back against her teeth. He felt warm blood trickle over his palm. Her other hand was beating at him now, clawing for purchase, but there was no purchase. There was none because he ... he was ...

Slick!

He threw her to the board floor. His hand came off her mouth, which was now smeared with blood, and she opened her mouth to scream again, but he landed on top of her, panting, grinning, and the air was driven out of her lungs in a soundless whoosh. She could feel him now, rock hard, gigantic and throbbing, and she quit trying to scream and went on struggling. Her fingers caught and slipped, caught and slipped. He forced her legs rudely apart and lay between them. One of her hands glanced off the bridge of his nose, making his eyes water.

'You nasty-fucker,' he whispered, and his hands closed on her throat. He began to throttle her, yanking her head up from the bandstand's board flooring and then

78

slamming it back down. Her eyes bulged. Her face went
pink, then red, then a congested purple. Her struggles
began to weaken.

'Nasty-fucker, nasty-fucker, nasty-fucker,' the killer
panted hoarsely. He really was the killer now, Alma
Frechette's days of rubbing her body all over people at
Serenity Hill were done now. Her eyes bugged out like
the eyes of some of those crazy dolls they sold along carnival midways. The killer panted hoarsely. Her hands
lay limp on the boards now. His fingers had almost disappeared from sight.

He let go of her throat, ready to grab her again if she
stirred. But she didn't. After a moment he ripped her
coat open with shaking hands and shoved the skirt of
her pink waitress uniform up.

The white sky looked down. The Castle Rock town
common was deserted. In fact, no one found the strangled,
violated corpse of Alma Frechette until the next day.
The sheriff's theory was that a drifter had done it. There
were statewide newspaper headlines, and in Castle Rock
there was general agreement with the sheriff's idea.

Surely no hometown boy could have done such a dreadful thing.

CHAPTER FIVE

1 ·

Herb and Vera Smith went back to Pownal and took up
the embroidery of their days. Herb finished a house in
Durham that December. Their savings did indeed melt
away, as Sarah had foreseen, and they applied to the
state for Extraordinary Disaster Assistance. That aged
Herb almost as much as the accident itself had done.
EDA was only a fancy way of saying 'welfare' or 'charity'
in his mind. He had spent a lifetime working hard and
honestly with his hands and had thought he would never

see the day when he would have to take a state dollar. But here that day was.

Vera subscribed to three new magazines which came through the mail at irregular intervals. All three were badly printed and might have been illustrated by talented children. *God's Saucers*, *The Coming Transfiguration*, and *God's Psychic Miracles*. *The Upper Room*, which still came monthly, now sometimes lay unopened for as long as three weeks at a stretch, but she read these others to tatters. She found a great many things in them that seemed to bear upon Johnny's accident, and she read these nuggets to her tired husband at supper in a high, piercing voice that trembled with exaltation. Herb found himself telling her more and more frequently to be quiet, and on occasion shouting at her to shut up that drivel and let him alone. When he did that, she would give him long-suffering, compassionate, and hurt glances – then slink upstairs to continue her studies. She began to correspond with these magazines, and to exchange letters with the contributors and with other pen-friends who had had similar experiences in their lives.

Most of her correspondents were good-hearted people like Vera herself, people who wanted to help and to ease the nearly insupportable burden of her pain. They sent prayers and prayer stones, they sent charms, they sent promises to include Johnny in their nightly devotions. Yet there were others who were nothing but con-men and women, and Herb was alarmed by his wife's increasing inability to recognize these. There was an offer to send her a sliver of the One True Cross of Our Lord for just $99.98. An offer to send a vial of water drawn from the spring at Lourdes, which would almost certainly work a miracle when rubbed into Johnny's forehead. That one was $110 plus postage. Cheaper (and more attractive to Vera) was a continuously playing cassette tape of the Twenty-third Psalm and the Lord's Prayer as spoken by southern evangelist Billy Humbarr. Played at Johnny's bedside over a period of weeks it would almost certainly effect a marvelous recovery, according to the pamphlet.

80

As an added blessing (For A Short Time Only) an auto-graphed picture of Billy Humbarr himself would be included.

Herb was forced to step in more and more frequently as her passion for these pseudoreligious geegaws grew. Sometimes he surreptitiously tore up her checks and simply readjusted the checkbook balance upward. But when the offer specified cash and nothing but, he simply had to put his foot down – and Vera began to draw away from him, to view him with distrust as a sinner and an unbeliever.

2 ·

Sarah Bracknell kept school during her days. Her after-noons and evenings were not much different than they had been following the breakup with Dan; she was in a kind of limbo, waiting for something to happen. In Paris, the peace talks were stalled. Nixon had ordered the bomb-ing of Hanoi continued in spite of rising domestic and foreign protests. At a press conference he produced pic-tures proving conclusively that American planes were surely not bombing North Vietnamese hospitals, but he went everywhere by Army helicopter. The investigation into the brutal rape-murder of a Castle Rock waitress was stalled following the release of a wandering sign painter who had once spent three years in the Augusta State Mental Hospital – against everyone's expectations, the sign painter's alibi had turned out to hold water. Janis Joplin was screaming the blues. Paris decreed (for the second year in a row) that hemlines would go down, but they didn't. Sarah was aware of all these things in a vague way, like voices from another room where some in-comprehensible party went on and on.

The first snow fell – just a dusting – then a second dusting, and ten days before Christmas there was a storm that closed area schools for the day and she sat home, looking out at the snow as it filled Flagg Street. Her brief thing with Johnny – she could not even properly call it an affair – was part of another season now, and she could

81

feel him beginning to slip away from her. It was a panicky feeling, as if a part of her was drowning. Drowning in days.

She read a good deal about head injuries, comas, and brain damage. None of it was very encouraging. She found out there was a girl in a small Maryland town who had been in a coma for six years; there had been a young man from Liverpool, England, who had been struck by a grappling hook while working on the docks and had remained in a coma for fourteen years before expiring. Little by little this brawny young dock-walloper had severed his connections with the world, wasting away, losing his hair, optic nerves degenerating into oatmeal behind his closed eyes, body gradually drawing up into a fetal position as his ligaments shortened. He had reversed time, had become a fetus again, swimming in the placental waters of coma as his brain degenerated. An autopsy following his death had shown that the folds and convolutions of his cerebrum had smoothed out, leaving the frontal and prefrontal lobes almost utterly smooth and blank.

Oh, Johnny, it just isn't fair, she thought, watching the snow fall outside, filling the world up with blank whiteness, burying fallen summer and red-gold autumn. *It isn't fair, they should let you go to whatever there is to go to.*

There was a letter from Herb Smith every ten days to two weeks – Vera had her pen-friends, and he had his. He wrote in a large, sprawling hand, using an old-fashioned fountain pen. 'We are both fine and well. Waiting to see what will happen next as you must be. Yes, I have been doing some reading and I know what you are too kind and thoughtful to say in your letter, Sarah. It looks bad. But of course we hope. I don't believe in God the way Vera does, but I do believe in him after my fashion, and wonder why he didn't take John outright if he was going to. Is there a reason? No one knows, I guess. We only hope.'

In another letter:

'I'm having to do most of the Xmas shopping this year as Vera has decided Xmas presents are a sinful custom. This is what I mean about her getting worse all the time. She's always thought it was a holy day instead of a holiday – if you see what I mean – and if she saw me calling it Xmas instead of Christmas I guess she'd "shoot me for a hoss-thief." She was always saying how we should remember it is the birthday of Jesus Christ and not Santa Claus, but she never minded the shopping before. In fact, she used to like it. Now ragging against it is all she talks about, seems like. She gets a lot of these funny ideas from the people she writes back and forth to. Golly I do wish she'd stop and get back to normal. But otherwise we are both fine and well. *Herb*.'

And a Christmas card that she had wept over a little: 'Best to you from both of us this holiday season, and if you'd like to come down and spend Xmas with a couple of "old fogies", the spare bedroom is made up. Vera and I are both fine and well. Hope the New Year is better for all of us, and am sure it will be. *Herb* and *Vera*.'

She didn't go down to Pownal over the Christmas vacation, partly because of Vera's continued withdrawal into her own world – her progress into that world could be read pretty accurately between the lines of Herb's letters – and partly because their mutual tie now seemed so strange and distant to her. The still figure in the Bangor hospital bed had once been seen in close-up, but now she always seemed to be looking at him through the wrong end of memory's telescope; like the balloon man, he was far and wee. So it seemed best to keep her distance.

Perhaps Herb sensed it as well. His letters became less frequent as 1970 became 1971. In one of them he came as close as he could to saying it was time for her to go on with her life, and closed by saying that he doubted a girl as pretty as she was lacked for dates.

But she hadn't had any dates, hadn't wanted them. Gene Sedecki, the math teacher who had once treated her to an evening that had seemed at least a thousand years long, had begun asking her out indecently soon after Johnny's accident, and he was a hard man to discourage, but she believed that he was finally beginning to get the point. It should have happened sooner.

Occasionally other men would ask her, and one of them, a law student named Walter Hazlett, attracted her quite a bit. She met him at Anne Strafford's New Year's Eve party. She had meant only to make an appearance, but she had stayed quite a while, talking primarily to Hazlett. Saying no had been surprisingly hard, but she had, because she understood the source of attraction too well – Walt Hazlett was a tall man with an unruly shock of brown hair and a slanted, half-cynical smile, and he reminded her strongly of Johnny. That was no basis on which to get interested in a man.

Early in February she was asked out by the mechanic who worked on her car at the Cleaves Mills Chevron. Again she almost said yes, and then backed away. The man's name was Arnie Tremont. He was tall, olive-skinned, and handsome in a smiling, predatory way. He reminded her a bit of James Brolin, the second banana on that Dr. Welby program, and even more of a certain Delta Tau Delta named Dan.

Better to wait. Wait and see if something was going to happen.

But nothing did.

3 ·

In that summer of 1971, Greg Stillson, sixteen years older and wiser than the Bible salesman who had kicked a dog to death in a deserted Iowa dooryard, sat in the back room of his newly incorporated insurance and real estate business in Ridgeway, New Hampshire. He hadn't aged much in the years between. There was a net of wrinkles around his eyes now, and his hair was longer (but still quite conservative). He was still a big man, and his swivel chair creaked when he moved.

He sat smoking a Pall Mall cigarette and looking at

84

the man sprawled comfortably in the chair opposite. Greg was looking at this man the way a zoologist might look at an interesting new specimen.

'See anything green?' Sonny Elliman asked.

Elliman topped six feet, five inches. He wore an ancient, grease-stiffened jeans jacket with the arms and buttons cut off. There was no shirt beneath. A Nazi iron cross, black dressed in white chrome, hung on his bare chest. The buckle of the belt running just below his considerable beer-belly was a great ivory skull. From beneath the pegged cuffs of his jeans poked the scuffed, square toes of a pair of Desert Driver boots. His hair was shoulder-length, tangled, and shining with an accumulation of greasy sweat and engine oil. From one earlobe there dangled a swastika earring, also black dressed in white chrome. He spun a coal-scuttle helmet on the tip of one blunt finger. Stitched on the back of his jacket was a leering red devil with a forked tongue. Above the devil was *The Devil's Dozen*. Below it: *Sonny Elliman, Prez.*

'No,' Greg Stillson said. 'I don't see anything green, but I do see someone who looks suspiciously like a walking asshole.'

Elliman stiffened a little, then relaxed and laughed. In spite of the dirt, the almost palpable body odor, and Nazi regalia, his eyes, a dark green, were not without intelligence and even a sense of humor.

'Rank me to the dogs and back, man,' he said. 'It's been done before. You got the power now.'

'You recognize that, do you?'

'Sure. I left my guys back in the Hamptons, came here alone. Be it on my own head, man.' He smiled. 'But if we should ever catch you in a similar position, you want to hope your kidneys are wearing combat boots.'

'I'll chance it,' Greg said. He measured Elliman. They were both big men. He reckoned Elliman had forty pounds on him, but a lot of it was beer muscle. 'I could take you, Sonny.'

Elliman's face crinkled in amiable good humor again. 'Maybe. Maybe not. But that's not the way we play it,

85

man. All that good American John Wayne stuff.' He leaned forward, as if to impart a great secret. 'Me personally, now, whenever I get me a piece of mom's apple pie, I make it my business to shit on it.'

'Foul mouth, Sonny,' Greg said mildly.

'What do you want with me?' Sonny asked. 'Why don't you get down to it? You'll miss your Jaycee's meeting.'

'No,' Greg said, still serene. 'The Jaycees meet Tuesday nights. We've got all the time in the world.'

Elliman made a disgusted blowing sound.

'Now what I thought,' Greg went on, 'is that *you'd* want something from *me*.' He opened his desk drawer and from it took three plastic Baggies of marijuana. Mixed in with the weed were a number of gel capsules. 'Found this in your sleeping bag,' Greg said. 'Nasty, nasty, nasty, Sonny. Bad boy. Do not pass go, do not collect two hundred dollars. Go directly to New Hampshire State Prison.'

'You didn't have any search warrant,' Elliman said. 'Even a kiddy lawyer could get me off, and you know it.'

'I don't know any such thing,' Greg Stillson said. He leaned back in his swivel chair and cocked his loafers, bought across the state line at L.L. Bean's in Maine, up on his desk. 'I'm a big man in this town, Sonny. I came into New Hampshire more or less on my uppers a few years back, and now I've got a nice operation here. I've helped the town council solve a couple of problems, including just what to do about all these kids the chief of police catches doing dope . . . oh, I don't mean bad-hats like you, Sonny, drifters like you we know what to do with when we catch them with a little treasure trove like that one right there on my desk . . . I mean the nice local kids. Nobody really wants to do anything to them at all, you know? I figured that out for them. Put them to work on community projects instead of sending them to jail, I said. It worked out real good. Now we've got the biggest head in the tri-town area coaching Little League and doing a real good job at it.'

Elliman was looking bored. Greg suddenly brought

his feet down with a crash, grabbed a vase with a UNH logo on the side, and threw it past Sonny Elliman's nose. It missed him by less than an inch, flew end over end across the room, and shattered against the file cabinets in the corner. For the first time Elliman looked startled. And for just a moment the face of this older, wiser Greg Stillson was the face of the younger man, the dog-bludgeoner.

'You want to listen when I talk,' he said softly. 'Because what we're discussing here is your career over the next ten years or so. Now if you don't have any interest in making a career out of stamping LIVE FREE OR DIE on license plates, you want to listen up, Sonny. You want to pretend this is the first day of school again, Sonny. You want to get it all right the first time. *Sonny.*'

Elliman looked at the smashed fragments of vase, then back at Stillson. His former uneasy calm was being replaced by a feeling of real interest. He hadn't been really interested in anything for quite a while now. He had made the run for beer because he was bored. He had come by himself because he was bored. And when this big guy had pulled him over, using a flashing blue light on the dashboard of his station wagon, Sonny Elliman had assumed that what he had to deal with was just another small-town Deputy Dawg, protecting his territory and rousting the big bad biker on the modified Harley-Davidson. But this guy was something else. He was ... was ...

He's crazy! Sonny realized, with dawning delight at the discovery. *He's got two public service awards on his wall, and pictures of him talking to the Rotarians and the Lions, and he's vice president of this dipshit town's Jaycees, and next year he'll be president, and he's just as crazy as a fucking bedbug!*

'Okay,' he said. 'You got my attention.'

'I have had what you might call a checkered career,' Greg told him. 'I've been up, but I've also been down. I've had a few scrapes with the law. What I'm trying to say, Sonny, is that I don't have any set feelings about you. Not like the other locals. They read in the *Union-Leader* about what you and your bikie friends are doing over in the Hamptons this summer and they'd like to castrate you with a rusty Gillette razor blade.'

'That's not the Devil's Dozen,' Sonny said. 'We came down on a run from upstate New York to get some beach-time, man. We're on vacation. We're not into trashing a bunch of honky-tonk bars. There's a bunch of Hell's Angels tearing ass, and a chapter of the Black Riders from New Jersey, but you know who it is mostly? A bunch of college kids.' Sonny's lip curled. 'But the papers don't like to report that, do they? They'd rather lay the rap on us than on Susie and Jim.'

'You're so much more colorful,' Greg said mildly. 'And William Loeb over at the *Union-Leader* doesn't like bike clubs.'

'That bald-headed creep,' Sonny muttered.

Greg opened his desk drawer and pulled out a flat pint of Leader's bourbon. 'I'll drink to that,' he said. He cracked the seal and drank half the pint at a draught. He blew out a great breath, his eyes watering, and held the pint across the desk. 'You?'

Sonny polished the pint off. Warm fire bellowed up from his stomach to his throat.

'Light me up, man,' he gasped.

Greg threw back his head and laughed. 'We'll get along, Sonny. I have a feeling we'll get along.'

'What do you want?' Sonny asked again, holding the empty pint.

'Nothing . . . not now. But I have a feeling . . .' Greg's eyes became far away, almost puzzled. 'I told you I'm a big man in Ridgeway. I'm going to run for mayor next time the office comes up, and I'll win. But that's . . .'

'Just the beginning?' Sonny prompted.

'It's a start, anyway.' That puzzled expression was still there. 'I get things done. People know it. I'm good at what I do. I feel like . . . there's a lot ahead of me. Sky's the limit. But I'm not . . . quite sure . . . what I mean. You know?'

Sonny only shrugged.

The puzzled expression faded. 'But there's a story, Sonny. A story about a mouse who took a thorn out of a lion's paw. He did it to repay the lion for not eating him a few years before. You know that story?'

'I might have heard it when I was a kid.'

Greg nodded. 'Well, it's a few years before . . . whatever it is, Sonny.' He shoved the plastic Baggies across the desk. 'I'm not going to eat you. I could if I wanted to, you know. A kiddie lawyer couldn't get you off. In this town, with the riots going on in Hampton less than twenty miles away, Clarence Fucking Darrow couldn't get you off in Ridgeway. These good people would love to see you go up.'

Elliman didn't reply, but he suspected Greg was right. There was nothing heavy in his dope stash – two Brown Bombers was the heaviest – but the collective parents of good old Susie and Jim would be glad to see him breaking rocks in Portsmouth, with his hair cut off his head.

'I'm not going to eat you,' Greg repeated. 'I hope you'll remember that in a few years if I get a thorn in my paw . . . or maybe if I have a job opportunity for you. Keep it in mind?'

Gratitude was not in Sonny Elliman's limited catalogue of human feelings, but interest and curiosity were. He felt both ways about this man Stillson. That craziness in his eyes hinted at many things, but boredom was not one of them.

'Who knows where we'll all be in a few years?' he murmured. 'We could all be dead, man.'

'Just keep me in mind. That's all I'm asking.'

Sonny looked at the broken shards of vase. 'I'll keep you in mind,' he said.

4 ·

1971 passed. The New Hampshire beach riots blew over, and the grumblings of the beachfront entrepreneurs were muted by the increased balances in their bankbooks. An obscure fellow named George McGovern declared for the presidency comically early. Anyone who followed politics knew that the nominee from the Democratic party in 1972 was going to be Edmund Muskie, and there were those who felt he might just wrestle the Troll of San Clemente off his feet and pin him to the mat.

In early June, just before school let out for the summer, Sarah met the young law student again. She was in Day's appliance store, shopping for a toaster, and he had been looking for a gift for his parents' wedding anniversary. He asked her if she'd like to go to the movies with him – the new Clint Eastwood, *Dirty Harry*, was in town. Sarah went. And the two of them had a good time. Walter Hazlett had grown a beard, and he no longer reminded her so much of Johnny. In fact, it had become increasingly difficult for her to remember just what Johnny did look like. His face only came clear in her dreams, dreams where he stood in front of the Wheel of Fortune, watching it spin, his face cold and his blue eyes darkened to that perplexing, and a little fearsome, dark violet shade, watching the Wheel as if it were his own private game preserve.

She and Walt began to see a lot of each other. He was easy to get along with. He made no demands – or, if he did, they were of such a gradually increasing nature as to be unnoticeable. In October he asked her if he could buy her a small diamond. Sarah asked him if she could have the weekend to think it over. That Saturday night she had gone to the Eastern Maine Medical Center, had gotten a special red-bordered pass at the desk, and had gone up to intensive care. She sat beside Johnny's bed for an hour. Outside, the fall wind howled in the dark, promising cold, promising snow, promising a season of death. It lacked sixteen days of a year since the fair, the Wheel, and the head-on collision near the Bog.

She sat and listened to the wind and looked at Johnny. The bandages were gone. The scar began on his forehead an inch above his right eyebrow and twisted up under the hairline. His hair there had gone white, making her think of that fictional detective in the 87th Precinct stories – Cotton Hawes, his name was. To Sarah's eyes there seemed to have been no degeneration in him, except for the inevitable weight loss. He was simply a young man she barely knew, fast asleep.

She bent over him and kissed his mouth softly, as if the old fairy tale could be reversed and her kiss could wake him. But Johnny only slept.

She left, went back to her apartment in Veazie, lay down on her bed and cried as the wind walked the dark world outside, throwing its catch of yellow and red leaves before it. On Monday she told Walt that if he really did want to buy her a diamond – a small one, mind – she would be happy and proud to wear it.

That was Sarah Bracknell's 1971.

In early 1972, Edmund Muskie burst into tears during an impassioned speech outside the offices of the man Sonny Elliman had referred to as 'that bald-headed creep'. George McGovern upset the primary, and Loeb announced gleefully in his paper that the people of New Hampshire didn't like crybabies. In July, McGovern was nominated. In that same month Sarah Bracknell became Sarah Hazlett. She and Walt were married in the First Methodist Church of Bangor.

Less than two miles away, Johnny Smith slept on. And the thought of him came to Sarah, suddenly and horribly, as Walt kissed her in front of the dearly beloved there assembled for the nuptials – *Johnny*, she thought, and saw him as she had when the lights went on, half Jekyll and half snarling Hyde. She stiffened in Walt's arms for a moment, and then it was gone. Memory, vision, whatever it had been, it was gone.

After long thought and discussion with Walt, she had invited Johnny's folks to the wedding. Herb had come alone. At the reception, she asked him if Vera was all right.

He glanced around, saw they were alone for the moment, and rapidly downed the remainder of his Scotch and soda. He had aged five years in the last eighteen months, she thought. His hair was thinning. The lines on his face were deeper. He was wearing glasses in the careful and self-conscious way of people who have just started wearing them, and behind the mild corrective lenses his eyes were wary and hurt.

'No . . . she really isn't, Sarah. The truth is, she's up in Vermont. On a farm. Waiting for the end of the world.'

'*What?*'

Herb told her that six months ago Vera had begun to correspond with a group of about ten people who called themselves The American Society of the Last Times. They were led by Mr. and Mrs. Harry L. Stonkers from Racine, Wisconsin. Mr. and Mrs. Stonkers claimed to have been picked up by a flying saucer while they were on a camping trip. They had been taken away to heaven, which was not out in the constellation Orion but on an earth-type planet that circled Arcturus. There they had communed with the society of angels and had seen Paradise. The Stonkerses had been informed that the Last Times were at hand. They were given the power of telepathy and had been sent back to Earth to gather a few fruitful together – for the first shuttle to heaven, as it were. And so the ten of them had gotten together, bought a farm north of St. Johnsbury, and had been settled in there for about seven weeks, waiting for the saucer to come and pick them up.

'It sounds . . .' Sarah began, and then closed her mouth.

'I know how it sounds,' Herb said. 'It sounds crazy. The place cost them nine thousand dollars. It's nothing but a crashed-in farmhouse with two acres of scrubland. Vera's share was seven hundred dollars – all she could put up. There was no way I could stop her . . . short of committal.' He paused, then smiled. 'But this is nothing to talk about at your wedding party, Sarah. You and your fellow are going to have all the best. I know you will.'

Sarah smiled back as best she could. 'Thank you, Herb. Will you . . . I mean, do you think she'll . . .'

'Come back? Oh yes. If the world doesn't end by winter, I think she'll be back.'

'Oh, I only wish you the best,' she said, and embraced him.

5 ·

The farm in Vermont had no furnace, and when the saucer had still not arrived by late October, Vera came home. The saucer had not come, she said, because they were not yet perfect – they had not burned away the non-essential and sinful dross of their lives. But she was up-lifted and spiritually exalted. She had had a sign in a dream. She was perhaps not meant to go to heaven in a saucer. She felt more and more strongly that she would be needed to guide her boy, show him the proper way, when he came out of his trance.

Herb took her in, loved her as best he could – and life went on. Johnny had been in his coma for two years.

6 ·

Nixon was reinaugurated. The American boys started coming home from Vietnam. Walter Hazlett took his bar exam and was invited to take it again at a later date. Sarah Hazlett kept school while he crammed for his tests. The students who had been silly, gawky freshmen the year she started teaching were now juniors. Flat-chested girls had become bosomy. Shrimps who hadn't been able to find their way around the building were now playing varsity basketball.

The second Arab-Israeli war came and went. The oil boycott came and went. Bruisingly high gasoline prices came and did not go. Vera Smith became convinced that Christ would return from below the earth at the South Pole. This intelligence was based on a new pamphlet (seventeen pages, price $4.50) entitled *God's Tropical Underground*. The startling hypothesis of the pamphleteer was that heaven was actually below our very feet, and that the easiest point of ingress was the South Pole. One of the sections of the pamphlet was 'Psychic Experiences of the South Pole Explorers'.

Herb pointed out to her that less than a year before she had been convinced that heaven was somewhere Out There, most probably circling Arcturus. 'I'd surely be more apt to believe that than this crazy South Pole stuff,' he told her. 'After all, the Bible says heaven's in the sky. That tropical place below the ground is supposed to be..'.

'Stop it!' she said sharply, lips pressed into thin white lines. 'No need to mock what you don't understand.'

'I wasn't mocking, Vera,' he said quietly.

'God knows why the unbeliever mocks and the heathen rages,' she said. That blank light was in her eyes. They were sitting at the kitchen table, Herb with an old plumbing J-bolt in front of him, Vera with a stack of old *National Geographics* which she had been gleaning for South Pole pictures and stories. Outside, restless clouds fled west to east and the leaves showered off the trees. It was early October again, and October always seemed to be her worst month. It was the month when that blank light came more frequently to her eyes and stayed longer. And it was always in October that his thoughts turned treacherously to leaving them both. His possibly certifiable wife and his sleeping son, who was probably already dead by any practical definition. Just now he had been turning the J-bolt over in his hands and looking out the window at that restless sky and thinking, *I could pack up. Just throw my things into the back of the pickup and go. Florida, maybe. Nebraska. California. A good carpenter can make good money any damn place. Just get up and go.*

But he knew he wouldn't. It was just that October was his month to think about running away, as it seemed to be Vera's month to discover some new pipeline to Jesus and the eventual salvation of the only child she had been able to nurture in her substandard womb.

Now he reached across the table and took her hand, which was thin and terribly bony – an old woman's hand. She looked up, surprised. 'I love you very much, Vera,' he said.

She smiled back, and for a glimmering moment she was a great deal like the girl he had courted and won, the girl who had goosed him with a hairbrush on their wedding night. It was a gentle smile, her eyes briefly clear

94

and warm and loving in return. Outside, the sun came out again, sending great shutter-shadows fleeing across their back field.

'I know you do, Herbert. And I love you.'

He put his other hand over hers and clasped it.

'Vera,' he said.

'Yes?' Her eyes were so clear ... suddenly she was with him, totally *with* him, and it made him realize how dreadfully far apart they had grown over the last three years.

'Vera, if he never does wake up ... God forbid, but if he doesn't ... we'll still have each other, won't we? I mean ...'

She jerked her hand away. His two hands, which had been holding it lightly, clapped on nothing.

'Don't you *ever* say that. Don't you *ever* say that Johnny isn't going to wake up.'

'All I meant was that we ...'

'Of course he's going to wake up,' she said, looking out the window to the field, where the shadows still crossed and crossed. 'It's God's plan for him. Oh yes. Don't you think I know? I *know*, believe me. God has great things in store for my Johnny. I have heard him in my heart.'

'Yes, Vera,' he said. 'Okay.'

Her fingers groped for the *National Geographics*, found them, and began to turn the pages again.

'I *know*,' she said in a childish, petulant voice.

'Okay,' he said quietly.

She looked at her magazines. Herb propped his chin in his palms and looked out at the sunshine and shadow and thought how soon winter came after golden, treacherous October. He wished Johnny would die. He had loved the boy from the very first. He had seen the wonder on his tiny face when Herb had brought a tiny tree frog to the boy's carriage and had put the small living thing in the boy's hands. He had taught Johnny how to fish and skate and shoot. He had sat up with him all night during his terrible bout with the flu in 1951, when the boy's temperature had crested at a giddy one hundred and five degrees. He had hidden tears in his hand when Johnny

95

graduated salutatorian of his high school class and had made his speech from memory without a slip. So many memories of him – teaching him to drive, standing on the bow of the *Bolero* with him when they went to Nova Scotia on vacation one year, Johnny eight years old, laughing and excited by the screwlike motion of the boat, helping him with his homework, helping him with his treehouse, helping him get the hang of his Silva compass when he had been in the Scouts. All the memories were jumbled together in no chronological order at all – Johnny was the single unifying thread, Johnny eagerly discovering the world that had maimed him so badly in the end. And now he wished Johnny would die, oh how he wished it, that he would die, that his heart would stop beating, that the final low traces on the EEG would go flat, that he would just flicker out like a guttering candle in a pool of wax: that he would die and release them.

7 ·

The seller of lightning rods arrived at Cathy's Roadhouse in Somersworth, New Hampshire, in the early afternoon of a blazing summer's day less than a week after the Fourth of July in that year of 1973; and somewhere not so far away there were, perhaps, storms only waiting to be born in the warm elevator shafts of summer's thermal updrafts.

He was a man with a big thirst, and he stopped at Cathy's to slake it with a couple of beers, not to make a sale. But from force of long habit, he glanced up at the roof of the low, ranch-style building, and the unbroken line he saw standing against the blistering gunmetal sky caused him to reach back in for the scuffed suede bag that was his sample case.

Inside, Cathy's was dark and cool and silent except for the muted rumble of the color TV on the wall. A few regulars were there, and behind the bar was the owner, keeping an eye on 'As The World Turns' along with his patrons.

The seller of lightning rods lowered himself onto a bar

stool and put his sample case on the stool to his left. The owner came over. 'Hi, friend. What'll it be?'

'A Bud,' the lightning rod salesman said. 'And draw another for yourself, if you're of a mind.'

'I'm always of a mind,' the owner said. He returned with two beers, took the salesman's dollar, and left three dimes on the bar. 'Bruce Carrick,' he said, and offered his hand.

The seller of lightning rods shook it. 'Dohay is the name,' he said, 'Andrew Dohay.' He drained off half his beer.

'Pleased to meet you,' Carrick said. He wandered off to serve a young woman with a hard face another Tequila Sunrise and eventually wandered back to Dohay. 'From out of town?'

'I am,' Dohay admitted. 'Salesman.' He glanced around. 'Is it always this quiet?'

'No. It jumps on the weekends and I do a fair trade through the week. Private parties is where we make our dough – if we make it. I ain't starving, but neither am I driving a Cadillac.' He pointed a pistol finger at Dohay's glass. 'Freshen that?'

'And another for yourself, Mr. Carrick.'

'Bruce.' He laughed. 'You must want to sell me something.'

When Carrick returned with the beers the seller of lightning rods said: 'I came in to lay the dust, not to sell anything. But now that you mention it ...' He hauled his sample case up onto the bar with a practiced jerk. Things jingled inside it.

'Oh, here it comes,' Carrick said, and laughed.

Two of the afternoon regulars, an old fellow with a wart on his right eyelid and a younger man in gray fatigues, wandered over to see what Dohay was selling. The hard-faced woman went on watching 'As The World Turns'.

Dohay took out three rods, a long one with a brass ball at the tip, a shorter one, and one with porcelain conductors.

'What the hell . . .' Carrick said.

'Lightning rods,' the old campaigner said, and cackled. 'He wants to save this ginmill from God's wrath, Brucie. You better listen to what he says.'

He laughed again, the man in the gray fatigues joined him, Carrick's face darkened, and the lightning rod salesman knew that whatever chance he had had of making a sale had just flown away. He was a good salesman, good enough to recognize that this queer combination of personalities and circumstances sometimes got together and queered any chance of a deal even before he had a chance to swing into his pitch. He took it philosophically and went into his spiel anyway, mostly from force of habit:

'As I was getting out of my car, I just happened to notice that this fine establishment wasn't equipped with lightning conductors – and that it's constructed of wood. Now for a very small price – and easy credit terms if you should want them – I can guarantee that . . .'

'That lightning'll strike this place at four this afternoon,' the man in the gray fatigues said with a grin. The old campaigner cackled.

'Mister, no offense,' Carrick said, 'but you see that?' He pointed to a golden nail on a small wooden plaque beside the TV near the glistening array of bottles. Spiked on the nail was a drift of papers. 'All of those things are bills. They got to be paid by the fifteenth of the month. They get written in red ink. Now you see how many people are in here drinking right now? I got to be careful. I got to . . .'

'Just my point,' Dohay broke in smoothly. 'You have to be careful. And the purchase of three or four lightning rods is a careful purchase. You've got a going concern here. You wouldn't want it wiped out by one stroke of lightning on a summer's day, would you?'

'He wouldn't mind,' the old campaigner said. 'He'd just collect the insurance and go down to Florida. Woon'tchoo, Brucie?'

Carrick looked at the old man with distaste.

98

'Well, then, let's talk about insurance,' the lightning rod salesman interposed. The man in the gray fatigues had lost interest and had wandered away. 'Your fire insurance premiums will go down . . .'

'The insurance is all lumped together,' Carrick said flatly. 'Look, I just can't afford the outlay. Sorry. Now if you was to talk to me again next year . . .'

'Well, perhaps I will,' the lightning rod salesman said, giving up. 'Perhaps I will.' No one thought they could be struck by lightning until they were struck; it was a constant fact of this business. You couldn't make a fellow like this Carrick see that it was the cheapest form of fire insurance he could buy. But Dohay was a philosopher. After all, he had told the truth when he said he came in to lay the dust.

To prove it, and to prove there were no hard feelings, he ordered another beer. But this time he did not match it with one for Carrick.

The old campaigner slid onto the stool beside him.

'About ten years ago there was a fella got hit by lightning out on the golf course,' he said. 'Killed him just as dead as shit. Now, there's a man could have used a lightning rod right up on his head, am I right?' He cackled, sending out a lot of stale beer-breath into Dohay's face. Dohay smiled dutifully. 'All the coins in his pockets were fused together. That's what I heard. Lightning's a funny thing. Sure is. Now, I remember one time . . .'

A funny thing, Dohay thought, letting the old man's words flow harmlessly over him, nodding in the right places out of instinct. A funny thing, all right, because it doesn't care who or what it hits. Or when.

He finished his beer and went out, carrying his satchelful of insurance against the wrath of God – maybe the only kind ever invented – with him. The heat struck him like a hammerblow, but still he paused for a moment in the mostly deserted parking lot, looking up at the unbroken line of roof-ridge. $19.95, $29.95 tops, and the man couldn't afford the outlay. He'd save seventy bucks on his combined insurance the first year, but he couldn't afford the outlay – and you couldn't tell him different with those clowns standing around yukking it up.

Maybe some day he would be sorry.

The seller of lightning rods got into his Buick, cranked up the air conditioning, and drove away west toward Concord and Berlin, his sample case on the seat beside him, running ahead of whatever storms might be whistling up the wind behind.

8 .

In early 1974 Walt Hazlett passed his bar exams. He and Sarah threw a party for all of his friends, her friends, and their mutual friends – more than forty people in all. The beer flowed like water, and after it was over Walt said they could count themselves damn lucky not to have been evicted. When the last of the guests were seen out (at three in the morning), Walt had come back from the door to find Sarah in the bedroom, naked except for her shoes and the diamond chip earrings he had gone into hock to give her for her birthday. They had made love not once but twice before falling into sodden slumber from which they awoke at nearly noon, with paralyzing hangovers. About six weeks later Sarah discovered that she was pregnant. Neither of them ever doubted that conception had occurred on the night of the big party.

In Washington, Richard Nixon was being pressed slowly into a corner, wrapped in a snarl of magnetic tapes. In Georgia, a peanut farmer, ex-Navy man and current governor named James Earl Carter had begun talking with a number of close friends about running for the job Mr. Nixon would soon be vacating.

In Room 619 of the Eastern Maine Medical Center, Johnny Smith still slept. He had begun to pull into a fetal shape.

Dr. Strawns, the doctor who had talked to Herb and Vera and Sarah in the conference room on the day following the accident, had died of burns in late 1973. His house had caught fire on the day after Christmas. The Bangor fire department had determined that the fire had been caused by a faulty set of Christmas tree ornaments. Two new doctors, Weizak and Brown, interested themselves in Johnny's case.

Four days before Nixon resigned, Herb Smith fell into the foundation of a house he was building in Gray, landed on a wheelbarrow, and broke his leg. The bone was a long time healing, and it never really felt good again. He limped, and on wet days he began to use a cane. Vera prayed for him, and insisted that he wrap a cloth that had been personally blessed by the Reverend Freddy Coltsmore of Bessemer, Alabama, around the leg each night when he went to bed. The price of the Blessed Coltsmore Cloth (as Herb called it) was $35. It did no good that he was aware of.

In the middle of October, shortly after Gerald Ford had pardoned the ex-president, Vera became sure that the world was going to end again. Herb realized what she was about barely in time; she had made arrangements to give what little cash and savings they had recouped since Johnny's accident to the Last Times Society of America. She had tried to put the house up for sale, and had made an arrangement with the Goodwill, which was going to send a van out in two days' time to pick up all the furniture. Herb found out when the realtor called him to ask if a prospective buyer could come and look at the house that afternoon.

For the first time he had genuinely lost his temper with Vera.

'What in *Christ's* name did you think you were doing?' he roared, after dragging the last of the incredible story out of her. They were in the living room. He had just finished calling Goodwill to tell them to forget the van. Outside, rain fell in monotonous gray sheets.

'Don't blaspheme the name of the Savior, Herbert. Don't...'

'Shut up! Shut up! I'm tired of listening to you rave about that *crap*!'

She drew in a startled gasp.

He limped over to her, his cane thumping the floor in counterpoint. She flinched back a little in her chair and then looked up at him with that sweet martyr's expression that made him want, God forgive him, to bust her one across the head with his own damn walking stick.

'You're not so far gone that you don't know what you're doing,' he said. 'You don't have that excuse. You snuck around behind my back, Vera. You...'

'I did not! That's a lie! I did no such...'

'*You did!*' he bellowed. 'Well, you listen to me, Vera. This is where I'm drawing the line. You pray all you want. Praying's free. Write all the letters you want, a stamp still only costs thirteen cents. If you want to take a bath in all the cheap, shitty lies those Jesus-jumpers tell, if you want to go on with the delusions and the make-believe, you go on. But I'm not a part of it. Remember that. *Do you understand me?*'

'Our-father-who-art-in-heaven-hallow'd-be-thy-name...'

'*Do you understand me?*'

'*You think I'm crazy!*' she shouted at him, and her face crumpled and squeezed together in a terrible way. She burst into the braying, ugly tears of utter defeat and dis-illusion.

'No,' he said more quietly. 'Not yet. But maybe it's time for a little plain talk, Vera, and the truth is, I think you will be if you don't pull out of this and start facing reality.'

'You'll see,' she said through her tears. 'You'll see. God knows the truth but waits.'

'Just as long as you understand that he's not going to have our furniture while he's waiting,' Herb said grimly. 'As long as we see eye to eye on that.'

'It's Last Times!' she told him. 'The hour of the Apocalypse is at hand.'

'Yeah? That and fifteen cents will buy you a cup of coffee, Vera.'

Outside the rain fell in steady sheets. That was the year Herb turned fifty-two, Vera fifty-one, and Sarah Hazlett twenty-seven.

Johnny had been in his coma for four years.

9 ·

The baby came on Halloween night. Sarah's labor lasted nine hours. She was given mild whiffs of gas when she needed them, and at some point in her extremity it occurred to her that she was in the same hospital as Johnny, and she called his name over and over again. Afterward she barely remembered this, and certainly never told Walt. She thought she might have dreamed it.

The baby was a boy. They named him Dennis Edward Hazlett. He and his mother went home three days later, and Sarah was teaching again after the Thanksgiving holiday. Walt had landed what looked like a fine job with a Bangor firm of lawyers, and if all went well they planned for Sarah to quit teaching in June of 1975. She wasn't all that sure she wanted to. She had grown to like it.

10 ·

On the first day of 1975, two small boys, Charlie Norton and Norm Lawson, both of Otisfield, Maine, were in the Nortons' back yard, having a snowball fight. Charlie was eight, Norm was nine. The day was overcast and drippy.

Sensing that the end of the snowball fight was nearing – it was almost time for lunch – Norm charged Charlie, throwing a barrage of snowballs. Ducking and laughing, Charlie was at first forced back, and then turned tail and ran, jumping the low stone wall that divided the Norton back yard from the woods. He ran down the path that led toward Strimmer's Brook. As he went, Norm caught him a damn good one on the back of the hood.

Then Charlie disappeared from sight.

Norm jumped the wall and stood there for a moment, looking into the snowy woods and listening to the drip of melt-water from the birches, pines, and spruces.

'Come on back, chicken!' Norm called, and made a series of high gobbling sounds.

Charlie didn't rise to the bait. There was no sign of him now, but the path descended steeply as it went down toward the brook. Norm gobbled again and shifted irresolutely from one foot to the other. These were Charlie's woods, not his. Charlie's territory. Norm loved a good snowball fight when he was winning, but he didn't really want to go down there if Charlie was lying in ambush for him with half a dozen good hard slushballs all ready to go.

Nonetheless he had taken half a dozen steps down the path when a high, breathless scream rose from below.

Norm Lawson went as cold as the snow his green gum-rubber boots were planted in. The two snowballs he had been holding dropped from his hands and plopped to the ground. The scream rose again, so thin it was barely audible.

Jeepers-creepers, he went and fell in the brook, Norm thought, and that broke the paralysis of his fear. He ran down the path, slipping and sliding, falling right on his can once. His heartbeat roared in his ears. Part of his mind saw him fishing Charlie from the brook just before he went down for the third time and getting written up in *Boys' Life* as a hero.

Three-quarters of the way down the slope the path doglegged, and when he got around the corner he saw that Charlie Norton hadn't fallen in Strimmer's Brook after all. He was standing at the place where the path leveled out, and he was staring at something in the melting snow. His hood had fallen back and his face was nearly as white as the snow itself. As Norm approached, he uttered that horrible gasping out-of-breath scream again.

'What is it?' Norm asked, approaching. 'Charlie, what's wrong?'

Charlie turned to him, his eyes huge, his mouth gaping. He tried to speak but nothing came out of his mouth but two inarticulate grunts and a silver cord of saliva. He pointed instead.

Norm came closer and looked. Suddenly all the strength went out of his legs and he sat down hard. The world swam around him.

Protruding from the melting snow were two legs clad in blue jeans. There was a loafer on one foot, but the other was bare, white, and defenseless. One arm stuck out of the snow, and the hand at the end of it seemed to plead for a rescue that had never come. The rest of the body was still mercifully hidden.

Charlie and Norm had discovered the body of seventeen-year-old Carol Dunbarger, the fourth victim of the Castle Rock Strangler.

It had been almost two years since he had last killed, and the people of Castle Rock (Strimmer's Brook formed the southern borderline between the towns of Castle Rock and Otisfield) had begun to relax, thinking the nightmare was finally over.

It wasn't.

CHAPTER SIX

1 ·

Eleven days after the discovery of the Dunbarger girl's body, a sleet-and-ice storm struck northern New England. On the sixth floor of the Eastern Maine Medical Center, everything was running just a little bit late in consequence. A lot of the staff had run into problems getting to work, and those that made it found themselves running hard just to stay even.

It was after nine A.M. when one of the aides, a young woman named Allison Conover, brought Mr. Starret his light breakfast. Mr. Starret was recovering from a heart attack and was 'doing his sixteen' in intensive care – a sixteen-day stay following a coronary was standard operating procedure. Mr. Starret was doing nicely. He was in Room 619, and he had told his wife privately that the

105

biggest incentive to his recovery was the prospect of getting away from the living corpse in the room's second bed. The steady whisper of the poor guy's respirator made it hard to sleep, he told her. After a while it got so you didn't know if you wanted it to go on whispering – or stop. Stop dead, so to speak.

The TV was on when Allison came in. Mr. Starret was sitting up in bed with his control button in one hand. 'Today' had ended, and Mr. Starret had not yet decided to blank out 'My Back Yard', the cartoon show that followed it. That would have left him alone with the sound of Johnny's respirator.

'I'd about given up on you this morning,' Mr. Starret said, looking at his breakfast tray of orange juice, plain yoghurt, and wheat flakes with no great joy. What he really craved was two cholesterol-filled eggs, fried over easy and sweating butter, with five slices of bacon on the side, not too crisp. The sort of fare that had, in fact, landed him here in the first place. At least according to his doctor – the birdbrain.

'The going's bad outside,' Allison said shortly. Six patients had already told her they had about given up on her this morning, and the line was getting old. Allison was a pleasant girl, but this morning she was feeling harried.

'Oh, sorry,' Mr. Starret said humbly. 'Pretty slippery on the roads, is it?'

'It sure is,' Allison said, thawing slightly. 'If I didn't have my husband's four-wheel drive today, I never would have made it.'

Mr. Starret pushed the button that raised his bed so he could eat his breakfast comfortably. The electric motor that raised and lowered it was small but loud. The TV was still quite loud – Mr. Starret was a little deaf, and as he had told his wife, the guy in the other bed had never complained about a little extra volume. Never asked to see what was on the other channels, either. He supposed a joke like that was in pretty poor taste, but when you'd had a heart attack and wound up in intensive care sharing a room with a human vegetable, you either learned a little black humor or you went crazy.

Allison raised her voice a little to be heard over the whining motor and the TV as she finished setting up Mr. Starret's tray. 'There were cars off the road all up and down State Street hill.'

In the other bed Johnny Smith said softly, 'The whole wad on nineteen. One way or the other. My girl's sick.'

'You know, this yogurt isn't half bad,' Mr. Starret said. He hated yogurt, but he didn't want to be left alone until absolutely necessary. When he was alone he kept taking his own pulse. 'It tastes a little bit like wild hickory n . . .'

'Did you hear something?' Allison asked. She looked around doubtfully.

Mr. Starret let go of the control button on the side of the bed and the whine of the electric motor died. On the TV, Elmer Fudd took a potshot at Bugs Bunny and missed.

'Nothing but the TV,' Mr. Starret said. 'What'd I miss?'

'Nothing, I guess. It must have been the wind around that window.' She could feel a stress headache coming on – too much to do and not enough people this morning to help her do it – and she rubbed at her temples, as if to drive the pain away before it could get properly seated.

On her way out she paused and looked down at the man in the other bed for a moment. Did he look different somehow? As if he had shifted position? Surely not.

Allison left the room and went on down the hall, pushing her breakfast cabinet ahead of her. It was as terrible a morning as she had feared it would be, everything out of kilter, and by noon her head was pounding. She had quite understandably forgotten all about anything she might have heard that morning in Room 619.

But in the days that followed she found herself looking more and more often at Smith, and by March Allison had become almost sure that he had straightened a bit – come

107

out of what the doctors called his prefetal position a little. Not much – just a little. She thought of mentioning it to someone, but in the end did not. After all, she was only an aide, little more than kitchen help.

It really wasn't her place.

2 .

It was a dream, he guessed.

He was in a dark, gloomy place – a hallway of some kind. The ceiling was too high to see. It was lost in the shadows. The walls were dark chromed steel. They opened out as they went upward. He was alone, but a voice floated up to where he stood, as if from a great distance. A voice he knew, words that had been spoken to him in another place, at another time. The voice frightened him. It was groaning and lost, echoing back and forth between that dark chromed steel like a trapped bird he remembered from his childhood. The bird had flown into his father's toolshed and hadn't the wit to get back out. It had panicked and had gone swooping back and forth, cheeping in desperate alarm, battering itself against the walls until it had battered itself to death. This voice had the same doomed quality as that long ago bird's cheeping. It was never going to escape this place.

'You plan all your life and you do what you can,' this spectral voice groaned. 'You never want nothing but the best, and the kid comes home with hair down to his asshole and says the president of the United States is a pig. A pig! Sheeyit, I don't . . .'

Look out, he wanted to say. He wanted to warn the voice, but he was mute. Look out for what? He didn't know. He didn't even know for sure who he was, although he had a suspicion that he had once been a teacher or a preacher.

'*Jeeeesus!*' The faraway voice screamed. Lost voice, doomed, drowned. '*Jeeeee* . . .'

Silence then. Echoes dying away. Then, in a little while, it would start again.

So after a while – he did not know how long, time

108

seemed to have no meaning or relevance in this place – he
began to grope his way down the hall, calling in return
(or perhaps only calling in his mind), perhaps hoping
that he and the owner of the voice could find their way
out together, perhaps only hoping to give some comfort
and receive some in return.

But the voice kept getting further and further away,
dimmer and fainter

(far and wee)

until it was just an echo of an echo. And then it was
gone. He was alone now, walking down this gloomy and
deserted hall of shadows. And it began to seem to him
that it wasn't an illusion or a mirage or a dream – at least
not of the ordinary kind. It was as if he had entered
limbo, a weird conduit between the land of the living and
that of the dead. But toward which end was he moving?

Things began to come back. Disturbing things. They
were like ghosts that joined him on his walk, fell in on
either side of him, in front of him, behind him, until
they circled him in an eldritch ring – weave a circle round
him thrice and touch his eyes with holy dread, was that
how it went? He could almost see them. All the whispering voices of purgatory. There was a Wheel turning and
turning in the night, a Wheel of the Future, red and
black, life and death, slowing. Where had he laid his bet?
He couldn't remember and he should be able to, because
the stakes were his existence. In and out? It had to be one
or the other. His girl was sick. He had to get her home.

After a while, the hallway began to seem brighter. At
first he thought it was imagination, a sort of dream within
a dream if that were possible, but after an unknown
length of time the brightness became too marked to be
an illusion. The whole experience of the corridor seemed
to become less dreamlike. The walls drew back until he
could barely see them, and the dull dark color changed
to a sad and misty gray, the color of twilight on a warm
and overcast March afternoon. It began to seem that he
was not in a hallway at all anymore, but in a room –
almost in a room, separated from it by the thinnest of

membranes, a sort of placental sac, like a baby waiting to be born. Now he heard other voices, not echoey but dull and thudding, like the voices of nameless gods speaking in forgotten tongues. Little by little these voices came clearer, until he could nearly make out what they were saying.

He began to open his eyes from time to time (or thought he did) and he could actually see the owners of those voices: bright, glowing, spectral shapes with no faces at first, sometimes moving about the room, sometimes bending over him. It didn't occur to him to try speaking to them, at least not at first. It came to him that this might be some sort of afterlife, and these bright shapes the shapes of angels.

The faces, like the voices, began to come clearer with time. He saw his mother once, leaning into his field of vision and slowly thundering something totally without meaning into his upturned face. His father was there another time. Dave Pelsen from school. A nurse he came to know; he believed her name was Mary or possibly Marie. Faces, voices, coming closer, jelling together.

Something else crept in: a feeling that he had *changed*. He didn't like the feeling. He distrusted it. It seemed to him that whatever the change was, it was nothing good. It seemed to him that it meant sorrow and bad times. He had gone into the darkness with everything, and now it felt to him that he was coming out of it with nothing at all – except for some secret strangeness.

The dream was ending. Whatever it had been, the dream was ending. The room was very real now, very *close*. The voices, the faces –

He was going to come into the room. And it suddenly seemed to him that what he wanted to do was turn and run – to go back down that dark hallway forever. The dark hallway was not good, but it was better than this new feeling of sadness and impending loss.

He turned and looked behind him and yes, it was there, the place where the room's walls changed to dark chrome, a corner beside one of the chairs where, unnoticed by the bright people who came and went, the room became a passageway into what he now suspected was eternity. The place where that other voice had gone, the voice of –

The cab driver.

Yes. That memory was all there now. The cab ride, the driver bemoaning his son's long hair, bemoaning the fact that his son thought Nixon was a pig. Then the head-lights breasting the hill, a pair on each side of the white line. The crash. No pain, but the knowledge that his thighs had connected with the taximeter hard enough to rip it out of its frame. There had been a sensation of cold wetness and then the dark hallway and now this.

Choose, something inside whispered. *Choose or they'll choose for you, they'll rip you out of this place, whatever and wherever it is, like doctors ripping a baby out of its mother's womb by cesarian section.*

And then Sarah's face came to him – she had to be out there someplace, although hers had not been one of the bright faces bending over his. She had to be out there, worried and scared. She was almost his, now. He felt that. He was going to ask her to marry him.

That feeling of unease came back, stronger than ever, and this time it was all mixed up with Sarah. But wanting her was stronger, and he made his decision. He turned his back on the dark place, and when he looked back over his shoulder later on, it had disappeared; there was nothing beside the chair but the smooth white wall of the room where he lay. Not long after he began to know where the room must be – it was a hospital room, of course. The dark hallway faded to a dreamy memory, never completely forgotten. But more important, more immediate, was the fact that he was John Smith, he had a girl named Sarah Bracknell, and he had been in a terrible car accident. He suspected that he must be very lucky to be alive, and he could only hope that all his original equipment was still there and still functioning. He might be in Cleaves Mills Community Hospital, but he guessed the EMMC was more likely. From the way he felt he guessed he had been here for some time – he might have been blacked out for as long as a week or ten days. It was time to get going again.

Time to get going again. That was the thought in Johnny's mind when things finally jelled all the way back together and he opened his eyes.

It was May 17, 1975. Mr. Starret had long since gone home with standing orders to walk two miles a day and mend his high-cholesterol ways. Across the room was an old man engaged in a weary fifteenth round with that all-time heavyweight champ, carcinoma. He slept the sleep of morphia, and the room was otherwise empty. It was 3:15 P.M. The TV screen was a drawn green shade.

'Here I am,' Johnny Smith croaked to no one at all. He was shocked by the weakness of his voice. There was no calendar in the room, and he had no way of knowing that he had been out of it four-and-a-half years.

3 ·

The nurse came in some forty minutes later. She went over to the old man in the other bed, changed his IV feed, went into the bathroom, and came out with a blue plastic pitcher. She watered the old man's flowers. There were over half a dozen bouquets, and a score of get-well cards standing open on his table and windowsill. Johnny watched her perform this homey chore, feeling as yet no urge to try his voice again.

She put the pitcher back and came over to Johnny's bed. *Going to turn my pillows,* he thought. Their eyes met briefly, but nothing in hers changed. *She doesn't know I'm awake. My eyes have been open before. It doesn't mean anything to her.*

She put her hand on the back of his neck. It was cool and comforting and Johnny knew she had three children and that the youngest had lost most of the sight of one eye last Fourth of July. A firecracker accident. The boy's name was Mark.

She lifted his head, flipped his pillow over, and settled him back. She started to turn away, adjusting her nylon

112

uniform at the hips, and then turned back, puzzled. Belatedly thinking that there had been something new in his eyes, maybe. Something that hadn't been there before.

She glanced at him thoughtfully, started to turn away again, and he said, 'Hello, Marie.'

She froze, and he could hear an ivory click as her teeth came suddenly and violently together. Her hand pressed against her chest just above the swell of her breasts. A small gold crucifix hung there. 'O-my-God,' she said. 'You're awake. I *thought* you looked different. How did you know my name?'

'I suppose I must have heard it.' It was hard to talk, terribly hard. His tongue was a sluggish worm, seemingly unlubricated by saliva.

She nodded. 'You've been coming up for some time now. I'd better go down to the nurses' station and have Dr. Brown or Dr. Weizak paged. They'll want to know you're back with us.' But she stayed a moment longer, looking at him with a frank fascination that made him uneasy.

'Did I grow a third eye?' he asked.

She laughed nervously. 'No ... of course not. Excuse me.'

His eye caught on his own window ledge and his table pushed up against it. On the ledge was a faded African violet and a picture of Jesus Christ – it was the sort of picture of Jesus his mother favored, with Christ looking as if he was ready to bat clean-up for the New York Yankees or something of a similar clean and athletic nature. But the picture was – yellow. *Yellow and beginning to curl at the corners.* Sudden fear dropped over him like a suffocating blanket. 'Nurse!' he called. 'Nurse!'

In the doorway she turned back.

'Where are my get-well cards?' Suddenly it was hard for him to breathe. 'That other guy's got ... didn't anyone send me a card?'

She smiled, but it was forced. It was the smile of someone who is hiding something. Suddenly Johnny wanted her by his bed. He would reach out and touch her. If he could touch her, he would know what she was hiding.

'I'll have the doctor paged,' she said, and left before he could say anything else. He looked at the African violet, at the aging picture of Jesus, baffled and afraid. After a little while, he drifted off to sleep again.

4 ·

'He *was* awake,' Marie Michaud said. 'He was completely coherent.'

'Okay,' Dr. Brown answered. 'I'm not doubting you. If he woke up once, he'll wake up again. Probably. It's just a matter of . . .'

Johnny moaned. His eyes opened. They were blank, half rolled up. Then he seemed to see Marie, and his eyes came into focus. He smiled a little. But his face was still slack, as if only his eyes were awake and the rest of him still slept. She had a sudden feeling that he was not looking at her but *into* her.

'I think he'll be okay,' Johnny said. 'Once they clean that impacted cornea, the eye'll be as good as new. Should be.'

Marie gasped harshly, and Brown glanced at her. 'What is it?'

'He's talking about my boy,' she whispered. 'My Mark.'

'No,' Brown said. 'He's talking in his sleep, that's all. Don't make a picture out of an inkblot, Nurse.'

'Yes. Okay. But he's not asleep now, is he?'

'Marie?' Johnny asked. He smiled tentatively. 'I dozed off, didn't I?'

'Yes,' Brown said. 'You were talking in your sleep. Gave Marie here a turn. Were you dreaming?'

'No-oo . . . not that I remember. What did I say? And who are you?'

'I'm Dr. James Brown. Just like the soul singer. Only I'm a neurologist. You said, "I think he'll be okay once they clean that impacted cornea." I think that was it, wasn't it, Nurse?'

'My boy's going to have that operation,' Marie said. 'My boy Mark.'

'I don't remember anything,' Johnny said. 'I guess I was sleeping.' He looked at Brown. His eyes were clear now, and scared. 'I can't lift my arms. Am I paralyzed?'

'Nope. Try your fingers.'

Johnny did. They all wiggled. He smiled.

'Superfine,' Brown said. 'Tell me your name.'

'John Smith.'

'Good, and your middle name?'

'I don't have one.'

'That's fine, who needs one? Nurse, go down to your station and find out who's in neurology tomorrow. I'd like to start a whole series of tests on Mr. Smith.'

'Yes, Doctor.'

'And you might call Sam Weizak. You'll get him at home or at the golf course.'

'Yes, Doctor.'

'And no reporters, please . . . for your life!' Brown was smiling but serious.

'No, of course not.' She left, white shoes squeaking faintly. Her little boy's going to be just fine, Johnny thought. I'll be sure to tell her.

'Dr. Brown,' he said, 'where are my get-well cards? Didn't anybody send me a card?'

'Just a few more questions,' Dr. Brown said smoothly. 'Do you recall your mother's name?'

'Of course I do. Vera.'

'Her maiden name?'

'Nason.'

'Your father's name?'

'Herbert. Herb. And why did you tell her no reporters?'

'Your mailing address?'

'RFD #1, Pownal,' Johnny said promptly, and then stopped. An expression of comic surprise passed across his face. 'I mean . . . well, I live in Cleaves Mills now, at

115

110 North Main Street. Why the hell did I give you my parents' address? I haven't lived there since I was eighteen.'

'And how old are you now?'

'Look it up on my driver's license,' Johnny said. 'I want to know why I don't have any get-well cards. How long have I been in the hospital, anyway? And which hospital is this?'

'It's the Eastern Maine Medical Center. And we'll get to all the rest of your questions if you'll just let me . . .'

Brown was sitting by the bed in a chair he had drawn over from the corner – the same corner where Johnny had once seen the passage leading away. He was making notes on a clipboard with a type of pen Johnny couldn't remember ever having seen before. It had a thick blue plastic barrel and a fibrous tip. It looked like the strange hybrid offspring of a fountain pen and a ballpoint.

Just looking at it made that formless dread come back, and without thinking about it, Johnny suddenly seized Dr. Brown's left hand in one of his own. His arm moved creakily, as if there were invisible sixty-pound weights tied to it – a couple below the elbow and a couple above. He captured the doctor's hand in a weak grip and pulled. The funny pen left a thick blue line across the paper.

Brown looked at him, at first only curious. Then his face drained of color. The sharp expression of interest left his eyes and was replaced with a muddy look of fear. He snatched his hand away – Johnny had no power to hold it – and for an instant a look of revulsion crossed the doctor's face, as if he had been touched by a leper.

Then it was gone, and he only looked surprised and disconcerted. 'What did you do that for? Mr. Smith . . .'

His voice faltered. Johnny's face had frozen in an expression of dawning comprehension. His eyes were the eyes of a man who has seen something terrible moving and shifting in the shadows, something too terrible to be described or even named.

But it was a fact. It had to be named.

116

'Fifty-five *months*?' Johnny asked hoarsely. 'Going on five *years*? *No*. Oh my God, *no*.'

'Mr. Smith,' Brown said, now totally flustered. 'Please, it's not good for you to excite . . .'

Johnny raised his upper body perhaps three inches from the bed and then slumped back, his face shiny with sweat. His eyes rolled helplessly in their sockets. 'I'm twenty-seven?' he muttered. 'Twenty-*seven*? Oh my *Jesus*.'

Brown swallowed and heard an audible click. When Smith had grabbed his hand, he had felt a sudden on-rush of bad feelings, childlike in their intensity; crude images of revulsion had assaulted him. He had found himself remembering a picnic in the country when he had been seven or eight, sitting down and putting his hand in something warm and slippery. He had looked around and had seen that he had put his hand into the maggoty remains of a woodchuck that had lain under a laurel bush all that hot August. He had screamed then, and he felt a little bit like screaming now – except that the feeling was fading, dwindling, to be replaced with a question: *How did he know? He touched me and he knew*.

Then twenty years of education rose up strongly in him, and he pushed the notion aside. There were cases without number of comatose patients who had awakened with a dreamlike knowledge of many of the things that had gone on around them while they were in coma. Like anything else, coma was a matter of degree. Johnny Smith had never been a vegetable; his EEG had never gone flat-line, and if it had, Brown would not be talking with him now. Sometimes being in a coma was a little like being behind a one-way glass. To the beholding eye the patient was completely conked out, but the patient's senses might still continue to function in some low, power-down fashion. And that was the case here, of course.

Marie Michaud came back in. 'Neurology is confirmed, and Dr. Weizak is on his way.'

'I think Sam will have to wait until tomorrow to meet

Mr. Smith,' Brown said. 'I want him to have five milligrams of Valium.'

'I don't want a sedative,' Johnny said. 'I want to get *out* of here. I want to know what happened!'

'You'll know everything in time,' Brown said. 'Right now it's important that you rest.'

'I've been resting for four-and-a-half years!'

'Then another twelve hours won't make much difference,' Brown said inexorably.

A few moments later the nurse swabbed his upper arm with alcohol, and there was the sting of a needle. Johnny began to feel sleepy almost at once. Brown and the nurse began to look twelve feet tall.

'Tell me one thing, at least,' he said. His voice seemed to come from far, far away. Suddenly it seemed terribly important. 'That pen. What do you call that pen?'

'This?' Brown held it out from his amazing height. Blue plastic body, fibrous tip. 'It's called a Flair. Now go to sleep, Mr. Smith.'

And Johnny did, but the word followed him down into his sleep like a mystic incantation, full of idiot meaning: *Flair . . . Flair . . . Flair . . .*

5 ·

Herb put the telephone down and looked at it. He looked at it for a long time. From the other room came the sound of the TV, turned up almost all the way. Oral Roberts was talking about football and the healing love of Jesus – there was a connection there someplace, but Herb had missed it. Because of the telephone call. Oral's voice boomed and roared. Pretty soon the show would end and Oral would close it out by confidently telling his audience that something *good* was going to happen to *them*. Apparently Oral was right.

My boy, Herb thought. While Vera had prayed for a miracle, Herb had prayed for his boy to die. It was Vera's prayer that had been answered. What did that mean, and where did it leave him? And what was it going to do to her?

118

He went into the living room. Vera was sitting on the couch. Her feet, encased in elastic pink mules, were up on a hassock. She was wearing her old gray robe. She was eating popcorn straight from the popper. Since Johnny's accident she had put on nearly forty pounds and her blood pressure had skyrocketed. The doctor wanted to put her on medication, but Vera wouldn't have it – if it was the will of the Lord for her to have the high blood, she said, then she would have it. Herb had once pointed out that the will of the Lord had never stopped her from taking Bufferin when she had a headache. She had answered with her sweetest long-suffering smile and her most potent weapon: silence.

'Who was on the phone?' she asked him, not looking away from the TV. Oral had his arm round the well-known quarterback of an NFC team. He was talking to a hushed multitude. The quarterback was smiling modestly.

'. . . and you have all heard this fine athlete tell you tonight how he abused his body, his Temple of God. And you have heard . . .'

Herb snapped it off.

'Herbert *Smith*!' She nearly spilled her popcorn sitting up. 'I was watching! That was . . .'

'Johnny woke up.'

'. . . Oral Roberts and . . .'

The words snapped off in her mouth. She seemed to crouch back in her chair, as if he had taken a swing at her. He looked back, unable to say more, wanting to feel joy but afraid. So afraid.

'Johnny's . . .' She stopped, swallowed, then tried again. 'Johnny . . . *our* Johnny?'

'Yes. He spoke with Dr. Brown for nearly fifteen minutes. Apparently it wasn't that thing they thought . . . false-waking . . . after all. He's coherent. He can move.'

'*Johnny's awake?*'

Her hands came up to her mouth. The popcorn popper, half-full, did a slow dipsy-doodle off her lap and thumped to the rug, spilling popcorn everywhere. Her hands covered the lower half of her face. Above them her eyes got wider and wider still until for a dreadful second, Herb was afraid that they might fall out and dangle by their stalks. Then they closed. A tiny mewing sound came from behind her hands.

'Vera? Are you all right?'

'O my God I thank You for Your will be done my Johnny You brought me my I knew You would, my Johnny, o dear God I will bring You my thanksgiving every day of my life for my Johnny *Johnny JOHNNY* –' Her voice was rising to an hysterical, triumphant scream. He stepped forward, grabbed the lapels of her robe, and shook her. Suddenly time seemed to have reversed, doubled back on itself like strange cloth – they might have been back on the night when the news of the accident came to them, delivered through that same telephone in that same nook.

By nook or by crook, Herb Smith thought crazily.

'O my precious God my Jesus oh my Johnny the miracle like I said the *miracle* . . .'

'*Stop it, Vera!*'

Her eyes were dark and hazy and hysterical. 'Are you sorry he's awake again? After all these years of making fun of me? Of telling people I was crazy?'

'Vera, I never told anyone you were crazy.'

'*You told them with your eyes!*' she shouted at him. 'But my God wasn't mocked. Was he, Herbert? *Was he?*'

'No,' he said. 'I guess not.'

'I told you. I told you God had a plan for my Johnny. Now you see his hand beginning to work.' She got up. 'I've got to go to him. I've got to tell him.' She walked toward the closet where her coat hung, seemingly unaware that she was in her robe and nightgown. Her face was stunned with rapture. In some bizarre and almost blasphemous way she reminded him of the way she had looked on the day they were married. Her pink mules crunched popcorn into the rug.

'Vera.'

'I've got to tell him that God's plan . . .'

120

'Vera.'

She turned to him, but her eyes were far away, with her Johnny.

He went to her and put his hands on her shoulders.

'You tell him that you love him . . . that you prayed . . . waited . . . watched. Who has a better right? You're his mother. You bled for him. Haven't I watched you bleed for him over the last five years? I'm not sorry he's back with us, you were wrong to say that. I don't think I can make of it what you do, but I'm not sorry. I bled for him, too.'

'Did you?' Her eyes were flinty, proud, and unbelieving.

'Yes. And I'm going to tell you something else, Vera. You're going to keep your trap shut about God and miracles and Great Plans until Johnny's up on his feet and able to . . .'

'I'll say what I have to say!'

'. . . and able to think what he's doing. What I'm saying is that you're going to give him a chance to make something of it for himself before you start in on him.'

'You have no right to talk to me that way! No right at all!'

'I'm exercising my right as Johnny's dad,' he said grimly. 'Maybe for the last time in my life. And you better not get in my way, Vera. You understand? Not you, not God, not the bleeding holy Jesus. You follow?'

She glared at him sullenly and said nothing.

'He's going to have enough to do just coping with the idea that he's been out like a light for four-and-a-half years. We don't know if he'll be able to walk again, in spite of the therapist that came in. We do know there'll have to be an operation on his ligaments, if he even wants to try; Weizak told us that. Probably more than one. And more therapy, and a lot of it's going to hurt him like hell. So tomorrow you're just going to be his mother.'

'Don't you dare talk to me that way! *Don't you dare!*'

'If you start sermonizing, Vera, I'll drag you out of his room by the hair of your head.'

She stared at him, white-faced and trembling. Joy and fury were at war in her eyes.

'You better get dressed,' Herb said. 'We ought to get going.'

It was a long, silent ride up to Bangor. The happiness they should have felt between them was not there; only Vera's hot and militant joy. She sat bolt upright in the passenger seat, her Bible in her lap, open to the twenty-third Psalm.

6 ·

At quarter of nine the next morning, Marie came into Johnny's room and said, 'Your mom and dad are here, if you're up to seeing them.'

'Yes, I'd like that.' He felt much better this morning, stronger and less disoriented. But the thought of seeing them scared him a little. In terms of his conscious recollection, he had seen them about five months ago. His father had been working on the foundation of a house that had now probably been standing for three years or more. His mom had fixed him home-baked beans and apple pie for dessert and had clucked over how thin he was getting.

He caught Marie's hand weakly as she turned to go.

'Do they look all right? I mean . . .'

'They look fine.'

'Oh. Good.'

'You can only have half an hour with them now. Some more time this evening if the neurology series doesn't prove too tiring.'

'Dr. Brown's orders?'

'And Dr. Weizak's.'

'All right. For a while. I'm not sure how long I want to be poked and prodded.'

Marie hesitated.

'Something?' Johnny asked.

'No . . . not now. You must be anxious to see your folks. I'll send them in.'

He waited, nervous. The other bed was empty; the

cancer patient had been moved out while Johnny slept off his Valium pop.

The door opened. His mother and father came in. Johnny felt simultaneous shock and relief: shock because they *had* aged, it *was* all true; relief because the changes in them did not yet seem mortal. And if that could be said of them, perhaps it could be said of him as well.

But something in him had changed, changed drastically – and it *might* be mortal.

That was all he had time to think before his mother's arms were around him, her violet sachet strong in his nostrils, and she was whispering: 'Thank God, Johnny, thank God, thank God you're awake.'

He hugged her back as best he could – his arms still had no power to grip and fell away quickly – and suddenly, in six seconds, he knew how it was with her, what she thought, and what was going to happen to her. Then it was gone, fading like that dream of the dark corridor. But when she broke the embrace to look at him, the look of zealous joy in her eyes had been replaced with one of thoughtful consideration.

The words seemed to come out of him of their own: 'Let them give you the medicine, Mom. That's best.'

Her eyes widened, she wet her lips – and then Herb was beside her, his eyes filled with tears. He had lost some weight – not as much as Vera had put on, but he was noticeably thinner. His hair was going fast but the face was the same, homely and plain and well-loved. He took a large brakeman's bandanna from his back pocket and wiped his eyes with it. Then he stuck out his hand.

'Hi, son,' he said. 'Good to have you back.'

Johnny shook his father's hand as well as he could; his pale and strengthless fingers were swallowed up in his father's red hand. Johnny looked from one to the other – his mother in a bulky powder-blue pantsuit, his father in a really hideous houndstooth jacket that looked as if it should belong to a vacuum-cleaner salesman in Kansas – and he burst into tears.

'I'm sorry,' he said. 'I'm sorry, it's just that . . .'

123

'You go on,' Vera said, sitting on the bed beside him. Her face was calm and clear now. There was more mother than madness in it. 'You go on and cry, sometimes that's best.'

And Johnny did.

7 ·

Herb told him his Aunt Germaine had died. Vera told him that the money for the Pownal Community Hall had finally been raised and the building had commenced a month ago, as soon as the frost was out of the ground. Herb added that he had put in a bid, but he guessed honest work cost too dear for them to want to pay. 'Oh, shush, you sore loser,' Vera said.

There was a little silence and then Vera spoke again. 'I hope you realize that your recovery is a miracle of God, Johnny. The doctors despaired. In Matthew, chapter nine, we read . . .'

'Vera,' Herb said warningly.

'Of course it was a miracle, Mom. I know that.'

'You . . . you do?'

'Yes. And I want to talk about it with you . . . hear your ideas about what that means . . . just as soon as I get on my feet again.'

She was staring at him, open-mouthed. Johnny glanced past her at his father and their eyes met for a moment. Johnny saw great relief in his father's eyes. Herb nodded imperceptibly.

'A Conversion!' Vera ejaculated loudly. 'My boy has had a Conversion! Oh, praise God!'

'Vera, hush,' Herb said. 'Best to praise God in a lower voice when you're in the hospital.'

'I don't see how anybody could not call it a miracle, Mom. And we're going to talk about it a lot. Just as soon as I'm out of here.'

'You're going to come home,' she said. 'Back to the house where you were raised. I'll nurse you back to health and we'll pray for understanding.'

He was smiling at her, but holding the smile was an

124

effort. 'You bet. Mom, would you go down to the nurses' station and ask Marie if I can have some juice? Or maybe some ginger ale? I guess I'm not used to talking, and my throat . . .'

'Of course I will.' She kissed his cheek and stood up. 'Oh, you're so thin. But I'll fix that when I get you home.' She left the room, casting a single victorious glance at Herb as she went. They heard her shoes tapping off down the hall.

'How long has she been that way?' Johnny asked quietly.

Herb shook his head. 'It's come a little at a time since your accident. But it had its start long before that. You know. You remember.'

'Is she . . .'

'I don't know. There are people down South that handle snakes. I'd call them crazy. She doesn't do that. How are you, Johnny? Really?'

'I don't know,' Johnny said. 'Daddy, where's Sarah?'

Herb leaned forward and clasped his hands between his knees. 'I don't like to tell you this, John, but . . .'

'She's married? She got *married*?'

Herb didn't answer. Without looking directly at Johnny, he nodded his head.

'Oh, God,' Johnny said hollowly. 'I was afraid of that.'

'She's been Mrs. Walter Hazlett for going on three years. He's a lawyer. They have a baby boy. John . . . no one really believed you were going to wake up. Except for your mother, of course. None of us had any *reason* to believe you would wake up.' His voice was trembling now, hoarse with guilt. 'The doctors said . . . ah, never mind what they said. Even I gave you up. I hate like hell to admit it, but it's true. All I can ask you is try to understand about me . . . and Sarah.'

He tried to say that he did understand, but all that would come out was a sickly sort of croak. His body felt sick and old, and suddenly he was drowning in his sense of loss. The lost time was suddenly sitting on him like a load of bricks – a real thing, not just a vague concept.

'Johnny, don't take on. There are other things. Good things.'

'It's . . . going to take some getting used to,' he managed.

'Yeah. I know.'

'Do you ever see her?'

'We write back and forth once in a while. We got acquainted after your accident. She's a nice girl, real nice. She's still teaching at Cleaves, but I understand she is getting done this June. She's happy, John.'

'Good,' he said thickly. 'I'm glad someone is.'

'Son . . .'

'I hope you're not telling secrets,' Vera Smith said brightly, coming back into the room. She had an ice-clogged pitcher in one hand. 'They said you weren't ready for fruit juice, Johnny, so I brought you the ginger ale.'

'That's fine, Mom.'

She looked from Herb to Johnny and back to Herb again. '*Have* you been telling secrets? Why the long faces?'

'I was just telling Johnny he's going to have to work hard if he wants to get out of here,' said Herb. 'Lots of therapy.'

'Now why would you want to talk about that now?' She poured ginger ale into Johnny's glass. 'Everything's going to be fine now. You'll see.'

She popped a flexible straw into the glass and handed it to him.

'Now you drink all of it,' she said, smiling. 'It's good for you.'

Johnny did drink all of it. It tasted bitter.

CHAPTER SEVEN

1 ·

'Close your eyes,' Dr. Weizak said.

He was a small, roly-poly man with an incredible styled head of hair and spade sideburns. Johnny couldn't get over all that hair. A man with a haircut like that in 1970 would have had to fight his way out of every bar in eastern Maine, and a man Weizak's age would have been considered ripe for committal.

All that hair. Man.

He closed his eyes. His head was covered with electrical contact points. The contacts went to wires that fed into a wall-console EEG. Dr. Brown and a nurse stood by the console, which was calmly extruding a wide sheet of graph paper. Johnny wished the nurse could have been Marie Michaud. He was a little scared.

Dr. Weizak touched his eyelids and Johnny jerked.

'Nuh ... hold still, Johnny. These are the last two. Just ... there.'

'All right, Doctor,' the nurse said.

A low hum.

'All right, Johnny. Are you comfortable?'

'Feels like there are pennies on my eyelids.'

'Yes? You'll get used to that in no time. Now let me explain to you this procedure. I am going to ask you to visualize a number of things. You will have about ten seconds on each, and there are twenty things to visualize in all. You understand?'

'Yes.'

'Very fine. We begin. Dr. Brown?'

'All ready.'

'Excellent. Johnny, I ask you to see a table. On this table there is an orange.'

Johnny thought about it. He saw a small card-table with folding steel legs. Resting on it, a little off-center, was a large orange with the word SUNKIST stamped on its pocky skin.

'Good,' Weizak said.

'Can that gadget see my orange?'

'Nuh ... well, yes; in a symbolic way it can. The machine is tracing your brainwaves. We are searching for blocks, Johnny. Areas of impairment. Possible indications of continuing intercranial pressure. Now I ask you to shush with the questions.'

'All right.'

'Now I ask you to see a television. It is on, but not receiving a station.'

Johnny saw the TV that was in his apartment – *had* been in his apartment. The screen was bright gray with snow. The tips of the rabbit ears were wrapped with tinfoil for better reception.

'Good.'

The series went on. For the eleventh item Weizak said, 'Now I ask you to see a picnic table on the left side of a green lawn.'

Johnny thought about it, and in his mind he saw a lawn chair. He frowned.

'Something wrong?' Weizak asked.

'No, not at all,' Johnny said. He thought harder. Picnics. Weiners, a charcoal brazier ... associate, dammit, associate. How hard can it be to see a picnic table in your mind, you've only seen a thousand of them in your life; associate your way to it. Plastic spoons and forks, paper plates, his father in a chef's hat, holding a long fork in one hand and wearing an apron with a motto printed across it in tipsy letters, THE COOK NEEDS A DRINK. His father making burgers and then they would all go sit at the –

Ah, here it came!

Johnny smiled, and then the smile faded. This time the image in his mind was of a hammock. 'Shit!'

'No picnic table?'

'It's the weirdest thing. I can't quite ... seem to think of it. I mean, I know what it is, but I can't see it in my mind. Is that weird, or is that weird?'

'Never mind. Try this one: a globe of the world, sitting on the hood of a pickup truck.'

That one was easy.

On the nineteenth item, a rowboat lying at the foot of a street sign (who thinks these things up? Johnny wondered), it happened again. It was frustrating. He saw a beachball lying beside a gravestone. He concentrated harder and saw a turnpike overpass. Weizak soothed him, and a few moments later the wires were removed from his head and eyelids.

'Why couldn't I see those things?' he asked, his eyes moving from Weizak to Brown. 'What's the problem?'

'Hard to say with any real certainty,' Brown said. 'It may be a kind of spot amnesia. Or it may be that the accident destroyed a small portion of your brain – and I mean a really microscopic bit. We don't really know what the problem is, but it's pretty obvious that you've lost a number of trace memories. We happened to strike two. You'll probably come across more.'

Weizak said abruptly, 'You sustained a head injury when you were a child, yes?'

Johnny looked at him doubtfully.

'There is an old scar,' Weizak said. 'There is a theory, Johnny, backed by a good deal of statistical research ...'

'Research that is nowhere near complete,' Brown said, almost primly.

'That is true. But this theory supposes that the people who tend to recover from long-term coma are people who have sustained some sort of brain injury at a previous time ... it is as though the brain has made some adaptation as the result of the first injury that allows it to survive the second.'

'It's not proven,' Brown said. He seemed to disapprove of Weizak even bringing it up.

'The scar is there,' Weizak said. 'Can you not remember what happened to you, Johnny? I would guess you must have blacked out. Did you fall down the stairs? A bicycle accident, perhaps? The scar says this happened to a young boy.'

Johnny thought hard, then shook his head. 'Have you asked my mom and dad?'

'Neither of them can remember any sort of head injury ... nothing occurs to you?'

For a moment, something did – a memory of smoke, black and greasy and smelling like rubber. Cold. Then it was gone. Johnny shook his head.

Weizak sighed, then shrugged. 'You must be tired.'

'Yes. A little bit.'

Brown sat on the edge of the examination table. 'It's quarter of eleven. You've worked hard this morning. Dr. Weizak and I will answer a few questions, if you like, then you go up to your room for a nap. Okay?'

'Okay,' Johnny said. 'The pictures you took of my brain ...'

'The CAT-scan,' Weizak nodded. 'Computerized Axial Tomography.' He took a box of Chiclets and shook three of them into his mouth. 'The CAT-scan is really a series of brain X-rays, Johnny. The computer highlights the pictures and ...'

'What did it tell you? How long have I got?'

'What is this how long have I got stuff?' Brown asked. 'It sounds like a line from an old movie.'

'I've heard that people who come out of long-term comas don't always last so long,' Johnny said. 'They lapse back. It's like a light bulb going really bright before it burns out for good.'

Weizak laughed hard. It was a hearty, bellowing laugh, and it was something of a wonder that he didn't choke on his gum. 'Oh, such melodrama.' He put a hand on Johnny's chest. 'You think Jim and I are babies in this field? Nuh. We are neurologists. What you Americans call high-priced talent. Which means we are only stupid about the functions of the human brain instead of out-

130

and-out ignoramuses. So I tell you, yes, there have been
lapse-backs. But you will not lapse. I think we can say
that, Jim, yes, okay?'

'Yes,' Brown said. 'We haven't been able to find very
much in the way of significant impairment. Johnny,
there's a guy in Texas who was in a coma for nine years.
Now he's a bank loan officer, and he's been doing that job
for six years. Before that he was a teller for two years.
There's a woman in Arizona who was down for twelve
years. Something went wrong with the anesthesia while
she was in labor. Now she's in a wheelchair, but she's
alive and aware. She came out of it in 1969 and met the
baby she had delivered twelve years before. The baby
was in the seventh grade and an honors student.'

'Am I going to be in a wheelchair?' Johnny asked. 'I
can't straighten my legs out. My arms are a little better,
but my legs . . .' He trailed off, shaking his head.

'The ligaments shorten,' Weizak said. 'Yes? That's why
comatose patients begin to pull into what we call the
prefetal position. But we know more about the physical
degeneration that occurs in coma than we used to, we are
better at holding it off. You have been exercised regularly
by the hospital physical therapist, even in your sleep. And
different patients react to coma in different ways. Your
deterioration has been quite slow, Johnny. As you say,
your arms are remarkably responsive and able. But there
has been deterioration. Your therapy will be long and . . .
should I lie to you? Nuh, I don't think so. It will be long
and painful. You will shed your tears. You may come to
hate your therapist. You may come to fall in love with
your bed. And there will be operations – only one if you
are very, very lucky, but perhaps as many as four – to
lengthen those ligaments. These operations are still new.
They may succeed completely, partially, or not at all.
And yet as God wills it, I believe you will walk again. I
don't believe you will ever ski or leap hurdles, but you
may run and you will certainly swim.'

'Thank you,' Johnny said. He felt a sudden wave of
affection for this man with the accent and the strange

haircut. He wanted to do something for Weizak in return – and with that feeling came the urge, almost the *need*, to touch him.

He reached out suddenly and took Weizak's hand in both of his own. The doctor's hand was big, deeply lined, warm.

'Yes?' Weizak said kindly. 'And what is this?'

And suddenly things changed. It was impossible to say how. Except that suddenly Weizak seemed very clear to him. Weizak seemed to ... to *stand forth*, outlined in a lovely, clear light. Every mark and mole and line on Weizak's face stood in relief. And every line told its own story. *He began to understand.*

'I want your wallet,' Johnny said.

'My ... ?' Weizak and Brown exchanged a startled glance.

'There's a picture of your mother in your wallet and I need to have it,' Johnny said. '*Please.*'

'How did you know that?'

'*Please!*'

Weizak looked into Johnny's face for a moment, and then slowly dug under his smock and produced an old Lord Buxton, bulgy and out of shape.

'How did you know I carry a picture of my mother? She is dead, she died when the Nazis occupied Warsaw ...'

Johnny snatched the wallet from Weizak's hand. Both he and Brown looked stunned. Johnny opened it, dismissed the plastic picture-pockets, and dug in the back instead, his fingers hurrying past old business cards, receipted bills, a canceled check, an old ticket to some political function. He came up with a small snapshot that had been laminated in plastic. The picture showed a young woman, her features plain, her hair drawn back under a kerchief. Her smile was radiant and youthful. She held the hand of a young boy. Beside her was a man in the uniform of the Polish army.

Johnny pressed the picture between his hands and

closed his eyes and for a moment there was darkness and then rushing out of the darkness came a wagon ... no, not a wagon, a hearse. A horse-drawn hearse. The lamps had been muffled in black sacking. Of course it was a hearse because they were

(dying by the hundreds, yes, by the thousands, no match for the panzers, the wehrmacht, nineteenth-century cavalry against the tanks and machine guns. explosions. screaming, dying men. a horse with its guts blown out and its eyes rolling wildly, showing the white, an overturned cannon behind it and still they come. weizak comes, standing in his stirrups, his sword held high in the slanting rain of late summer 1939, his men following him, stumbling through the mud. the turret gun of the nazi tiger tank tracks him, braces him, brackets him, fires, and suddenly he is gone below the waist, the sword flying out of his hand; and down the road is warsaw. the nazi wolf is loose in europe)

'Really, we have to put a stop to this,' Brown said, his voice faraway and worried. 'You're overexciting yourself, Johnny.'

The voices came from far away, from a hallway in time.

'He's put himself in some kind of trance,' Weizak said.

Hot in here. He was sweating. He was sweating because *(the city's on fire, thousands are fleeing, a truck is roaring from side to side down a cobbled street, and the back of the truck is full of waving german soldiers in coalscuttle helmets and the young woman is not smiling now, she is fleeing, no reason not to flee. the child has been sent away to safety and now the truck jumps the curb, the mudguard strikes her, shattering her hip and sending her flying through a plateglass window and into a clock shop and everything begins to chime. chime because of the time. the chime time is)*

'Six o'clock,' Johnny said thickly. His eyes had rolled up to straining, bulging whites. 'September 2, 1939, and all the cuckoo birds are singing.'

'Oh my God, what is it we have?' Weizak whispered. The nurse had backed up against the EEG console, her face pale and scared. Everyone is scared now because death is in the air. It's always in the air in this place, this

(*hospital. smell of ether. they're screaming in the place of death. poland is dead, poland has fallen before the lightning warfare wehrmacht blitzkreig. shattered hip. the man in the next bed calling for water, calling, calling, calling. she remembers 'THE BOY IS SAFE.' what boy? she doesn't know. what boy? what is her name? she doesn't remember. only that*)

'The boy is safe,' Johnny said thickly. 'Uh-huh. Uh-huh.'

'We have to put a stop to this,' Brown repeated.

'How do you suggest we do that?' Weizak asked, his voice brittle. 'It has gone too far to . . .'

Voices fading. The voices are under the clouds. Everything is under the clouds. Europe is under the clouds of war. Everything is under the clouds but the peaks, the mountain peaks of

(*switzerland. switzerland and now her name is BORENTZ. her name is JOHANNA BORENTZ and her husband is an engineer or an architect, whichever it is that builds the bridges. he builds in switzerland and there is goat's milk, goat's cheese. a baby. ooooh the labor! the labor is terrible and she needs drugs, morphine, this JOHANNA BORENTZ, because of the hip. the broken hip. it has mended, it has gone to sleep, but now it awakes and begins to scream as her pelvis spreads to let the baby out, one baby. two. and three. and four. they don't come all at once, no – they are a harvest of years, they are*)

'The babies,' Johnny lilted, and now he spoke in a woman's voice, not his own voice at all. It was the voice of a woman. Then gibberish in song came from his mouth.

'What in the name of God . . .' Brown began.

'Polish, it is Polish!' Weizak cried. His eyes were bulging, his face pale. 'It is a cradle song and it is in Polish,

134

my God, my Christ, what is it we have here?'

Weizak leaned forward as if to cross the years with Johnny, as if to leap them, as if to

(bridge, a bridge, it's in turkey. then a bridge somewhere hot in the far east, is it Laos? can't tell, lost a man there, we lost HANS there, then a bridge in virginia, a bridge over the RAPPAHANNOCK RIVER and another bridge in california. we are applying for citizenship now and we go to classes in a hot little room in the back of a post-office where it always smells of glue. it is 1963, november, and when we hear kennedy has been killed in dallas we weep and when the little boy salutes his dead father's coffin she thinks 'THE BOY IS SAFE' and it brings back memories of some burning, some great burning and sorrow, what boy? she dreams about the boy, it makes her head hurt. and the man dies, HELMUT BORENTZ dies and she and the children live in carmel california. in a house on. on. on. can't see the street sign, it's in the dead zone, like the rowboat, like the picnic table on the lawn. it's in the dead zone. like warsaw. the children go away, she goes to their graduation ceremonies one by one, and her hip hurts. one dies in vietnam. the rest of them are fine. one of them is building bridges. her name is JOHANNA BORENTZ and late at night alone now she sometimes thinks in the ticking darkness: 'THE BOY IS SAFE.')

Johnny looked up at them. His head felt strange. That peculiar light around Weizak had gone. He felt like himself again, but weak and a little pukey. He looked at the picture in his hands for a moment and then handed it back.

'Johnny?' Brown said. 'Are you all right?'

'Tired,' he muttered.

'Can you tell us what happened to you?'

He looked at Weizak. 'Your mother is alive,' he said.

'No, Johnny. She died many years ago. In the war.'

'A German trooptruck knocked her through a plate-glass show window and into a clock shop,' Johnny said. 'She woke up in a hospital with amnesia. She had no identification, no papers. She took the name Johanna . . . somebody. I didn't get that, but when the war was over she went to Switzerland and married a Swiss . . . engineer, I think. His specialty was building bridges, and his name was Helmut Borentz. So her married name was – is – Johanna Borentz.'

The nurse's eyes were getting bigger and bigger. Dr. Brown's face was tight, either because he had decided Johnny was having them all on or perhaps just because he didn't like to see his neat schedule of tests disrupted. But Weizak's face was still and thoughtful.

'She and Helmut Borentz had four children,' Johnny said in that same, calm, washed-out voice. 'His job took him all over the world. He was in Turkey for a while. Somewhere in the Far East, Laos, I think, maybe Cambodia. Then he came here. Virginia first, then some other places I didn't get, finally California. He and Johanna became U.S. citizens. Helmut Borentz is dead. One of the children they had is also dead. The others are alive and fine. But she dreams about you sometimes. And in the dreams she thinks, 'the boy is safe'. But she doesn't remember your name. Maybe she thinks it's too late.'

'California?' Weizak said thoughtfully.

'Sam,' Dr. Brown said. 'Really, you mustn't encourage this.'

'Where in California, John?'

'Carmel. By the sea. But I couldn't tell which street. It was there, but I couldn't tell. It was in the dead zone. Like the picnic table and the rowboat. But she's in Carmel, California. Johanna Borentz. She's not old.'

'No, of course she would not be old,' Sam Weizak said in that same thoughtful, distant tone. 'She was only twenty-four when the Germans invaded Poland.'

'Dr. Weizak, I have to insist,' Brown said harshly.

Weizak seemed to come out of a deep study. He looked around as if noticing his younger colleague for the first time. 'Of course,' he said. 'Of course you must. And John has had his question-and-answer period . . . although I believe he has told us more than we have told him.'

'That's nonsense,' Brown said curtly, and Johnny thought: *He's scared. Scared spitless.*

Weizak smiled at Brown, and then at the nurse. She was eyeing Johnny as if he were a tiger in a poorly built cage. 'Don't talk about this, Nurse. Not to your supervisor, your mother, your brother, your lover, or your priest. Understood?'

'Yes, Doctor,' the nurse said. *But she'll talk,* Johnny thought, and then glanced at Weizak. *And he knows it.*

2 ·

He slept most of the afternoon. Around four P.M. he was rolled down the corridor to the elevator, taken down to neurology, and there were more tests. Johnny cried. He seemed to have very little control over the functions adults are supposed to be able to control. On his way back up, he urinated on himself and had to be changed like a baby. The first (but far from the last) wave of deep depression washed over him, carried him limply away, and he wished himself dead. Self-pity accompanied the depression and he thought how unfair this was. He had done a Rip van Winkle. He couldn't walk. His girl had married another man and his mother was in the grip of a religious mania. He couldn't see anything ahead that looked worth living for.

Back in his room, the nurse asked him if he would like anything. If Marie had been on duty, Johnny would have asked for ice water. But she had gone off at three.

'No,' he said, and rolled over to face the wall. After a little while, he slept.

CHAPTER EIGHT

1 ·

His father and mother came in for an hour that evening, and Vera left a bundle of tracts.

'We're going to stay until the end of the week,' Herb

said, 'and then, if you're still doing fine, we'll be going back to Pownal for a while. But we'll be back up every weekend.'

'I want to stay with my boy,' Vera said loudly.

'It's best that you don't, Mom,' Johnny said. The depression had lifted a little bit, but he remembered how black it had been. If his mother started to talk about God's wonderful plan for him while he was in that state, he doubted if he would be able to hold back his cackles of hysterical laughter.

'You need me, John. You need me to explain ...'

'First I need to get well,' Johnny said. 'You can explain after I can walk. Okay?'

She didn't answer. There was an almost comically stubborn expression on her face – except there was nothing very funny about it. Nothing at all. *Nothing but a quirk of fate, that's all. Five minutes earlier or later on that road would have changed everything. Now look at us, all of us fucked over royally. And she believes it's God's plan. It's either that or go completely crazy, I suppose.*

To break the awkward silence, Johnny said: 'Well, did Nixon get reelected, dad? Who ran against him?'

'He got reelected,' Herb said. 'He ran against McGovern.'

'Who?'

'McGovern. George McGovern. Senator from South Dakota.'

'Not Muskie?'

'No. But Nixon's not president anymore. He resigned.'

'*What?*'

'He was a liar,' Vera said dourly. 'He became swollen with pride and the Lord brought him low.'

'Nixon resigned?' Johnny was flabbergasted. '*Him?*'

'It was either quit or be fired,' Herb said. 'They were getting ready to impeach him.'

Johnny suddenly realized that there had been some great and fundamental upheaval in American politics – almost surely as a result of the war in Vietnam – and he had missed it. For the first time he really *felt* like Rip

138

van Winkle. How much had things changed? He was almost afraid to ask. Then a really chilling thought occurred.

'Agnew . . . Agnew's president?'

'Ford,' Vera said. 'A good, honest man.'

'*Henry Ford is president of the United States?*'

'Not Henry,' she said. 'Jerry.'

He stared from one to the other, more than half convinced that all this was a dream or a bizarre joke.

'Agnew resigned, too,' Vera said. Her lips were pressed thin and white. 'He was a thief. He accepted a bribe right in his office. That's what they say.'

'He didn't resign over the bribe,' Herb said. 'He resigned over some mess back in Maryland. He was up to his neck in it, I guess. Nixon nominated Jerry Ford to become vice president. Then Nixon resigned last August and Ford took over. *He* nominated Nelson Rockefeller to be vice president. And that's where we are now.'

'A divorced man,' Vera said grimly. 'God forbid he ever becomes the president.'

'What did Nixon do?' Johnny asked. 'Jesus Christ, I . . .' He glanced at his mother, whose brow had clouded instantly. 'I mean, holy crow, if they were going to impeach him . . .'

'You needn't take the Savior's name in vain over a bunch of crooked politicians,' Vera said. 'It was Watergate.'

'Watergate? Was that an operation in Vietnam? Something like that?'

'The Watergate Hotel in Washington,' Herb said. 'Some Cubans broke into the offices of the Democratic Committee there and got caught. Nixon knew about it. He tried to cover it up.'

'Are you kidding?' Johnny managed at last.

'It was the tapes,' Vera said. 'And that John Dean. Nothing but a rat deserting a sinking ship, that's what I think. A common tattletale.'

'Daddy, can you explain this to me?'

'I'll try,' Herb said, 'but I don't think the whole story

has come out, even yet. And I'll bring you the books. There's been about a million books written on it already, and I guess there'll be a million more before it's finally done. Just before the election, in the summer of 1972 ...'

2 ·

It was ten-thirty and his parents were gone. The lights on the ward had been dimmed. Johnny couldn't sleep. It was all dancing around in his head, a frightening jumble of new input. The world had changed more resoundingly than he would have believed possible in so short a time. He felt out of step and out of tune.

Gas prices had gone up nearly a hundred percent, his father had told him. At the time of his accident, you could buy regular gas for thirty or thirty-two cents a gallon. Now it was fifty-four cents and sometimes there were lines at the pumps. The legal speed limit all over the country was fifty-five miles an hour and the long-haul truckers had almost revolted over that.

But all of that was nothing. Vietnam was over. It had ended. The country had finally gone Communist. Herb said it had happened just as Johnny began to show signs that he might come out of his coma. After all those years and all that bloodshed, the heirs of Uncle Ho had rolled up the country like a windowshade in a matter of days.

The president of the United States had been to Red China. Not Ford, but Nixon. He had gone before he resigned. *Nixon*, of all people, the old witch-hunter himself. If anyone but his dad had told him that, Johnny would have flatly refused to believe.

It was all too much, it was too scary. Suddenly he didn't want to know any more, for fear it might drive him totally crazy. That pen Dr. Brown had had, that Flair – how many other things were there like that? How many hundreds of little things, all of them making the point over and over again: You lost part of your life, almost six percent, if the actuarial tables are to be believed. You're behind the times. You missed out.

'John?' The voice was soft. 'Are you asleep, John?'

He turned over. A dim silhouette stood in his doorway. A small man with rounded shoulders. It was Weizak.

'No. I'm awake.'

'I hoped so. May I come in?'

'Yes. Please do.'

Weizak looked older tonight. He sat by Johnny's bed.

'I was on the phone earlier,' he said. 'I called directory assistance for Carmel, California. I asked for a Mrs. Johanna Borentz. Do you think there was such a number?'

'Unless it's unlisted or she doesn't have a phone at all,' Johnny said.

'She has a phone. I was given the number.'

'Ah,' Johnny said. He was interested because he liked Weizak, but that was all. He felt no need to have his knowledge of Johanna Borentz validated, because he knew it was valid knowledge – he knew it the same way he knew he was right-handed.

'I sat for a long time and thought about it,' Weizak said. 'I told you my mother was dead, but that was really only an assumption. My father died in the defense of Warsaw. My mother simply never turned up, nuh? It was logical to assume that she had been killed in the shelling ... during the occupation ... you understand. She never turned up, so it was logical to assume that. Amnesia ... as a neurologist I can tell you that permanent, general amnesia is very, very rare. Probably rarer than true schizophrenia. I have never read of a documented case lasting thirty-five years.'

'She recovered from her amnesia long ago,' Johnny said. 'I think she simply blocked everything out. When her memory did come back, she had remarried and was the mother of two children ... possibly three. Remembering became a guilt trip, maybe. But she dreams of you. "The boy is safe." Did you call her?'

'Yes,' Weizak said. 'I dialed it direct. Did you know you could do that now? Yes. It is a great convenience. You dial one, the area code, the number. Eleven digits and you can be in touch with any place in the country.

It is an amazing thing. In some ways a frightening thing. A boy – no, a young man – answered the telephone. I asked if Mrs. Borentz was at home. I heard him call, "Mom, it's for you." Clunk went the receiver on the table or desk or whatever. I stood in Bangor, Maine, not forty miles from the Atlantic Ocean and listened to a young man put the phone down on a table in a town on the Pacific Ocean. My heart ... it was pounding so hard it frightened me. The wait seemed long. Then she picked up the phone and said, "Yes? Hello?" '

'What did you say? How did you handle it?'

'I did not, as you say, handle it,' Weizak replied, and smiled crookedly. 'I hung up the telephone. And I wished for a strong drink, but I did not have one.'

'Are you satisfied it was her?'

'John, what a naive question! I was nine years old in 1939. I had not heard my mother's voice since then. She spoke only Polish when I knew her. I speak only English now ... I have forgotten much of my native language, which is a shameful thing. How could I be satisfied one way or the other?'

'Yes, but *were* you?'

Weizak scrubbed a hand slowly across his forehead. 'Yes,' he said. 'It was her. It was my mother.'

'But you couldn't talk to her?'

'Why should I?' Weizak asked, sounding almost angry. 'Her life is her life, nuh? It is as you said. The boy is safe. Should I upset a woman that is just coming into her years of peace? Should I take the chance of destroying her equilibrium forever? Those feelings of guilt you mentioned ... should I set them free? Or even run the risk of so doing?'

'I don't know,' Johnny said. They were troublesome questions, and the answers were beyond him – but he felt that Weizak was trying to say something about what he had done by articulating the questions. The questions he could not answer.

'The boy is safe, the woman is safe in Carmel. The country is between them, and we let that be. But what

142

about you, John? What are we going to do about you?'

'I don't understand what you mean.'

'I will spell it out for you then, nuh? Dr. Brown is angry. He is angry at me, angry at you, and angry at himself, I suspect, for half-believing something he has been sure is total poppycock for his whole life. The nurse who was a witness will never keep her silence. She will tell her husband tonight in bed, and it may end there, but her husband may tell his boss, and it is very possible that the papers will have wind of this by tomorrow evening. "Coma Patient Re-Awakens with Second Sight." '

'Second sight,' Johnny said. 'Is that what it is?'

'I don't know what it is, not really. Is it psychic? Seer? Handy words that describe nothing, nothing at all. You told one of the nurses that her son's optic surgery was going to be successful . . .'

'Marie,' Johnny murmured. He smiled a little. He liked Marie.

'. . . and that is already all over the hospital. Did you see the future? Is that what second sight is? I don't know. You put a picture of my mother between your hands and were able to tell me where she lives today. Do you know where lost things and lost people may be found? Is *that* what second sight is? I don't know. Can you read thoughts? Influence objects of the physical world? Heal by the laying on of hands? These are all things that some call "psychic". They are all related to the idea of "second sight". They are things that Dr. Brown laughs at. Laughs? No. He doesn't laugh. He scoffs.'

'And you don't?'

'I think of Edgar Cayce. And Peter Hurkos. I tried to tell Dr. Brown about Hurkos and he scoffed. He doesn't want to talk about it; he doesn't want to know about it.'

Johnny said nothing.

'So . . . what are we going to do about you?'

'Does something need to be done?'

'I think so,' Weizak said. He stood up. 'I'll leave you to think it out for yourself. But when you think, think about

143

this: some things are better not seen, and some things are better lost than found.'

He bade Johnny good night and left quietly. Johnny was very tired now, but still sleep did not come for a long time.

CHAPTER NINE

1 ·

Johnny's first surgery was scheduled for May 28. Both Weizak and Brown had explained the procedure carefully to him. He would be given a local anesthetic – neither of them felt a general could be risked. This first operation would be on his knees and ankles. His own ligaments, which had shortened during his long sleep, would be lengthened with a combination of plastic wonder-fibers. The plastic to be used was also employed in heart valve bypass surgery. The question was not so much one of his body's acceptance or rejection of the artificial ligaments, Brown told him, as it was a question of his legs' ability to adjust to the change. If they had good results with the knees and the ankles, three more operations were on the boards: one on the long ligaments of his thighs, one on the elbow-strap ligaments, and possibly a third on his neck, which he could barely turn at all. The surgery was to be performed by Raymond Ruopp, who had pioneered the technique. He was flying in from San Francisco.

'What does this guy Ruopp want with me, if he's such a superstar?' Johnny asked. *Superstar* was a word he had learned from Marie. She had used it in connection with a balding, bespectacled singer with the unlikely name of Elton John.

'You're underestimating your own superstar qualities,' Brown answered. 'There are only a handful of people in the United States who have recovered from comas as long as yours was. And of that handful, your recovery from

144

the accompanying brain damage has been the most radical and pleasing.'

Sam Weizak was more blunt. 'You're a guinea pig, nuh?'

'What?'

'Yes. Look into the light, please.' Weizak shone a light into the pupil of Johnny's left eye. 'Did you know I can look right at your optic nerve with this thing? Yes. The eyes are more than the windows of the soul. They are one of the brain's most crucial maintenance points.'

'Guinea pig,' Johnny said morosely, staring into the savage point of light.

'Yes.' The light snapped off. 'Don't feel so sorry for yourself. Many of the techniques to be employed in your behalf – and some of those already employed – were perfected during the Vietnam war. No shortage of guinea pigs in the V.A. hospitals, nuh? A man like Ruopp is interested in you because you are unique. Here is a man who has slept four-and-a-half years. Can we make him walk again? An interesting problem. He sees the monograph he will write on it for *The New England Journal of Medicine.* He looks forward to it the way a child looks forward to new toys under the Christmas tree. He does not see you, he does not see Johnny Smith in his pain, Johnny Smith who must take the bedpan and ring for the nurse to scratch if his back itches. That's good. His hands will not shake. Smile, Johnny. This Ruopp looks like a bank clerk, but he is maybe the best surgeon in North America.'

But it was hard for Johnny to smile.

He had read his way dutifully through the tracts his mother had left him. They depressed him and left him frightened all over again for her sanity. One of them, by a man named Salem Kirban, struck him as nearly pagan in its loving contemplation of a bloody apocalypse and the yawning barbecue pits of hell. Another described the coming Antichrist in pulp-horror terms. The others were a dark carnival of craziness: Christ was living under the South Pole, God drove flying saucers, New York was

Sodom, L.A. was Gomorrah. They dealt with exorcism, with witches, with all manner of things seen and unseen. It was impossible for him to reconcile the pamphlets with the religious yet earthy woman he had known before his coma.

Three days after the incident involving Weizak's snapshot of his mother, a slim and dark-haired reporter from the Bangor *Daily News* named David Bright showed up at the door of Johnny's room and asked if he could have a short interview.

'Have you asked the doctors?' Johnny asked.

Bright grinned. 'Actually, no.'

'All right,' Johnny said. 'In that case, I'd be happy to talk to you.'

'You're a man after my own heart,' Bright said. He came in and sat down.

His first questions were about the accident and about Johnny's thoughts and feelings upon slipping out of the coma and discovering he had misplaced nearly half a decade. Johnny answered these questions honestly and straightforwardly. Then Bright told him that he had heard from 'a source' that Johnny had gained some sort of sixth sense as a result of the accident.

'Are you asking me if I'm psychic?'

Bright smiled and shrugged. 'That'll do for a start.'

Johnny had thought carefully about the things Weizak had said. The more he thought, the more it seemed to him that Weizak had done exactly the right thing when he hung up the phone without saying anything. Johnny had begun to associate it in his mind with that W. W. Jacobs story, 'The Monkey's Paw'. The paw was for wishing, but the price you paid for each of your three wishes was a black one. The old couple had wished for one hundred pounds and had lost their son in a mill accident – the mill's compensation had come to exactly one hundred pounds. Then the old woman had wished for her son back and he had come – but before she could open the door and see what a horror she had summoned out of its grave, the old man had used the last wish to send it back. As Weizak had said, maybe some things were better lost than found.

'No,' he said. 'I'm no more psychic than you are.'

'According to my source, you . . .'

'No, it isn't true.'

Bright smiled a trifle cynically, seemed to debate pressing the matter further, then turned to a fresh page in his notebook. He began to ask about Johnny's prospects for the future, his feelings about the road back, and Johnny also answered these questions as honestly as he could.

'So what are you going to do when you get out of here?' Bright asked, closing his notebook.

'I haven't really thought about that. I'm still trying to adjust to the idea that Gerald Ford is the president.'

Bright laughed. 'You're not alone in that, my friend.'

'I suppose I'll go back to teaching. It's all I know. But right now that's too far ahead to think about.'

Bright thanked him for the interview and left. The article appeared in the paper two days later, the day before his leg surgery. It was on the bottom of the front page, and the headline read: JOHN SMITH, MODERN RIP VAN WINKLE, FACES LONG ROAD BACK. There were three pictures, one of them Johnny's picture for the Cleaves Mills High School yearbook (it had been taken barely a week before the accident), a picture of Johnny in his hospital bed, looking thin and twisted with his arms and legs in their bent positions. Between these two was a picture of the almost totally demolished taxi, lying on its side like a dead dog. There was no mention in Bright's article of sixth senses, precognitive powers, or wild talents.

'How did you turn him off the ESP angle?' Weisak asked him that evening.

Johnny shrugged. 'He seemed like a nice guy. Maybe he didn't want to stick me with it.'

'Maybe not,' Weizak said. 'But he won't forget it. Not if he's a good reporter, and I understand that he is.'

'You understand?'

'I asked around.'

147

'Looking out for my best interests?'

'We all do what we can, nuh? Are you nervous about tomorrow, Johnny?'

'Not nervous, no. Scared is a more accurate word.'

'Yes, of course you are. I would be.'

'Will you be there?'

'Yes, in the observation section of the operating theater. You won't be able to tell me from the others in my greens, but I will be there.'

'Wear something,' Johnny said. 'Wear something so I'll know it's you.'

Weizak looked at him, and smiled. 'All right. I'll pin my watch to my tunic.'

'Good,' Johnny said. 'What about Dr. Brown? Will he be there?'

'Dr. Brown is in Washington. Tomorrow he will present you to the American Society of Neurologists. I have read his paper. It is quite good. Perhaps overstated.'

'You weren't invited?'

Weizak shrugged. 'I don't like to fly. That is something that scares me.'

'And maybe you wanted to stay here?'

Weizak smiled crookedly, spread his hands, and said nothing.

'He doesn't like me much, does he?' Johnny asked. 'Dr. Brown?'

'No, not much,' Weizak said. 'He thinks you are having us on. Making things up for some reason of your own. Seeking attention, perhaps. Don't judge him solely on that, John. His cast of mind makes it impossible for him to think otherwise. If you feel anything for Jim, feel a little pity. He is a brilliant man, and he will go far. Already he has offers, and someday soon he will fly from these cold north woods and Bangor will see him no more. He will go to Houston or Hawaii or possibly even to Paris. But he is curiously limited. He is a mechanic of the brain. He has cut it to pieces with his scalpel and found no soul. Therefore there is none. Like the Russian astronauts who circled the earth and did not see God. It is the empiricism of the mechanic, and a mechanic is only a child with superior motor control. You must never tell him I said that.'

'No.'

'And now you must rest. Tomorrow you have a long day.'

2 ·

All Johnny saw of the world-famous Dr. Ruopp during the operation was a pair of thick horn-rimmed glasses and a large wen at the extreme left side of the man's forehead. The rest of him was capped, gowned, and gloved.

Johnny had been given two preop injections, one of demerol and one of atropine, and when he was wheeled in he was as high as a kite. The anesthetist approached with the biggest novocaine needle Johnny had ever seen in his life. He expected that the injection would hurt, and he was not wrong. He was injected between L4 and L5, the fourth and fifth lumbar vertebrae, high enough up to avoid the *cauda equina*, that bundle of nerves at the base of the spine that vaguely resembles a horse's tail.

Johnny lay on his stomach and bit his arm to keep from screaming.

After an endless time, the pain began to fade to a dull sensation of pressure. Otherwise, the lower half of his body was totally gone.

Ruopp's face loomed over him. The green bandit, Johnny thought. Jesse James in horn-rims. Your money or your life.

'Are you comfortable, Mr. Smith?' Ruopp asked.

'Yes. But I'd just as soon not go through that again.'

'You may read magazines, if you like. Or you may watch in the mirror, if you feel it will not upset you.'

'All right.'

'Nurse, give me a blood pressure, please.'

'One-twenty over seventy-six, Doctor.'

'That's lovely. Well, group, shall we begin?'

'Save me a drumstick,' Johnny said weakly, and was

149

surprised by the hearty laughter. Ruopp patted his sheet-covered shoulder with one thinly gloved hand.

He watched Ruopp select a scalpel and disappear behind the green drapes hung over the metal hoop that curved above Johnny. The mirror was convex, and Johnny had a fairly good if slightly distorted view of everything.

'Oh yes,' Ruopp said. 'Oh yes, dee-de-dee ... here's what we want ... hum-de-hum ... okay ... clamp, please, Nurse, come on, wake up for Christ's sake ... yes sir ... now I believe I'd like one of those ... no, hold it ... don't give me what I ask for, give me what I need ... yes, okay. Strap, please.'

With forceps, the nurse handed Ruopp something that looked like a bundle of thin wires twisted together. Ruopp picked them delicately out of the air with tweezers.

Like an Italian dinner, Johnny thought, *and look at all that spaghetti sauce*. That was what made him feel ill, and he looked away. Above him, in the gallery, the rest of the bandit gang looked down at him. Their eyes looked pale and merciless and frightening. Then he spotted Weizak, third from the right, his watch pinned neatly to the front of his gown.

Johnny nodded.

Weizak nodded back.

That made it a little better.

3 ·

Ruopp finished the connections between his knees and calves, and Johnny was turned over. Things continued. The anesthesiologist asked him if he felt all right. Johnny told her he thought he felt as well as possible under the circumstances. She asked him if he would like to listen to a tape and he said that would be very nice. A few moments later the clear, sweet voice of Joan Baez filled the operating room. Ruopp did his thing. Johnny grew sleepy and dozed off. When he woke up the operation was still going on. Weizak was still there. Johnny raised one hand, acknowledging his presence, and Weizak nodded again.

4 ·
An hour later it was done. He was wheeled into a recovery room where a nurse kept asking him if he could tell her how many of his toes she was touching. After a while, Johnny could.

Ruopp came in, his bandit's mask hanging off to one side.

'All right?' he asked.

'Yes.'

'It went very well,' Ruopp said. 'I'm optimistic.'

'Good.'

'You'll have some pain,' Ruopp said. 'Quite a lot of it, perhaps. The therapy itself will give you a lot of pain at first. Stick with it.'

'Stick with it,' Johnny muttered.

'Good afternoon,' Ruopp said, and left. Probably, Johnny thought, to play a quick nine on the local golf course before it got too dark.

5 ·
Quite a lot of pain.

By nine P.M. the last of the local had worn off, and Johnny was in agony. He was forbidden to move his legs without the help of two nurses. It felt as if nail-studded belts had been looped around his knees and then cinched cruelly tight. Time slowed to an inchworm's crawl. He would glance at his watch, sure that an hour had passed since the last time he had looked at it, and would see instead that it had only been four minutes. He became sure he couldn't stand the pain for another minute, then the minute would pass, and he would be sure he couldn't stand it for another minute.

He thought of all the minutes stacked up ahead, like coins in a slot five miles high, and the blackest depression he had ever known swept over him in a smooth solid wave and carried him down. They were going to torture

151

him to death. Operations on his elbows, thighs, his neck. Therapy. Walkers, wheelchairs, canes.

You're going to have pain ... stick with it.

No, you *stick with it,* Johnny thought. *Just leave me alone. Don't come near me again with your butchers' knives. If this is your idea of helping, I want no part of it.*

Steady throbbing pain, digging into the meat of him.

Warmth on his belly, trickling.

He had wet himself.

Johnny Smith turned his face toward the wall and cried.

6 ·

Ten days after that first operation and two weeks before the next one was scheduled, Johnny looked up from the book he was reading – Woodward and Bernstein's *All the President's Men* – and saw Sarah standing in the doorway, looking at him hesitantly.

'Sarah,' he said. 'It is you, isn't it?'

She let out her breath shakily. 'Yes. It's me, Johnny.'

He put the book down and looked at her. She was smartly dressed in a light-green linen dress, and she held a small, brown clutch bag in front of her like a shield. She had put a streak in her hair and it looked good. It also made him feel a sharp and twisting stab of jealousy – had it been her idea, or that of the man she lived and slept with? She was beautiful.

'Come in,' he said. 'Come in and sit down.'

She crossed the room and suddenly he saw himself as she must see him – too thin, his body slumped a little to one side in the chair by the window, his legs stuck out straight on the hassock, dressed in a johnny and a cheap hospital bathrobe.

'As you can see, I put on my tux,' he said.

'You look fine.' She kissed his cheek and a hundred memories shuffled brightly through his mind like a doubled pack of cards. She sat in the other chair, crossed her legs, and tugged at the hem of her dress.

They looked at each other without saying anything.

He saw that she was very nervous. If someone were to touch her on the shoulder, she would probably spring right out of her seat.

'I didn't know if I should come,' she said, 'but I really wanted to.'

'I'm glad you did.'

Like strangers on a bus, he thought dismally. *It's got to be more than this, doesn't it?*

'So how're you doing?' she asked.

He smiled. 'I've been in the war. Want to see my battle scars?' He raised his gown over his knees, showing the S-shaped incisions that were now beginning to heal. They were still red and hashmarked with stitches.

'Oh, my Lord, what are they *doing* to you?'

'They're trying to put Humpty Dumpty back together again,' Johnny said. 'All the king's horses, all the king's men, and all the king's doctors. So I guess . . .' And then he stopped, because she was crying.

'Don't say it like that, Johnny,' she said. 'Please don't say it like that.'

'I'm sorry. It was just . . . I was trying to joke about it.' Was that it? Had he been trying to laugh it off or had it been a way of saying, *Thanks for coming to see me, they're cutting me to pieces?*

'Can you? Can you joke about it?' She had gotten a Kleenex from the clutch bag and was wiping her eyes with it.

'Not very often. I guess seeing you again . . . the defenses go up, Sarah.'

'Are they going to let you out of here?'

'Eventually. It's like running the gauntlet in the old days, did you ever read about that? If I'm still alive after every Indian in the tribe has had a swing at me with his tomahawk, I get to go free.'

'This summer?'

'No, I . . . I don't think so.'

'I'm so sorry it happened,' she said, so low he could barely hear her. 'I try to figure out why . . . or how things could have changed . . . and it just robs me of sleep. If I

hadn't eaten that bad hot dog . . . if you had stayed instead of going back . . .' She shook her head and looked at
him, her eyes red. 'It seems sometimes there's no percent-
age.'

Johnny smiled. 'Double zero. House spin. Hey, you remember that? I clobbered that Wheel, Sarah.'

'Yes. You won over five hundred dollars.'

He looked at her, still smiling, but now the smile was
puzzled, wounded almost. 'You want to know something
funny? My doctors think maybe the reason I lived was
because I had some sort of head injury when I was young.
But I couldn't remember any, and neither could my mom
and dad. But it seems like every time I think of it, I flash
on that Wheel of Fortune . . . and a smell like burning
rubber.'

'Maybe you were in a car accident . . .' she began doubtfully.

'No, I don't think that's it. But it's like the Wheel was
my warning . . . and I ignored it.'

She shifted a little and said uneasily, 'Don't, Johnny.'

He shrugged. 'Or maybe it was just that I used up four
years of luck in one evening. But look at this, Sarah.'
Carefully, painfully, he took one leg off the hassock, bent
it to a ninety-degree angle, then stretched it out on the
hassock again. 'Maybe they can put Humpty back together again. When I woke up, I couldn't do that, and I
couldn't get my legs to straighten out as much as they
are now, either.'

'And you can *think*, Johnny,' she said. 'You can *talk*.
We all thought that . . . you know.'

'Yeah, Johnny the turnip.' A silence fell between them
again, awkward and heavy. Johnny broke it by saying
with forced brightness, 'So how's by you?'

'Well . . . I'm married. I guess you knew that.'

'Dad told me.'

'He's such a fine man,' Sarah said. And then, in a burst,
'I couldn't wait, Johnny. I'm sorry about that, too. The
doctors said you'd never come out of it, that you'd get
lower and lower until you just . . . just slipped away. And

154

even if I had known . . .' She looked up at him with an uneasy expression of defense on her face. 'Even if I had known, Johnny, I don't think I could have waited. Four-and-a-half years is a long time.'

'Yeah, it is,' he said. 'That's a hell of a long time. You want to hear something morbid? I got them to bring me four years worth of news magazines just so I could see who died. Truman. Janis Joplin. Jimi Hendrix – Jesus, I thought of him doing "Purple Haze" and I could hardly believe it. Dan Blocker. And you and me. We just slipped away.'

'I feel so bad about it,' she said, nearly whispering. 'So damn guilty. But I love the guy, Johnny. I love him a lot.'

'Okay, that's what matters.'

'His name is Walt Hazlett, and he's a . . .'

'I think I'd rather hear about your kid,' Johnny said. 'No offense, huh?'

'He's a peach,' she said, smiling. 'He's seven months old now. His name is Dennis but we call him Denny. He's named after his paternal grandfather.'

'Bring him in sometime. I'd like to see him.'

'I will,' Sarah said, and they smiled at each other falsely, knowing that nothing of the kind was ever going to happen. 'Johnny, is there anything that you need?'

Only you, babe. And the last four-and-a-half years back again.

'Nah,' he said. 'You still teachin?'

'Still teachin, for a while yet,' she agreed.

'Still snortin that wicked cocaine?'

'Oh Johnny, you haven't changed. Same old tease.'

'Same old tease,' he agreed, and the silence fell between them again with an almost audible thump.

'Can I come see you again?'

'Sure,' he said. 'That would be fine, Sarah.' He hesitated, not wanting it to end so inconclusively, not wanting to hurt her or himself if it could be avoided. Wanting to say something honest.

'Sarah,' he said, 'you did the right thing.'

'Did I?' she asked. She smiled, and it trembled at the

155

corners of her mouth. 'I wonder. It all seems so cruel and
... I can't help it, so *wrong*. I love my husband and my
baby, and when Walt says that someday we're going to be
living in the finest house in Bangor, I believe him. He
says someday he's going to run for Bill Cohen's seat in the
House, and I believe that, too. He says someday someone
from Maine is going to be elected president, and I can
almost believe that. And I come in here and look at your
poor legs . . .' She was beginning to cry again now. 'They
look like they went through a Mixmaster or something
and you're so *thin* . . .'

'No, Sarah, don't.'

'You're so thin and it seems wrong and cruel and I *hate*
it, I *hate* it, because it isn't right at all, none of it!'

'Sometimes nothing is right, I guess,' he said. 'Tough
old world. Sometimes you just have to do what you can
and try to live with it. You go and be happy, Sarah. And
if you want to come and see me, come on and come. Bring
a cribbage board.'

'I will,' she said. 'I'm sorry to cry. Not very cheery for
you, huh?'

'It's all right,' he said, and smiled. 'You want to get off
that cocaine, baby. Your nose'll fall off.'

She laughed a little. 'Same old Johnny,' she said. Suddenly she bent and kissed his mouth. 'Oh, Johnny, be well
soon.'

He looked at her thoughtfully as she drew away.

'Johnny?'

'You didn't leave it,' he said. 'No, you didn't leave it
at all.'

'Leave what?' She was frowning in puzzlement.

'Your wedding ring. You didn't leave it in Montreal.'

He had put his hand up to his forehead and was rubbing the patch of skin over his right eye with his fingers.
His arm cast a shadow and she saw with something very
like superstitious fear that his face was half-light, half-
dark. It made her think of the Halloween mask he had
scared her with. She and Walt had honeymooned in
Montreal, but how could Johnny know that? Unless may-

be Herb had told him. Yes, that was almost certainly it. But only she and Walt knew that she had lost her wedding ring somewhere in the hotel room. No one else knew because he had bought her another ring before they flew home. She had been too embarrassed to tell anyone, even her mother.

'How . . .'

Johnny frowned deeply, then smiled at her. His hand fell away from his forehead and clasped its mate in his lap.

'It wasn't sized right,' he said. 'You were packing, don't you remember, Sarah? He was out buying something and you were packing. He was out buying . . . buying . . . don't know. It's in the dead zone.'

Dead zone?

'He went out to a novelty shop and bought a whole bunch of silly stuff as souvenirs. Whoopee cushions and things like that. But Johnny, how could you know I lost my r . . .'

'You were packing. The ring wasn't sized right, it was a lot too big. You were going to have it taken care of when you got back. But in the meantime, you . . . you . . .' That puzzled frown began to return, then cleared immediately. He smiled at her. 'You stuffed it with toilet paper!'

There was no question about the fear now. It was coiling lazily in her stomach like cold water. Her hand crept up to her throat and she stared at him, nearly hypnotized. *He's got the same look in his eyes, that same cold amused look that he had when he was beating the Wheel that night. What's happened to you, Johnny? What are you?* The blue of his eyes had darkened to a near violet, and he seemed far away. She wanted to run. The room itself seemed to be darkening, as if he were somehow tearing the fabric of reality, pulling apart the links between past and present.

'It slipped off your finger,' he said. 'You were putting his shaving stuff into one of those side pockets and it just slipped off. You didn't notice you'd lost it until later, and

157

so you thought it was somewhere in the room.' He laughed, and it was a high, tinkling, tripping sound – not like Johnny's usual laugh at all – but cold . . . cold. 'Boy, you two turned that room upside down. But you packed it. It's still in that suitcase pocket. All this time. You go up in the attic and look, Sarah. You'll see.'

In the corridor outside, someone dropped a water glass or something and cursed in surprise when it broke. Johnny glanced toward the sound, and his eyes cleared. He looked back, saw her frozen, wide-eyed face, and frowned with concern.

'What? Sarah, did I say something wrong?'

'How did you know?' she whispered. 'How could you know those things?'

'I don't know,' he said. 'Sarah, I'm sorry if I . . .'

'Johnny, I ought to go, Denny's with the sitter.'

'All right. Sarah, I'm sorry I upset you.'

'How could you know about my ring, Johnny?'

He could only shake his head.

7 ·

Halfway down the first-floor corridor, her stomach began to feel strange. She found the ladies' just in time. She hurried in, closed the door of one of the stalls, and threw up violently. She flushed and then stood with her eyes closed, shivering, but also close to laughter. The last time she had seen Johnny she had thrown up, too. Rough justice? Brackets in time, like bookends? She put her hands over her mouth to stifle whatever might be trying to get out – laughter or maybe a scream. And in the darkness the world seemed to tilt irrationally, like a dish. Like a spinning Wheel of Fortune.

8 ·

She had left Denny with Mrs. Labelle, so when she got home the house was silent and empty. She went up the narrow stairway to the attic and turned the switch that controlled the two bare, dangling light bulbs. Their luggage was stacked up in one corner, the Montreal travel

158

stickers still pasted to the sides of the orange Grants' suit-cases. There were three of them. She opened the first, felt through the elasticized side pouches, and found nothing. Likewise the second. Likewise the third.

She drew in a deep breath and then let it out, feeling foolish and a little disappointed – but mostly relieved. Overwhelmingly relieved. No ring. Sorry, Johnny. But on the other hand, I'm not sorry at all. It would have been just a little bit too spooky.

She started to slide the suitcases back into place between a tall pile of Walt's old college texts and the floor lamp that crazy woman's dog had knocked over and which Sarah had never had the heart to throw out. And as she dusted off her hands preparatory to putting the whole thing behind her, a small voice far inside her whispered, almost too low to hear, *Sort of a flying search, wasn't it? Didn't really want to find anything, did you, Sarah?*

No. No, she really hadn't wanted to find anything. And if that little voice thought she was going to open all those suitcases again, it was crazy. She was fifteen minutes in picking up Denny. Walt was bringing home one of the senior partners in his firm for dinner (a *very* big deal), and she owed Bettye Hackman a letter – from the Peace Corps in Uganda, Bettye had gone directly into marriage with the son of a staggeringly rich Kentucky horse breeder. Also, she ought to clean both bathrooms, set her hair, and give Denny a bath. There was really too much to do to be frigging around up in this hot, dirty attic.

So she pulled all three suitcases open again and this time she searched the side pockets *very* carefully, and tucked all the way down in the corner of the third suit-case she found her wedding ring. She held it up to the glare of one of the naked bulbs and read the engraving inside, still as fresh as it had been on the day Walt slipped the ring on her finger: WALTER AND SARAH HAZ-LETT – JULY 9, 1972.

Sarah looked at it for a long time.

Then she put the suitcases back, turned off the lights,

and went back downstairs. She changed out of the linen dress, which was now streaked with dust, and into slacks and a light top. She went down the block to Mrs. Labelle's and picked up her son. They went home and Sarah put Denny in the living room, where he crawled around vigorously while she prepared the roast and peeled some potatoes. With the roast in the oven, she went into the living room and saw that Denny had gone to sleep on the rug. She picked him up and put him in his crib. Then she began to clean the toilets. And in spite of everything, in spite of the way the clock was racing toward dinnertime, her mind never left the ring. Johnny had known. She could even pinpoint the moment he had come by this knowledge. When she had kissed him before leaving.

Just thinking about him made her feel weak and strange, and she wasn't sure why. It was all mixed up. His crooked smile, so much the same, his body, so terribly changed, so light and undernourished, the lifeless way his hair lay against his scalp contrasting so blindingly with the rich memories she still held of him. She had *wanted* to kiss him.

'Stop it,' she murmured to herself. Her face in the bathroom mirror looked like a stranger's face. Flushed and hot and – let's face it, gang, sexy.

Her hand closed on the ring in the pocket of her slacks, and almost – but not quite – before she was aware of what she was going to do, she had thrown it into the clean, slightly blue water of the toilet bowl. All sparkly clean so that if Mr. Treaches of Baribault, Treaches, Moorehouse, and Gendron had to take a leak sometime during the dinner party, he wouldn't be offended by any unsightly ring around the bowl, who knows what roadblocks may stand in the way of a young man on his march toward the counsels of the mighty, right? Who knows anything in this world?

It made a tiny splash and sank slowly to the bottom of the clear water, turning lazily over and over. She thought she heard a small clink when it struck the porcelain at the bottom, but that was probably just imagination. Her head throbbed. The attic had been hot and stale and musty. But Johnny's kiss – that had been sweet. So sweet.

Before she could think about what she was doing (and thus allow reason to reassert itself), she reached out and flushed the toilet. It went with a bang and a roar. It seemed louder, maybe, because her eyes were squeezed shut. When she opened them, the ring was gone. It had been lost, and now it was lost again.

Suddenly her legs felt weak and she sat down on the edge of the tub and put her hands over her face. Her hot, hot face. She wouldn't go back and see Johnny again. It wasn't a good idea. It had upset her. Walt was bringing home a senior partner and she had a bottle of Mondavi and a budget-fracturing roast, those were the things she would think about. She should be thinking about how much she loved Walt, and about Denny asleep in his crib. She should think about how, once you made your choices in this crazy world, you had to live with them. And she would not think about Johnny Smith and his crooked, charming smile anymore.

9 ·

The dinner that night was a great success.

CHAPTER TEN

1 ·

The doctor put Vera Smith on a blood-pressure drug called Hydrodiural. It didn't lower her blood pressure much ('not a dime's worth,' she was fond of writing in her letters), but it did make her feel sick and weak. She had to sit down and rest after vacuuming the floor. Climbing a flight of stairs made her stop at the top and pant like a doggy on a hot August afternoon. If Johnny hadn't told her it was for the best, she would have thrown the pills out the window right then.

The doctor tried her on another drug, and that made her heart race so alarmingly that she did stop taking it.

'This is a trial-and-error procedure,' the doctor said. 'We'll get you fixed up eventually, Vera. Don't worry.'

'I don't worry,' Vera said. 'My faith is in the Lord God.'

'Yes, of course it is. Just as it should be, too.'

By the end of June, the doctor had settled on a combination of Hydrodiural and another drug called Aldomet – fat, yellow, expensive pills, nasty things. When she started taking the two drugs together, it seemed like she had to make water every fifteen minutes. She had headaches. She had heart palpitations. The doctor said her blood pressure was down into the normal range again, but she didn't believe him. What good were doctors, anyway? Look what they were doing to her Johnny, cutting him up like butcher's meat, three operations already, he looked like a monster with stitches all over his arms and legs and neck, and he still couldn't get around without one of those walkers, like old Mrs. Sylvester had to use. If her blood pressure was down, why did she feel so crummy all the time?

'You've got to give your body time enough to get used to the medication,' Johnny said. It was the first Saturday in July, and his parents were up for the weekend. Johnny had just come back from hydrotherapy, and he looked pale and haggard. In each hand he held a small lead ball, and he was raising them and then lowering them into his lap as they talked, flexing his elbows, building up his biceps and triceps. The healing scars which ran like slashmarks across his elbows and forearms expanded and contracted.

'Put your faith in God, Johnny,' Vera said. 'There's no need of all this foolishness. Put your faith in God and he'll help you.'

'Vera . . .' Herb began.

'Don't you Vera me. This is *foolishness*! Doesn't the Bible say, ask and it shall be given, knock and it shall be opened unto you? There's no need for me to take that evil medicine and no need for my boy to let those doctors

162

go on torturing him. It's wrong, it's not helping, and *it's sinful!*'

Johnny put the balls of lead shot on the bed. The muscles in his arms were trembling. He felt sick to his stomach and exhausted and suddenly furious at his mother.

'The Lord helps those who help themselves,' he said. 'You don't want the Christian God at all, Mom. You want a magic genie that's going to come out of a bottle and give you three wishes.'

'Johnny!'

'Well, it's true.'

'Those doctors put that idea in your head! All of these crazy ideas!' Her lips were trembling; her eyes wide but tearless. 'God brought you out of that coma to do his will, John. These others, they're just...'

'Just trying to get me back on my feet so I won't have to do God's will from a wheelchair the rest of my life.'

'Let's not have an argument,' Herb said. 'Families shouldn't argue.' And hurricanes shouldn't blow, but they do every year, and nothing he could say was going to stop this. It had been coming.

'If you put your trust in God, Johnny...' Vera began, taking no notice of Herb at all.

'I don't trust anything anymore.'

'I'm sorry to hear you say that,' she said. Her voice was stiff and distant. 'Satan's agents are everywhere. They'll try to turn you from your destiny. Looks like they are getting along with it real well.'

'You have to make some kind of... of eternal thing out of it, don't you? I'll tell you what it was, it was a stupid accident, a couple of kids were dragging and I just happened to get turned into dog meat. You know what I want, Mom? I want to get out of here. That's all I want. And I want you to go on taking your medicine and... and try to get your feet back on the ground. That's all I want.'

'I'm leaving.' She stood up. Her face was pale and drawn. 'I'll pray for you, Johnny.'

163

He looked at her helpless, frustrated, and unhappy. His anger was gone. He had taken it out on her. 'Keep taking your medicine!' he said.

'I pray that you'll see the light.'

She left the room, her face set and as grim as stone.

Johnny looked helplessly at his father.

'John, I wish you hadn't done that,' Herb said.

'I'm tired. It doesn't do a thing for my judgment. Or my temper.'

'Yeah,' Herb said. He seemed about to say more and didn't.

'Is she still planning to go out to California for that flying saucer symposium or whatever it is?'

'Yes. But she may change her mind. You never know from one day to the next, and it's still a month away.'

'You ought to do something.'

'Yeah? What? Put her away? Commit her?'

Johnny shook his head. 'I don't know. But maybe it's time you thought about that seriously instead of just acting like it's out of the question. She's sick. You have to see that.'

Herb said loudly: 'She was all right before you . . .'

Johnny winced, as if slapped.

'Look, I'm sorry. John, I didn't mean that.'

'Okay, Dad.'

'No, I really didn't.' Herb's face was a picture of misery. 'Look, I ought to go after her. She's probably leafleting the hallways by now.'

'Okay.'

'Johnny, just try to forget this and concentrate on getting well. She does love you, and so do I. Don't be hard on us.'

'No. It's all right, dad.'

Herb kissed Johnny's cheek. 'I have to go after her.'

'All right.'

Herb left. When they were gone, Johnny got up and tottered the three steps between his chair and the bed. Not much. But something. A start. He wished more than his father knew that he hadn't blown up at his mother like that. He wished it because an odd sort of certainty was growing in him that his mother was not going to live much longer.

2 .

Vera stopped taking her medication. Herb talked to her, then cajoled, finally demanded. It did no good. She showed him the letters of her 'correspondents in Jesus', most of them scrawled and full of misspellings, all of them supporting her stand and promising to pray for her. One of them was from a lady in Rhode Island who had also been at the farm in Vermont, waiting for the end of the world (along with her pet Pomeranian, Otis). '*GOD* is the best medicine,' this lady wrote, 'ask *GOD* and YOU WILL BE HEALED, not DRS who OSURP the POWER of *GOD*, it is DRS who have caused all the CANCER in this evil world with there DEVIL'S MEDDLING, anyone who has had SURGERY for instance, even MINOR like TONSILS OUT, sooner or later they will end up with CANCER, this is a proven fact, so ask *GOD*, pray *GOD*, merge YOUR WILL with HIS WILL and YOU WILL BE *HEALED*¦¦'

Herb talked to Johnny on the phone, and the next day Johnny called his mother and apologized for being so short with her. He asked her to please start taking the medicine again – for him. Vera accepted his apology, but refused to go back to the medication. If God needed her treading the earth, then he would see she continued to tread it. If God wanted to call her home, he would do that even if she took a barrel of pills a day. It was a seamless argument, and Johnny's only possible rebuttal was the one that Catholics and Protestants alike have rejected for eighteen hundred years: that God works His will through the mind of man as well as through the spirit of man.

'Momma,' he said, 'haven't you thought that God's will was for some doctor to invent that drug so you could live longer? Can't you even consider that idea?'

Long distance was no medium for theological argument. She hung up.

The next day Marie Michaud came into Johnny's room, put her head on his bed, and wept.

'Here, here,' Johnny said, startled and alarmed. 'What's this? What's wrong?'

'My boy,' she said, still crying. 'My Mark. They operated on him and it was just like you said. He's fine. He's going to see out of his bad eye again. Thank God.'

She hugged Johnny and he hugged her back as best he could. With her warm tears on his own cheek, he thought that whatever had happened to him wasn't all bad. Maybe some things should be told, or seen, or found again. It wasn't even so farfetched to think that God *was* working through him, although his own concept of God was fuzzy and ill-defined. He held Marie and told her how glad he was. He told her to remember that he wasn't the one who had operated on Mark, and that he barely remembered what it was that he had told her. She left shortly after that, drying her eyes as she went, leaving Johnny alone to think.

3 ·

Early in August, Dave Pelsen came to see Johnny. The Cleaves Mills High assistant principal was a small, neat man who wore thick glasses and Hush Puppies and a series of loud sports jackets. Of all the people who came to see Johnny during that almost endless summer of 1975, Dave had changed the least. The gray was speckled a little more fully through his hair, but that was all.

'So how are you doing? Really?' Dave asked, when they had finished the amenities.

'Not so bad,' Johnny said. 'I can walk alone now if I don't overdo it. I can swim six laps in the pool. I get headaches sometimes, real killers, but the doctors say I can expect that to go on for some time. Maybe the rest of my life.'

'Mind a personal question?'

'If you're going to ask me if I can still get it up,' Johnny

166

said with a grin, 'that's affirmative.'

'That's good to know, but what I wanted to know about is the money. Can you pay for this?'

Johnny shook his head. 'I've been in the hospital for going on five years. No one but a Rockefeller could pay for that. My father and mother got me into some sort of state-funded program. Total Disaster, or something like that.'

Dave nodded. 'The Extraordinary Disaster program. I figured that. But how did they keep you out of the state hospital, Johnny? That place is the pits.'

'Dr. Weizak and Dr. Brown saw to that. And they're largely responsible for my having been able to come back as far as I have. I was a . . . a guinea pig, Dr. Weizak says. How long can we keep this comatose man from turning into a total vegetable? The physical therapy unit was working on me the last two years I was in coma. I had megavitamin shots . . . my ass still looks like a case of smallpox. Not that they expected any return on the project from me personally. I was assumed to be a terminal case almost from the time I came in. Weizak says that what he and Brown did with me is "aggressive life support". He thinks it's the beginning of a response to all the criticism about sustaining life after hope of recovery is gone. Anyway, they couldn't continue to use me if I'd gone over to the state hospital, so they kept me here. Eventually, they would have finished with me and then I *would* have gone to the state hospital.'

'Where the most sophisticated care you would have gotten would have been a turn every six hours to prevent bedsores,' Dave said. 'And if you'd waked up in 1980, you would have been a basket case.'

'I think I would have been a basket case no matter what,' Johnny said. He shook his head slowly. 'I think if someone proposes one more operation on me, I'll go nuts. And I'm still going to have a limp and I'll never be able to turn my head all the way to the left.'

'When are they letting you out?'

'In three weeks, God willing.'

167

'Then what?'

Johnny shrugged. 'I'm going down home, I guess. To Pownal. My mother's going to be in California for a while on a . . . a religious thing. Dad and I can use the time to get reacquainted. I got a letter from one of the big literary agents in New York . . . well, not *him*, exactly, but one of his assistants. They think there might be a book in what happened to me. I thought I'd try to do two or three chapters and an outline, maybe this guy or his assistants can sell it. The money would come in pretty damn handy, no kidding there.'

'Has there been any other media interest?'

'Well, the guy from the Bangor *Daily News* who did that original story . . .'

'Bright? He's good.'

'He'd like to come down to Pownal after I blow this joint and do a feature story. I like the guy, but right now I'm holding him off. There's no money in it for me, and right now, frankly, that's what I'm looking for. I'd go on "To Tell the Truth" if I thought I could make two hundred bucks out of it. My folks' savings are gone. They sold their car and bought a clunker. Dad took a second mortgage on the house when he should have been thinking about retiring and selling it and living on the proceeds.'

'Have you thought about coming back into teaching?'

Johnny glanced up. 'Is that an offer?'

'It ain't chopped liver.'

'I'm grateful,' Johnny said. 'But I'm just not going to be ready in September, Dave.'

'I wasn't thinking about September. You must remember Sarah's friend, Anne Strafford?' Johnny nodded. 'Well, she's Anne Beatty now, and she's going to have a baby in December. So we need an English teacher second semester. Light schedule. Four classes, one senior study hall, two free periods.'

'Are you making a firm offer, Dave?'

'Firm.'

'That's pretty damn good of you,' Johnny said hoarsely.

'Hell with that,' Dave said easily. 'You were a pretty damn good teacher.'

'Can I have a couple of weeks to think it over?'

'Until the first of October, if you want,' Dave said. 'You'd still be able to work on your book, I think. If it looks like there might be a possibility there.'

Johnny nodded.

'And you might not want to stay down there in Pownal too long,' Dave said. 'You might find it ... uncomfortable.'

Words rose to Johnny's lips and he had to choke them off.

Not for long, Dave. You see, my mother's in the process of blowing her brains out right now. She's just not using a gun. She's going to have a stroke. She'll be dead before Christmas unless my father and I can persuade her to start taking her medicine again, and I don't think we can. And I'm a part of it – how much of a part I don't know. I don't think I want to know.

Instead he replied, 'News travels, huh?'

Dave shrugged. 'I understand through Sarah that your mother has had problems adjusting. She'll come around, Johnny. In the meantime, think about it.'

'I will. In fact, I'll give you a tentative yes right now. It would be good to teach again. To get back to normal.'

'You're my man,' Dave said.

After he left, Johnny lay down on his bed and looked out the window. He was very tired. *Get back to normal.* Somehow he didn't think that was ever really going to happen.

He felt one of his headaches coming on.

4 ·

The fact that Johnny Smith had come out of his coma with something extra finally did get into the paper, and it made page one under David Bright's by-line. It happened less than a week before Johnny left the hospital.

He was in physical therapy, lying on his back on a

169

floorpad. Resting on his belly was a twelve-pound medicine ball. His physical therapist, Eileen Magown, was standing above him and counting off situps. He was supposed to do ten of them, and he was currently struggling over number eight. Sweat was streaming down his face, and the healing scars on his neck stood out bright red.

Eileen was a small, homely woman with a whipcord body, a nimbus of gorgeous, frizzy red hair, and deep green eyes flecked with hazel. Johnny sometimes called her – with a mixture of irritation and amusement – the world's smallest Marine D.I. She had ordered and cajoled and demanded him back from a bed-fast patient who could barely hold a glass of water to a man who could walk without a cane, do three chinups at a time, and do a complete turn around the hospital pool in fifty-three seconds – not Olympic time, but not bad. She was unmarried and lived in a big house on Center Street in Oldtown with her four cats. She was slate-hard and she wouldn't take no for an answer.

Johnny collapsed backward. 'Nope,' he panted. 'Oh, I don't think so, Eileen.'

'Up, boy!' she cried in high and sadistic good humor. 'Up! Up! Just three more and you can have a Coke!'

'Give me my ten-pound ball and I'll give you two more.'

'That ten-pound ball is going into the *Guinness Book of Records* as the world's biggest suppository if you don't give me three more. *Up!*'

'*Urrrrrrgrah!*' Johnny cried, jerking through number eight. He flopped back down, then jerked up again.

'Great!' Eileen cried. 'One more, one more!'

'*OOOOARRRRRRRRUNCH!*' Johnny screamed, and sat up for the tenth time. He collapsed to the mat, letting the medicine ball roll away. 'I ruptured myself, are you happy, all my guts just came loose, they're floating around inside me, I'll sue you, you goddam harpy.'

'Jeez, what a baby,' Eileen said, offering him her hand. 'This is nothing compared to what I've got on for next time.'

'Forget it,' Johnny said. 'All I'm gonna do next time is swim in the . . .'

He looked at her, an expression of surprise spreading over his face. His grip tightened on her hand until it was almost painful.

'Johnny? What's wrong? Is it a charley horse?'

'Oh gosh,' Johnny said mildly.

'*Johnny?*'

He was still gripping her hand, looking into her face with a faraway, dreamy contemplation that made her feel nervous. She had heard things about Johnny Smith, rumors that she had disregarded with her own brand of hard-headed pragmatism. There was a story that he had predicted Marie Michaud's boy was going to be all right, even before the doctors were one hundred percent sure they wanted to try the risky operation. Another rumor had something to do with Dr. Weizak; it was said Johnny had told him his mother was not dead but living someplace on the West Coast under another name. As far as Eileen Magown was concerned, the stories were so much eyewash, on a par with the confession magazines and sweet-savage love stories so many nurses read on station. But the way he was looking at her now made her feel afraid. It was as if he was looking inside her.

'Johnny, are you okay?' They were alone in the physical therapy room. The big double doors with the frosted glass panels which gave on the pool area were closed.

'Gosh sakes,' Johnny said. 'You better . . . yes, there's still time. Just about.'

'What are you talking about?'

He snapped out of it then. He let go of her hand . . . but he had gripped it tightly enough to leave white indentations along the back.

'Call the fire department,' he said. 'You forgot to turn off the burner. The curtains are catching on fire.'

'What . . . ?'

'The burner caught the dish towel and the dish towel caught the curtains,' Johnny said impatiently. 'Hurry up and call them. Do you want your house to burn down?'

'Johnny, you can't know . . .'

'Never mind what you can't know,' Johnny said, grabbing her elbow. He got her moving and they walked across to the doors. Johnny was limping badly on his left leg, as he always did when he was tired. They crossed the room that housed the swimming pool, their heels clacking hollowly on the tiles, then went out into the first floor hallway and down to the nurses' station. Inside, two nurses were drinking coffee and a third was on the phone, telling someone on the other end how she had redone her apartment.

'Are you going to call or should I?' Johnny asked.

Eileen's mind was in a whirl. Her morning routine was as set as a single person's is apt to be. She had gotten up and boiled herself a single egg while she ate a whole grapefruit, unsweetened, and a bowl of All-Bran. After breakfast she had dressed and driven to the hospital. *Had* she turned off the burner? Of course she had. She couldn't specifically remember doing it, but it was habit. She must have.

'Johnny, really, I don't know where you got the idea . . .'

'Okay, I will.'

They were in the nurses' station now, a glassed-in booth furnished with three straight-backed chairs and a hot plate. The little room was dominated by the callboard – rows of small lights that flashed red when a patient pushed his call button. Three of them were flashing now. The two nurses went on drinking their coffee and talking about some doctor who had turned up drunk at Benjamin's. The third was apparently talking with her beautician.

'Pardon me, I have to make a call,' Johnny said.

The nurse covered the phone with her hand. 'There's a pay phone in the lob . . .'

'Thanks,' Johnny said, and took the phone out of her hand. He pushed for one of the open lines and dialed O. He got a busy signal. 'What's wrong with this thing?'

'Hey!' The nurse who had been talking to her beautician cried. 'What the hell do you think you're doing? Give me that!'

Johnny remembered that he was in a hospital with its own switchboard and dialed 9 for an outside line. Then he redialed the 0.

The deposed nurse, her cheeks flaming with anger, grabbed for the phone. Johnny pushed her away. She whirled, saw Eileen, and took a step toward her. 'Eileen, what's with this crazy guy?' she asked stridently. The other two nurses had put down their coffee cups and were staring gape-mouthed at Johnny.

Eileen shrugged uncomfortably. 'I don't know, he just . . .'

'Operator.'

'Operator, I want to report a fire in Oldtown,' Johnny said. 'Can you give me the correct number to call, please?'

'Hey,' one of the nurses said. 'Whose house is on fire?'

Eileen shifted her feet nervously. 'He says mine is.'

The nurse who had been talking about her apartment to her beautician did a double take. 'Oh my God, it's *that* guy,' she said.

Johnny pointed at the callboard, where five or six lights were flashing now. 'Why don't you go see what those people want?'

The operator had connected him with the Oldtown Fire Department.

'My name is John Smith and I need to report a fire. It's at . . .' He looked at Eileen. 'What's your address?'

For a moment Johnny didn't think she was going to tell him. Her mouth worked, but nothing came out. The two coffee-drinkers had now forsaken their cups and withdrawn to the station's far corner. They were whispering together like little girls in a grammar school john. Their eyes were wide.

'Sir?' the voice on the other end asked.

'Come *on*,' Johnny said, 'do you want your cats to fry?'

'624 Center Street,' Eileen said reluctantly. 'Johnny, you've wigged out.'

173

Johnny repeated the address into the phone. 'It's in the kitchen.'

'Your name, sir?'

'John Smith. I'm calling from the Eastern Maine Medical Center in Bangor.'

'May I ask how you came by your information?'

'We'd be on the phone the rest of the day. My information is correct. Now go put it out.' He banged the phone down.

'. . . and he said Sam Weizak's mother was still . . .'

She broke off and looked at Johnny. For a moment he felt all of them looking at him, their eyes lying on his skin like tiny, hot weights, and he knew what would come of this and it made his stomach turn.

'Eileen,' he said.

'What?'

'Do you have a friend next door?'

'Yes . . . Burt and Janice are next door . . .'

'Either of them home?'

'I guess Janice probably would be, sure.'

'Why don't you give her a call?'

Eileen nodded, suddenly understanding what he was getting at. She took the phone from his hand and dialed an 827 exchange number. The nurses stood by watching avidly, as if they had stepped into a really exciting TV program by accident.

'Hello? Jan? It's Eileen. Are you in your kitchen? . . . Would you take a look out your window and tell me if everything looks, well, all right over at my place? . . . Well, a friend of mine says . . . I'll tell you after you go look, okay?' Eileen was blushing. 'Yes, I'll wait.' She looked at Johnny and repeated, 'You've wigged out, Johnny.'

There was a pause that seemed to go on and on. Then Eileen began listening again. She listened for a long time and then said in a strange, subdued voice totally unlike her usual one: 'No, that's all right, Jan. They've been called. No . . . I can't explain right now but I'll tell you later.' She looked at Johnny. 'Yes, it is funny how I could

174

have known ... but I can explain. At least I think I can. Good-bye.'

She hung up the telephone. They all looked at her, the nurses with avid curiosity, Johnny with only dull certainty.

'Jan says there's smoke pouring out of my kitchen window,' Eileen said, and all three nurses sighed in unison. Their eyes, wide and somehow accusing, turned to Johnny again. *Jury's eyes*, he thought dismally.

'I ought to go home,' Eileen said. The aggressive, cajoling, positive physical therapist was gone, replaced by a small woman who was worried about her cats and her house and her things. 'I ... I don't know how to thank you, Johnny ... I'm sorry I didn't believe you, but ...' She began to weep.

One of the nurses moved toward her, but Johnny was there first. He put an arm around her and led her out into the hall.

'You really can,' Eileen whispered. 'What they said ...'

'You go on,' Johnny said. 'I'm sure it's going to be fine. There's going to be some minor smoke and water damage, and that's all. That movie poster from *Butch Cassidy and the Sundance Kid*, I think you're going to lose that, but that's all.'

'Yes, okay. Thank you, Johnny. God bless you.' She kissed him on the cheek and then began to trot down the hall. She looked back once, and the expression on her face was very much like superstitious dread.

The nurses were lined up against the glass of the nurses' station, staring at him. Suddenly they reminded him of crows on a telephone line, crows staring down at something bright and shiny, something to be pecked at and pulled apart.

'Go on and answer your calls,' he said crossly, and they flinched back at the sound of his voice. He began to limp up the hall toward the elevator, leaving them to start the gossip on its way. He was tired. His legs hurt. His hip joints felt as if they had broken glass in them. He wanted to go to bed.

CHAPTER ELEVEN

1 .

'What are you going to do?' Sam Weizak asked.

'Christ, I don't know,' Johnny said. 'How many did you say are down there?'

'About eight. One of them is the northern New England AP stringer. And there are people from two of the TV stations with cameras and lights. The hospital director is quite angry with you, Johnny. He feels you have been naughty.'

'Because a lady's house was going to burn down?' Johnny asked. 'All I can say is it must have been one frigging slow news day.'

'As a matter of fact it wasn't. Ford vetoed two bills. The P.L.O. blew up a restaurant in Tel Aviv. And a police dog sniffed out four hundred pounds of marijuana at the airport.'

'Then what are they doing here?' Johnny asked. When Sam had come in with the news that reporters were gathering in the lobby, his first sinking thought was what his mother might make of this. She was with his father in Pownal, making ready for her California pilgrimage, which began the following week. Neither Johnny nor his father believed the trip was a good idea, and the news that her son had somehow turned psychic might make her cancel it, but in this case Johnny was very much afraid that the cure might be the greater of two evils. Something like this could set her off for good.

On the other hand – this thought suddenly blossomed in his mind with all the force of inspiration – it might persuade her to start taking her medicine again.

'They're here because what happened is news,' Sam said. 'It has all the classic ingredients.'

'I didn't do anything, I just . . .'

'You just told Eileen Magown her house was on fire

and it was,' Sam said softly. 'Come on, Johnny, you must have known this was going to happen sooner or later.'

'I'm no publicity hound,' Johnny said grimly.

'No. I didn't mean to suggest you were. An earthquake is no publicity hound. But the reporters cover it. People want to know.'

'What if I just refuse to talk to them?'

'That is not much of an option,' Sam replied. 'They will go away and publish crazy rumors. Then, when you leave the hospital, they will fall on you. They will shove microphones in your face as if you were a senator or a crime boss, nuh?'

Johnny thought about it. 'Is Bright down there?'

'Yes.'

'Suppose I ask him to come up? He can get the story and give it to the rest of them.'

'You can do that, but it would make the rest of them extremely unhappy. And an unhappy reporter will be your enemy. Nixon made them unhappy and they tore him to pieces.'

'I'm not Nixon,' Johnny said.

Weizak grinned radiantly. 'Thank God,' he said.

'What do you suggest?' Johnny asked.

2 ·

The reporters stood up and crowded forward when Johnny stepped through the swing doors and into the west lobby. He was wearing a white shirt, open at the collar, and a pair of blue jeans that were too big for him. His face was pale but composed. The scars from the tendon operations stood out clearly on his neck. Flashbulbs popped warm fire at him and made him wince. Questions were babbled.

'Here! Here!' Sam Weizak shouted. 'This is a convalescent patient! He wants to make a brief statement and he will answer some of your questions, but only if you behave in an orderly fashion! Now fall back and let him breathe!'

Two sets of TV light bars flashed on, bathing the lobby

in an unearthly glare. Doctors and nurses had gathered by the lounge doorway to watch. Johnny winced away from the lights, wondering if this was what they meant by the limelight. He felt as if all of it might be a dream.

'Who're you?' one of the reporters yelled at Weizak.

'I am Samuel Weizak, this young man's doctor, and that name is spelled with two X's.'

There was general laughter and the mood eased a little.

'Johnny, you feel all right?' Weizak asked. It was early evening, and his sudden insight that Eileen Magown's kitchen was catching fire seemed distant and unimportant, the memory of a memory.

'Sure,' he said.

'What's your statement?' one of the reporters called.

'Well,' Johnny said, 'it's this. My physical therapist is a woman named Eileen Magown. She's a very nice lady, and she's been helping me get my strength back. I was in an accident, you see, and ...' One of the TV cameras moved in, goggling at him blankly, throwing him off-stride for a moment '... and I got pretty weak. My muscles sort of collapsed. We were in the physical therapy room this morning, just finishing up, and I got the feeling that her house was on fire. That is, to be more specific ...' *Jesus, you sound like an asshole!* 'I felt that she had forgotten to turn off her stove and that the curtains in the kitchen were about to catch fire. So we just went and called the fire department and that's all there was to it.'

There was a moment's gaping pause as they digested that – *I sort of got the feeling, and that's all there was to it* – and then the barrage of questions came again, everything mixed together into a meaningless stew of human voices. Johnny looked around helplessly, feeling disoriented and vulnerable.

'One at a time!' Weizak yelled. 'Raise your hands! Were you never schoolchildren?'

Hands waved, and Johnny pointed at David Bright.

'Would you call this a psychic experience, Johnny?'

178

'I would call it a feeling,' Johnny answered. 'I was doing situps and I finished. Miss Magown took my hand to help me up and I just knew.'

He pointed at someone else.

'Mel Allen, Portland *Sunday Telegram,* Mr. Smith. Was it like a picture? A picture in your head?'

'No, not at all,' Johnny said, but he was not really able to remember what it *had* been like.

'Has this happened to you before, Johnny?' A young woman in a slacksuit asked.

'Yes, a few times.'

'Can you tell us about the other incidents?'

'No, I'd rather not.'

One of the TV reporters raised his hand and Johnny nodded at him. 'Did you have any of these flashes *before* your accident and the resulting coma, Mr. Smith?'

Johnny hesitated.

The room seemed very still. The TV lights were warm on his face, like a tropical sun. 'No,' he said.

Another barrage of questions. Johnny looked helplessly at Weizak again.

'Stop! Stop!' He bellowed. He looked at Johnny as the roar subsided. 'You are done, Johnny?'

'I'll answer two more questions,' Johnny said. 'Then . . . really . . it's been a long day for me . . . yes, Ma'am?'

He was pointing to a stout woman who had wedged herself in between two young reporters. 'Mr. Smith,' she said in a loud, carrying, tubalike voice, 'who will be the Democrats' nominee for president next year?'

'I can't tell you that,' Johnny said, honestly surprised at the question. 'How could I tell you that?'

More hands were raised. Johnny pointed to a tall, sober-faced man in a dark suit. He took one step forward. There was something prim and coiled about him.

'Mr. Smith, I'm Roger Dussault, from the Lewiston *Sun*, and I would like to know if you have any idea why you should have such an extraordinary ability as this . . . if indeed you do. Why you, Mr. Smith?'

179

Johnny cleared his throat. 'As I understand your question ... you're asking me to justify something I don't understand. I can't do that.'

'Not justify, Mr. Smith. Just explain.'

He thinks I'm hoaxing them. Or trying.

Weizak stepped up beside Johnny. 'I wonder if I might answer that,' he said. 'Or at least attempt to explain why it cannot be answered.'

'Are you psychic, too?' Dussault asked coldly.

'Yes, all neurologists must be, it's a requirement,' Weizak said. There was a burst of laughter and Dussault flushed.

'Ladies and gentlemen of the press. This man spent four-and-a-half years in a coma. We who study the human brain have no idea why he did, or why he came out of it, and this is for the simple reason that we do not understand what a coma really is, any more than we understand sleep or the simple act of waking. Ladies and gentlemen, we do not understand the brain of a frog or the brain of an ant. You may quote me on these things ... you see I am fearless, nuh?'

More laughter. They liked Weizak. But Dussault did not laugh.

'You may also quote me as saying I believe this man is now in possession of a very new human ability, or a very old one. Why? If I and my colleagues do not understand the brain of an ant, can I tell you why? I cannot. I can suggest some interesting things to you, however, things which may or may not have bearing. A part of John Smith's brain has been damaged beyond repair – a very small part, but all parts of the brain may be vital. He calls this his "dead zone", and there, apparently, a number of trace memories were stored. All of these wiped-out memories seem to be part of a "set" – that of street, road, and highway designations. A subset of a larger overall set, that of where it is. This is a small but total aphasia which seems to include both language and vizualization skills.

'Balancing this off, another tiny part of John Smith's

180

brain appears to have *awakened*. A section of the cerebrum within the parietal lobe. This is one of the deeply grooved sections of the "forward" or "thinking" brain. The electrical responses from this section of Smith's brain are way out of line from what they should be, nuh? Here is one more thing. The parietal lobe has something to do with the sense of touch – how much or how little we are not completely sure – and it is very near to that area of the brain that sorts and identifies various shapes and textures. And it has been my own observation that John's "flashes" are always preceded by some sort of touching.'

Silence. Reporters were scribbling madly. The TV cameras, which had moved in to focus on Weizak, now pulled back to include Johnny in the picture.

'Is that it, Johnny?' Weizak asked again.

'I guess...'

Dussault suddenly shouldered his way through the knot of reporters. For a bemused moment Johnny thought he was going to join them in front of the doors, possibly for the purpose of rebuttal. Then he saw that Dussault was slipping something from around his neck.

'Let's have a demonstration,' he said. He was holding a medallion on a fine-link gold chain. 'Let's see what you can do with this.'

'We'll see no such thing,' Weizak said. His bushy salt-and-pepper eyebrows had drawn thunderously together and he stared down at Dussault like Moses. 'This man is not a carnival performer, sir!'

'You sure could have fooled me,' Dussault said. 'Either he can or he can't, right? While you were busy suggesting things, I was busy suggesting something to myself. What I was suggesting was that these guys can never perform on demand, because they're all as genuine as a pile of three-dollar bills.'

Johnny looked at the other reporters. Except for Bright, who looked rather embarrassed, they were watching avidly. They looked like the nurses peering at him through the glass. Suddenly he felt like a Christian in a pitful of lions. They win either way, he thought. If I can

181

tell him something, they've got a front-page story. If I can't, or if I refuse to try, they've got another kind of story.

'Well?' Dussault asked. The medallion swung back and forth below his fist.

Johnny looked at Weizak, but Weizak was looking away, disgusted.

'Give it to me,' Johnny said.

Dussault handed it over. Johnny put the medallion in his palm. It was a St. Christopher medal. He dropped the fine-link chain on top of it in a crisp little yellow heap and closed his hand over it.

Dead silence fell in the room. The handful of doctors and nurses standing by the lounge doorway had been joined by half a dozen others, some of them dressed in streetclothes and on their way out of the hospital for the night. A crowd of patients had gathered at the end of the hallway leading to the first-floor TV and game lounge. The people who had come for the regular early evening visiting hours had drifted over from the main lobby. A feeling of thick tension lay in the air like a humming power cable.

Johnny stood silently, pale and thin in his white shirt and oversized blue jeans. The St. Christopher medal was clamped so tightly in his right hand that the cords in his wrist stood out clearly in the glare of the TV light bars. In front of him, sober, impeccable, and judgmental in his dark suit, Dussault stood in the adversary position. The moment seemed to stretch out interminably. No one coughed or whispered.

'Oh,' Johnny said softly . . . then: 'Is that it?'

His fingers loosened slowly. He looked at Dussault.

'Well?' Dussault asked, but the authority was suddenly gone from his voice. The tired, nervous young man who had answered the reporters' questions seemed also to be gone. There was a half-smile on Johnny's lips, but there was nothing warm about it. The blue of his eyes had darkened. They had grown cold and distant. Weizak saw it and felt a chill of gooseflesh. He later told his wife that it had been the face of a man looking through a high-powered microscope and observing an interesting species of paramecium.

'It's your sister's medallion,' he said to Dussault. 'Her name was Anne but everyone called her Terry. Your older sister. You loved her. You almost worshiped the ground she walked on.'

Suddenly, terribly, Johnny Smith's voice began to climb and change. It became the cracked and unsure voice of an adolescent.

'It's for when you cross Lisbon Street against the lights, Terry, or when you're out parking with one of those guys from E.L. Don't forget, Terry . . . don't forget . . .'

The plump woman who had asked Johnny who the Democrats would nominate next year uttered a frightened little moan. One of the TV cameramen muttered 'Holy Jesus!' in a hoarse voice.

'Stop it,' Dessault whispered. His face had gone a sick shade of gray. His eyes bulged and spittle shone like chrome on his lower lip in this harsh light. His hands moved for the medallion, which was now looped on its fine gold chain over Johnny's fingers. But his hands moved with no power or authority. The medallion swung back and forth, throwing off hypnotic gleams of light.

'Remember me, Terry,' the adolescent voice begged. 'Stay clean, Terry . . . please, for God's sake stay clean . . .'

'*Stop it! Stop it, you bastard!*'

Now Johnny spoke in his own voice again. 'It was speed, wasn't it? Then meth. She died of a heart attack at twenty-seven. But she wore it ten years, Rog. She remembered you. She never forgot. Never forgot . . . never . . . never . . . never.'

The medallion slipped from his fingers and struck the floor with a small, musical sound. Johnny stared away into emptiness for a moment, his face calm and cool and distant. Dussault grubbed at his feet for the medallion, sobbing hoarsely in the stunned silence.

A flashbulb popped, and Johnny's face cleared and became his own again. Horror touched it, and then pity. He knelt clumsily beside Dussault.

'I'm sorry,' he said. 'I'm sorry, I didn't mean . . .'

'You cheapjack, bastard hoaxer!' Dussault screamed at him. 'It's a lie! All a lie! All a *lie!*' He struck Johnny a clumsy, open-handed blow on the neck and Johnny fell over, striking his head on the floor, hard. He saw stars.

Uproar.

He was dimly aware that Dussault was pushing his way blindly through the crowd and toward the doors. People milled around Dussault, around Johnny. He saw Dussault through a forest of legs and shoes. Then Weizak was beside him, helping him to sit up.

'John, are you all right? Did he hurt you?'

'Not as bad as I hurt him. I'm okay.' He struggled to his feet. Hands – maybe Weizak's, maybe someone else's – helped him. He felt dizzy and sick; almost revolted. This had been a mistake, a terrible mistake.

Someone screamed piercingly – the stout woman who had asked about the Democrats. Johnny saw Dussault pitch forward to his knees, grope at the sleeve of the stout woman's print blouse and then slide tiredly forward onto the tile near the doorway he had been trying to reach. The St. Christopher medal was still in one hand.

'Fainted,' someone said. 'Fainted dead away. I'll be damned.'

'My fault,' Johnny said to Sam Weizak. His throat felt close and tight with shame, with tears. 'All my fault.'

'No,' Sam said. 'No, John.'

But it was. He shook loose of Weizak's hands and went to where Dussault lay, coming around now, eyes blinking dazedly at the ceiling. Two of the doctors had come over to where he lay.

'Is he all right?' Johnny asked. He turned toward the woman reporter in the slacksuit and she shrank away from him. A cramp of fear passed over her face.

Johnny turned the other way, toward the TV reporter who had asked him if he'd had any flashes before his

184

accident. It suddenly seemed very important that he explained to someone. 'I didn't mean to hurt him,' he said. 'Honest to God, I never meant to hurt him. I didn't know . . .'

The TV reporter backed up a step. 'No,' he said. 'Of course you didn't. He was asking for it, anybody could see that. Just . . . don't touch me, huh?'

Johnny looked at him dumbly, lips quivering. He was still in shock but beginning to understand. Oh yes. He was beginning to understand. The TV reporter tried to smile and could only produce a death's-head rictus.

'Just don't touch me, Johnny. Please.'

'It's not like that,' Johnny said – or tried to. Later, he was never sure if any sound had come out.

'Don't touch me, Johnny, okay?'

The reporter backed up to where his cameraman was packing his gear. Johnny stood and watched him. He began to shake all over.

3 ·

'It's for your own good, John,' Weizak said. The nurse stood behind him, a white ghost, a sorcerer's apprentice with her hands hovering above the small, wheeled medication table, a junkie's paradise of sweet dreams.

'No,' Johnny said. He was still shaking, and now there was cold sweat as well. 'No more shots. I've had it up to here with shots.'

'A pill, then.'

'No more pills, either.'

'To help you sleep.'

'Will *he* be able to sleep? That man Dussault?'

'He asked for it,' the nurse murmured, and then flinched as Weizak turned toward her. But Weizak smiled crookedly.

'She is right, nuh?' he said. 'The man asked for it. He thought you were selling empty bottles, John. A good night's sleep and you'll be able to put this in perspective.'

'I'll sleep on my own.'

'Johnny, please.'

It was quarter past eleven. The TV across the room had just gone off. Johnny and Sam had watched the filmed story together; it had been second-lined right after the bills Ford had vetoed. My own story made better theater, Johnny thought with morbid amusement. Film footage of a bald-headed Republican mouthing platitudes about the national budget just didn't compare with the film clip that WABI camera man had gotten here earlier this evening. The clip had ended with Dussault plunging across the floor with his sister's medal clutched in his hand and then crashing down in a faint, clutching at the woman reporter the way a drowning man might clutch at a straw.

When the TV anchorman went on to the police dog and the four hundred pounds of pot, Weizak had left briefly and had come back with the news that the hospital switchboard had jammed up with calls for him even before the report was over. The nurse with the medication had shown up a few minutes later, leading Johnny to believe that Sam had gone down to the nurses' station to do more than check on incoming calls.

At that instant, the telephone rang.

Weizak swore softly under his breath. 'I told them to hold them all. Don't answer it, John, I'll . . .'

But Johnny already had it. He listened for a moment, then nodded. 'Yes, that was right.' He put a hand over the receiver. 'It's my dad,' he said. He uncovered the receiver. 'Hi, Dad. I guess you . . .' He listened. The small smile on his lips faded and was replaced by an expression of dawning horror. His lips moved silently.

'John, what is it?' Weizak asked sharply.

'All right, Daddy,' Johnny said, almost in a whisper. 'Yes. Cumberland General. I know where it is. Just above Jerusalem's Lot. Okay. All right. Daddy . . .'

His voice broke. His eyes were tearless but glistening.

'I know that, Daddy. I love you too. I'm sorry.'

Listened.

'Yes. Yes it was,' Johnny said. 'I'll see you, Daddy. Yes. Good-bye.'

He hung up the phone, put the heels of his hands to his eyes, and pressed.

'Johnny?' Sam leaned forward, took one of his hands away and held it gently. 'Is it your mother?'

'Yeah. It's my mother.'

'Heart attack?'

'Stroke,' Johnny said, and Sam Weizak made a small, pained hissing between his teeth. 'They were watching the TV news ... neither of them had any idea ... and I came on ... and she had a stroke. Christ. She's in the hospital. Now if something happens to my dad, we got a triple play.' He uttered a high scream of laughter. His eyes rolled wildly from Sam to the nurse and back to Sam again. 'It's a good talent,' he said. 'Everybody should have it.' The laugh came again, so like a scream.

'How bad is she?' Sam asked.

'He doesn't know.' Johnny swung his legs out of bed. He had changed back to a hospital gown and his feet were bare.

'What do you think you are doing?' Sam asked sharply.

'What does it look like?'

Johnny got up, and for a moment it seemed that Sam would push him back onto the bed. But he only watched Johnny limp over to the closet. 'Don't be ridiculous. You're not ready for this, John.'

Unmindful of the nurse – they had seen his bare tail enough times, God knew – Johnny let the gown drop around his feet. The thick, twisting scars stood out on the backs of his knees and dimpled into the scant swell of his calves. He began to rummage in the closet for clothes, and came up with the white shirt and jeans he had worn to the news conference.

'John, I absolutely forbid this. As your doctor and your friend. I tell you, it is madness.'

'Forbid all you want, I'm going,' Johnny said. He began to dress. His face wore that expression of distant preoccupation that Sam associated with his trances. The nurse gawped.

'Nurse, you might as well go back to your station,' Sam said.

She backed to the door, stood there for a moment, and then left. Reluctantly.

'Johnny,' Sam said. He got up, went to him, and put a hand on his shoulder. 'You didn't do it.'

Johnny shook the hand off. 'I did it, all right,' he said. 'She was watching me when it happened.' He began to button the shirt.

'You urged her to take her medicine and she stopped.'

Johnny looked at Weizak for a moment and then went back to buttoning his shirt.

'If it hadn't happened tonight, it would have happened tomorrow, next week, next month . . .'

'Or next year. Or in ten years.'

'No. It would not have been ten years, or even one. And you know it. Why are you so anxious to pin this tail on yourself? Because of that smug reporter? Is it maybe an inverted kind of self-pity? An urge to believe that you have been cursed?'

Johnny's face twisted. 'She was watching *me* when it happened. Don't you get that? Are you so fucking soft you don't get that?'

'She was planning a strenuous trip, all the way to California and back, you told me that yourself. A symposium of some kind. A highly emotional sort of thing, from what you have said. Yes? Yes. It would almost certainly have happened then. A stroke is not lightning from a blue sky, Johnny.'

Johnny buttoned the jeans and then sat down as if the act of dressing had tired him out too much to do more. His feet were still bare. 'Yeah,' he said. 'Yeah, you may be right.'

'Sense! He sees sense! Thank the Lord!'

'But I still have to go, Sam.'

Weizak threw up his hands. 'And do what? She is in the hands of her doctors and her God. That is the situation. Better than anyone else, you must understand.'

'My dad will need me,' Johnny said softly. 'I understand that, too.'

'How will you go? It's nearly midnight.'

'By bus. I'll grab a cab over to Peter's Candlelighter.
The Greyhounds still stop there, don't they?'

'You don't have to do that,' Sam said.

Johnny was groping under the chair for his shoes and
not finding them, Sam got them from under the bed and
handed them to him.

'I'll drive you down.'

Johnny looked up at him. 'You'd do that?'

'If you'll take a mild tranquilizer, yes.'

'But your wife . . .' He realized in a confused sort of
way that the only concrete thing he knew about Weizak's
personal life was that his mother was living in California.

'I am divorced,' Weizak said. 'A doctor has to be out at
all hours of the night . . . unless he is a pediatrist or a
dermatologist, nuh? My wife saw the bed as half-empty
rather than half-full. So she filled it with a variety of
men.'

'I'm sorry,' Johnny said, embarrassed.

'You spend far too much time being sorry, John.' Sam's
face was gentle, but his eyes were stern. 'Put on your
shoes.'

CHAPTER TWELVE

1 ·

Hospital to hospital, Johnny thought dreamily, flying
gently along on the small blue pill he had taken just before he and Sam left the EMMC and climbed into Sam's
'75 El Dorado. *Hospital to hospital, person to person,
station to station.*

In a queer, secret way, he enjoyed the trip – it was his
first time out of the hospital in almost five years. The
night was clear, the Milky Way sprawled across the sky in
an unwinding clockspring of light, a half-moon followed

189

them over the dark tree line as they fled south through Palmyra, Newport, Pittsfield, Benton, Clinton. The car whispered along in near total silence. Low music, Haydn, issued from the four speakers of the stereo tape player.

Came to one hospital in the Cleaves Mills Rescue Squad ambulance, went to another in a Cadillac, he thought. He didn't let it bother him. It was just enough to ride, to float along on the track, to let the problem of his mother, his new ability, and the people who wanted to pry into his soul (*He asked for it . . . just don't touch me, huh?*) rest in a temporary limbo. Weizak didn't talk. Occasionally he hummed snatches of the music.

Johnny watched the stars. He watched the turnpike, nearly deserted this late. It unrolled ceaselessly in front of them. They went through the tollgate at Augusta and Weizak took a time-and-toll ticket. Then they went on again – Gardener, Sabbatus, Lewiston.

Nearly five years, longer than some convicted murderers spend in the slam.

He slept.

Dreamed.

'Johnny,' his mother said in his dream. 'Johnny, make me better, make me well.' She was in a beggar's rags. She was crawling toward him over cobblestones. Her face was white. Thin blood ran from her knees. White lice squirmed in her thin hair. She held shaking hands out to him. 'It's the power of God working in you,' she said. 'It's a great responsibility, Johnny. A great trust. You must be worthy.'

He took her hands, closed his own over them, and said, 'Spirits, depart from this woman.'

She stood up. 'Healed!' she cried in a voice that was filled with a strange and terrible triumph. '*Healed! My son has healed me! His work is great upon the earth!*'

He tried to protest, to tell her that he didn't want to do great works, or heal, or speak in tongues, to divine the future, or find those things that had been lost. He tried to tell her, but his tongue wouldn't obey the command of his brain. Then she was past him, striding off down the

cobbled street, her posture cringing and servile but somehow arrogant at the same time; her voice belled like a
clarion: 'Saved! Savior! Saved! Savior!'

And to his horror he saw that there had been thousands
of others behind her, maybe millions, all of them maimed
or deformed or in terror. The stout lady reporter was
there, needing to know who the Democrats would nominate for the presidency in 1976; there was a death-eyed
farmer in biballs with a picture of his son, a smiling
young man in Air Force blues, who had been reported
MIA over Hanoi in 1972, he needed to know if his son
was dead or alive; a young woman who looked like Sarah
with tears on her smooth cheeks, holding up a baby with
a hydrocephalic head on which blue veins were traced
like runes of doom; an old man with his fingers turned
into clubs by arthritis; others. They stretched for miles,
they would wait patiently, they would kill him with their
mute, bludgeoning need.

'Saved!' His mother's voice carried back imperatively.
'Savior! Saved! Saved!'

He tried to tell them that he could neither heal nor
save, but before he could open his mouth to make the
denial, the first had laid hands on him and was shaking
him.

The shaking was real enough. It was Weizak's hand on
his arm. Bright orange light filled the car, turning the
interior as bright as day – it was nightmare light, turning
Sam's kind face into the face of a hobgoblin. For a moment he thought the nightmare was still going on and
then he saw the light was coming from parking-lot lamps.
They had changed those, too, apparently, while he was
in his coma. From hard white to a weird orange that lay
on the skin like paint.

'Where are we?' he asked thickly.

'The hospital,' Sam said. 'Cumberland General.'

'Oh. All right.'

He sat up. The dream seemed to slide off him in fragments, still littering the floor of his mind like something
broken and not yet swept up.

191

'Are you ready to go in?'

'Yes,' Johnny said.

They crossed the parking lot amid the soft creak of summer crickets in the woods. Fireflies stitched through the darkness. The image of his mother was very much on him – but not so much that he was unable to enjoy the soft and fragrant smell of the night and the feel of the faint breeze against his skin. There was time to enjoy the health of the night, and the feeling of health coming inside him. In the context of why he was here, the thought seemed almost obscene – but only almost. And it wouldn't go away.

2 ·

Herb came down the hallway to meet them, and Johnny saw that his father was wearing old pants, shoes with no socks, and his pajama shirt. It told Johnny a lot about the suddenness with which it had come. It told him more than he wanted to know.

'Son,' he said. He looked smaller, somehow. He tried to say more and couldn't. Johnny hugged him and Herb burst into tears. He sobbed against Johnny's shirt.

'Daddy,' he said. 'That's all right, Daddy, that's all right.'

His father put his arms on Johnny's shoulders and wept. Weizak turned away and began to inspect the pictures on the walls, indifferent water colors by local artists.

Herb began to recover himself. He swiped his arm across his eyes and said, 'Look at me, still in my pj top. I had time to change before the ambulance came. I guess I never thought of it. Must be getting senile.'

'No, you're not.'

'Well.' He shrugged. 'Your doctor friend brought you down? That was nice of you, Dr. Weizak.'

Sam shrugged. 'It was nothing.'

Johnny and his father walked toward the small waiting room and sat down. 'Daddy, is she . . .'

'She's sinking,' Herb said. He seemed calmer now. 'Conscious, but sinking. She's been asking for you,

Johnny. I think she's been holding on for you.'

'My fault,' Johnny said. 'All this is my f . . .'

The pain in his ear startled him, and he stared at his father, astonished. Herb had seized his ear and twisted it firmly. So much for the role reversal of having his father cry in his arms. The old twist-the-ear trick had been a punishment Herb had reserved for the gravest of errors. Johnny couldn't remember having his ear twisted since he was thirteen, and had gotten fooling around with their old Rambler. He had inadvertently pushed in the clutch and the old car had rumbled silently downhill to crash into their back shed.

'Don't you ever say that,' Herb said.

'*Jeez Dad!*'

Herb let go, a little smile lurking just below the corners of his mouth. 'Forgot all about the old twist-the-ear, huh? Probably thought I had, too. No such luck, Johnny.'

Johnny stared at his father, still dumbfounded.

'Don't you *ever* blame yourself.'

'But she was watching that damned . . .'

'News, yes. She was ecstatic, she was thrilled . . . then she was on the floor, her poor old mouth opening and closing like she was a fish out of water.' Herb leaned closer to his son. 'The doctor won't come right out and tell me, but he asked me about "heroic measures". I told him none of that stuff. She committed her own kind of sin, Johnny. She presumed to know the mind of God. So don't you ever blame yourself for her mistake.' Fresh tears glinted in his eyes. His voice roughened. 'God knows I spent my life loving her and it got hard in the late going. Maybe this is just the best thing.'

'Can I see her?'

'Yes, she's at the end of the hall, Room 35. They're expecting you, and so is she. Just one thing, Johnny. Agree with anything and everything she might say. Don't . . . let her die thinking it was all for nothing.'

'No.' He paused. 'Are you coming with me?'

'Not now. Maybe later.'

Johnny nodded and walked up the hall. The lights

were turned down low for the nighttime. The brief moment in the soft, kind summer night seemed far away now, but his nightmare in the car seemed very close.

Room 35. VERA HELEN SMITH, the little card on the door read. Had he known her middle name was Helen? It seemed he must have, although he couldn't remember. But he could remember other things: her bringing him an ice-cream bar wrapped in her handkerchief one bright summer day at Old Orchard Beach, smiling and gay. He and his mother and father playing rummy for matches – later, after the religion business began to deepen its hold on her, she wouldn't have cards in the house, not even to play cribbage with. He remembered the day the bee had stung him and he ran to her, bawling his head off, and she had kissed the swelling and pulled out the stinger with tweezers and then had wrapped the wound in a strip of cloth that had been dipped in baking soda.

He pushed the door open and went in. She was a vague hump in the bed and Johnny thought, *That's what I looked like.* A nurse was taking her pulse; she turned when the door opened and the dim hall lights flashed on her spectacles.

'Are you Mrs. Smith's son?'

'Yes.'

'*Johnny?*' The voice rose from the hump in the bed, dry and hollow, rattling with death as a few pebbles will rattle in an empty gourd. The voice – God help him – made his skin crawl. He moved closer. Her face was twisted into a snarling mask on the left-hand side. The hand on the counterpane was a claw. *Stroke*, he thought. *What the old people call a shock. Yes. That's better. That's what she looks like. Like she's had a bad shock.*

'Is that you, John?'

'It's me, Ma.'

'Johnny? Is that you?'

'Yes, Ma.'

He came closer yet, and forced himself to take the bony claw.

194

'I want my Johnny,' she said querulously.

The nurse shot him a pitying look, and he found himself wanting to smash his fist through it.

'Would you leave us alone?' he asked.

'I really shouldn't while . . .'

'Come on, she's my mother and I want some time alone with her,' Johnny said. 'What about it?'

'Well . . .'

'Bring me my juice, Dad!' his mother cried hoarsely. 'Feel like I could drink a quart!'

'Would you get *out* of here?' he cried at the nurse. He was filled with a terrible sorrow of which he could not even find the focus. It seemed like a whirlpool going down into darkness.

The nurse left.

'Ma,' he said, sitting beside her. That weird feeling of doubled time, of reversal, would not leave him. How many times had she sat over his bed like this, perhaps holding his dry hand and talking to him? He recalled the timeless period when the room had seemed so close to him – seen through a gauzy placental membrane, his mother's face bending over him, thundering senseless sounds slowly into his upturned face.

'Ma,' he said again, and kissed the hook that had replaced her hand.

'Gimme those nails, I can do that,' she said. Her left eye seemed frozen in its orbit; the other rolled wildly. It was the eye of a gutshot horse. 'I want Johnny.'

'Ma, I'm here.'

'John-ny! John-ny! JOHN-NY!'

'Ma,' he said, afraid the nurse would come back.

'You . . .' She broke off and her head turned toward him a little. 'Bend over here where I can see,' she whispered.

He did as she asked.

'You came,' she said. 'Thank you. Thank you.' Tears began to ooze from the good eye. The bad one, the one on the side of her face that had been frozen by the shock, stared indifferently upward.

195

'Sure I came.'

'I saw you,' she whispered. 'What a power God has given you, Johnny! Didn't I tell you? Didn't I say it was so?'

'Yes, you did.'

'He has a job for you,' she said. 'Don't run from him, Johnny. Don't hide away in a cave like Elijah or make him send a big fish to swallow you up. Don't do that, John.'

'No. I won't.' He held her claw-hand. His head throbbed.

'Not the potter but the potter's clay, John. Remember.'

'All right.'

'*Remember that!*' she said stridently, and he thought, *She's going back into nonsense land.* But she didn't; at least she went no further into nonsense land than she had been since he came out of his coma.

'Heed the still, small voice when it comes,' she said.

'Yes, Ma. I will.'

Her head turned a tiny bit on the pillow, and – was she *smiling*?

'You think I'm crazy, I guess.' She twisted her head a little more, so she could look directly at him. 'But that doesn't matter. You'll know the voice when it comes. It'll tell you what to do. It told Jeremiah and Daniel and Amos and Abraham. It'll come to you. It'll tell you. And when it does, Johnny . . . *do your duty.*'

'Okay, Ma.'

'What a power,' she murmured. Her voice was growing furry and indistinct. 'What a power God has given you . . . I knew . . . I always knew . . .' Her voice trailed off. The good eye closed. The other stared blankly forward.

Johnny sat with her another five minutes, then got up to leave. His hand was on the doorknob and he was easing the door open when her dry, rattling voice came again, chilling him with its implacable, positive command.

'*Do your duty, John.*'

'Yes, Ma.'

It was the last time he ever spoke to her. She died at

five minutes past eight on the morning of August 20. Somewhere north of them, Walt and Sarah Hazlett were having a discussion about Johnny that was almost an argument, and somewhere south of them, Greg Stillson was cutting himself some prime asshole.

CHAPTER THIRTEEN

1 ·

'You don't understand,' Greg Stillson said in a voice of utter, reasonable patience to the kid sitting in the lounge at the back of the Ridgeway police station. The kid, shirtless, was tilted back in a padded folding chair and drinking a bottle of Pepsi. He was smiling indulgently at Greg Stillson, not understanding that twice was all Greg Stillson ever repeated himself, understanding that there was one prime asshole in the room, but not yet understanding who it was.

That realization would have to be brought home to him.

Forcibly, if necessary.

Outside, the late August morning was bright and warm. Birds sang in the trees. And Greg felt his destiny was closer than ever. That was why he would be careful with this prime asshole. That was no long-haired bike-freak with a bad case of bowlegs and B.O.; this kid was a college boy, his hair was moderately long but squeaky clean, and he was George Harvey's nephew. Not that George cared for him much (George had fought his way across Germany in 1945, and he had two words for these long-haired freaks, and those two words were not Happy Birthday), but he was blood. And George was a man to be reckoned with on the town council. *See what you can do with him*, George had told Greg when Greg informed him that Chief Wiggins had arrested his sister's kid. But his eyes said, *Don't hurt him. He's blood.*

The kid was looking at Greg with lazy contempt. 'I

197

understand,' he said. 'Your Deputy Dawg took my shirt
and I want it back. And *you* better understand something.
If I don't get it back, I'm going to have the American
Civil Liberties Union down on your red neck.'

Greg got up, went to the steel-gray file cabinet opposite
the soda machine, pulled out his keyring, selected a key,
and opened the cabinet. From atop a pile of accident and
traffic forms, he took a red T-shirt. He spread it open so
the legend on it was clear: BABY LET'S FUCK.

'You were wearing this,' Greg said in that same mild
voice. 'On the street.'

The kid rocked on the back legs of his chair and
swigged some more Pepsi. The little indulgent smile
playing around his mouth – almost a sneer – did not
change. 'That's right,' he said. 'And I want it back. It's
my property.'

Greg's head began to ache. This smartass didn't realize
how easy it would be. The room was soundproofed, and
there had been times when that soundproofing had
muffled screams. No – he didn't realize. He didn't *understand.*

*But keep your hand on it. Don't go overboard. Don't
upset the applecart.*

Easy to think. Usually easy to do. But sometimes, his
temper – his temper got out of hand.

Greg reached into his pocket and pulled out his Bic
lighter.

'So you just go tell your gestapo chief and my fascist
uncle that the First Amendment . . .' He paused, eyes
widening a little. 'What are you . . . ? Hey! *Hey!*'

Taking no notice and at least outwardly calm, Greg
struck a light. The Bic's gas flame vroomed upward, and
Greg lit the kid's T-shirt on fire. It burned quite well,
actually.

The front legs of the kid's chair came down with a
bang and he leaped toward Greg with his bottle of Pepsi
still in his hand. The self-satisfied little smirk was gone,
replaced with a look of wide-eyed shock and surprise –

and the anger of a spoiled brat who has had everything his own way for too long.

No one ever called him *runt,* Greg Stillson thought, and his headache worsened. Oh, he was going to have to be careful.

'Gimme that!' the kid shouted. Greg was holding the shirt out, pinched together in two fingers at the neck, ready to drop it when it got too hot. 'Gimme that, you asshole! That's mine! That's...'

Greg planted his hand in the middle of the kid's bare chest and shoved him as hard as he could – which was hard indeed. The kid went flying across the room, the anger dissolving into total shock, and – at last – what Greg needed to see: fear.

He dropped the shirt on the tile floor, picked up the kid's Pepsi, and poured what was left in the bottle onto the smouldering T-shirt. It hissed balefully.

The kid was getting up slowly, his back pressed against the wall. Greg caught his eyes with his own. The kid's eyes were brown and very, very wide.

'We're going to reach an understanding,' Greg said, and the words seemed distant to him, behind the sick thud in his head. 'We're going to have a little seminar right here in this back room about just who's the asshole. You got my meaning? We're gonna reach some conclusions. Isn't that what you college boys like to do? Reach conclusions?'

The kid drew breath in hitches. He wet his lips, seemed about to speak, and then he yelled: '*Help!*'

'Yeah, you need help, all right,' Greg said. 'I'm going to give you some, too.'

'You're crazy,' George Harvey's nephew said, and then yelled again, louder: 'HELP!'

'I may be,' Greg said. 'Sure. But what we got to find out, Sonny, is who the prime asshole is. See what I mean?'

He looked down at the Pepsi bottle in his hand, and suddenly he swung it savagely against the corner of the steel cabinet. It shattered, and when the kid saw the

199

scatter of glass on the floor and the jagged neck in Greg's hand pointing toward him, he screamed. The crotch of his jeans, faded almost white, suddenly darkened. His face went the color of old parchment. And as Greg walked toward him, gritting glass under the workboots he wore summer and winter, he cringed against the wall.

'When I go out on the street, I wear a white shirt,' Greg said. He was grinning, showing white teeth. 'Sometimes a tie. When you go out on the street, you wear some rag with a filthy saying on it. So who's the asshole, kiddo?'

George Harvey's nephew whined something. His bulging eyes never left the spears of glass jutting from the bottle neck in Greg's hand.

'I'm standing here high and dry,' Greg said, coming a little closer, 'and you got piss running down both legs into your shoes. So who's the asshole?'

He began to jab the bottle neck lightly toward the kid's bare and sweaty midriff, and George Harvey's nephew began to cry. This was the sort of kid that was tearing the country in two, Greg thought. The thick wine of fury buzzed and coursed in his head. Stinking yellowbelly crybaby assholes like this.

Ah, but don't hurt him – don't kick over the applecart –

'I sound like a human being,' Greg said, 'and you sound like a pig in a grease-pit, boy. So who's the asshole?'

He jabbed with the bottle again: one of the jagged glass points dimpled the kid's skin just below the right nipple and brought a tiny bead of blood. The kid howled.

'I'm talking to you,' Greg said. 'You better answer up, same as you'd answer up one of your professors. Who's the asshole?'

The kid sniveled but made no coherent sound.

'You answer up if you want to pass this exam,' Greg said. 'I'll let your guts loose all over this floor, boy.' And in that instant, he meant it. He couldn't look directly at this welling drop of blood; it would send him crazy if he did, George Harvey's nephew or not. 'Who's the asshole?'

'Me,' the kid said, and began to sob like a small child afraid of the bogeyman, the Allamagoosalum that waits behind the closet door in the dead hours of the night.

Greg smiled. The headache thumped and flared. 'Well, that's pretty good, you know. That's a start. But it's not quite good enough. I want you to say, "I'm an asshole." '

'I'm an asshole,' the kid said, still sobbing. Snot flowed from his nose and hung there in a runner. He wiped it away with the back of his hand.

'Now I want you to say, "I'm a prime asshole." '

'I . . . I'm a prime asshole.'

'Now you just say one more thing and maybe we can be done here. You say, "Thank you for burning up that dirty shirt, Mayor Stillson." '

The kid was eager now. The kid saw his way clear. 'Thanks for burning up that dirty shirt.'

In a flash, Greg ran one of the jagged points from left to right across the kid's soft belly, bringing a line of blood. He barely broke the skin, but the kid howled as if all the devils of hell were behind him.

'You forgot to say "Mayor Stillson",' Greg said, and just like that it broke. The headache gave one more massive beat right between his eyes and was gone. He looked down stupidly at the bottle neck in his hand and could barely remember how it had gotten there. Stupid damn thing. He had almost thrown everything away over one numbnuts kid.

'Mayor Stillson!' The kid was screaming. His terror was perfect and complete. 'Mayor Stillson! Mayor Stillson! Mayor Still . . .'

'That's good,' Greg said.

'. . . son! Mayor Stillson! Mayor Stillson! Mayor . . .'

Greg whacked him hard across the face, and the kid rapped his head on the wall. He fell silent, his eyes wide and blank.

Greg stepped very close to him. He reached out. He closed one hand around each of the kid's ears. He pulled the kid's face forward until their noses were touching. Their eyes were less than half an inch apart.

'Now, your uncle is a power in this town,' he said softly, holding the kid's ears like handles. The kid's eyes were huge and brown and swimming. 'I'm a power too – coming to be one – but I ain't no George Harvey. He was born here, raised here, everything. And if you was to tell your uncle what went on in here, he might take a notion to finish me in Ridgeway.'

The kid's lips were twitching in a nearly soundless blubber. Greg shook the boy's head slowly back and forth by the ears, banging their noses together.

'He might not . . . he was pretty damn mad about that shirt. But he might. Blood ties are strong ties. So you think about this, son. If you was to tell your uncle what went on here and your uncle squeezed me out, I guess I would come along and kill you. Do you believe that?'

'Yeah,' the kid whispered. His cheeks were wet, gleaming.

' "Yes sir, Mayor Stillson." '

'Yessir, Mayor Stillson.'

Greg let go of his ears. 'Yeah,' he said. 'I'd kill you, but first I'd tell anybody that'd listen about how you pissed yourself and stood there crying with snot running out of your nose.'

He turned and walked away quickly, as if the kid smelled bad, and went to the cabinet again. He got a box of Band-Aids from one of the shelves and tossed them across to the kid, who flinched back and fumbled them. He hastened to pick them up off the floor, as if Stillson might attack him again for missing.

Greg pointed. 'Bathroom over there. You clean yourself up. I'm gonna leave you a Ridgeway PAL sweatshirt. I want it mailed back, clean, no bloodstains. You understand?'

'Yes,' the kid whispered.

'SIR!' Stillson screamed at him. '*SIR! SIR! SIR! Can't you remember that?*'

'Sir,' the kid moaned. 'Yessir, yessir.'

'They don't teach you kids respect for *nothing*,' Greg said. 'Not for *nothing*.'

The headache was trying to come back. He took several deep breaths and quelled it – but his stomach felt miserably upset. 'Okay, that's the end. I just want to offer you one good piece of advice. Don't you make the mistake of getting back to your damn college this fall or whenever and start thinking this was some way it wasn't. Don't you try to kid yourself about Greg Stillson. Best forgotten, kid. By you, me, and George. Working this around in your mind until you think you could have another swing at it would be the worst mistake of your life. Maybe the last.'

With that Greg left, taking one last contemptuous look at the kid standing there, his chest and belly caked with a few minor smears of dried blood, his eyes wide, his lips trembling. He looked like an overgrown ten-year-old who has struck out in the Little League playoffs.

Greg made a mental bet with himself that he would never see or hear from this particular kid again, and it was a bet he won. Later that week, George Harvey stopped by the barbershop where Greg was getting a shave and thanked him for 'talking some sense' into his nephew. 'You're good with these kids, Greg,' he said. 'I dunno . . . they seem to respect you.'

Greg told him not to mention it.

2 ·

While Greg Stillson was burning a shirt with an obscene saying on it in New Hampshire, Walt and Sarah Hazlett were having a late breakfast in Bangor, Maine. Walt had the paper.

He put his coffee cup down with a clink and said, 'Your old boyfriend made the paper, Sarah.'

Sarah was feeding Denny. She was in her bathrobe, her hair something of a mess, her eyes still only about a quarter open. Eighty percent of her mind was still asleep. There had been a party last night. The guest of honor had been Harrison Fisher, who had been New Hampshire's third district congressman since dinosaurs walked the earth, and a sure candidate for reelection next year.

It had been politic for her and Walt to go. *Politic*. That was a word that Walt used a lot lately. He had had lots more to drink than she had, and this morning he was dressed and apparently chipper while she felt buried in a pile of sludge. It wasn't fair.

'Blue!' Denny remarked, and spat back a mouthful of mixed fruit.

'That's not nice,' Sarah said to Denny. To Walt: 'Are you talking about Johnny Smith?'

'The one and only.'

She got up and came around to Walt's side of the table. 'He's all right, isn't he?'

'Feeling good and kicking up dickens by the sound of this,' Walt said dryly.

She had a hazy idea that it might be related to what had happened to her when she went to see Johnny, but the size of the headline shocked her: REAWAKENED COMA PATIENT DEMONSTRATES PSYCHIC ABILITY AT DRAMATIC NEWS CONFERENCE. The story was under David Bright's by-line. The accompanying photo showed Johnny, still looking thin and, in the unsparing glare of the flash, pitifully confused, standing over the sprawled body of a man the caption identified as Roger Dussault, a reporter for the Lewiston paper. *Reporter Faints after Revelation*, the caption read.

Sarah sank down into the chair next to Walt and began to read the article. This did not please Denny, who began to pound on the tray of his highchair for his morning egg.

'I believe you're being summoned,' Walt said.

'Would you feed him, honey? He eats better for you anyway.' *Story Continued Page 9, Col. 3.* She folded the paper open to page nine.

'Flattery will get you everywhere,' Walt said agreeably. He slipped off his sports coat and put on her apron. 'Here it comes, guy,' he said, and began feeding Denny his egg.

When she had finished the story, Sarah went back and read it again. Her eyes were drawn again and again to the picture, to Johnny's confused, horror-struck face. The people loosely grouped around the prone Dussault were looking at Johnny with an expression close to fear. She could understand that. She remembered kissing him, and the strange, preoccupied look that had slipped over his face. And when he told her where to find the lost wedding ring, *she* had been afraid.

But Sarah, what you were afraid of wasn't quite the same thing, was it?

'Just a little more, big boy,' Walt was saying, as if from a thousand miles away. Sarah looked up at them, sitting together in a bar of mote-dusted sunlight, her apron flapping between Walt's knees, and she was suddenly afraid again. She saw the ring sinking to the bottom of the toilet bowl, turning over and over. She heard the small clink as it struck the porcelain. She thought of Halloween masks, of the kid saying, *I love to see this guy take a beatin.* She thought of promises made and never kept, and her eyes went to his thin newsprint face, looking out at her with such haggard, wretched surprise.

'... gimmick, anyway,' Walt said, hanging up her apron. He had gotten Denny to eat the egg, every bit of it, and now their son and heir was sucking contentedly away at a juice-bottle.

'Huh?' Sarah looked up as he came over to her.

'I said that for a man who must have almost half a million dollars' worth of hospital bills outstanding, it's a helluva good gimmick.'

'What are you *talking* about? What do you mean, *gimmick?*'

'Sure,' he said, apparently missing her anger. 'He could make seven, maybe ten thousand dollars doing a book about the accident and the coma. But if he came out of the coma psychic, the sky's the limit.'

'That's one *hell* of an allegation!' Sarah said, and her voice was thin with fury.

He turned to her, his expression first one of surprise and then of understanding. The understanding look made her angrier than ever. If she had a nickel for every time Walt Hazlett had thought he understood her, they could fly first-class to Jamaica.

'Look, I'm sorry I brought it up,' he said.

'Johnny would no more lie than the Pope would ... would ... you know.'

He bellowed laughter, and in that moment she nearly picked up his own coffee cup and threw it at him. Instead, she locked her hands together tightly under the table and squeezed them. Denny goggled at his father and then burst into his own peal of laughter.

'Honey,' Walt said. 'I have nothing against him, I have nothing against what he's doing. In fact, I respect him for it. If that fat old mossback Fisher can go from a broke lawyer to a millionaire during fifteen years in the House of Representatives, then this guy should have a perfect right to pick up as much as he can playing psychic...'

'Johnny doesn't lie,' she repeated tonelessly.

'It's a gimmick for the blue-rinse brigade who read the weekly tabloids and belong to the Universe Book Club,' he said cheerily. 'Although I will admit that a little second sight would come in handy during jury selection in this damn Timmons trial.'

'Johnny Smith doesn't lie,' she repeated, and heard him saying: *It slipped off your finger. You were putting his shaving stuff into one of those side pockets and it just slipped off ... you go up in the attic and look, Sarah. You'll see.* But she couldn't tell Walt that. Walt didn't know she had been to see Johnny.

Nothing wrong in going to see him, her mind offered uneasily.

No, but how would he react to the news that she had thrown her original wedding ring into the toilet and flushed it away? He might not understand the sudden twitch of fear that had made her do it – the same fear she saw mirrored on those other newsprint faces, and, to some degree, on Johnny's own. No, Walt might not understand that at all. After all, throwing your wedding ring into the toilet and then pushing the flush did suggest a certain vulgar symbolism.

'All right,' Walt was saying, 'he doesn't lie. But I just don't believe . . .'

Sarah said softly, 'Look at the people behind him, Walt. Look at their faces. *They* believe.'

Walt gave them a cursory glance. 'Sure, the way a kid believes in a magician as long as the trick is ongoing.'

'You think this fellow Dussault was a, what-do-you-call-it, a shill? According to the article, he and Johnny had never met before.'

'That's the only way the illusion will work, Sarah,' Walt said patiently. 'It doesn't do a magician any good to pull a bunny out of a rabbit hutch, only out of a hat. Either Johnny Smith knew something or he made a terribly good guess based on this guy Dussault's behavior at the time. But I repeat, I respect him for it. He got a lot of mileage out of it. If it turns him a buck, more power to him.'

In that moment she hated him, loathed him, this good man she had married. There was really nothing so terrible on the reverse side of his goodness, his steadiness, his mild good humor – just the belief, apparently grounded in the bedrock of his soul, that everybody was looking out for number one, each with his or her own little racket. This morning he could call Harrison Fisher a fat old mossback; last night he had been bellowing with laughter at Fisher's stories about Greg Stillson, the funny mayor of some-town-or-other and who might just be crazy enough to run as an independent in the House race next year.

No, in the world of Walt Hazlett, no one had psychic powers and there were no heroes and the doctrine of *we-have-to-change-the-system-from-within* was all-powerful. He was a good man, a steady man, he loved her and Denny, but suddenly her soul cried out for Johnny and the five years together of which they had been robbed. Or the lifetime together. A child with darker hair.

'You better get going, babe,' she said quietly. 'They'll have your guy Timmons in stocks and bonds, or whatever they are.'

'Sure.' He smiled at her, the summation done, session adjourned. 'Still friends?'

'Still friends.' *But he knew where the ring was. He* knew.

Walt kissed her, his right hand resting lightly on the back of her neck. He always had the same thing for breakfast, he always kissed her the same way, some day they were going to Washington, and no one was psychic.

Five minutes later he was gone, backing their little red Pinto out onto Pond Street, giving his usual brief toot on the horn, and putting away. She was left alone with Denny, who was in the process of strangling himself while he tried to wriggle under his highchair tray.

'You're going at that all wrong, Sluggo,' Sarah said, crossing the kitchen and unlatching the tray.

'Blue!' Denny said, disgusted with the whole thing.

Speedy Tomato, their tomcat, sauntered into the kitchen at his usual slow, hipshot juvenile delinquent's stride, and Denny grabbed him, making little chuckling noises. Speedy laid his ears back and looked resigned.

Sarah smiled a little and cleared the table. Inertia. A body at rest tends to remain at rest, and she was at rest. Never mind Walt's darker side; she had her own. She had no intention of doing more than sending Johnny a card at Christmas. It was better, safer, that way – because a body in motion tends to keep moving. Her life here was good. She had survived Dan, she had survived Johnny, who had been so unfairly taken from her (but so much in this world was unfair), she had come through her own personal rapids to this smooth water, and here she would stay. This sunshiny kitchen was not a bad place. Best to forget county fairs, Wheels of Fortune, and Johnny Smith's face.

As she ran water into the sink to do the dishes she turned on the radio and caught the beginning of the news. The first item made her freeze with a just-washed plate in one hand, her eyes looking out over their small backyard in startled contemplation. Johnny's mother had had a stroke while watching a TV report on her son's press conference. She had died this morning, not an hour ago.

Sarah dried her hands, snapped off the radio, and pried Speedy Tomato out of Denny's hands. She carried her boy into the living room and popped him into his playpen. Denny protested this indignity with loud, lusty howls of which she took no notice. She went to the telephone and called the EMMC. A switchboard operator who sounded tired of repeating the same piece of intelligence over and over again told her that John Smith had discharged himself the night before, slightly before midnight.

She hung up the phone and sat down in a chair. Denny continued to cry from his playpen. Water ran into the kitchen sink. After a while she got up, went into the kitchen, and turned it off.

CHAPTER FOURTEEN

1 ·

The man from *Inside View* showed up on October 16, not long after Johnny had walked up to get the mail.

His father's house was set well back from the road; their graveled driveway was nearly a quarter of a mile long, running through a heavy stand of second-growth spruce and pine. Johnny did the total round trip every day. At first he had returned to the porch trembling with exhaustion, his legs on fire, his limp so pronounced that he was really lurching along. But now, a month and a half after the first time (when the half a mile had taken him an hour to do), the walk had become one of his day's pleasures, something to look forward to. Not the mail, but the walk.

He had begun splitting wood for the coming winter, a chore Herb had been planning to hire out since he himself had landed a contract to do some inside work on a new housing project in Libertyville. 'You know when old

209

age has started lookin over your shoulder, John,' he had said with a smile. 'It's when you start lookin for inside work as soon as fall rolls around.'

Johnny climbed the porch and sat down in the wicker chair beside the glider, uttering a small sound of relief. He propped his right foot on the porch railing, and with a grimace of pain, used his hands to lift his left leg over it. That done, he began to open his mail.

It had tapered off a lot just lately. During the first week he had been back here in Pownal, there had sometimes been as many as two dozen letters and eight or nine packages a day, most of them forwarded through the EMMC, a few of them sent to General Delivery, Pownal (and assorted variant spellings: Pownell, Poenul, and, in one memorable case, Poonuts).

Most of them were from dissociated people who seemed to be drifting through life in search of any rudder. There were children who wanted his autograph, women who wanted to sleep with him, both men and women seeking advice to the lovelorn. Some sent lucky charms. Some sent horoscopes. A great many of the letters were religious in nature, and in these badly spelled missives, usually written in a large and careful handwriting but one step removed from the scrawl of a bright first-grader, he seemed to feel the ghost of his mother.

He was a prophet, these letters assured him, come to lead the weary and disillusioned American people out of the wilderness. He was a sign that the Last Times were at hand. To this date, October 16, he had received eight copies of Hal Lindsey's *The Late Great Planet Earth* – his mother surely would have approved of that one. He was urged to proclaim the divinity of Christ and put a stop to the loose morals of youth.

These letters were balanced off by the negative contingent, which was smaller but just as vocal – if usually anonymous. One correspondent, writing in grubby pencil on a sheet of yellow legal paper proclaimed him the Antichrist and urged him to commit suicide. Four or five of the letter writers had inquired about how it felt to murder your own mother. A great many wrote to accuse him of perpetrating a hoax. One wit wrote, 'PRECOGNITION, TELEPATHY, BULLSHIT! EAT MY DONG, YOU EXTRASENSORY TURKEY!'

And they sent *things*. That was the worst of it.

Every day on his way home from work, Herb would stop at the Pownal post office and pick up the packages that were too big to fit in their mailbox. The notes accompanying the things were all essentially the same; a low-grade scream. *Tell me, tell me, tell me.*

This scarf belonged to my brother, who disappeared on a fishing trip in the Allagash in 1969. I feel very strongly that he is still alive. Tell me where he is.

This lipstick came from my wife's dressing table. I think she's having an affair, but I'm not sure. Tell me if she is.

This is my son's ID bracelet. He never comes home after school anymore, he stays out until all hours, I'm worried sick. Tell me what he's doing.

A woman in North Carolina – God knew how she had found out about him; the press conference in August had not made the national media – sent a charred piece of wood. Her house had burned down, her letter explained, and her husband and two of her five children had died in the blaze. The Charlotte fire department said it was faulty wiring, but she simply couldn't accept that. It had to be arson. She wanted Johnny to feel the enclosed blackened relic and tell her who had done it, so the monster would spend the rest of his life rotting in prison.

Johnny answered none of the letters and returned all the objects (even the charcoaled hunk of wood) at his cost and with no comment. He *did* touch some of them. Most, like the charred piece of wallboard from the grief-stricken woman in Charlotte, told him nothing at all. But when he touched a few of them, disquieting images came, like waking dreams. In most cases there was barely a trace; a picture would form and fade in seconds, leaving him with nothing concrete at all, only a feeling. But one of them . . .

It had been the woman who sent the scarf in hopes of

finding out what had happened to her brother. It was a white knitted scarf, no different from a million others. But as he handled it, the reality of his father's house had suddenly been gone, and the sound of the television in the next room rose and flattened, rose and flattened, until it was the sound of drowsing summer insects and the faraway babble of water.

Woods smells in his nostrils. Green shafts of sunlight falling through great old trees. The ground had been soggy for the last three hours or so, squelchy, almost swamplike. He was scared, plenty scared, but he had kept his head. If you were lost in the big north country and panicked, they might as well carve your headstone. He had kept pushing south. It had been two days since he had gotten separated from Stiv and Rocky and Logan. They had been camping near

(but that wouldn't come, it was in the dead zone)

some stream, trout-fishing, and it had been his own damn fault; he had been pretty damn drunk.

Now he could see his pack leaning against the edge of an old and moss-grown blowdown, white deadwood poking through the green here and there like bones, he could see his pack, yes, but he couldn't reach it because he had walked a few yards away to take a leak and he had walked into a really squelchy place, mud almost to the tops of his L.L. Bean's boots, and he tried to back out, find a dryer place to do his business, but he couldn't get out. He couldn't get out because it wasn't mud at all. It was . . . something else.

He stood there, looking around fruitlessly for something to grab onto, almost laughing at the idiocy of having walked right into a patch of quicksand while looking for a place to take a piss.

He stood there, at first positive that it must be a shallow patch of quicksand, at the very worst over his boot-tops, another tale to tell when he was found.

He stood there, and real panic did not begin to set in until the quicksand oozed implacably over his knees. He began to struggle then, forgetting that if you got your stupid self into quicksand you were supposed to remain very still. In no time at all the quicksand was up to his waist and now it was chest-high, sucking at him like great brown lips, constricting his breathing; he began to scream and no one came, nothing came except for a fat brown squirrel that picked its way down the side of the mossy deadfall and perched on his pack and watched him with his bright, black eyes.

Now it was up to his neck, the rich, brown smell of it in his nose and his screams became thin and gasping as the quicksand implacably pressed the breath out of him. Birds flew swooping and cheeping and scolding, and green shafts of sunlight like tarnished copper fell through the trees, and the quicksand rose over his chin. Alone, he was going to die alone, and he opened his mouth to scream one last time and there was no scream because the quicksand flowed into his mouth, it flowed over his tongue, it flowed between his teeth in thin ribbons, he was *swallowing* quicksand and the scream was never uttered –

Johnny had come out of that in a cold sweat, his flesh marbled into goosebumps, the scarf wrapped tightly between his hands, his breath coming in short, strangled gasps. He had thrown the scarf on the floor where it lay like a twisted white snake. He would not touch it again. His father had put it in a return envelope and sent it back.

But now, mercifully, the mail was beginning to taper off. The crazies had discovered some fresher object for their public and private obsessions. Newsmen no longer called for interviews, partly because the phone number had been changed and unlisted, partly because the story was old hat.

Roger Dussault had written a long and angry piece for his paper, of which he was the feature editor. He proclaimed the whole thing a cruel and tasteless hoax. Johnny had undoubtedly boned up on incidents from the pasts of several reporters who were likely to attend the press conference, just in case. Yes, he admitted, his sister Anne's nickname had been Terry. She had died fairly young, and amphetamines might have been a contributing cause. But all of that was accessible information to anyone who wanted to dig it up. He made it all seem quite logical. The article did not explain how Johnny, who had not been out of the hospital, could have come by this 'accessible information', but that was a point most readers seemed to have overlooked. Johnny could not have cared less. The incident was closed, and he had no intention of creating new ones. What good could it possibly do to write the lady who had sent the scarf and tell her that her brother had drowned, screaming, in quicksand because he had gone the wrong way while looking for a place to take a piss? Would it ease her mind or help her live her life any better?

Today's mail was a mere six letters. A power bill. A card from Herb's cousin out in Oklahoma. A lady who had sent Johnny a crucifix with MADE IN TAIWAN stamped on Christ's feet in tiny gold letters. There was a brief note from Sam Weizak. And a small envelope with a return address that made him blink and sit up straighter. *S. Hazlett, 12 Pond Street, Bangor.*

Sarah. He tore it open.

He had received a sympathy card from her two days after the funeral services for his mother. Written on the back of it in her cool, back-slanting hand had been: 'Johnny – I'm so sorry that this has happened. I heard on the radio that your mom had passed away – in some ways that seemed the most unfair thing of all, that your private grief should have been made a thing of public knowledge. You may not remember, but we talked a little about your mom the night of your accident. I asked you what she'd do if you brought home a lapsed Catholic and you said she would smile and welcome me in and slip me a few tracts. I could see your love for her in the way you smiled. I know from your father that she had changed, but much of the change was because she loved you so much and just couldn't accept what had happened. And in the end I guess her faith was rewarded. Please accept my warm sympathy, and if there's anything I can do, now or later on, please count on your friend – *Sarah*.'

That was one note he had answered, thanking her for both the card and the thought. He had written it carefully, afraid that he might betray himself and say the wrong thing. She was a married woman now, that was beyond his control or ability to change. But he *did* remember their conversation about his mother – and so many other things about that night. Her note had summoned up the whole evening, and he answered in a bittersweet mood that was more bitter than sweet. He still loved Sarah Bracknell, and he had to remind himself constantly that she was gone, replaced by another woman who was five years older and the mother of a small boy.

Now he pulled a single sheet of stationery out of the envelope and scanned it quickly. She and her boy were headed down to Kennebunk to spend a week with Sarah's freshman and sophomore roommate, a girl named Stephanie Constantine now, Stephanie Carsleigh then. She said that Johnny might remember her, but Johnny didn't. Anyway, Walt was stuck in Washington for three weeks on combined firm and Republican party business, and Sarah thought she might take one afternoon and come by Pownal to see Johnny and Herb, if it was no trouble.

'You can reach me at Steph's number, 814–6219, any time between Oct. 17th and the 23rd. Of course, if it would make you feel uncomfortable in any way, just call me and say so, either up here or down there in K'bunk. I'll understand. Much love to both of you – *Sarah*.'

Holding the letter in one hand, Johnny looked across the yard and into the woods, which had gone russet and gold, seemingly just in the last week. The leaves would be falling soon, and then it would be time for winter.

Much love to both of you – Sarah. He ran his thumb across the words thoughtfully. It would be better not to call, not to write, not to do anything, he thought. She would get the message. Like the woman who mailed the scarf – what possible good could it do? Why kick a sleeping dog? Sarah might be able to use that phrase, much love, blithely, but he could not. He wasn't over the hurt of the past. For him, time had been crudely folded, stapled, and mutilated. In the progression of his own interior time, she had been his girl only six months ago. He could accept the coma and the loss of time in an intellectual way, but his emotions stubbornly resisted. Answering her condolence note had been difficult, but with a note it was always possible to crumple the thing up and start again if it began to go in directions it shouldn't go, if it began to overstep the bounds of friendship, which was all they were now allowed to share. If he saw her, he might do or say something stupid. Better not to call. Better just to let it sink.

But he would call, he thought. Call and invite her over. Troubled, he slipped the note back into the envelope.

The sun caught on bright chrome, twinkled there, and tossed an arrow of light back into his eyes. A Ford sedan was crunching its way down the driveway. Johnny squinted and tried to make out if it was a familiar car. Company out here was rare. There had been lots of mail, but people had only stopped by on three or four occasions. Pownal was small on the map, hard to find. If the car did belong to some seeker after knowledge, Johnny would send him or her away quickly, as kindly as possible, but firmly. That had been Weizak's parting advice. Good advice, Johnny thought.

'Don't let anyone rope you into the role of consulting swami, John. Give no encouragement and they will forget. It may seem heartless to you at first – most of them are misguided people with too many problems and only the best of intentions – but it is a question of your life, your privacy. So be firm.' And so he had been.

The Ford pulled into the turnaround between the shed and the woodpile, and as it swung around, Johnny saw the small Hertz sticker in the corner of the windshield. A very tall man in very new blue jeans and a red plaid hunting shirt that looked as if it had just come out of an L.L. Bean box got out of the car and glanced around. He had the air of a man who is not used to the country, a man who knows there are no more wolves or cougars in New England, but who wants to make sure all the same. A city man. He glanced up at the porch, saw Johnny, and raised one hand in greeting.

'Good afternoon,' he said. He had a flat city accent as well – Brooklyn, Johnny thought – and he sounded as if he were talking through a Saltine box.

'Hi,' Johnny said. 'Lost?'

'Boy, I hope not,' the stranger said, coming over to the foot of the steps. 'You're either John Smith or his twin brother.'

Johnny grinned. 'I don't have a brother, so I guess you found your way to the right door. Can I do something for you?'

'Well, maybe we can do something for each other.' The stranger mounted the porch steps and offered his hand. Johnny shook it. 'My name is Richard Dees. *Inside View* magazine.'

His hair was cut in a fashionable ear-length style, and it was mostly gray. Dyed gray, Johnny thought with some amusement. What could you say about a man who sounded as if he were talking through a Saltine box and dyed his hair gray?

'Maybe you've seen the magazine.'

'Oh, I've seen it. They sell it at the checkout counters in the supermarket. I'm not interested in being interviewed. Sorry you had to make a trip out here for nothing.' They sold it in the supermarket, all right. The headlines did everything but leap off the pulp-stock pages and try to mug you. CHILD KILLED BY CREATURES FROM SPACE, DISTRAUGHT MOTHER CRIES. THE FOODS THAT ARE POISONING YOUR CHILDREN. 12 PSYCHICS PREDICT CALIFORNIA EARTHQUAKE BY 1978.

'Well now, an interview wasn't exactly what we were thinking of,' Dees said. 'May I sit down?'

'Really, I . . .'

'Mr. Smith, I've flown all the way up from New York,

and from Boston I came on a little plane that had me wondering what would happen to my wife if I died intestate.'

'Portland-Bangor Airways?' Johnny asked, grinning.

'That's what it was,' Dees agreed.

'All right,' Johnny said. 'I'm impressed with your valor and your dedication to your job. I'll listen, but only for fifteen minutes or so. I'm supposed to sleep every afternoon.' This was a small lie in a good cause.

'Fifteen minutes should be more than enough.' Dees leaned forward. 'I'm just making an educated guess, Mr. Smith, but I'd estimate that you must owe somewhere in the neighborhood of two hundred thousand dollars. That roll somewhere within putting distance of the pin, does it?'

Johnny's smile thinned. 'What I owe or don't owe,' he said, 'is my business.'

'All right, of course, sure. I didn't mean to offend, Mr. Smith. *Inside View* would like to offer you a job. A rather lucrative job.'

'No. Absolutely not.'

'If you'll just give me a chance to lay this out for you . . .'

Johnny said, 'I'm not a practicing psychic. I'm not a Jeanne Dixon or an Edgar Cayce or an Alex Tannous. That's over with. The last thing I want to do is rake it up again.'

'Can I have just a few moments?'

'Mr Dees, you don't seem to understand what I'm . . .'

'Just a few moments?' Dees smiled winningly.

'How did you find out where I was, anyway?'

'We have a stringer on a mid-Maine paper called the Kennebec *Journal*. He said that although you'd dropped out of the public view, you were probably staying with your father.'

'Well, I owe him a real debt of thanks, don't I?'

'Sure,' Dees said easily. 'I'm betting you'll think so when you hear the whole deal. May I?'

'All right,' Johnny said. 'But just because you flew up

here on Panic Airlines, I'm not going to change my mind.'

'Well, however you see it. It's a free country, isn't it? Sure it is. *Inside View* specializes in a psychic view of things, Mr. Smith, as you probably know. Our readers, to be perfectly frank, are out of their gourds for this stuff. We have a weekly circulation of three million. Three million readers every week, Mr. Smith, how's that for a long shot straight down the fairway? How do we do it? We stick with the upbeat, the spiritual . . .'

'Twin Babies Eaten By Killer Bear,' Johnny murmured.

Dees shrugged. 'Sure, well, it's a tough old world, isn't it? People have to be informed about these things. It's their right to know. But for every downbeat article we've got three others telling our readers how to lose weight painlessly, how to find sexual happiness and compatibility, how to get closer to God . . .'

'Do you believe in God, Mr. Dees?'

'Actually, I don't,' Dees said, and smiled his winning smile. 'But we live in a democracy, greatest country on earth, right? Everyone is the captain of his own soul. No, the point is, our *readers* believe in God. They believe in angels and miracles . . .'

'And exorcisms and devils and Black Masses . . .'

'Right, right, right. You catch. It's a *spiritual* audience. They *believe* all this psychic bushwah. We have a total of ten psychics under contract, including Kathleen Nolan, the most famous seer in America. We'd like to put you under contract, Mr. Smith.'

'Would you?'

'Indeed we would. What would it mean for you? Your picture and a short column would appear roughly twelve times a year, when we run one of our All-Psychic issues. *Inside View*'s Ten Famous Psychics Preview the Second Ford Administration, that sort of thing. We always do a New Year's issue, and one each Fourth of July on the course of America over the next year – that's always a very informative issue, lots of chip shots on foreign policy

219

and economic policy in that one – plus assorted other goodies.'

'I don't think you understand,' Johnny said. He was speaking very slowly, as if to a child. 'I've had a couple of precognitive bursts – I suppose you could say I "saw the future" – but I don't have any control over it. I could no more come up with a prediction for the second Ford administration – if there ever is one – than I could milk a bull.'

Dees looked horrified. 'Who said you could? Staff writers do all those columns.'

'Staff . . . ?' Johnny gaped at Dees, finally shocked.

'Of course,' Dees said impatiently. 'Look. One of our most popular guys over the last couple of years has been Frank Ross, the guy who specializes in natural disasters. Hell of a nice guy, but Jesus Christ, he quit school in the ninth grade. He did two hitches in the Army and was swamping out Greyhound buses at the Port Authority terminal in New York when we found him. You think we'd let him write his own column? He'd misspell cat.'

'But the predictions . . .'

'A free hand, nothing but a free hand. But you'd be surprised how often these guys and gals get stuck for a real whopper.'

'Whopper,' Johnny repeated, bemused. He was a little surprised to find himself getting angry. His mother had bought *Inside View* for as long as he could remember, all the way back to the days when they had featured pictures of bloody car wrecks, decapitations, and bootlegged execution photos. She had sworn by every word. Presumably the greater part of *Inside View*'s other 2,999,999 readers did as well. And here sat this fellow with his dyed gray hair and his forty-dollar shoes and his shirt with the store-creases still in it, talking about *whoppers*.

'But it all works out,' Dees was saying. 'If you ever get stuck, all you have to do is call us collect and we all take it into the pro-shop together and come up with something. We have the right to anthologize your columns in our yearly book, *Inside Views of Things to Come*. You're perfectly free to sign any contract you can get with a book publisher, however. All we get is first refusal on the magazine rights, and we hardly ever refuse, I can tell you. And we pay very handsomely. That's over and above whatever figure we contract for. Gravy on your mashed potatoes, you might say.' Dees chuckled.

'And what might that figure be?' Johnny asked slowly. He was gripping the arms of his rocker. A vein in his right temple pulsed rhythmically.

'Thirty thousand dollars per year for two years,' Dees said. 'And if you prove popular, that figure would become negotiable. Now, all our psychics have some area of expertise. I understand that you're good with objects.' Dees's eyes became half-lidded, dreamy. 'I see a regular feature. Twice monthly, maybe – we don't want to run a good thing into the ground. "John Smith invites *Inside View*-ers to send in personal belongings for psychic examination . . ." Something like that. We'd make it clear, of course, that they should send in inexpensive stuff because nothing could be returned. But you'd be surprised. Some people are crazy as bedbugs, God love em. You'd be surprised at some of the stuff that would come in. Diamonds, gold coins, wedding rings . . . and we could attach a rider to the contract specifying that all objects mailed in would become your personal property.'

Now Johnny began to see tones of dull red before his eyes. 'People would send things in and I'd just keep them. That's what you're saying.'

'Sure, I don't see any problem with that. It's just a question of keeping the ground rules clear up front. A little extra gravy for those mashed potatoes.'

'Suppose,' Johnny said, carefully keeping his voice even and modulated, 'suppose I got . . . stuck for a whopper, as you put it . . . and I just called in and said President Ford was going to be assassinated on September 31, 1976? Not because I felt he was, but because I was stuck?'

'Well, September only has thirty days, you know,' Dees said. 'But otherwise, I think it's a hole in one. You're going to be a natural, Johnny. You think big. That's good. You'd be surprised how many of these people think small. Afraid to put their mouths where their money is, I suppose. One of our guys – Tim Clark out in Idaho – wrote in two weeks ago and said he'd had a flash that Earl Butz was going to be forced to resign next year. Well pardon my French, but who gives a fuck? Who's Earl Butz to the American housewife? But you have good waves, Johnny. You were made for this stuff.'

'Good waves,' Johnny muttered.

Dees was looking at him curiously. 'You feel all right, Johnny? You look a little white.'

Johnny was thinking of the lady who had sent the scarf. Probably she read *Inside View*, too. 'Let me see if I can summarize this,' he said. 'You'd pay me thirty thousand dollars a year for my name . . .'

'And your picture, don't forget.'

'*And* my picture, for a few ghost-written columns. Also a feature where I tell people what they want to know about objects they send in. As an extra added attraction, I get to keep the stuff . . .'

'If the lawyers can work it out . . .'

'. . . as my personal property. That the deal?'

'That's the *bare bones* of the deal, Johnny. The way these things feed each other, it's just amazing. You'll be a household word in six months, and after that, the sky is the limit. The Carson show. Personal appearances. Lecture tours. Your book, of course, pick your house, they're practically throwing money at psychics along Publisher's Row. Kathy Nolan started with a contract like the one we're offering you, and she makes over two hundred thou a year now. Also, she founded her own church and the IRS can't touch dime-one of her money. She doesn't miss a trick, does our Kathy.' Dees leaned forward, grinning. 'I tell you, Johnny, the sky is the limit.'

'I'll bet.'

'Well? What do you think?'

Johnny leaned forward toward Dees. He grabbed the sleeve of Dees's new L.L. Bean shirt in one hand and the collar of Dees's new L.L. Bean shirt in the other.

'Hey! What the hell do you think you're d . . .'

Johnny bunched the shirt in both hands and drew Dees forward. Five months of daily exercise had toned up the muscles in his hands and arms to a formidable degree.

'You asked me what I thought,' Johnny said. His head was beginning to throb and ache. 'I'll tell you. I think you're a ghoul. A grave robber of people's dreams. I think someone ought to put you to work at Roto-Rooter. I think your mother should have died of cancer the day after she conceived you. If there's a hell, I hope you burn there.'

'You can't talk to me like that!' Dees cried. His voice rose to a fishwife's shriek. 'You're fucking crazy! Forget it! Forget the whole thing, you stupid hick sonofabitch! You had your chance! Don't come crawling around . . .'

'Furthermore, you sound like you're talking through a Saltine box,' Johnny said, standing up. He lifted Dees with him. The tails of his shirt popped out of the waistband of his new jeans, revealing a fishnet undershirt beneath. Johnny began to shake Dees methodically back and forth. Dees forgot about being angry. He began to blubber and roar.

Johnny dragged him to the porch steps, raised one foot and planted it squarely in the seat of the new Levi's. Dees went down in two big steps, still blubbering and roaring. He fell in the dirt and sprawled full length. When he got up and turned around to face Johnny, his country-cousin duds were caked with dooryard dust. It made them look more real, somehow, Johnny thought, but doubted if Dees would appreciate that.

'I ought to put the cops on you,' he said hoarsely. 'And maybe I will.'

'You do whatever turns you on,' Johnny said. 'But the law around here doesn't take too kindly to people who stick their noses in where they haven't been invited.'

Dees's face worked in an uneasy contortion of fear, anger, and shock. 'God help you if you ever need us,' he said.

Johnny's head was aching fiercely now, but he kept his voice even. 'That's just right,' he said. 'I couldn't agree more.'

'You're going to be sorry, you know. Three million readers. That cuts both ways. When we get done with you the people in this country wouldn't believe you if you predicted spring in April. They wouldn't believe you if you said the World Series is going to come in October. They wouldn't believe you if ... if ...' Dees spluttered, furious.

'Get out of here, you cheap cocksucker,' Johnny said.

'*You can kiss off that book!*' Dees screamed, apparently summoning up the worst thing he could think of. With his working, knotted face and his dust-caked shirt, he looked like a kid having a class-A tantrum. His Brooklyn accent had deepened and darkened to the point where it was almost a patois. 'They'll laugh you out of every publishing house in New York! Nightstand Readers wouldn't touch you when I get done with you! There are ways of fixing smart guys like you and we got em, fuckhead! We...'

'I guess I'll go get my Remmy and shoot myself a trespasser,' Johnny remarked.

Dees retreated to his rental car, still shouting threats and obscenities. Johnny stood on the porch and watched him, his head thudding sickly. Dees got in, revved the car's engine mercilessly, and then screamed out, throwing dirt into the air in clouds. He let the car drift just enough on his way out to knock the chopping block by the shed flying. Johnny grinned a little at that in spite of his bad head. He could set up the chopping block a lot more easily than Dees was going to be able to explain the big dent in that Ford's front fender to the Hertz people.

Afternoon sun twinkled on chrome again as Dees sprayed gravel all the way up the driveway to the road. Johnny sat down in the rocker again and put his forehead in his hand and got ready to wait out the headache.

'You're going to do *what*?' the banker asked. Outside
and below, traffic passed back and forth along the bucolic
main street of Ridgeway, New Hampshire. On the walls
of the banker's pine-panelled, third-floor office were
Frederick Remington prints and photographs of the
banker at local functions. On his desk was a lucite cube,
and embedded in this cube were pictures of his wife and
son.

'I'm going to run for the House of Representatives next
year,' Greg Stillson repeated. He was dressed in khaki
suntan pants, a blue shirt with the sleeves rolled up, and
a black tie with a single blue figure. He looked out of
place in the banker's office, somehow, as if at any moment he might rise to his feet and begin an aimless,
destructive charge around the room, knocking over furniture, sweeping the expensively framed Remington
prints to the floor, pulling the drapes from their rods.

The banker, Charles 'Chuck' Gendron, president of the
local Lions Club, laughed – a bit uncertainly. Stillson
had a way of making people feel uncertain. As a boy he
had been scrawny, perhaps; he liked to tell people that 'a
high wind woulda blowed me away'; but in the end his
father's genes had told, and sitting here in Gendron's
office, he looked very much like the Oklahoma oilfield
roughneck that his father had been.

He frowned at Gendron's chuckle.

'I mean, George Harvey might have something to say
about that, mightn't he, Greg?' George Harvey, besides
being a mover and a shaker in town politics, was the
third district Republican godfather.

'George won't say boo,' Greg said calmly. There was a
salting of gray in his hair, but his face suddenly looked
very much like the face of the man who long ago had
kicked a dog to death in an Iowa farmyard. His voice
was patient. 'George is going to be on the sidelines, but
he's gonna be on my side of the sidelines, if you get my
meaning. I ain't going to be stepping on his toes, because
I'm going to run as an independent. I don't have twenty

years to spend learning the ropes and licking boots.'

Chuck Gendron said hesitantly, 'You're kidding, aren't you, Greg?'

Greg's frown returned. It was forbidding. 'Chuck, I never kid. People . . . they *think* I kid. The *Union-Leader* and those yo-yos on the *Daily Democrat*, they think I kid. But you go see George Harvey. You ask *him* if I kid around, or if I get the job done. You ought to know better, too. After all, we buried some bodies together, didn't we, Chuck?'

The frown metamorphosed into a somehow chilling grin – chilling to Gendron, perhaps, because he had allowed himself to be pulled along on a couple of Greg Stillson's development schemes. They had made money, yes, of course they had, that wasn't the problem. But there had been a couple of aspects of the Sunningdale Acres development (and the Laurel Estates deal as well, to be honest) that hadn't been – well, strictly legal. A bribed EPA agent for one thing, but that wasn't the worst thing.

On the Laurel Estates thing there had been an old man out on the Back Ridgeway Road who hadn't wanted to sell, and first the old man's fourteen-or-so chickens had died of some mysterious ailment and second there had been a fire in the old man's potato house and third when the old man came back from visiting his sister, who was in a nursing home in Keene, one weekend not so long ago, someone had smeared dogshit all over the old man's living room and dining room and fourth the old man had sold and fifth Laurel Estates was now a fact of life.

And, maybe sixth: That motorcycle spook, Sonny Elliman, was hanging around again. He and Greg were good buddies, and the only thing that kept that from being town gossip was the counterbalancing fact that Greg was seen in the company of a lot of heads, hippies, freaks, and cyclists – as a direct result of the Drug Counselling Center he had set up, plus Ridgeway's rather unusual program for young drug, alcohol, and road offenders. Instead of fining them or locking them up, the town took out their services in trade. It had been Greg's idea – and a good one, the banker would be the first to admit. It had been one of the things that had helped Greg to get elected mayor.

But this – this was utter craziness.

Greg had said something else. Gendron wasn't sure what.

'Pardon me,' he said.

'I asked you how you'd like to be my campaign manager,' Greg repeated.

'Greg ...' Gendron had to clear his throat and start again. 'Greg, you don't seem to understand. Harrison Fisher is the Third District representative in Washington. Harrison Fisher is Republican, respected, and probably eternal.'

'No one is eternal,' Greg said.

'Harrison is damn close,' Gendron said. 'Ask Harvey. They went to school together. Back around 1800, I think.'

Greg took no notice of this thin witticism. 'I'll call myself a Bull Moose or something ... and everyone will think I'm kidding around ... and in the end, the good people of the Third District are going to laugh me all the way to Washington.'

'Greg, you're crazy.'

Greg's smile disappeared as if it had never been there. Something frightening happened to his face. It became very still, and his eyes widened to show too much of the whites. They were like the eyes of a horse that smells bad water.

'You don't want to say something like that, Chuck. *Ever.*'

The banker felt more than chilled now.

'Greg, I apologize. It's just that ...'

'No, you don't ever want to say that to me, unless you want to find Sonny Elliman waiting for you some afternoon when you go out to get your big fucking Imperial.'

Gendron's mouth moved but no sound came out.

Greg smiled again, and it was like the sun suddenly breaking through threatening clouds. 'Never mind. We don't want to be kicking sand if we're going to be working together.'

'Greg . . .'

'I want you because you know every damn businessman in this part of New Hampshire. We're gonna have plenty good money once we get this thing rolling, but I figure we'll have to prime the pump. Now's the time for me to expand a little, and start looking like the state's man as well as Ridgeway's man. I figure fifty thousand dollars ought to be enough to fertilize the grass roots.'

The banker, who had worked for Harrison Fisher in his last four canvasses, was so astounded by Greg's political naiveté that at first he was at a loss on how to proceed. At last he said, 'Greg. Businessmen contribute to campaigns not out of the goodness of their hearts but because the winner ends up owing them something. In a close campaign they'll contribute to any candidate who has a chance of winning, because they can write off the loser as a tax loss as well. But the operant phrase is *chance of winning*. Now Fisher is a . . .'

'Shoo-in,' Greg supplied. He produced an envelope from his back pocket. 'Want you to look at these.'

Gendron looked doubtfully at the envelope, then up at Greg. Greg nodded encouragingly. The banker opened the envelope.

There was a long silence in the pine-panelled office after Gendron's initial gasp for breath. It was unbroken except for the faint hum of the digital clock on the banker's desk and the hiss of a match as Greg lit a Phillies cheroot. On the walls of the office were Frederick Remington pictures. In the lucite cube were family pictures. Now, spread on the desk, were pictures of the banker with his head buried between the thighs of a young woman with black hair – or it might have been red, the pictures were high-grain black-and-white glossies and it was hard to tell. The woman's face was very clear. It was not the face of the banker's wife. Some residents of Ridgeway would have recognized it as the face of one of the waitresses at Bobby Strang's truckstop two towns over.

The pictures of the banker with his head between the legs of the waitress were the safe ones – her face was clear but his was not. In others, his own grandmother would have recognized him. There were pictures of Gendron and the waitress involved in a whole medley of sexual delights – hardly all the positions of the Kama Sutra, but there were several positions represented that had never made the 'Sexual Relationships' chapter of the Ridgeway High health textbook.

Gendron looked up, his face cheesy, his hands trembling. His heart was galloping in his chest. He feared a heart attack.

Greg was not even looking at him. He was looking out the window at the bright blue slice of October sky visible between the Ridgeway Five and Ten and the Ridgeway Card and Notion Shoppe.

'The winds of change have started to blow,' he said, and his face was distant and preoccupied; almost mystical. He looked back at Gendron. 'One of those drug-freaks down at the Center, you know what he gave me?'

Chuck Gendron shook his head numbly. With one of his shaking hands he was massaging the left side if his chest – just in case. His eyes kept falling to the photographs. The damning photographs. What if his secretary came in right now? He stopped massaging his chest and began gathering up the pictures, stuffing them back into the envelope.

'He gave me Chairman Mao's little red book,' Greg said. A chuckle rumbled up from the barrel chest that had once been so thin, part of a body that had mostly disgusted his idolized father. 'And one of the proverbs in there ... I can't remember exactly how it went, but it was something like, "The man who senses the wind of change should build not a windbreak but a windmill." That was the flavor of it, anyway.'

He leaned forward.

'Harrison Fisher's not a shoo-in, he's a has-been. Ford is a has-been. Muskie's a has-been. Humphrey's a has-been. A lot of local and state politicians all the way across this country are going to wake up the day after election day and find out that they're as dead as dodo birds. They forced Nixon out, and the next year they forced out the people who stood behind him in the impeachment hearings, and next year they'll force out Jerry Ford for the same reason.'

Greg Stillson's eyes blazed at the banker.

'You want to see the wave of the future? Look up in Maine at this guy Longley. The Republicans ran a guy named Erwin and the Democrats ran a guy named Mitchell and when they counted the votes for governor, they both got a big surprise, because the people went and elected themselves an insurance man from Lewiston that didn't want any part of either party. Now they're talking about him as a dark horse candidate for president.'

Gendron still couldn't talk.

Greg drew in his breath. 'They're all gonna think I'm kiddin, see? They thought *Longley* was kiddin. But I'm not kiddin. I'm building windmills. And you're gonna supply the building materials.'

He ceased. Silence fell in the office, except for the hum of the clock. At last Gendron whispered, 'Where did you get these pictures? Was it that Elliman?'

'Aw, hey. You don't want to talk about that. You forget all about those pictures. Keep them.'

'And who keeps the negatives?'

'Chuck,' Greg said earnestly, 'you don't understand. I'm offering you Washington. Sky's the limit, boy! I'm not even asking you to raise that much money. Like I said, just a bucket of water to help prime the pump. When we get rolling, plenty of money is going to come in. Now, you know the guys that have money. You have lunch with them down at the Caswell House. You play poker with them. You have written them commercial loans tied to the prime rate at no more than their say so. And you know how to put an armlock on them.'

'Greg you don't understand, you don't . . .'

Greg stood up. 'The way I just put an armlock on you,' he said.

The banker looked up at him. His eyes rolled helplessly. Greg Stillson thought he looked like a sheep that had been led neatly to the slaughter.

'Fifty thousand dollars,' he said. 'You find it.'

He walked out, closing the door gently behind him. Gendron heard his booming voice even through the thick walls, bandying with his secretary. His secretary was a sixty-year-old flat-chested biddy, and Stillson probably had her giggling like a schoolgirl. He was a buffoon. It was that as much as his programs for coping with youthful crime that had made him mayor of Ridgeway. But the people didn't elect buffoons to Washington.

Well – hardly ever.

That wasn't his problem. Fifty thousand dollars in campaign contributions, that was his problem. His mind began to scurry around the problem like a trained white rat scurrying around a piece of cheese on a plate. It could probably be done. Yes, it could probably be done – but would it end there?

The white envelope was still on his desk. His smiling wife looked at it from her place in the lucite cube. He scooped the envelope up and jammed it into the inner pocket of his suitcoat. It had been Elliman, somehow Elliman had found out and had taken the pictures, he was sure of it.

But it had been Stillson who told him what to do.

Maybe the man wasn't such a buffoon after all. His assessment of the political climate of 1975–76 wasn't completely stupid. *Building windmills instead of windbreaks . . . the sky's the limit.*

But that wasn't his problem.

Fifty thousand dollars was his problem.

Chuck Gendron, president of the Lions and all-round good fellow (last year he had ridden one of those small, funny motorcycles in the Ridgeway Fourth of July parade), pulled a yellow legal tablet out of the top drawer of his desk and began jotting down a list of names. The trained white rat at work. And down on Main Street Greg Stillson turned his face up into the

strong autumn sunlight and congratulated himself on a
job well-done – or well-begun.

CHAPTER FIFTEEN

1 ·

Later, Johnny supposed that the reason he ended up
finally making love to Sarah – almost five years to the
day after the fair – had a lot to do with the visit of
Richard Dees, the man from *Inside View*. The reason he
finally weakened and called Sarah and invited her to
come and visit was little more than a wistful urge to have
someone nice to come to call and take the nasty taste out
of his mouth. Or so he told himself.

He called her in Kennebunk and got the former roommate, who said Sarah would be right with him. The
phone clunked down and there was a moment of silence
when he contemplated (but not very seriously) just hanging up and closing the books for good. Then Sarah's
voice was in his ear.

'Johnny? Is it you?'

'The very same.'

'How are you?'

'Fine. How's by you?'

'I'm fine,' she said. 'Glad you called. I . . . didn't know
if you would.'

'Still sniffin that wicked cocaine?'

'No, I'm on heroin now.'

'You got your boy with you?'

'I sure do. Don't go anywhere without him.'

'Well, why don't the two of you truck on out here
some day before you have to go back up north?'

'I'd like that, Johnny,' she said warmly.

'Dad's working in Westbrook and I'm chief cook and
bottlewasher. He gets home around four-thirty and we
eat around five-thirty. You're welcome to stay for dinner,

but be warned: all my best dishes use Franco-American spaghetti as their base.'

She giggled. 'Invitation accepted. Which day is best?'

'What about tomorrow or the day after, Sarah?'

'Tomorrow's fine,' she said after the briefest of hesitations. 'See you then.'

'Take care, Sarah.'

'You too.'

He hung up thoughtfully, feeling both excited and guilty – for no good reason at all. But your mind went where it wanted to, didn't it? And where his mind wanted to go now was to examine possibilities maybe best left unconsidered.

Well, she knows the thing she needs to know. She knows what time dad comes home – what else does she need to know?

And his mind answered itself: *What you going to do if she shows up at noon?*

Nothing, he answered, and didn't wholly believe it. Just thinking about Sarah, the set of her lips, the small, upward tilt of her green eyes – those were enough to make him feel weak and sappy and a little desperate.

Johnny went out to the kitchen and slowly began to put together this night's supper, not so important, just for two. Father and son batching it. It hadn't been all that bad. He was still healing. He and his father had talked about the four-and-a-half years he had missed, about his mother – working around that carefully but always seeming to come a little closer to the center, in a tightening spiral. Not needing to understand, maybe, but needing to come to terms. No, it hadn't been that bad. It was a way to finish putting things together. For both of them. But it would be over in January when he returned to Cleaves Mills to teach. He had gotten his half-year contract from Dave Pelsen the week before, had signed it and sent it back. What would his father do then? Go on, Johnny supposed. People had a way of doing that, just going on, pushing through with no particular drama, no big drumrolls. He would get down to visit Herb as often as he could, every weekend, if that felt like the right thing to do. So many things had gotten strange so fast that all he could do was feel his way slowly along, groping like a blind man in an unfamiliar room.

He put the roast in the oven, went into the living room, snapped on the TV, then snapped it off again. He sat down and thought about Sarah. *The baby*, he thought. *The baby will be our chaperon if she comes early.* So that was all right, after all. All bases covered.

But his thoughts were still long and uneasily speculative.

2 ·

She came at quarter past twelve the next day, wheeling a snappy little red Pinto into the driveway and parking it, getting out, looking tall and beautiful, her dark blonde hair caught in the mild October wind.

'Hi, Johnny!' she called, raising her hand.

'Sarah!' He came down to meet her; she lifted her face and he kissed her cheek lightly.

'Just let me get the emperor,' she said, opening the passenger door.

'Can I help?'

'Naw, we get along just fine together, don't we, Denny? Come on, kiddo.' Moving deftly, she unbuckled the straps holding a pudgy little baby in the car seat. She lifted him out. Denny stared around the yard with wild, solemn interest, and then his eyes fixed on Johnny and held there. He smiled.

'Vig!' Denny said, and waved both hands.

'I think he wants to go to you,' Sarah said. 'Very unusual. Denny has his father's Republican sensibilities – he's rather standoffish. Want to hold him?'

'Sure,' Johnny said, a little doubtfully.

Sarah grinned. 'He won't break and you won't drop him,' she said, and handed Denny over. 'If you did, he'd probably bounce right up like Silly Putty. *Disgustingly* fat baby.'

'Vun bunk!' Denny said, curling one arm nonchalantly around Johnny's neck and looking comfortably at his mother.

'It really is amazing,' Sarah said. 'He never takes to people like . . . Johnny? *Johnny?*'

When the baby put his arm around Johnny's neck, a confused rush of feelings had washed over him like mild warm water. There was nothing dark, nothing troubling. Everything was very simple. There was no concept of the future in the baby's thoughts. No feeling of trouble. No sense of past unhappiness. And on words, only strong images: warmth, dryness, the mother, the man that was himself.

'Johnny?' She was looking at him apprehensively.

'Hmmmm?'

'Is everything all right?'

She's asking me about Denny, he realized. Is everything all right with Denny? Do you see trouble? Problems?

'Everything's fine,' he said. 'We can go inside if you want, but I usually roost on the porch. It'll be time to crouch around the stove all day long soon enough.'

'I think the porch will be super. And Denny looks as if he'd like to try out the yard. *Great* yard, he says. Right, kiddo?' She ruffled his hair and Denny laughed.

'He'll be okay?'

'As long as he doesn't try to eat any of those wood-chips.'

'I've been splitting stove-lengths,' Johnny said, setting Denny down as carefully as a Ming vase. 'Good exercise.'

'How are you? Physically?'

'I think,' Johnny said, remembering the heave-ho he had given Richard Dees a few days ago, 'that I'm doing as well as could be expected.'

'That's good. You were kinda low the last time I saw you.'

Johnny nodded. 'The operations.'

'Johnny?'

He glanced at her and again felt that odd mix of specu-lation, guilt, and something like anticipation in his viscera. Her eyes were on his face, frankly and openly.

'Yeah?'

'Do you remember . . . about the wedding ring?'

He nodded.

'It was there. Where you said it would be. I threw it away.'

'Did you?' He was not completely surprised.

'I threw it away and never mentioned it to Walt.' She shook her head. 'And I don't know why. It's bothered me ever since.'

'Don't let it.'

They were standing on the steps, facing each other. Color had come up in her cheeks, but she didn't drop her eyes.

'There's something I'd like to finish,' she said simply. 'Something we never had the chance to finish.'

'Sarah . . .' he began, and stopped. He had absolutely no idea what to say next. Below them, Denny tottered six steps and then sat down hard. He crowed, not put out of countenance at all.

'Yes,' she said. 'I don't know if it's right or wrong. I love Walt. He's a good man, easy to love. Maybe the one thing I know is a good man from a bad one. Dan – that guy I went with in college – was one of the bad guys. You set my mouth for the other kind, Johnny. Without you, I never could have appreciated Walt for what he is.'

'Sarah, you don't have to . . .'

'I *do* have to,' Sarah contradicted. Her voice was low and intense. 'Because things like this you can only say once. And you either get it wrong or right, it's the end either way, because it's too hard to ever try to say again.' She looked at him pleadingly. 'Do you understand?'

· 'Yes, I suppose I do.'

'I love you, Johnny,' she said. 'I never stopped. I've tried to tell myself that it was an act of God that split us up. I don't know. Is a bad hot dog an act of God? Or two kids dragging on a back road in the middle of the night? All I want . . .' Her voice had taken on a peculiar flat emphasis that seemed to beat its way into

236

the cool October afternoon like an artisan's small hammer into thin and precious foil, '... all I want is what was taken from us.' Her voice faltered. She looked down. 'And I want it with all my heart, Johnny. Do you?'

'Yes,' he said. He put his arms out and was confused when she shook her head and stepped away.

'Not in front of Denny,' she said. 'It's stupid, maybe, but that would be a little bit too much like public infidelity. I want everything, Johnny.' Her color rose again, and her pretty blush began to feed his own excitement. 'I want you to hold me and kiss me and love me,' she said. Her voice faltered, nearly broke. 'I think it's wrong, but I can't help it. It's wrong but it's right. It's *fair*.'

He reached out one finger and brushed away a tear that was moving slowly down her cheek.

'And it's only this once, isn't it?'

She nodded. 'Once will have to put paid to everything. Everything that would have been, if things hadn't gone wrong.' She looked up, her eyes brighter green than ever, swimming with tears. 'Can we put paid to everything with only the one time, Johnny?'

'No,' he said, smiling. 'But we can try, Sarah.'

She looked fondly down at Denny, who was trying to climb up onto the chopping block without much success. 'He'll sleep,' she said.

3 ·

They sat on the porch and watched Denny play in the yard under the high blue sky. There was no hurry, no impatience between them, but there was a growing electricity that they both felt. She had opened her coat and sat on the porch glider in a powder-blue wool dress, her ankles crossed, her hair blown carelessly on her shoulders where the wind had spilled it. The blush never really left her face. And high white clouds fled across the sky, west to east.

They talked of inconsequential things – there was no hurry. For the first time since he had come out of it, Johnny felt that time was not his enemy. Time had provided them with this little air pocket in exchange for the main flow of which they had been robbed, and it would be here for as long as they needed it. They talked about people who had been married, about a girl from Cleaves Mills who had won a Merit scholarship, about Maine's independent governor. Sarah said he looked like Lurch on the old Addams Family show and thought like Herbert Hoover, and they both laughed over that.

'Look at him,' Sarah said, nodding toward Denny.

He was sitting on the grass by Vera Smith's ivy trellis, his thumb in his mouth, looking at them sleepily.

She got his car-bed out of the Pinto's back seat.

'Will he be okay on the porch?' she asked Johnny. 'It's so mild. I'd like to have him nap in the fresh air.'

'He'll be fine on the porch,' Johnny said.

She set the bed in the shade, popped him into it, and pulled the two blankets up to his chin. 'Sleep, baby,' Sarah said.

He smiled at her and promptly closed his eyes.

'Just like that?' Johnny asked.

'Just like that,' she agreed. She stepped close to him and put her arms around his neck. Quite clearly he could hear the faint rustle of her slip beneath her dress. 'I'd like you to kiss me,' she said calmly. 'I've waited five years for you to kiss me again, Johnny.'

He put his arms around her waist and kissed her gently. Her lips parted.

'Oh, Johnny,' she said against his neck. 'I love you.'

'I love you too, Sarah.'

'Where do we go?' she asked, stepping away from him. Her eyes were as clear and dark as emeralds now. 'Where?'

4 ·

He spread the faded army blanket, which was old but clean, on the straw of the second loft. The smell was fragrant and sweet. High above them there was the mysterious coo and flutter of the barn swallows, and then they settled down again. There was a small, dusty window which looked down on the house and porch. Sarah wiped a clean place on the glass and looked down at Denny.

'It's okay?' Johnny asked.

'Yes. Better here than in the house. That would have been like . . .' She shrugged.

'Making my dad a part of it?'

'Yes. This is between us.'

'Our business.'

'Our business,' she agreed. She lay on her stomach, her face turned to one side on the faded blanket, her legs bent at the knee. She pushed her shoes off, one by one. 'Unzip me, Johnny.'

He knelt beside her and pulled the zipper down. The sound was loud in the stillness. Her back was the color of coffee with cream against the whiteness of her slip. He kissed her between the shoulder blades and she shivered.

'Sarah,' he murmured.

'What?'

'I have to tell you something.'

'What?'

'The doctor made a mistake during one of those operations and gelded me.'

She punched him on the shoulder. 'Same old Johnny,' she said. 'And you had a friend once who broke his neck on the crack-the-whip at Topsham Fair.'

'Sure,' he said.

Her hand touched him like silk, moving gently up and down.

'It doesn't feel like they did anything terminal to you,' she said. Her luminous eyes searched his. 'Not at all. Shall we look and see?'

There was the sweet smell of the hay. Time spun out. There was the rough feel of the army blanket, the smooth feel of her flesh, the naked reality of her. Sinking into her was like sinking into an old dream that had never been quite forgotten.

'Oh, Johnny, my dear . . .' Her voice in rising excitement. Her hips moving in a quickening tempo. Her voice

239

was far away. The touch of her hair was like fire on his shoulder and chest. He plunged his face deeply into it, losing himself in that dark-blonde darkness.

Time spinning out in the sweet smell of hay. The rough-textured blanket. The sound of the old barn creaking gently, like a ship, in the October wind. Mild white light coming in through the roof chinks, catching motes of chaff in half a hundred pencil-thin sunbeams. Motes of chaff dancing and revolving.

She cried out. At some point she cried out his name, again and again and again, like a chant. Her fingers dug into him like spurs. Rider and ridden. Old wine decanted at last, a fine vintage.

Later they sat by the window, looking out into the yard. Sarah slipped her dress on over bare flesh and left him for a little bit. He sat alone, not thinking, content to watch her reappear in the window, smaller, and cross the yard to the porch. She bent over the baby bed and re-adjusted the blankets. She came back, the wind blowing her hair out behind her and tugging playfully at the hem of her dress.

'He'll sleep another half hour,' she said.

'Will he?' Johnny smiled. 'Maybe I will, too.'

She walked her bare toes across his belly. 'You better not.'

And so again, and this time she was on top, almost in an attitude of prayer, her head bent, her hair swinging forward and obscuring her face. Slowly. And then it was over.

5 ·

'Sarah . . .'

'No, Johnny. Better not say it. Time's up.'

'I was going to say that you're beautiful.'

'Am I?'

'You are,' he said softly. 'Dear Sarah.'

'Did we put paid to everything?' she asked him.

Johnny smiled. 'Sarah, we did the best we could.'

Herb didn't seem surprised to see Sarah when he got home from Westbrook. He welcomed her, made much of the baby, and then scolded Sarah for not bringing him down sooner.

'He has your color and complexion,' Herb said. 'And I think he's going to have your eyes, when they get done changing.'

'If only he has his father's brains,' Sarah said. She had put an apron on over the blue wool dress. Outside, the sun was going down. Another twenty minutes and it would be dark.

'You know, the cooking is supposed to be Johnny's job,' Herb said.

'Couldn't stop her. She put a gun to my head.'

'Well, maybe it's all for the best,' Herb said. 'Everything you make comes out tasting like Franco-American spaghetti.'

Johnny shied a magazine at him and Denny laughed, a high, piercing sound that seemed to fill the house.

Can he see? Johnny wondered. *It feels like it's written all over my face.* And then a startling thought came to him as he watched his father digging in the entryway closet for a box of Johnny's old toys that he had never let Vera give away: *Maybe he understands.*

They ate. Herb asked Sarah what Walt was doing in Washington and she told them about the conference he was attending, which had to do with Indian land claims. The Republican meetings were mostly wind-testing exercises, she said.

'Most of the people he's meeting with think that if Reagan is nominated over Ford next year, it's going to mean the death of the party,' Sarah said. 'And if the Grand Old Party dies, that means Walt won't be able to run for Bill Cohen's seat in 1978 when Cohen goes after Bill Hathaway's Senate seat.

Herb was watching Denny eat string beans, seriously, one by one, using all six of his teeth on them. 'I don't think Cohen will be able to wait until '78 to get in the

Senate. He'll run against Muskie next year.'

'Walt says Bill Cohen's not that big a dope,' Sarah said.
'He'll wait. Walt says his own chance is coming, and I'm starting to believe him.'

After supper they sat in the living room, and the talk turned away from politics. They watched Denny play with the old wooden cars and trucks that a much younger Herb Smith had made for his own son over a quarter of a century ago. A younger Herb Smith who had been married to a tough, good-humored woman who would sometimes drink a bottle of Black Label beer in the evening. A man with no gray in his hair and nothing but the highest hopes for his son.

He does understand, Johnny thought, sipping his coffee. *Whether he knows what went on between Sarah and me this afternoon, whether or not he suspects what might have gone on, he understands the basic cheat. You can't change it or rectify it, the best you can do is try to come to terms. This afternoon she and I consummated a marriage that never was. And tonight he's playing with his grandson.*

He thought of the Wheel of Fortune, slowing, stopping. *House number. Everyone loses.*

Gloom was trying to creep up, a dismal sense of finality, and he pushed it away. This wasn't the time; he wouldn't let it be the time.

By eight-thirty Denny had begun to get scratchy and cross and Sarah said, 'Time for us to go, folks. He can suck a bottle on our way back to Kennebunk. About three miles from here, he'll have corked off. Thanks for having us.' Her eyes, brilliant green, found Johnny's for a moment.

'Our pleasure entirely,' Herb said, standing up. 'Right, Johnny?'

'Right,' he said. 'Let me carry that car-bed out for you, Sarah.'

At the door, Herb kissed the top of Denny's head (and Denny grabbed Herb's nose in his chubby fist and honked it hard enough to make Herb's eyes water) and Sarah's

242

cheek. Johnny carried the car-bed down to the red Pinto and Sarah gave him the keys so he could put everything in the back.

When he finished, she was standing by the driver's door, looking at him. 'It was the best we could do,' she said, and smiled a little. But the brilliance of her eyes told him the tears were close again.

'It wasn't so bad at all,' Johnny said.

'We'll stay in touch?'

'I don't know, Sarah. Will we?'

'No, I suppose not. It would be too easy, wouldn't it?'

'Pretty easy, yes.'

She stepped close and stretched to kiss his cheek. He could smell her hair, clean and fragrant.

'Take care,' she whispered. 'I'll think about you.'

'Be good, Sarah,' he said, and touched her nose.

She turned then, got in behind the wheel, a smart young matron whose husband was on the way up. I doubt like hell if they'll be driving a Pinto next year, Johnny thought.

The lights came on, then the little sewing machine motor roared. She raised a hand to him and then she was pulling out of the driveway. Johnny stood by the chopping block, hands in his pockets, and watched her go. Something in his heart seemed to have closed. It was not a major feeling. That was the worst of it – it wasn't a major feeling at all.

He watched until the taillights were out of sight and then he climbed the porch steps and went back into the house. His dad was sitting in the big easy chair in the living room. The TV was off. The few toys he had found in the closet were scattered on the rug and he was looking at them.

'Good to see Sarah,' Herb said. 'Did you and she have . . .' there was the briefest, most minute hesitation . . . 'a nice visit?'

'Yes,' Johnny said.

'She'll be down again?'

'No, I don't think so.'

He and his father were looking at each other.

'Well now, maybe that's for the best,' Herb said finally.

'Yes. Maybe so.'

'You played with these toys,' Herb said, getting down on his knees and beginning to gather them up. 'I gave a bunch of them to Lottie Gedreau when she had her twins, but I knew I had a few of them left. I saved a few back.'

He put them back in the box one at a time, turning each of them over in his hands, examining them. A race car. A bulldozer. A police car. A small hook-and-ladder truck from which most of the red paint had been worn away where a small hand would grip. He took them back to the entryway closet and put them away.

Johnny didn't see Sarah Hazlett again for three years.

CHAPTER SIXTEEN

1 ·

The snow came early that year. There were six inches on the ground by November 7, and Johnny had taken to lacing on a pair of old green gumrubber boots and wearing his old parka for the trek up to the mailbox. Two weeks before, Dave Pelsen had mailed down a package containing the texts he would be using in January, and Johnny had already begun making tentative lesson plans. He was looking forward to getting back. Dave had also found him an apartment on Howland Street in Cleaves. 24 Howland Street. Johnny kept that on a scrap of paper in his wallet, because the name and number had an irritating way of slipping his mind.

On this day the skies were slatey and lowering, the temperature hovering just below the twenty-degree mark. As Johnny tramped up the driveway, the first spats of snow began to drift down. Because he was alone, he didn't feel too self-conscious about running his tongue out and trying to catch a flake on it. He was hardly limp-

ing at all, and he felt good. There hadn't been a headache in two weeks or more.

The mail consisted of an advertising circular, a *Newsweek*, and a small manila envelope addressed to John
Smith, no return address. Johnny opened it on the way
back, the rest of the mail stuffed into his hip pocket. He
pulled out a single page of newsprint, saw the words
Inside View at the top, and came to a halt halfway back
to the house.

It was page three of the previous week's issue. The
headline story dealt with a reporter's 'exposé' on the
handsome second banana of a TV crime show; the second
banana had been suspended from high school twice
(twelve years ago) and busted for possession of cocaine
(six years ago). Hot news for the *hausfraus* of America.
There was also an all-grain diet, a cute baby photo, and
a story of a nine-year-old girl who had been miraculously
cured of cerebral palsy at Lourdes (DOCTORS MYS-
TIFIED, the headline trumpeted gleefully). A story near
the bottom of the page had been circled. MAINE 'PSY-
CHIC' ADMITS HOAX, the headline read. The story
was not by-lined.

IT HAS ALWAYS BEEN THE POLICY of *Inside
View* not only to bring you the fullest coverage of the
psychics which the so-called 'National Press' ignores,
but to expose the tricksters and charlatans who have
held back true acceptance of legitimate psychic phenomena for so long.

One of these tricksters admitted his own hoax to an
Inside View source recently. This so-called 'psychic',
John Smith of Pownal, Maine, admitted to our source
that 'it was all a gimmick to pay back my hospital bills.
If there's a book in it, I might come out with enough
to pay off what I owe and retire for a couple of years
in the bargain,' Smith grinned. 'These days, people
will believe anything – why shouldn't I get on the
gravy train?'

Thanks to *Inside View*, which has always cautioned

readers that there are two phony psychics for each real one, John Smith's gravy train has just been derailed. And we reiterate our standing offer of $1000 to anyone who can prove that any nationally known psychic is a fraud.

Hoaxers and charlatans be warned!

Johnny read the article twice as the snow began to come down more heavily. A reluctant grin broke over his features. The ever-vigilant press apparently didn't enjoy being thrown off some bumpkin's front porch, he thought. He tucked the tear sheet back into its envelope and stuffed it into his back pocket with the rest of the mail.

'Dees,' he said aloud, 'I hope you're still black and blue.'

2 ·

His father was not so amused. Herb read the clipping and then slammed it down on the kitchen table in disgust. 'You ought to sue that son of a whore. That's nothing but slander, Johnny. A deliberate hatchet job.'

'Agreed and agreed,' Johnny said. It was dark outside. This afternoon's silently falling snow had developed into tonight's early winter blizzard. The wind shrieked and howled around the eaves. The driveway had disappeared under a dunelike progression of drifts. 'But there was no third party when we talked, and Dees damn well knows it. It's his word against mine.'

'He didn't even have the guts to put his own name to this lie,' Herb said. 'Look at this "an *Inside View* source". What's this source? Get him to name it, that's what I say.'

'Oh, you can't do that,' Johnny said, grinning. 'That's like walking up to the meanest street-fighter on the block with a KICK ME HARD sign taped to your crotch. Then they turn it into a holy war, page one and all. No thanks. As far as I'm concerned, they did me a favor. I don't want to make a career out of telling people where gramps hid

246

his stock certificates or who's going to win the fourth at Scarborough Downs. Or take this lottery.' One of the things that had most surprised Johnny on coming out of his coma was to discover that Maine and about a dozen other states had instituted a legal numbers game. 'In the last month I've gotten sixteen letters from people who want me to tell them what the number's going to be. It's insane. Even if I could tell them, which I couldn't, what good would it do them? You can't pick your own number in the Maine lottery, you get what they give you. But still I get the letters.'

'I don't see what that has to do with this crappy article.'

'If people think I'm a phony, maybe they'll leave me alone.'

'Oh,' Herb said. 'Yeah, I see what you mean.' He lit his pipe. 'You've never really been comfortable with it, have you?'

'No,' Johnny said. 'We never talk much about it, either, which is something of a relief. It seems like the only thing other people *do* want to talk about.' And it wasn't just that they wanted to talk; that wouldn't have bothered him so much. But when he was in Slocum's Store for a sixpack or a loaf of bread, the girl would try to take his money without touching his hand, and the frightened, skittish look in her eyes was unmistakable. His father's friends would give him a little wave instead of a hand-shake. In October Herb had hired a local high school girl to come in once a week to do some dusting and vacuum the floors. After three weeks she had quit for no stated reason at all – probably someone at her high school had told her who she was cleaning for. It seemed that for everyone who was anxious to be touched, to be informed, to be in contact with Johnny's peculiar talent, there was another who regarded him as a kind of leper. At times like these, Johnny would think of the nurses staring at him the day he had told Eileen Magown that her house was on fire, staring at him like magpies on a telephone wire. He would think of the way the TV reporter had drawn back from him after the press conference's unexpected conclusion, agreeing with everything he said but not wanting to be touched. Unhealthy either way.

'No, we don't talk about it,' Herb agreed. 'It makes me think of your mother, I suppose. She was so sure you'd been given the ... the whatever-it-is for some reason. Sometimes I wonder if she wasn't right.'

Johnny shrugged. 'All I want is a normal life. I want to bury the whole damn thing. And if this little squib helps me do it, so much the better.'

'But you still can do it, can't you?' Herb asked. He was looking closely at his son.

Johnny thought about a night not quite a week ago. They had gone out to dinner, a rare happening on their strapped budget. They had gone to Cole's Farm in Gray, probably the best restaurant in the area, a place that was always packed. The night had been cold, the dining room cheery and warm. Johnny had taken his father's coat and his own into the cloakroom, and as he thumbed through the racked coats, looking for empty hangers, a whole series of clear impressions had cascaded through his mind. It was like that sometimes, and on another occasion he could have handled every coat for twenty minutes and gotten nothing at all. Here was a lady's coat with a fur collar. She was having an affair with one of her husband's poker buddies, was scared sick about it, but didn't know how to close it off. A man's denim jacket, sheepskin-lined. This guy was also worried – about his brother, who had been badly hurt on a construction project the week before. A small boy's parka – his grandmother in Durham had given him a Snoopy transistor radio just today and he was mad because his father hadn't let him bring it into the dining room with him. And another one, a plain, black topcoat, that had turned him cold with terror and robbed him of his appetite. The man who owned this coat was going mad. So far he had kept up appearances – not even his wife suspected – but his vision of the world was being slowly darkened by a series of increasingly paranoid fantasies. Touching that coat had been like touching a writhing coil of snakes.

'Yes, I can still do it,' Johnny said briefly. 'I wish to hell I couldn't.'

'You really mean that?'

Johnny thought of the plain, black topcoat. He had only picked at his meal, looking this way and that, trying to single the man out of the crowd, unable to do so.

'Yes,' he said. 'I mean it.'

'Best forgotten then,' Herb said, and clapped his son on the shoulder.

3 ·

And for the next month or so it seemed that it would be forgotten. Johnny drove north to attend a meeting at the high school for midyear teachers and to take a load of his personal things up to his new apartment, which he found small but liveable.

He went in his father's car, and as he was getting ready to leave Herb asked him, 'You're not nervous? About driving?'

Johnny shook his head. Thoughts of the accident itself troubled him very little now. If something was going to happen to him, it would. And deep down he felt confident that lightning would not strike in the same place again – when he died, he didn't believe it would be in a car accident.

In fact, the long trip was quiet and soothing, the meeting a little bit like Old Home Week. All of his old colleagues who were still teaching at CMHS dropped by to wish him the best. But he couldn't help noticing how few of them actually shook hands with him, and he seemed to sense a certain reserve, a wariness in their eyes. Driving home, he convinced himself it was probably imagination. And if not, well . . . even that had its amusing side. If they had read their *Inside View*, they would know he was a hoax and nothing to worry about.

The meeting over, there was nothing to do but go back to Pownal and wait for the Christmas holidays to come and go. The packages containing personal objects stopped coming, almost as if a switch had been thrown – the power of the press, Johnny told his father. They were replaced by a brief spate of angry – and mostly anonymous – letters and cards from people who seemed to feel personally cheated.

'You ort to burn in H I E I L I L I for your slimey skeems to bilk this American Republic,' a typical one read. It had been written on a crumpled sheet of Ramada Inn stationery and was postmarked York, Pennsylvania. 'You are nothing but a *Con Artist* and a *dirty rotten cheet*. I bless God for that paper that saw thru you. You ort to be ashamed of yourself Sir. The Bible says an ordinery sinner will be cast into the Lake of F I I I R I E I and be consomed but a F I A I L I S I E P I R I O I F I I I T I shall burn *forever* and *EVER* I That's you a False Profit who sold your Immortal Soul for a few cheep bucks. So thats the end of my letter and I hope for your sake I never catch you out on the Streets of your Home Town. Signed, A FRIEND (of God not you Sir) I '

Over two dozen letters in this approximate vein came in during the course of about twenty days following the appearance of the *Inside View* story. Several enterprising souls expressed an interest in joining in with Johnny as partners. 'I used to be a magician's assistant,' one of these latter missives bragged, 'and I could trick an old whore out of her g-string. If you're planning a mentalist gig, you need me in I '

Then the letters dried up, as had the earlier influx of boxes and packages. On a day in late November when he had checked the mailbox and found it empty for the third afternoon in a row, Johnny walked back to the house remembering that Andy Warhol had predicted that a day would come when everyone in America would be famous for fifteen minutes. Apparently his fifteen minutes had come and gone, and no one was any more pleased about it than he was.

But as things turned out, it wasn't over yet.

'Smith?' The telephone voice asked. 'John Smith?'

'Yes.' It wasn't a voice he knew, or a wrong number. That made it something of a puzzle since his father had had the phone unlisted about three months ago. This was December 17, and their tree stood in the corner of the living room, its base firmly wedged into the old tree stand Herb had made when Johnny was just a kid. Outside it was snowing.

'My name is Bannerman. Sheriff George Bannerman, from Castle Rock.' He cleared his throat. 'I've got a ... well, I suppose you'd say I've got a proposal for you.'

'How did you get this number?'

Bannerman cleared his throat again. 'Well, I could have gotten it from the phone company, I suppose, it being police business. But actually I got it from a friend of yours. Doctor by the name of Weizak.'

'Sam Weizak gave you my number?'

'That's right.'

Johnny sat down in the phone nook, utterly perplexed. Now the name Bannerman meant something to him. He had come across the name in a Sunday supplement article only recently. He was the sheriff of Castle County, which was considerably west of Pownal, in the Lakes region. Castle Rock was the county seat, about thirty miles from Norway and twenty from Bridgton.

'Police business?' he repeated.

'Well, I guess you'd say so, ayuh. I was wondering if maybe the two of us could get together for a cup of coffee ...'

'It involves Sam?'

'No. Dr. Weizak has nothing to do with it,' Bannerman said. 'He gave me a call and mentioned your name. That was ... oh, a month ago, at least. To be frank, I thought he was nuts. But now we're just about at our wits' end.'

'About what? Mr. – *Sheriff* – Bannerman, I don't understand what you're talking about.'

'It'd really be a lot better if we could get together for

SOLIHULL S.F.C
JBRARY

coffee,' Bannerman said. 'Maybe this evening? There's a place called Jon's on the main drag in Bridgton. Sort of halfway between your town and mine.'

'No, I'm sorry,' Johnny said. 'I'd have to know what it was about. And how come Sam never called me?'

Bannerman sighed. 'I guess you're a man who doesn't read the papers,' he said.

But that wasn't true. He had read the papers compulsively since he had regained consciousness, trying to pick up on the things he had missed. And he had seen Bannerman's name just recently. Sure. Because Bannerman was on a pretty hot seat. He was the man in charge of –

Johnny held the phone away from his ear and looked at it with sudden understanding. He looked at it the way a man might look at a snake he has just realized is poisonous.

'Mr. Smith?' It squawked tinnily. 'Hello, Mr. Smith?'

'I'm here,' Johnny said putting the phone back to his ear. He was conscious of a dull anger at Sam Weizak, Sam who had told him to keep his head down only this summer, and then had turned around and given this local-yokel sheriff an earful – behind Johnny's back.

'It's that strangling business, isn't it?'

Bannerman hesitated a long time. Then he said, 'Could we talk, Mr. Smith?'

'No. Absolutely not.' The dull anger had ignited into sudden fury. Fury and something else. He was scared.

'Mr. Smith, it's important. Today . . .'

'No. I want to be left alone. Besides, don't you read the goddam *Inside View*? I'm a fake anyway.'

'Dr. Weizak said . . .'

'He had no business saying anything!' Johnny shouted. He was shaking all over. 'Good-bye!' He slammed the phone into its cradle and got out of the phone nook quickly, as if that would prevent it from ringing again. He could feel a headache beginning in his temples. Dull drill-bits. Maybe I should call his mother out there in

California, he thought. Tell her where her little sonny-buns is. Tell her to get in touch. Tit for tat.

Instead he hunted in the address book in the phone-table drawer, found Sam's office number in Bangor, and called it. As soon as it rang once on the other end he hung up, scared again. Why had Sam done that to him? Goddammit, why?

He found himself looking at the Christmas tree.

Same old decorations. They had dragged them down from the attic again and taken them out of their tissue-paper cradles again and hung them up again, just two evenings ago. It was a funny thing about Christmas decorations. There weren't many things that remained intact year after year as a person grew up. Not many lines of continuity, not many physical objects that could easily serve both the states of childhood and adulthood. Your kid clothes were handed down or packed off to the Salvation Army; your Donald Duck watch sprung its mainspring; your Red Ryder cowboy boots wore out. The wallet you made in your first camp handicrafts class got replaced by a Lord Buxton, and you traded your red wagon and your bike for more adult toys – a car, a tennis racket, maybe one of those new TV hockey games. There were only a few things you could hang onto. A few books, maybe, or a lucky coin, or a stamp collection that had been preserved and improved upon.

Add to that the Christmas tree ornaments in your parents' house.

The same chipped angels year after year, and the same tinsel star on top; the tough surviving platoon of what had once been an entire battalion of glass balls (and we never forget the honored dead, he thought – this one died as a result of a baby's clutching hand, this one slipped as dad was putting it on and crashed to the floor, the red one with the Star of Bethlehem painted on it was simply and mysteriously broken one year when we took them down from the attic, and I cried); the tree stand itself. But sometimes, Johnny thought, absently massaging his temples, it seemed it would be better, more merciful, if you lost touch with even these last vestiges of childhood. You could never discover the books that had first turned you on in quite the same way. The lucky coin had not protected you from any of the ordinary whips and scorns and scrapes of an ordinary life. And when you looked at the ornaments you remembered that there had once been a mother in the place to direct the tree-trimming operation, always ready and willing to piss you off by saying 'a little higher' or 'a little lower' or 'I think you've got too much tinsel on that left side, dear.' You looked at the ornaments and remembered that just the two of you had been around to put them up this year, just the two of you because your mother went crazy and then she died, but the fragile Christmas tree ornaments were still here, still hanging around to decorate another tree taken from the small back woodlot and didn't they say more people committed suicide around Christmas than at any other time of the year? By God, it was no wonder.

What a power God has given you, Johnny.

Sure, that's right, God's a real prince. He knocked me through the windshield of a cab and I broke my legs and spent five years or so in a coma and three people died. The girl I loved got married. She had the son who should have been mine by a lawyer who's breaking his ass to get to Washington so he can help run the big electric train set. If I'm on my feet for more than a couple of hours at a time it feels like somebody took a long splinter and rammed it straight up my leg to my balls. God's a real sport. He's such a sport that he fixed up a funny comic-opera world where a bunch of glass Christmas tree globes could outlive you. Neat world, and a really first-class God in charge of it. He must have been on our side during Vietnam, because that's the way he's been running things ever since time began.

He has a job for you, Johnny.

Bailing some half-assed country cop out of a jam so he can get re-elected next year.

Don't run from him, Johnny. Don't hide away in a cave.

He rubbed his temples. Outside, the wind was rising. He hoped dad would be careful coming home from work.

Johnny got up and pulled on a heavy sweatshirt. He went out into the shed, watching his breath frost the air ahead of him. To the left was a large pile of wood he had split in the autumn just past, all of it cut into neat stove lengths. Next to it was a box of kindling, and beside that was a stack of old newspapers. He squatted down and began to thumb through them. His hands went numb quickly but he kept going, and eventually he came to the one he was looking for. The Sunday paper from three weeks ago.

He took it into the house, slapped it down on the kitchen table, and began to root through it. He found the article he was looking for in the features section and sat down to reread it.

The article was accompanied by several photos, one of them showing an old woman locking a door, another showing a police car cruising a nearly deserted street, two others snowing a couple of businesses that were nearly deserted. The headline read: THE HUNT FOR THE CASTLE ROCK STRANGLER GOES ON ... AND ON.

Five years ago, according to the story, a young woman named Alma Frechette who worked at a local restaurant had been raped and strangled on her way home from work. A joint investigation of the crime had been conducted by the state attorney general's office and the Castle County sheriff's department. The result had been a total zero. A year later an elderly woman, also raped and strangled, had been discovered in her tiny third-floor apartment on Carbine Street in Castle Rock. A month later the killer had struck again; this time the victim had been a bright young junior high school girl.

There had been a more intensive investigation. The investigative facilities of the FBI had been utilized, all to no result. The following November Sheriff Carl M. Kelso, who had been the county's chief law officer since approximately the days of the Civil War, had been voted out and George Bannerman had been voted in, largely on an aggressive campaign to catch the 'Castle Rock Strangler'.

Two years passed. The strangler had not been apprehended, but no further murders occurred, either. Then, last January, the body of seventeen-year-old Carol Dunbarger had been found by two small boys. The Dunbarger girl had been reported as a missing person by her parents. She had been in and out of trouble at Castle Rock High School where she had a record of chronic tardiness and truancy, she had been busted twice for shoplifting, and had run away once before, getting as far as Boston. Both Bannerman and the state police assumed she had been thumbing a ride – and the killer had picked her up. A midwinter thaw had uncovered her body near Strimmer's Brook, where two small boys had found it. The state medical examiner said she had been dead about two months.

Then, this November 2, there had been yet another murder. The victim was a well-liked Castle Rock grammar school teacher named Etta Ringgold. She was a lifetime member of the local Methodist church, holder of an M.B.S. in elementary education, and prominent in local charities. She had been fond of the works of Robert Browning, and her body had been found stuffed into a culvert that ran beneath an unpaved secondary road. The uproar over the murder of Miss Ringgold had rumbled over all of northern New England. Comparisons to Albert DeSalvo, the Boston Strangler, were made – comparisons that did nothing to pour oil on the troubled waters. William Loeb's *Union-Leader* in not-so-distant Manchester, New Hampshire, had published a helpful editorial titled THE DO-NOTHING COPS IN OUR SISTER STATE.

This Sunday supplement article, now nearly six weeks old and smelling pungently of shed and woodbox, quoted two local psychiatrists who had been perfectly happy to blue-sky the situation as long as their names weren't printed. One of them mentioned a particular sexual aberration – the urge to commit some violent act at the moment of orgasm. Nice, Johnny thought, grimacing. He strangled them to death as he came. His headache was getting worse all the time.

The other shrink pointed out the fact that all five murders had been committed in late fall or early winter. And while the manic-depressive personality didn't conform to any one set pattern, it was fairly common for such a person to have mood-swings closely paralleling the change of the seasons. He might have a 'low' lasting from mid-April until about the end of August and then begin to climb, 'peaking' at around the time of the murders.

During the manic or 'up' state, the person in question was apt to be highly sexed, active, daring, and optimistic. 'He would be likely to believe the police unable to catch him,' the unnamed psychiatrist had finished. The article concluded by saying that, so far, the person in question had been right.

Johnny put the paper down, glanced at the clock, and saw his father should be home almost anytime, unless the snow was holding him up. He took the old newspaper over to the wood stove and poked it into the firebox.

Not my business. Goddam Sam Weizak anyway.

Don't hide away in a cave, Johnny.

He wasn't hiding away in a cave, that wasn't it at all. It just so happened that he'd had a fairly tough break. Losing a big chunk of your life, that qualified you for tough-break status, didn't it?

And all the self-pity you can guzzle?

'Fuck you,' he muttered to himself. He went to the window and looked out. Nothing to see but snow falling in heavy, wind-driven lines. He hoped dad was being careful, but he also hoped his father would show up soon and put an end to this useless rat-run of introspection. He went over to the telephone again and stood there, undecided.

Self-pity or not, he *had* lost a goodish chunk of his

life. His *prime*, if you wanted to put it that way. He had worked hard to get back. Didn't he deserve some ordinary privacy? Didn't he have a right to what he had just been thinking of a few minutes ago – an ordinary life?

There is no such thing, my man.

Maybe not, but there was such a thing as an *abnormal* life. That thing at Cole's Farm. Feeling people's clothes and suddenly knowing their little dreads, small secrets, petty triumphs – that was abnormal. It wasn't a talent, it was a curse.

Suppose he did meet this sheriff? There was no guarantee he could tell him a thing. And suppose he could? Just suppose he could hand him his killer on a silver platter? It would be the hospital press conference all over again, a three-ring circus raised to the grisly nth power.

A little song began to run maddeningly through his aching head, little more than a jingle, really. A Sunday-school song from his early childhood: *This little light of mine ... I'm gonna let it shine ... this little light of mine ... I'm gonna let it shine ... let it shine, shine, shine, let it shine ...*

He picked up the phone and dialed Weizak's office number. Safe enough now, after five. Weizak would have gone home, and big-deal neurologists don't list their home phones. The phone rang six or seven times and Johnny was going to put it down when it was answered and Sam himself said, 'Hi? Hello?'

'Sam?'

'John Smith?' The pleasure in Sam's voice was unmistakable – but was there also an undercurrent of unease in it.

'Yeah, it's me.'

'How do you like this snow?' Weizak said, maybe a little heartily. 'Is it snowing where you are?'

'It's snowing.'

'Just started here about an hour ago. They say ... John? Is it the sheriff? Is that why you sound so cold?'

'Well, he called me,' Johnny said, 'and I've been sort of wondering what happened. Why you gave him my name?

Why you didn't call me and say you had . . . and why you didn't call me first and ask if you could.'

Weizak sighed. 'Johnny, I could maybe give you a lie, but that would be no good. I didn't ask you first because I was afraid you would say no. And I didn't tell you I'd done it afterward because the sheriff laughed at me. When someone laughs at one of my suggestions, I assume, nuh, that the suggestion is not going to be taken.'

Johnny rubbed at one aching temple with his free hand and closed his eyes. 'But why, Sam? You know how I feel about that. You were the one who told me to keep my head down and let it blow over. You told me that yourself.'

'It was the piece in the paper,' Sam said. 'I said to myself, Johnny lives down that way. And I said to myself, five dead women. Five.' His voice was slow, halting, and embarrassed. It made Johnny feel much worse to hear Sam sounding like this. He wished he hadn't called.

'Two of them teen-age girls. A young mother. A teacher of young children who loved Browning. All of it so corny, nuh? So corny I suppose they would never make a movie or a TV show out of it. But nonetheless true. It was the teacher I thought about most. Stuffed into a culvert like a bag of garbage . . .'

'You had no damn right to bring me into your guilt fantasies,' Johnny said thickly.

'No, perhaps not.'

'No perhaps about it!'

'Johnny, are you all right? You sound . . .'

'I'm fine!' Johnny shouted.

'You don't sound fine.'

'I've got a shitter of a headache, is that so surprising? I wish to *Christ* you'd left this alone. When I told you about your mother you didn't call her. Because you said . . .'

'I said some things are better lost than found. But that is not always true, Johnny. This man, whoever he is, has a terribly disturbed personality. He may kill himself. I am sure that when he stopped for two years the police thought he had. But a manic-depressive sometimes has long level periods – it is called a "plateau of normality" – and then goes back to the same mood-swings. He may have killed himself after murdering that teacher last month. But if he hasn't, what then? He may kill another one. Or two. Or four. Or . . .'

'Stop it.'

Sam said, 'Why did Sheriff Bannerman call you? What made him change his mind?'

'I don't know. I suppose the voters are after him.'

'I'm sorry I called him, Johnny, and that this has upset you so. But even more I am sorry that I did not call you and tell you what I had done. I was wrong. God knows you have a right to live your life quietly.'

Hearing his own thoughts echoed did not make him feel better. Instead he felt more miserable and guilty than ever.

'All right,' he said. 'That's okay, Sam.'

'I'll not say anything to anyone again. I suppose that is like putting a new lock on the barn door after a horse theft, but it's all I can say. I was indiscreet. In a doctor, that's bad.'

'All right,' Johnny said again. He felt helpless, and the slow embarrassment with which Sam spoke made it worse.

'I'll see you soon?'

'I'll be up in Cleaves next month to start teaching. I'll drop by.'

'Good. Again, my sincere apologies, John.'

Stop saying that!

They said their good-byes and Johnny hung up, wishing he hadn't called at all. Maybe he hadn't wanted Sam to agree so readily that what he had done was wrong. Maybe what he had really wanted Sam to say was, *Sure I called him. I wanted you to get off your ass and do something.*

He wandered across to the window and looked out into the blowing darkness. *Stuffed into a culvert like a bag of garbage.*

God, how his head ached.

Herb got home half an hour later, took one look at Johnny's white face and said, 'Headache?'

'Yeah.'

'Bad?'

'Not too bad.'

'We want to watch the national news,' Herb said. 'Glad I got home in time. Bunch of people from NBC were over in Castle Rock this afternoon, filming. That lady reporter you think is so pretty was there. Cassie Mackin.'

He blinked at the way Johnny turned on him. For a moment it seemed that Johnny's face was all eyes, staring out at him and full of a nearly inhuman pain.

'Castle Rock? Another murder?'

'Yeah. They found a little girl on the town common this morning. Saddest damn thing you ever heard of. I guess she had a pass to go across the common to the library for some project she was working on. She got to the library but she never got back ... Johnny, you look terrible, boy.'

'How old was she?'

'Just nine,' Herb said. 'A man who'd do a thing like that should be strung up by the balls. That's my view on it.'

'Nine,' Johnny said, and sat down heavily. 'Stone the crows.'

'Johnny, you sure you feel okay? You're white as paper.'

'Fine. Turn on the news.'

Shortly, John Chancellor was in front of them, bearing his nightly satchel of political aspirations (Fred Harris's campaign was not catching much fire), government edicts (the cities of America would just have to learn common budgetary sense, according to President Ford), international incidents (a nationwide strike in France), the Dow Jones (up), and a 'heartwarming' piece about a boy with cerebral palsy who was raising a 4-H cow.

'Maybe they cut it,' Herb said.

But after a commercial, Chancellor said: 'In western

Maine, there's a townful of frightened, angry people to-night. The town is Castle Rock, and over the last five years there have been five nasty murders – five women ranging in age from seventy-one to fourteen have been raped and strangled. Today there was a sixth murder in Castle Rock, and the victim was a nine-year-old girl. Catherine Mackin is in Castle Rock with the story.'

And there she was, looking like a figment of make-believe carefully superimposed on a real setting. She was standing across from the Town Office Building. The first of that afternoon's snow which had developed into to-night's blizzard was powdering the shoulders of her coat and her blonde hair.

'A sense of quietly mounting hysteria lies over this small New England mill town this afternoon,' she began. 'The townspeople of Castle Rock have been nervous for a long time over the unknown person the local press calls "the Castle Rock Strangler" or sometimes "the November Killer". That nervousness has changed to terror – no one here thinks that word is too strong – fol-lowing the discovery of Mary Kate Hendrasen's body on the town common, not far from the bandstand where the body of the November Killer's first victim, a waitress named Alma Frechette, was discovered.'

A long panning shot of the town common, looking bleak and dead in the falling snow. This was replaced with a school photograph of Mary Kate Hendrasen, grin-ning brashly through a heavy set of braces. Her hair was a fine white-blonde. Her dress was an electric blue. Most likely her best dress, Johnny thought sickly. Her mother put her into her best dress for her school photo.

The report went on – now they were recapitulating the past murders – but Johnny was on the phone, first to directory assistance and then to the Castle Rock town offices. He dialed slowly, his head thudding.

Herb came out of the living room and looked at him curiously. 'Who are you calling, son?'

Johnny shook his head and listened to the phone ring

on the other end. It was picked up. 'Castle County sheriff's office.'

'I'd like to talk to Sheriff Bannerman, please.'

'Could I have your name?'

'John Smith, from Pownal.'

'Hold on, please.'

Johnny turned to look at the TV and saw Bannerman as he had been that afternoon, bundled up in a heavy parka with county sheriff patches on the shoulders. He looked uncomfortable and dogged as he fielded the reporters' questions. He was a broad-shouldered man with a big, sloping head capped with curly dark hair. The rimless glasses he wore looked strangely out of place, as spectacles always seem to look out of place on very big men.

'We're following up a number of leads,' Bannerman said.

'Hello? Mr. Smith?' Bannerman said.

Again that queer sense of doubling. Bannerman was in two places at one time. Two *times* at one time, if you wanted to look at it that way. Johnny felt an instant of helpless vertigo. He felt the way, God help him, you felt on one of those cheap carnival rides, the Tilt-A-Whirl or the Crack-The-Whip.

'Mr. Smith? Are you there, man?'

'Yes, I'm here.' He swallowed. 'I've changed my mind.'

'Good boy! I'm damned glad to hear it.'

'I still may not be able to help you, you know.'

'I know that. But . . . no venture, no gain.' Bannerman cleared his throat. 'They'd run me out of this town on a rail if they knew I was down to consulting a psychic.'

Johnny's face was touched with a ghost of a grin. 'And a *discredited* psychic, at that.'

'Do you know where Jon's in Bridgton is?'

'I can find it.'

'Can you meet me there at eight o'clock?'

'Yes, I think so.'

'Thank you, Mr. Smith.'

263

'All right.'

He hung up. Herb was watching him closely. Behind him, the 'Nightly News' credits were rolling.

'He called you earlier, huh?'

'Yeah, he did. Sam Weizak told him I might be able to help.'

'Do you think you can?'

'I don't know,' Johnny said, 'but my headache feels a little better.'

6 ·

He was fifteen minutes late getting to Jon's Restaurant in Bridgton; it seemed to be the only business establishment on Bridgton's main drag that was still open. The plows were falling behind the snow, and there were drifts across the road in several places. At the junction of Routes 302 and 117, the blinker light swayed back and forth in the screaming wind. A police cruiser with CASTLE COUNTY SHERIFF in gold leaf on the door was parked in front of Jon's. He parked behind it and went inside.

Bannerman was sitting at a table in front of a cup of coffee and a bowl of chili. The TV had misled. He wasn't a big man; he was a huge man. Johnny walked over and introduced himself.

Bannerman stood up and shook the offered hand. Looking at Johnny's white, strained face and the way his thin body seemed to float inside his Navy pea jacket, Bannerman's first thought was: *This guy is sick – he's maybe not going to live too long.* Only Johnny's eyes seemed to have any real life – they were a direct, piercing blue, and they fixed firmly on Bannerman's own with sharp, honest curiosity. And when their hands clasped, Bannerman felt a peculiar kind of surprise, a sensation he would later describe as a *draining*. It was a little like getting a shock from a bare electrical wire. Then it was gone.

'Glad you could come,' Bannerman said. 'Coffee?'

'Yes.'

'How about a bowl of chili? They make a great damn

chili here. I'm not supposed to eat it because of my ulcer, but I do anyway.' He saw the look of surprise on Johnny's face and smiled. 'I know, it doesn't seem right, a great big guy like me having an ulcer, does it?'

'I guess anyone can get one.'

'You're damn tooting,' Bannerman said. 'What changed your mind?'

'It was the news. The little girl. Are you sure it was the same guy?'

'It was the same guy. Same M.O. And the same sperm type.'

He watched Johnny's face as the waitress came over. 'Coffee?' she asked.

'Tea,' Johnny said.

'And bring him a bowl of chili, Miss,' Bannerman said. When the waitress had gone he said, 'This doctor, he says that if you touch something, sometimes you get ideas about where it came from, who might have owned it, that sort of thing.'

Johnny smiled. 'Well,' he said, 'I just shook your hand and I know you've got an Irish setter named Rusty. And I know he's old and going blind and you think it's time he was put to sleep, but you don't know how you'd explain it to your girl.'

Bannerman dropped his spoon back into his chili – *plop*. He stared at Johnny with his mouth open. 'By God,' he said. 'You got that from me? Just now?'

Johnny nodded.

Bannerman shook his head and muttered, 'It's one thing to hear something like that and another to ... doesn't it tire you out?'

Johnny looked at Bannerman, surprised. It was a question he had never been asked before. 'Yes. Yes, it does.'

'But you knew. I'll be *damned*.'

'But look, Sheriff.'

'George. Just plain George.'

'Okay, I'm Johnny, just plain Johnny. George, what I don't know about you would fill about five books. I don't know where you grew up or where you went to police

265

school or who your friends are or where you live. I know you've got a little girl, and her name's something like Cathy, but that's not quite it. I don't know what you did last week or what beer you favor or what your favorite TV program is.'

'My daughter's name is Katrina,' Bannerman said softly. 'She's nine, too. She was in Mary Kate's class.'

'What I'm trying to say is that the . . . the knowing is sometimes a pretty limited thing. Because of the dead zone.'

'Dead zone?'

'It's like some of the signals don't conduct,' Johnny said. 'I can never get streets or addresses. Numbers are hard but they sometimes come.' The waitress returned with Johnny's tea and chili. He tasted the chili and nodded at Bannerman. 'You're right. It's good. Especially on a night like this.'

'Go to it,' Bannerman said. 'Man, I love good chili. My ulcer hollers bloody hell about it. Fuck you, ulcer, I say. Down the hatch.'

They were quiet for a moment. Johnny worked on his chili and Bannerman watched him curiously. He supposed Smith could have found out he had a dog named Rusty. He even could have found out that Rusty was old and nearly blind. Take it a step farther: if he knew Katrina's name, he might have done that 'something like Cathy but that's not quite it' routine just to add the right touch of hesitant realism. But *why*? And none of that explained that queer, zapped feeling he'd gotten in his head when Smith touched his hand. If it was a con, it was a damned good one.

Outside, the wind gusted to a low shriek that seemed to rock the small building on its foundations. A flying veil of snow lashed the Pondicherry Bowling Lanes across the street.

'Listen to that,' Bannerman said. 'Supposed to keep up all night. Don't tell *me* the winters're getting milder.'

'Have you got something?' Johnny asked. 'Something that belonged to the guy you're looking for?'

'We think we might,' Bannerman said, and then shook his head. 'But it's pretty thin.'

'Tell me.'

Bannerman laid it out for him. The grammar school and the library sat facing each other across the town common. It was standard operating procedure to send students across when they needed a book for a project or a report. The teacher gave them a pass and the librarian initialed it before sending them back. Near the center of the common, the land dipped slightly. On the west side of the dip was the town bandstand. In the dip itself were two dozen benches where people sat during band concerts and football rallies in the fall.

'We think he just sat himself down and waited for a kid to come along. He would have been out of sight from both sides of the common. But the footpath runs along the north side of the dip, close to those benches.'

Bannerman shook his head slowly.

'What makes it worse is that the Frechette woman was killed right *on* the bandstand. I am going to face a shit-storm about that at town meeting in March – that is, if I'm still around in March. Well, I can show them a memo I wrote to the town manager, requesting adult crossing guards on the common during school hours. Not that it was this killer that I was worried about, Christ, no. Never in my wildest dreams did I think he'd go back to the same spot a second time.'

'The town manager turned down the crossing guards?'

'Not enough money,' Bannerman said. 'Of course, he can spread the blame around to the town selectmen, and they'll try to spread it back on me, and the grass will grow on Mary Kate Hendrasen's grave and . . .' He paused for a moment, or perhaps choked on what he was saying. Johnny gazed at his lowered head sympathetically.

'It might not have made any difference anyhow,' Bannerman went on in a dryer voice. 'Most of the crossing guards we use are women, and this fuck we're after doesn't seem to care how old or young they are.'

'But you think he waited on one of those benches?'

Bannerman did. They had found an even dozen fresh cigarette butts near the end of one of the benches, and four more behind the bandstand itself, along with an empty box. Marlboros, unfortunately – the second or third most popular brand in the country. The cellophane on the box had been dusted for prints and had yielded none at all.

'None at all?' Johnny said. 'That's a little funny, isn't it?'

'Why do you say so?'

'Well, you'd guess the killer was wearing gloves even if he wasn't thinking about prints – it was cold out – but you'd think the guy that sold him the cigarettes . . .'

Bannerman grinned. 'You've got a head for this work,' he said, 'but you're not a smoker.'

'No,' Johnny said. 'I used to smoke a few cigarettes when I was in college, but I lost the habit after my accident.'

'A man keeps his cigarettes in his breast pocket. Take them out, get a cigarette, put the pack back. If you're wearing gloves and not leaving fresh prints every time you get a butt, what you're doing is polishing that cellophane wrapper? Get it? And you missed one other thing, Johnny. Need me to tell you?'

Johnny thought it over and then said, 'Maybe the pack of cigarettes came out of a carton. And those cartons are packed by machine.'

'That's it,' Bannerman said. 'You *are* good at this.'

'What about the tax stamp on the package?'

'Maine,' Bannerman said.

'So if the killer and the smoker were the same man . . .' Johnny said thoughtfully.

Bannerman shrugged. 'Sure, there's the technical possibility that they weren't. But I've tried to imagine who else would want to sit on a bench in the town common on a cold, cloudy winter morning long enough to smoke twelve or sixteen cigarettes, and I come up a blank.'

Johnny sipped his tea. 'None of the other kids that crossed saw anything?'

'Nothing,' Bannerman said. 'I've talked to every kid that had a library pass this morning.'

'That's a lot weirder than the fingerprint business. Doesn't it strike you that way?'

'It strikes me as goddam scary. Look, the guy is sitting there, and what he's waiting for is one kid – one *girl* – by herself. He can hear the kids as they come along. And each time he fades back behind the bandstand ...'

'Tracks,' Johnny said.

'Not this morning. There was no snow-cover this morning. Just frozen ground. So here's this crazy shitbag that ought to have his own testicles carved off and served to him for dinner, here he is, skulking behind the bandstand. At about 8 : 50 A.M., Peter Harrington and Melissa Loggins come along. School has been in session about twenty minutes at that time. When they're gone, he goes back to his bench. At 9 : 15 he fades back behind the bandstand again. This time it's two little girls, Susan Flarhaty and Katrina Bannerman.'

Johnny set his mug down with a bang. Bannerman had taken off his spectacles and was polishing them savagely.

'Your *daughter* crossed this morning? Jesus!'

Bannerman put his glasses on again. His face was dark and dull with fury. And he's afraid, Johnny saw. Not afraid that the voters would turn him out, or that the *Union-Leader* would publish another editorial about nitwit cops in western Maine, but afraid because, if his daughter had happened to go to the library alone this morning –

'My daughter,' Bannerman agreed softly. 'I think she passed within forty feet of that ... that animal. You know what that makes me feel like?'

'I can guess,' Johnny said.

'No, I don't think you can. It makes me feel like I almost stepped into an empty elevator shaft. Like I passed up the mushrooms at dinner and someone else died of toadstool poisoning. And it makes me feel dirty. It makes me feel *filthy*. I guess maybe it also explains why I finally

269

called you. I'd do anything right now to nail this guy. Anything at all.'

Outside, a giant orange plow loomed out of the snow like something from a horror movie. It parked and two men got out. They crossed the street to Jon's and sat at the counter. Johnny finished his tea. He no longer wanted the chili.

'This guy goes back to his bench,' Bannerman resumed, 'but not for long. Around 9 : 25 he hears the Harrington boy and the Loggins girl coming back from the library. So he goes back behind the bandstand again. It must have been around 9.25 because the librarian signed them out at 9 : 18. At 9.45 three boys from the fifth grade went past the bandstand on their way to the library. One of them thinks he might have seen "some guy" standing on the other side of the bandstand. That's our whole description. "Some guy." We ought to put it out on the wire, what do you think? Be on the lookout for some guy.'

Bannerman uttered a short laugh like a bark.

'At 9 : 55 my daughter and her friend Susan go by on their way back to school. Then, about 10 : 05, Mary Kate Hendrasen came along . . . by herself. Katrina and Sue met her going down the school steps as they were going up. They all said hi.'

'Dear God,' Johnny muttered. He ran his hands through his hair.

'Last of all, 10 : 30 A.M. The three fifth-grade boys are coming back. One of them sees something on the bandstand. It's Mary Kate, with her leotard and her underpants yanked down, blood all over her legs, her face . . . her face . . .'

'Take it easy,' Johnny said, and put a hand on Bannerman's arm.

'No, I can't take it easy,' Bannerman said. He spoke almost apologetically. 'I've never seen anything like that, not in eighteen years of police work. He raped that little girl and that would have been enough . . . enough to, you know, kill her . . . the medical examiner said the way he did it . . . he ruptured something and it . . . yeah, it probably would have, well . . . killed her . . . but then he had to go on and choke her. Nine years old and choked and left . . . left on the bandstand with her underpants pulled down.'

Suddenly Bannerman began to cry. The tears filled his eyes behind his glasses and then rolled down his face in two streams. At the counter the two guys from the Bridgton road crew were talking about the Superbowl. Bannerman took his glasses off again and mopped his face with his handkerchief. His shoulders shook and heaved. Johnny waited, stirring his chili aimlessly.

After a little while, Bannerman put his handkerchief away. His eyes were red, and Johnny thought how oddly naked his face looked without his glasses.

'I'm sorry, man,' he said. 'It's been a very long day.'

'It's all right,' Johnny said.

'I knew I was going to do that, but I thought I could hold on until I got home to my wife.'

'Well, I guess that was just too long to wait.'

'You're a sympathetic ear.' Bannerman slipped his glasses back on. 'No, you're more than that. You've got something. I'll be damned if I know just what it is, but it's something.'

'What else have you got to go on?'

'Nothing. I'm taking most of the heat, but the state police haven't exactly distinguished themselves. Neither has the attorney general's special investigator, or our pet FBI man. The county M.E. has been able to type the sperm, but that's no good to us at this stage of the game. The thing that bothers me the most is the lack of hair or skin under the victim's fingernails. They all must have struggled, but we don't have as much as a centimeter of skin. The devil must be on this guy's side. He hasn't dropped a button or a shopping list or left a single damn track. We got a shrink from Augusta, also courtesy of the state A.G., and he tells us all these guys give themselves away sooner or later. Some comfort. What if it's later . . . say about twelve bodies from now?'

'The cigarette pack is in Castle Rock?'

'Yes.'

Johnny stood up. 'Well, let's take a ride.'

'My car?'

Johnny smiled a little as the wind rose, shrieking, outside. 'On a night like this, it pays to be with a policeman,' he said.

7 ·

The snowstorm was at its height and it took them an hour and a half to get over to Castle Rock in Bannerman's cruiser. It was twenty past ten when they came in through the foyer of the Town Office Building and stamped the snow off their boots.

There were half a dozen reporters in the lobby, most of them sitting on a bench under a gruesome oil portrait of some town founding father, telling each other about previous night watches. They were up and surrounding Bannerman and Johnny in no time.

'Sheriff Bannerman, is it true there has been a break in the case?'

'I have nothing for you at this time,' Bannerman said stolidly.

'There's been a rumor that you've taken a man from Oxford into custody, Sheriff, is that true?'

'No. If you folks will pardon us . . .'

But their attention had turned to Johnny, and he felt a sinking sensation in his belly as he recognized at least two faces from the press conference at the hospital.

'Holy God!' one of them exclaimed. 'You're John Smith, aren't you?'

Johnny felt a crazy urge to take the fifth like a gangster at a Senate committee hearing.

'Yes,' he said. 'That's me.'

'The psychic guy?' another asked.

'Look, let us pass!' Bannerman said, raising his voice. 'Haven't you guys got anything better to do than . . .'

'According to *Inside View*, you're a fake,' a young man in a heavy topcoat said. 'Is that true?'

'All I can say about that is *Inside View* prints what they want,' Johnny said. 'Look, really . . .'

'You're denying the *Inside View* story?'

'Look, I really can't say anything more.'

As they went through the frosted glass door and into the sheriff's office, the reporters were racing toward the two pay phones on the wall by the dog warden's office.

'Now the shit has truly hit the fan,' Bannerman said unhappily. 'I swear before God I never thought they'd still be here on a night like this. I should have brought you in the back.'

'Oh, didn't you know?' Johnny asked bitterly. 'We love the publicity. All of us psychics are in it for the publicity.'

'No, I don't believe that,' Bannerman said. 'At least not of you. Well, it's happened. Can't be helped now.'

But in his mind, Johnny could visualize the headlines: a little extra seasoning in a pot of stew that was already bubbling briskly. CASTLE ROCK SHERIFF DEPUTIZES LOCAL PSYCHIC IN STRANGLER CASE. 'NOVEMBER KILLER' TO BE INVESTIGATED BY SEER. HOAX ADMISSION STORY A FABRICATION, SMITH PROTESTS.

There were two deputies in the outer office, one of them snoozing, the other drinking coffee and looking glumly through a pile of reports.

'His wife kick him out or something?' Bannerman asked sourly, nodding toward the sleeper.

'He just got back from Augusta,' the deputy said. He was little more than a kid himself, and there were dark circles of weariness under his eyes. He glanced over at Johnny curiously.

'Johnny Smith, Frank Dodd. Sleeping beauty over there is Roscoe Fisher.'

Johnny nodded hello.

'Roscoe says the A.G. wants the whole case,' Dodd told Bannerman. His look was angry and defiant and somehow pathetic. 'Some Christmas present, huh?'

Bannerman put a hand on the back of Dodd's neck

and shook him gently. 'You worry too much, Frank. Also, you're spending too much time on the case.'

'I just keep thinking there must be something in these reports . . .' He shrugged and then flicked them with one finger. '*Something*.'

'Go home and get some rest, Frank. And take sleeping beauty with you. All we need is for one of those photographers to get a picture of him. They'd run it in the papers with a caption like "In Castle Rock the Intensive Investigation Goes On," and we'd all be out sweeping streets.'

Bannerman led Johnny into his private office. The desk was awash in paperwork. On the windowsill was a triptych showing Bannerman, his wife, and his daughter Katrina. His degree hung neatly framed on the wall, and beside it, in another frame, the front page of the Castle Rock *Call* which had announced his election.

'Coffee?' Bannerman asked him, unlocking a file cabinet.

'No thanks. I'll stick to tea.'

'Mrs. Sugarman guards her tea jealously,' Bannerman said. 'Takes it home with her every day, sorry. I'd offer you a tonic, but we'd have to run the gauntlet out there again to get to the machine. Jesus Christ, I wish they'd go home.'

'That's okay.'

Bannerman came back with a small clasp envelope. 'This is it,' he said. He hesitated for a moment, then handed the envelope over.

Johnny held it but did not immediately open it. 'As long as you understand that nothing comes guaranteed. I can't promise. Sometimes I can and sometimes I can't.'

Bannerman shrugged tiredly and repeated: 'No venture, no gain.'

Johnny undid the clasp and shook an empty Marlboro cigarette box out into his hand. Red and white box. He held it in his left hand and looked at the far wall. Gray wall. Industrial gray wall. Red and white box. Industrial gray box. He put the cigarette package in his other hand, then cupped it in both. He waited for something, anything to come. Nothing did. He held it longer, hoping against hope, ignoring the knowledge that when things come, they came at once.

At last he handed the cigarette box back. 'I'm sorry,' he said.

'No soap, huh?'

'No.'

There was a perfunctory tap at the door and Roscoe Fisher stuck his head in. He looked a bit shamefaced. 'Frank and I are going home, George. I guess you caught me coopin.'

'As long as I don't catch you doing it in your cruiser,' Bannerman said. 'Say hi to Deenie for me.'

'You bet.' Fisher glanced at Johnny for a moment and then closed the door.

'Well,' Bannerman said. 'It was worth the try, I guess. I'll run you back . . .'

'I want to go over to the common,' Johnny said abruptly.

'No, that's no good. It's under a foot of snow.'

'You can find the place, can't you?'

'Of course I can. But what'll it gain?'

'I don't know. But let's go across.'

'Those reporters are going to follow us, Johnny. Just as sure as God made little fishes.'

'You said something about a back door.'

'Yeah, but it's a fire door. Getting in that way is okay, but if we use it to go out, the alarm goes off.'

Johnny whistled through his teeth. 'Let them follow along, then.'

Bannerman looked at him thoughtfully, for several moments and then nodded. 'Okay.'

8 ·

When they came out of the office, the reporters were up and surrounding them immediately. Johnny was reminded of a rundown kennel over in Durham where a strange old woman kept collies. The dogs would all run out at

275

you when you went past with your fishing pole, yapping and snarling and generally scaring the hell out of you. They would nip but not actually bite.

'Do you know who did it, Johnny?'

'Have any ideas at all?'

'Got any brainwaves, Mr. Smith?'

'Sheriff, was calling in a psychic your idea?'

'Do the state police and the A.G.'s office know about this development, Sheriff Bannerman?'

'Do you think you can break the case, Johnny?'

'Sheriff, have you deputized this guy?'

Bannerman pushed his way slowly and solidly through them, zipping his coat. 'No comment, no comment.' Johnny said nothing at all.

The reporters clustered in the foyer as Johnny and Bannerman went down the snowy steps. It wasn't until they bypassed the cruiser and began wading across the street that one of them realized they were going to the common. Several of them ran back for their topcoats. Those who had been dressed for outside when Bannerman and Johnny emerged from the office now floundered down the Town Office steps after them, calling like children.

9 ·

Flashlights bobbing in the snowy dark. The wind howled, blowing snow past them this way and that in errant sheets.

'You're not gonna be able to see a damn thing,' Bannerman said. 'You w ... *holy shit*!' He was almost knocked off his feet as a reporter in a bulky overcoat and a bizarre tam o'shanter sprawled into him.

'Sorry, Sheriff,' he said sheepishly. 'Slippery. Forgot my galoshes.'

Up ahead a yellow length of nylon rope appeared out of the gloom. Attached to it was a wildly swinging sign reading POLICE INVESTIGATION.

'You forgot your brains, too,' Bannerman said. 'Now you keep back, all of you! Keep right back!'

'Town common's public property, Sheriff!' one of the reporters cried.

'That's right, and this is police business. You stay behind this rope here or you'll spend the night in my holding cell.'

With the beam of his flashlight he traced the course of the rope for them and then held it up so Johnny could pass beneath. They walked down the slope toward the snow-mounded shapes of the benches. Behind them the reporters gathered at the rope, pooling their few lights so that Johnny and George Bannerman walked in a dull sort of spotlight.

'Flying blind,' Bannerman said.

'Well, there's nothing to see, anyway,' Johnny said. 'Is there?'

'No, not now. I told Frank he could take that rope down anytime. Now I'm glad he didn't get around to it. You want to go over to the bandstand?'

'Not yet. Show me where the cigarette butts were.'

They went on a little farther and then Bannerman stopped. 'Here,' he said, and shone his light on a bench that was little more than a vague hump poking out of a drift.

Johnny took off his gloves and put them in his coat pockets. Then he knelt and began to brush the snow away from the seat of the bench. Again Bannerman was struck by the haggard pallor of the man's face. On his knees before the bench he looked like a religious penitent, a man in desperate prayer.

Johnny's hands went cold, then mostly numb. Melted snow ran off his fingers. He got down to the splintered, weatherbeaten surface of the bench. He seemed to see it very clearly, almost with magnifying power. It had once been green, but now much of the paint had flaked and eroded away. Two rusted steel bolts held the seat to the backrest.

He seized the bench in both hands, and sudden weirdness flooded him – he had felt nothing so intense before and would feel something so intense only once ever again.

277

He stared down at the bench, frowning, gripping it tightly in his hands. It was . . .

(*A summer bench*)

How many hundreds of different people had sat here at one time or another, listening to 'God Bless America', to 'Stars and Stripes Forever' ('*Be kind to your web-footed friends . . . for a duck may be somebody's moooother . . .*'), to the Castle Rock Cougars' fight song? Green summer leaves, smoky haze of fall like a memory of cornhusks and men with rakes in mellow dusk. The thud of the big snare drum. Mellow gold trumpets and trombones. School band uniforms . . .

(*for a duck . . . may be . . . somebody's mother . . .*)

Good summer people sitting here, listening, applauding, holding programs that had been designed and printed in the Castle Rock High School graphic arts shop.

But this morning a killer had been sitting here. Johnny could *feel* him.

Dark tree branches etched against a gray snow-sky like runes. He(I) am sitting here, smoking, waiting, feeling good, feeling like he(I) could jump right over the roof of the world and land lightly on two feet. Humming a song. Something by the Rolling Stones. Can't get that, but very clearly everything is . . . is what?

All right. *Everything is all right, everything is gray and waiting for snow, and I'm . . .*

'Slick,' Johnny muttered. 'I'm slick, I'm so slick.'

Bannerman leaned forward, unable to catch the words over the howling wind. 'What?'

'Slick,' Johnny repeated. He looked up at Bannerman and the Sheriff involuntarily took a step backward. Johnny's eyes were cool and somehow inhuman. His dark hair blew wildly around his white face, and overhead the winter wind screamed through the black sky. His hands seemed welded to the bench.

'*I'm so fucking slick,*' he said clearly. A triumphant smile had formed on his lips. His eyes stared through Bannerman. Bannerman believed. No one could be acting this, or putting it on. And the most terrible part of it was ... he was *reminded* of someone. The smile ... the tone of voice ... Johnny Smith was gone; he seemed to have been replaced by a human blank. And lurking behind the planes of his ordinary features, almost near enough to touch, was another face. The face of the killer.

The face of someone he *knew*.

'Never catch me because I'm too slick for you.' A little laugh escaped him, confident, lightly taunting. 'I put it on every time, and if they scratch ... or bite ... they don't get a bit of me ... because *I'm so SLICK!*' His voice rose to a triumphant, crazy shriek that competed with the wind, and Bannerman fell back another step, his flesh crawling helplessly, his balls tight and cringing against his guts.

Let it stop, he thought. *Let it stop now. Please.*

Johnny bent his head over the bench. Melting snow dripped between his bare fingers.

(*Snow. Silent snow, secret snow –*)

(*She put a clothespin on it so I'd know how it felt. How it felt when you got a disease. A disease from one of those nasty-fuckers, they're all nasty-fuckers, and they have to be stopped, yes, stopped, stop them, stop, the stop, the STOP – OH MY GOD THE STOP SIGN –!*)

He was little again. Going to school through the silent, secret snow. And there was a man looming out of the shifting whiteness, a terrible man, a terrible black grinning man with eyes as shiny as quarters, and there was a red STOP sign clutched in one gloved hand ... him! ... him! ... *him!*

(*OH MY GOD DON'T ... DON'T LET HIM GET ME ... MOMMA ... DON'T LET HIM GET MEEEEE ...*)

Johnny screamed and fell away from the bench, his hands suddenly pressed to his cheeks. Bannerman crouched beside him, badly frightened. Behind the rope the reporters stirred and murmured.

'Johnny! Snap out of it! Listen, Johnny ...'

'Slick,' Johnny muttered. He looked up at Bannerman with hurt, frightened eyes. In his mind he still saw that black shape with the shiny-quarter eyes looming out of the snow. His crotch throbbed dully from the pain of the clothespin the killer's mother had made him wear. He hadn't been the killer then, oh no, not an animal, not a pusbag or a shitbag or whatever Bannerman had called him, he'd only been a scared little boy with a clothespin on his . . . his . . .

'Help me get up,' he muttered.

Bannerman helped him to his feet.

'The bandstand now,' Johnny said.

'No, I think we ought to go back, Johnny.'

Johnny pushed past him blindly and began to flounder toward the bandstand, a big circular shadow up ahead. It bulked and loomed in the darkness, the death place. Bannerman ran and caught up to him.

'Johnny, who is it? Do you know who . . . ?'

'You never found any scraps of tissue under their fingernails because he was wearing a raincoat,' Johnny said. He panted the words out. 'A raincoat with a hood. A slick vinyl raincoat. You go back over the reports. You go back over the reports and you'll see.. It was raining or snowing every time. They clawed at him, all right. They fought him. Sure they did. But their fingers just slipped and slid over it.'

'Who, Johnny? Who?'

'I don't know. But I'm going to find out.'

He stumbled over the lowest of the six steps leading up to the bandstand, fumbled for his balance, and would have lost it if Bannerman had not gripped his arm. Then they were up on the stage. The snow was thin here, a bare dusting, kept off by the conical roof. Bannerman trained his flashlight beam on the floor and Johnny dropped to his hands and knees and began to crawl slowly across it. His hands were bright red. Bannerman thought they must be like chunks of raw meat by now.

Johnny stopped suddenly and stiffened like a dog on point. 'Here,' he muttered. 'He did it right here.'

Images and textures and sensations flooded in. The copper taste of excitement, the possibility of being seen adding to it. The girl was squirming, trying to scream. He had covered her mouth with one gloved hand. Awful excitement. Never catch me, I'm the Invisible Man, is it dirty enough for you now, momma?

Johnny began to moan, shaking his head back and forth.

Sound of clothes ripping. Warmth. Something flowing. Blood? Semen? Urine?

He began to shudder all over. His hair hung in his face. His face. His smiling, open face caught inside the circular border of the raincoat's hood as his (my) hands close around the neck at the moment of orgasm and squeeze . . . and squeeze . . . and squeeze.

The strength left his arms as the images began to fade. He slipped forward, now lying on the stage full-length, sobbing. When Bannerman touched his shoulder he cried out and tried to scramble away, his face crazy with fear. Then, little by little, it loosened. He put his head back against the waist-high bandstand railing and closed his eyes. Shudders raced through his body like whippets. His pants and coat were sugared with snow.

'I know who it is,' he said.

10 ·

Fifteen minutes later Johnny sat in Bannerman's inner office again, stripped to his shorts and sitting as close as he could to a portable electric heater. He still looked cold and miserable, but he had stopped shaking.

'Sure you don't want some coffee?'

Johnny shook his head. 'I can't abide the stuff.'

'Johnny . . .' Bannerman sat down. 'Do you really know something?'

'I know who killed them. You would have gotten him eventually. You were just too close to it. You've even seen him in his raincoat, that shiny all-over raincoat. Because he crosses the kids in the morning. He has a stop sign on a stick and he crosses the kids in the morning.'

Bannerman looked at him, thunderstruck. 'Are you

281

talking about Frank? Frank *Dodd*? You're nuts!'

'Frank Dodd killed them,' Johnny said. 'Frank Dodd killed them all.'

Bannerman looked as though he didn't know whether to laugh at Johnny or deal him a good swift kick. 'That's the craziest goddam thing I've ever heard,' he said finally. 'Frank Dodd's a fine officer and a fine man. He's crossing over next November to run for municipal chief of police, and he'll do it with my blessing.' Now his expression was one of amusement mixed with tired contempt. 'Frank's twenty-five. That means he would have had to have started this crazy shit when he was just nineteen. He lives at home very quietly with his mother, who isn't very well – hypertension, thyroid, and a semidiabetic condition. Johnny, you put your foot in the bucket. Frank Dodd is no murderer. I'd stake my life on that.'

'The murders stopped for two years,' Johnny said. 'Where was Frank Dodd then? Was he in town?'

Bannerman turned toward him, and now the tired amusement had left his face and he only looked hard. Hard and angry. 'I don't want to hear any more about this. You were right the first time – you're nothing but a fake. Well, you got your press coverage, but that doesn't mean I have to listen to you malign a good officer, a man I ...'

'A man you think of as your son,' Johnny said quietly.

Bannerman's lips thinned, and a lot of the color that had risen in his cheeks during their time outside now faded out of his face. He looked like a man who has been punched low. Then it passed and his face was expressionless.

'Get out of here,' he said. 'Get one of your reporter friends to give you a ride home. You can hold a press conference on your way. But I swear to God, I swear to *holy God* that if you mention Frank Dodd's name, I'll come for you and I'll break your back. Understood?'

'Sure, my buddies from the press!' Johnny shouted at him suddenly. 'That's right! Didn't you see me answering all their questions? Posing for their pictures and making sure they got my good side? Making sure they spelled my name right?'

Bannerman looked startled, then hard again. 'Lower your voice.'

'No, I'll be goddamned if I will!' Johnny said, and his voice rose even higher in pitch and volume. 'I think you forgot who called who! I'll refresh your recollection for you. It was *you*, calling *me*. That's how eager I was to get over here!'

'That doesn't mean you're . . .'

Johnny walked over to Bannerman, pointing his index finger like a pistol. He was several inches shorter and probably eighty pounds lighter, but Bannerman backed up a step – as he had done on the common. Johnny's cheeks had flushed a dull red. His lips were drawn back slightly from his teeth.

'No, you're right, you calling me doesn't mean shit in a tin bucket,' he said. 'But you don't *want* it to be Dodd, do you? It can be somebody else, then we'll at least look into it, but it can't be good old Frank Dodd. Because Frank's upstanding, Frank takes care of his mother, Frank looks up to good old Sheriff George Bannerman, oh, Frank's bloody Christ down from the cross except when he's raping and strangling old ladies and little girls, and it could have been your *daughter*, Bannerman, don't you understand it could have been your *own dau* . . .'

Bannerman hit him. At the last moment he pulled the punch, but it was still hard enough to knock Johnny backward; he stumbled over the leg of a chair and then sprawled on the floor. Blood trickled from his cheek where Bannerman's Police Academy ring had grazed him.

'You had that coming,' Bannerman said, but there was no real conviction in his voice. It occurred to him that for the first time in his life he had hit a cripple – or the next thing to a cripple.

Johnny's head felt light and full of bells. His voice seemed to belong to someone else, a radio announcer or a B-movie actor. 'You ought to get down on your knees and thank God that he really didn't leave any clues, because you would have overlooked them, feeling like you do about Dodd. And then you could have held yourself responsible in Mary Kate Hendrasen's death, as an accessory.'

'That is nothing but a damnable lie,' Bannerman said slowly and clearly. 'I'd arrest my own brother if he was the guy doing this. Get up off the floor. I'm sorry I hit you.'

He helped Johnny to his feet and looked at the scrape on his cheek.

'I'll get the first-aid kit and put some iodine on that.'

'Forget it,' Johnny said. The anger had left his voice. 'I guess I kind of sprang it on you, didn't I?'

'I'm telling you, it can't be Frank. You're not a publicity hound, okay. I was wrong about that. Heat of the moment, okay? But your vibes or your astral plane or whatever it is sure gave you a bum steer this time.'

'Then check,' Johnny said. He caught Bannerman's eyes with his own and held them. '*Check it out.* Show me I got it wrong.' He swallowed. 'Check the times and dates against Frank's work schedule. Can you do that?'

Grudgingly, Bannerman said, 'The time cards in the back closet there go back fourteen or fifteen years. I guess I could check it.'

'Then do it.'

'Mister . . .' He paused. 'Johnny, if you *knew* Frank, you'd laugh at yourself. I mean it. It's not just me, you ask anybody . . .'

'If I'm wrong, I'll be glad to admit it.'

'This is crazy,' Bannerman muttered, but he went to the storage closet where the old time cards were kept and opened the door.

11 ·

Two hours passed. It was now nearly one o'clock in the morning. Johnny had called his father and told him he would find a place to sleep in Castle Rock; the storm had leveled off at a single furious pitch, and driving back would be next to impossible.

284

'What's going on over there?' Herb asked. 'Can you tell me?'

'I better not over the phone, Dad.'

'All right, Johnny. Don't exhaust yourself.'

'No.'

But he *was* exhausted. He was more tired than he could remember being since those early days in physical therapy with Eileen Magown. A nice woman, he thought randomly. A nice *friendly* woman, at least until I told her that her house was burning down. After that she had become distant and awkward. She had thanked him, sure, but – had she ever touched him after that? Actually touched him? Johnny didn't think so. And it would be the same with Bannerman when this thing was over. Too bad. Like Eileen, he was a fine man. But people get very nervous around people who can just touch things and know all about them.

'It doesn't prove a thing,' Bannerman was saying now. There was a sulky, little-boy rebelliousness in his voice that made Johnny want to grab him and shake him until he rattled. But he was too tired.

They were looking down at a rough chart Johnny had made on the back of a circular for used state police interceptors. Stacked untidily by Bannerman's desk were seven or eight cartons of old time cards, and sitting in the top half of Bannerman's in/out basket were Frank Dodd's cards, going back to 1971, when he had joined the sheriff's department. The chart looked like this:

THE MURDERS	FRANK DODD
Alma Frechette (waitress) 3 : 00 PM, 11/12/70	Then working at Main Street Gulf Station
Pauline Toothaker 10 : 00 AM, 11/17/71	Off-duty
Cheryl Moody (J.H.S. student) 2 : 00 PM, 12/16/71	Off-duty

285

Carol Dunbarger (H.S. student)	Two-week vacation period
11/?/74	
Etta Ringgold (teacher)	Regular duty tours
10/29(?)/75	
Mary Kate Hendrasen	Off-duty
10:10 AM, 12/17/75	

*All times are 'estimated time of death' figures
supplied by State Medical Examiner*

'No, it doesn't prove anything,' Johnny agreed, rubbing his temples. 'But it doesn't exactly rule him out, either.'

Bannerman tapped the chart. 'When Miss Ringgold was killed, he was on duty.'

'Yeah, if she really was killed on the twenty-ninth of October. But it might have been the twenty-eighth, or the twenty-seventh. And even if he was on duty, who suspects a cop?'

Bannerman was looking at the little chart very carefully.

'What about the gap?' Johnny said. 'The two-year gap?'

Bannerman thumbed the time cards. 'Frank was right here on duty all during 1973 and 1974. You saw that.'

'So maybe the urge didn't come on him that year. At least, so far as we know.'

'So far as we know, we don't know anything,' Bannerman contradicted quickly.

'But what about 1972? Late 1972 and early 1973? There are no time cards for that period. Was he on vacation?'

'No,' Bannerman said. 'Frank and a guy named Tom Harrison took a semester course in Rural Law Enforcement at a branch of the University of Colorado in Pueblo. It's the only place in the country where they offer a deal like that. It's an eight-week course. Frank and

Tom were out there from October 15 until just about Christmas. The state pays part, the county pays part, and the U.S. government pays part under the Law Enforcement Act of 1971. I picked Harrison – he's chief of police over in Gates Falls now – and Frank. Frank almost didn't go, because he was worried about his mother being alone. To tell you the truth, I think she tried to persuade him to stay home. I talked him into it. He wants to be a career officer, and something like the Rural Law Enforcement course looks damn good on your record. I remember that when he and Tom got back in December, Frank had a low-grade virus and he looked terrible. He'd lost twenty pounds. Claimed no one out there in cow country could cook like his mom.'

Bannerman fell silent. Something in what he had just said seemed to disturb him.

'He took a week's sick leave around the holidays and then he was okay,' Bannerman resumed, almost defensively. 'He was back by the fifteenth of January at the latest. Check the time cards for yourself.'

'I don't have to. Any more than I have to tell you what your next step is.'

'No,' Bannerman said. He looked at his hands. 'I told you that you had a head for this stuff. Maybe I was righter than I knew. Or wanted to be.'

He picked up the telephone and pulled out a thick directory with a plain blue cover from the bottom drawer of his desk. Paging through it without looking up, he told Johnny, 'This is courtesy of that same Law Enforcement Act. Every sheriff's office in every county of the United States.' He found the number he wanted and made his call.

Johnny shifted in his seat.

'Hello,' Bannerman said. 'Am I talking to the Pueblo sheriff's office? ... All right. My name is George Bannerman, I'm the county sheriff of Castle County, in western Maine ... yes, that's what I said. State of Maine. Who am I talking to, please? ... All right, Officer Taylor, this is the situation. We've had a series of murders out here, rape-stranglings, six of them in the past five years. All of them have taken place in the late fall or early winter. We have a ...' He looked up at Johnny for a moment, his eyes hurt and helpless. Then he looked down at the phone again. 'We have a suspect who was in Pueblo from October 15 of 1972 until ... uh, December 17, I think. What I'd like to know is if you have an unsolved homicide on your books during that period, victim female, no particular age, raped, cause of death, strangulation. Further, I would like to know the perpetrator's sperm type if you have had such a crime and a sperm sample was obtained. What? ... Yes, okay. Thanks ... I'll be right here, waiting. Good-bye, Officer Taylor.'

He hung up. 'He's going to verify my bona fides, then check it through, then call me back. You want a cup of ... no, you don't drink it, do you?'

'No,' Johnny said. 'I'll settle for a glass of water.'

He went over to the big glass cooler and drew a paper cupful of water. Outside the storm howled and pounded.

Behind him, Bannerman said awkwardly: 'Yeah, okay. You were right. He's the son I'd've liked to have had. My wife had Katrina by cesarian. She can never have another one, the doctor said it would kill her. She had the Band-Aid operation and I had a vasectomy. Just to be sure.'

Johnny went to the window and looked out on darkness, his cup of water in his hand. There was nothing to see but snow, but if he turned around, Bannerman would break off – you didn't have to be psychic to know that.

'Frank's dad worked on the B&M line and died in an accident when Frank was five or so. He was drunk, tried to make a coupling in a state where he probably would have pissed down his own leg and never known it. He got crushed between two flatcars. Frank's had to be the man of the house ever since. Roscoe says he had a girl in high school, but Mrs. Dodd put paid to that in a hurry.'

I bet she did, Johnny thought. *A woman who would do that thing ... that clothespin thing ... to her own son*

288

. . . that sort of woman would stop at nothing. She must be almost as crazy as he is.

'He came to me when he was sixteen and asked if there was such a thing as a part-time policeman. Said it was the only thing he'd ever really wanted to do or be since he was a kid. I took a shine to him right off. Hired him to work around the place and paid him out of my own pocket. Paid him what I could, you know, he never complained about the wages. He was the sort of kid who would have worked for free. He put in an application for full-time work the month before he graduated from high school, but at that time we didn't have any vacancies. So he went to work at Donny Haggar's Gulf and took a night course in police work at the university down in Gorham. I guess Mrs. Dodd tried to put paid to that, too – felt she was alone too much of the time, or something – but that time Frank stood up to her . . . with my encouragement. We took him on in July of 1971 and he's been with the department ever since. Now you tell me this and I think of Katrina being out yesterday morning, walking right past whoever did it . . . and it's like some dirty kind of incest, almost. Frank's been at our house, he's eaten our food, babysat Katie once or twice . . . and you tell me . . .'

Johnny turned around. Bannerman had taken off his glasses and was wiping his eyes again.

'If you really can see such things, I pity you. You're a freak of God, no different from a two-headed cow I once saw in the carnival. I'm sorry. That's a shit thing to say, I know.'

'The Bible says God loves all his creatures,' Johnny said. His voice was a bit unsteady.

'Yeah?' Bannerman nodded and rubbed the red places on the sides of his nose where his glasses sat. 'Got a funny way of showing it, doesn't he?'

12 ·

About twenty minutes later the telephone rang and Bannerman answered it smartly. Talked briefly. Listened.

Johnny watched his face get old. He hung up and looked at Johnny for a long time without speaking.

'November 12, 1972,' he said. 'A college girl. They found her in a field out by the turnpike. Ann Simons, her name was. Raped and strangled. Twenty-three years old. No semen type obtained. It's still not proof, Johnny.'

'I don't think, in your own mind, you need any more proof,' Johnny said. 'And if you confront him with what you have, I think he'll break down.'

'And if he doesn't?'

Johnny remembered the vision on the bandstand. It whirled back at him like a crazy, lethal boomerang. The tearing sensation. The pain that was pleasant, the pain that recalled the pain of the clothespin, the pain that reconfirmed everything.

'Get him to drop his pants,' Johnny said.

Bannerman looked at him.

13 ·

The reporters were still out in the lobby. In truth, they probably wouldn't have moved even had they not suspected a break in the case – or at least a bizarre new development. The roads out of town were impassable.

Bannerman and Johnny went out the supply closet window.

'Are you sure this is the way to do it?' Johnny asked, and the storm tried to rip the words out of his mouth. His legs hurt.

'No,' Bannerman said simply, 'but I think you should be in on it. Maybe I think he should have the chance to look you in the face, Johnny. Come on. The Dodds are only two blocks from here.'

They set off, hooded and booted, a pair of shadows in the driving snow. Beneath his coat Bannerman was wearing his service pistol. His handcuffs were clipped to his belt. Before they had gone a block through the deep snow Johnny was limping badly, but he kept his mouth grimly shut about it.

But Bannerman noticed. They stopped in the doorway of the Castle Rock Western Auto.

'Son, what's the matter with you?'

'Nothing,' Johnny said. His head was starting to ache again, too.

'It sure is something. You act like you're walking on two broken legs.'

'They had to operate on my legs after I came out of the coma. The muscles had atrophied. Started to melt is how Dr. Brown put it. The joints were decayed. They fixed it up the best they could with synthetics . . .'

'Like the Six Million Dollar Man, huh?'

Johnny thought of the neat piles of hospital bills back home, sitting in the top drawer of the dining room hutch.

'Yes, something like that. When I'm on them too long, they stiffen up. That's all.'

'You want to go back?'

You bet I do. Go back and not have to think about this hellacious business anymore. Wish I'd never come. Not my problem. This is the guy who compared me to a two-headed cow.

'No, I'm okay,' he said.

They stepped out of the doorway and the wind grabbed them and tried to bowl them along the empty street. They struggled through the harsh, snow-choked glare of arc-sodium streetlights, bent into the wind. They turned onto a side street and five houses down Bannerman stopped in front of a small and neat New England salt-box. Like the other houses on the street, it was dark and battened down.

'This is the house,' Bannerman said, his voice oddly colorless. They worked their way through the snowdrift that the wind had thrown against the porch and mounted the steps.

14 ·

Mrs. Henrietta Dodd was a big woman who was carrying a dead weight of flesh on her frame. Johnny had never seen a woman who looked any sicker. Her skin was a yellowish-gray. Her hands were nearly reptilian with an eczemalike rash. And there was something in her eyes, narrowed to glittering slits in their puffy sockets, that reminded him unpleasantly of the way his mother's eyes had sometimes looked when Vera Smith was transported into one of her religious frenzies.

She had opened the door to them after Bannerman had rapped steadily for nearly five minutes. Johnny stood beside him on his aching legs, thinking that this night would never end. It would just go on and on until the snow had piled up enough to avalanche down and bury them all.

'What do you want in the middle of the night, George Bannerman?' she asked suspiciously. Like many fat women, her voice was a high, buzzy reed instrument – it sounded a bit like a fly or a bee caught in a bottle.

'Have to talk to Frank, Henrietta.'

'Then talk to him in the morning,' Henrietta Dodd said, and started to close the door in their faces.

Bannerman stopped the door's swing with a gloved hand. 'I'm sorry, Henrietta. Has to be now.'

'Well, I'm not going to wake him up!' she cried, not moving from the doorway. 'He sleeps like the dead anyway! Some nights I ring my bell for him, the palpitations are terrible sometimes, and does he come? No, he sleeps right through it and he could wake up some morning to find me dead of a heart attack in my bed instead of getting him his goddam runny poached egg! Because you work him too hard!'

She grinned in a sour kind of triumph; the dirty secret exposed and hats over the windmill.

'All day, all night, swing shift, chasing after drunks in the middle of the night and any one of them could have a .32 gun under the seat, going out to the ginmills and honky-tonks, oh, they're a rough trade out there but a lot you mind! I guess I know what goes on in those places, those cheap slutty women that'd be happy to give a nice boy like my Frank an incurable disease for the price of a quarter beer!'

Her voice, that reed instrument, swooped and buzzed. Johnny's head pumped and throbbed in counterpoint. He wished she would shut up. It was a hallucination, he knew, just the tiredness and stress of this awful night catching up, but it began to seem more and more to him that this was his mother standing here, that at any moment she would turn from Bannerman to him and begin to huckster him about the wonderful talent God had given him.

'Mrs. Dodd ... Henrietta ...' Bannerman began patiently.

Then she did turn to Johnny, and regarded him with her smart-stupid little pig's eyes.

'Who's this?'

'Special deputy,' Bannerman said promptly. 'Henrietta, I'll take the responsibility for waking Frank up.'

'Oooh, the *responsibility*!' she cooed with monstrous, buzzing sarcasm, and Johnny finally realized she was afraid. The fear was coming off her in pulsing, noisome waves – that was what was making his headache worse. Couldn't Bannerman feel it? 'The ree-spon-si-*bil*-i-tee! Isn't that *biiig* of you, my God yes! Well, I won't have my boy waked up in the middle of the night, George Bannerman, so you and your *special deputy* can just go peddle your goddam papers!'

She tried to shut the door again and this time Bannerman shoved it all the way open. His voice showed tight anger and beneath that a terrible tension. 'Open up, Henrietta, I mean it, now.'

'You can't do this!' she cried. 'This isn't no police state! I'll have your job! Let's see your warrant!'

'No, that's right, but I'm going to talk to Frank,' Bannerman said, and pushed past her.

Johnny, barely aware of what he was doing, followed. Henrietta Dodd made a grab for him. Johnny caught her wrist – and a terrible pain flared in his head, dwarfing the sullen thud of the headache. *And the woman felt it, too.* The two of them stared at each other for a moment that seemed to last forever, an awful, perfect understanding. For that moment they seemed welded together. Then she fell back, clutching at her ogre's bosom.

'My heart . . . my heart . . .' She scrabbled at her robe pocket and pulled out a phial of pills. Her face had gone to the color of raw dough. She got the cap off the phial and spilled tiny pills all over the floor getting one into her palm. She slipped it under her tongue. Johnny stood staring at her in mute horror. His head felt like a swelling bladder full of hot blood.

'You *knew*?' he whispered.

Her fat, wrinkled mouth opened and closed, opened and closed. No sound came out. It was the mouth of a beached fish.

'All of this time *you knew*?'

'You're a devil!' she screamed at him. 'You're a monster . . . devil . . . oh my heart . . . oh, I'm dying . . . think I'm dying . . . call the doctor . . . *George Bannerman don't you go up there and wake my baby!*'

Johnny let go of her, and unconsciously rubbing his hand back and forth on his coat as if to free it of a stain, he stumbled up the stairs after Bannerman. The wind outside sobbed around the eaves like a lost child. Halfway up he glanced back. Henrietta Dodd sat in a wicker chair, a sprawled mountain of meat, gasping and holding a huge breast in each hand. His head still felt as if it were swelling and he thought dreamily: *Pretty soon it'll just pop and that'll be the end. Thank God.*

An old and threadbare runner covered the narrow hall floor. The wallpaper was watermarked. Bannerman was pounding on a closed door. It was at least ten degrees colder up here.

'Frank? Frank! It's George Bannerman! Wake up, Frank!'

There was no response. Bannerman turned the knob and shoved the door open. His hand had fallen to the butt of his gun, but he had not drawn it. It could have been a fatal mistake, but Frank Dodd's room was empty.

The two of them stood in the doorway for a moment,

looking in. It was a child's room. The wallpaper – also watermarked – was covered with dancing clowns and rocking horses. There was a child-sized chair with a Raggedy Andy sitting in it, looking back at them with its shiny blank eyes. In one corner was a toybox. In the other was a narrow maple bed with the covers thrown back. Hooked over one of the bedposts and looking out of place was Frank Dodd's holstered gun.

'My God,' Bannerman said softly. 'What is this?'

'Help,' Mrs. Dodd's voice floated up. 'Help me . . .'

'She knew,' Johnny said. 'She knew from the very beginning, from the Frechette woman. He told her. And she covered up for him.'

Bannerman backed slowly out of the room and opened another door. His eyes were dazed and hurt. It was a guest bedroom, unoccupied. He opened the closet, which was empty except for a neat tray of D-Con rat-killer on the floor. Another door. This bedroom was unfinished and cold enough to show Bannerman's breath. He looked around. There was another door, this one at the head of the stairs. He went to it, and Johnny followed. This door was locked.

'Frank? Are you in there?' He rattled the knob. 'Open it, Frank!'

There was no answer. Bannerman raised his foot and kicked out, connecting with the door just below the knob. There was a flat cracking sound that seemed to echo in Johnny's head like a steel platter dropped on a tile floor.

'Oh God,' Bannerman said in a flat, choked voice. 'Frank.'

Johnny could see over his shoulder, could see too much. Frank Dodd was propped on the lowered seat of the toilet. He was naked except for a shiny black raincoat, which he had looped over his shoulders; the raincoat's black hood (*executioner's hood*, Johnny thought dimly) dangled down on the top of the toilet tank like some grotesque, deflated black pod. He had somehow managed to cut his own throat – Johnny would not have thought

295

that possible. There was a package of Wilkinson Sword Blades on the edge of the washbasin. A single blade lay on the floor, glittering wickedly. Drops of blood had beaded on its edge. The blood from his severed jugular vein and carotid artery had splashed everywhere. There were pools of it caught in the folds of the raincoat which dragged on the floor. It was on the shower curtain, which had a pattern of paddling ducks with umbrellas held over their heads. It was on the ceiling.

Around Frank Dodd's neck on a string was a sign crayoned in lipstick. It read: I CONFESS.

The pain in Johnny's head began to climb to a sizzling, insupportable peak. He groped out with a hand and found the doorjamb.

Knew, he thought incoherently. *Knew somehow when he saw me. Knew it was all over. Came home. Did this.*

Black rings overlaying his sight, spreading like evil ripples.

What a talent God has given you, Johnny.

(I CONFESS)

'Johnny?'

From far away.

'Johnny, are you all . . .'

Fading. Everything fading away. That was good. Would have been better if he had never come out of the coma at all. Better for all concerned. Well, he had had his chance.

'– Johnny –'

Frank Dodd had come up here and somehow he had slit his throat from the ear to the proverbial ear while the storm howled outside like all the dark things of the earth let loose. Gone a gusher, as his father had said that winter twelve years or so ago, when the pipes in the basement had frozen and burst. Gone a gusher. Sure as hell had. All the way up to the ceiling.

He believed that he might have screamed then, but afterward was never sure. It might only have been in his own head that he screamed. But he had *wanted* to scream;

to scream out all the horror and pity and agony in his heart.

Then he was falling forward into darkness, and grateful to go. Johnny blacked out.

15 ·

From the *New York Times*, December 19, 1975:

MAINE PSYCHIC DIRECTS SHERIFF TO KILLER DEPUTY'S HOME AFTER VISITING SCENE OF THE CRIME

(Special to the Times) John Smith of Pownal may not actually be psychic, but one would have difficulty persuading Sheriff George F. Bannerman of Castle County, Maine, to believe that. Desperate after a sixth assault-murder in the small western Maine town of Castle Rock, Sheriff Bannerman called Mr. Smith on the phone and asked him to come over to Castle Rock and lend a hand, if possible. Mr. Smith, who received national attention earlier this year when he recovered from a deep coma after fifty-five months of unconsciousness, had been condemned by the weekly tabloid *Inside View* as a hoaxer, but at a press conference yesterday Sheriff Bannerman would only say, 'We don't put a whole lot of stock up here in Maine in what those New York reporters think.'

According to Sheriff Bannerman, Mr. Smith crawled on his hands and knees around the scene of the sixth murder, which occurred on the Castle Rock town common. He came up with a mild case of frostbite and the murderer's name – Sheriff's Deputy Franklin Dodd, who had been on the Castle County Sheriff's payroll five years, as long as Bannerman himself.

Earlier this year Mr. Smith stirred controversy in his native state when he had a psychic flash that his physical therapist's house had caught fire. The flash turned out to be nothing but the truth. At a press conference following, a reporter challenged him to . . .

From *Newsweek*, page 41, week of December 24, 1975:

THE NEW HURKOS

It may be that the first genuine psychic since Peter Hurkos has been uncovered in this country – Hurkos was the German-born seer who has been able to tell questioners all about their private lives by touching their hands, silverware, or items from their handbags.

John Smith is a shy and unassuming young man from the south-central Maine town of Pownal. Earlier this year he returned to consciousness after a period of more than four years in a deep coma following a car accident (see photo). According to the consulting neurologist in the case, Dr. Samuel Weizak, Smith made a 'perfectly astounding recovery'. Today he is recovering from a mild case of frostbite and a four-hour blackout following the bizarre resolution of a long-unsolved multiple murder case in the town of . . .

December 27, 1975

Dear Sarah,

Dad and I both enjoyed your letter, which arrived just this afternoon. I'm really fine, so you can stop worrying, okay? But I thank you for your concern. The 'frostbite' was greatly exaggerated in the press. Just a couple of patches on the tips of three fingers of my left hand. The blackout was really nothing much more than a fainting spell 'brought on by emotional overload', Weizak says. Yes, he came down himself and insisted on driving me to the hospital in Portland. Just watching him in action is nearly worth the price of admission. He bullied them into giving him a consultation room and an EEG machine and a technician to run it. He says he can find no new brain damage or signs of progressive brain damage. He wants to do a whole series of tests, some of them sound utterly inquisitorial – 'Renounce, heretic, or we'll give you another pneumo-brainscan!' (Ha-ha, and are

298

you still sniffin' that wicked cocaine, darlin'?) Anyway, I turned down the kind offer to be pumped and prodded some more. Dad is rather pissed at me about turning the tests down, keeps trying to draw a parallel between my refusal to have them and my mother's refusal to take her hypertension medicine. It's very hard to make him see that, if Weizak did find something, the odds would be nine-to-one against him being able to do anything about it.

Yes, I saw the Newsweek *article. That picture of me is from the press conference, only cropped. Don't look like anyone you'd like to meet in a dark alley, do I? Ha-ha! Holy Gee (as your buddy Anne Strafford is so fond of saying), but I wish they hadn't run that story. The packages, cards, and letters have started coming again. I don't open any of them anymore unless I recognize the return address, just mark them 'Return to Sender'. They are too pitiful, too full of hope and hate and belief and unbelief, and somehow they all remind me of the way my Mom was.*

Well, I don't mean to sound so gloomy, it ain't all that bad. But I don't want to be a practicing psychic, I don't want to go on tour or appear on TV (some yahoo from NBC got our phone number, who knows how, and wanted to know if I'd consider 'doing the Carson show'. Great idea, huh? Don Rickles could insult some people, some starlet could show her jugs, and I could make a few predictions. All brought to you by General Foods.). I don't want to do any of that S*H*I*T. What I am really looking forward to is getting back to Cleaves Mills and sinking into the utter obscurity of the H.S. English teacher. And save the psychic flashes for football pep rallies.

Guess that's all for this time. Hope you and Walt and Denny had yourself a merry little Christmas and are looking forward eagerly (from what you said I'm sure Walt is, at the very least) to the Brave Bicentennial Election Year now stretching before us. Glad to hear your spouse has been picked to run for the state senate seat there, but cross your fingers, Sarey — '76 doesn't exactly

299

look like a banner year for elephant-lovers. Send your thanks for that one across to San Clemente.

My dad sends best and wants me to tell you thanks for the picture of Denny, who really impressed him. I send my best, also. Thanks for writing, and for your misplaced concern (misplaced, but very welcome). I'm fine, and looking forward to getting back in harness.

Love and good wishes,
Johnny

P.S. For the last time, kiddo, get off that cocaine.

J.

December 29, 1975

Dear Johnny,

I think this is the hardest, bitterest letter I've had to write in my sixteen years of school administration – not only because you're a good friend but because you're a damned good teacher. There is no way to gild the lily on this, so guess I won't even try.

There was a special meeting of the school board last evening (at the behest of two members I won't name, but they were on the board when you were teaching here and I think you can probably guess the names), and they voted 5–2 to ask that your contract be withdrawn. The reason: you're too controversial to be effective as a teacher. I came very close to tendering my own resignation; I was that disgusted. If it wasn't for Maureen and the kids, I think I would have. This abortion isn't even on a par with tossing Rabbit, Run or Catcher in the Rye out of the classroom. This is worse. It stinks.

I told them that, but I might as well have been talking in Esperanto or igpay atinlay. All they can see is that your picture was in Newsweek and the New York Times

*and that the Castle Rock story was on the national net-
work news broadcasts. Too controversial! Five old men in
trusses, the kind of men who are more interested in hair
length than in textbooks, more involved in finding out
who might smoke pot on the faculty than in finding out
how to get some twentieth-century equipment for the
Sci Wing.*

*I have written a strong letter of protest to the board-
at-large, and with a little arm-twisting I believe I can get
Irving Finegold to cosign it with me. But I'd also be less
than truthful if I told you there was a hope in hell of
getting those five old men to change their minds.*

*My honest advice to you is to get yourself a lawyer,
Johnny. You signed that blueback in good faith, and I
believe you can squeeze them for every last cent of your
salary, whether you ever step into a Cleaves Mills classroom or not. And call me when you feel like talking.*

With all my heart, I'm sorry.

> *Your friend,*
> *Dave Pelsen*

16 ·
*Johnny stood beside the mailbox with Dave's letter in
his hand, looking down at it unbelievingly. It was the
last day of 1975, clear and bitingly cold. His breath came
out of his nostrils in fine white jets of smoke.*

'Shit,' he whispered. 'Oh man, oh shit.'

*Numbly, still not assimilating it totally, he leaned
down to see what else the mailman had brought him. As
usual, the box was crammed full. It had just been luck
that Dave's letter had been sticking out the end.*

*There was a white, fluttering slip of paper telling him
to call at the post office for the packages, the inevitable
packages. My husband deserted me in 1969, here is a pair
of his socks, tell me where he is so I can get child-support
out of the bastard. My baby choked to death last year,
here is his rattle, please write and tell me if he is happy
with the angels. I didn't have him baptized because his*

301

father did not approve and now my heart is breaking.
The endless litany.

What a talent God has given you, Johnny.

The reason: You're too controversial to be effective as
a teacher.

In a sudden vicious spasm he began to rake letters and
manila envelopes out of the box, dropping some in the
snow. The inevitable headache began to form around his
temples like two dark clouds that would slowly draw together, enveloping him in pain. Sudden tears began to
slip down his cheeks, and in the deep, still cold, they
froze to glittering tracks almost immediately.

He bent and began to pick up the letters he had
dropped; he saw one, doubled and trebled through the
prisms of his tears, addressed in heavy dark pencil to
JOHN SMITH SIKIK SEER.

Sikik seer, that's me. His hands began to tremble wildly
and he dropped everything, including Dave's letter. It
fluttered down like a leaf and landed print side up among
the other letters, all the other letters. Through his helpless tears he could see the letterhead, and the motto below the torch:

TO TEACH, TO LEARN, TO KNOW, TO SERVE.

'Serve my ass, you cheap bastards,' Johnny said. He
fell on his knees and began to gather up the letters,
sweeping them together with his mittens. His fingers
ached dully, a reminder of the frostbite, a reminder of
Frank Dodd riding a dead toilet seat into eternity, blood
in his all-American blond hair. I CONFESS.

He swept the letters up and heard himself muttering
over and over, like a defective record: 'Killing me, you
people are killing me, let me alone, can't you see you're
killing me?'

He made himself stop. This was no way to behave. Life
would go on. One way or another, life would most certainly go on.

Johnny started back to the house, wondering what he
could do now. Perhaps something would come along. At
any rate, he had fulfilled his mother's prophecy. If God

had had a mission for him, then he had done it. No matter now that it had been a kamikaze mission. He had done it.

He was quits.

PART TWO

The Laughing Tiger

CHAPTER SEVENTEEN

1 ·

The boy read slowly, following the words with his finger,
his long brown football-player's legs stretched out on the
chaise by the pool in the bright clear light of June.

' "Of course young Danny Ju ... Juniper ... young
Danny Juniper was dead, and I suh ... suppose that there
were few in the world who would say he had not de ...
duh ... dee ..." Oh, shit, I don't know.'

' "Few in the world who would say he had not deserved
his death," ' Johnny Smith said. 'Only a slightly fancier
way of saying that most would agree that Danny's death
was a good thing.'

Chuck was looking at him, and the familiar mix of
emotions was crossing his usually pleasant face: amusement, resentment, embarrassment, and a trace of sullenness. Then he sighed and looked down at the Max Brand
Western again.

' "Deserved his death. But it was my great trah ...
truhjud ..." '

'Tragedy,' Johnny supplied.

' "But it was my great *tragedy* that he had died just as
he was about to redeem some of his e-e-evil work by one
great service to the world.

' "Of course that ... suh ... that sih ... sih ..." '

Chuck closed the book, looked up at Johnny, and
smiled brilliantly.

'Let's quit for the day, Johnny, what do you say?'
Chuck's smile was his most winning, the one that had
probably tumbled cheerleaders into bed all over New
Hampshire. 'Doesn't that pool look good? You bet it does.
The sweat is running right off your skinny, malnourished
little bod.'

Johnny had to admit – at least to himself – that the
pool did look good. The first couple of weeks of the Bi-

centennial Summer of '76 had been uncommonly hot and sticky. From behind them, around on the other side of the big, gracious white house, came the soporific drone of the riding lawnmower as Ngo Phat, the Vietnamese groundsman, mowed what Chuck called the front forty. It was a sound that made you want to drink two glasses of cold lemonade and then nod off to sleep.

'No derogatory comments about my skinny bod,' he said. 'Besides, we just started the chapter.'

'Sure, but we read two before it.' Wheedling.

Johnny sighed. Usually he could keep Chuck at it, but not this afternoon. And today the kid had fought his way gamely through the way John Sherburne had set up his net of guards around the Amity jail and the way the evil Red Hawk had broken through and killed Danny Juniper.

'Yeah, well, just finish this page, then,' he said. 'That word you're stuck on's "sickened". No teeth in that one, Chuck.'

'Good man!' The grin widened. 'And no questions, right?'

'Well . . . maybe just a few.'

Chuck scowled, but it was a put-on; he was getting off easy and knew it. He opened the paperback with the picture of the gunslinger shouldering his way through a set of saloon batwings again and began to read in his slow, halting voice . . . a voice so different from his normal speaking voice that it could have belonged to a different young man altogether.

' "Of course that suh . . . sickened me at once. But it was . . . was nothing to what waited for me at the bedside of poor Tom Keyn . . . Kenyon.

' "He had been shot through the body and he was fast drying when I . . ." '

'Dying,' Johnny said quietly. 'Context, Chuck. Read for context.'

'Fast drying,' Chuck said, and giggled. Then he resumed: ' " . . . and he was fast *dying* when I ar-ar . . . when I arrived." '

Johnny felt a sadness for Chuck steal over him as he watched the boy, hunched over the paperback copy of *Fire Brain*, a good oat opera that should have read like the wind – and instead, here was Chuck, following Max Brand's simple point-to-point prose with a laboriously moving finger. His father, Roger Chatsworth, owned Chatsworth Mills and Weaving, a very big deal indeed in southern New Hampshire. He owned this sixteen-room house in Durham, and there were five people on the staff, including Ngo Phat, who went down to Portsmouth once a week to take United States citizenship classes. Chatsworth drove a restored 1957 Cadillac convertible. His wife, a sweet, clear-eyed woman of forty-two, drove a Mercedes. Chuck had a Corvette. The family fortune was in the neighborhood of five million dollars.

And Chuck, at seventeen, was what God had really meant when he breathed life into the clay, Johnny often thought. He was a physically lovely human being. He stood six-two and weighed a good muscular one hundred and ninety pounds. His face was perhaps not quite interesting enough to be truly handsome, but it was acne- and pimple-free and set off by a pair of striking green eyes – which had caused Johnny to think that the only other person he knew with really green eyes was Sarah Hazlett. At his high school, Chuck was the apotheosis of the BMOC, almost ridiculously so. He was captain of the baseball and football teams, president of the junior class during the school year just ended, and president-elect of the student council this coming fall. And most amazing of all, none of it had gone to his head. In the words of Herb Smith, who had been down once to check out Johnny's new digs, Chuck was 'a regular guy'. Herb had no higher accolade in his vocabulary. In addition, he was someday going to be an exceedingly rich regular guy.

And here he sat, bent grimly over his book like a machine gunner at a lonely outpost, shooting the words down one by one as they came at him. He had taken Max Brand's exciting, fast-moving story of drifting John 'Fire

Brain' Sherburne and his confrontation with the outlaw Comanche Red Hawk and had turned it into something that sounded every bit as exciting as a trade advertisement for semiconductors or radio components.

But Chuck wasn't stupid. His math grades were good, his retentive memory was excellent, and he was manually adept. His problem was that he had great difficulty storing printed words. His oral vocabulary was fine, and he could grasp the theory of phonics but apparently not its practice; and he would sometimes reel a sentence off flawlessly and then come up totally blank when you asked him to rephrase it. His father had been afraid that Chuck was dyslexic, but Johnny didn't think so – he had never met a dyslexic child that he was aware of, although many parents seized on the words to explain or excuse the reading problems of their children. Chuck's problem seemed more general – a loose, across-the-board reading phobia.

It was a problem that had become more and more apparent over the last five years of Chuck's schooling, but his parents had only begun to take it seriously – as Chuck had – when his sports eligibility became endangered. And that was not the worst of it. This winter would be Chuck's last good chance to take the Scholastic Achievement Tests, if he expected to start college in the fall of 1977. The maths were not much of a problem, but the rest of the exam . . . well . . . if he could have the questions read aloud to him, he would do an average-to-good job. Five hundreds, no sweat. But they don't let you bring a reader with you when you take the SATs, not even if your dad is a biggie in the world of New Hampshire business.

' "But I found him a ch . . . changed man. He knew what lay before him and his courage was supp . . . supper . . . superb. He asked for nothing; he regretted nothing. All the terror and the nerv . . . nervousness which had puss . . . possett . . . *possessed* him so long as he was cuh . . . cuh . . . cuhfronted . . . *confronted* by an unknown fate . . ." '

Johnny had seen the ad for a tutor in the *Maine Times* and had applied without too much hope. He had moved down to Kittery in mid-February, needing more than anything else to get away from Pownal, from the boxful of mail each day, the reporters who had begun to find their way to the house in ever-increasing numbers, the nervous women with the wounded eyes who had just 'dropped by' because 'they just happened to be in the neighborhood' (one of those who had just dropped by because she just happened to be in the neighborhood had a Maryland license plate; another was driving a tired old Ford with Arizona tags). Their hands, stretching out to touch him . . .

In Kittery he had discovered for the first time that an anonymous name like John-no-middle-initial-Smith had its advantages. His third day in town he had applied for a job as a short-order cook, putting down his experience in the UMO commons and one summer cooking at a boys' camp in the Rangely Lakes as experience. The diner's owner, a tough-as-nails widow named Ruby Pelletier, had looked over his application and said, 'You're a teensy bit overeducated for slinging hash. You know that, don't you, slugger?'

'That's right,' Johnny said. 'I went and educated myself right out of the job market.'

Ruby Pelletier put her hands on her scrawny hips, threw her head back, and bellowed laughter. 'You think you can keep your shit together at two in the morning when twelve CB cowboys pull in all at once and order scrambled eggs, bacon, sausage, french toast, and flapjacks?'

'I guess maybe,' Johnny said.

'I guess maybe you don't know what the eff I'm talking about just yet,' Ruby said, 'but I'll give you a go, college boy. Go get yourself a physical so we're square with the board of health and bring me back a clean bill. I'll put you right on.'

He had done that, and after a harum-scarum first two weeks (which included a painful rash of blisters on his right hand from dropping a french-fry basket into a well of boiling fat a little too fast), he had been riding the job instead of the other way around. When he saw Chatsworth's ad, he had sent his resumé to the box number. In the course of the resumé he had listed his special ed credentials, which included a one-semester seminar in learning disabilities and reading problems.

In late April, as he was finishing his second month at the diner, he had gotten a letter from Roger Chatsworth, asking him to appear for an interview on May 5. He made the necessary arrangements to take the day off, and at 2 : 10 on a lovely midspring afternoon he had been sitting in Chatsworth's study, a tall, ice-choked glass of Pepsi-Cola in one hand, listening to Stuart talk about his son's reading problems.

'That sound like dyslexia to you?' Stuart asked.

'No. It sounds like a general reading phobia.'

Chatsworth had winced a little. 'Jackson's Syndrome?'

Johnny had been impressed – as he was no doubt supposed to be. Michael Carey Jackson was a reading-and-grammar specialist from the University of Southern California who had caused something of a stir nine years ago with a book called *The Unlearning Reader*. The book described a loose basket of reading problems that had since become known as Jackson's Syndrome. The book was a good one if you could get past the dense academic jargon. The fact that Chatsworth apparently had done so told Johnny a good deal about the man's commitment to solving his son's problem.

'Something like it,' Johnny agreed. 'But you understand I haven't even met your son yet, or listened to him read.'

'He's got course work to make up from last year. American Writers, a nine-week history block, and *civics*, of all things. He flunked his final exam there because he couldn't read the beastly thing. Have you got a New Hampshire teacher's certificate?'

'No,' Johnny said, 'but getting one is no problem.'

'And how would you handle the situation?'

Johnny outlined the way he would deal with it. A lot of oral reading on Chuck's part, leaning heavily on high-impact materials such as fantasy, science fiction, Westerns, and boy-meets-car juvenile novels. Constant questioning on what had just been read. And a relaxation technique described in Jackson's book. 'High achievers often suffer the most,' Johnny said. 'They try too hard and reinforce the block. It's a kind of mental stutter that . . .'

'Jackson says that?' Chatsworth interposed sharply.

Johnny smiled. 'No, I say that,' he said.

'Okay. Go on.'

'Sometimes, if the student can totally blank his mind right after reading and not feel the pressure to recite back right away, the circuits seem to clear themselves. When that begins to happen, the student begins to re-think his line of attack. It's a positive thinking kind of thing . . .'

Chatsworth's eyes had gleamed. Johnny had just touched on the linchpin of his own personal philosophy – probably the linchpin for the beliefs of most self-made men. 'Nothing succeeds like success,' he said.

'Well, yes. Something like that.'

'How long would it take you to get a New Hampshire certificate?'

'No longer than it takes them to process my application. Two weeks, maybe.'

'Then you could start on the twentieth?'

Johnny blinked. 'You mean I'm hired?'

'If you want the job, you're hired. You can stay in the guest house, it'll keep the goddam relatives at bay this summer, not to mention Chuck's friends – and I want him to really buckle down. I'll pay you six hundred dol-lars a month, not a king's ransom, but if Chuck gets along, I'll pay you a substantial bonus. Substantial.'

Chatsworth removed his glasses and rubbed a hand across his face. 'I love my boy, Mr. Smith. I only want the best for him. Help us out a little if you can.'

'I'll try.'

Chatsworth put his glasses back on and picked up

Johnny's resumé again. 'You haven't taught for a helluva long time. Didn't agree with you?'

Here it comes, Johnny thought.

'It agreed,' he said, 'but I was in an accident.'

Chatsworth's eyes had gone to the scars on Johnny's neck where the atrophied tendons had been partially repaired. 'Car crash?'

'Yes.'

'Bad one?'

'Yes.'

'You seem fine now,' Chatsworth said. He picked up the resumé, slammed it into a drawer and, amazingly, that had been the end of the questions. So after five years Johnny was teaching again, although his student load was only one.

2 ·

' "As for me, who had i ... indirectly br ... brog ... brought his death upon him, he took my hand with a weak grip and smiled his for ... forgiveness up to me. It was a hard moment, and I went away feeling that I had done more harm in the world than I could ever ma ... make up to it." '

Chuck snapped the book closed. 'There. Last one in the pool's a green banana.'

'Hold it a minute, Chuck.'

'Ahhhhhhh ...' Chuck sat down again, heavily, his face composing itself into what Johnny already thought of as his *now the questions* expression. Long-suffering good humor predominated, but beneath it he could sometimes see another Chuck: sullen, worried, and scared. Plenty scared. Because it was a reader's world, the unlettered of America were dinosaurs lumbering down a blind alley, and Chuck was smart enough to know it. And he was plenty afraid of what might happen to him when he got back to school this fall.

'Just a couple of questions, Chuck.'

'Why bother? You know I won't be able to answer them.'

314

'Oh yes. This time you'll be able to answer them all.'

'I can never understand what I read, you ought to know that by now.' Chuck looked morose and unhappy. 'I don't even know what you stick around for, unless it's the chow.'

'You'll be able to answer these questions because they're not about the book.'

Chuck glanced up. 'Not about the book? Then why ask em? I thought . . .'

'Just humor me, okay?'

Johnny's heart was pounding hard, and he was not totally surprised to find that he was scared. He had been planning this for a long time, waiting for just the right confluence of circumstances. This was as close as he was ever going to get. Mrs. Chatsworth was not hovering around anxiously, making Chuck that much more nervous. None of his buddies were splashing around in the pool, making him feel self-conscious about reading aloud like a backward fourth grader. And most important, his father, the man Chuck wanted to please above all others in the world, was not here. He was in Boston at a New England Environmental Commission meeting on water pollution.

From Edward Stanney's *An Overview of Learning Disabilities*:

'*The subject, Rupert J., was sitting in the third row of a movie theater. He was closest to the screen by more than six rows, and was the only one in a position to observe that a small fire had started in the accumulated litter on the floor. Rupert J. stood up and cried "F-F-F-F-F –" while the people behind him shouted for him to sit down and be quiet.*

'*"How did that make you feel?" I asked Rupert J.*

'*"I could never explain in a thousand years how it made me feel," he answered. "I was scared, but even more than being scared, I was frustrated. I felt inadequate, not fit to be a member of the human race. The stuttering always made me feel that way, but now I felt impotent, too."*

' "Was there anything else?"
' "Yes, I felt jealousy, because someone else would see the fire and – you know –"
' "Get the glory of reporting it?"
' "Yes, that's right. I saw the fire starting, I was the only one. And all I could say was F-F-F-F like a stupid broken record. Not fit to be a member of the human race describes it best."
' "And how did you break the block?"
' "The day before had been my mother's birthday. I got her half a dozen roses at the florist's. And I stood there with all of them yelling at me and I thought: I am going to open my mouth and scream ROSES! just as loud as I can. I got that word all ready."
' "Then what did you do?"
' "I opened my mouth and screamed FIRE! at the top of my lungs." '

It had been eight years since Johnny had read that case history in the introduction to Stanney's text, but he had never forgotten it. He had always thought that the key word in Rupert J.'s recollection of what had happened was *impotent*. If you feel that sexual intercourse is the most important thing on earth at this point in time, your risk of coming up with a limp penis increases ten or a hundredfold. And if you feel that reading is the most important thing on earth . . .

'What's your middle name, Chuck?' he asked casually.

'Murphy,' Chuck said with a little grin. 'How's that for bad? My mother's maiden name. You tell Jack or Al that, and I'll be forced to do gross damage to your skinny body.'

'No fear,' Johnny said. 'When's your birthday?'

'September 8.'

Johnny began to throw the questions faster, not giving Chuck a chance to think – but they weren't questions you had to think about.

'What's your girl's name?'

'Beth. You know Beth, Johnny . . .'

'What's her middle name?'

316

Chuck grinned. 'Alma. Pretty horrible, right?'

'What's your paternal grandfather's name?'

'Richard.'

'Who do you like in the American League East this year?'

'Yankees. In a walk.'

'Who do you like for president?'

'I'd like to see Jerry Brown get it.'

'You planning to trade that Vette?'

'Not this year. Maybe next.'

'Your mom's idea?'

'You bet. She says it outraces her peace of mind.'

'How did Red Hawk get past the guards and kill Danny Jupiter?'

'Sherburne didn't pay enough attention to that trapdoor leading into the jail attic,' Chuck said promptly, without thinking, and Johnny felt a sudden burst of triumph that hit him like a knock of straight bourbon. It had worked. He had gotten Chuck talking about roses, and he had responded with a good, healthy yell of *fire*!

Chuck was looking at him in almost total surprise.

'Red Hawk got into the attic through the skylight. Kicked open the trapdoor. Shot Danny Jupiter. Shot Tom Kenyon, too.'

'That's right, Chuck.'

'I remembered,' he muttered, and then looked up at Johnny, eyes widening, a grin starting at the corners of his mouth. 'You tricked me into remembering!'

'I just took you by the hand and led you around the side of whatever has been in your way all this time,' Johnny said. 'But whatever it is, it's still there, Chuck. Don't kid yourself. Who was the girl Sherburne fell for?'

'It was . . .' His eyes clouded a little, and he shook his head reluctantly. 'I don't remember.' He struck his thigh with sudden viciousness. 'I can't remember *anything*! I'm so fucking *stupid*!'

'Can you remember ever having been told how your dad and mom met?'

Chuck looked up at him and smiled a little. There was

an angry red place on his thigh where he had struck himself. 'Sure. She was working for Avis down in Charleston, South Carolina. She rented my dad a car with a flat tire.' Chuck laughed. 'She still claims she only married him because number two tries harder.'

'And who was that girl Sherburne got interested in?'

'Jenny Langhorne. Big-time trouble for him. She's Gresham's girl. A redhead. Like Beth. She . . .' He broke off, staring at Johnny as if he had just produced a rabbit from the breast pocket of his shirt. 'You did it again !'

'No. You did it. It's a simple trick of misdirection. Why do you say Jenny Langhorne is big-time trouble for John Sherburne?'

'Well, because Gresham's the big wheel there in that town . . .'

'What town?'

Chuck opened his mouth, but nothing came out. Suddenly he cut his eyes away from Johnny's face and looked at the pool. Then he smiled and looked back. 'Amity. The same as in the flick *Jaws*.'

'Good ! How did you come up with the name?'

Chuck grinned. 'This makes no sense at all, but I started thinking about trying out for the swimming team, and there it was. What a trick. What a great trick.'

'Okay. That's enough for today, I think.' Johnny felt tired, sweaty, and very, very good. 'You just made a breakthrough, in case you didn't notice. Let's swim: Last one in's a green banana.'

'Johnny?'

'What?'

'Will that always work?'

'If you make a habit of it, it will,' Johnny said. 'And every time you go around that block instead of trying to bust through the middle of it, you're going to make it a little smaller. I think you'll begin to see an improvement in your word-to-word reading before long, also. I know a couple of other little tricks. He fell silent. What he had just given Chuck was less the truth than a king of hypnotic suggestion.

'Thanks, Chuck said. The mask of long-suffering good humor was gone, replaced by naked gratitude. 'If you get me over this, I'll . . . well, I guess I'd get down and kiss your feet if you wanted me to. Sometimes I get so scared, I feel like I'm letting my dad down . . .'

'Chuck, don't you know that's part of the problem?'

'It is?'

'Yeah. You're . . . you're overswinging. Overthrowing. Overeverything. And it may not be just a psychological block, you know. There are people who believe that some reading problems, Jackson's Syndrome, reading phobias, all of that, may be some kind of . . . mental birthmark. A fouled circuit, a faulty relay, a d . . .' He shut his mouth with a snap.

'A what?' Chuck asked.

'A dead zone,' Johnny said slowly. 'Whatever. Names don't matter. Results do. The misdirection trick really isn't a trick at all. It's educating a fallow part of your brain to do the work of that small faulty section. For you, that means getting into an oral-based train of thought every time you hit a snag. You're actually changing the location in your brain from which your thought is coming. It's learning to switch-hit.'

'But can I do it? You think I can do it?'

'I know you can,' Johnny said.

'All right. Then I will.' Chuck dived low and flat into the pool and came up, shaking water out of his long hair in a fine spray of droplets. 'Come on in! It's fine!'

'I will,' Johnny said, but for the moment he was content just to stand on the pool's tile facing and watch Chuck swim powerfully toward the pool's deep end to savor this success. There had been no good feeling like this when he had suddenly known Eileen Magown's kitchen curtains were taking fire, no good feeling like this when he had uncovered the name of Frank Dodd. If God had given him a talent, it was teaching, not knowing things he had no business knowing. This was the sort of thing he had been made for, and when he had been teaching at Cleaves Mills back in 1970, he had known it. More important, the kids had known it and responded to it, as Chuck had done just now.

'You gonna stand there like a dummy?' Chuck asked.

Johnny dived into the pool.

CHAPTER EIGHTEEN

Warren Richardson came out of his small office building at quarter to five as he always did. He walked around to the parking lot and hoisted his two-hundred-pound bulk behind the wheel of his Chevy Caprice and started the engine. All according to routine. What was not according to routine was the face that appeared suddenly in the rear-view mirror – an olive-skinned, stubbled face framed by long hair and set off by eyes every bit as green as those of Sarah Hazlett or Chuck Chatsworth. Warren Richardson had not been so badly scared since he was a kid, and his heart took a great, unsteady leap in his chest.

'Howdy,' said Sonny Elliman, leaning over the seat.

'Who . . .' was all Richardson managed, uttering the word in a terrified hiss of breath. His heart was pounding so hard that dark specks danced and pulsed before his eyes in rhythm with its beat. He was afraid he might have a heart attack.

'Easy,' the man who had been hiding in his back seat said. 'Go easy, man. Lighten up.'

And Warren Richardson felt an absurd emotion. It was gratitude. The man who had scared him wasn't going to scare him anymore. He must be a nice man, he must be –

'Who are you?' he managed this time.

'A friend,' Sonny said.

Richardson started to turn and fingers as hard as pincers bit into the sides of his flabby neck. The pain was excruciating. Richardson drew breath in a convulsive, heaving whine.

'You don't need to turn around, man. You can see me as well as you need to see me in your rear-view. Can you dig that?'

'Yes,' Richardson gasped. 'Yes yes yes just let me go!'

The pincers began to ease up, and again he felt that irrational sense of gratitude. But he no longer doubted that the man in the back seat was dangerous, or that he was in this car on purpose although he couldn't think why anyone would –

And then he *could* think why someone would, at least why someone *might*, it wasn't the sort of thing you'd expect any ordinary candidate for office to do, but Greg Stillson wasn't ordinary, Greg Stillson was a crazy man, and –

Very softly, Warren Richardson began to blubber.

'Got to talk to you, man,' Sonny said. His voice was kind and regretful, but in the rear-view mirror his eyes glittered green amusement. 'Got to talk to you like a Dutch uncle.'

'It's Stillson, isn't it? It's . . .'

The pincers were suddenly back, the man's fingers were buried in his neck, and Richardson uttered a high-pitched shriek.

'No names,' the terrible man in the back seat told him in that same kind-yet-regretful voice. 'You draw your own conclusions, Mr. Richardson, but keep the names to yourself. I've got one thumb just over your carotid artery and my fingers are over by your jugular, and I can turn you into a human turnip, if I want to.'

'What do you want?' Richardson asked. He did not exactly moan, but it was a near thing; he had never felt more like moaning in his life. He could not believe that this was happening in the parking lot behind his real estate office in Capital City, New Hampshire, on a bright summer's day. He could see the clock set into the red brick of the town hall tower. It said ten minutes to five. At home, Norma would be putting the pork chops, nicely coated with Shake 'n Bake, into the oven to broil. Sean would be watching Sesame Street on TV. And there was a man behind him threatening to cut off the flow of blood to his brain and turn him into an idiot. No, it wasn't real; it was like a nightmare. The sort of nightmare that makes you moan in your sleep.

'I don't want anything,' Sonny Elliman said. 'It's all a matter of what you want.'

'I don't understand what you're talking about.' But he was terribly afraid that he did.

'That story in the New Hampshire *Journal* about funny real estate deals,' Sonny said. 'You surely did have a lot to say, Mr. Richardson, didn't you? Especially about . . . certain people.'

'I . . .'

'That stuff about the Capital Mail, for instance. Hinting around about kickbacks and payoffs and one hand washing the other. All that *horseshit*.' The fingers tightened on Richardson's neck again, and this time he did moan. But he hadn't been identified in the story, he had just been 'an informed source'. How had they known? How had *Greg Stillson* known?

The man behind him began to speak rapidly into Warren Richardson's ear now, his breath warm and ticklish.

'You could get certain people into trouble talking horseshit like that, Mr. Richardson, you know it? People running for public office, let's say. Running for office, it's like playing bridge, you dig it? You're vulnerable. People can sling mud and it sticks, especially these days. Now, there's no trouble yet. I'm happy to tell you that, because if there *was* trouble, you might be sitting here picking your teeth out of your nose instead of having a nice little talk with me.'

In spite of his pounding heart, in spite of his fear, Richardson said: 'This . . . this person . . . young man, you're crazy if you think you can protect him. He's played it as fast and loose as a snake-oil salesman in a southern town. Sooner or later . . .'

A thumb slammed into his ear, grinding. The pain was immense, unbelievable. Richardson's head slammed into his window and he cried out. Blindly, he groped for the horn ring.

'You blow that horn, I'll kill you,' the voice whispered. Richardson let his hands drop. The thumb eased up.

'You ought to use Q-tips in there, man,' the voice said. 'I got wax all over my thumb. Pretty gross.'

Warren Richardson began to cry weakly. He was powerless to stop himself. Tears coursed down his fat cheeks. 'Please don't hurt me anymore,' he said. 'Please don't. Please.'

'It's like I said,' Sonny told him. 'It's all a matter of what you want. Your job isn't to worry what someone else might say about these ... these certain people. Your job is to watch what comes out of your own mouth. Your job is to think before you talk the next time that guy from the *Journal* comes around. You might think about how easy it is to find out who "an informed source" is. Or you might think about what a bummer it would be if your house burned down. Or you might think about how you'd pay for plastic surgery if someone threw some battery acid in your wife's face.'

The man behind Richardson was panting now. He sounded like an animal in a jungle.

'Or you might think, you know, dig it, how easy it would be for someone to come along and pick up your son on his way home from kindergarten.'

'Don't you say that!' Richardson cried hoarsely. 'Don't you say that, you slimy bastard!'

'All I'm saying is that you want to think about what you want,' Sonny said. 'An election, it's an all-American thing, you know? Especially in a Bicentennial year. Everyone should have a good time. No one has a good time if numb fucks like you start telling a lot of lies. Numb *jealous* fucks like you.'

The hand went away altogether. The rear door opened. Oh thank God, thank God.

'You just want to think,' Sonny Elliman repeated. 'Now do we have an understanding?'

'Yes,' Richardson whispered. 'But if you think Gr . . . a certain person can be elected using these tactics, you're badly mistaken.'

'No,' Sonny said. 'You're the one who's mistaken. Because everyone's having a good time. Make sure that you're not left out.'

Richardson didn't answer. He sat rigid behind the steering wheel, his neck throbbing, staring at the clock on the Town Office Building as if it were the only sane thing left in his life. It was now almost five of five. The pork chops would be in by now.

The man in the back seat said one more thing and then he was gone, striding away rapidly, his long hair swinging against the collar of his shirt, not looking back. He went around the corner of the building and out of sight.

The last thing he had said to Warren Richardson was: 'Q-Tips.'

Richardson began to shake all over and it was a long time before he could drive. His first clear feeling was anger – terrible anger. The impulse that came with it was to drive directly to the Capital City police department (housed in the building below the clock) and report what had happened – the threats on his wife and son, the physical abuse – and on whose behalf it had been done.

You might think about how you'd pay for plastic surgery . . . or how easy it would be for someone to come along and pick up your son . . .

But why? Why take the chance? What he had said to that thug was just the plain, unvarnished truth. Everyone in southern New Hampshire real estate knew that Stillson had been running a shell game, reaping short-term profits that would land him in jail, not sooner or later, but sooner or even sooner. His campaign was an exercise in idiocy. And now strong-arm tactics! No one could get away with that for long in America – and especially not in New England.

But let someone else blow the whistle.

Someone with less to lose.

Warren Richardson started his car and went home to his pork chops and said nothing at all. Someone else would surely put a stop to it.

CHAPTER NINETEEN

1 ·

On a day not long after Chuck's first breakthrough, Johnny Smith stood in the bathroom of the guest house, running his Norelco over his cheeks. Looking at himself closeup in a mirror always gave him a weird feeling these days, as if he were looking at an older brother instead of himself. Deep horizontal lines had grooved themselves across his forehead. Two more bracketed his mouth. Strangest of all, there was that streak of white, and the rest of his hair was beginning to go gray. It seemed to have started almost overnight.

He snapped off the razor and went out into the combination kitchen-living room. Lap of luxury, he thought, and smiled a little. Smiling was starting to feel natural again. He turned on the TV, got a Pepsi out of the fridge, and settled down to watch the news. Roger Chatsworth was due back later in the evening, and tomorrow Johnny would have the distinct pleasure of telling him that his son was beginning to make real progress.

Johnny had been up to see his own father every two weeks or so. He was pleased with Johnny's new job and listened with keen interest as Johnny told him about the Chatsworths, the house in the pleasant college town of Durham, and Chuck's problems. Johnny, in turn, listened as his father told him about the gratis work he was doing at Charlene MacKenzie's house in neighboring New Gloucester.

'Her husband was a helluva doctor but not much of a handyman,' Herb said. Charlene and Vera had been friends before Vera's deepening involvement in the stranger offshoots of fundamentalism. That had separated them. Her husband, a GP, had died of a heart attack in 1973. 'Place was practically falling down around that woman's ears,' Herb said. 'Least I could do. I go up on Saturdays and she gives me a dinner before I come back home. I have to tell the truth, Johnny, she cooks better than you do.'

'Looks better, too,' Johnny said blandly.

'Sure, she's a fine-looking woman, but it's nothing like *that*, Johnny. Your mother not even in her grave a year . . .'

But Johnny suspected that maybe it *was* something like that, and secretly couldn't have been more pleased. He didn't fancy the idea of his father growing old alone.

On the television, Walter Cronkite was serving up the evening's political news. Now, with the primary season over and the conventions only weeks away, it appeared that Jimmy Carter had the Democratic nomination sewed up. It was Ford who was in a scrap for his political life with Ronald Reagan, the ex-governor of California and ex-host of 'GE Theater'. It was close enough to have the reporters counting individual delegates, and in one of her infrequent letters Sarah Hazlett had written: 'Walt's got his fingers (and toes!) crossed that Ford gets in. As a candidate for state senate up here, he's already thinking about coattails. And he says that, in Maine at least, Reagan hasn't any.'

While he was short-order cooking in Kittery, Johnny had gotten into the habit of going down to Dover or Portsmouth or any number of smaller towns in New Hampshire a couple of times a week. All of the candidates for president were in and out, and it was a unique opportunity to see those who were running closeup and without the nearly regal trappings of authority that might later surround any one of them. It became something of a hobby, although of necessity a short-lived one; when New Hampshire's first-in-the-nation primary was over, the candidates would move on to Florida without a glance back. And of course a few of their number would bury their political ambitions somewhere between Ports-

mouth and Keene. Never a political creature before –
except during the Vietnam era – Johnny became an avid
politician-watcher in the healing aftermath of the Castle
Rock business – and his own particular talent, affliction,
whatever it was, played a part in that, too.

He shook hands with Morris Udall and Henry Jackson. Fred Harris clapped him on the back. Ronald
Reagan gave him a quick and practiced politico's double-pump and said, 'Get out to the polls and help us if you
can.' Johnny had nodded agreeably enough, seeing no
point in disabusing Mr. Reagan of his notion that he was
a bona fide New Hampshire voter.

He had chatted with Sarge Shriver just inside the main
entrance to the monstrous Newington Mall for nearly
fifteen minutes. Shriver, his hair freshly cut and smelling
of after-shave and perhaps desperation, was accompanied
by a single aide with his pockets stuffed full of leaflets,
and a Secret Service man who kept scratching furtively
at his acne. Shriver had seemed inordinately pleased to
be recognized. A minute or two before Johnny said good-bye, a candidate in search of some local office had approached Shriver and asked him to sign his nominating
papers. Shriver had smiled gently.

Johnny had sensed things about all of them, but little
of a specific nature. It was as if they had made the act of
touching such a ritual that their true selves were buried
beneath a layer of tough, clear lucite. Although he saw
most of them – with the exception of President Ford –
Johnny had felt only once that sudden, electrifying snap
of knowledge that he associated with Eileen Magown –
and, in an entirely different way, with Frank Dodd.

It was a quarter of seven in the morning. Johnny had
driven down to Manchester in his old Plymouth. He had
worked from ten the evening before until six this morning. He was tired, but the quiet winter dawn had been
too good to sleep through. And he liked Manchester,
Manchester with its narrow streets and timeworn brick
buildings, the gothic textile mills strung along the river
like mid-Victorian beads. He had not been consciously

politician-hunting that morning; he thought he would cruise the streets for a while, until they began to get crowded, until the cold and silent spell of February was broken, then go back to Kittery and catch some sacktime.

He turned a corner and there had been three non-descript sedans pulled up in front of a shoe factory in a no-parking zone. Standing by the gate in the cyclone fencing was Jimmy Carter, shaking hands with the men and women going on shift. They were carrying lunch buckets or paper sacks, breathing out white clouds, bundled into heavy coats, their faces still asleep. Carter had a word for each of them. His grin, then not so publicized as it became later, was tireless and fresh. His nose was red with the cold.

Johnny parked half a block down and walked toward the factory gate, his shoes crunching and squeaking on the packed snow. The Secret Service agent with Carter sized him up quickly and then dismissed him – or seemed to.

'I'll vote for anyone who's interested in cutting taxes,' a man in an old ski parka was saying. The parka had a constellation of what looked like battery-acid burns in one sleeve. 'The goddam taxes are killing me, I kid you not.'

'Well, we're gonna see about that,' Carter said. 'Lookin over the tax situation is gonna be one of our first priorities when I get into the White House.' There was a serene self-confidence in his voice that struck Johnny and made him a little uneasy.

Carter's eyes, bright and almost amazingly blue, shifted to Johnny. 'Hi there,' he said.

'Hello, Mr. Carter,' Johnny said. 'I don't work here. I was driving by and saw you.'

'Well I'm glad you stopped. I'm running for President.'

'I know.'

Carter put his hand out. Johnny shook it.

Carter began: 'I hope you'll . . .' And broke off.

The flash came, a sudden, powerful zap that was like sticking his finger in an electric socket. Carter's eyes sharpened. He and Johnny looked at each other for what seemed a very long time.

The Secret Service guy didn't like it. He moved toward Carter, and suddenly he was unbuttoning his coat. Somewhere behind them, a million miles behind them, the shoe factory's seven o'clock whistle blew its single note into the crisp blue morning.

Johnny let go of Carter's hand, but still the two of them looked at each other.

'What the *hell* was that?' Carter asked, very softly.

'You've probably got someplace to go, don't you?' the Secret Service guy said suddenly. He put a hand on Johnny's shoulder. It was a very big hand. 'Sure you do.'

'It's all right,' Carter said.

'You're going to be president,' Johnny said.

The agent's hand was still on Johnny's shoulder, more lightly now but still there, and he was getting something from him, too. The Secret Service guy

(*eyes*)

didn't like his eyes. He thought they were

(*assassin's eyes, psycho's eyes*)

cold and strange, and if this guy put so much as one hand in his coat pocket, if he even looked as if he might be going in that direction, he was going to put him on the sidewalk. Behind the Secret Service guy's second-to-second evaluation of the situation there ran a simple, maddening litany of thought:

(*laurel maryland laurel maryland laurel maryland laurel*)

'Yes,' Carter said.

'It's going to be closer than anyone thinks ... closer than *you* think, but you'll win. He'll beat himself. Poland. Poland will beat him.'

Carter only looked at him, half-smiling.

'You've got a daughter. She's going to go to a public school in Washington. She's going to go to ...' But it was in the dead zone. 'I think ... it's a school named after a freed slave.'

'Fellow, I want you to move on,' the agent said.

329

Carter looked at him and the agent subsided.

'It's been a pleasure meeting you,' Carter said. 'A little disconcerting, but a pleasure.'

Suddenly, Johnny was himself again. It had passed. He was aware that his ears were cold and that he had to go to the bathroom. 'Have a good morning,' he said lamely.

'Yes. You too, now.'

He had gone back to his car, aware of the Secret Service guy's eyes still on him. He drove away, bemused. Shortly after, Carter had put away the competition in New Hampshire and went on to Florida.

2 ·

Walter Cronkite finished with the politicians and went on to the civil war in Lebanon. Johnny got up and freshened his glass of Pepsi. He tipped the glass at the TV. *Your good health, Walt. To the three Ds – death, destruction, and destiny. Where would we be without them?*

There was a light tap at the door. 'Come in,' Johnny called, expecting Chuck, probably with an invitation to the drive-in over in Somersworth. But it wasn't Chuck. It was Chuck's father.

'Hi, Johnny,' he said. He was wearing wash-faded jeans and an old cotton sports shirt, the tails out. 'May I come in?'

'Sure. I thought you weren't due back until late.'

'Well, Shelley gave me a call.' Shelley was his wife. Roger came in and shut the door. 'Chuck came to see her. Burst into tears, just like a little kid. He told her you were doing it, Johnny. He said he thought he was going to be all right.'

Johnny put his glass down. 'We've got a ways to go,' he said.

'Chuck met me at the airport. I haven't seen him looking like he did since he was ... what? Ten? Eleven? When I gave him the .22 he'd been waiting for for five years. He read me a story out of the newspaper. The improvement is ... almost eerie. I came over to thank you.'

'Thank Chuck,' Johnny said. 'He's an adaptable boy.

A lot of what's happening to him is positive reinforcement. He's psyched himself into believing he can do it and now he's tripping on it. That's the best way I can put it.'

Roger sat down. 'He says you're teaching him to switch-hit.'

Johnny smiled. 'Yeah, I guess so.'

'Is he going to be able to take the SATs?'

'I don't know. And I'd hate to see him gamble and lose. The SATs are a heavy pressure situation. If he gets in that lecture hall with an answer sheet in front of him and an IBM pencil in his hand and then freezes up, it's going to be a real setback for him. Have you thought about a good prep school for a year? A place like Pittsfield Academy?'

'We've kicked the idea around, but frankly I always thought of it as just postponing the inevitable.'

'That's one of the things that's been giving Chuck trouble. This feeling that he's in a make-or-break situation.'

'I've never pressured Chuck.'

'Not on purpose, I know that. So does he. On the other hand, you're a rich, successful man who graduated from college *summa cum laude*. I think Chuck feels a little bit like he's batting after Hank Aaron.'

'There's nothing I can do about that, Johnny.'

'I think a year at a prep school, away from home, after his senior year might put things in perspective for him. And he wants to go to work in one of your mills next summer. If he were my kid and if they were my mills, I'd let him.'

'Chuck wants to do that? How come he never told me?'

'Because he didn't want you to think he was ass-kissing,' Johnny said.

'He told you that?'

'Yes. He wants to do it because he thinks the practical experience will be helpful to him later on. The kid wants to follow in your footsteps, Mr. Chatsworth. You've left some big ones behind you. That's what a lot of the read-

331

ing block has been about. He's having buck fever.'

In a sense, he had lied. Chuck had hinted around these things, and even mentioned some of them obliquely, but he had not been as frank as Johnny had led Roger Chatsworth to believe. Not verbally, at least. But Johnny had touched him from time to time, and he had gotten signals that way. He had looked through the pictures Chuck kept in his wallet and knew how Chuck felt about his dad. There were things he could never tell this pleasant but rather distant man sitting across from him. Chuck idolized the ground his father walked on. Beneath his easy-come easy-go exterior (an exterior that was very similar to Roger's), the boy was eaten up by the secret conviction that he could never measure up. His father had built a ten percent interest in a failing woolen mill into a New England textile empire. He believed that the issue of his father's love hung on his own ability to move similar mountains. To play sports. To get into a good college. To *read*.

'How sure are you about all of this?' Roger asked.

'I'm pretty sure. But I'd appreciate it if you never mentioned to Chuck that we talked this way. They're his secrets I'm telling.' *And that's truer than you'll ever know.*

'All right. And Chuck and his mother and I will talk over the prep school idea. In the meantime, this is yours.' He took out a plain white business envelope from his back pocket and passed it to Johnny.

'What is it?'

'Open it and see.'

Johnny opened it. Inside the envelope was a cashier's check for five hundred dollars.

'Oh, hey . . . ! I can't take this.'

'You can, and you will. I promised you a bonus if you could perform, and I keep my promises. There'll be another when you leave.'

'Really, Mr. Chatsworth, I just . . .'

'Shh. I'll tell you something, Johnny.' He leaned forward. He was smiling a peculiar little smile, and Johnny

332

suddenly felt he could see beneath the pleasant exterior to the man who had made all of this happen – the house, the grounds, the pool, the mills. And, of course, his son's reading phobia, which could probably be classified a hysterical neurosis.

'It's been my experience that ninety-five percent of the people who walk the earth are simply inert, Johnny. One percent are saints, and one percent are assholes. The other three percent are the people who do what they say they can do. I'm in that three percent, and so are you. You earned that money. I've got people in the mills that take home eleven thousand dollars a year for doing little more than playing with their dicks. But I'm not bitching. I'm a man of the world, and all that means is I understand what powers the world. The fuel mix is one part high-octane to nine parts pure bull-shit. You're no bull-shitter. So you put that money in your wallet and next time try to value yourself a little higher.'

'All right,' Johnny said. 'I can put it to good use, I won't lie to you about that.'

'Doctor bills?'

Johnny looked up at Roger Chatsworth, his eyes narrowed.

'I know all about you,' Roger said. 'Did you think I wouldn't check back on the guy I hired to tutor my son?'

'You know about...'

'You're supposed to be a psychic of some kind. You helped to solve a murder case in Maine. At least, that's what the papers say. You had a teaching job lined up for last January, but they dropped you like a hot potato when your name got in the papers.'

'You *knew*? For how long?'

'I knew before you moved in.'

'And you still hired me?'

'I wanted a tutor, didn't I? You looked like you might be able to pull it off. I think I showed excellent judgment in engaging your services.'

'Well, thanks,' Johnny said. His voice was hoarse.

'I told you you didn't have to say that.'

333

As they talked, Walter Cronkite had finished up with the real news of the day and had gone on to the man-bites-dog stories that sometimes turn up near the end of a newscast. He was saying, '... voters in western New Hampshire have an independent running in the third district this year ...'

'Well, the cash will come in handy,' Johnny said. 'That's ...'

'Shh. I want to hear this.'

Chatsworth was leaning forward, hands dangling between his knees, a pleasant smile of expectation on his face. Johnny turned to look at the TV.

'... Stillson,' Cronkite said. 'This forty-three-year-old insurance and real estate agent is surely running one of the most eccentric races of Campaign '76, but both the third-district Republican candidate, Harrison Fisher, and his Democratic opponent, David Bowes, are running scared, because the polls have Greg Stillson running comfortably ahead. George Herman has the story.'

'Who's Stillson?' Johnny asked.

Chatsworth laughed. 'Oh, you gotta see this guy, Johnny. He's as crazy as a rat in a drainpipe. But I do believe the sober-sided electorate of the third district is going to send him to Washington this November. Unless he actually falls down and starts frothing at the mouth. And I wouldn't completely rule that out.'

Now the TV showed a picture of a handsome young man in a white open-throated shirt. He was speaking to a small crowd from a bunting-hung platform in a super-market parking lot. The young man was exhorting the crowd. The crowd looked less than thrilled. George Herman voiced over: 'This is David Bowes, the Democratic candidate – sacrificial offering, some would say – for the third-district seat in New Hampshire. Bowes expected an uphill fight because New Hampshire's third district has *never* gone Democratic, not even in the great LBJ blitz of 1964. But he expected his competition to come from this man.'

Now the TV showed a man of about sixty-five. He was

334

speaking to a plushy fund-raising dinner. The crowd had that plump, righteous, and slightly constipated look that seems the exclusive province of businessmen who belong to the GOP. The speaker bore a remarkable resemblance to Edward Gurney of Florida, although he did not have Gurney's slim, tough build.

'This is Harrison Fisher,' Herman said. 'The voters of the third district have been sending him to Washington every two years since 1960. He is a powerful figure in the house, sitting on five committees and chairing the House Committee on Parks and Waterways. It had been expected that he would beat young David Bowes handily. But neither Fisher nor Bowes counted on a wild card in the deck. This wild card.'

The picture switched.

'Holy God!' Johnny said.

Beside him, Chatsworth roared laughter and slapped his thighs. 'Can you *believe* that guy?'

No lackadaisical supermarket parking-lot crowd here. No comfy fund raiser in the Granite State Room of the Portsmouth Hilton, either. Greg Stillson was standing on a platform outside in Ridgeway, his home town. Behind him there loomed the statue of a Union soldier with his rifle in his hand and his kepi tilted down over his eyes. The street was blocked off and crowded with wildly cheering people, predominantly young people. Stillson was wearing faded jeans and a two-pocket Army fatigue shirt with the words GIVE PEACE A CHANCE embroidered on one pocket and MOM'S APPLE PIE on the other. There was a hi-impact construction worker's helmet cocked at an arrogant, rakish angle on his head, and plastered to the front of it was a green American flag ecology sticker. Beside him was a stainless steel cart of some kind. From the twin loudspeakers came the sound of John Denver singing 'Thank God I'm a Country Boy.'

'What's that cart?' Johnny asked.

'You'll see,' Roger said, still grinning hugely.

Herman said: 'The wild card is Gregory Ammas Stillson, forty-three, ex-salesman for the TruthWay Bible Company of America, ex-housepainter, and, in Oklahoma, where he grew up, one-time rainmaker.'

'Rainmaker,' said Johnny, bemused.

'Oh, that's one of his planks,' Roger said. 'If he's elected, we'll have rain whenever we need it.'

George Herman went on: 'Stillson's platform is ... well, refreshing.'

John Denver finished singing with a yell that brought answering cheers from the crowd. Then Stillson started talking, his voice booming at peak amplification. His PA system at least was sophisticated; there was hardly any distortion. His voice made Johnny vaguely uneasy. The man had the high, hard, pumping delivery of a revival preacher. You could see a fine spray of spittle from his lips as he talked.

'What are we gonna do in Washington? Why do we want to go to Washington?' Stillson roared. 'What's our platform? Our platform got five boards, my friends n neighbors, five old boards! And what are they? I'll tell you up front! First board: *THROW THE BUMS OUT!*'

A tremendous roar of approval ripped out of the crowd. Someone threw double handfuls of confetti into the air and someone else yelled, '*Yaaaah-HOO!*' Stillson leaned over his podium.

'You wanna know why I'm wearing this helmet, friends n neighbors? I'll tell you why. I'm wearin it because when you send me up to Washington, I'm gonna go through them like *you-know-what* through a canebrake! Gonna go through em *just like this!*'

And before Johnny's wondering eyes, Stillson put his head down and began to charge up and down the podium stage like a bull, uttering a high, yipping Rebel yell as he did so. Roger Chatsworth simply dissolved in his chair, laughing helplessly. The crowd went wild. Stillson charged back to the podium, took off his construction helmet, and spun it into the crowd. A minor riot over possession of it immediately ensued.

'Second board!' Stillson yelled into the mike. 'We're gonna throw out anyone in the government, from the highest to the lowest, who is spending time in bed with some gal who ain't his wife! If they wanna sleep around, they ain't gonna do it on the public tit!'

'What did he say?' Johnny asked, blinking.

'Oh, he's just getting warmed up,' Roger said. He wiped his streaming eyes and went off into another gale of laughter. Johnny wished it seemed that funny to him.

'Third board!' Stillson roared. 'We're gonna send all the pollution right into outer space! Gonna put it in Hefty bags! Gonna put it in Glad bags! Gonna send it to Mars, to Jupiter, and the rings of Saturn! We're gonna have clean air and we're gonna have clean water and we're gonna have it in *SIX MONTHS!*'

The crowd was in paroxysms of joy. Johnny saw many people in the crowd who were almost killing themselves laughing, as Roger Chatsworth was presently doing.

'Fourth board! We're gonna have all the gas and oil we need! We're gonna stop playing games with these Arabs and get down to brass tacks! Ain't gonna be no old people in New Hampshire turned into Popsicles this coming winter like there was last winter!'

This brought a solid roar of approval. The winter before an old woman in Portsmouth had been found frozen to death in her third-floor apartment, apparently following a turn-off by the gas company for nonpayment.

'We got the muscle, friends n neighbors, we can do it! Anybody out there think we can't do it?'

'*NO!*' The crowd bellowed back.

'Last board,' Stillson said, and approached the metal cart. He threw back the hinged lid and a cloud of steam puffed out. '*HOT DOGS!!*'

He began to grab double handfuls of hot dogs from the cart, which Johnny now recognized as a portable steam table. He threw them into the crowd and went back for more. Hot dogs flew everywhere. 'Hot dogs for every man, woman, and child in America! And when you put

337

Greg Stillson in the House of Representatives, you gonna say *HOT DOG! SOMEONE GIVES A RIP AT LAST!'*

The picture changed. The podium was being dismantled by a crew of long-haired young men who looked like rock band roadies. Three more of them were cleaning up the litter the crowd had left behind. George Herman resumed: 'Democratic candidate David Bowes calls Stillson a practical joker who is trying to throw a monkeywrench into the workings of the democratic process. Harrison Fisher is stronger in his criticism. He calls Stillson a cynical carnival pitchman who is playing the whole idea of the free election as a burlesque-house joke. In speeches, he refers to independent candidate Stillson as the only member of the American Hot Dog party. But the fact is this: the latest CBS poll in New Hampshire's third district showed David Bowes with twenty percent of the vote, Harrison Fisher with twenty-six — and maverick Greg Stillson with a whopping forty-two percent. Of course election day is still quite a way down the road, and things may change. But for now, Greg Stillson has captured the hearts — if not the minds — of New Hampshire's third-district voters.'

The TV showed a shot of Herman from the waist up. Both hands had been out of sight. Now he raised one of them, and in it was a hot dog. He took a big bite.

'This is George Herman, CBS News, in Ridgeway, New Hampshire.'

Walter Cronkite came back on in the CBS newsroom, chuckling. 'Hot dogs,' he said, and chuckled again. 'And that's the way it is . . .'

Johnny got up and snapped off the set. 'I just can't believe that,' he said. 'That guy's really a candidate? It's not a joke?'

'Whether it's a joke or not is a matter of personal interpretation,' Roger said, grinning, 'but he really is running. I'm a Republican myself, born and bred, but I must admit I get a kick out of that guy Stillson. You know he hired half a dozen ex-motorcycle outlaws as bodyguards?

Real iron horsemen. Not Hell's Angels or anything like that, but I guess they were pretty rough customers. He seems to have reformed them.'

Motorcycle freaks as security. Johnny didn't like the sound of that very much. The motorcycle freaks had been in charge of security when the Rolling Stones gave their free concert at Altamont Speedway in California. It hadn't worked out so well.

'People put up with a . . . a motorcycle goon squad?'

'No, it really isn't like that. They're quite clean-cut. And Stillson has a helluva reputation around Ridgeway for reforming kids in trouble.'

Johnny grunted doubtfully.

'You saw him,' Roger said, gesturing at the TV set. 'The man is a clown. He goes charging around the speaking platform, like that at every rally. Throws his helmet into the crowd – I'd guess he's gone through a hundred of them by now – and gives out hot dogs. He's a clown, so what? Maybe people need a little comic relief from time to time. We're running out of oil, the inflation is slowly but surely getting out of control, the average guy's tax load has never been heavier, and we're apparently getting ready to elect a fuzzy-minded Georgia cracker president of the United States. So people want a giggle or two. Even more, they want to thumb their noses at a political establishment that doesn't seem able to solve anything. Stillson's harmless.'

'He's in orbit,' Johnny said, and they both laughed.

'We have plenty of crazy politicians around,' Roger said. 'In New Hampshire we've got Stillson, who wants to hot dog his way into the House of Representatives, so what? Out in California they've got Hayakawa. Or take our own governor, Meldrim Thomson. Last year he wanted to arm the New Hampshire National Guard with tactical nuclear weapons. I'd call that big-time crazy.'

'Are you saying it's okay for those people in the third district to elect the village fool to represent them in Washington?'

'You don't get it,' Chatsworth said patiently. 'Take a voter's-eye-view, Johnny. Those third-district people are mostly all blue-collars and shopkeepers. The most rural parts of the district are just starting to develop some recreational potential. Those people look at David Bowes and they see a hungry young kid who's trying to get elected on the basis of some slick talk and a passing resemblance to Dustin Hoffman. They're supposed to think he's a man of the people because he wears blue jeans.

'Then take Fisher. My man, at least nominally. I've organized fund raisers for him and the other Republican candidates around this part of New Hampshire. He's been on the Hill so long he probably thinks the Capitol dome would split in two pieces if he wasn't around to give it moral support. He's never had an original thought in his life, he never went against the party line in his life. There's no stigma attached to his name because he's too stupid to be very crooked, although he'll probably wind up with some mud on him from this Koreagate thing. His speeches have all the excitement of the copy of the National Plumbers Wholesale Catalogue. People don't *know* all those things, but they can sense them sometimes. The idea that Harrison Fisher is doing anything for his constituency is just plain ridiculous.'

'So the answer is to elect a loony?'

Chatsworth smiled indulgently. 'Sometimes these loonies turn out doing a pretty good job. Look at Bella Abzug. There's a damn fine set of brains under those crazy hats. But even if Stillson turns out to be as crazy in Washington as he is down in Ridgeway, he's only renting the seat for two years. They'll turn him out in '78 and put in someone who understands the lesson.'

'The lesson?'

Roger stood up. 'Don't fuck the people over for too long,' he said. 'That's the lesson. Adam Clayton Powell found out. Agnew and Nixon did, too. Just . . . don't fuck the people for too long.' He glanced at his watch. 'Come on over to the big house and have a drink, Johnny.

340

Shelley and I are going out later on, but we've got time for a short one.'

Johnny smiled and got up. 'Okay,' he said. 'You twisted my arm.'

CHAPTER TWENTY

1 ·

In mid-August, Johnny found himself alone at the Chatsworth estate except for Ngo Phat, who had his own quarters over the garage. The Chatsworth family had closed up the house and had gone to Montreal for three weeks of r & r before the new school year and the fall rush at the mills began.

Roger had left Johnny the keys to his wife's Mercedes and he motored up to his dad's house in Pownal, feeling like a potentate. His father's negotiations with Charlene MacKenzie had entered the critical stage, and Herb was no longer bothering to protest that his interest in her was only to make sure that the house didn't fall down on top of her. In fact, he was in full courting plumage and made Johnny a little nervous. After three days of it Johnny went back to the Chatsworth house, caught up on his reading and his correspondence, and soaked up the quiet.

He was sitting on a rubber chair-float in the middle of the pool, drinking a Seven-Up and reading the *New York Times Book Review*, when Ngo came over to the pool's apron, took off his zori, and dipped his feet into the water.

'Ahhhh,' he said. 'Much better.' He smiled at Johnny. 'Quiet, huh?'

'Very quiet,' Johnny agreed. 'How goes the citizenship class, Ngo?'

'Very nice going,' Ngo said. 'We are having a field trip on Saturday. First one. Very exciting. The whole class will be tripping.'

'Going,' Johnny said, smiling at an image of Ngo

Phat's whole citizenship class freaking on LSD or psilo-cybin.

'Pardon?' He raised his eyebrows politely.

'Your whole class will be going.'

'Yes, thanks. We are going to the political speech and rally in Trimbull. We are all thinking how lucky it is to be taking the citizenship class in an election year. It is most instructive.'

'Yes, I'll bet it is. Who are you going to see?'

'Greg Stirrs ...' He stopped and pronounced it again, very carefully. 'Greg Stillson, who is running independ-ently for a seat in the U.S. House of Representatives.'

'I've heard of him,' Johnny said. 'Have you discussed him in class at all, Ngo?'

'Yes, we have had some conversation of this man. Born in 1933. A man of many jobs. He came to New Hamp-shire in 1964. Our instructor has told us that now he is here long enough so people do not see him as a carpet-fogger.'

'Bagger,' Johnny said.

Ngo looked at him with blank politeness.

'The term is carpetbagger.'

'Yes, thanks.'

'Do you find Stillson a bit odd?'

'In America perhaps he is odd,' Ngo said. 'In Vietnam there were many like him. People who are ...' He sat thinking, swishing his small and delicate feet in the blue-green water of the pool. Then he looked up at Johnny again.

'I do not have the English for what I wish to say. There is a game the people of my land play, it is called the Laughing Tiger. It is old and much loved, like your base-ball. One child is dressing up as the tiger, you see. He puts on a skin. And the other children tries to catch him as he runs and dances. The child in the skin laughs, but he is also growling and biting, because that is the game. In my country, before the Communists, many of the vil-lage leaders played the Laughing Tiger. I think this Still-son knows that game, too.'

Johnny looked over at Ngo, disturbed.

Ngo did not seem disturbed at all. He smiled. 'So we will all go and see for ourselves. After, we are having the picnic foods. I myself am making two pies. I think it will be nice.'

'It sounds great.'

'It will be very great,' Ngo said, getting up. 'Afterward, in class, we will talk over all we saw in Trimbull. Maybe we will be writing the compositions. It is much easier to write the compositions, because one can look up the exact word. *Le mot juste.*'

'Yes, sometimes writing can be easier. But I never had a high school comp class that would believe it.'

Ngo smiled. 'How does it go with Chuck?'

'He's doing quite well.'

'Yes, he is happy now. Not just pretending. He is a good boy.' He stood up. 'Take a rest, Johnny. I'm going to take a nap.'

'All right.'

He watched Ngo walk away, small, slim, and lithe in blue jeans and a faded chambray work shirt.

The child in the skin laughs, but he is also growling and biting, because that is the game ... I think this Stillson knows that game, too.

That thread of disquiet again.

The pool chair bobbed gently up and down. The sun beat pleasantly on him. He opened his *Book Review* again, but the article he had been reading no longer engaged him. He put it down and paddled the little rubber float to the edge of the pool and got out. Trimbull was less than thirty miles away. Maybe he would just hop into Mrs. Chatsworth's Mercedes and drive down this Saturday. See Greg Stillson in person. Enjoy the show. Maybe ... maybe shake his hand.

No. No!

But why not? After all, he had more or less made politicians his hobby this election year. What could possibly be so upsetting about going to see one more?

But he *was* upset, no question about that. His heart

343

was knocking harder and more rapidly than it should have been, and he managed to drop his magazine into the pool. He fished it out with a curse before it was saturated.

Somehow, thinking about Greg Stillson made him think about Frank Dodd.

Utterly ridiculous. He couldn't have any feeling at all about Stillson one way or the other from having just seen him on TV.

Stay away.

Well, maybe he would and maybe he wouldn't. Maybe he would go down to Boston this Saturday instead. See a film.

But a strange, heavy feeling of fright had settled on him by the time he got back to the guest house and changed his clothes. In a way the feeling was like an old friend – the sort of old friend you secretly hate. Yes, he would go down to Boston on Saturday. That would be better.

Although he relived that day over and over in the months afterward, Johnny could never remember exactly how or why it was that he ended up in Trimbull after all. He had set out in another direction, planning to go down to Boston and take in the Red Sox at Fenway Park, then maybe go over to Cambridge and nose through the bookshops. If there was enough cash left over (he had sent four hundred dollars of Chatsworth's bonus to his father, who in turn sent it on to Eastern Maine Medical – a gesture tantamount to a spit in the ocean) he planned to go to the Orson Welles Cinema and see that reggae movie, *The Harder They Come.* A good day's program, and a fine day to implement it; that August 19 had dawned hot and clear and sweet, the distillation of the perfect New England summer's day.

He had let himself into the kitchen of the big house and made three hefty ham-and-cheese sandwiches for lunch, put them in an old-fashioned wicker picnic basket he found in the pantry, and after a little soul-searching, had topped off his haul with a sixpack of Tuborg Beer. At that point he had been feeling fine, absolutely first-rate. No thought of either Greg Stillson or his homemade bodyguard corps of iron horsemen had so much as crossed his mind.

He put the picnic basket on the floor of the Mercedes and drove southeast toward I-95. All clear enough up to that point. But then other things had begun to creep in. Thoughts of his mother on her deathbed first. His mother's face, twisted into a frozen snarl, the hand on the counterpane hooked into a claw, her voice sounding as if it were coming through a big mouthful of cotton wadding.

Didn't I tell you? Didn't I say it was so?

Johnny turned the radio up louder. Good rock 'n' roll poured out of the Mercedes's stereo speakers. He had been asleep for four-and-a-half years but rock 'n' roll had remained alive and well, thank you very much. Johnny sang along.

He has a job for you. Don't run from him, Johnny.

The radio couldn't drown out his dead mother's voice. His dead mother was going to have her say. Even from beyond the grave she was going to have her say.

Don't hide away in a cave or make him have to send a big fish to swallow you.

But he had been swallowed by a big fish. Its name was not leviathan but coma. He had spent four-and-a-half years in that particular fish's black belly, and that was enough.

The entrance ramp to the turnpike came up – and then slipped behind him. He had been so lost in his thoughts that he had missed his turn. The old ghosts just wouldn't give up and let him alone. Well, he would turn around and go back as soon as he found a good place.

Not the potter but the potter's clay, Johnny.

'Oh, come on,' he muttered. He had to get this crap off his mind, that was all. His mother had been a religious crazy, not a very kind way of putting it, but true all the same. Heaven out in the constellation Orion, angels driving flying saucers, kingdoms under the earth. In her way she had been at least as crazy as Greg Stillson was in his.

345

Oh for Christ's sake, don't get off on that guy.

'And when you send Greg Stillson to the House of Representatives, you gonna say HOT DOG! SOMEONE GIVES A RIP AT LAST!'

He came to New Hampshire Route 63. A left turn would take him to Concord, Berlin, Ridder's Mill, Trimbull. Johnny made the turn without even thinking about it. His thoughts were elsewhere.

Roger Chatsworth, no babe in the woods, had laughed over Greg Stillson as if he were this year's answer to George Carlin and Chevy Chase all rolled up into one. *He's a clown, Johnny.*

And if that was *all* Stillson was, then there was no problem, was there? A charming eccentric, a piece of blank paper on which the electorate could write its message: *You other guys are so wasted that we decided to elect this fool for two years instead.* That was probably all Stillson was, after all. Just a harmless crazy, there was no need at all to associate him with the patterned, destructive madness of Frank Dodd. And yet . . . somehow . . . he did.

The road branched ahead. Left branch to Berlin and Ridder's Mill, right branch to Trimbull and Concord. Johnny turned right.

But it wouldn't hurt to just shake his hand, would it?

Maybe not. One more politician for his collection. Some people collected stamps, some coins, but Johnny Smith collects handshakes and —

— and admit it. You've been looking for a wild card in the deck all along.

The thought shook him so badly that he almost pulled over to the side of the road. He caught a glimpse of himself in the rear-view mirror and it wasn't the contented, everything-is-resting-easy face he had gotten up with that morning. Now it was the press conference face, and the face of the man who had crawled through the snow of the Castle Rock town common on his hands and knees. The skin was too white, the eyes circled with bruised-looking brown rings, the lines etched too deep.

346

No. It isn't true.

But it was. Now that it was out, it couldn't be denied. In the first twenty-three years of his life he had shaken hands with exactly one politician; that was when Ed Muskie had come to talk to his high school government class in 1966. In the last seven months he had shaken hands with over a dozen big names. And hadn't the thought flashed across the back of his mind as each one stuck out his hand – *What's this guy all about? What's he going to tell me?*

Hadn't he been looking, all along, for the political equivalent of Frank Dodd?

Yes. It was true.

But the fact was, none of them except Carter had told him much of anything, and the feelings that he had gotten from Carter were not particularly alarming. Shaking hands with Carter had not given him that sinking feeling he had gotten just from watching Greg Stillson on TV. He felt as if Stillson might have taken the game of the Laughing Tiger a step further: inside the beast-skin, a man, yes.

But inside the man-skin, a beast.

2 ·

Whatever the progression had been, Johnny found himself eating his picnic lunch in the Trimbull town park instead of the Fenway bleachers. He had arrived shortly after noon and had seen a sign on the community notice board announcing the rally at three P.M.

He drifted over to the park, expecting to have the place pretty much to himself so long before the rally was scheduled to begin, but others were already spreading blankets, unlimbering Frisbees, or settling down to their own lunches.

Up front, a number of men were at work on the bandstand. Two of them were decorating the waist-high railings with bunting. Another was on a ladder, hanging colorful crepe streamers from the bandstand's circular eave. Others were setting up the sound system, and as

347

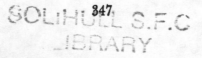
SOLIHULL S.F.C
LIBRARY

Johnny had guessed when he watched the CBS newsclip, it was no four-hundred-dollar podium PA set. The speakers were Altec-Lansings, and they were being carefully placed to give surround-sound.

The advance men (but the image that persisted was that of roadies setting up for an Eagles or Geils band concert) went about their work with businesslike precision. The whole thing had a practiced, professional quality to it that jarred with Stillson's image of the amiable Wild Man of Borneo.

The crowd mostly spanned about twenty years, from midteens to mid-thirties. They were having a good time. Babies toddled around clutching melting Dairy Queens and Slush Puppies. Women chatted together and laughed. Men drank beer from styrofoam cups. A few dogs bounced around, grabbing what there was to be grabbed, and the sun shone benignly down on everyone.

'Test,' one of the men on the bandstand said laconically into the two mikes. 'Test-one, test-two . . .' One of the speakers in the park uttered a loud feedback whine, and the guy on the podium motioned that he wanted it moved backward.

This isn't the way you set up for a political speech and rally, Johnny thought. *They're setting up for a love-feast . . . or a group grope.*

'Test-one, test-two . . . test, test, test.'

They were *strapping* the big speakers to the trees, Johnny saw. Not *nailing* them but *strapping* them. Stillson was an ecology booster, and someone had told his advance men not to hurt so much as one tree in one town park. The operation gave him the feeling of having been honed down to the smallest detail. This was no grab-it-and-run-with-it deal.

Two yellow school buses pulled into the turnaround left of the small (and already full) parking lot. The doors folded open and men and women got out, talking animatedly to one another. They were in sharp contrast to those already in the park because they were dressed in their best – men in suits or sports coats, ladies in crisp skirt-and-blouse combinations or smart dresses. They were gazing around with expressions of nearly childlike wonder and anticipation, and Johnny grinned. Ngo's citizenship class had arrived.

He walked over to them. Ngo was standing with a tall man in a corduroy suit and two women, both Chinese.

'Hi, Ngo,' Johnny said.

Ngo grinned broadly. 'Johnny!' he said. 'Good to see you, man! It is being a great day for the state of New Hampshire, right?'

'I guess so,' Johnny said.

Ngo introduced his companions. The man in the corduroy suit was Polish. The two women were sisters from Taiwan. One of the women told Johnny that she was much hoping for shaking hands with the candidate after the program and then, shyly, she showed Johnny the autograph book in her handbag.

'I am so glad to be here in America,' she said. 'But it is strange, is it not, Mr. Smith?'

Johnny, who thought the whole thing was strange, agreed.

The citizenship class's two instructors were calling the group together. 'I'll see you later, Johnny,' Ngo said. 'I've got to be tripping.'

'Going,' Johnny said.

'Yes, thanks.'

'Have a fine time, Ngo.'

'Oh, yes, I am sure I will.' And Ngo's eyes seemed to glint with a secret amusement. 'I am sure it will be most entertaining, Johnny.'

The group, about forty in all, went over to the south side of the park to have their picnic lunch. Johnny went back to his own place and made himself eat one of his sandwiches. It tasted like a combination of paper and library paste.

A thick feeling of tension had begun to creep into his body.

349

By two-thirty the park was completely full; people were jammed together nearly shoulder to shoulder. The town police, augmented by a small contingent of State Police, had closed off the streets leading to the Trimbull town park. The resemblance to a rock concert was stronger than ever. Bluegrass music poured from the speakers, cheery and fast. Fat white clouds drifted across the innocent blue sky.

Suddenly, people started getting to their feet and craning their necks. It was a ripple effect passing through the crowd. Johnny got up too, wondering if Stillson was going to be early. Now he could hear the steady roar of motorcycle engines, the beat swelling to fill the summer afternoon as they grew closer. Johnny got an eyeful of sun-arrows reflecting off chrome, and a few moments later about ten cycles swung into the turnaround where the citizenship buses were parked. There was no car with them. Johnny guessed they were an advance guard.

His feeling of disquiet deepened. The riders were neat enough, dressed for the most part in clean, faded jeans and white shirts, but the bikes themselves, mostly Harleys and BSAs, had been customized almost beyond recognition: ape-hanger handlebars, raked chromium manifolds, and strange fairings abounded.

Their owners killed the engines, swung off, and moved away toward the bandstand in single file. Only one of them looked back. His eyes moved without haste over the big crowd; even from some distance away Johnny could see that the man's irises were a brilliant bottle green. He seemed to be counting the house. He glanced left, at four or five town cops leaning against the chain-link backstop of the Little League ballfield. He waved. One of the cops leaned over and spit. The act had a feeling of ceremony to it, and Johnny's disquiet deepened further. The man with the green eyes sauntered to the bandstand.

Above the disquiet, which now lay like an emotional floor to his other feelings, Johnny felt predominantly a wild mix of horror and hilarity. He had a dreamlike sense of having somehow entered one of those paintings where steam engines are coming out of brick fireplaces or clockfaces are lying limply over tree limbs. The cyclists looked like extras in an American-International bike movie who had all decided to Get Clean For Gene. Their fresh, faded jeans were snugged down over square-toed engineer boots, and on more than one pair Johnny could see chromed chains strapped down over the insteps. The chrome twinkled savagely in the sun. Their expressions were nearly all the same: a sort of vacuous good humor that seemed directed at the crowd. But beneath it there might have been simple contempt for the young mill workers, the summer students who had come over from UNH in Durham, and the factory workers who were standing to give them a round of applause. Each of them wore a pair of political buttons. One of them showed a construction worker's yellow hard hat with a green ecology sticker on the front. The other bore the motto STILL-SON'S GOT 'EM IN A FULL-NELSON.

And sticking out of every right hip pocket was a sawed-off pool cue.

Johnny turned to the man next to him, who was with his wife and small child. 'Are those things legal?' he asked.

'Who the hell cares,' the young guy responded, laughing. 'They're just for show, anyway.' He was still applauding. '*Go-get-em-Greg!*' he yelled.

The motorcycle honor guard deployed themselves around the bandstand in a circle and stood at parade rest.

The applause tapered off, but conversation went on at a louder level. The crowd's mass mouth had received the meal's appetizer and had found it good.

Brownshirts, Johnny thought, sitting down. *Brownshirts is all they are.*

Well, so what? Maybe that was even good. Americans had a rather low tolerance for the fascist approach – even rock-ribbed righties like Reagan didn't go for that stuff; nothing but a pure fact no matter how many tantrums the New Left might want to throw or how many songs Joan Baez wrote. Eight years before, the fascist tactics of the Chicago police had helped lose the election for Hubert Humphrey. Johnny didn't care how clean-cut these fellows were; if they were in the employ of a man running for the House of Representatives, then Stillson couldn't be more than a few paces from overstepping himself. *If it wasn't quite so weird, it really would be funny.*

All the same, he wished he hadn't come.

4 ·

Just before three o'clock, the thud of a big bass drum impressed itself on the air, felt through the feet before actually heard by the ears. Other instruments gradually began to surround it, and all of them resolved into a marching band playing a Sousa tune. Small-town election hoopla, all of a summer's day.

The crowd came to its feet again and craned in the direction of the music. Soon the band came in sight – first a baton-twirler in a short skirt, high-stepping in white kidskin boots with pompons on them, then two majorettes, then two pimply boys with grimly set faces carrying a banner that proclaimed this was THE TRIMBULL HIGH SCHOOL MARCHING BAND and you had by-God better not forget it. Then the band itself, resplendent and sweaty in blinding white uniforms and brass buttons.

The crowd cleared a path for them, and then broke into a wave of applause as they began to march in place. Behind them was a white Ford van, and standing spread-legged on the roof, face sunburned and split into a mammoth grin under his cocked-back construction hat, was the candidate himself. He raised a battery-powered bullhorn and shouted into it with leather-lunged enthusiasm: '*HI, Y'ALL!*'

'*Hi, Greg!*' The crowd gave it right back.

Greg, Johnny thought a little hysterically. *We're on first-name terms with the guy.*

Stillson leaped down from the roof of the van, managing to make it look easy. He was dressed as Johnny had seen him on the news, jeans and a khaki shirt. He began to work the crowd on his way to the bandstand, shaking hands, touching other hands outstretched over the heads of those in the first ranks. The crowd lurched and swayed deliriously toward him, and Johnny felt an answering lurch in his own guts.

I'm not going to touch him. No way.

But in front of him the crowd suddenly parted a little and he stepped into the gap and suddenly found himself in the front row. He was close enough to the tuba player in the Trimbull High School Marching Band to have reached out and rapped his knuckles on the bell of his horn, had he wanted to.

Stillson moved quickly through the ranks of the band to shake hands on the other side, and Johnny lost complete sight of him except for the bobbing yellow helmet. He felt relief. That was all right, then. No harm, no foul. Like the pharisee in that famous story, he was going to pass by on the other side. Good. Wonderful. And when he made the podium, Johnny was going to gather up his stuff and steal away into the afternoon. Enough was enough.

The bikies had moved up on both sides of the path through the crowd to keep it from collapsing in on the candidate and drowning him in people. All the chunks of pool cue were still in the back pockets, but their owners looked tense and alert for trouble. Johnny didn't know exactly what sort of trouble they expected – a Brownie Delight thrown in the candidate's face, maybe – but for the first time the bikies looked really interested.

Then something did happen, but Johnny was unable to tell exactly what it had been. A female hand reached for the bobbing yellow hard hat, maybe just to touch it for good luck, and one of Stillson's fellows moved in quickly. There was a yell of dismay and the woman's hand disappeared quickly. But it was all on the other side of the marching band.

The din from the crowd was enormous, and he thought

again of the rock concerts he had been to. This was what it would be like if Paul McCartney or Elvis Presley decided to shake hands with the crowd.

They were screaming his name, chanting it: '*GREG ... GREG ... GREG ...*'

The young guy who had billeted his family next to Johnny was holding his son up over his head so the kid could see. A young man with a large, puckered burn scar on one side of his face was waving a sign that read: LIVE FREE OR DIE, HERE'S GREG IN YER EYE! An achingly beautiful girl of maybe eighteen was waving a chunk of watermelon, and pink juice was running down her tanned arm. It was all mass confusion. Excitement was humming through the crowd like a series of high-voltage electrical cables.

And suddenly there was Greg Stillson, darting back through the band, back to Johnny's side of the crowd. He didn't pause, but still found time to give the tuba player a hearty clap on the back.

Later, Johnny mulled it over and tried to tell himself that there really hadn't been any chance or time to melt back into the crowd; he tried to tell himself that the crowd had practically *heaved* him into Stillson's arms. He tried to tell himself that Stillson had done everything but abduct his hand. None of it was true. There was time, because a fat woman in absurd, yellow clamdiggers threw her arms around Stillson's neck and gave him a hearty kiss, which Stillson returned with a laugh and a 'You bet I'll remember *you*, hon.' The fat woman screamed laughter.

Johnny felt the familiar compact coldness come over him, the trance feeling. The sensation that nothing mattered except to *know*. He even smiled a little, but it wasn't his smile. He put his hand out, and Stillson seized it in both of his and began to pump it up and down.

'Hey, man, hope you're gonna support us in ...'

Then Stillson broke off. The way Eileen Magown had. The way Dr. James (just like the soul singer) Brown had. The way Roger Dussault had. His eyes went wide, and

354

then they filled with – fright? No. It was *terror* in Stillson's eyes.

The moment was endless. Objective time was replaced
by something else, a perfect cameo of time as they stared
into each other's eyes. For Johnny it was like being in that
dull chrome corridor again, only this time Stillson was
with him and they were sharing . . . sharing

(*everything*)

For Johnny it had never been this strong, never. Everything came at him at once, crammed together and screaming like some terrible black freight train highballing
through a narrow tunnel, a speeding engine with a single
glaring headlamp mounted up front, and the headlamp
was *knowing everything*, and its light impaled Johnny
Smith like a bug on a pin. There was nowhere to run
and perfect knowledge ran him down, plastered him as
flat as a sheet of paper while that night-running train
raced over him.

He felt like screaming, but had no taste for it, no voice
for it.

The one image he never escaped

(*as the blue filter began to creep in*)

was Greg Stillson taking the oath of office. It was being
administered by an old man with the humble, frightened
eyes of a fieldmouse trapped by a terribly proficient,
battlescarred

(*tiger*)

barnyard tomcat. One of Stillson's hands clapped over a
Bible, one upraised. It was years in the future because
Stillson had lost most of his hair. The old man was speak-
ing, Stillson was following. Stillson was saying

(*the blue filter is deepening, covering things, blotting
them out bit by bit, merciful blue filter, Stillson's face is
behind the blue . . . and the yellow . . . the yellow like
tiger-stripes*)

he would do it 'So help him God.' His face was solemn,
grim, even, but a great hot joy clapped in his chest and
roared in his brain. Because the man with the scared

fieldmouse eyes was the Chief Justice of the United States Supreme Court and

(*oh dear God the filter the filter the blue filter the yellow stripes*)

now all of it began to disappear slowly behind that blue filter – except it wasn't a filter; it was something real. It was

(*in the future in the dead zone*)

something in the future. His? Stillson's? Johnny didn't know.

There was the sense of flying – flying through the blue – above scenes of utter desolation that could not quite be seen. And cutting through this came the disembodied voice of Greg Stillson, the voice of a cut-rate God or a comic-opera engine of the dead: '*I'M GONNA GO THROUGH THEM LIKE BUCKWHEAT THROUGH A GOOSE! GONNA GO THROUGH THEM LIKE SHIT THROUGH A CANEBRAKE!*'

'The tiger,' Johnny muttered thickly. 'The tiger's behind the blue. Behind the yellow.'

Then all of it, pictures, images, and words, broke up in the swelling, soft roar of oblivion. He seemed to smell some sweet, coppery scent, like burning high-tension wires. For a moment that inner eye seemed to open even wider, searching; the blue and yellow that had obscured everything seemed about to solidify into . . . into something, and from somewhere inside, distant and full of terror, he heard a woman shriek: '*Give him to me, you bastard!*'

Then it was gone.

How long did we stand together like that? he would ask himself later. His guess was maybe five seconds. Then Stillson was pulling his hand away, *ripping* it away, staring at Johnny with his mouth open, the color draining away from beneath the deep tan of the summertime campaigner. Johnny could see the fillings in the man's back teeth.

His expression was one of revolted horror.

356

Good! Johnny wanted to scream. *Good! Shake yourself to pieces! Total yourself! Destruct! Implode! Disintegrate! Do the world a favor!*

Two of the motorcycle guys were rushing forward and now the sawed-off pool cues *were* out and Johnny felt a stupid kind of terror because they were going to hit him, hit him over the head with their cues, they were going to make believe Johnny Smith's head was the eight ball and they were going to blast it right into the side pocket, right back into the blackness of coma and he would never come out of it this time, he would never be able to tell anyone what he had seen or change anything.

That sense of destruction – God! It had been *everything!*

He tried to backpedal. People scattered, pressed back, yelled with fear (or perhaps with excitement). Stillson was turning toward his bodyguards, already regaining his composure, shaking his head, restraining them.

Johnny never saw what happened next. He swayed on his feet, head lowered, blinking slowly like a drunk at the bitter end of a week-long binge. Then the soft, swelling roar of oblivion overwhelmed him and Johnny let it; he gladly let it. He blacked out.

CHAPTER TWENTY-ONE

1 ·

'No,' the Trimbull chief of police said in answer to Johnny's question, 'you're not charged with anything. You're not under detention. And you don't have to answer any questions. We'd just be very grateful if you would.'

'*Very* grateful,' the man in the conservative business suit echoed. His name was Edgar Lancte. He was with the Boston office of the Federal Bureau of Investigation. He thought that Johnny Smith looked like a very sick man. There was a puffed bruise above his left eyebrow that was rapidly turning purple. When he blacked out, Johnny had come down very hard – either on the shoe of a marching-bandsman or on the squared-off toe of a motorcycle boot. Lancte mentally favored the latter possibility. And possibly the motorcycle boot had been in motion at the instant of contact.

Smith was too pale, and his hands trembled badly as he drank the paper cup of water that Chief Bass had given him. One eyelid was ticking nervously. He looked like the classic would-be assassin, although the most deadly thing in his personal effects had been a nailclipper. Still, Lancte would keep that impression in mind, because he was what he was.

'What can I tell you?' Johnny asked. He had awakened on a cot in an unlocked cell. He'd had a blinding headache. It was draining away now, leaving him feeling strangely hollow inside. He felt a little as if his legitimate innards had been scooped out and replaced with Reddi Wip. There was a high, constant sound in his ears – not precisely a ringing; more like a high, steady hum. It was nine P.M. The Stillson entourage had long since swept out of town. All the hot dogs had been eaten.

'You can tell us exactly what happened back there,' Bass said.

'It was hot. I guess I got overexcited and fainted.'

'You an invalid or something?' Lancte asked casually.

Johnny looked at him steadily. 'Don't play games with me, Mr. Lancte. If you know who I am, then say so.'

'I know,' Lancte said. 'Maybe you *are* psychic.'

'Nothing psychic about guessing an FBI agent might be up to a few games,' Johnny said.

'You're a Maine boy, Johnny. Born and bred. What's a Maine boy doing down in New Hampshire?'

'Tutoring.'

'The Chatsworth boy?'

'For the second time: if you know, why ask? Unless you suspect me of something.'

Lancte lit a Vantage Green. 'Rich family.'

'Yes. They are.'

358

'You a Stillson fan, are you, Johnny?' Bass asked. Johnny didn't like fellows who used his first name on first acquaintance, and both of these fellows were doing it. It made him nervous.

'Are you?' he asked.

Bass made an obscene blowing sound. 'About five years ago we had a day-long folk-rock concert in Trimbull. Out on Hake Jamieson's land. Town council had their doubts, but they went ahead because the kids have got to have something. We thought we were going to have maybe two hundred local kids in Hake's east pasture listening to music. Instead we got sixteen hundred, all of em smoking pot and drinking hard stuff straight out from the neck of the bottle. They made a hell of a mess and the council got mad and said there'd never be another one and they turned around all hurt and wet-eyed and said, "Whassa matter? No one got hurt, did they?" It was supposed to be okay to make a helluva mess because no one got hurt. I feel the same way about this guy Stillson. I remember once . . .'

'You don't have any sort of grudge against Stillson, do you, Johnny?' Lancte asked. 'Nothing personal between you and him?' He smiled a fatherly, you-can-get-it-off-your-chest-if-you-want-to smile.

'I didn't even know who he was until six weeks ago.'

'Yes, well, but that really doesn't answer my question, does it?'

Johnny sat silent for a little while. 'He disturbs me,' he said finally.

'That doesn't really answer my question, either.'

'Yes, I think it does.'

'You're not being as helpful as we'd like,' Lancte said regretfully.

Johnny glanced over at Bass. 'Does anybody who faints in your town at a public gathering get the FBI treatment, Chief Bass?'

Bass looked uncomfortable. 'Well . . . no. Course not.'

'You were shaking hands with Stillson when you keeled

359

over,' Lancte said. 'You looked sick. Stillson himself looked scared green. You're a very lucky young man, Johnny. Lucky his goodbuddies there didn't turn your head into a votive urn. They thought you'd pulled a piece on him.'

Johnny was looking at Lancte with dawning surprise. He looked at Bass, then back to the FBI man. 'You were *there*,' he said. 'Bass didn't call you up on the phone. You were *there*. At the rally.'

Lancte crushed out his cigarette. 'Yes. I was.'

'Why is the FBI interested in Stillson?' Johnny nearly barked the question.

'Let's talk about you, Johnny. What's your . . .'

'No, let's talk about Stillson. Let's talk about his good-buddies, as you call them. Is it legal for them to carry around sawed-off pool cues?'

'It is,' Bass said. Lancte threw him a warning look, but Bass either didn't see it or ignored it. 'Cues, baseball bats, golf clubs. No law against any of them.'

'I heard someone say those guys used to be iron riders. Bike gang members.'

'Some of them used to be with a New Jersey club, some used to be with a New York club, that's . . .'

'Chief Bass,' Lancte interrupted, 'I hardly think this is the time . . .'

'I can't see the harm of telling him,' Bass said. 'They're bums, rotten apples, hairbags. Some of them ganged together in the Hamptons back four or five years ago, when they had the bad riots. A few of them were affiliated with a bike club called the Devil's Dozen that disbanded in 1972. Stillson's ramrod is a guy named Sonny Elliman. He used to be the president of the Devil's Dozen. He's been busted half a dozen times but never convicted of anything.'

'You're wrong about that, Chief,' Lancte said, lighting a fresh cigarette. 'He was cited in Washington State in 1973 for making an illegal left turn against traffic. He signed the waiver and paid a twenty-five-dollar fine.'

Johnny got up and went slowly across the room to the water cooler, where he drew himself a fresh cup of water. Lancte watched him go with interest.

'So you just fainted, right?' Lancte said.

'No,' Johnny said, not turning around. 'I was going to shoot him with a bazooka. Then, at the critical moment, all my bionic circuits blew.'

Lancte sighed.

Bass said, 'You're free to go any time.'

'Thank you.'

'But I'll tell you just the same way Mr. Lancte here would tell you. In the future, I'd stay away from Stillson rallies, if I were you. If you want to keep a whole skin, that is. Things have a way of happening to people Greg Stillson doesn't like . . .'

'Is that so?' Johnny asked. He drank his water.

'Those are matters outside your bailiwick, Chief Bass,' Lancte said. His eyes were like hazy steel and he was looking at Bass very hard.

'All right,' Bass said mildly.

'I don't see any harm in telling you that there have been other rally incidents,' Lancte said. 'In Ridgeway a young pregnant woman was beaten so badly she miscarried. This was just after the Stillson rally there that CBS filmed. She said she couldn't ID her assailant, but we feel it may have been one of Stillson's bikies. A month ago a kid, he was fourteen, got himself a fractured skull. He had a little plastic squirtgun. He couldn't ID his assailant, either. But the squirtgun makes us believe it may have been a security overreaction.'

How nicely put, Johnny thought.

'You couldn't find anyone who saw it happen?'

'Nobody who would talk.' Lancte smiled humorlessly and tapped the ash off his cigarette. 'He's the people's choice.'

Johnny thought of the young guy holding his son up so that the boy could see Greg Stillson. *Who the hell cares? They're just for show, anyway.*

'So he's got his own pet FBI agent.'

361

Lancte shrugged and smiled disarmingly. 'Well, what can I say? Except, FYI, it's no tit assignment, Johnny. Sometimes I get scared. The guy generates one hell of a lot of magnetism. If he pointed me out from the podium and told the crowd at one of those rallies who I was, I think they'd run me up the nearest lamppost.'

Johnny thought of the crowd that afternoon, and of the pretty girl hysterically waving her chunk of watermelon. 'I think you might be right,' he said.

'So if there's something you know that might help me . . .' Lancte leaned forward. The disarming smile had become slightly predatory. 'Maybe you even had a psychic flash about him. Maybe that's what messed you up.'

'Maybe I did,' Johnny said, unsmiling.

'Well?'

For one wild moment Johnny considered telling them everything. Then he rejected it. 'I saw him on TV. I had nothing in particular to do today, so I thought I'd come over here and check him out in person. I bet I wasn't the only out-of-towner who did that.'

'You sure *wasn't*,' Bass said vehemently.

'And that's all?' Lancte asked.

'That's all,' Johnny said, and then hesitated. 'Except . . . I think he's going to win his election.'

'We're sure he is,' Lancte said. 'Unless we can get something on him. In the meantime, I'm in complete agreement with Chief Bass. Stay away from Stillson rallies.'

'Don't worry.' Johnny crumpled up his paper cup and threw it away. 'It's been nice talking to you two gentlemen, but I've got a long drive back to Durham.'

'Going back to Maine soon, Johnny?' Lancte asked casually.

'Don't know.' He looked from Lancte, slim and impeccable, tapping out a fresh cigarette on the blank face of his digital watch, to Bass, a big, tired man with a basset hound's face. 'Do either of you think he'll run for higher office? If he gets this seat in the House of Representatives?'

'Jesus wept,' Bass muttered, and rolled his eyes.

'These guys come and go,' Lancte said. His eyes, so brown they were nearly black, had never stopped studying Johnny. 'They're like one of those rare radioactive elements that are so unstable that they don't last long. Guys like Stillson have no permanent political base, just a temporary coalition that holds together for a little while and then falls apart. Did you see that crowd today? College kids and mill hands yelling for the same guy? That's not politics, that's something on the order of hula hoops or coonskin caps or Beatle wigs. He'll get his term in the House and he'll free-lunch until 1978 and that'll be it. Count on it.'

But Johnny wondered.

2 ·

The next day, the left side of Johnny's forehead had become very colorful. Dark purple – almost black – above the eyebrow shaded to red and then to a morbidly gay yellow at the temple and hairline. His eyelid had puffed slightly, giving him a leering sort of expression, like the second banana in a burlesque review.

He did twenty laps in the pool and then sprawled in one of the deck chairs, panting. He felt terrible. He had gotten less than four hours' sleep the night before, and all of what he had gotten had been dream-haunted.

'Hi, Johnny . . . how you doing, man?'

He turned around. It was Ngo, smiling gently. He was dressed in his work clothes and wearing gardening gloves. Behind him was a child's red wagon filled with small pine trees, their roots wrapped in burlap. Recalling what Ngo called the pines, he said: 'I see you're planting more weeds.'

Ngo wrinkled his nose. 'Sorry, yes. Mr. Chatsworth is loving them. I tell him, but they are junk trees. Everywhere there are these trees in New England. His face goes like this . . .' Now Ngo's whole face wrinkled and he looked like a caricature of some late show monster. '. . . and he says to me, "Just plant them." '

Johnny laughed. That was Roger Chatsworth, all right.

He liked things done his way. 'How did you enjoy the rally?'

Ngo smiled gently. 'Very instructive,' he said. There was no way to read his eyes. He might not have noticed the sunrise on the side of Johnny's face. 'Yes, very instructive, we are all enjoying ourselves.'

'Good.'

'And you?'

'Not so much,' Johnny said, and touched the bruise lightly with his fingertips. It was very tender.

'Yes, too bad, you should put a beefsteak on it,' Ngo said, still smiling gently.

'What did you think about him, Ngo? What did your class think? Your Polish friend? Or Ruth Chen and her sister?'

'Going back we did not talk about it, at our instructors' request. Think about what you have seen, they say. Next Tuesday we will write in class, I think. Yes, I am thinking very much that we will. A class composition.'

'What will you say in your composition?'

Ngo looked at the blue summer sky. He and the sky smiled at each other. He was a small man with the first threads of gray in his hair. Johnny knew almost nothing about him; didn't know if he had been married, had fathered children, if he had fled before the Vietcong, if he had been from Saigon or from one of the rural provinces. He had no idea what Ngo's political leanings were.

'We talked of the game of the Laughing Tiger,' Ngo said. 'Do you remember?'

'Yes,' Johnny said.

'I will tell you of a real tiger. When I was a boy there was a tiger who went bad near my village. He was being *le manger d'homme*, eater of men, you understand, except he was not that, he was an eater of boys and girls and old women because this was during the war and there were no men to eat. Not the war you know of, but the Second World War. He had gotten the taste for human meat, this tiger. Who was there to kill such an awful creature in a humble village where the youngest

364

man is being sixty and with only one arm, and the oldest
boy is myself, only seven years of age? And one day this
tiger was found in a pit that had been baited with the
body of a dead woman. It is a terrible thing to bait a trap
with a human being made in the image of God, I will say
in my composition, but it is more terrible to do nothing
while a bad tiger carries away small children. And I will
say in my composition that this bad tiger was still alive
when we found it. It was having a stake pushed through
its body but it was still alive. We beat it to death with
hoes and sticks. Old men and women and children, some
children so excited and frightened they are wetting themselves in their pants. The tiger fell in the pit and we beat
it to death with our hoes because the men of the village
had gone to fight the Japanese. I am thinking that this
Stillson is like that bad tiger with its taste for human
meat. I think a trap should be made for him, and I think
he should be falling into it. And if he still lives, I think
he should be beaten to death.'

He smiled gently at Johnny in the clear summer sunshine.

'Do you really believe that?' Johnny asked.

'Oh, yes,' Ngo said. He spoke lightly, as if it were a
matter of no consequence. 'What my teacher will say
when I am handing in such a composition, I don't know.'
He shrugged his shoulders. 'Probably he will say, "Ngo,
you are not ready for the American Way." But I will say
the truth of what I feel. What did *you* think, Johnny?'
His eyes moved to the bruise, then moved away.

'I think he's dangerous,' Johnny said. 'I . . . I know he's
dangerous.'

'Do you?' Ngo remarked. 'Yes, I believe you do know
it. Your fellow New Hampshires, they see him as an engaging clown. They set him the way many of this world
are seeing this black man, Idi Amin Dada. But you do
not.'

'No,' Johnny said. 'But to suggest he should be
killed . . .'

'*Politically* killed,' Ngo said, smiling. 'I am only sug-

365

gesting he should be politically killed.'

'And if he can't be politically killed?'

Ngo smiled at Johnny. He unfolded his index finger, cocked his thumb, and then snapped it down. 'Bam,' he said softly. 'Bam, bam, bam.'

'No,' Johnny said, surprised at the hoarseness in his own voice. 'That's never an answer. *Never.*'

'No? I thought it was an answer you Americans used quite often.' Ngo picked up the handle of the red wagon. 'I must be planting these weeds, Johnny. So long, man.'

Johnny watched him go, a small man in suntans and moccasins, pulling a wagonload of baby pines. He disappeared around the corner of the house.

No. Killing only sows more dragon's teeth. I believe that. I believe it with all my heart.

3 ·

On the first Tuesday in November, which happened to be the second day in the month, Johnny Smith sat slumped in the easy chair of his combined kitchen-living room and watched the election returns. Chancellor and Brinkley were featuring a large electronic map that showed the results of the presidential race in a color-code as each state came in. Now, at nearly midnight, the race between Ford and Carter looked very close. But Carter would win; Johnny had no doubt of it.

Greg Stillson had also won.

His victory had been extensively covered on the local newsbreaks, but the national reporters had also taken some note of it, comparing his victory to that of James Longley, Maine's independent governor, two years before.

Chancellor said, 'Late polls showing that the Republican candidate and incumbent Harrison Fisher was closing the gap were apparently in error; NBC predicts that Stillson, who campaigned in a construction worker's hard hat and on a platform that included the proposal that all pollution be sent into outer space, ended up with forty-

366

six percent of the vote, to Fisher's thirty-one percent. In a district where the Democrats have always been poor relations, David Bowes could only poll twenty-three percent of the vote.'

'And so,' Brinkley said, 'it's hot dog time down in New Hampshire . . . for the next two years, at least.' He and Chancellor grinned. A commercial came on. Johnny didn't grin. He was thinking of tigers.

The time between the Trimbull rally and election night had been busy for Johnny. His work with Chuck had continued, and Chuck continued to improve at a slow but steady pace. He had taken two summer courses, passed them both, and retained his sports eligibility. Now, with the football season just ending, it looked very much as if he would be named to the Gannett newspaper chain's All New England team. The careful, almost ritualistic visits from the college scouts had already begun, but they would have to wait another year; the decision had already been made between Chuck and his father that he would spend a year at Stovington Prep, a good private school in Vermont. Johnny thought Stovington would probably be delirious at the news. The Vermont school regularly fielded great soccer teams and dismal football teams. They would probably give him a full scholarship and a gold key to the girl's dorm in the bargain. Johnny felt that it had been the right decision. After it had been reached and the pressure on Chuck to take the SATs right away had eased off, his progress had taken another big jump.

In late September, Johnny had gone up to Pownal for the weekend and after an entire Friday night of watching his father fidget and laugh uproariously at jokes on TV that weren't particularly funny, he had asked Herb what the trouble was.

'No trouble,' Herb said, smiling nervously and rubbing his hands together like an accountant who has discovered that the company he just invested his life savings with is bankrupt. 'No trouble at all, what makes you think that, son?'

367

'Well, what's on your mind, then?'

Herb stopped smiling, but he kept rubbing his hands together. 'I don't really know how to tell you, Johnny. I mean . . .'

'Is it Charlene?'

'Well, yes. It is.'

'You popped the question.'

Herb looked at Johnny humbly. 'How do you feel about coming into a stepmother at the age of twenty-nine, John?'

Johnny grinned. 'I feel fine about it. Congratulations, Dad.'

Herb smiled, relieved. 'Well, thanks. I was a little scared to tell you, I don't mind admitting it. I know what you said when we talked about it before, but people sometimes feel one way when something's maybe and another way when it's gonna be. I loved your mom, Johnny. And I guess I always will.'

'I know that, dad.'

'But I'm alone and Charlene's alone and . . . well, I guess we can put each other to good use.'

Johnny went over to his father and kissed him. 'All the best. I know you'll have it.'

'You're a good son, Johnny.' Herb took his handkerchief out of his back pocket and swiped at his eyes with it. 'We thought we'd lost you. I did, anyway. Vera never lost hope. She always believed. Johnny, I . . .'

'Don't, Daddy. It's over.'

'I have to,' he said. 'It's been in my gut like a stone for a year and a half now. I prayed for you to die, Johnny. My own son, and I prayed for God to take you.' He wiped his tears again and put his handkerchief away. 'Turned out God knew a smidge more than I did. Johnny . . . would you stand up with me? At my wedding?'

Johnny felt something inside that was almost but not quite like sorrow. 'That would be my pleasure,' he said.

'Thanks. I'm glad I've . . . that I've said everything that's on my mind. I feel better than I have in a long, long time.'

'Have you set a date?'

'As a matter of fact, we have. How does January 2 sound to you?'

'Sounds good,' Johnny said. 'You can count on me.'

'We're going to put both places on the market, I guess,' Herb said. 'We've got our eye on a farm in Biddeford. Nice place. Twenty acres. Half of it woodlot. A new start.'

'Yes. A new start, that's good.'

'You wouldn't have any objections to us selling the home place?' Herb asked anxiously.

'A little tug,' Johnny said. 'That's all.'

'Yeah, that's what I feel. A little tug.' He smiled. 'Somewhere around the heart, that's where mine is. What about you?'

'About the same,' Johnny said.

'How's it going down there for you?'

'Good.'

'Your boy's getting along?'

'Amazin well,' Johnny said, using one of his father's pet expressions and grinning.

'How long do you think you'll be there?'

'Working with Chuck? I guess I'll stick with it through the school year, if they want me. Working one-on-one has been a new kind of experience. I like it. And this has been a really good job. Atypically good, I'd say.'

'What are you going to do after?'

Johnny shook his head. 'I don't know yet. But I know one thing.'

'What's that?'

'I'm going out for a bottle of champagne. We're going to get bombed.'

His father had stood up on that September evening and clapped him on the back. 'Make it two,' he said.

He still got the occasional letter from Sarah Hazlett. She and Walt were expecting their second child in April. Johnny wrote back his congratulations and his good wishes for Walt's canvass. And he thought sometimes about his afternoon with Sarah, the long, slow afternoon.

It wasn't a memory he allowed himself to take out too often; he was afraid that constant exposure to the sunlight of recollection might cause it to wash out and fade, like the reddish-tinted proofs they used to give you of your graduation portraits.

He had gone out a few times this fall, once with the older and newly divorced sister of the girl Chuck was seeing, but nothing had developed from any of those dates.

Most of his spare time that fall he had spent in the company of Gregory Ammas Stillson.

He had become a Stillsonphile. He kept three looseleaf notebooks in his bureau under his socks and underwear and T-shirts. They were filled with notes, speculations, and Xerox copies of news items.

Doing this had made him uneasy. At night, as he wrote around the pasted-up clippings with a fine-line Pilot pen, he sometimes felt like Arthur Bremmer or the Moore woman who had tried to shoot Jerry Ford. He knew that if Edgar Lancte, Fearless Minion of the Effa Bee Eye, could see him doing this, his phone, living room, and bathroom would be tapped in a jiffy. There would be an Acme Furniture van parked across the street, only instead of being full of furniture it would be loaded with cameras and mikes and God knew what else.

He kept telling himself that he wasn't Bremmer, that Stillson wasn't an obsession, but that got harder to believe after the long afternoons at the UNH library, searching through old newspapers and magazines and feeding dimes into the photocopier. It got harder to believe on the nights he burned the midnight oil, writing out his thoughts and trying to make valid connections. It grew well-nigh impossible to believe on those graveyard-ditch three A.M.s when he woke up sweating from the recurring nightmare.

The nightmare was nearly always the same, a naked replay of his handshake with Stillson at the Trimbull rally. The sudden blackness. The feeling of being in a tunnel filled with the glare of the onrushing headlight, a headlight bolted to some black engine of doom. The old man with the humble, frightened eyes administering an unthinkable oath of office. The nuances of feeling, coming and going like tight puffs of smoke. And a series of brief images, strung together in a flapping row like the plastic pennants over a used-car dealer's lot. His mind whispered to him that these images were all related, that they told a picture-story of a titanic approaching doom, perhaps even the Armageddon of which Vera Smith had been so endlessly confident.

But what were the images? What were they exactly? They were hazy, impossible to see except in vague outline, because there was always that puzzling blue filter between, the blue filter that was sometimes cut by those yellow markings like tiger stripes.

The only clear image in these dream-replays came near the end: the screams of the dying, the smell of the dead. And a single tiger padding through miles of twisted metal, fused glass, and scorched earth. This tiger was always laughing, and it seemed to be carrying something in its mouth – something blue and yellow and dripping blood.

There had been times in the fall when he thought that dream would send him mad. Ridiculous dream; the possibility it seemed to point to was impossible, after all. Best to drive it totally out of his mind.

But because he couldn't, he researched Gregory Stillson and tried to tell himself it was only a harmless hobby and not a dangerous obsession.

Stillson had been born in Tulsa. His father had been an oil-field roughneck who drifted from job to job, working more often than some of his colleagues because of his tremendous size. His mother might once have been pretty, although there was only a hint of that in the two pictures that Johnny had been able to unearth. If she had been, the times and the man she had been married to had dimmed her prettiness quickly. The pictures showed little more than another dustbowl face, a southeast United States depression woman who was wearing a faded print dress and holding a baby – Greg – in her scrawny arms, and squinting into the sun.

His father had been a domineering man who didn't think much of his son. As a child, Greg had been pallid and sickly. There was no evidence that his father had abused the boy either mentally or physically, but there was the suggestion that at the very least, Greg Stillson had lived in a disapproving shadow for the first nine years of his life. The one picture Johnny had of the father and son together was a happy one, however; it showed them together in the oil fields, the father's arm slung around the son's neck in a careless gesture of comradeship. But it gave Johnny a little chill all the same. Harry Stillson was dressed in working clothes, twill pants and a double-breasted khaki shirt, and his hard hat was cocked jauntily back on his head.

Greg had begun school in Tulsa, then had been switched to Oklahoma City when he was ten. The previous summer his father had been killed in an oil-derrick flameout. Mary Lou Stillson had gone to Okie City with her boy because it was where her mother lived, and where the war work was. It was 1942, and good times had come around again.

Greg's grades had been good until high school, and then he began to get into a series of scrapes. Truancy, fighting, hustling snooker downtown, maybe hustling stolen goods uptown, although that had never been proved. In 1949, when he had been a high-school junior, he had pulled a two-day suspension for putting a cherry-bomb fire-cracker in a locker-room toilet.

In all of these confrontations with authority, Mary Lou Stillson took her son's part. The good times – at least for the likes of the Stillsons – had ended with the war work in 1945, and Mrs. Stillson seemed to think of it as a case of her and her boy against the rest of the world. Her mother had died, leaving her the small frame house and nothing else. She hustled drinks in a roughneck bar for a while, then waited table in an all-light beanery. And when her boy got in trouble, she went to bat for him, never checking (apparently) to see if his hands were dirty or clean.

The pale sickly boy that his father had nicknamed Runt was gone by 1949. As Greg Stillson's adolescence progressed, his father's physical legacy came out. The boy shot up six inches and put on seventy pounds between thirteen and seventeen. He did not play organized school sports but somehow managed to acquire a Charles Atlas bodybuilding gym and then a set of weights. The Runt became a bad guy to mess with.

Johnny guessed he must have come close to dropping out of school on dozens of occasions. He had probably avoided a bust out of sheer dumb luck. If only he *had* taken at least one serious bust, Johnny thought often. It would have ended all these stupid worries, because a convicted felon can't aspire to high public office.

Stillson had graduated – near the bottom of his class, it was true – in June, 1951. Grades notwithstanding, there was nothing wrong with his brains. His eye was on the main chance. He had a glib tongue and a winning manner. He worked briefly that summer as a gas jockey. Then, in August of that year, Greg Stillson had gotten Jesus at a tent-revival in Wildwood Green. He quit his job at the 76 station and went into business as a rainmaker 'through the power of Jesus Christ our Lord'.

Coincidentally or otherwise, that had been one of the driest summers in Oklahoma since the days of the dust bowl. The crops were already a dead loss, and the livestock would soon follow if the shallowing wells went dry. Greg had been invited to a meeting of the local ranchers' association. Johnny had found a great many stories about what had followed; it was one of the high points of Stillson's career. None of these stories completely jibed, and Johnny could understand why. It had all the attributes of an American myth, not much different from some of the stories about Davy Crockett, Pecos Bill, Paul Bunyan. That *something* had happened was undeniable. But the strict truth of it was already beyond reach.

One thing seemed sure. That meeting of the ranchers' association must have been one of the strangest ever held. The ranchers had invited over two dozen rainmakers from various parts of the southeast and southwest. About half of them were Negroes. Two were Indians – a half-breed Pawnee and a full-blooded Apache. There was a peyote-chewing Mexican. Greg was one of about nine white fellows, and the only home-town boy.

The ranchers heard the proposals of the rainmakers and dowsers one by one. They gradually and naturally divided themselves into two groups: those who would take half of their fee up front (nonrefundable) and those who wanted their entire fee up front (nonrefundable).

When Greg Stillson's turn came, he stood up, hooked his thumbs into the belt loops of his jeans, and was supposed to have said: 'I guess you fellows know I got in the way of being able to make it rain after I gave my heart to Jesus. Before that I was deep in sin and the ways of sin. Now one of the main ways of sin is the way we've seen tonight, and you spell that kind of sinning mostly with dollar signs.'

The ranchers were interested. Even at nineteen Stillson had been something of a comic spellbinder. And he had made them an offer they couldn't refuse. Because he was a born-again Christian and because he knew that the love of money was the root of all evil, he would make it rain and afterward they could pay him whatever they thought the job had been worth.

He was hired by acclamation, and two days later he was down on his knees in the back of a flatbed farm truck, cruising slowly along the highways and byways of central Oklahoma, dressed in a black coat and a preacher's low-crowned hat, praying for rain through a pair of loudspeakers hooked up to a Delco tractor battery. People turned out by the thousands to get a look at him.

The end of the story was predictable but satisfying. The skies grew cloudy during the afternoon of Greg's second day on the job, and the next morning the rains came. The rains came for three days and two nights, flash floods killed four people, whole houses with chickens perched on the roof peaks were washed down the Greenwood River, the wells were filled, the livestock was saved, and The Oklahoma Ranchers' and Cattlemen's Association decided it probably would have happened anyway. They passed the hat for Greg at their next meeting and the young rainmaker was given the princely sum of seventeen dollars.

Greg was not put out of countenance. He used the seventeen dollars to place an ad in the Oklahoma City *Herald*. The ad pointed out that about the same sort of thing had happened to a certain rat-catcher in the town of Hamlin. Being a Christian, the ad went on, Greg Stillson was not in the way of taking children, and he surely knew he had no legal recourse against a group as large and powerful as the Oklahoma Ranchers' and Cattlemen's Association. But fair was fair, wasn't it? He had his elderly mother to support, and she was in failing health. The ad suggested that he had prayed his ass off for a bunch of rich, ungrateful snobs, the same sort of men that had tractored poor folks like the Joads off their land in the thirties. The ad suggested that he had saved tens of thousands of dollars' worth of livestock and had got seventeen dollars in return. Because he was a good Christian, this sort of ingratitude didn't bother him, but maybe it ought to give the good citizens of the county some pause. Right-thinking people could send contributions to Box 471, care of the *Herald*.

Johnny wondered how much Greg Stillson had actually received as a result of that ad. Reports varied. But that fall, Greg had been tooling around town in a brand-new Mercury. Three years' worth of back taxes were paid on the small house left to them by Mary Lou's mother. Mary Lou herself (who was not particularly sickly and no older than forty-five), blossomed out in a new raccoon coat. Stillson had apparently discovered one of the great hidden muscles of principle which move the earth: if those who receive will not pay, those who have not often will, for no good reason at all. It may be the same principle that assures the politicians there will always be enough young men to feed the war machine.

The ranchers discovered they had stuck their collective hand into a hornets' nest. When members came into town, crowds often gathered and jeered at them. They were denounced from pulpits all across the county. They found it suddenly difficult to sell the beef the rain had saved without shipping it a considerable distance.

In November of that memorable year, two young men with brass knucks on their hands and nickel-plated .32s in their pockets had turned up on Greg Stillson's doorstep, apparently hired by the Ranchers' and Cattlemen's Association to suggest – as strenuously as necessary – that Greg would find the climate more congenial elsewhere. Both of them ended up in the hospital. One of them had a concussion. The other had lost four of his teeth and was suffering a rupture. Both had been found on the corner of Greg Stillson's block, *sans* pants. Their brass knucks had been inserted in an anatomical location most commonly associated with sitting down, and in the case of one of these two young men, minor surgery was necessary to remove the foreign objects.

The Association cried off. At a meeting in early December, an appropriation of $700 was made from its general fund, and a check in that amount was forwarded to Greg Stillson.

He got what he wanted.

In 1953 he and his mother moved to Nebraska. The rainmaking business had gone bad, and there were some who said the pool-hall hustling had also gone bad. Whatever the reason for moving, they turned up in Omaha where Greg opened a house-painting business that went bust two years later. He did better as a salesman for the TruthWay Bible Company of America. He crisscrossed the cornbelt, taking dinner with hundreds of hard-working, God-fearing farm families, telling the story of his conversion and selling Bibles, plaques, luminous plastic Jesuses, hymn books, records, tracts, and a rabidly right-wing paperback called *America the TruthWay: The Communist-Jewish Conspiracy Against Our United States*. In 1957 the aging Mercury was replaced with a brand-new Ford ranch wagon.

In 1958 Mary Lou Stillson died of cancer, and late that year Greg Stillson got out of the born-again Bible business and drifted east. He spent a year in New York City before moving upstate to Albany. His year in New York had been devoted to an effort at cracking the acting business. It was one of the few jobs (along with house painting) that he hadn't been able to turn a buck at. But probably not from lack of talent, Johnny thought cynically.

In Albany he had gone to work for Prudential, and he had stayed in the capital city until 1965. As an insurance salesman he was an aimless sort of success. There was no offer to join the company at the executive level, no outbursts of Christian fervor. During that five-year period, the brash and brassy Greg Stillson of yore seemed to have gone into hibernation. In all of his checkered career, the only woman in his life had been his mother. He had never married, had not even dated regularly as far as Johnny had been able to find out.

In 1965, Prudential had offered him a position in Ridgeway, New Hampshire, and Greg had taken it. At about the same time, his period of hibernation seemed to end. The go-go Sixties were gathering steam. It was the era of the short skirt and do your own thing. Greg became active in Ridgeway community affairs. He joined the Chamber of Commerce and the Rotary Club. He got state-wide coverage in 1967, during a controversy over the parking meters downtown. For six years, various factions had been wrangling over them. Greg suggested that all the meters be taken out and that collection boxes be put up in their stead. Let people pay what they want. Some people had said that was the craziest idea they had ever heard. Well, Greg responded, you might just be

377

surprised. Yes sir. He was persuasive. The town finally adopted the proposal on a provisional basis, and the ensuing flood of nickels and dimes had surprised everyone but Greg. He had discovered the principle years ago.

In 1969 he made New Hampshire news again when he suggested, in a long and carefully worked-out letter to the Ridgeway newspaper, that drug offenders be put to work on town public works projects such as parks and bike paths, even weeding the grass on the traffic islands. That's the craziest idea I ever heard, many said. Well, Greg responded, try her out and if she don't work, chuck her. The town tried it out. One pothead reorganized the entire town library from the outmoded Dewey decimal system to the more modern Library of Congress cataloguing system, at no charge to the town. A number of hippies busted at an hallucinogenic house party relandscaped the town park into an area showplace, complete with duckpond and a playground scientifically designed to maximize effective playtime and minimize danger. As Greg pointed out, most of these drug-users got interested in all those chemicals in college, but that was no reason why they shouldn't utilize all the other things they had learned in college.

At the same time Greg was revolutionizing his adopted home town's parking regulations and its handling of drug offenders, he was writing letters to the Manchester *Union-Leader*, the Boston *Globe*, and the *New York Times*, espousing hawkish positions on the war in Vietnam, mandatory felony sentences for heroin addicts, and a return to the death penalty, especially for heroin pushers. In his campaign for the House of Representatives, he had claimed on several occasions to have been against the war from 1970 on, but the man's own published statements made that a flat lie.

In 1970, Greg Stillson had opened his own insurance and realty company. He was a great success. In 1973 he and three other businessmen had financed and built a shopping mall on the outskirts of Capital City, the county seat of the district he now represented. That was the year

of the Arabian oil boycott, also the year Greg started
driving a Lincoln Continental. It was also the year he
ran for mayor of Ridgeway.

The mayor enjoyed a two-year term, and two years
before, in 1971, he had been asked by both the Republicans and Democrats of the largish (population 8,500)
New England town to run. He had declined both of them
with smiling thanks. In '73 he ran as an independent,
taking on a fairly popular Republican who was vulnerable because of his fervent support of President Nixon,
and a Democratic figurehead. He donned his construction helmet for the first time. His campaign slogan was
Let's Build A Better Ridgeway! He won in a landslide. A
year later, in New Hampshire's sister state of Maine, the
voters turned away from both the Democrat, George
Mitchell, and the Republican, James Erwin, and elected
an insurance man from Lewiston named James Longley
their governor.

The lesson had not been lost on Gregory Ammas Stillson.

4 ·

Around the Xerox clippings were Johnny's notes and the
questions he regularly asked himself. He had been over
his chain of reasoning so often that now, as Chancellor
and Brinkley continued to chronicle the election results,
he could have spouted the whole thing word for word.

First, Greg Stillson shouldn't have been able to get
elected. His campaign promises were, by and large, jokes.
His background was all wrong. His education was all
wrong. It stopped at the twelfth-grade level, and, until
1965, he had been little more than a drifter. In a country
where the voters have decided that the lawyers should
make the laws, Stillson's only brushes with that force had
been from the wrong side. He wasn't married. And his
personal history was decidedly freaky.

Second, the press had left him almost completely – and
very puzzlingly – alone. In an election year when Wilbur
Mills had admitted to a mistress, when Wayne Hays had

379

been dislodged from his barnacle-encrusted House seat because of his, when even those in the houses of the mighty had not been immune from the rough-and-ready frisking of the press, the reporters should have had a field day with Stillson. His colorful, controversial personality seemed to stir only amused admiration from the national press, and he seemed to make no one – except maybe Johnny Smith – nervous. His bodyguards had been Harley-Davidson beach-hoppers only a few years ago, and people had a way of getting hurt at Stillson rallies, but no investigative reporter had done an in-depth study of that. At a campaign rally in Capital City – at that same mall Stillson had had a hand in developing – an eight-year-old girl had suffered a broken arm and a dislocated neck; her mother swore hysterically that one of those 'motorcycle maniacs' had pushed her from the stage when the girl tried to climb up on the podium and get the Great Man's signature for her autograph book. Yet there had only been a squib in the paper – *Girl Hurt at Stillson Rally* – quickly forgotten.

Stillson had made a financial disclosure that Johnny thought too good to be true. In 1975 Stillson had paid $11,000 in Federal taxes on an income of $36,000 – no state income tax at all, of course; New Hampshire didn't have one. He claimed all of his income came from his insurance and real estate agency, plus a small pittance that was his salary as mayor. There was no mention of the lucrative Capital City mall. No explanation of the fact that Stillson lived in a house with an assessed value of $86,000, a house he owned free and clear. In a season when the president of the United States was being dunned over what amounted to greens fees, Stillson's weird financial disclosure statement raised zero eyebrows.

Then there was his record as mayor. His performance on the job was a lot better than his campaign performances would have led anyone to expect. He was a shrewd and canny man with a rough but accurate grasp of human, corporate, and political psychology. He had wound up his term in 1975 with a fiscal surplus for the first time in ten years, much to the delight of the taxpayers. He pointed with justifiable pride to his parking program and what he called his Hippie Work-Study Program. Ridgeway had also been one of the first towns in the whole country to organize a Bicentennial Committee. A company that made filing cabinets had located in Ridgeway, and in recessionary times, the unemployment rate locally was an enviable 3.2 percent. All very admirable.

It was some of the other things that had happened while Stillson was mayor that made Johnny feel scared.

Funds for the town library had been cut from $11,500 to $8,000, and then, in the last year of Stillson's term, to $6,500. At the same time, the municipal police appropriation had risen by forty percent. Three new police cruisers had been added to the town motor pool, and a collection of riot equipment. Two new officers had also been added, and the town council had agreed, at Stillson's urging, to institute a 50/50 policy on purchasing officers' personal sidearms. As a result, several of the cops in this sleepy New England town had gone out and bought .357 Magnums, the gun immortalized by Dirty Harry Callahan. Also during Stillson's term as mayor, the teen rec center had been closed, a supposedly voluntary but police-enforced ten o'clock curfew for people under sixteen had been instituted, and welfare had been cut by thirty-five percent.

Yes, there were lots of things about Greg Stillson that scared Johnny.

The domineering father and laxly approving mother. The political rallies that felt more like rock concerts. The man's way with a crowd, his bodyguards –

Ever since Sinclair Lewis people had been crying woe and doom and beware of the fascist state in America, and it just didn't happen. Well, there had been Huey Long down there in Louisiana, but Huey Long had –

Had been assassinated.

Johnny closed his eyes and saw Ngo cocking his finger. Bam, bam, bam. Tiger, tiger, burning bright, in the forests of the night. What fearful hand or eye –

But you don't sow dragon's teeth. Not unless you want to get right down there with Frank Dodd in his hooded vinyl raincoat. With the Oswalds and the Sirhans and the Bremmers. Crazies of the world, unite. Keep your paranoid notebooks up-to-date and thumb them over at midnight and when things start to reach a head inside you, send away the coupon for the mail-order gun. Johnny Smith, meet Squeaky Fromme, Nice to meet you, Johnny, everything you've got in that notebook makes perfect sense to me. Want you to meet my spiritual master. Johnny, meet Charlie. Charlie, this is Johnny. When you finish with Stillson, we're going to get off together and off the rest of the pigs so we can save the redwoods.

His head was swirling. The inevitable headache was coming on. It always led to this. Greg Stillson always led him to this. It was time to go to sleep and please God, no dreams.

Still: The Question.

He had written it in one of the notebooks and kept coming back to it. He had written it in neat letters and then had drawn a triple circle around it, as if to keep it in. The Question was this: *If you could jump into a time machine and go back to 1932, would you kill Hitler?*

Johnny looked at his watch. Quarter of one. It was November 3 now, and the Bicentennial election was a part of history. Ohio was still undecided, but Carter was leading. No contest, baby. The hurly burly's done, the election's lost and won. Jerry Ford could hang up his jock, at least until 1980.

Johnny went to the window and looked out. The big house was dark, but there was a light burning in Ngo's apartment over the garage. Ngo, who would shortly be an American citizen, was still watching the great American quadrennial ritual: Old Bums Exit There, New Bums Enter Here. Maybe Gordon Strachan hadn't given the Watergate Committee such a bad answer at that.

Johnny went to bed. After a long time he slept.

And dreamed of the laughing tiger.

CHAPTER TWENTY-TWO

1 ·

Herb Smith took Charlene MacKenzie as his second wife on the afternoon of January 2, 1977, just as planned. The ceremony took place in the Congregational Church at Southwest Bend. The bride's father, an eighty-year-old gentleman who was almost blind, gave her away. Johnny stood up with his dad and produced the ring flawlessly at the proper moment. It was a lovely occasion.

Sarah Hazlett attended with her husband and their son, who was leaving his babyhood behind now. Sarah was pregnant and radiant, a picture of happiness and fulfillment. Looking at her, Johnny was surprised by a stab of bitter jealousy like an unexpected attack of gas. After a few moments it went away, and Johnny went over and spoke to them at the reception following the wedding.

It was the first time he had met Sarah's husband. He was a tall, good-looking man with a pencil-line moustache and prematurely graying hair. His canvass for the Maine state senate had been successful, and he held forth on what the national elections had really meant, and the difficulties of working with an independent governor, while Denny pulled at the leg of his trousers and demanded more-drink, Daddy, more-drink, more-*drink*!

Sarah said little, but Johnny felt her brilliant eyes on him – an uncomfortable sensation, but somehow not unpleasant. A little sad, maybe.

The liquor at the reception flowed freely, and Johnny went two drinks beyond his usual two-drink stopping point – the shock of seeing Sarah again, maybe, this time with her family, or maybe only the realization, written on Charlene's radiant face, that Vera Smith really was gone,

383

and for all time. So when he approached Hector Mac-
Kenzie, father of the bride, some fifteen minutes after the
Hazletts had left, he had a pleasant buzz on.

The old man was sitting in the corner by the demolished remains of the wedding cake, his arthritis-gnarled
hands folded over his cane. He was wearing dark glasses.
One bow had been mended with black electrician's tape.
Beside him there stood two empty bottles of beer and
another that was half-full. He peered closely at Johnny.

'Herb's boy, ain't you?'

'Yes, sir.'

A longer scrutiny. Then Hector MacKenzie said, 'Boy,
you don't look well.'

'Too many late nights, I guess.'

'Look like you need a tonic. Something to build you
up.'

'You were in World War I, weren't you?' Johnny
asked. A number of medals, including a Croix de Guerre,
were pinned to the old man's blue serge suit coat.

'Indeed I was,' MacKenzie said, brightening. 'Served
under Black Jack Pershing. AEF, 1917 and 18. We went
through the mud and the crud. The wind blew and the
shit flew. Belleau Wood, my boy. Belleau Wood. It's just
a name in the history books now. But I was there. I saw
men die there. The wind blew and the shit flew and up
from the trenches came the whole damn crew.'

'And Charlene said that your boy . . . her brother . . .'

'Buddy. Yep. Would have been your stepuncle, boy.
Did we love that boy? I guess we did. His name was Joe,
but everyone called him Buddy almost from the day he
was born. Charlie's mother started to die the day the
telegram came.'

'Killed in the war, wasn't he?'

'Yes, he was,' the old man said slowly. 'St. Lô, 1944. Not
that far from Belleau Wood, not the way we measure
things over here, anyway. They ended Buddy's life with
a bullet. The Nazis.'

'I'm working on an essay,' Johnny said, feeling a certain drunken cunning at having brought the coversation

around to his real object at last. 'I'm hoping to sell it to the *Atlantic* or maybe *Harper's* . . .'

'Writer, are you?' The dark glasses glinted up at Johnny with renewed interest.

'Well, I'm trying,' Johnny said. Already he was beginning to regret his glibness. *Yes, I'm a writer. I write in my notebooks, after the dark of night has fallen.* 'Anyway, the essay's going to be about Hitler.'

'Hitler? What about Hitler?'

'Well . . . suppose . . . just suppose you could hop into a time machine and go back to the year 1932. In Germany. And suppose you came across Hitler. Would you kill him or let him live?'

The old man's blank black glasses tilted slowly up to Johnny's face. And now Johnny didn't feel drunk or glib or clever at all. Everything seemed to depend on what this old man had to say.

'Is it a joke, boy?'

'No. No joke.'

One of Hector MacKenzie's hands left the head of his cane. It went to the pocket of his suit pants and fumbled there for what seemed an eternity. At last it came out again. It was holding a bone-handled pocket knife that had been rubbed as smooth and mellow as old ivory over the course of years. The other hand came into play, folding the knife's one blade out with all the incredible delicacy of arthritis. It glimmered with bland wickedness under the light of the Congregational parish hall: a knife that had traveled to France in 1917 with a boy, a boy who had been part of a boy-army ready and willing to stop the dirty hun from bayoneting babies and raping nuns, ready to show the Frenchies a thing or two in the bargain; and the boys had been machine-gunned, the boys had gotten dysentery and the killer flu, the boys had inhaled mustard gas and phosgene gas, the boys had come out of Belleau Wood looking like haunted scarecrows who had seen the face of Lord Satan himself. And it had all turned out to be for nothing; it turned out that it all had to be done over again.

Somewhere music was playing. People were laughing. People were dancing. A flashbar popped warm light. Somewhere far away. Johnny stared at the naked blade, transfixed, hypnotized by the play of the light over its honed edge.

'See this?' MacKenzie asked softly.

'Yes,' Johnny breathed.

'I'd seat this in his black, lying, murderer's heart,' MacKenzie said. 'I'd put her in as far as she'd go . . . and then I'd twist her.' He twisted the knife slowly in his hand, first clock, then counterclock. He smiled, showing baby-smooth gums and one leaning yellow tooth.

'But first,' he said, 'I'd coat the blade with rat poison.'

2 ·

'Kill Hitler?' Roger Chatsworth said, his breath coming out in little puffs. The two of them were snowshoeing in the woods behind the Durham house. The woods were very silent. It was early March, but this day was as smoothly and coldly silent as deep January.

'Yes, that's right.'

'Interesting question,' Roger said. 'Pointless, but interesting. No. I wouldn't. I think I'd join the party instead. Try to change things from within. It might have been possible to purge him or frame him, always granting the foreknowledge of what was going to happen.'

Johnny thought of the sawed-off pool cues. He thought of the brilliant green eyes of Sonny Elliman.

'It might also be possible to get yourself killed!' he said. 'Those guys were doing more than singing beer-hall songs back in 1933.'

'Yes, that's true enough.' He cocked an eyebrow at Johnny. 'What would you do?'

'I really don't know,' Johnny said.

Roger dismissed the subject. 'How did your dad and his wife enjoy their honeymoon?'

Johnny grinned. They had gone to Miami Beach, hotel-workers' strike and all. 'Charlene said she felt right at home, making her own bed. My dad says he feels like a freak, sporting a sunburn in March. But I think they both enjoyed it.'

'And they've sold the houses?'

'Yes, both on the same day. Got almost what they wanted, too. Now if it wasn't for the goddam medical bills still hanging over my head, it'd be plain sailing.'

'Johnny . . .'

'Hmmm?'

'Nothing. Let's go back. I've got some Chivas Regal, if you've got a taste.'

'I believe I do,' Johnny said.

3 ·

They were reading *Jude the Obscure* now, and Johnny had been surprised at how quickly and naturally Chuck had taken to it (after some moaning and groaning over the first forty pages or so). He confessed he had been reading ahead at night on his own, and he intended to try something else by Hardy when he finished. For the first time in his life he was reading for pleasure. And like a boy who has just been initiated into the pleasures of sex by an older woman, he was wallowing in it.

Now the book lay open but facedown in his lap. They were by the pool again, but it was still drained and both he and Johnny were wearing light jackets. Overhead, mild white clouds scudded across the sky, trying desultorily to coalesce enough to make rain. The feel of the air was mysterious and sweet; spring was somewhere near. It was April 16.

'Is this one of those trick questions?' Chuck asked.

'Nope.'

'Well, would they catch me?'

'Pardon?' That was a question none of the others had asked.

'If I killed him. Would they catch me? Hang me from a lamppost? Make me do the funky chicken six inches off the ground?'

'Well, I don't know,' Johnny said slowly. 'Yes, I suppose they would catch you.'

'I don't get to escape in my time machine to a gloriously changed world, huh? Back to good old 1977?'

'No, I don't think so.'

'Well, it wouldn't matter. I'd kill him anyway.'

'Just like that?'

'Sure.' Chuck smiled a little. 'I'd rig myself up with one of those hollow teeth filled with quick-acting poison or a razor blade in my shirt collar or something like that. So if I did get caught they couldn't do anything too gross to me. But I'd do it. If I didn't, I'd be afraid all those millions of people he ended up killing would haunt me to my grave.'

'To your grave,' Johnny said a little sickly.

'Are you okay, Johnny?'

Johnny made himself return Chuck's smile. 'Fine. I guess my heart just missed a beat or something.'

Chuck went on with *Jude* under the milky cloudy sky.

4 ·
May.

The smell of cut grass was back for yet another return engagement – also those long-running favorites, honeysuckle, dust, and roses. In New England spring really only comes for one priceless week and then the deejays drag out the Beach Boys golden oldies, the buzz of the cruising Honda is heard throughout the land, and summer comes down with a hot thud.

On one of the last evenings of that priceless spring week, Johnny sat in the guest house, looking out into the night. The spring dark was soft and deep. Chuck was off at the senior prom with his current girl friend, a more intellectual type than the last half-dozen. She *reads*, Chuck had confided to Johnny, one man of the world to another.

Ngo was gone. He had gotten his citizenship papers in late March, had applied for a job as head groundskeeper at a North Carolina resort hotel in April, had gone down for an interview three weeks ago, and had been hired on the spot. Before he left, he had come to see Johnny.

'You worry too much about tigers that are not there, I think,' he said. 'The tiger has stripes that will fade into the background so he will not be seen. This makes the worried man see tigers everywhere.'

'There's a tiger,' Johnny had answered.

'Yes,' Ngo agreed. 'Somewhere. In the meantime, you grow thin.'

Johnny got up, went to the fridge, and poured himself a Pepsi. He went outside with it to the little deck. He sat down and sipped his drink and thought how lucky everyone was that time travel was a complete impossibility. The moon came up, an orange eye above the pines, and beat a bloody path across the swimming pool. The first frogs croaked and thumped. After a little while Johnny went inside and poured a hefty dollop of Ron Rico into his Pepsi. He went back outside and sat down again, drinking and watching as the moon rose higher in the sky, changing slowly from orange to mystic, silent silver.

CHAPTER TWENTY-THREE

1 ·

On June the 23rd, 1977, Chuck graduated from high school. Johnny, dressed in his best suit, sat in the hot auditorium with Roger and Shelley Chatsworth and watched as he graduated forty-third in his class. Shelley cried.

Afterward, there was a lawn party at the Chatsworth home. The day was hot and humid. Thunderheads with purple bellies had formed in the west; they dragged slowly back and forth across the horizon, but seemed to come no closer. Chuck, flushed with three screwdrivers, came over with his girl friend, Patty Strachan, to show Johnny his graduation present from his parents – a new Pulsar watch.

'I told them I wanted that R2D2 robot, but this was the best they could do,' Chuck said, and Johnny laughed.

They talked a while longer and then Chuck said with almost rough abruptness: 'I want to thank you, Johnny. If it hadn't been for you, I wouldn't be graduating today at all.'

'No, that isn't true,' Johnny said. He was a little alarmed to see that Chuck was on the verge of tears. 'Class always tells, man.'

'That's what I keep telling him,' Chuck's girl said. Behind her glasses, a cool and elegant beauty was waiting to come out.

'Maybe,' Chuck said. 'Maybe it does. But I think I know which side my diploma is buttered on. Thanks a hell of a lot.' He put his arms around Johnny and gave him a hug.

It came suddenly – a hard, bright bolt of image that made Johnny straighten up and clap his hand against the side of his head as if Chuck had struck him instead of hugging him. The image sank into his mind like a picture done by electroplate.

'No,' he said. 'No *way*. You two stay right away from there.'

Chuck drew back uneasily. He had felt *something*. Something cold and dark and incomprehensible. Suddenly he didn't want to touch Johnny; at that moment he never wanted to touch Johnny again. It was as if he had found out what it would be like to lie in his own coffin and watch the lid nailed down.

'Johnny,' he said, and then faltered. 'What's ... what's ...'

Roger had been on his way over with drinks, and now he paused, puzzled. Johnny was looking over Chuck's shoulder, at the distant thunderheads. His eyes were vague and hazy.

He said: 'You want to stay away from that place. There are no lightning rods.'

'*Johnny* ...' Chuck looked at his father, frightened. 'It's like he's having some kind of ... *fit*, or something.'

'Lightning,' Johnny proclaimed in a carrying voice. People turned their heads to look at him. He spread his

hands. 'Flash fire. The insulation in the walls. The doors
... jammed. Burning people smell like hot pork.'

'What's he talking about?' Chuck's girl cried, and conversation trickled to a halt. Now everyone was looking
at Johnny, as they balanced plates of food and glasses.

Roger stepped over. 'John! Johnny! What's wrong?
Wake up!' He snapped his fingers in front of Johnny's
vague eyes. Thunder muttered in the west, the voice of
giants over gin rummy, perhaps. 'What's wrong?'

Johnny's voice was clear and moderately loud, carrying
to each of the fifty-some people who were there – businessmen and their wives, professors and their wives, Durham's upper middle class. 'Keep your son home tonight or
he's going to burn to death with the rest of them. There
is going to be a fire, a terrible fire. Keep him away from
Cathy's. It's going to be struck by lightning and it will
burn flat before the first fire engine can arrive. The insulation will burn. They will find charred bodies six and
seven deep in the exits and there will be no way to
identify them except by their dental work. It ... it ...'

Patty Strachan screamed then, her hand going to her
mouth, her plastic glass tumbling to the lawn, the ice
cubes spilling out onto the grass and gleaming there like
diamonds of improbable size. She stood swaying for a
moment and then she fainted, going down in a pastel
billow of party dress, and her mother ran forward, crying
at Johnny as she passed: 'What's *wrong* with you? What
in God's name is *wrong* with you?'

Chuck stared at Johnny. His face was paper-white.

Johnny's eyes began to clear. He looked around at the
staring knots of people. 'I'm sorry,' he muttered.

Patty's mother was on her knees, holding her daughter's head in her arms and patting her cheeks lightly. The
girl began to stir and moan.

'Johnny?' Chuck whispered, and then, without waiting
for an answer, went to his girl.

It was very still on the Chatsworth back lawn. Everyone was looking at him. They were looking at him because it had happened again. They were looking at him

391

the way the nurses had. And the reporters. They were crows strung out on a telephone line. They were holding their drinks and their plates of potato salad and looking at him as if he were a bug, a freak. They were looking at him as if he had suddenly opened his pants and exposed himself to them.

He wanted to run, he wanted to hide. He wanted to puke.

'Johnny,' Roger said, putting an arm around him. 'Come on in the house. You need to get off your feet for . . .'

Thunder rumbled, far off.

'What's Cathy's?' Johnny said harshly, resisting the pressure of Roger's arm over his shoulders. 'It isn't someone's house, because there were exit signs. What is it? Where is it?'

'Can't you get him out of here?' Patty's mother nearly screamed. 'He's upsetting her all over again!'

'Come on, Johnny.'

'But . . .'

'*Come on.*'

He allowed himself to be led away toward the guest house. The sound of their shoes on the gravel drive was very loud. There seemed to be no other sound. They got as far as the pool, and then the whispering began behind them.

'Where's Cathy's?' Johnny asked again.

'How come you don't know?' Roger asked. 'You seemed to know everything else. You scared poor Patty Strachan into a faint.'

'I can't see it. It's in the dead zone. What is it?'

'Let's get you upstairs first.'

'I'm not sick!'

'Under strain, then,' Roger said. He spoke softly and soothingly, the way people speak to the hopelessly mad. The sound of his voice made Johnny afraid. And the headache started to come. He willed it back savagely. They went up the stairs to the guest house.

392

'Feel any better?' Roger asked.

'What's Cathy's?'

'It's a very fancy steakhouse and lounge in Somersworth. Graduation parties at Cathy's are something of a tradition. God knows why. Sure you don't want these aspirin?'

'No. Don't let him go, Roger. It's going to be hit by lightning. It's going to burn flat.'

'Johnny,' Roger Chatsworth said, slowly and very kindly, 'you can't know a thing like that.'

Johnny drank ice water a small sip at a time and set the glass back down with a hand that shook slightly. 'You said you checked into my background. I thought . . .'

'Yes, I did. But you're drawing a mistaken conclusion. I knew you were supposed to be a psychic or something, but I didn't want a psychic. I wanted a tutor. You've done a fine job as a tutor. My personal belief is that there isn't any difference between good psychics and bad ones, because I don't believe in any of that business. It's as simple as that. I don't believe it.'

'That makes me a liar, then.'

'Not at all,' Roger said in that same kind, low voice. 'I have a foreman at the mill in Sussex who won't light three on a match, but that doesn't make him a bad foreman. I have friends who are devoutly religious, and although I don't go to church myself, they're still my friends. Your belief that you can see into the future or sight things at a distance never entered into my judgment of whether or not to hire you. No . . . that isn't quite true. It never entered into it once I'd decided that it wouldn't interfere with your ability to do a good job with Chuck. It hasn't. But I no more believe that Cathy's is going to burn down tonight than I believe the moon is green cheese.'

'I'm not a liar, just crazy,' Johnny said. In a dull sort of way, it was interesting. Roger Dussault and many of the people who wrote Johnny letters had accused him of trickery, but Chatsworth was the first to accuse him of having a Jeanne d'Arc complex.

'Not that, either,' Roger said. 'You're a young man who was involved in a terriible accident and who has fought his way back against terrible odds at what has probably been a terrible price. That isn't a thing I'd ever flap my jaw about freely, Johnny, but if any of those people out there on the lawn – including Patty's mother – want to jump to a lot of stupid conclusions they'll be invited to shut their mouths about things they don't understand.'

'Cathy's,' Johnny said suddenly. 'How did I know the name, then? And how did I know it wasn't someone's house?'

'From Chuck. He's talked about the party a lot this week.'

'Not to me.'

Roger shrugged. 'Maybe he said something to Shelley or me while you were in earshot. Your subconscious happened to pick it up and file it away . . .'

'That's right,' Johnny said bitterly. 'Anything we don't understand, anything that doesn't fit into our scheme of the way things are, we'll just file it under S for subconscious, right? The twentieth-century god. How many times have you done that when something ran counter to your pragmatic view of the world, Roger?'

Roger's eyes might have flickered a little – or it might have been imagination.

'You associated lightning with the thunderstorm that's coming,' he said. 'Don't you see that? It's perfectly sim . . .'

'Listen,' Johnny said. 'I'm telling you this as simply as I can. That place is going to be struck by lightning. It's going to burn down. *Keep Chuck home.*'

Ah, God, the headache was coming for him. Coming like a tiger. He put his hand to his forehead and rubbed it unsteadily.

'Johnny, you've been pushing much too hard.'

'Keep him home,' Johnny repeated.

'It's his decision, and I wouldn't presume to make it for him. He's free, white, and eighteen.'

There was a tap at the door. 'Johnny?'

'Come in,' Johnny said, and Chuck himself came in. He looked worried.

'How are you?' Chuck asked.

'I'm all right,' Johnny said. 'I've got a headache, that's all. Chuck . . . please stay away from that place tonight. I'm asking you as a friend. Whether you think like your dad or not. *Please.*'

'No problem, man,' Chuck said cheerfully, and whumped down on the sofa. He hooked a hassock over with one foot. 'Couldn't drag Patty within a mile of that place with a twenty-foot towin chain. You put a scare into her.'

'I'm sorry,' Johnny said. He felt sick and chilly with relief. 'I'm sorry but I'm glad.'

'You had some kind of a flash, didn't you?' Chuck looked at Johnny, then at his father, and then slowly back to Johnny. 'I felt it. It was bad.'

'Sometimes people do. I understand it's sort of nasty.'

'Well, I wouldn't want it to happen again,' Chuck said. 'But hey . . . that place isn't really going to burn down, is it?'

'Yes,' Johnny said. 'You want to just keep away.'

'But . . .' He looked at his father, troubled. 'The senior class reserved the whole damn place. The school encourages that, you know. It's safer than twenty or thirty different parties and a lot of people drinking on the back roads. There's apt to be . . .' Chuck fell silent for a moment and then began to look frightened. 'There's apt to be two hundred couples there,' he said. 'Dad . . .'

'I don't think he believes any of this,' Johnny said.

Roger stood up and smiled. 'Well, let's take a ride over to Somersworth and talk to the manager of the place,' he said. 'It was a dull lawn party, anyway. And if you two still feel the same coming back, we can have everyone over here tonight.'

He glanced at Johnny.

'Only condition being that you have to stay sober and help chaperon, fellow.'

'I'll be glad to,' Johnny said. 'But why, if you don't believe it?'

'For your peace of mind,' Roger said, 'and for Chuck's. And so that, when nothing happens tonight, I can say I told you so and then just laaaugh my ass off.'

'Well, whatever, thanks.' He was trembling worse than ever now that the relief had come, but his headache had retreated to a dull throb.

'One thing up front, though,' Roger said. 'I don't think we stand a snowball's chance in hell of getting the owner to cancel on your unsubstantiated word, Johnny. This is probably one of his big business nights each year.'

Chuck said, 'Well, we could work something out . . .'

'Like what?'

'Well, we could tell him a story . . . spin some kind of yarn . . .'

'Lie, you mean? No, I won't do that. Don't ask me, Chuck.'

Chuck nodded. 'All right.'

'We better get going,' Roger said briskly. 'It's quarter of five. We'll take the Mercedes over to Somersworth.'

3 ·

Bruce Carrick, the owner-manager, was tending bar when the three of them came in at five-forty. Johnny's heart sank a little when he read the sign posted outside the lounge doors: PRIVATE PARTY THIS EVENING ONLY 7 PM TO CLOSING SEE YOU TOMORROW.

Carrick was not exactly being run into the ground. He was serving a few workmen who were drinking beer and watching the early news, and three couples who were having cocktails. He listened to Johnny's story with a face that grew ever more incredulous. When he had finished, Carrick said: 'You say Smith's your name?'

'Yes, that's right.'

'Mr. Smith, come on over to this window with me.'

He led Johnny to the lobby window, by the cloakroom door.

'Look out there, Mr. Smith, and tell me what you see.'

Johnny looked out, knowing what he would see. Route 9 ran west, now drying from a light afternoon sprinkle. Above, the sky was perfectly clear. The thunderheads had passed.

'Not much. At least, not now. But . . .'

'But nothing,' Bruce Carrick said. 'You know what I think? You want to know frankly? I think you're a nut. Why you picked me for this royal screwing I don't know or care. But if you got a second, sonny, I'll tell you the facts of life. The senior class has paid me six hundred and fifty bucks for this bash. They've hired a pretty good rock 'n roll band, Oak, from up in Maine. The food's out there in the freezer, all ready to go into the micro-wave. The salads are on ice. Drinks are extra, and most of these kids are over eighteen and can drink all they want . . . and tonight they will, who can blame them, you only graduate from a high school once. I'll take in two thousand dollars in the lounge tonight, no sweat. I got two extra barmen coming in. I got six waitresses and a hostess. If I should cancel this thing now, I lose the whole night, plus I got to pay back the six-fifty I already took for the meal. I don't even get my regular dinner crowd because that sign's been there all week. Do you get the picture?'

'Are there lightning rods on this place?' Johnny asked.

Carrick threw his hands up. 'I tell this guy the facts of life and he wants to discuss lightning rods! Yeah, I got lightning rods! A guy came in here, before I added on, must be five years ago now. He gave me a song-and-dance about improving my insurance rates. So I bought the goddam lightning rods! Are you happy? Jesus *Christ*!' He looked at Roger and Chuck. 'What are you two guys doing? Why are you letting this asshole run around loose? Get out, why don't you? I got a business to run.'

'Johnny . . .' Chuck began.

397

'Never mind,' Roger said. 'Let's go. Thank you for your time, Mr. Carrick, and for your polite and sympathetic attention.'

'Thanks for nothing,' Carrick said. 'Bunch of nuts!' He strode back toward the lounge.

The three of them went out. Chuck looked doubtfully at the flawless sky. Johnny started toward the car, looking only at his feet, feeling stupid and defeated. His headache thudded sickly against his temples. Roger was standing with his hands in his back pockets, looking up at the long, low roof of the building.

'What are you looking at, Dad?' Chuck asked.

'There are no lightning rods up there,' Roger Chatsworth said thoughtfully. 'No lightning rods at all.'

4 ·

The three of them sat in the living room of the big house, Chuck by the telephone. He looked doubtfully at his father. 'Most of them won't want to change their plans this late,' he said.

'They've got plans to go out, that's all,' Roger said. 'They can just as easily come here.'

Chuck shrugged and began dialing.

They ended up with about half the couples who had been planning to go to Cathy's that graduation evening, and Johnny was never really sure why they came. Some probably came simply because it sounded like a more interesting party and because the drinks were on the house. But word traveled fast, and the parents of a good many of the kids here had been at the lawn party that afternoon – as a result, Johnny spent much of the evening feeling like an exhibit in a glass case. Roger sat in the corner on a stool, drinking a vodka martini. His face was a studied mask.

Around quarter of eight he walked across the big bar/playroom combination that took up three-quarters of the basement level, bent close to Johnny and bellowed over the roar of Elton John, 'You want to go upstairs and play some cribbage?'

398

Johnny nodded gratefully.

Shelley was in the kitchen, writing letters. She looked up when they came in, and smiled. 'I thought you two masochists were going to stay down there all night. It's not really necessary, you know.'

'I'm sorry about all of this,' Johnny said. 'I know how crazy it must seem.'

'It does seem crazy,' Shelley said. 'No reason not to be candid about that. But having them here is really rather nice. I don't mind.'

Thunder rumbled outside. Johnny looked around. Shelley saw it and smiled a little. Roger had left to hunt for the cribbage board in the dining room welsh dresser.

'It's just passing over, you know,' she said. 'A little thunder and a sprinkle of rain.'

'Yes,' Johnny said.

She signed her letter in a comfortable sprawl, folded it, sealed it, addressed it, stamped it. 'You really experienced something, didn't you, Johnny?'

'Yes.'

'A momentary faintness,' she said. 'Possibly caused by a dietary deficiency. You're much too thin, Johnny. It might have been a hallucination, mightn't it?'

'No, I don't think so.'

Outside, thunder growled again, but distantly.

'I'm just as glad to have him home. I don't believe in astrology and palmistry and clairvoyance and all of that, but . . . I'm just as glad to have him home. He's our only chick . . . a pretty damned big chick now, I suspect you're thinking, but it's easy to remember him riding the little kids' merry-go-round in the town park in his short pants. Too easy, perhaps. And it's nice to be able to share the . . . the last rite of his boyhood with him.'

'It's nice that you feel that way,' Johnny said. Suddenly he was frightened to find himself close to tears. In the last six or eight months it seemed to him that his emotional control had slipped several notches.

'You've been good for Chuck. I don't mean just teaching him to read. In a lot of ways.'

'I like Chuck.'

'Yes,' she said quietly. 'I know you do.'

Roger came back with the cribbage board and a transistor radio tuned to WMTQ, a classical station that broadcast from the top of Mount Washington.

'A little antidote for Elton John, Aerosmith, Foghat, et al,' he said. 'How does a dollar a game sound, Johnny?'

'It sounds fine.'

Roger sat down, rubbing his hands. 'Oh, you're goin home poor,' he said.

6 .

They played cribbage and the evening passed. Between each game one of them would go downstairs and make sure no one had decided to dance on the pool table or go out back for a little party of their own. 'No one is going to impregnate anyone else at this party if I can help it,' Roger said.

Shelley had gone into the living room to read. Once an hour the music on the radio would stop and the news would come on and Johnny's attention would falter a little. But there was nothing about Cathy's in Somersworth – not at eight, nine, or ten.

After the ten o'clock news, Roger said: 'Getting ready to hedge your prediction a little, Johnny?'

'No.'

The weather forecast was for scattered thundershowers, clearing after midnight.

The steady bass signature of K.C. and the Sunshine Band came up through the floor.

'Party's getting loud,' Johnny remarked.

'The hell with that,' Roger said, grinning. 'The party's getting drunk. Spider Parmeleau is passed out in the corner and somebody's using him for a beer coaster. Oh, they'll have big heads in the morning, you want to believe it. I remember at my own graduation party . . .'

'Here is a bulletin from the WMTQ newsroom,' the radio said.

Johnny, who had been shuffling, sprayed cards all over the floor.

'Relax, it's probably just something about that kidnapping down in Florida.'

'I don't think so,' Johnny said.

The broadcaster said: 'It appears at this moment that the worst fire in New Hampshire history has claimed more than seventy-five young lives in the border town of Somersworth, New Hampshire. The fire occurred at a restaurant-lounge called Cathy's. A graduation party was in progress when the fire broke out. Somersworth fire chief Milton Hovey told reporters they have no suspicions of arson; they believe that the fire was almost certainly caused by a bolt of lightning.'

Roger Chatsworth's face was draining of all color. He sat bolt upright in his kitchen chair, his eyes fixed on a point somewhere above Johnny's head. His hands lay loosely on the table. From below them came the babble of conversation and laughter, intermingled now with the sound of Bruce Springsteen.

Shelley came into the room. She looked from her husband to Johnny and then back again. 'What is it? What's wrong?'

'Shut up,' Roger said.

'. . . is still blazing, and Hovey said that a final tally of the dead will probably not be known until early morning. It is known that over thirty people, mostly members of the Durham High School senior class, have been taken to hospitals in surrounding areas to be treated for burns. Forty people, also mostly graduating students, escaped from small bathroom windows at the rear of the lounge, but others were apparently trapped in fatal pile-ups at the . . .'

'Was it Cathy's?' Shelley Chatsworth screamed. '*Was it that place?*'

'Yes,' Roger said. He seemed eerily calm. 'Yes, it was.'

Downstairs there had been a momentary silence. It was

401

followed by a running thud of footsteps coming up the stairs. The kitchen door burst open and Chuck came in, looking for his mother.

'Mom? What is it? What's wrong?'

'It appears that we may owe you for our son's life,' Roger said in that same eerily calm voice. Johnny had never seen a face that white. Roger looked like a ghastly living waxwork.

'It *burned?*' Chuck's voice was incredulous. Behind him, others were crowding up the stairs now, whispering in low, affrighted voices. 'Are you saying it burned *down?*'

No one answered. And then, suddenly, from somewhere behind him, Patty Strachan began to talk in a high, hysterical voice. 'It's his fault, that guy there! He made it happen! He set it on fire by his mind, just like in that book *Carrie*. You murderer! Killer! You . . .'

Roger turned toward her. '*SHUT UP!*' He roared.

Patty collapsed into wild sobs.

'Burned?' Chuck repeated. He seemed to be asking himself now, inquiring if that could possibly be the right word.

'Roger?' Shelley whispered. 'Rog? Honey?'

There was a growing mutter on the stairs, and in the playroom below, like a stir of leaves. The stereo clicked off. The voices murmured.

Was Mike there? Shannon went, didn't she? Are you sure? Yes, I was all ready to leave when Chuck called me. My mother was there when that guy freaked out and she said she felt like a goose was walking on her grave, she asked me to come here instead. Was Casey there? Was Ray there? Was Maureen Ontello there? Oh my God, was she? Was . . .

Roger stood up slowly and turned around. 'I suggest,' he said, 'that we find the soberest people here to drive and that we all go down to the hospital. They'll need blood donors.'

Johnny sat like a stone. He found himself wondering if he would ever move again. Outside, thunder rumbled.

And followed on its heels like an inner clap, he heard his dying mother's voice:

Do your duty, John.

CHAPTER TWENTY-FOUR

August 12, 1977

Dear Johnny,

Finding you wasn't much of a trick – I sometimes think if you have enough free cash, you can find anyone in this country, and the cash I got. Maybe I'm risking your resentment stating it as baldly as that, but Chuck and Shelley and I owe you too much to tell you less than the truth. Money buys a lot, but it can't buy off the lightning. They found twelve boys still in the men's room opening off the restaurant, the one where the window had been nailed shut. The fire didn't reach there but the smoke did, and all twelve of them were suffocated. I haven't been able to get that out of my mind, because Chuck could have been one of those boys. So I had you 'tracked down', as you put it in your letter. And for the same reason, I can't leave you alone as you requested. At least not until the enclosed check comes back canceled with your endorsement on the back.

You'll notice that it's a considerably smaller check than the one you returned about a month ago. I got in touch with the EMMC Accounts Department and paid your outstanding hospital bills with the balance of it. You're free and clear that way, Johnny. That I could do, and I did it – with great pleasure, I might add.

You protest you can't take the money. I say you can and you will. You will, Johnny. I traced you to Ft. Lauderdale, and if you leave there I will trace you to the next place you go, even if you decide on Nepal. Call me a louse who won't let go if you want to; I see myself more as 'the Hound of Heaven'. I don't want to hound

you, Johnny. I remember you telling me that day not to
sacrifice my son. I almost did. And what about the others?
Eighty-one dead, thirty more terribly maimed and
burned. I think of Chuck saying maybe we could work
out some kind of a story, spin a yarn or something, and
me saying with all the righteousness of the totally stupid,
'I won't do that, Chuck. Don't ask me." Well, I could
have done something. That's what haunts me. I could
have given that butcher Carrick $3,000 to pay off his
help and shut down for the night. It would have come to
about $37 a life. So believe me when I say I don't want
to hound you; I'm really too busy hounding myself to
want to spare the time. I think I'll be doing it for quite a
few years to come. I'm paying up for refusing to believe
anything I couldn't touch with one of my five senses. And
please don't believe that paying the bills and tendering
this check is just a sop to my conscience. Money can't
buy off the lightning, and it can't buy an end to bad
dreams, either. The money is for Chuck, although he
knows nothing about it.

Take the check and I'll leave you in peace. That's the
deal. Send it on to UNICEF, if you want, or give it to a
home for orphan bloodhounds, or blow it all on the
ponies. I don't care. Just take it.

I'm sorry you felt you had to leave in such a hurry, but
I believe I understand. We all hope to see you soon.
Chuck leaves for Stovington Prep on September 4.

Johnny, take the check. Please.

All regards,
Roger Chatsworth

September 1, 1977

Dear Johnny,

Will you believe that I'm not going to let this go?
Please. Take the check.

Regards,
Roger

404

Dear Johnny,

Charlie and I were both so glad to know where you are, and it was a relief to get a letter from you that sounded so natural and like yourself. But there was one thing that bothered me very much, son. I called up Sam Weizak and read him that part of your letter about the increasing frequency of your headaches. He advises you to see a doctor, Johnny, without delay. He is afraid that a clot may have formed around the old scar tissue. So that worries me, and it worries Sam, too. You've never looked really healthy since you came out of the coma, Johnny, and when I last saw you in early June, I thought you looked very tired. Sam didn't say, but I know what he'd really like you to do is to catch a plane out of Phoenix and come on home and let him be the one to look at you. You certainly can't plead poverty now!

Roger Chatsworth has called here twice, and I tell him what I can. I think he's telling the truth when he says it isn't conscience-money or a reward for saving his son's life. I believe your mother would have said that the man is doing penance the only way he knows how. Anyway, you've taken it, and I hope you don't mean it when you say you only did it to 'get him off your back'. I believe you have too much grit in you to do anything for a reason like that.

Now this is very hard for me to say, but I will do the best I can. Please come home, Johnny. The publicity has died down again – I can hear you saying, 'Oh bullshit, it will never die down again, not after this' and I suppose you are right in a way, but you are also wrong. Over the phone Mr. Chatsworth said, 'If you talk to him, try to make him understand that no psychic except Nostradamus has ever been much more than a nine-days' wonder.' I worry about you a lot, son. I worry about you blaming yourself for the dead instead of blessing yourself for the living, the ones you saved, the ones that were at the Chatsworths' house that night. I worry and I miss

405

you, too. 'I miss you like the dickens,' as your grand-mother used to say. So please come home as soon as you can.

Dad

P.S. I'm sending the clippings about the fire and about your part in it. Charlie collected them up. As you will see, you were correct in guessing that 'everyone who was at that lawn party will spill their guts to the papers'. I suppose these clippings may just upset you more, and if they do, just toss them away. But Charlie's idea was that you may look at them and say, 'That wasn't as bad as I thought, I can face that.' I hope it turns out that way.

Dad

September 29, 1977

Dear Johnny,

I got your address from my dad. How is the great American desert. Seen any redskins (ha-ha)? Well here I am at Stovington Prep. This place isn't so tough. I am taking sixteen hours of credit. Advanced chemistry is my favorite although it's really something of a tit after the course at DHS. I always had the feeling that our teacher there, old Fearless Farnham, would really have been more happy making doomsday weapons and blowing up the world. In English we are reading three things by J. D. Salinger this first four weeks, Catcher in the Rye, Franny and Zooey, and Raise High the Roof Beams, Carpenters. I like him a lot. Our teacher told us he still lives over in N.H. but has given up writing. That blows my mind. Why would someone just give up when they are going great guns? Oh well. The football team here really sucks but I'm learning to like soccer. The coach says soccer is football for smart people and football is football for ass-holes. I can't figure out yet if he's right or just jealous.

I'm wondering if it would be ok to give out your ad-

406

dress to some people who were at our party graduation night. They want to write and say thanks. One of them is Patty Strachan's mother, you will remember her, the one that made such a pisshead of herself when her 'precious daughter' fainted at the lawn party that afternoon. She now figures that you're an ok person. I'm not going with Patty anymore, by the way. I'm not much on long-distance courtships at my 'tender age' (ha-ha), and Patty is going to Vassar, as you might have expected. I've met a foxy little chick here.

Well, write when you can, my man. My dad made it sound like you were really 'bummed out' for what reason I do not know since it seems to me that you did everything you could to make things turn out right. He's wrong, isn't he, Johnny? You're really not that bummed out, are you? Please write and tell me you are ok, I worry about you. That's a laugh, isn't it, the original Alfred E. Neuman worried about you, but I am.

When you write, tell me why Holden Caulfield always has to have the blues so much when he isn't even black.

Chuck

P.S. The foxy chick's name is Stephanie Wyman, and I have already turned her on to Something Wicked This Way Comes. She also likes a punk-rock group called The Ramones, you should hear them, they are hilarious.

C

October 17, 1977

Dear Johnny,

Okay, that's better, you sound ok. Laughed my ass off about your job with the Phoenix Public Works Dept. I have no sympathy at all for your sunburn after four outings as a Stovington Tiger. Coach is right, I guess, football is football for assholes, at least at this place. Our record is 1–3 and in the game we won I scored three

407

touchdowns, hyperventilated my stupid self and blacked out. Scared Steff into a tizzy (ha-ha).

I waited to write so I could answer your question about how the Home Folks feel about Greg Stillson now that he is 'on the job'. I was home this last weekend, and I'll tell you all I can. Asked my dad first and he said, 'Is Johnny still interested in that guy?' I said, 'He's showing his fundamental bad taste by wanting your opinion.' Then he goes to my mother, 'See, prep school is turning him into a smartass. I thought it would.'

Well, to make a long story short, most people are pretty surprised by how well Stillson's doing. My dad said this: 'If people of a congressman's home district had to give a report card on how well the guy was doing after 10 months, Stillson would get mostly Bs, plus an A for his work on Carter's energy bill and his own home heating-oil ceiling bill. Also an A for effort.' Dad told me to tell you that maybe he was wrong about Stillson being the village fool.

Other comments from people I talked to when I was home: they like it around here that he doesn't dress up in a business suit. Mrs. Jarvis who runs the Quik-Pik (sorry about the spelling, man, but that's what they call it) says she thinks Stillson is not afraid of 'the big interests'. Henry Burke, who runs The Bucket – that el scuzzo tavern downtown – says he thinks Stillson has done 'a double-damn good job'. Most other comments are similar. They contrast what Stillson has done with what Carter hasn't done, most of them are really disappointed in him and are kicking themselves for having voted for him. I asked some of them if they weren't worried that those iron horsemen were still hanging around and that fellow Sonny Elliman was serving as one of Stillson's aides. None of them seemed too upset. The guy who runs the Record Rock put it to be this way: 'If Tom Hayden can go straight and Eldridge Cleave can get Jesus, why can't some bikies join the establishment? Forgive and forget.'

So there you are. I would write more, but football prac-

*tice is coming up. This weekend we are scheduled to be
trounced by the Barre Wildcats. I just hope I survive the
season. Keep well, my man.*

Chuck

From the *New York Times*, March 4, 1978:

FBI AGENT MURDERED IN OKLAHOMA

Special to the Times – Edgar Lancte, 37, a ten-year
veteran of the FBI, was apparently murdered last night
in an Oklahoma City parking garage. Police say that a
dynamite bomb wired to the ignition of his car exploded when Mr. Lancte turned the key. The gang-
land-style execution was similar in style to the murder
of Arizona investigative reporter Don Bolles two years
ago, but FBI chief William Webster would not specu-
late on any possible connection. Mr. Webster would
also neither confirm nor deny that Mr. Lancte had
been investigating shady land deals and possible links
to local politicians.

There appears to be some mystery surrounding exactly what Mr. Lancte's current assignment was, and
one source in the Justice Department claims that Mr.
Lancte was not investigating possible land fraud at all
but a national security matter.

Mr. Lancte joined the Federal Bureau of Investigation in 1968 and ...

CHAPTER TWENTY-FIVE

1 .

The notebooks in Johnny's bureau drawer grew from
four to five, and by the fall of 1978 to seven. In the fall of
1978, between the deaths of two popes in rapid succession,
Greg Stillson had become national news.

He was reelected to the House of Representatives in a landslide, and with the country tending toward Proposition 13 conservativism, he had formed the America Now party. Most startling, several members of the House had reneged on their original party standing and had 'jined up', as Greg liked to put it. Most of them held very similar beliefs, which Johnny had defined as superficially liberal on domestic issues and moderate to very conservative on issues of foreign policy. There was not a one of them who had voted on the Carter side of the Panama Canal treaties. And when you peeled back the liberal veneer on domestic positions, they turned out to be pretty conservative, too. The America Now party wanted bad trouble for big-time dopers, they wanted the cities to have to sink or swim on their own ('There is no need for a struggling dairy farmer to have to subsidize New York City's methadone programs with his taxes,' Greg proclaimed), they wanted a crackdown on welfare benefits to whores, pimps, bums, and people with a felony bust on their records, they wanted sweeping tax reforms to be paid for by sweeping social services cutbacks. All of it was an old song, but Greg's America Now party had set it to a pleasing new tune.

Seven congressmen swung over before the off-year elections, and two senators. Six of the Congressmen were reelected, and both of the senators. Of the nine, eight had been Republicans whose base had been whittled away to a pinhead. Their switch of party and subsequent reelections, one wag had quipped, was a better trick than the one that had followed 'Lazarus, come forth!'

Some were already saying that Greg Stillson might be a power to be reckoned with, and not that many years down the road, either. He had not been able to send all the world's pollution out to Jupiter and the rings of Saturn, but he had succeeded in running at least two of the rascals out – one of them a congressman who had been feathering his nest as the silent partner in a parking-lot kickback scheme, and one of them a presidential aide with a penchant for gay bars. His oil-ceiling bill had shown vision and boldness, and his careful guidance of its passage from committee to final vote had shown a down-home country-boy shrewdness. Nineteen-hundred eighty would be too early for Greg, and 1984 might be too tempting to resist, but if he managed to stay cool until 1988, if he continued to build his base and the winds of change did not shift radically enough to blow his fledgling party away, why, anything might happen. The Republicans had fallen to squabbling splinters, and assuming that Mondale or Jerry Brown or even Howard Baker might follow Carter as president, who was to follow then? Even 1992 might not be too late for him. He was a relatively young man. Yes, 1992 sounded about right . . .

There were several political cartoons in Johnny's notebooks. All of them showed Stillson's infectious slantwise grin, and in all of them he was wearing his construction helmet. One by Oliphant showed Greg rolling a barrel of oil marked PRICE CEILINGS straight down the middle aisle of the House, the helmet cocked back on his head. Up front was Jimmy Carter, scratching his head and looking puzzled; he was not looking Greg's way at all and the implication seemed to be that he was going to get run down. The caption read: OUTTA MY WAY, JIMMY!

The helmet. The helmet somehow bothered Johnny more than anything else. The Republicans had their elephant, the democrats their donkey, and Greg Stillson had his construction helmet. In Johnny's dreams it sometimes seemed that Stillson was wearing a motorcycle helmet. And sometimes it was a coal-scuttle helmet.

2 ·

In a separate notebook he kept the clippings his father had sent him concerning the fire at Cathy's. He had gone over them again and again, although for reasons that Sam, Roger, or even his father could not have suspected. PSYCHIC PREDICTS FIRE. 'MY DAUGHTER WOULD HAVE DIED TOO,' TEARFUL, THANK-

411

FUL MOM PROCLAIMS (the tearful, thankful mom in question had been Patty Strachan's). *Psychic Who Cracked Castle Rock Murders Predicts Flash Fire.* ROADHOUSE DEATH-TOLL REACHES 90. FATHER SAYS JOHNNY SMITH HAS LEFT NEW ENGLAND, REFUSES TO SAY WHERE. Pictures of him. Pictures of his father. Pictures of that long-ago wreck on Route 6 in Cleaves Mills, back in the days when Sarah Bracknell had been his girl. Now Sarah was a woman, the mother of two, and in his last letter Herb had said Sarah was showing a few gray hairs. It seemed impossible to believe that he himself was thirty-one. Impossible, but true.

Around all these clippings were his own jottings, his painful efforts to get it straight in his mind once and for all. None of them understood the true importance of the fire, its implication on the much larger matter of what to do about Greg Stillson.

He had written: 'I have to do something about Stillson. I *have* to. I was right about Cathy's, and I'm going to be right about this. There is absolutely no question in my mind. He is going to become president and he is going to start a war – or cause one through simple mismanagement of the office, which amounts to the same thing.

'The question is: *How drastic are the measures that need to be taken?*

'Take Cathy's as a test-tube case. It almost could have been sent to me as a sign, God I'm starting to sound like my mother, but there it is. Okay, I *knew* there was going to be a fire and that people were going to die. Was that sufficient to save them? Answer: it was not sufficient to save *all* of them, because *people only truly believe after the fact.* The ones who came to the Chatsworth house instead of going to Cathy's were saved, but it's important to remember that R.C. didn't have the party because he believed my prediction. He was very upfront about that. He had the party because he thought it would help me have peace of mind. He was . . . humoring me. He believed *after.* Patty Strachan's mother believed *after.* After-

after-after. By then it was too late for the dead and the burned.

'So, Question 2: Could I have changed the outcome?

'Yes. I could have driven a car right through the front of the place. Or, I could have burned it down myself that afternoon.

'Question 3: What would the results of either action have been to me?

'Imprisonment, probably. If I took the car option and then lightning struck it later that night, I suppose I could have argued ... no, it doesn't wash. Common experience may recognize some sort of psychic ability in the human mind, but the law sure as hell doesn't. I think now, if I had it to do over again, I would do one of those things and never mind the consequences to me. Is it possible that I didn't completely believe my own prediction?

'The matter of Stillson is horribly similar in all respects, except, thank God, that I have a lot more lead time.

'So, back to square one. I don't want Greg Stillson to become President. How can I change that outcome?

'1. Go back to New Hampshire and "jine up", as he puts it. Try to throw a few monkey wrenches into the America Now party. Try to sabotage *him*. There's dirt enough under the rug. Maybe I could sweep some of it out.

'2. Hire someone else to get the dirt on him. There's enough of Roger's money left over to hire someone good. On the other hand, I got the feeling that Lancte was pretty good. And Lancte's dead.

'3. Wound or cripple him. The way Arthur Bremmer crippled Wallace, the way whoever-it-was crippled Larry Flynt.

'4. Kill him. Assassinate him.

'Now, some of the drawbacks. The first option isn't sure enough. I could end up doing nothing more constructive than getting myself trounced, the way Hunter Thompson did when he was researching his first book, that one on the Hell's Angels. Even worse, this fellow

Elliman may be familiar with what I look like, as a result of what happened at the Trimbull rally. Isn't it more or less S.O.P. to keep a file on people who may be dangerous to your guys? I wouldn't be surprised to find out that Stillson had one guy on his payroll whose only job was to keep updated files on weird people and kooks. Which definitely includes me.

'Then there's the second option. Suppose all the dirt has already come out? If Stillson has already formed his higher political aspirations – and all his actions seem to point that way – he may already have cleaned up his act. And another thing: dirt under the rug is only as dirty as the press wants to make it, and the press likes Stillson. He cultivates them. In a novel I suppose I would turn private detective myself and "get the goods on him", but the sad fact is that I wouldn't know where to begin. You could argue that my ability to "read" people, to find things out that have been lost (to quote Sam) would give me a boost. If I could find out something about Lancte, that would turn the trick. But isn't it likely that Stillson delegates all that to Sonny Elliman? And I cannot even be sure, despite my suspicions, that Edgar Lancte was still on Stillson's trail when he was murdered. It is possible that I might hang Sonny Elliman and still not finish Stillson.

'Overall, the second alternative *is just not sure enough*. The stakes are *enormous*, so much so that I don't even dare let myself think about "the big picture" very often. It brings on a very bitch-kitty of a headache every time.

'I have even considered, in my wilder moments, trying to hook him on drugs the way the character Gene Hackman played in *The French Connection II* was, or driving him batty with LSD slipped into his Dr Pepper or whatever it is he drinks. But all of that is cop-show make-believe. Gordon Liddy shit. The problems are so great that this "option" doesn't even bear much talking about. Maybe I could kidnap him. After all, the guy is only a U.S. representative. I wouldn't know where to get heroin or morphine, but I could get plenty of LSD from Larry

McNaughton right here in the good old Phoenix Public Works Department. He has pills for every purpose. But suppose (if we're willing to suppose the foregoing) that he just enjoyed his trip(s)?

'Shooting and crippling him? Maybe I could and maybe I couldn't. I guess under the right circumstances, I could – like the rally in Trimbull. Suppose I did. After what happened in Laurel, George Wallace was never really a potent political force again. On the other hand, FDR campaigned from his wheelchair and even turned it into an asset.

'That leaves assassination, the Big Casino. This is the one unarguable alternative. You can't run for president if you're a corpse.

'If I could pull the trigger.

'And if I could, what would the results be to me?

'As Bob Dylan says, "Honey, do you have to ask me that?"'

There were a great many other notes and jottings, but the only other really important one was written out and neatly boxed : 'Suppose outright murder does turn out to be the only alternative? And suppose it turned out that I could pull the trigger? Murder is still wrong. Murder is wrong. Murder is wrong. There may yet be an answer. Thank God there's years of time.'

3 ·

But for Johnny, there wasn't.

In early December of 1978, shortly after another congressman, Leo Ryan of California, had been shot to death on a jungle airstrip in the South American country of Guayana, Johnny Smith discovered he had almost run out of time.

CHAPTER TWENTY-SIX

1 .

At 2 : 30 P.M. on December 26, 1978, Bud Prescott waited on a tall and rather haggard-looking young man with graying hair and badly bloodshot eyes. Bud was one of three clerks working in the 4th Street Phoenix Sporting Goods Store on the day after Christmas, and most of the business was exchanges – but this fellow was a paying customer.

He said he wanted to buy a good rifle, light-weight, bolt-action. Bud showed him several. The day after Christmas was a slow one on the gun-counter; when men got guns for Christmas, very few of them wanted to exchange them for something else.

This fellow looked them all over carefully and finally settled on a Remington 700, .243 caliber, a very nice gun with a light kick and a flat trajectory. He signed the gun-book John Smith and Bud thought, *If I never saw me an alias before in my life, there's one there.* 'John Smith' paid cash – took the twenties right out of a wallet that was bulging with them. Took the rifle right over the counter. Bud, thinking to poke him a little, told him he could have his initials burned into the stock, no extra charge. 'John Smith' merely shook his head.

When 'Smith' left the store, Bud noticed that he was limping noticeably. Would never be any problem identifying that guy again, he thought, not with that limp and those scars running up and down his neck.

2 .

At 10: 30 A.M. on December 27, a thin man who walked with a limp came into Phoenix Office Supply, Inc., and approached Dean Clay, a salesman there. Clay said later that he noticed what his mother had always called a 'fire-spot' in one of the man's eyes. The customer said he wanted to buy a large attaché case, and eventually picked out a handsome cowhide item, top of the line, priced at $149.95. And the man with the limp qualified for the cash discount by paying with new twenties. The whole transaction, from looking to paying, took no more than ten minutes. The fellow walked out of the store, and turned right toward the downtown area, and Dean Clay never saw him again until he saw his picture in the Phoenix *Sun.*

3 ·

Late that same afternoon a tall man with graying hair approached Bonita Alvarez's window in the Phoenix Amtrak terminal and inquired about traveling from Phoenix to New York by train. Bonita showed him the connections. He followed them with his finger and then carefully jotted them all down. He asked Bonnie Alvarez if she could ticket him to depart on January 3. Bonnie danced her fingers over her computer console and said that she could.

'Then why don't you ...' the tall man began, and then faltered. He put one hand up to his head.

'Are you all right, sir?'

'Fireworks,' the tall man said. She told the police later on that she was quite sure that was what he said. *Fireworks.*

'Sir? Are you all right?'

'Headache,' he said. 'Excuse me.' He tried to smile, but the effort did not improve his drawn, young-old face much.

'Would you like some aspirin? I have some.'

'No, thanks. It'll pass.'

She wrote the tickets and told him he would arrive at New York's Grand Central Station on January 6, at mid-afternoon.

'How much is that?'

She told him and added: 'Will that be cash or charge, Mr. Smith?'

417

'Cash,' he said, and pulled it right out of his wallet – a whole handful of twenties and tens.

She counted it, gave him his change, his receipt, his tickets. 'Your train leaves at 10:30 A.M., Mr. Smith,' she said. 'Please be here and ready to entrain at 10:10.'

'All right,' he said. 'Thank you.'

Bonnie gave him the big professional smile, but Mr. Smith was already turning away. His face was very pale, and to Bonnie he looked like a man who was in a great deal of pain.

She was very sure that he had said *fireworks*.

4 ·

Elton Curry was a conductor on Amtrak's Phoenix–Salt Lake run. The tall man appeared promptly at 10:00 A.M. on January 3, and Elton helped him up the steps and into the car because he was limping quite badly. He was carrying a rather old tartan traveling bag with scuffmarks and fraying edges in one hand. In the other he carried a brand-new cowhide attaché case. He carried the attaché case as if it were quite heavy.

'Can I help you with that, sir?' Elton asked, meaning the attaché case, but it was the traveling bag that the passenger handed him, along with his ticket.

'No, I'll take that when we're underway, sir.'

'All right. Thank you.'

A very polite sort of fellow, Elton Curry told the FBI agents who questioned him later. And he tipped well.

5 ·

January 6, 1979, was a gray, overcast day in New York – snow threatened but did not fall. George Clements' taxi was parked in front of the Biltmore Hotel, across from Grand Central.

The door opened and a fellow with graying hair got in, moving carefully and a little painfully. He placed a traveling bag and an attaché case beside him on the seat, closed the door, then put his head back against the seat

418

and closed his eyes for a moment, as if he was very, very tired.

'Where we goin, my friend?' George asked.

His fare looked at a slip of paper. 'Port Authority Terminal,' he said.

George got going. 'You look a little white around the gills, my friend. My brother-in-law looked like that when he was havin his gallstone attacks. You got stones?'

'No.'

'My brother-in-law, he says gallstones hurt worse than anything. Except maybe kidney stones. You know what I told him? I told him he was full of shit. Andy, I says, you're a great guy, I love ya, but you're full of shit. You ever had cancer, Andy? I says. I asks him that, you know, did he ever have cancer. I mean, everybody knows cancer's the worst.' George took a long look in his rear-view mirror. 'I'm asking you sincerely, my friend ... are you okay? Because, I'm telling you the truth, you look like death warmed over.'

The passenger answered, 'I'm fine. I was ... thinking of another taxi ride. Several years ago.'

'Oh, right,' George said sagely, exactly as if he knew what the man was talking about. Well, New York was full of kooks, there was no denying that. And after this brief pause for reflection, he went on talking about his brother-in-law.

6 ·

'Mommy, is that man sick?'

'Shhh.'

'Yeah, but is he?'

'Danny, be quiet.'

She smiled at the man on the other side of the Greyhound's aisle, an apologetic, kids-will-say-anything-won't-they smile, but the man appeared not to have heard. The poor guy did look sick. Danny was only four, but he was right about that. The man was looking listlessly out at the snow that had begun to fall shortly after they crossed the Connecticut state line. He was much too pale, much too thin, and there was a hideous Frankenstein scar running up out of his coat collar to just under his jaw. It was as if someone had tried taking his head clean off at sometime in the not-too-distant past – tried and almost succeeded.

The Greyhound was on its way to Portsmouth, New Hampshire, and they would arrive at 9 : 30 tonight if the snow didn't slow things down too much. Julie Brown and her son were going to see Julie's mother-in-law, and as usual the old bitch would spoil Danny rotten – and Danny didn't have far to go.

'I wanna go see him.'

'No, Danny.'

'I wanna see if he's sick.'

'No!'

'Yeah, but what if he's *dine*, ma?' Danny's eyes positively glowed at this entrancing possibility. 'He might be dine right now!'

'Danny, shut up.'

'Hey, mister!' Danny cried. 'You dine, or anything?'

'Danny, you *shut your mouth*!' Julie hissed, her cheeks burning with embarrassment.

Danny began to cry then, not real crying but that snotty, I-can't-get-my-own-way whining that always made her want to grab him and pinch his arms until he *really* had something to cry about. At times like this, riding the bus into evening through another cruddy snowstorm with her son whining beside her, she wished her own mother had sterilized her several years before she had reached the age of consent.

That was when the man across the aisle turned his head and smiled at her – a tired, painful smile, but rather sweet for all that. She saw that his eyes were terribly bloodshot, as if he had been crying. She tried to smile back, but it felt false and uneasy on her lips. That red left eye – and the scar running up his neck – made that half of his face look sinister and unpleasant.

She hoped that the man across the aisle wasn't going all the way to Portsmouth, but as it turned out, he was.

She caught sight of him in the terminal as Danny's gram swept the boy, giggling happily, into her arms. She saw him limping toward the terminal doors, a scuffed traveling bag in one hand, a new attaché case in the other. And for just a moment, she felt a terrible chill cross her back. It was really worse than a limp – it was very nearly a headlong lurch. But there was something implacable about it, she told the New Hampshire state police later. It was as if he knew exactly where he was going and nothing was going to stop him from getting there.

Then he passed out into the darkness and she lost sight of him.

7 ·

Timmesdale, New Hampshire, is a small town west of Durham, just inside the third congressional district. It is kept alive by the smallest of the Chatsworth Mills, which hulks like a soot-stained brick ogre on the edge of Timmesdale Stream. Its one modest claim to fame (according to the local Chamber of Commerce) is that it was the first town in New Hampshire to have electric streetlights.

One evening in early January, a young man with prematurely graying hair and a limp walked into the Timmesdale Pub, the town's only beer joint. Dick O'Donnell, the owner, was tending the bar. The place was almost empty because it was the middle of the week and another norther was brewing. Two or three inches had piled up out there already, and more was on the way.

The man with the limp stamped off his shoes, came to the bar, and ordered a Pabst. O'Donnell served him. The fellow had two more, making them last, watching the TV over the bar. The color was going bad, had been for a couple of months now, and The Fonz looked like an aging Rumanian ghoul. O'Donnell couldn't remember having seen this guy around.

'Like another?' O'Donnell asked, coming back to the bar after serving the two old bags in the corner.

'One more won't hurt,' the fellow said. He pointed to a spot above the TV. 'You met him, I guess.'

It was a framed blowup of a political cartoon. It showed Greg Stillson, his construction helmet cocked back on his head, throwing a fellow in a business suit down the Capitol steps. The fellow in the business suit was Louis Quinn, the congressman who had been caught taking kickbacks in the parking-lot scam some fourteen months ago. The cartoon was titled GIVING EM THE BUM'S RUSH, and across the corner it had been signed in a scrawling hand: *For Dick O'Donnell, who keeps the best damn saloon in the third district! Keep drawing them, Dick – Greg Stillson.*

'Betcha butt I did,' O'Donnell said. 'He gave a speech in here the last time he canvassed for the House. Had signs out all over town, come on into the Pub at two o'clock Saturday afternoon and have one on Greg. That was the best damn day's business I've ever done. People was only supposed to have one on him, but he ended up grabbing the whole tab. Can't do much better than that, can you?'

'Sounds like you think he's one hell of a guy.'

'Yeah, I do,' O'Donnell said. 'I'd be tempted to put my bare knuckles on anyone who said the other way.'

'Well, I won't try you.' The fellow put down three quarters. 'Have one on me.'

'Well, okay. Don't mind if I do. Thanks, mister . . . ?'

'Johnny Smith is my name.'

'Why, pleased to meet you, Johnny. Dicky O'Donnell, that's me.' He drew himself a beer from the tap. 'Yeah, Greg's done this part of New Hampshire a lotta good. And there's a lotta people afraid to come right out and say it, but I'm not. I'll say it right out loud. Some day Greg Stillson's apt to be president.'

'You think so?'

'I do,' O'Donnell said, coming back to the bar. 'New Hampshire's not big enough to hold Greg. He's one hell of a politician, and coming from me, that's something. I thought the whole crew was nothin but a bunch of crooks and lollygags. I still do, but Greg's an exception to the

422

rule. He's a square shooter. If you told me five years ago I'd be sayin somethin like that, I woulda laughed in your face. You'd be more likely to find me readin poitry than seein any good in a politician, I woulda said. But, goddammit, he's a man.'

Johnny said, 'Most of these guys want to be your buddy while they're running for office, but when they get in its fuck you, Jack, I got mine until the next election. I come from Maine myself, and the one time I wrote Ed Muskie, you know what I got? A form letter!'

'Ah, that's a Polack for you,' O'Donnell said. 'What do you expect from a Polack? Listen, Greg comes back to the district every damn weekend! Now does that sound like fuck you, Jack, I got mine, to you?'

'Every weekend, huh?' Johnny sipped his beer. 'Where? Trimbull? Ridgeway? The big towns?'

'He's got a system,' O'Donnell said in the reverent tones of a man who has never been able to work one out for himself. 'Fifteen towns, from the big places like Capital City right down to the little burgs like Timmes-dale and Coorter's Notch. He hits one a week until he's gone through the whole list and then he starts at the top again. You know how big Coorter's Notch is? They got eight hundred souls up there. So what do you think about a guy who takes a weekend off from Washington and comes down to Coorter's Notch to freeze his balls off in a cold meetin hall? Does that sound like fuck you, Jack, I got mine, to you?'

'No, it doesn't,' Johnny said truthfully. 'What does he do? Just shake hands?'

'No, he's got a hall in every town. Reserves it for all day Saturday. He gets in there about ten in the morning, and people can come by and talk to him. Tell him their idears, you know. If they got questions, he answers them. If he can't answer them, he goes back to Washington and *finds* the answer!' He looked at Johnny triumphantly.

'When was he here in Timmesdale last?'

'Couple of months ago,' O'Donnell said. He went to

the cash register and rummaged through a pile of papers beside it. He came up with a dog-eared clipping and laid it on the bar beside Johnny.

'Here's the list. You just take a look at that and see what you think.'

The clipping was from the Ridgeway paper. It was fairly old now. The story was headlined STILLSON AN-NOUNCES 'FEEDBACK CENTERS'. The first para-graph looked as though it might have been lifted straight from the Stillson press kit. Below it was the list of towns where Greg would be spending his weekends, and the proposed dates. He was not due in Timmesdale again until mid-March.

'I think it looks pretty good,' Johnny said.

'Yeah, I think so. Lotta people think so.'

'By this clipping, he must have been in Coorter's Notch just last weekend.'

'That's right,' O'Donnell said, and laughed. 'Good old Coorter's Notch. Want another beer, Johnny?'

'Only if you'll join me,' Johnny said, and laid a couple of bucks on the bar.

'Well, I don't care if I do.'

One of the two bar-bags had put some money in the juke and Tammy Wynette, sounding old and tired and not happy to be here, began singing, 'Stand By Your Man.'

'Hey Dick!' the other cawed. 'You ever hear of service in this place?'

'Shut your head!' he hollered back.

'Fuck – *YOU*,' she called, and cackled.

'Goddammit, Clarice, I told you about saying the eff-word in my bar! I told you . . .'

'Oh get off it and let's have some beer.'

'I hate those two old cunts,' O'Donnell muttered to Johnny. 'Couple of old alky diesel-dykes, that's what they are. They been here a million years, and I wouldn't be surprised if they both lived to spit on my grave. It's a hell of a world sometimes.'

'Yes, it is.'

'Pardon me, I'll be right back. I got a girl, but she only comes in Fridays and Saturdays in the winter.'

O'Donnell drew two schooners of beer and brought them over to the table. He said something to them and Clarice replied 'Fuck – *YOU!*' and cackled again. The beerjoint was filled with the ghosts of dead hamburgers. Tammy Wynette sang through the popcorn-crackle of an old record. The radiators thudded dull heat into the room and outside snow spatted dryly against the glass. Johnny rubbed his temples. He had been in this bar before, in a hundred other small towns. His head ached. When he had shaken O'Donnell's hand he knew that the barkeep had a big old mongrel dog that he had trained to sic on command. His one great dream was that some night a burglar would break into his house and he would legally be able to sic that big old dog onto him, and there would be one less goddam hippie pervo junkie in the world.

Oh, his head ached.

O'Donnell came back, wiping his hands on his apron. Tammy Wynette finished up and was replaced with Red Sovine, who had a CB call for the Teddy Bear.

'Thanks again for the suds,' O'Donnell said, drawing two.

'My pleasure,' Johnny said, still studying the clipping. 'Coorter's Notch last week, Jackson this coming weekend. I never heard of that one. Must be a pretty small town, huh?'

'Just a burg,' O'Donnell agreed. 'They used to have a ski resort, but it went broke. Lotta unemployment up that way. They do some wood-pulping and a little shirt-tail farming. But he goes up there, by the Jesus. Talks to em. Listens to their bitches. Where you from up in Maine, Johnny?'

'Lewiston,' Johnny lied. The clipping said that Greg Stillson would meet with interested persons at the town hall.

'Guess you came down for the skiing, huh?'

'No, I hurt my leg a while back. I don't ski anymore.

Just passing through. Thanks for letting me look at this.'
Johnny handed the clipping back. 'It's quite interesting.'

O'Donnell put it carefully back with his other papers.
He had an empty bar, a dog back home that would sic
on command, and Greg Stillson. Greg had been in his
bar.

Johnny found himself abruptly wishing himself dead.
If this talent was a gift from God, then God was a dangerous lunatic who ought to be stopped. If God wanted
Greg Stillson dead, why hadn't he sent him down the
birth canal with the umbilical cord wrapped around his
throat? Or strangled him on a piece of meat? Or electro-
cuted him while he was changing the radio station?
Drowned him in the ole swimming hole? Why did God
have to have Johnny Smith to do his dirty work? It
wasn't his responsibility to save the world, that was for
the psychos and only psychos would presume to try it. He
suddenly decided he would let Greg Stillson live and
spit in God's eye.

'You okay, Johnny?' O'Donnell asked.

'Huh? Yeah, sure.'

'You looked sorta funny for just a second there.'

Chuck Chatsworth saying: *If I didn't, I'd be afraid all
those people he killed would haunt me to my grave.*

'Out woolgathering, I guess,' Johnny said. 'I want you
to know it's been a pleasure drinking with you.'

'Well, the same goes back to you,' O'Donnell said,
looking pleased. 'I wish more people passing through
felt that way. They go through here headed for the ski
resorts, you know. The big places. That's where they
take their money. If I thought they'd stop in, I'd fix this
place up like they'd like. Posters, you know, of Switzerland and Colorado. A fireplace. Load the juke up with
rock 'n' roll records instead of that shitkicking music.
I'd ... you know, I'd like that.' He shrugged. 'I'm not a
bad guy, hell.'

'Of course not,' Johnny said, getting off the stool and
thinking about the dog trained to sic, and the hoped-for
hippie junkie burglar.

'Well, tell your friends I'm here,' O'Donnell said.

'For sure,' Johnny said.

'Hey Dick!' one of the bar-bags hollered. 'Ever hear of service-with-a-smile in this place?'

'Why don't you get stuffed?' O'Donnell yelled at her, flushing.

'Fuck – *YOU!*' Clarice called back, and cackled.

Johnny slipped quietly out into the gathering storm.

8 .

He was staying at the Holiday Inn in Portsmouth. When he got back that evening, he told the desk clerk to have his bill ready for checkout in the morning.

In his room, he sat down at the impersonal Holiday Inn writing desk, took out all the stationery, and grasped the Holiday Inn pen. His head was throbbing, but there were letters to be written. His momentary rebellion – if that was what it had been – had passed. His unfinished business with Greg Stillson remained.

I've gone crazy, he thought. *That's really it. I've gone entirely off my chump.* He could see the headlines now. PSYCHO SHOOTS N.H. REP. MADMAN ASSASSIN-ATES STILLSON. HAIL OF BULLETS CUTS DOWN U.S. REPRESENTATIVE IN NEW HAMPSHIRE. And *Inside View*, of course, would have a field day. SELF-PROCLAIMED 'SEER' KILLS STILLSON, 12 NOTED PSYCHIATRISTS TELL WHY SMITH DID IT. With a sidebar by that fellow Dees, maybe, telling how Johnny had threatened to get his shotgun and 'shoot me a trespasser'.

Crazy.

The hospital debt was paid, but this would leave a new bill of particulars behind, and his father would have to pay for it. He and his new wife would spend a lot of days in the limelight of his reflected notoriety. They would get the hate mail. Everyone he had known would be interviewed – the Chatsworths, Sam, Sheriff George Bannerman. Sarah? Well, maybe they wouldn't get as far as Sarah. After all, it wasn't as though he were planning to

427

shoot the president. At least, not yet. *There's a lotta people afraid to come right out and say it, but I'm not. I'll say it right out loud. Some day Greg Stillson's apt to be president.*

Johnny rubbed his temples. The headache came in low, slow waves, and none of this was getting his letters written. He drew the first sheet of stationery toward him, picked up the pen, and wrote *Dear Dad*. Outside, snow struck the window with that dry, sandy sound that means serious business. Finally the pen began to move across the paper, slowly at first, then gaining speed.

CHAPTER TWENTY-SEVEN

1 ·

Johnny came up wooden steps that had been shoveled clear of snow and salted down. He went through a set of double doors and into a foyer plastered with specimen ballots and notices of a special town meeting to be held here in Jackson on the third of February. There was also a notice of Greg Stillson's impending visit and a picture of The Man Who himself, hard hat cocked back on his head, grinning that hard slantwise 'We're wise to em, ain't we, pard?' grin. Set a little to the right of the green door leading into the meeting hall itself was a sign that Johnny hadn't expected, and he pondered it in silence for several seconds, his breath pluming white from his lips. DRIVER EXAMINATIONS TODAY, this sign read. It was set on a wooden easel. HAVE PAPERS READY.

He opened the door, went into the stuporous glow of heat thrown by a big woodstove, and there sat a cop at a desk. The cop was wearing a ski parka, unzipped. There were papers scattered across his desk, and there was also a gadget for examining visual acuity.

The cop looked up at Johnny, and he felt a sinking sensation in his gut.

'Can I help you, sir?'

Johnny fingered the camera slung around his neck. 'Well, I wondered if it would be all right to look around a little bit,' he said. 'I'm on assignment from *Yankee* magazine. We're doing a spread on town hall architecture in Maine, New Hampshire, and Vermont. Taking a lot of pictures, you know.'

'Go right to it,' the cop said. 'My wife reads *Yankee* all the time. Puts me to sleep.'

Johnny smiled. 'New England architecture has a tendency toward . . . well, starkness.'

'Starkness,' the cop repeated doubtfully, and then let it go. 'Next, please.'

A young man approached the desk the cop was sitting behind. He handed an examination sheet to the cop, who took it and said, 'Look into the viewer, please, and identify the traffic signs and signals which I will show you.'

The young man peered into the viewing machine. The cop put an answer-key over the young man's exam sheet. Johnny moved down the center aisle of the Jackson town hall and clicked a picture of the rostrum at the front.

'Stop sign,' the young man said from behind him. 'The next one's a yield sign . . . and the next one is a traffic information sign . . . no right turn, no left turn, like that . . .'

He hadn't expected a cop in the town hall; he hadn't even bothered to buy film for the camera he was using as a prop. But now it was too late to back out anyway. This was Friday, and Stillson would be here tomorrow if things went the way they were supposed to go. He would be answering questions and listening to suggestions from the good people of Jackson. There would be a fair-sized entourage with him. A couple of aides, a couple of advisors – and several others, young men in sober suits and sports jackets who had been wearing jeans and riding motorcycles not so long ago. Greg Stillson was still a firm believer in guards for the body. At the Trimbull rally they had been carrying sawed-off pool cues. Did they

carry guns now? Would it be so difficult for a U.S. representative to get a permit to carry a concealed weapon?
Johnny didn't think so. He could count on one good
chance only; he would have to make the most of it. So it
was important to look the place over, to try and decide
if he could take Stillson in here or if it would be better
to wait in the parking lot with the window rolled down
and the rifle on his lap.

So he had come and here he was, casing the joint while
a state cop gave driver-permit exams not thirty feet away.

There was a bulletin board on his left, and Johnny
snapped his unloaded camera at it – why in God's name
hadn't he taken another two minutes and bought himself a roll of film? The board was covered with chatty
small-town intelligence concerning baked-bean suppers,
an upcoming high school play, dog-licensing information,
and, of course, more on Greg. A file card said that Jackson's first selectman was looking for someone who could
take shorthand, and Johnny studied this as though it
were of great interest to him while his mind moved into
high gear.

Of course if Jackson looked impossible – or even
chancy – he could wait until next week, where Stillson
would be doing the whole thing all over again in the
town of Upson. Or the week after, in Trimbull. Or the
week after that. Or never.

It should be this week. It ought to be tomorrow.

He snapped the big woodstove in the corner, and then
glanced upward. There was a balcony up there. No – not
precisely a balcony, more like a gallery with a waist-high
railing and wide, white-painted slats with small, decora-
tive diamonds and curlicues cut into the wood. It would
be very possible for a man to crouch behind that railing
and look through one of those doodads. At the right moment, he could just stand up and –

'What kind of camera is that?'

Johnny looked around, sure it was the cop. The cop
would ask to see his filmless camera – and then he would
want to see some ID – and then it would be all over.

But it wasn't the cop. It was the young man who had been taking his driver's permit test. He was about twenty-two, with long hair and pleasant, frank eyes. He was wearing a suede coat and faded jeans.

'A Nikon,' Johnny said.

'Good camera, man. I'm a real camera nut. How long have you been working for *Yankee*?'

'Well, I'm a free lance,' Johnny said. 'I do stuff for them, sometimes for *Country Journal*, sometimes for *Downeast*, you know.'

'Nothing national, like *People* or *Life*?'

'No. At least, not yet.'

'What f-stop do you use in here?'

What in hell is an f-stop?

Johnny shrugged. 'I play it mostly by ear.'

'By eye, you mean,' the young man said, smiling.

'That's right, by eye.' *Get lost, kid, please get lost.*

'I'm interested in free-lancing myself,' the young man said, and grinned. 'My big dream is to take a picture some day like the flag-raising at Iwo Jima.'

'I heard that was staged,' Johnny said.

'Well, maybe. Maybe. But it's a classic. Or how about the first picture of a UFO coming in for a landing? I'd sure like that. Anyway, I've got a portfolio of stuff I've taken around here. Who's your contact at *Yankee*?'

Johnny was sweating now. 'Actually, they contacted me on this one,' he said. 'It was a . . .'

'Mr. Clawson, you can come over now,' the cop said, sounding impatient. 'I'd like to go over these answers with you.'

'Whoops, his master's voice,' Clawson said. 'See you later, man.' He hurried off and Johnny let out his breath in a silent, whispering sigh. It was time to get out, and quickly.

He snapped another two or three 'pictures' just so it wouldn't look like a complete rout, but he was barely aware of what he was looking at through the view-finder. Then he left.

The young man in the suede jacket – Clawson – had

431

forgotten all about him. He had apparently flunked the written part of his exam. He was arguing strenuously with the cop, who was only shaking his head.

Johnny paused for a moment in the town hall's entryway. To his left was a cloakroom. To his right was a closed door. He tried it and found it unlocked. A narrow flight of stairs led upward into dimness. The actual offices would be up there, of course. And the gallery.

2 ·

He was staying at the Jackson House, a pleasant little hotel on the main drag. It had been carefully renovated and the renovations had probably cost a lot of money, but the place would pay for itself, the owners must have reckoned, because of the new Jackson Mountain ski resort. Only the resort had gone bust and now the pleasant little hotel was barely hanging on. The night clerk was dozing over a cup of coffee when Johnny went out at four o'clock on Saturday morning, the attaché case in his left hand.

He had slept little last night, slipping into a short, light doze after midnight. He had dreamed. It was 1970 again. It was carnival time. He and Sarah stood in front of the Wheel of Fortune and again he had that feeling of crazy, enormous power. In his nostrils he could smell burning rubber.

'Come on,' a voice said softly behind him, 'I love to watch this guy take a beatin.' He turned and it was Frank Dodd, dressed in his black vinyl raincoat, his throat slit from ear to ear in a wide red grin, his eyes sparkling with dead vivaciousness. He turned back to the booth, scared – but now the pitchman was Greg Stillson, grinning knowingly at him, his yellow hard hat tipped cockily back on his skull. 'Hey-hey-hey,' Stillson chanted, his voice deep and resonant and ominous, 'Lay em down where you want em down, fella. What do you say? Want to shoot the moon?'

Yes, he wanted to shoot the moon. But as Stillson set the Wheel in motion he saw that the entire outer circle

432

had turned green. Every number was double-zero. Every number was a house number.

He had jerked awake and spent the rest of the night looking out the frost-rimmed window into darkness. The headache he'd had ever since arriving in Jackson the day before was gone, leaving him feeling weak but composed. He sat with his hands in his lap. He didn't think about Greg Stillson; he thought about the past. He thought about his mother putting a Band-Aid on a scraped knee; he thought about the time the dog had torn off the back of Grandma Nellie's absurd sundress and how he had laughed and how Vera had swatted him one and cut his forehead with the stone in her engagement ring; he thought about his father showing him how to bait a fishing hook and saying, *It doesn't hurt the worms, Johnny ... at least, I don't think it does.* He thought about his father giving him a pocketknife for Christmas when he was seven and saying very seriously, *I'm trusting you, Johnny.* All those memories had come back in a flood.

Now he stepped off into the deep cold of the morning, his shoes squeaking on the path shoveled through the snow. His breath plumed out in front of him. The moon was down but the stars were sprawled across the black sky in idiot's profusion. God's jewel box, Vera always called it. *You're looking into God's jewel box, Johnny.*

He walked down Main Street, and he stopped in front of the tiny Jackson post office and fumbled the letters out of his coat pocket. Letters to his father, to Sarah, to Sam Weizak, to Bannerman. He set the attaché case down between his feet, opened the mailbox that stood in front of the neat little brick building, and after one brief moment of hesitation, dropped them in. He could hear them drop down inside, surely the first letters mailed in Jackson this new day, and the sound gave him a queer sense of finality. The letters were mailed, there was no stopping now.

He picked up the case again and walked on. The only sound was the squeak of his shoes on the snow. The big thermometer over the door of the Granite State Savings Bank stood at 3 degrees, and the air had that feeling of total silent inertia that belongs exclusively to cold New Hampshire mornings. Nothing moved. The roadway was empty. The windshields of the parked cars were blinded with cataracts of frost. Dark windows, drawn shades. To Johnny it all seemed somehow dreadful and at the same time holy. He fought the feeling. This was no holy business he was on.

He crossed Jasper Street and there was the town hall, standing white and austerely elegant behind its plowed banks of twinkling snow.

What are you going to do if the front door's locked, smart guy?

Well, he would find a way to cross that bridge if he had to. Johnny looked around, but there was no one to see him. If this had been the president coming for one of his famous town meetings, everything would have been different, of course. The place would have been blocked off since the night before, and men would be stationed inside already. But this was only a U.S. representative, one of over four hundred, no big deal. No big deal yet.

Johnny went up the steps and tried the door. The knob turned easily and he stepped into the cold entryway and pulled the door shut behind him. Now the headache was coming back, pulsing along with the steady thick beat of his heart. He set his case down and massaged his temples with his gloved fingers.

There was a sudden low scream. The coat-closet door was opening, very slowly, and then something white was falling out of the shadows toward him.

Johnny barely held back a cry. For one moment he thought it was a body, falling out of the closet like something from a spook movie. But it was only a heavy cardboard sign that read PLEASE HAVE PAPERS IN ORDER BEFORE APPEARING FOR EXAMINATION.

He set it back in place and then turned to the doorway giving upon the stairs.

This door was now locked.

He leaned down to get a better look at it in the dim

434

white glow of the streetlight that filtered in the one window. It was a spring lock, and he thought he might be able to open it with a coat hanger. He found one in the coat closet and hooked the neck of it into the crack between the door and the jamb. He worked it down to the lock and began to fumble around. His head was thudding fiercely now. At last he heard the bolt snap back as the wire caught it. He pulled the door open. He picked up his attaché case and went through, still holding the coat hanger. He pulled the door closed behind him and heard it lock again. He went up the narrow stairs, which creaked and groaned under his weight.

At the top of the stairs there was a short hallway with several doors on either side. He walked down the hall, past TOWN MANAGER and TOWN SELECTMEN, past TAX ASSESSOR and MEN'S and O'SEER OF THE POOR and LADIES'.

There was an unmarked door at the end. It was unlocked and he came out onto the gallery above the rear of the meeting hall, which was spread out below him in a crazy quilt of shadows. He closed the door behind him and shivered a little at the soft stir of echoes in the empty hall. His footfalls also echoed back as he walked to the right along the rear gallery, then turned left. Now he was walking along the right-hand side of the hall, about twenty-five feet above the floor. He stopped at a point above the woodstove and directly across from the podium where Stillson would be standing in about five-and-a-half hours.

He sat down cross-legged and rested for a while. Tried to get in control of the headache with some deep breathing. The woodstove wasn't operating and he felt the cold settling steadily against him – and then into him. Previews of the winding shroud.

When he had begun to feel a little better, he thumbed the catches on the attaché case. The double click echoed back as his footfalls had done, and this time it was the sound of cocking pistols.

Western justice, he thought, for no reason at all. That

435

was what the prosecutor had said when the jury found Claudine Longet guilty of shooting her lover. *She's found out what western justice means.*

Johnny looked down into the case and rubbed his eyes. His vision doubled briefly and then things came together again. He was getting an impression from the very wood he was sitting on. A very old impression; if it had been a photograph, it would have been sepia-toned. Men standing here and smoking cigars, talking and laughing and waiting for town meeting to begin. Had it been 1920? 1902? There was something ghostly about it that made him feel uneasy. One of them had been talking about the price of whiskey and cleaning his nose with a silver toothpick and

(*and two years before he had poisoned his wife*)

Johnny shivered. Whatever the impression was, it didn't matter. It was an impression of a man who was long dead now.

The rifle gleamed up at him.

When men do it in wartime, they give them medals, he thought.

He began to assemble the rifle. Each *click!* echoed back, just once, solemnly, the sound of a cocking pistol.

He loaded the Remington with five bullets.

He placed it across his knees.

And waited.

3 ·

Dawn came slowly. Johnny dozed a little, but he was too cold now to do more than doze. Thin, sketchy dreams haunted what sleep he did get.

He came fully awake at a little past seven. The door below was thrown open with a crash, and he had to bite his tongue to keep from crying out, *Who's there?*

It was the custodian. Johnny put his eye to one of the diamond shapes cut into the balustrade and saw a burly man who was bundled up in a thick Navy pea coat. He was coming up the center aisle with an armload of firewood. He was humming 'Red River Valley'. He dropped the armload of wood into the woodbox with a crash and then disappeared below Johnny. A second later he heard the thin screeing noise of the stove's firebox door being swung open.

Johnny suddenly thought of the plume of vapor he was producing every time he exhaled. Suppose the custodian looked up? Would he be able to see that?

He tried to slow the rate of his breathing, but that made his head ache worse and his vision doubled alarmingly.

Now there was the crackle of paper being crumpled, then the scratch of a match. A faint whiff of sulphur in the cold air. The custodian went on humming 'Red River Valley', and then broke into loud and tuneless song: 'From this valley they say you are going . . . we will miss your bright eyes and sweet smiiiiile . . .'

Now a different crackling sound. Fire.

'That's got it, you sucker,' the custodian said from directly below Johnny, and then there was the sound of the firebox door being slammed shut again. Johnny pressed both hands over his mouth like a bandage, suddenly afflicted with suicidal amusement. He saw himself rising up from the floor of the gallery, as thin and white as any self-respecting ghost. He saw himself spreading his arms like wings and his fingers like talons and calling down in hollow tones: 'That's got *you*, you sucker.'

He held the laughter behind his hands. His head throbbed like a tomato full of hot, expanding blood. His vision jittered and blurred crazily. Suddenly he wanted very badly to move away from the impression of the man who had been cleaning his nose with the silver toothpick, but he didn't dare make a sound. Dear Jesus, what if he had to sneeze?

Suddenly, with no warning, a terrible wavering shriek filled the hall, drilling into Johnny's ears like thin silver nails, climbing, making his head vibrate. He opened his mouth to scream –

It cut off.

437

'Oh, you whore,' the custodian said conversationally.

Johnny looked through the diamond and saw the custodian standing behind the podium and fiddling with a microphone. The mike cord snaked down to a small portable amp. The custodian went down the few steps from the podium to the floor and pulled the amplifier farther from the mike, then fooled with the dials on top of it. He went back to the mike and turned it on again. There was another feedback whine, this one lower and then tapering away entirely. Johnny pressed his hands tight against his forehead and rubbed them back and forth.

The custodian tapped on the mike with his thumb, and the sound filled the big empty room. It sounded like a fist knocking on a coffin lid. Then his voice, still tuneless, but now amplified to the point of monstrosity, a giant's voice bludgeoning into Johnny's head: *'FROM THIS VAL-LEEE THEY SAY YOU ARE GOING ...'*

Stop it, Johnny wanted to scream. *Oh, please stop it, I'm going crazy, can't you stop it?*

The singing ended with a loud, amplified *snap!* and the custodian said in his own voice, 'That's got you, whore.'

He walked out of Johnny's line of sight again. There was a sound of tearing paper and the low popping sounds of twine being snapped. Then the custodian reappeared, whistling and holding a large stack of booklets. He began to place them at close intervals along the benches.

When he had finished that chore, the custodian buttoned his coat and left the hall. The door slammed hollowly shut behind him. Johnny looked at his watch. It was 7:45. The town hall was warming up a little. He sat and waited. The headache was still very bad, but oddly enough, it was easier to bear than it had ever been before. All he had to do was tell himself that he wouldn't have to bear it for long.

438

4 ·

The doors slammed open again promptly at nine o'clock, startling him out of a catnap. His hands clamped tightly over the rifle and then relaxed. He put his eye to the diamond-shaped peephole. Four men this time. One of them was the custodian, the collar of his pea coat turned up against his neck. The other three were wearing top-coats with suits underneath. Johnny felt his heartbeat quicken. One of them was Sonny Elliman. His hair was cut short now and handsomely styled, but the brilliant green eyes had not changed.

'Everything set?' he asked.

'Check for yourself,' the custodian said.

'Don't be offended, Dad,' one of the others replied. They were moving to the front of the hall. One of them clicked the amplifier on and then clicked it off again, satisfied.

'People round these parts act like he was the bloody emperor,' the custodian grumbled.

'He is, he is,' the third man said – Johnny thought he also recognized this fellow from the Trimbull rally. 'Haven't you got wise to that yet, Pop?'

'Have you been upstairs?' Elliman asked the custodian, and Johnny went cold.

'Stairway door's locked,' the custodian answered. 'Same as always. I gave her a shake.'

Johnny silently gave thanks for the spring lock on the door.

'Ought to check it out,' Elliman said.

The custodian uttered an exasperated laugh. 'I don't know about you guys,' he said. 'Who are you expecting? The Phantom of the Opera?'

'Come on Sonny,' the fellow Johnny thought he recognized said. 'There's nobody up there. We just got time for a coffee if we shag ass down to that resrunt on the corner.'

'That's not coffee,' Sonny said. 'Fucking mud is all that is. Just run upstairs first and make sure no one's there, Moochie. We go by the book.'

439

Johnny licked his lips and clutched the gun. He looked up and down the narrow gallery. To his right it ended in a blank wall. To his left it went back to the suite of offices, and either way it made no difference. If he moved, they would hear him. This empty, the town hall served as a natural amplifier. He was stuck.

There were footfalls down below. Then the sound of the door between the hall and the entryway being opened and closed. Johnny waited, frozen and helpless. Just below him the custodian and the other two were talking, but he heard nothing they said. His head had turned on his neck like some slow engine and he stared down the length of the gallery, waiting for the fellow Sonny Elliman had called Moochie to appear at the end of it. His bored expression would suddenly turn to shock and incredulity, his mouth would open: *Hey Sonny, there's a guy up here!*

Now he could hear the muffled sound of Moochie climbing the stairs. He tried to think of something, anything. Nothing came. They were going to discover him, it was less than a minute away now, and he didn't have any idea of how to stop it from happening. No matter what he did, his one chance was on the verge of being blown.

Doors began to open and close, the sound of each drawing closer and less muffled. A drop of sweat spilled from Johnny's forehead and darkened the leg of his jeans. He could remember each door he had come past on his way here. Moochie had checked TOWN MANAGER and TOWN SELECTMEN and TAX ASSESSOR. Now he was opening the door of MEN'S, now he was glancing through the office that belonged to the O'SEER OF THE POOR, now the LADIES' room. The next door would be the one leading to the galleries.

It opened.

There was the sound of two footfalls as Moochie approached the railing of the short gallery that ran along the back of the hall. 'Okay, Sonny? You satisfied?'

'Everything look good?'

'Looks like a fucking dump,' Moochie responded, and there was a burst of laughter from below.

'Well, come on down and let's go for coffee,' the third man said. And incredibly, that was it. The door slammed to. The footsteps retreated back down the hall, and then down the steps to the first floor.

Johnny went limp and for a moment everything swam away from him into shades of gray. The slam of the entryway door as they went out for their coffee brought him partially out of it.

Below, the custodian presented his judgment: 'Bunch of whores.' Then he left, too, and for the next twenty minutes or so, there was only Johnny.

5 ·

Around 9:30 A.M., the people of Jackson began to file into their town hall. The first to appear was a trio of old ladies dressed in formal black, chattering together like magpies. Johnny watched them pick seats close to the stove – almost entirely out of the field of his vision – and pick up the booklets that had been left on the seats. The booklets appeared to be filled with glossy pictures of Greg Stillson.

'I just love that man,' one of the three said. 'I've gotten his autograph three times and I'll get it again today, I'll be bound.'

That was all the talk there was about Greg Stillson. The ladies went on to discuss the impending Old Home Sunday at the Methodist Church.

Johnny, almost directly over the stove, went from very cold to very hot. He had taken advantage of the slack tide between the departure of Stillson's security people and the arrival of the first townfolk, using it to shed both his jacket and his outer shirt. He kept wiping sweat from his face with a handkerchief, and the linen was streaked with blood as well as sweat. His bad eye was kicking up again, and his vision was constantly blurred and reddish.

The door below opened, there was the hearty tromp-

tromp-tromp of men stamping snow from their pacs, and then four men in checked woolen jackets came down the aisle and sat in the front row. One of them launched immediately into a Frenchman joke.

A young woman of about twenty-three arrived with her son, who looked about four. The boy was wearing a blue snowmobile suit with bright yellow markings, and he wanted to know if he could talk into the microphone.

'No, dear,' the woman said, and they went down behind the men. The boy immediately began to kick his feet against the bench in front of him, and one of the men glanced back over his shoulder.

'Sean, stop that,' she said.

Quarter of ten now. The door was opening and closing with a steady regularity. Men and women of all types and occupations and ages were filling up the hall. There was a drifting hum of conversation, and it was edged with an indefinable sense of anticipation. They weren't here to quiz their duly-elected representative; they were waiting for a bona-fide star turn in their small community. Johnny knew that most 'meet-your-candidate' and 'meet-your-representative' sessions were attended by a handful of die-hards in the nearly empty meeting halls. During the election of 1976 a debate between Maine's Bill Cohen and his challenger, Leighton Cooney, had attracted all of twenty-six people, press aside. The skull-sessions were so much window-dressing, a self-testimonial to wave when election time came around again. Most could have been held in a middling-sized closet. But by 10 A.M., every seat in the town hall was taken, and there were twenty or thirty standees at the back. Every time the door opened, Johnny's hands tensed down on the rifle. And he was still not positive he could do it, no matter what the stakes.

Five past, ten past. Johnny began to think Stillson had been held up, or was perhaps not coming at all. And the feeling which moved stealthily through him was one of relief.

Then the door opened again and a hearty voice called: 'Hey! How ya doin, Jackson, N.H.?'

A startled, pleased murmur. Someone called ecstatically, 'Greg! How are you?'

'Well, I'm feeling perky,' Stillson came right back. 'How the heck are you?'

A spatter of applause quickly swelled to a roar of approval.

'Hey, all right!' Greg shouted over it. He moved quickly down the aisle, shaking hands, toward the podium.

Johnny watched him through his loophole. Stillson was wearing a heavy rawhide coat with a sheepskin collar, and today the hard hat had been replaced with a woolen ski cap with a bright red tassel. He paused at the head of the aisle and waved at the three or four press in attendance. Flashbulbs popped and the applause got its second wind, shaking the rafters.

And Johnny Smith suddenly knew it was now or never.

The feelings he had had about Greg Stillson at the Trimbull rally suddenly swept over him again with a certain and terrible clarity. Inside his aching, tortured head he seemed to hear a dull wooden sound, two things coming together with a terrible force at one single moment. It was, perhaps, the sound of destiny. It would be too easy to delay, to let Stillson talk and talk. Too easy to let him get away, to sit up here with his head in his hands, waiting as the crowd thinned out, waiting as the custodian returned to dismantle the sound system and sweep up the litter, all the time kidding himself that there would be next week in another town.

The time was now, indisputably now, and every human being on earth suddenly had a stake in what happened in this backwater meetinghouse.

That thudding sound in his head, like poles of destiny coming together.

Stillson was mounting the steps to the podium. The area behind him was clear. The three men in their open topcoats were lounging against the far wall.

Johnny stood up.

6 ·

Everything seemed to happen in slow motion.

There were cramps in his legs from sitting so long. His knees popped like dud firecrackers. Time seemed frozen, the applause went on and on even though heads were turning, necks were craning; someone screamed through the applause and still it went on; someone had screamed because there was a man in the gallery and the man was holding a rifle and this was something they had all seen on TV, it was a situation with classic elements that they all recognized. In its own way, it was as American as *The Wonderful World of Disney*. The politician and the man in a high place with the gun.

Greg Stillson turned toward him, his thick neck craning, wrinkling into creases. The red puff on the top of his ski cap bobbed.

Johnny put the rifle to his shoulder. It seemed to float up there and he felt the thud as it socketed home next to the joint there. He thought of shooting partridge with his dad as a boy. They had gone deer-hunting but the only time Johnny had ever seen one he had not been able to pull the trigger; the buck fever had gotten him. It was a secret, as shameful as masturbation, and he had never told anyone.

There was another scream. One of the old ladies was clutching her mouth and Johnny saw there was artificial fruit scattered along the wide brim of her black hat. Faces turned up to him, big white zeros. Open mouths, small black zeros. The little boy in the snowmobile suit was pointing. His mother was trying to shield him. Stillson was in the gunsight suddenly and Johnny remembered to flick off the rifle's safety. Across the way the men in the topcoats were reaching inside their jackets and Sonny Elliman, his green eyes blazing, was hollering: *Down! Greg, get DOWN!'*

But Stillson stared up into the gallery and for the second time their eyes locked together in a perfect sort of understanding, and Stillson only ducked at the same instant Johnny fired. The rifle's roar was loud, filling the place, and the slug took away nearly one whole corner of the podium, peeling it back to the bare, bright wood. Splinters flew. One of them struck the microphone, and there was another monstrous whine of feedback that suddenly ended in a guttural, low-key buzzing.

Johnny pumped another cartridge into the chamber and fired again. This time the slug punched a hole through the dusty carpeting of the dais.

The crowd had started to move, panicky as cattle. They all drove into the center aisle. The people who had been standing at the rear escaped easily, but then a bottleneck of cursing, screaming men and women formed in the double doorway.

There were popping noises from the other side of the hall, and suddenly part of the gallery railing splintered up in front of Johnny's eyes. Something screamed past his ear a second later. Then an invisible finger gave the collar of his shirt a flick. All three of them across the way were holding handguns, and because Johnny was up in the gallery, their field of fire was crystal clear – but Johnny doubted if they would have bothered overmuch about innocent bystanders anyway.

One of the trio of old women grabbed Moochie's arm. She was sobbing, trying to ask something. He flung her away and steadied his gun in both hands. There was a stink of gunpowder in the hall now. It had been about twenty seconds since Johnny had stood up.

'Down! Down, Greg!'

Stillson was still standing at the edge of the dais, crouching slightly, looking up. Johnny brought the rifle down, and for an instant Stillson was dead-bang in front sight. Then a pistol-slug grooved his neck, knocking him backward, and his own shot went wild into the air. The window across the way dissolved in a tinkling rain of glass. Thin screams drifted up from below. Blood poured down and across his shoulder and chest.

Oh, you're doing a great job of killing him, he thought hysterically, and pushed back to the railing again. He levered another cartridge into the breech and threw it to

445

his shoulder again. Now Stillson was on the move. He darted down the steps to floor-level and then glanced up at Johnny again.

Another bullet whizzed by his temple. *I'm bleeding like a stuck pig,* he thought. *Come on. Come on and get this over.*

The bottleneck at the entryway broke, and now people began to pour out. A puff of smoke rose from the barrel of one of the pistols across the way, there was a bang, and the invisible finger that had flicked his collar a few seconds ago now drew a line of fire across the side of Johnny's head. It didn't matter. Nothing mattered except taking Stillson. He brought the rifle down again.

Make this one count —

Stillson moved with good speed for such a big man. The dark-haired young woman Johnny had noticed earlier was about halfway up the center aisle, holding her crying son in her arms, still trying to shield him with her body. And what Stillson did then so dumbfounded Johnny that he almost dropped the rifle altogether. He snatched the boy from his mother's arms, whirled toward the gallery, holding the boy's body in front of him. It was no longer Greg Stillson in the front sight, but a small squirming figure in

(*the filter blue filter yellow stripes tiger stripes*)

a dark blue snowmobile suit with bright yellow piping.

Johnny's mouth dropped open. It was Stillson, all right. The tiger. *But he was behind the filter now.*

What does it mean? Johnny screamed, but no sound passed his lips.

The mother screamed shrilly then; but Johnny had heard it all somewhere before. '*Tommy! Give him to me! TOMMY! GIVE HIM TO ME, YOU BASTARD!*'

Johnny's head was swelling blackly, expanding like a bladder. Everything was starting to fade. The only brightness left was centered around the notched gunsight, the gunsight now laid directly over the chest of that blue snowmobile suit.

446

*Do it, oh for Christ's sake you have to do it he'll get
away –*

And now – perhaps it was only his blurring eyesight
that made it seem so – the blue snowmobile suit began
to spread, its color washing out to the light robin's-egg
color of the vision, the dark yellow stretching, striping,
until everything began to be lost in it.

*(behind the filter. yes, he's behind the filter, but what
does it mean? does it mean it's safe or just that he's beyond my reach? what does it)*

Warm fire flashed somewhere below and was gone.
Some dim part of Johnny's mind registered it as a flashbulb.

Stillson shoved the woman away and backed toward
the door, eyes squeezed into calculating pirate's slits. He
held the squirming boy firmly by the neck and the crotch.

Can't. Oh dear God forgive me, I can't.

Two more bullets struck him then, one high in the
chest, driving him back against the wall and bouncing
him off it, the second into the left side of his midsection,
spinning him around into the gallery railing. He was
dimly aware that he had lost the rifle. It struck the gallery
floor and discharged point-blank into the wall. Then his
upper thighs crashed into the ballustrade and he was
falling. The town hall turned over twice before his eyes
and then there was a splintering crash as he struck two
of the benches, breaking his back and both legs.

He opened his mouth to scream, but what came out
was a great gush of blood. He lay in the splintered remains of the benches he had struck and thought: *It's
over. I punked out. Blew it.*

Hands were on him, not gentle. They were turning
him over. Elliman, Moochie, and the other guy were
there. Elliman was the one who had turned him over.

Stillson came, shoving Moochie aside.

'Never mind this guy,' he said harshly. 'Find the son
of a bitch that took that picture. Smash his camera.'

Moochie and the other guy left. Somewhere close by
the woman with the dark hair was crying out: '...

behind a kid, hiding behind a kid and I'll tell every-
body . . .'

'Shut her up, Sonny,' Stillson said.

'Sure,' Sonny said, and left Stillson's side.

Stillson got down on his knees above Johnny. 'Do we
know each other, fella? No sense lying. You've had the
course.'

Johnny whispered, 'We knew each other.'

'It was that Trimbull rally, wasn't it?'

Johnny nodded.

Stillson got up abruptly, and with the last bit of his
strength Johnny reached out and grasped his ankle. It
was only for a second; Stillson pulled free easily. But it
was long enough.

Everything had changed.

People were drawing near him now, but he saw only
feet and legs, no faces. It didn't matter. *Everything had
changed.*

He began to cry a little. Touching Stillson this time
had been like touching a blank. Dead battery. Fallen
tree. Empty house. Bare bookshelves. Wine bottles ready
for candles.

Fading. Going away. The feet and legs around him
were becoming misty and indistinct. He heard their
voices, the excited gabble of speculation, but not the
words. Only the sound of the words, and even that was
fading, blurring into a high, sweet humming sound.

He looked over his shoulder and there was the corridor
he had emerged from so long ago. He had come out of
that corridor and into this bright placental place. Only
then his mother had been alive and his father had been
there, calling him by name, until he broke through to
them. Now it was only time to go back. Now it was right
to go back.

*I did it. Somehow I did it. I don't understand how, but
I have.*

He let himself drift toward that corridor with the dark
chrome walls, not knowing if there might be something
at the far end of it or not, content to let time show him

that. The sweet hum or the voices faded. The misty brightness faded. But he was still *he* – Johnny Smith – intact.

Get into the corridor, he thought. *All right.*

He thought that if he could get into that corridor, he
would be able to walk.

PART THREE

Notes from the Dead Zone

1 ·

Portsmouth, N.H.
January 23, 1979

Dear Dad,

*This is a terrible letter to have to write, and I will try
to keep it short. When you get it, I guess I will probably
be dead. An awful thing has happened to me, and I think
now that it may have started a long time before the car
accident and the coma. You know about the psychic business, of course, and you may remember Mom swearing
on her deathbed that God had meant for it to be this way,
that God had something for me to do. She asked me not
to run from it, and I promised her that I wouldn't – not
meaning it seriously, but wanting her mind to be easy.
Now it looks as if she was right, in a funny sort of way. I
still don't really believe in God, not in a real Being who
plans for us and gives us all little jobs to do, like Boy
Scouts winning merit badges on The Great Hike of Life.
But neither do I believe that all the things that have
happened to me are blind chance.*

*In the summer of 1976, Dad, I went to a Greg Stillson
rally in Trimbull, which is in New Hampshire's third
district. He was running for the first time then, you may
recall. When he was on his way to the speaker's rostrum
he shook a lot of hands, and one of them was mine. This
is the part you may find hard to believe, even though you
have seen the ability in action. I had one of my 'flashes',
only this one was no flash, Dad. It was a vision, either in
the biblical sense or in something very near it. Oddly
enough, it wasn't as clear as some of my other 'insights'
have been – there was a puzzling blue glow over everything that has never been there before – but it was incredibly powerful. I saw Greg Stillson as president of the
United States. How far in the future I can't say, except
that he had lost most of his hair. I would say fourteen*

453

years, or perhaps eighteen at the most. Now, my ability is to see and not to interpret, and in this case my ability to see was impeded by that funny blue filter, but I saw enough. If Stillson becomes president, he's going to worsen an international situation that is going to be pretty awful to begin with. If Stillson becomes president, he is going to end up precipitating a full-scale nuclear war. I believe that the initial flashpoint for this war is going to be in South Africa. And I also believe that in the short, bloody course of this war, it's not going to be just two or three nations throwing warheads, but maybe as many as twenty – plus terrorist groups.

Daddy, I know how crazy this must look. It looks crazy to me. But I have no doubts, no urge to look back over my shoulder and try to second-guess this thing into something less real and urgent than it is. You never knew – no one did – but I didn't run away from the Chatsworths because of that restaurant fire. I guess I was running away from Greg Stillson and the thing I am supposed to do. Like Elijah hiding in his cave or Jonah, who ended up in the fish's belly. I thought I would just wait and see, you know. Wait and see if the preconditions for such a horrible future began to come into place. I would probably be waiting still, but in the fall of last year the headaches began to get worse, and there was an incident on the road-crew I was working with. I guess Keith Strang, the foreman, would remember that . . .

2 .

Excerpt from testimony given before the so-called 'Stillson Committee', chaired by Senator William Cohen of Maine. The questioner is Mr. Norman D. Verizer, the Committee's Chief Counsel. The witness is Mr. Keith Strang, of 1421 Desert Boulevard, Phoenix, Arizona.

Date of testimony: August 17, 1979.

Verizer: And at this time, John Smith was in the employ of the Phoenix Public Works Department, was he not?

Strang: Yes, Sir, he was.

V.: This was early December of 1978.

S.: Yes, Sir.

V.: And did something happen on December 7 that you particularly remember? Something concerning John Smith?

S.: Yes, Sir. It sure did.

V.: Tell the Committee about that, if you would.

S.: Well, I had to go back to the central motor pool to get two forty-gallon drums of orange paint. We were lining roads, you understand. Johnny – that's Johnny Smith – was out on Rosemont Avenue on the day you're talking about, putting down new lane markings. Well, I got back out there at approximately four-fifteen – about forty-five minutes before knocking-off time – and this fellow Herman Joellyn that you've already talked to, he comes up to me and says, 'You better check on Johnny, Keith. Something's wrong with Johnny. I tried to talk to him and he acted like he didn't hear. He almost run me down. You better get him straight.' That's what he said. So I said, 'What's wrong with him, Hermie?' And Hermie says, 'Check it out for yourself, there's something offwhack with that dude.' So I drove on up the road, and at first everything was all right, and then – wow!

V.: What did you see?

S.: Before I saw Johnny, you mean.

V.: Yes, that's right.

S.: The line he was putting down started to go haywire. Just a little bit at first – a jig here and there, a little bubble – it wasn't perfectly straight, you know. And Johnny had always been the best liner on the whole crew. Then it started to get really bad. It started to go all over the road in these big loops and swirls. Some places it was like he'd gone right round in circles a few times. For about a hundred yards he'd put the stripe right along the dirt shoulder.

V.: What did you do?

S.: I stopped him. That is, eventually I stopped him. I pulled up right beside the lining machine and started yelling at him. Must have yelled half a dozen times. It

455

was like he didn't hear. Then he swooped that thing toward me and put a helluva ding in the side of the car I was driving. Highway Department property, too. So I laid on the horn and yelled at him again, and that seemed to get through to him. He threw it in neutral and looked over at me. I asked him what in the name of God he thought he was doing.

V.: And what was his response?

S.: He said hi. That was all. 'Hi, Keith.' Like everything was hunky-dory.

V.: And your response was . . . ?

S.: My response was pretty blue. I was mad. And Johnny is just standing there, looking all around and holding onto the side of the liner like he would fall down if he let go. That was when I realized how sick he looked. He was always thin, you know, but now he looked as white as paper, and the side of his mouth was kind of . . . you know . . . drawn down. At first he didn't even seem to get what I was saying. Then he looked around and saw the way that line was – all over the road.

V.: And he said . . . ?

S.: Said he was sorry. Then he kind of – I don't know – staggered, and put one hand up to his face. So I asked him what was wrong with him and he said . . . oh, a lot of confused stuff. It didn't mean anything.

Cohen: Mr. Strang, the Committee is particularly interested in *anything* Mr. Smith said that might cast a light on this matter. Can you remember what he said?

S.: Well, at first he said there was nothing wrong except that it smelled like rubber tires. Tires on fire. Then he said, 'That battery will explode if you try to jump it.' And something like, 'I got potatoes in the chest and both radios are in the sun. So it's all out for the trees.' That's the best I can remember. Like I say, it was all confused and crazy.

V.: What happened then?

S.: He started to fall down. So I grabbed him by the shoulder and his hand – he had been holding it against the side of his face – it came away. And I saw his right eye was full of blood. Then he passed out.

V.: But he said one more thing before he passed out, did he not?

S.: Yes, Sir, he did.

V.: And what was that?

S.: He said, 'We'll worry about Stillson later, Daddy, he's in the dead zone now.'

V.: Are you sure that's what he said?

S.: Yes, Sir, I am. I'll never forget it.

3 ·

... and when I woke up I was in the small equipment shed at the base of Rosemont Drive. Keith said I'd better get to see a doctor right away, and I wasn't to come back to work until I did. I was scared, Dad, but not for the reasons Keith thought, I guess. Anyway, I made an appointment to see a neurologist that Sam Weizak had mentioned to me in a letter he wrote in early November. You see, I had written to Sam telling him that I was afraid to drive a car because I was having some incidents of double vision. Sam wrote back right away and told me to go see this Dr. Vann – said he considered the symptoms very alarming, but wouldn't presume to diagnose long-distance.

I didn't go right away. I guess your mind can screw you over pretty well, and I kept thinking – right up to the incident with the road-lining machine – that it was just a phase I was going through and that it would get better. I guess I just didn't want to think about the alternative. But the road-lining incident was too much. I went, because I was getting scared – not just for myself, because of what I knew.

So I went to see this Dr. Vann, and he gave me the tests, and then he laid it out for me. It turned out I didn't have as much time as I thought, because ...

4 ·

Excerpt from testimony given before the so-called 'Stillson Committee', chaired by Senator William Cohen of

Maine. The questioner is Mr. Norman D. Verizer, the Committee's Chief Counsel. The witness is Dr. Quentin M. Vann, of 17 Parkland Drive, Phoenix, Arizona.

Date of testimony: August 22, 1979.

Verizer: After your tests were complete and your diagnosis was complete, you saw John Smith in your office, didn't you?

Vann: Yes. It was a difficult meeting. Such meetings are always difficult.

Ve: Can you give us the substance of what passed between you?

Va: Yes. Under these unusual circumstances, I believe that the doctor-patient relationship may be waived. I began by pointing out to Smith that he had had a terribly frightening experience. He agreed. His right eye was still extremely bloodshot, but it was better. He had ruptured a small capillary. If I may refer to the chart . . .

(Material deleted and condensed at this point)

Ve: And after making this explanation to Smith?

Va: He asked me for the bottom line. That was his phrase; 'the bottom line'. In a quiet way he impressed me with his calmness and his courage.

Ve: And the bottom line was what, Dr. Vann?

Va: Ah? I thought that would be clear by now. John Smith had an extremely well-developed brain tumor in the parietal lobe.

(Disorder among spectators; short recess)

Ve: Doctor, I'm sorry about this interruption. I'd like to remind the spectators that this Committee is in session, and that it is an investigatory body, not a freak-show. I'll have order or I'll have the Sergeant-at-Arms clear the room.

Va: That is quite all right, Mr. Verizer.

Ve: Thank you, Doctor. Can you tell the Committee how Smith took the news?

Va: He was calm. Extraordinarily calm. I believe that in

458

his heart he had formed his own diagnosis, and that his and mine happened to coincide. He said that he was badly scared, however. And he asked me how long he had to live.

Ve: What did you tell him?

Va: I said that at that point such a question was meaningless, because our options were all still open. I told him he would need an operation. I should point out that at this time I had no knowledge of his coma and his extraordinary – almost miraculous – recovery.

Ve: And what was his response?

Va: He said there would be no operation. He was quiet but very, very firm. No operation. I said that I hoped he would reconsider, because to turn such an operation down would be to sign his own death-warrant.

Ve: Did Smith make any response to this?

Va: He asked me to give him my best opinion on how long he could live without such an operation.

Ve: Did you give him your opinion?

Va: I gave him a ballpark estimate, yes. I told him that tumors have extremely erratic growth patterns, and that I had known patients whose tumors had fallen dormant for as long as two years, but that such a dormancy was quite rare. I told him that without an operation he might reasonably expect to live from eight to twenty months.

Ve: But he still declined the operation, is that right?

Va: Yes, that is so.

Ve: Did something unusual happen as Smith was leaving?

Va: I would say it was extremely unusual.

Ve: Tell the Committee about that, if you would.

Va: I touched his shoulder, meaning to restrain him, I suppose. I was unwilling to see the man leave under those circumstances, you understand. And I felt something coming from him when I did . . . it was a sensation like an electric shock, but it was also an oddly draining, debilitating sensation. As if he were *drawing* something from me. I will grant you that this is an

459

extremely subjective description, but it comes from a man trained in the art and craft of professional observation. It was not pleasant, I assure you. I ... drew away from him ... and he suggested I call my wife because Strawberry had hurt himself seriously.

Ve: Strawberry?

Va: Yes, that's what he said. My wife's brother ... his name is Stanbury Richards. My youngest son always called him Uncle Strawberry when he was very small. That association didn't occur until later, by the way. That evening I suggested to my wife that she call her brother, who lives in the town of Coose Lake, New York.

Ve: Did she call him?

Va: Yes, she did. They had a very nice chat.

Ve: And was Mr. Richards – your brother-in-law – was he all right?

Va: Yes, he was fine. But the following week he fell from a ladder while painting his house and broke his back.

Ve: Dr. Vann, do you believe John Smith saw that happen? Do you believe that he had a precognitive vision concerning your wife's brother?

Va: I don't know. But I believe ... that it may have been so.

Ve: Thank you, Dr. ...

Va: May I say one more thing?

Ve: Of course.

Va: If he did have such a curse – yes, I would call it a curse – I hope God will show pity to that man's tortured soul.

5 ·

... and I know, Dad, that people are going to say that I did what I am planning to do because of the tumor, but Daddy, don't believe them. It isn't true. The tumor is only the accident finally catching up with me, the accident which I now believe never stopped happening. The tumor lies in the same area that was injured in the crash,

the same area that I now believe was probably bruised when I was a child and took a fall one day while skating on Runaround Pond. That was when I had the first of my 'flashes', although even now I cannot remember exactly what it was. And I had another just before the accident, at the Esty Fair. Ask Sarah about that one; I'm sure she remembers. The tumor lies in that area which I always called 'the dead zone'. And that turned out to be right, didn't it? All too bitterly right. God ... destiny ... providence ... fate ... whatever you want to call it, seems to be reaching out with its steady and unarguable hand to put the scales back in balance again. Perhaps I was meant to die in that car-crash, or even earlier, that day on the Runaround. And I believe that when I've finished what I have to finish, the scales will come completely back into balance again.

Daddy, I love you. The worst thing, next to the belief that the gun is the only way out of this terrible deadlock I find myself in, is knowing that I'll be leaving you behind to bear the grief and hate of those who have no reason to believe Stillson is anything but a good and just man ...

6 ·

Excerpt from testimony given before the so-called 'Stillson Committee', chaired by Senator William Cohen of Maine. The questioner is Mr. Albert Renfrew, the Committee's Deputy Counsel. The witness is Dr. Samuel Weizak, of 26 Harlow Court, Bangor, Maine.

Date of testimony: August 23, 1979.

Renfrew: We are now approaching the hour of adjournment, Dr. Weizak, and on behalf of the Committee, I would like to thank you for the last four long hours of testimony. You have offered a great deal of light on the situation.

Weizak: That is quite all right.

R.: I have one final question for you, Dr. Weizak, one which seems to me to be of nearly ultimate importance;

it speaks to an issue which John Smith himself raised in the letter to his father which has been entered into evidence. That question is...

W.: No.

R.: I beg your pardon?

W.: You are preparing to ask me if Johnny's tumor pulled the trigger that day in New Hampshire, are you not?

R.: In a manner of speaking, I suppose...

W.: The answer is no. Johnny Smith was a thinking, reasoning human being until the end of his life. The letter to his father shows this; his letter to Sarah Hazlett also shows this. He was a man with a terrible, Godlike power – perhaps a curse, as my colleague Dr. Vann has called it – but he was neither unhinged nor acting upon fantasies caused by cranial pressure – if such a thing is even possible.

R.: But isn't it true that Charles Witman, the so-called 'Texas Tower Sniper', had...

W.: Yes, yes, he had a tumor. So did the pilot of the Eastern Airlines airplane that crashed in Florida some years ago. And it has never been suggested that the tumor was a precipitating cause in either case. I would point out to you that other infamous creatures – Richard Speck; the so-called 'Son of Sam', and Adolf Hitler – needed no brain tumors to cause them to act in a homicidal manner. Or Frank Dodd, the murderer Johnny himself uncovered in the town of Castle Rock. However misguided this Committee may find Johnny's act to have been, it was the act of a man who was sane. In great mental agony, perhaps... but sane.

7 ·

... and most of all, don't believe that I did this without the longest and most agonizing reflection. If by killing him I could be sure that the human race was gaining another four years, another two, even another eight months in which to think it over, it would be worth it. It's wrong, but it may turn out right. I don't know. But I won't play

*Hamlet any longer. I know how dangerous Stillson is.
Daddy, I love you very much. Believe it.*

*Your son,
Johnny*

8 .

Excerpt from testimony given before the so-called 'Stillson Committee', chaired by Senator William Cohen of Maine. The questioner is Mr. Albert Renfrew, the Committee's Deputy Counsel. The witness is Mr. Stuart Clawson, of the Blackstrap Road in Jackson, New Hampshire.

Renfrew: And you say you just happened to grab your camera, Mr. Clawson?

Clawson: Yeah! Just as I went out the door. I almost didn't even go that day, even though I like Greg Stillson – well, I did like him before all of this, anyway. The town hall just seemed like a bummer to me, you know?'

R.: Because of your driver's exam.

C.: You got it. Flunking that permit test was one colossal bummer. But at the end, I said what the hell. And I got the picture. Wow! I got it. That picture's going to make me rich, I guess. Just like the flag-raising on Iwo Jima.

R.: I hope you don't get the idea that the entire thing was staged for your benefit, young man.

C.: Oh, no! Not at all! I only meant . . . well . . . I don't know what I meant. But it happened right in front of me, and . . . I don't know. Jeez, I was just glad I had my Nikon, that's all.

R.: You just snapped the photo when Stillson picked up the child?

C.: Matt Robeson, yessir.

R.: And this is a blowup of that photo?

C.: That's my picture, yes.

R.: And after you took it, what happened?

C.: Two of those goons ran after me. They were yelling 'Give us the camera, kid! Drop it.' Shi – uh, stuff like that.

463

R.: And you ran.

C.: Did I run? Holy God, I guess I ran. They chased me almost all the way to the town garage. One of them almost had me, but he slipped on the ice and fell down.

Cohen: Young man, I'd like to suggest that you won the most important footrace of your life when you outran those two thugs.

C.: Thank you, Sir. What Stillson did that day . . . maybe you had to be there, but . . . holding a little kid in front of you, that's pretty low. I bet the people in New Hampshire wouldn't vote for that guy for dog-catcher. Not for . . .

R.: Thank you, Mr. Clawson. The witness is excused.

9 ·

October again.

Sarah had avoided this trip for a very long time, but now the time had come and it could be put off no longer. She felt that. She had left both children with Mrs. Ablanap – they had house-help now, and two cars instead of the little red Pinto; Walt's income was scraping near thirty thousand dollars a year – and had come by herself to Pownal through the burning blaze of late autumn.

Now she pulled over on the shoulder of a pretty litle country road, got out, and crossed to the small cemetery on the other side. A small, tarnished plaque on one of the stone posts announced that this was THE BIRCHES. It was enclosed by a rambling rock wall, and the grounds were neatly kept. A few faded flags remained from Memorial Day five months ago. Soon they would be buried under snow.

She walked slowly, not hurrying, the breeze catching the hem of her dark green skirt and fluttering it. Here were generations of BOWDENS; here was a whole family of MARSTENS; here, grouped around a large marble memorial, were PILLSBURYS going back to 1750.

And near the rear wall, she found a relatively new stone, which read simply JOHN SMITH. Sarah knelt

464

beside it, hesitated, touched it. She let her fingertips skate
thoughtfully over its polished surface.

10 ·

January 23, 1979

Dear Sarah,

*I've just written my father a very important letter, and
it took me nearly an hour and a half to work my way
through it. I just don't have the energy to repeat the
effort, so I am going to suggest that you call him* as soon
as you receive this. *Go do it now, Sarah, before you read
the rest of this.*

*So now, in all probability, you know. I just wanted to
tell you that I've been thinking a lot about our date at
the Esty Fair just recently. If I had to guess the two things
that you remember most about it, I'd guess the run of
luck I had on the Wheel of Fortune (remember the kid
who kept saying 'I love to see this guy take a beatin'?),
and the mask I wore to fool you. That was supposed to be
a big joke, but you got mad and our date damn near went
right down the drain. Maybe if it had, I wouldn't be here
now and that taxi driver would still be alive. On the
other hand, maybe nothing at all of importance changes
in the future, and I would have been handed the same
bullet to eat a week or a month or a year later.*

*Well, we had our chance and it came up on one of the
house numbers – double zero, I guess. But I wanted you
to know that I think of you, Sarah. For me there really
hasn't been anyone else, and that night was the best night
for us ...*

11 ·

'Hello, Johnny,' she murmured, and the wind walked
softly through the trees that burned and blazed; a red
leaf flipped its way across the bright blue sky and landed,
unnoticed, in her hair. 'I'm here. I finally came.'

Speaking out loud should have also seemed wrong;
speaking to the dead in a graveyard was the act of a crazy

465

person, she would have said once. But now emotion surprised her, emotion of such force and intensity that it caused her throat to ache and her hands to suddenly clap shut. It was all right to speak to him, maybe; after all, it had been nine years, and this was the end of it. After this there would be Walt and the children and lots of smiles from one of the chairs behind her husband's speaking podium; the endless smiles from the background and an occasional feature article in the Sunday supplements, if Walt's political career skyrocketed as he so calmly expected it to do. The future was a little more gray in her hair each year, never going braless because of the sag, becoming more careful about makeup; the future was exercise classes at the YWCA in Bangor and shopping and taking Denny to the first grade and Janis to nursery school; the future was New Year's Eve parties and funny hats as her life rolled into the science-fiction decade of the 1980s and also into a queer and almost unsuspected state – middle age.

She saw no county fairs in her future.

The first slow, scalding tears began to come. 'Oh, Johnny,' she said. 'Everything was supposed to be different, wasn't it? It wasn't supposed to end like this.'

She lowered her head, her throat working painfully – and to no effect. The sobs came anyway, and the bright sunlight broke into prisms of light. The wind, which had seemed so warm and Indian summery, now seemed as chill as February on her wet cheeks.

'Not *fair!*' she cried into the silence of BOWDENS and MARSTENS and PILLSBURYS, that dead congregation of listeners who testified to nothing more or less than life is quick and dead is dead. 'Oh God, not *fair!*'

And that was when the hand touched her neck.

12 ·

... and that night was the best night for us, although there are still times when it's hard for me to believe there ever was such a year as 1970 and upheaval on the campuses and Nixon was president, no pocket calculators,

*no home video tape recorders, no Bruce Springsteen or
punk-rock bands either. And at other times it seems like
that time is only a handsbreadth away, that I can almost
touch it, that if I could put my arms around you or touch
your cheek or the back of your neck, I could carry you
away with me into a different future with no pain or
darkness or bitter choices.*

*Well, we all do what we can, and it has to be good
enough ... and if it isn't good enough, it has to do. I
only hope that you will think of me as well as you can,
dear Sarah. All my best,*

and all my love,
Johnny

13 ·

She drew her breath in raggedly, her back straightening,
her eyes going wide and round. 'Johnny ... ?'

It was gone.

Whatever it had been, it was gone. She stood and
turned around and of course there was nothing there.
But she could see him standing there, his hands jammed
deep into his pockets, that easy, crooked grin on his
pleasant-rather-than-handsome face, leaning lanky and
at ease against a monument or one of the stone gateposts
or maybe just a tree gone red with fall's dying fire. No big
deal, Sarah – you still sniffin that wicked cocaine?

Nothing there but Johnny; somewhere near, maybe
everywhere.

*We all do what we can, and it has to be good enough
... and if it isn't good enough, it has to do. Nothing is
ever lost, Sarah. Nothing that can't be found.*

'Same old Johnny,' she whispered, and walked out of
the cemetery and crossed the road. She paused for a moment, looking back. The warm October wind gusted
strongly and great shades of light and shadow seemed to
pass across the world. The trees rustled secretly.

Sarah got in her car and drove away.

CUJO

ONCE UPON A TIME, not so long ago, a monster came to the small town of Castle Rock, Maine. He killed a waitress named Alma Frechette in 1970; a woman named Pauline Toothaker and a junior high school student named Cheryl Moody in 1971; a pretty girl named Carol Dunbarger in 1974; a teacher named Etta Ringgold in the fall of 1975; finally, a grade-schooler named Mary Kate Hendrasen in the early winter of that same year.

He was not werewolf, vampire, ghoul, or unnameable creature from the enchanted forest or from the snowy wastes; he was only a cop named Frank Dodd with mental and sexual problems. A good man named John Smith uncovered his name by a kind of magic, but before he could be captured – perhaps it was just as well – Frank Dodd killed himself.

There was some shock, of course, but mostly there was rejoicing in that small town, rejoicing because the monster which had haunted so many dreams was dead, dead at last. A town's nightmares were buried in Frank Dodd's grave.

Yet even in this enlightened age, when so many parents are aware of the psychological damage they may do to their children, surely there was one parent somewhere in Castle Rock – or perhaps one grandmother – who quieted the kids by telling them that Frank Dodd would get them if they didn't watch out, if they weren't good. And surely a hush fell as children looked toward their dark windows and thought of Frank Dodd in his shiny black vinyl raincoat, Frank Dodd who had choked . . . and choked . . . and choked.

He's out there, I can hear the grandmother whispering as the wind whistles down the chimney pipe and snuffles around the old pot lid crammed in the stove hole. *He's out there, and if you're not good, it may be* his *face you see looking in your bedroom window after everyone in the house is asleep except* you; *it may be* his *smiling face you see peeking at you from the closet in the middle of the night, the STOP sign he held up when he crossed the little children in one hand, the razor he used to kill himself in the other . . . so shhh, children . . . shhhh . . . shhhh. . . .*

But for most, the ending was the ending. There were nightmares to be sure, and children who lay wakeful to be sure, and the empty Dodd house (for his mother had a stroke shortly afterwards and died) quickly gained a reputation as a haunted house and was avoided; but these were passing phenomena – the perhaps unavoidable side effects of a chain of senseless murders.

But time passed. Five years of time.

The monster was gone, the monster was dead. Frank Dodd moldered inside his coffin.

Except that the monster never dies. Werewolf, vampire, ghoul, unnameable creature from the wastes. The monster never dies.

It came to Castle Rock again in the summer of 1980.

Tad Trenton, four years old, awoke one morning not long after midnight in May of that year, needing to go to the bathroom. He got out of bed and walked half asleep toward the white light thrown in a wedge through the half-open door, already lowering his pajama pants. He urinated forever, flushed, and went back to bed. He pulled the covers up, and that was when he saw the creature in his closet.

Low to the ground it was, with huge shoulders bulking above its cocked head, its eyes amber-glowing pits – a thing that might have been half man, half wolf. And its eyes rolled to follow him as he sat up, his scrotum crawling, his hair standing on end, his breath a thin winter-whistle in his throat: mad eyes that laughed, eyes that promised horrible death and the music of screams that went unheard; something in the closet.

He heard its purring growl; he smelled its sweet carrion breath.

Tad Trenton clapped his hands to his eyes, hitched in breath, and screamed.

A muttered exclamation in another room – his father.

A scared cry of 'What was that?' from the same room – his mother.

Their footfalls, running. As they came in, he peered through his fingers and saw it there in the closet, snarling, promising dreadfully that they might come, but they would surely go, and that when they did –

The light went on. Vic and Donna Trenton came to his bed, exchanging a look of concern over his chalky face and his staring eyes, and his mother said – no, snapped, 'I told you three hot dogs was too many, Vic!'

And then his daddy was on the bed, Daddy's arm around his back, asking what was wrong.

Tad dared to look into the mouth of his closet again.

The monster was gone. Instead of whatever hungry beast he had seen, there were two uneven piles of blankets, winter bedclothes which Donna had not yet gotten around to taking up to the cut-off third floor. These were stacked on the chair which Tad used to stand on when he needed something from the high closet shelf. Instead of the shaggy, triangular head, cocked sideways in a kind of predatory questioning gesture, he saw his teddybear on the taller of the two piles of blankets. Instead of pitted and baleful amber eyes, there were the friendly brown glass balls from which his Teddy observed the world.

'What's wrong, Tadder?' his daddy asked him again.

'There was a monster!' Tad cried. 'In my closet!' And he burst into tears.

His mommy sat with him; they held him between them, soothed him as best they could. There followed the ritual of parents. They explained there were no monsters; that he had just had a bad dream. His mommy explained how shadows could sometimes look like the bad things they sometimes showed on TV or in the comic books, and Daddy told him everything was all right, fine, that nothing in their good house could hurt him. Tad nodded and agreed that it was so, although he knew it was not.

His father explained to him how, in the dark, the two uneven piles of blankets had looked like hunched shoulders, how the teddybear had looked like a cocked head, and how the bathroom light, reflecting from Teddy's glass eyes, had made them seem like the eyes of a real live animal.

'Now look,' he said. 'Watch me close, Tadder.'

Tad watched.

His father took the two piles of blankets and put them far back in Tad's closet. Tad could hear the coathangers jingling softly, talking about Daddy in their coathanger language. That was funny, and he smiled a little. Mommy caught his smile and smiled back, relieved.

His daddy came out of the closet, took Teddy, and put him in Tad's arms.

'And last but not least, Daddy said with a flourish and a bow that made both Tad and Mommy giggle, 'ze chair.'

He closed the closet door firmly and then put the chair against the door. When he came back to Tad's bed he was still smiling, but his eyes were serious.

'Okay, Tad?'

'Yes,' Tad said, and then forced himself to say it. 'But it was there, Daddy. I saw it. Really.'

'Your *mind* saw something, Tad,' Daddy said, and his big, warm hand stroked Tad's hair. 'But you didn't see a monster in your closet, not a real one. There are no monsters, Tad. Only in stories, and in your mind.'

He looked from his father to his mother and back again — their big, well-loved faces.

'Really?'

'Really,' his mommy said. 'Now I want you to get up and go pee, big guy.'

'I did. That's what woke me up.'

'Well,' she said, because parents never believed you, 'humor me then, what do you say?'

So he went in and she watched while he did four drops and she smiled and said, 'See? You *did* have to go.'

Resigned, Tad nodded. Went back to bed. Was tucked in. Accepted kisses.

And as his mother and father went back to the door the fear settled on him again like a cold coat full of mist. Like a shroud stinking of hopeless death. *Oh please*, he thought, but there was no more, just that: *Oh please oh please oh please.*

Perhaps his father caught his thought, because Vic turned back, one hand on the light switch, and repeated: 'No monsters, Tad.'

'No, Daddy,' Tad said, because in that instant his father's eyes seemed shadowed and far, as if he needed to be convinced. 'No monsters.' *Except for the one in my closet.*

The light snapped off.

'Good night, Tad.' His mother's voice trailed back to him lightly, softly, and in his mind he cried out, *Be careful, Mommy, they eat the ladies! In all the movies they catch the ladies and carry them off and eat them! Oh please oh please oh please –*

But they were gone.

So Tad Trenton, four years old, lay in his bed, all wires and stiff Erector Set braces. He lay with the covers pulled up to his chin and one arm crushing Teddy against his chest, and there was Luke Skywalker on one wall; there was a chipmunk standing on a blender on another wall, grinning cheerily (IF LIFE HANDS YOU LEMONS, MAKE LEMONADE! the cheeky, grinning chipmunk was saying); there was the whole motley Sesame Street crew on a third: Big Bird, Bert, Ernie, Oscar, Grover. Good totems; good magic. But oh the wind outside, screaming over the roof and skating down black gutters! He would sleep no more this night.

But little by little the wires unsnarled themselves and stiff Erector Set muscles relaxed. His mind began to drift. . . .

And then a new screaming, this one closer than the nightwind outside, brought him back to staring wakefulness again.

The hinges on the closet door.

Creeeeeeeeeeee –

That thin sound, so high that perhaps only dogs and small boys awake in the night could have heard it. His closet door swung open slowly and steadily, a dead mouth opening on darkness inch by inch and foot by foot.

The monster was in that darkness. It crouched where it had crouched before. It grinned at him, and its huge shoulders bulked above its cocked head, and its eyes glowed amber, alive with stupid cunning. *I told you they'd go away, Tad,* it whispered. *They always do, in the end. And then I can come back. I like to come back. I like you, Tad. I'll come back every night now, I think, and every night I'll come a little closer to your bed . . . and a little closer . . . until one night, before you can scream for them, you'll hear something growling, something growling right beside you, Tad, it'll be me, and I'll pounce, and then I'll eat you and you'll be in me.*

Tad stared at the creature in his closet with drugged, horrified fascination. There was something that . . . was almost familiar. Something he almost knew. And that was the worst, that almost knowing. Because –

Because I'm crazy, Tad. I'm here. I've been here all along. My name was Frank Dodd once, and I killed the ladies and maybe I ate them, too. I've been here all along, I stick around, I keep my ear to the ground. I'm the monster, Tad, the old monster, and I'll have you soon, Tad. Feel me getting closer . . . and closer. . . .

Perhaps the thing in the closet spoke to him in its own hissing breath, or perhaps its voice was the wind's voice. Either way, neither way, it didn't matter. He listened to its words, drugged with terror, near fainting (but oh so wide awake); he looked upon its shadowed, snarling face, which he almost knew. He would sleep no more tonight; perhaps he would never sleep again.

But sometime later, sometime between the striking of half past midnight and the hour of one, perhaps because he was small, Tad drifted away again. Thin sleep in which hulking, furred creatures with white teeth chased him deepened into dreamless slumber.

The wind held long conversations with the gutters. A rind of white spring moon rose in the sky. Somewhere far away, in some still meadow of night or along some pine-edged corridor of forest, a dog barked furiously and then fell silent.

And in Tad Trenton's closet, something with amber eyes held watch.

'Did you put the blankets back?' Donna asked her husband the next morning. She was standing at the stove, cooking bacon. Tad was in the other room, watching *The New Zoo Revue* and eating a bowl of Twinkles. Twinkles was a Sharp cereal, and the Trentons got all their Sharp cereals free.

'Hmmm?' Vic asked. He was buried deep in the sports pages. A transplanted New Yorker, he had so far successfully resisted Red Sox fever. But he was masochistically pleased to see that the Mets were off to another superlatively cruddy start.

'The blankets. In Tad's closet. They were back in there. The chair was back in there, too, and the door was open again.' She brought the bacon, draining on a paper towel and still sizzling, to the table. 'Did you put them back on his chair?'

'Not me,' Vic said, turning a page. 'It smells like a mothball convention back there.'

'That's funny. *He* must have put them back.'

He put the paper aside and looked up at her. 'What are you talking about, Donna?'

'You remember the bad dream last night —'

'Not apt to forget. I thought the kid was dying. Having a convulsion or something.'

She nodded. 'He thought the blankets were some kind of —' She shrugged.

'Bogeyman,' Vic said, grinning.

'I guess so. And you gave him his teddybear and put those blankets in the back of the closet. But they were back on the chair when I went to make his bed.' She laughed. 'I looked in, and for just a second there I thought –'

'*Now* I know where he gets it,' Vic said, picking up the newspaper again. He cocked a friendly eye at her. 'Three hot dogs, my ass.'

Later, after Vic had shot off to work, Donna asked Tad why he had put the chair back in the closet with the blankets on it if they had scared him in the night.

Tad looked up at her, and his normally animated, lively face seemed pale and watchful – too old. His *Star Wars* coloring book was open in front of him. He had been doing a picture from the interstellar cantina, using his green Crayola to color Greedo.

'I didn't,' he said.

'But Tad, if you didn't, and Daddy didn't, and *I* didn't –'

'The monster did it,' Tad said. 'The monster in my closet.' He bent to his picture again.

She stood looking at him, troubled, a little frightened. He was a bright boy, and perhaps too imaginative. This was not such good news. She would have to talk to Vic about it tonight. She would have to have a long talk with him about it.

'Tad, remember what your father said,' she told him now. 'There aren't any such things as monsters.'

'Not in the daytime, anyway,' he said, and smiled at her so openly, so beautifully, that she was charmed out of her fears. She ruffled his hair and kissed his cheek.

She meant to talk to Vic, and then Steve Kemp came while Tad was at nursery school, and she forgot, and Tad screamed that night too, screamed that it was in his closet, the monster, the monster!

The closet door hung ajar, blankets on the chair. This time Vic took them up to the third floor and stacked them in the closet up there.

'Locked it up, Tadder,' Vic said, kissing his son. 'You're all set now. Go back to sleep and have a good dream.'

But Tad did not sleep for a long time, and before he did the closet door swung clear of its latch with a sly little snicking sound, the dead mouth opened on the dead dark – the dead dark where something furry and sharp-toothed and -clawed waited, something that smelled of sour blood and dark doom.

Hello, Tad, it whispered in its rotting voice, and the moon peered in Tad's window like the white and slitted eye of a dead man.

The oldest living person in Castle Rock that late spring was Evelyn Chalmers, known as Aunt Evvie by the town's older residents, known as 'that old loudmouth bitch' by George Meara, who had to deliver her mail – which mostly consisted of catalogues and offers from the *Reader's Digest* and prayer folders from the Crusade of the Eternal Christ – and listen to her endless monologues. 'The only thing that old loudmouth bitch is any good at is telling the weather,' George had been known to allow when in his cups and in the company of his cronies down at the Mellow Tiger. It was one stupid name for a bar, but since it was the only one Castle Rock could boast, it looked like they were pretty much stuck with it.

There was general agreement with George's opinion. As the oldest resident of Castle Rock, Aunt Evvie had held the *Boston Post* cane for the last two years, ever since Arnold Heebert, who had been one hundred and one and so far gone in senility that talking to him held all the intellectual challenge of talking to an empty catfood can, had doddered off the back patio of the Castle Acres Nursing Home and broken his neck exactly twenty-five minutes after whizzing in his pants for the last time.

Aunt Evvie was nowhere near as senile as Arnie Heebert had been, and nowhere near as old, but at ninety-three she was old enough, and, as she was fond of bawling at a resigned (and often hung-over) George Meara when he delivered the mail, she hadn't been stupid enough to lose her home the way Heebert had done.

But she was good at the weather. The town consensus –

among the older people, who cared about such things –
was that Aunt Evvie was never wrong about three things:
the week when the first hay-cutting would happen in the
summertime, how good (or how bad) the blueberries would
be, and what the weather would be like.

One day early that June she shuffled out to the mailbox
at the end of the driveway, leaning heavily on her *Boston
Post* cane (which would go to Vin Marchant when the
loudmouthed old bitch popped off, George Meara thought,
and good riddance to *you*, Evvie) and smoking a Herbert
Tareyton. She bellowed a greeting at Meara – her deafness
had apparently convinced her that everyone else in the
world had gone deaf in sympathy – and then shouted that
they were going to have the hottest summer in thirty years.
Hot early and hot late, Evvie bellowed leather-lunged into
the drowsy eleven-o'clock quiet, and hot in the middle.

'That so?' George asked.

'*What?*'

'*I said, "Is that so?"*' That was the other thing about Aunt
Evvie; she got you shouting right along with her. A man
could pop a blood vessel.

'*I should hope to smile and kiss a pig if it ain't!*' Aunt
Evvie screamed. The ash of her cigarette fell on the shoulder
of George Meara's uniform blouse, freshly dry-cleaned and
just put on clean this morning; he brushed it off resignedly.
Aunt Evvie leaned in the window of his car, all the better to
bellow in his ear. Her breath smelled like sour cucumbers.

'*Fieldmice has all gone outta the root cellars! Tommy
Neadeau seen deer out by Moosuntic Pond rubbin velvet
off'n their antlers ere the first robin showed up! Grass under
the snow when she melted! Green grass, Meara!*'

'That so, Evvie?' George replied, since some reply seemed
necessary. He was getting a headache.

'*What?*'

'*THAT SO, AUNT EVVIE?*' George Mear screamed.
Saliva flew from his lips.

'*Oh, ayuh!*' Aunt Evvie howled back contentedly. '*And I
seen heat lightnin last night late! Bad sign, Meara! Early*

heat's a bad sign! Be people die of the heat this summer! It's gonna be a bad un!'

'*I got to go, Aunt Evvie!*' George yelled. '*Got a Special Delivery for Stringer Beaulieu!*'

Aunt Evvie Chalmers threw her head back and cackled at the spring sky. She cackled until she was fit to choke and more cigarette ashes rolled down the front of her housedress. She spat the last quarter inch of cigarette out of her mouth, and it lay smoldering in the driveway by one of her old-lady shoes – a shoe as black as a stove and as tight as a corset; a shoe for the ages.

'*You got a Special Delivery for Frenchy Beaulieu? Why, he couldn't read the name on his own tombstone!*'

'*I got to go, Aunt Evvie!*' George said hastily, and threw his car in gear.

'*Frenchy Beaulieu is a stark natural-born fool if God ever made one!*' Aunt Evvie hollered, but by then she was hollering into George Meara's dust; he had made good his escape.

She stood there by her mailbox for a minute, watching him go. There was no personal mail for her; these days there rarely was. Most of the people she knew who had been able to write were now dead. She would follow soon enough, she suspected. The oncoming summer gave her a bad feeling, a scary feeling. She could speak of the mice leaving the root cellars early, or of heat lightning in a spring sky, but she could not speak of the heat she sensed somewhere just over the horizon, crouched like a scrawny yet powerful beast with mangy fur and red, smoldering eyes; she could not speak of her dreams, which were hot and shadowless and thirsty; she could not speak of the morning when tears had come for no reason, tears that did not relieve but stung the eyes like August-mad sweat instead. She smelled lunacy in a wind that had not arrived.

'George Meara, you're an old fart,' Aunt Evvie said, giving the word a juicy Maine resonance which built it into something that was both cataclysmic and ludicrous: *faaaaaat.*

She began working her way back to the house, leaning on her *Boston Post* cane, which had been given her at a Town Hall ceremony for no more than the stupid accomplishment of growing old successfully. No wonder, she thought, the goddamned paper had gone broke.

She paused on her stoop, looking at a sky which was still spring-pure and pastel soft. Oh, but she sensed it coming: something hot. Something foul.

A year before that summer, when Vic Trenton's old Jaguar developed a distressing clunking sound somewhere inside the rear left wheel, it had been George Meara who recommended that he take it up to Joe Camber's Garage on the outskirts of Castle Rock. 'He's got a funny way of doing things for around here,' George told Vic that day as Vic stood by his mailbox. 'Tells you what the job's gonna cost, then he does the job, and then he charges you what he said it was gonna cost. Funny way to do business, huh?' And he drove away, leaving Vic to wonder if the mailman had been serious or if he (Vic) had just been on the receiving end of some obscure Yankee joke.

But he had called Camber, and one day in July (a much cooler July than the one which would follow a year later), he and Donna and Tad had driven out to Camber's place together. It really was far out; twice Vic had to stop and ask directions, and it was then that he began to call those farthest reaches of the township East Galoshes Corners.

He pulled into the Camber dooryard, the back wheel clunking louder than ever. Tad, then three, was sitting on Donna Trenton's lap, laughing up at her; a ride in Daddy's 'no-top' always put him in a fine mood, and Donna was feeling pretty fine herself.

A boy of eight or nine was standing in the yard, hitting an old baseball with an even older baseball bat. The ball would travel through the air, strike the side of the barn, which Vic assumed was also Mr. Camber's garage, and then roll most of the way back.

'Hi,' the boy said. 'Are you Mr. Trenton?'

'That's right,' Vic said.

'I'll get my dad,' the boy said, and went into the barn.

The three Trentons got out, and Vic walked around to the back of his Jag and squatted by the bad wheel, not feeling very confident. Perhaps he should have tried to nurse the car into Portland after all. The situation out here didn't look very promising; Camber didn't even have a sign hung out.

His meditations were broken by Donna, calling his name nervously. And then: 'Oh my *God*, Vic —'

He got up quickly and saw a huge dog emerging from tne barn. For one absurd moment he wondered if it really was a dog, or maybe some strange and ugly species of pony. Then, as the dog padded out of the shadows of the barn's mouth, he saw its sad eyes and realized it was a Saint Bernard.

Donna had impulsively snatched up Tad and retreated toward the hood of the Jag, but Tad was struggling impatiently in her arms, trying to get down.

'Want to see the doggy, Mom . . . want to see the *doggy*!'

Donna cast a nervous glance at Vic, who shrugged, also uneasy. Then the boy came back and ruffled the dog's head as he approached Vic. The dog wagged a tail that was absolutely huge, and Tad redoubled his struggles.

'You can let him down, ma'am,' the boy said politely. 'Cujo likes kids. He won't hurt him.' And then, to Vic: 'My dad's coming right out. He's washing his hands.'

'All right,' Vic said. 'That's one hell of a big dog, son. Are you sure he's safe?'

'He's safe,' the boy agreed, but Vic found himself moving up beside his wife as his son, incredibly small, toddled toward the dog. Cujo stood with his head cocked, that great brush of a tail waving slowly back and forth.

'Vic —' Donna began.

'It's all right,' Vic said, thinking, *I hope*. The dog looked big enough to swallow the Tadder in a single bite.

Tad stopped for a moment, apparently doubtful. He and the dog looked at each other.

'Doggy?' Tad said.

'Cujo,' Camber's boy said, walking over to Tad. 'His name's Cujo.'

'Cujo,' Tad said, and the dog came to him and began to lick his face in great, goodnatured, slobbery swipes that had Tad giggling and trying to fend him off. He turned back to his mother and father, laughing the way he did when one of them was tickling him. He took a step toward them and his feet tangled in each other. He fell down, and suddenly the dog was moving toward him, over him, and Vic, who had his arm around Donna's waist, felt his wife's gasp as well as he heard it. He started to move forward . . . and then stopped.

Cujo's teeth had clamped on the back of Tad's Spider-Man T-shirt. He pulled the boy up – for a moment Tad looked like a kitten in its mother's mouth – and set the boy on his feet.

Tad ran back to his mother and father. 'Like the doggy! Mom! Dad! I like the doggy!'

Camber's boy was watching this with mild amusement, his hands stuffed into the pockets of his jeans.

'Sure, it's a great dog,' Vic said. He was amused, but his heart was still beating fast. For just one moment there he had really believed that the dog was going to bite off Tad's head like a lollipop. 'It's a Saint Bernard, Tad,' he said.

'Saint . . . Bennart!' Tad cried, and ran back toward Cujo, who was now sitting outside the mouth of the barn like a small mountain. 'Cujo! *Coooojo!*'

Donna tensed beside Vic again. 'Oh, Vic, do you think –'

But now Tad was with Cujo again, first hugging him extravagantly and then looking closely at his face. With Cujo sitting down (his tail thumping on the gravel, his tongue lolling out pinkly), Tad could almost look into the dog's eyes by standing on tiptoe.

'I think they're fine,' Vic said.

Tad had now put one of his small hands into Cujo's mouth and was peering in like the world's smallest dentist. That gave Vic another uneasy moment, but then Tad was running back to them again. 'Doggy's got teeth,' he told Vic.

'Yes,' Vic said. 'Lots of teeth.'

He turned to the boy, meaning to ask him where he had come up with that name, but then Joe Camber was coming out of the barn, wiping his hands on a piece of waste so he could shake without getting Vic greasy.

Vic was pleasantly surprised to find that Camber knew exactly what he was doing. He listened carefully to the clunking sound as he and Vic drove down to the house at the bottom of the hill and then back up to Camber's place.

'Wheel bearing's going,' Camber said briefly. 'You're lucky it ain't froze up on you already.'

'Can you fix it?' Vic asked.

'Oh, ayuh. Fix it right now if you don't mind hanging around for a couple of hours.'

'That'd be all right, I guess,' Vic said. He looked toward Tad and the dog. Tad had gotten the baseball Camber's son had been hitting. He would throw it as far as he could (which wasn't very far), and the Cambers' Saint Bernard would obediently get it and bring it back to Tad. The ball was looking decidedly slobbery. 'Your dog is keeping my son amused.'

'Cujo likes kids,' Camber agreed. 'You want to drive your car into the barn, Mr. Trenton?'

The doctor will see you now, Vic thought, amused, and drove the Jag in. As it turned out, the job only took an hour and a half and Camber's price was so reasonable it was startling.

And Tad ran through that cool, overcast afternoon, calling the dog's name over and over again: '*Cujo . . . Cooojo . . . heeere, Cujo. . . .*' Just before they left, Camber's boy, whose name was Brett, actually lifted Tad onto Cujo's back and held him around the waist while Cujo padded obediently up and down the gravel dooryard twice. As it passed Vic, the dog caught his eye . . . and Vic would have sworn it was laughing.

Just three days after George Meara's bellowed conversation with Aunt Evvie Chalmers, a little girl who was exactly Tad Trenton's age stood up from her place at the breakfast table — said breakfast table being in the breakfast nook of a tidy little house in Iowa City, Iowa — and announced: 'Oh, Mamma, I don't feel so good. I feel like I'm going to be sick.'

Her mother looked around, not exactly surprised. Two days before, Marcy's bigger brother had been sent from school with a raging case of stomach flu. Brock was all right now, but he had spent a lousy twenty-four hours, his body enthusiastically throwing off ballast from both ends.

'Are you sure, honey?' Marcy's mother said.

'Oh, I —' Marcy moaned loudly and lurched toward the downstairs hall, her hands laced over her stomach. Her mother followed her, saw Marcy buttonhook into the bathroom, and thought, *Oh, boy, here we go again. If I don't catch this it'll be a miracle.*

She heard the retching sounds begin and turned into the bathroom her mind already occupied with the details: clear liquids, bed rest, the chamber-pot, some books; Brock could take the portable TV up to her room when he got back from school and —

She looked, and these thoughts were driven from her mind with the force of a roundhouse slap.

The toilet bowl where her four-year-old daughter had vomited was full of blood; blood splattered the white porcelain lip of the bowl; blood beaded the tiles.

'Oh, Mommy, I don't feel good —'

Her daughter turned, her daughter turned, turned, and there was blood all over her mouth, it was down her chin, it was matting her blue sailor dress, blood, oh dear God dear Jesus Joseph and Mary so much *blood* —

'Mommy —'

And her daughter did it again, a huge bloody mess flying from her mouth to patter down everywhere like sinister rain, and then Marcy's mother gathered her up and ran with her, ran for the phone in the kitchen to dial the emergency unit.

Cujo knew he was too old to chase rabbits.

He wasn't *old*; no, not even for a dog. But at five, he was well past his puppyhood, when even a butterfly had been enough to set off an arduous chase through the woods and meadows behind the house and barn. He was five, and if he had been a human, he would have been entering the youngest stage of middle age.

But it was the sixteenth of June, a beautiful early morning, the dew still on the grass. The heat Aunt Evvie had predicted to George Meara had indeed arrived – it was the warmest early June in years – and by two that afternoon Cujo would be lying in the dusty dooryard (or in the barn, if THE MAN would let him in, which he sometimes did when he was drinking, which was most of the time these days), panting under the hot sun. But that was later.

And the rabbit, which was large, brown, and plump, didn't have the slightest idea Cujo was there, down near the end of the north field, a mile from the house. The wind was blowing the wrong way for Br'er Rabbit.

Cujo worked toward the rabbit, out for sport rather than meat. The rabbit munched happily away at new clover that would be baked and brown under the relentless sun a month later. If he had only covered half the original distance between himself and the rabbit when the rabbit saw him and bolted, Cujo would have let it go. But he had actually got to within fifteen yards of it when the rabbit's head and ears came up. For a moment the rabbit did not move at all; it was a frozen rabbit sculpture with black walleyes bulging comically. Then it was off.

Barking furiously, Cujo gave chase. The rabbit was very small and Cujo was very big, but the *possibility* of the thing put an extra ration of energy in Cujo's legs. He actually got close enough to paw at the rabbit. The rabbit zigged. Cujo came around more ponderously, his claws digging black meadow dirt, losing some ground at first, making it up quickly. Birds took wing at his heavy, chopping bark; if it is possible for a dog to grin, Cujo was grinning then. The rabbit zagged, then made straight across the north field.

Cujo pelted after it, already suspecting this was one race he wasn't going to win.

But he tried hard, and he was gaining on the rabbit again when it dropped into a small hole in the side of a small and easy hill. The hole was overgrown by long grasses, and Cujo didn't hesitate. He lowered his big tawny body into a kind of furry projectile and let his forward motion carry him in . . . where he promptly stuck like a cork in a bottle.

Joe Camber had owned Seven Oaks Farm out at the end of Town Road No. 3 for seventeen years, but he had no idea this hole was here. He surely would have discovered it if farming was his business, but it wasn't. There was no livestock in the big red barn; it was his garage and auto-body shop. His son Brett rambled the fields and woods behind the home place frequently, but he had never noticed the hole either, although on several occasions he had nearly put his foot in it, which might have earned him a broken ankle. On clear days the hole could pass for a shadow; on cloudy days, overgrown with grass as it was, it disappeared altogether.

John Mousam, the farm's previous owner, had known about the hole but had never thought to mention it to Joe Camber when Joe bought the place in 1963. He might have mentioned it, as a caution, when Joe and his wife, Charity, had their son in 1970, but by then the cancer had carried old John off.

It was just as well Brett had never found it. There's nothing in the world quite so interesting to a small boy as a hole in the ground, and this one opened on a small natural limestone cave. It was about twenty feet deep at its deepest, and it would have been quite possible for a small squirty boy to eel his way in, slide to the bottom, and then find it impossible to get out. It had happened to other small animals in the past. The cave's limestone surface made a good slide but a bad climb, and its bottom was littered with bones: a woodchuck, a skunk, a couple of chipmunks, a couple of squirrels, and a housecat. The housecat's name had been Mr. Clean. The Cambers had lost him two years before and assumed he had been hit by a car or had just run off. But here he was, along with the bones of the good-sized fieldmouse he had chased inside.

Cujo's rabbit had rolled and slid all the way to the bottom and now quivered there, ears up and nose vibrating like a tuning fork, as Cujo's furious barking filled the place. The echoes made it sound as though there was a whole pack of dogs up there.

The small cave had also attracted bats from time to time – never many, because the cave was only a small one, but its rough ceiling made a perfect place for them to roost upside down and snooze the daylight away. The bats were another good reason that Brett Camber had been lucky, especially this year. This year the brown insectivorous bats inhabiting the small cave were crawling with a particularly virulent strain of rabies.

Cujo had stuck at the shoulders. He dug furiously with his back legs to no effect at all. He could have reversed and pulled himself back out, but for now he still wanted the rabbit. He sensed it was trapped, his for the taking. His eyes were not particularly keen, his large body blocked out almost all the light anyway, and he had no sense of the drop just beyond his front paws. He could smell damp, and he could smell bat guano, both old and fresh . . . but most important of all, he could smell rabbit. Hot and tasty. Dinner is served.

His barking roused the bats. They were terrified. Something had invaded their home. They flew en masse toward the exit, squeaking. But their sonar recorded a puzzling and distressing fact: the entrance was no longer there. The predator was where the entrance had been.

They wheeled and swooped in the darkness, their membranous wings sounding like small pieces of clothing – diapers, perhaps – flapping from a line in a gusty wind. Below them, the rabbit cringed and hoped for the best.

Cujo felt several of the bats flutter against the third of him that had managed to get into the hole, and he became frightened. He didn't like their scent or their sound; he didn't like the odd heat that seemed to emanate from them.

He barked louder and snapped at the things that were wheeling and squeaking around his head. His snapping jaws closed on one brown-black wing. Bones thinner than those in a baby's hand crunched. The bat slashed and bit at him, slicing open the skin of the dog's sensitive muzzle in a long, curving wound that was shaped like a question mark. A moment later it went skittering and cartwheeling down the limestone slope, already dying. But the damage had been done; a bite from a rabid animal is most serious around the head, for rabies is a disease of the central nervous system. Dogs, more susceptible than their human masters, cannot even hope for complete protection from the inactivated-virus vaccine which every veterinarian administers. And Cujo had never had a single rabies shot in his life.

Not knowing this, but knowing that the unseen thing he had bitten had tasted foul and horrible, Cujo decided the game was not worth the candle. With a tremendous yank of his shoulders he pulled himself out of the hole, causing a little avalanche of dirt. He shook himself, and more dirt and smelly crumbled limestone flew from his pelt. Blood dripped from his muzzle. He sat down, tilted his head skyward, and uttered a single low howl.

The bats exited their hole in a small brown cloud, whirled confusedly in the bright June sunshine for a couple of seconds, and then went back in to roost. They were brainless things, and within the course of two or three minutes they had forgotten all about the barking interloper and were sleeping again, hung from their heels with their wings wrapped around their ratty little bodies like the shawls of old women.

Cujo trotted away. He shook himself again. He pawed helplessly at his muzzle. The blood was already clotting, drying to a cake, but it hurt. Dogs have a sense of self-consciousness that is far out of proportion to their intelligence, and Cujo was disgusted with himself. He didn't want to go home. If he went home, one of his trinity – THE MAN, THE WOMAN, or THE BOY – would see that he had done something to himself. It was possible that one of them might call him BADDOG. And at this particular moment he certainly considered himself to be a BADDOG.

So instead of going home, Cujo went down to the stream that separated Camber land from the property of Gary Pervier, the Cambers' nearest neighbour. He waded upstream; he drank deeply; he rolled over in the water, trying to get rid of the nasty taste in his mouth, trying to get rid of the dirt and the watery green stink of limestone, trying to get rid of that BADDOG feeling.

Little by little, he began to feel better. He came out of the stream and shook himself, the spray of water forming a momentary rainbow of breathless clarity in the air.

The BADDOG feeling was fading, and so was the pain in his nose. He started up toward the house to see if THE BOY might be around. He had gotten used to the big yellow schoolbus that came to pick THE BOY up every morning and which dropped him back off again in midafternoon, but this last week the schoolbus had not shown up with its flashing eyes and its yelling cargo of children. THE BOY was always at home. Usually he was out in the barn, doing things with THE MAN. Maybe the yellow schoolbus had come again today. Maybe not. He would see. He had forgotten about the hole and the nasty taste of the batwing. His nose hardly hurt at all now.

Cujo breasted his way easily through the high grass of the north field, driving up an occasional bird but not bothering to give chase. He had had his chase for the day, and his body remembered even if his brain did not. He was a Saint Bernard in his prime, five years old, nearly two hundred pounds in weight, and now, on the morning of June 16, 1980, he was pre-rabid.

Seven days later and thirty miles from Seven Oaks Farm in Castle Rock, two men met in a downtown Portland restaurant called the Yellow Submarine. The Sub featured a large selection of hero sandwiches, pizzas, and Dagwoods in Lebanese pouches. There was a pinball machine in the back.

There was a sign over the counter saying that if you could eat two Yellow Sub Nightmares, you ate free; below that, in parentheses, the codicil IF YOU PUKE YOU PAY had been added.

Ordinarily there was nothing Vic Trenton would have liked better than one of the Yellow Sub's meatball heroes, but he suspected he would get nothing from today's but a really good case of acid burn.

'Looks like we're going to lose the ball, doesn't it?' Vic said to the other man, who was regarding a Danish ham with a marked lack of enthusiasm. The other man was Roger Breakstone, and when he looked at food without enthusiasm, you knew that some sort of cataclysm was at hand. Roger weighed two hundred and seventy pounds and had no lap when he sat down. Once, when the two of them had been in bed with a kids-at-camp case of the giggles, Donna had told Vic she thought Roger's lap had been shot off in Vietnam.

'It looks piss-poor,' Roger admitted. 'It looks so fucking piss-poor you wouldn't believe it, Victor old buddy.'

'You really think making this trip will solve anything?'

'Maybe not,' Roger said, 'but we're going to lose the Sharp account for sure if we don't go. Maybe we can salvage something. Work our way back in.' He bit into his sandwich.

'Closing up for ten days is going to hurt us.'

'You think we're not hurting now?'

'Sure, we're hurting. But we've got those Book Folks spots to shoot down at Kennebunk Beach —'

'Lisa can handle that.'

'I'm not entirely convinced that Lisa can handle her own love-life, let along the Book Folks spots,' Vic said. 'But even supposing she *can* handle it, the Yor Choice Blueberries series is still hanging fire ... Casco Bank and Trust ... and you're supposed to meet with the head honcho from the Main Realtors' Association—'

'Huh-uh, that's yours.'

'Fuck you it's mine,' Vic said. 'I break up every time I think of those red pants and white shoes. I kept wanting to look in the closet to see if I could find the guy a sandwich board.'

'It doesn't matter, and you know it doesn't. None of them bills a tenth of what Sharp bills. What else can I say? You know Sharp and the kid are going to want to talk to both of us. Do I book you a seat or not?'

The thought of ten days, five in Boston and five in New York, gave Vic a mild case of the cold sweats. He and Roger had both worked for the Ellison Agency in New York for six years. Vic now had a home in Castle Rock. Roger and Althea Breakstone lived in neighboring Bridgton, about fifteen miles away.

For Vic, it had been a case of never even wanting to look back. He felt he had never come fully alive, had never really known what he was for, until he and Donna moved to Maine. And now he had a morbid sense that New York had only been waiting these last three years to get him in its clutches again. The plane would skid off the runway coming in and be engulfed in a roaring firecloud of hi-test jet fuel. Or there would be a crash on the Triborough Bridge, their Checker crushed into a bleeding yellow accordion. A mugger would use his gun instead of just waving it. A gas main would explode and he would be decapitated by a manhole cover flying through the air like a deadly ninety-pound Frisbee. Something. If he went back, the city would kill him.

'Rog,' he said, putting down his meatball sandwich after one small bite, 'have you ever thought that it might not be the end of the world if we *did* lose the Sharp account?'

'The world will go on,' Roger said, pouring a Busch down the side of a pilsner glass, 'but will we? Me, I've got seventeen years left on a twenty-year mortgage and twin girls who have their hearts set on Bridgton Academy. You've got your own mortgage, your own kid, plus that old Jag sportster that's going to half-buck you to death.'

'Yes, but the local economy —'

'The local economy *sucks*!' Roger exclaimed violently, and set his pilsner glass down with a bang.

SOLIHULL S.F.C.
LIBRARY

A party of four at the next table, three in UMP tennis shirts and one wearing a faded T-shirt with the legend DARTH VADER IS GAY written across the front, began to applaud.

Roger waved a hand at them impatiently and leaned toward Vic. 'We're not going to make it happen doing campaigns for Yor Choice Blueberries and the Main Realtors, and you know it. If we lose the Sharp account, we're going to go under without a ripple. On the other hand, if we can keep even a piece of Sharp over the next two years, we'll be in line for some of the Department of Tourism budget, maybe even a crack at the state lottery if they don't mismanage it into oblivion by then. Juicy pies, Vic. We can wave so long to Sharp and their crappy cereals and there's happy endings all around. The big bad wolf has to go somewhere else to get his dinner; these little piggies are home free.'

'All contingent on us being able to save something,' Vic said, 'which is about as likely as the Cleveland Indians winning the World Series this fall.'

'I think we better try, buddy.'

Vic sat silent, looking at his congealing sandwich and thinking. It was totally unfair, but he could live with unfairness. What really hurt was the whole situation's crazed absurdity. It had blown up out of a clear sky like a killer tornado that lays a zigzagging trail of destruction and then disappears. He and Roger and Ad Worx itself were apt to be numbered among the fatalities no matter what they did; he could read it on Roger's round face, which had not looked so pallidly serious since he and Althea had lost their boy, Timothy, to the crib-death syndrome when the infant was only nine days old. Three weeks after that happened, Roger had broken down and wept, his hands plastered to his fat face in a kind of terrible hopeless sorrow that had squeezed Vic's heart into his throat. That had been bad. But the incipient panic he saw in Roger's eyes now was bad, too.

Tornadoes blew out of nowhere in the advertising business from time to time. A bit outfit like the Ellison

Agency, which billed in the millions, could withstand them. A little one like Ad Worx just couldn't. They had been carrying one basket with a lot of little eggs in it and another basket with one big egg – the Sharp account – and it now remained to be seen whether the big egg had been lost entirely or if it could at least be scrambled. None of it had been their fault, but ad agencies make lovely whipping boys.

Vic and Roger had teamed naturally together ever since their first joint effort at the Ellison Agency, six years ago. Vic, tall and skinny and rather quiet, had formed the perfect yin for Roger Breakstone's fat, happy, and extroverted yang. They had clicked on a personal basis and on a professional one. That first assignment had been a minor one, to submit a magazine ad campaign for United Cerebral Palsy.

They had come up with a stark black-and-white ad that showed a small boy in huge, cruel leg braces standing in foul territory by the first-base line of a Little League ballfield. A New York Mets cap was perched on his head, and his expression – Roger had always maintained that it had been the boy's expression which sold the ad – wasn't sad at all; it was simply dreamy. Almost happy, in fact. The copy read simply: BILLY BELLAMY IS NEVER GOING TO BAT CLEANUP. Beneath: BILLY HAS CEREBRAL PALSY. Beneath that, smaller type: *Give Us a Hand, Huh?*

CP donations had taken a noticeable leap. Good for them, good for Vic and Roger. The team of Trenton and Breakstone had been off and running. Half a dozen successful campaigns had followed, Vic dealing most commonly with broad-scope conception, Roger dealing with actual execution.

For the Sony Corporation, a picture of a man sitting cross-legged on the median strip of a sixteen-lane superhighway in a business suit, a big Sony radio on his lap, a seraphic smile on his kisser. The copy read: POLICE BAND, THE ROLLING STONES, VIVALDI, MIKE WALLACE, THE KINGSTON TRIO, PAUL HARVEY. PATTI SMITH, JERRY FALWELL. And below that: HELLO, LA!

For the Voit people, makers of swim equipment, an ad that showed a man who was the utter antithesis of the Miami beachboy. Standing arrogantly hipshot on the golden beach of some tropical paradise, the model was a fifty-year-old man with tattoos, a beer belly, slab-muscled arms and legs, and a puckered scar high across one thigh. In his arms this battered soldier of fortune was cradling a pair of Voit swimfins. MISTER, the copy for this one read, I DIVE FOR A LIVING. I DON'T MESS AROUND. There was a lot more underneath, stuff Roger always referred to as the blah-blah, but the copy set in boldface was the real hooker. Vic and Roger had wanted it to read I DON'T SCREW AROUND, but they hadn't been able to sell the Voit people on that. Pity, Vic was fond of saying over drinks. They could have sold a lot more swimfins.

Then there was Sharp.

The Sharp Company of Cleveland had stood twelfth in the Great American Bakestakes when old man Sharp reluctantly came to the Ellison Agency in New York after more than twenty years with a hometown ad agency. Sharp had been bigger than Nabisco before World War II, the old man was fond of pointing out. His son was just as fond of pointing out that World War II had ended thirty years ago.

The account – on a six-month trial basis at first – had been handed over to Vic Trenton and Roger Breakstone. At the end of the trial period, Sharp had vaulted from twelfth in the cookies-cakes-and-cereals market to ninth. A year later, when Vic and Roger pulled up stakes and moved to Maine to open up their own business, the Sharp Company had climbed to seventh.

Their campaign had been a sweeping one. For Sharp Cookies, Vic and Roger had developed the Cookie Sharpshooter, a bumbling Western peace officer whose six-guns shot cookies instead of bullets, courtesy of the special-effects people – Chocka Chippers in some spots, Ginger Snappies in others, Oh Those Oatmeals in still others. The spots always ended with the Sharpshooter standing sadly in a pile of cookies with his guns out. 'Well, the bad guys got away,' he'd tell millions of Americans every day or so, 'but I got the cookies. Best cookies in the West . . . or anywhere else, I reckon.' The Sharpshooter bites into a cookie. His expression suggests that he is experiencing the gastronomic equivalent of a boy's first orgasm. Fadeout.

For the prepared cakes – sixteen different varieties ranging from pound to crumb to cheese – there was what Vic called the George and Gracie spot. We fade in on George and Gracie leaving a posh dinner party where the buffet table groans with every possible delicacy. We dissolve to a dingy little cold-water flat, starkly lighted. George is sitting at a plain kitchen table with a checked tablecloth. Gracie takes a Sharp Pound Cake (or Cheese Cake or Crumb Cake) from the freezer of their old refrigerator and sets it on the table. They are both still in their evening clothes. They smile into each other's eyes with warmth and love and under-standing, two people who are utterly in sync with each other. Fade to these words, on black: SOMETIMES ALL YOU WANT IS A SHARP CAKE. Not a word spoken in the entire spot. That one had won a Clio.

As had the Sharp Cereal Professor, hailed in the trades as 'the most responsible advertisement ever produced for children's programming.' Vic and Roger had considered it their crowning achievement . . . but now it was the Sharp Cereal Professor who had come back to haunt them.

Played by a character actor in late middle age, the Sharp Cereal Professor was a low-key and daringly adult advertisement in a sea of animated kiddie-vid ads selling bubble gum, adventure toys, dolls, action figures . . . and rival cereals.

The ad faded in on a deserted fourth- or fifth-grade classroom, a scene Saturday-morning viewers of *The Bugs Bunny/Roadrunner Hour* and *The Drac Pack* could readily identify with. The Sharp Cereal Professor was wearing a suit, a V-necked sweater, and a shirt open at the collar. Both in looks and in speech he was mildly authoritarian; Vic and Roger had talked to some forty teachers and half a dozen child psychiatrists and had discovered that this was the sort of parental role model that the majority of kids feel most comfortable with, and the sort that so few actually have in their homes.

The Cereal Professor was sitting on a teacher's desk, hinting at some informality – the soul of a real pal hidden somewhere beneath that gray-green tweed, the young viewer might assume – but he spoke slowly and gravely. He did not command. He did not talk down. He did not wheedle. He did not cajole or extol. He spoke to the millions of T-shirted, cereal-slurping, cartoon-watching Saturday-morning viewers as though they were *real people*.

'Good morning, children,' the Professor said quietly. 'This is a commercial for cereal. Listen to me carefully, please. I know a lot about cereals, because I'm the Sharp Cereal Professor. Sharp Cereals – Twinkles, Cocoa Bears, Bran-16, and Sharp All-Grain Blend – are the best-tasting cereals in America. And they're good for you.' A beat of silence, and then the Sharp Cereal Professor grinned . . . and when he grinned, you *knew* there was the soul of a real pal in there. 'Believe me, because I know. Your mom knows; I just thought you'd like to know too.'

A young man came into the ad at that point, and he handed the Sharp Cereal Professor a bowl of Twinkles or Cocoa Bears or whatever. The Sharp Cereal Professor dug in, then looked straight into every living room in the country and said: 'Nope, nothing wrong here.'

Old man Sharp hadn't cared for that last line, or the idea that anything *could* be wrong with one of his cereals. Eventually Vic and Roger had worn him down, but not with rational arguments. Making ads was not a rational business. You often did what felt right, but that didn't mean you could understand *why* it felt right. Both Vic and Roger felt that the Professor's final line had a power which was both simple and enormous. Coming from the Cereal Professor, it was the final, total comfort, a complete security blanket. I'll never hurt you, it implied. In a world where parents get divorced, where older kids sometimes beat the shit out of you for no rational reason, where the rival Little League team sometimes racks the crap out of your pitching, where the good guys don't always win like they do on TV, where you don't always get invited to the *good* birthday party, in a world where so *much* goes wrong, there will always be Twinkles and Cocoa Bears and All-Grain Blend, and they'll always taste good. 'Nope, nothing wrong here.'

With a little help from Sharp's son (later on, Roger said, you would have believed the kid thought the ad up and wrote it himself), the Cereal Professor concept was approved and saturated Saturday-morning TV, plus such weekly syndicated programs as *Star Blazers, U.S. of Archie, Hogan's Heroes*, and *Gilligan's Island*. Sharp Cereals surged even more powerfully than the rest of the Sharp line, and the Cereal Professor became an American institution. His tag line, 'Nope, nothing wrong here,' became one of those national catch phrases, meaning roughly the same thing as 'Stay cool' and 'No sweat'.

When Vic and Roger decided to go their own way, they had observed strict protocol and had not gone to any of their previous clients until their connections with the Ellison Agency were formally – and amicably – severed. Their first six months in Portland had been a scary, pressure-cooker time for all of them. Vic and Donna's boy, Tad, was only a year old. Donna, who missed New York badly, was by turns sullen, petulant, and just plain scared. Roger had an old ulcer – a battle scar from his years in the Big Apple advertising wars – and when he and Althea lost the baby the ulcer had flared up again, turning him into a closet Gelusil chugger. Althea bounced back as well as possible under the circumstances, Vic thought; it was Donna who pointed out to him that placid Althea's single weak drink before dinner had turned into two before and three after. The two couples had vacationed in Maine, separately and together, but neither Vic nor Roger had realized how many doors are initially closed to folks who have moved in, as Mainers say, from 'outta state'.

They would indeed have gone under, as Roger pointed out, if Sharp hadn't decided to stay with them. And at the company's Cleveland headquarters, positions had done an ironic flip-flop. Now it was the old man who wanted to stick with Vic and Roger and it was the kid (by this time forty years old) who wanted to jettison them, arguing with some logic that it would be madness to hand their account over to a two-bit ad agency six hundred miles north of the New York pulsebeat. The fact that Ad Worx was affiliated with a New York market-analysis firm cut zero ice with the kid, as it had cut zero ice with the other firms for which they had put together campaigns in the past few years.

'If loyalty was toilet paper,' Roger had said bitterly, 'we'd be hard-pressed to wipe our asses, old buddy.'

But Sharp had come along, providing the margin they had so desperately needed. 'We made do with an ad agency here in town for forty years,' old man Sharp said, 'and if those two boys want to move out of that Christless city, they're just showing good old common sense.'

That was that. The old man had spoken. The kid shut up. And for the last two and a half years, the Cookie Sharp-shooter had gone on shooting, George and Gracie had gone on eating Sharp Cakes in their cold-water flat, and the Sharp Cereal Professor had gone on telling kids that there was nothing wrong here. Actual spot production was handled by a small independent studio in Boston, the New York market-analysis firm went on doing its thing competently, and three or four times a year either Vic or Roger flew to Cleveland to confer with Carroll Sharp and his kid – said kid now going decidedly gray around the temples. All the rest of the client-agency intercourse was handled by the U.S. Post Office and Ma Bell. The process was perhaps strange, certainly cumbersome, but it seemed to work fine.

Then along came Red Razberry Zingers.

Vic and Roger had known about Zingers for some time, of course, although it had only gone on the general market some two months ago, in April of 1980. Most of the Sharp cereals were lightly sweetened or not sweetened at all. All-Grain Blend, Sharp's entry in the 'natural' cereal arena, had been quite successful. Red Razberry Zingers, however, was aimed at a segment of the market with a sweeter tooth: at those prepared-cereal eaters who bought such cereals as Count Chocula, Frankenberry, Lucky Charms, and similar pre-sweetened breakfast foods which were somewhere in the twilight zone between cereal and candy.

In the late summer and early fall of 1979, Zingers had been successfully test-marketed in Boise, Idaho, Scranton, Pennsylvania, and in Roger's adopted Maine hometown of Bridgton. Roger had told Vic with a shudder that he wouldn't let the twins near it with a ten-foot pole (although he had been pleased when Althea told him the kids had clamored for it when they saw it shelved at Gigeure's Market). 'It's got more sugar than whole grain in it, and it looks like the side of a firebarn.'

Vic had nodded and replied innocently enough, with no sense of prophecy, 'The first time I looked in one of those boxes, I thought it was full of blood.'

'So what do you think?' Roger repeated. He had made it halfway through his sandwich as Vic reviewed the dismal train of events in his mind. He was becoming more and more sure that in Cleveland old man Sharp and his aging kid were looking again to shoot the messenger for the message.

'Guess we better try.'

Roger clapped him on the shoulder. 'My man,' he said. 'Now eat up.'

But Vic wasn't hungry.

The two of them had been invited to Cleveland to attend an 'emergency meeting' that was to be held three weeks after the Fourth of July – a good many of the Sharp regional sales managers and executives were vacationing, and it would take at least that long to get them all together. One of the items on the agenda had to do directly with Ad Worx: 'an assessment of the association to this point,' the letter had said. Which meant, Vic assumed, that the kid was using the Zingers debacle to dump them at last.

About three weeks after Red Razberry Zingers went

national, enthusiastically – if gravely – pitched by the Sharp Cereal Professor ('Nope, nothing wrong here'), the first mother had taken her little one to the hospital, nearly hysterical and sure the child was bleeding internally. The little girl, victim of nothing more serious than a low-grade virus, had thrown up what her mother had first believed to be a huge amount of blood.

Nope, nothing wrong here.

That had been in Iowa City, Iowa. The following day there had been seven more cases. The day after, twenty-four. In all cases the parents of children afflicted with vomiting or diarrhea had rushed the kids to the hospital, believing them to be suffering internal bleeding. After that, the cases had skyrocketed – first into the hundreds, then into the thousands. In none of these cases had the vomiting and/or diarrhea been caused by the cereal, but that was generally overlooked in the growing furor.

Nope, not a single thing wrong here.

The cases had spread west to east. The problem was the food dye that gave Zingers its zingy red color. The dye itself was harmless, but that was also mostly overlooked. Something had gone wrong, and instead of assimilating the red dye, the human body simply passed it along. The goofed-up dye had only gotten into one batch of cereal, but it had been a whopper of a batch. A doctor told Vic that if a child who had just died after ingesting a big bowl of Red Razberry Zingers were the subject of an autopsy, the postmortem would reveal a digestive tract as red as a stop sign. The effect was strictly temporary, but that had been overlooked too.

Roger wanted them to go down with all guns firing, if they were to go down. He had proposed marathon conferences with the Image-Eye people in Boston, who actually did the spots. He wanted to talk with the Sharp Cereal Professor himself, who had gotten so involved with his role that he was mentally and emotionally torn up over what had happened. Then on to New York, to talk to the marketing people. Most important, it would be almost two weeks at Boston's Ritz-Carlton and at New York's UN Plaza, two weeks Vic and Roger would spend mostly in each other's hip pockets, digesting the input and brainstorming as they had in the old days. What Roger hoped would come out of it was a rebound campaign that would blow the socks off both old man Sharp and the kid. Instead of going to Cleveland with their necks shaved for the drop of the guillotine blade, they would show up with battle plans drawn to reverse the effects of the Zingers snafu. That was the theory. In practice, they both realized that their chances were about as good as they were for a pitcher who deliberately sets out to throw a no-hitter.

Vic had other problems. For the last eight months or so, he had sensed that he and his wife were drifting slowly apart. He still loved her, and he damn near idolized Tad, but things had gone from a little uneasy to bad, and he sensed that there were worse things – and worse times – waiting. Just over the horizon, maybe. This trip, a grand tour from Boston to New York to Cleveland, coming at what should have been their at-home season, their doing-things-together season, was maybe not such a hot idea. When he looked at her face lately he saw a stranger lurking just below its planes and angles and curves.

And the question. It played over and over in his mind on nights when he wasn't able to sleep, and such nights had become more common lately. Had she taken a lover? They sure didn't sleep together much any more. Had she done it? He hoped it wasn't so, but what did he think? Really? Tell the truth, Mr. Trenton, or you'll be forced to pay the consequences.

He wasn't sure. He didn't want to be sure. He was afraid that if he became sure, the marriage would end. He was still completely gone on her, had never so much as considered an extramarital fling, and he could forgive her much. But not being cuckolded in his own home. You don't want to wear those horns; they grow out of your ears, and kids laugh at the funny man on the street. He –

'What?' Vic said, emerging from his reverie. 'I missed it, Rog.'

'I said, "That goddam red cereal." Unquote. My exact words.'

'Yeah,' Vic said. 'I'll drink to that.'

Roger raised his pilsner glass. 'Do it,' he said.

Vic did.

Gary Pervier sat out on his weedy front lawn at the bottom of Seven Oaks Hill on Town Road No. 3 about a week after Vic and Roger's depressing luncheon meeting at the Yellow Sub, drinking a screwdriver that was 25 percent Bird's Eye frozen orange juice and 75 percent Popov vodka. He sat in the shade of an elm that was in the last stages of rampant Dutch elm disease, his bottom resting against the frayed straps of a Sears, Roebuck mail-order lawn chair that was in the last stages of useful service. He was drinking Popov because Popov was cheap. Gary had purchased a large supply of it in New Hampshire, where booze was cheaper, on his last liquor run. Popov was cheap in Maine, but it was *dirt* cheap in New Hampshire, a state which took its stand for the finer things in life – a fat state lottery, cheap booze, cheap cigarettes, and tourist attractions like Santa's Village and Six-Gun City. New Hampshire was a great old place. The lawn chair had slowly settled into his run-to-riot lawn, digging deep divots. The house behind the lawn had also run to riot; it was a gray, paint-peeling, roof-sagging shambles. Shutters hung. The chimney hooked at the sky like a drunk trying to get up from a tumble. Singles blown off in the previous winter's last big storm still hung limply from some of the branches of the dying elm. It ain't the Taj Mahal, Gary sometimes said, but who gives a shit?

Gary was, on this swelteringly hot late-June day, as drunk as a coot. This was not an uncommon state of affairs with him. He did not know Roger Breakstone from shit. He did not know Vic Trenton from shit. He didn't know Donna Trenton from shit, and if he had known her, he wouldn't have given a shit if the visiting team was throwing line drives into her catcher's mitt. He did know the Cambers and their dog Cujo; the family lived up the hill, at the end of Town Road No. 3. He and Joe Camber did a good deal of drinking together, and in a rather foggy fashion Gary realized that Joe Camber was already a goodly way down the road to alcoholism. It was a road Gary himself had toured extensively.

'Just a good-for-nothing drunk and I don't give a shit!' Gary told the birds and the singles in the diseased elm. He tipped his glass. He farted. He swatted a bug. Sunlight and shadow dappled his face. Behind the house, a number of disemboweled cars had almost disappeared in the tall weeds. The ivy which grew on the west side of his house had gone absolutely apeshit, almost covering it. One window peeked out – barely – and on sunny days it glittered like a dirty diamond. Two years ago, in a drunken frenzy, Gary had uprooted a bureau from one of the upstairs rooms and had thrown it out a window – he could not remember why now. He had reglazed the window himself because it had let in one crotch of a draft come winter, but the bureau rested exactly where it had fallen. One drawer was popped out like a tongue.

In 1944, when Gary Pervier had been twenty, he had single-handedly taken a German pillbox in France and, following that exploit, had led the remains of his squad ten miles farther before collapsing with the six bullet wounds he had suffered in his charge of the machine-gun emplacement. For this he had been awarded one of his grateful country's highest honors, the Distinguished Service Cross. In 1968 he had gotten Buddy Torgeson down in Castle Falls to turn the medal into an ashtray. Buddy had been shocked. Gary told Buddy he would have gotten him to make it into a toilet bowl so he could shit in it, but it wasn't big enough. Buddy spread the story, and maybe that had been Gary's intention, or maybe it hadn't.

Either way, it had driven the local hippies crazy with admiration. In the summer of '68 most of these hippies were on vacation in the Lakes Region with their wealthy parents before returning to their colleges in September, where they were apparently studying up on Protest, Pot, and Pussy.

After Gary had his DSC turned into an ashtray by Buddy Torgeson, who did custom welding in his spare time and who worked days down to the Castle Falls Esso (they were all Exxon stations now, and Gary Pervier didn't give a shit), a version of the story found its way into the Castle Rock *Call*. The story was written by a local-yokel reporter who construed the act as an antiwar gesture. That was when the hippies started to show up at Gary's place on Town Road No. 3. Most of them wanted to tell Gary he was 'far out'. Some of them wanted to tell him he was 'some kind of heavy'. A few wanted to tell him that he was 'too fucking much'.

Gary showed them all the same thing, which was his Winchester .30-.06. He told them to get off his property. As far as he was concerned they were all a bunch of long-haired muff-diving crab-crawling asshole pinko fucksticks. He told them he didn't give a shit if he blew their guts from Castle Rock to Fryeburg. After a while they stopped coming, and that was the end of the DSC affair.

One of those German bullets had taken Gary Pervier's right testicle off; a medic had found most of it splattered across the seat of his GI-issue underwear. Most of the other one survived, and sometimes he could still get a pretty respectable bone-on. Not, he had frequently told Joe Camber, that he gave much of a shit one way or the other. His grateful country had given him the Distinguished Service Cross. A grateful hospital staff in Paris had discharged him in February 1945 with an 80-percent disability pension and a gold-plated monkey on his back. A grateful hometown gave him a parade on the Fourth of July 1945 (by then he was twenty-one instead of twenty, able to vote, his hair graying around the temples, and he felt all of seven hundred, thank you very much). The grateful town selectmen had remanded the property taxes on the Pervier place in perpetuity. That was good, because he would have lost it twenty years ago otherwise. He had replaced the morphine he could no longer obtain with high-tension booze and had then proceeded to get about his life's work, which was killing himself as slowly and as pleasantly as he could.

Now, in 1980, he was fifty-six years old, totally gray, and meaner than a bull with a jackhandle up its ass. About the only three living creatures he could stand were Joe Camber, his boy Brett, and Brett's big Saint Bernard, Cujo.

He tilted back in the decaying lawn chair, almost went over on his back, and used up some more of his screwdriver. The screwdriver was in a glass he had gotten free from a McDonald's restaurant. There was some sort of purple animal on the glass. Something called a Grimace. Gary ate a lot of his meals at the Castle Rock McDonald's, where you could still get a cheap hamburger. Hamburgers were good. But as for the Grimace . . . and Mayor McCheese . . . and Monsieur Ronald Fucking McDonald . . . Gary Pervier didn't give a shit for any of them.

A broad, tawny shape was moving through the high grass to his left, and a moment later Cujo, on one of his rambles, emerged into Gary's tattered front yard. He saw Gary and barked once, politely. Then he came over, wagging his tail.

'Cuje, you old sonofawhore,' Gary said. He put his screwdriver down and began digging methodically through his pockets for dog biscuits. He always kept a few on hand for Cujo, who was one of your old-fashioned, dyed-in-the-wool good dogs.

He found a couple in his shirt pocket and held them up. 'Sit boy. Sit up.'

No matter how low or how mean he was feeling, the sight of that two-hundred-pound dog sitting up like a rabbit never failed to tickle him.

Cujo sat up, and Gary saw a short but ugly-looking scratch healing on the dog's muzzle. Gary tossed him the biscuits, which were shaped like bones, and Cujo snapped them effortlessly out of the air. He dropped one between his forepaws and began to gnaw the other one.

'Good dog,' Gary said, reaching out to pat Cujo's head. 'Good —'

Cujo began to growl. Deep in his throat. It was a rumbling, almost reflective sound. He looked up at Gary, and there was something cold and speculative in the dog's eyes that gave Gary a chill. He took his hand back to himself quickly. A dog as big as Cujo was nothing to get screwing around with. Not unless you wanted to spend the rest of your life wiping your ass with a hook.

'What's got into you, boy?' Gary asked. He had never heard Cujo growl, not in all the years the Cambers had had him. To tell the truth, he wouldn't have believed ole Cuje had a growl in him.

Cujo wagged his tail a little bit and came over to Gary to be patted, as if ashamed of his momentary lapse.

'Hey, that's more like it,' Gary said, ruffling the big dog's fur. It had been one scorcher of a week, and more coming, according to George Meara, who had heard it from Aunt Evvie Chalmers. He supposed that was it. Dogs felt the heat even more than people did, and he guessed there was no rule against a mutt getting testy once in a while. But it sure had been funny, hearing Cujo growl like that. If Joe Camber had told him, Gary wouldn't have believed it.

'Go get your other biscuit,' Gary said, and pointed.

Cujo turned around, went to the biscuit, picked it up, mouthed it – a long string of saliva depending from his mouth – and then dropped it. He looked at Gary apologetically.

'You, turnin down chow?' Gary said unbelievingly. 'You?'

Cujo picked up the dog biscuit again and ate it.

'That's better,' Gary said. 'A little heat ain't gonna killya. Ain't gonna kill me either, but it bitches the *shit* outta my hemorrhoids. Well, I don't give a shit if they get as big as fucking golfballs. You know it?' He swatted a mosquito.

Cujo lay down beside Gary's chair as Gary picked up his screwdriver again. It was almost time to go in and freshen it up, as the country-club cunts said.

'Freshen up my ass,' Gary said. He gestured at the roof of his house, and a sticky mixture of orange juice and vodka trickled down his sunburned, scrawny arm. 'Look at that chimbly, Cuje ole guy. Fallin right the fuck down. And you know what? I don't give a shit. The whole place could fall flat and I wouldn't fart sideways to a dime. You know that?'

Cujo thumped his tail a little. He didn't know what this MAN was saying, but the rhythms were familiar and the patterns were soothing. These polemics had gone on a dozen times a week since . . . well, as far as Cujo was concerned, since forever. Cujo liked this MAN, who always had food. Just lately Cujo didn't seem to want food, but if THE MAN wanted him to eat, he would. Then he could lie here – as he was now – and listen to the soothing talk. All in all, Cujo didn't feel very well. He hadn't growled at THE MAN because he was hot but simply because he didn't feel good. For a moment there – just a moment – he had felt like biting THE MAN.

'Got your nose in the brambles, looks like,' Gary said. 'What was you after? Woodchuck? Rabbit?'

Cujo thumped his tail a little. Crickets sang in the rampant bushes. Behind the house, honeysuckle grew in a wild drift, calling the somnolent bees of a summer afternoon. Everything in Cujo's life should have been right, but somehow it wasn't. He just didn't feel good at all.

'I don't even give a shit if all that Georgia redneck's teeth fall out, and all of Ray-Gun's teeth too,' Gary said, and stood up unsteadily. The lawn chair fell over and collapsed itself. If you had guessed that Gary Pervier didn't give a shit, you would have been right. 'Scuse me, boy.' He went inside and built himself another screwdriver. The kitchen was buzzing, fly-blown horror of split-open green garbage bags, empty cans, and empty liquor bottles.

When Gary came back out again, fresh drink in hand, Cujo had left.

On the last day of June, Donna Trenton came back from downtown Castle Rock (the locals called it 'downstreet', but at least she hadn't picked up *that* particular Maine-ism yet), where she had dropped Tad off at his afternoon daycamp and picked up a few groceries at the Agway Market. She was hot and tired, and the sight of Steve Kemp's battered Ford Econoline van with the gaudy desert murals painted on the sides suddenly turned her furious.

Anger had simmered all day. Vic had told her about the impending trip at breakfast, and when she had protested being left alone with Tad for what might be ten days or two weeks or God only knew, he made it clear to her exactly what the stakes were. He had thrown a scare into her, and she didn't like to be frightened. Up until this morning she had treated the Red Razberry Zingers affair as a joke – a rather good one at Vic and Roger's expense. She had never dreamed that such an absurd thing could have such serious consequences.

Then Tad had been scratchy about going off to the daycamp, complaining that a bigger boy had pushed him down last Friday. The bigger boy's name was Stanley Dobson, and Tad was afraid that Stanley Dobson might push him down again today. He had cried and clutched onto her when she got him to the American Legion field where the camp was held, and she'd had to pry his fingers loose from her blouse finger by finger, making her feel more like a Nazi than a mom: *You vill go to daykemp, ja? Ja, mein Mamma!* Sometimes Tad seemed so *young* for his age, so vulnerable. Weren't only children supposed to be precocious and resourceful? His fingers had been chocolatey and had left fingerprints on her blouse. They reminded her of the bloodstained handprints you sometimes saw in cheap detective magazines.

To add to the fun, her Pinto had started to act funny on the way home from the market, jerking and hitching, as if it had an automotive case of the hiccups. It had smoothed out after a bit, but what could happen once could happen again, and –

– and, just to put a little icing on the cake, here was Steve Kemp.

'Well, no bullshit,' she muttered, grabbed her bag of

groceries, and got out, a pretty, dark-haired woman of twenty-nine, tall, gray-eyed. She somehow managed to look tolerably fresh in spite of the relentless heat, her Tad-printed blouse, and academy-gray shorts that felt pasted to her hips and fanny.

She went up the steps quickly and into the house by the porch door. Steve was sitting in Vic's living-room chair. He was drinking one of Vic's beers. He was smoking a cigarette – presumably one of his own. The TV was on, and the agonies of *General Hospital* played out there, in living color.

'The princess arrives,' Steve said with the lopsided grin she had once found so charming and interestingly dangerous. 'I thought you were never going to – '

'I want you out of here, you son of a bitch,' she said tonelessly, and went through into the kitchen. She put the grocery bag down on the counter and started putting things away. She could not remember when she had last been so angry, so furious that her stomach had tied itself in a gripping, groaning knot. One of the endless arguments with her mother, maybe. One of the real horrorshows before she had gone away to school. When Steve came up behind her and slipped his tanned arms around her bare midriff, she acted with no thought at all; she brought her elbow back into his lower chest. Her temper was not cooled by the obvious fact that he had anticipated her. He played a lot of tennis, and her elbow felt as if it had struck a stone wall coated with a layer of hard rubber.

She turned around and looked into his grinning, bearded face. She stood five-eleven and was an inch taller than Vic when she wore heels, but Steve was nearly six-five.

'Didn't you hear me? I want you *out* of here!'

'Now, what for?' he asked. 'The little one is off making beaded loincloths or shooting apples off the heads of counselors with his little bow and arrow . . . or whatever they do . . . and hubby is busting heavies at the office . . . and now is the time for Castle Rock's prettiest *hausfrau* and Castle Rock's resident poet and tennis bum to make all the bells of sexual congress chime in lovely harmony.'

'I see you parked out in the driveway,' Donna said. 'Why not just tape a big sign to the side of your van? I'M FUCKING DONNA TRENTON, or something witty like that?'

'I've got every reason to park in the driveway,' Steve said, still grinning. 'I've got that dresser in the back. Stripped clean. Even as I wish you were yourself, my dear.'

'You can put it on the porch. I'll take care of it. While you're doing that, I'll write you a check.'

His smile faded a little. For the first time since she had come in, the surface charm slipped a little and she could see the real person underneath. It was a person she didn't like at all, a person that dismayed her when she thought of him in connection with herself. She had lied to Vic, gone behind his back, in order to go to bed with Steve Kemp. She wished that what she felt now could be something as simple as rediscovering herself, as after a nasty bout of fever. Or rediscovering herself as Vic's mate. But when you took the bark off it, the simple fact was that Steve Kemp – publishing poet, itinerant furniture stripper and refinisher, chair caner, fair amateur tennis player, excellent afternoon lover – was a turd.

'Be serious,' he said.

'Yeah, no one could reject handsome, sensitive Steven Kemp,' she said. 'It's got to be a joke. Only it's not. So what you do, handsome, sensitive Steven Kemp, is put the dresser on the porch, get your check, and blow.'

'Don't talk to me like that, Donna.' His hand moved to her breast and squeezed. It hurt. She began to feel a little scared as well as angry. [But hadn't she been a little scared all along? Hadn't that been part of the nasty, scuzzy little thrill of it?]

She slapped his hand away.

'Don't you get on my case, Donna.' He wasn't smiling now. 'It's too goddam hot.'

'*Me?* On *your* case? You were here when I came in.' Being frightened of him had made her angrier than ever. He wore a heavy black beard that climbed high on his cheekbones, and it occurred to her suddenly that although she had seen his penis close up – had had it in her mouth – she had never really seen what his face looked like.

'What you mean,' he said, 'is that you had a little itch and now it's scratched, so fuck off. Right? Who gives a crap about how I feel?'

'You're breathing on me,' she said, and pushed him away to take the milk to the refrigerator.

He was not expecting it this time. Her shove caught him off balance, and he actually stumbled back a step. His forehead was suddenly divided by lines, and a dark flush flared high on his cheekbones. She had seen him look this way on the tennis courts behind the Bridgton Academy buildings, sometimes. When he blew an easy point. She had watched him play several times – including two sets during which he had mopped up her panting, puffing husband with ease – and on the few occasions she had seen him lose, his reaction had made her extremely uneasy about what she had gotten into with him. He had published poems in over two dozen little magazines, and a book, *Chasing Sundown*, had been published by an outfit in Baton Rouge called The Press over the Garage. He had graduated from Drew, in New Jersey; he held strong opinions on modern art, the upcoming nuclear referendum question in Maine, the films of Andy Warhol, and he took a double fault the way Tad took the news it was bedtime.

Now he came after her, grabbed her shoulder, and spun her around to face him. The carton of milk fell from her hand and split open on the floor.

'There, look at that,' Donna said. 'Nice going, hotshot.'

'Listen, I'm not going to be pushed around. Do you –'

'*You get out of here!*' she screamed into his face. Her spittle sprayed his cheeks and his forehead. '*What do I have to do to convince you? Do you need a picture? You're not welcome here! Go be God's gift to some other woman!*'

'You cheap, cockteasing little bitch,' he said. His voice was sullen, his face ugly. He didn't let go of her arm.

'And take the bureau with you. Pitch it in the dump'.

She pulled free of him and got the washrag from its place, hung over the sink faucet. Her hands were trembling, her stomach was upset, and she was starting to get a headache. She thought that soon she would vomit.

She got down on her hands and knees and began wiping up the spilt milk.

'Yeah, you think you're something,' he said. 'When did your crotch turn to gold? You loved it. You screamed for more.'

'You've got the right tense, anyway, champ,' she said, not looking up. Her hair hung in her face and she liked it that way just fine. She didn't want him to see how pale and sick her face was. She felt as if someone had pushed her into a nightmare. She felt that if she looked at herself in a mirror at this moment she would see an ugly, capering witch. 'Get out, Steve. I'm not going to tell you again.'

'And what if I don't? You going to call Sheriff Bannerman? Sure. Just say, "Hi, there George, this is Mr. Businessman's wife, and the guy I've been screwing on the side won't leave. Would you please come on up here and roust him?" That what you're going to say?'

The fright went deep now. Before marrying Vic, she had been a librarian in the Westchester school system, and her own private nightmare had always been telling the kids for the third time – in her loudest speaking voice – to quiet down *at once*, please. When she did that, they always had – enough for her to get through the period, at least – but what if they wouldn't? That was her nightmare. What if they absolutely wouldn't? What did that leave? The question scared her. It scared her that such a question should ever have to be asked, even to oneself, in the dark of night. She had been afraid to use her loudest voice, and had done so only when it became absolutely necessary. Because that was where civilization came to an abrupt, screeching halt. That was the place where the tar turned to dirt. If they wouldn't listen when you used your very loudest voice, a scream became your only recourse.

This was the same sort of fear. The only answer to the

man's question, of course, was that she would scream if he came near her. But would she?

'Go,' she said in a lower voice. 'Please. It's over.'

'What if I decide it isn't? What if I decide to just rape you there on the floor in that damned spilt milk?'

She looked up at him through the tangle of hair. Her face was still pale, and her eyes were too big, ringed with white flesh. 'Then you'll have a fight on your hands. And if I get a chance to tear your balls off or put one of your eyes out, I won't hesitate.'

For just a moment, before his face closed up, she thought he looked uncertain. He knew she was quick, in pretty good shape. He could beat her at tennis, but she made him sweat to do it. His balls and his eyes were probably safe, but she might very well put some furrows in his face. It was a question of how far he wanted to go. She smelled something thick and unpleasant in the air of her kitchen, some whiff of the jungle, and realized with dismay that it was a mixture of her fear and his rage. It was coming out of their pores.

'I'll take the bureau back to my shop,' he said. 'Why don't you send your handsome hubby down for it, Donna? He and I can have a nice talk. About stripping.'

He left then, pulling the door which communicated between the living room and the porch to behind him almost hard enough to break the glass. A moment later the engine of his van roared, settled into a ragged idle, and then dropped to a working pitch as he threw it in gear. He screeched his tires as he left.

Donna finished wiping the milk up slowly, rising from time to time to wring out her rag in the stainless steel sink. She watched the threads of milk run down the drain. She was trembling all over, partly from reaction, partly from relief. She had barely heard Steve's implied threat to tell Vic. She could only think, over and over again, about the chain of events that had led to such an ugly scene.

She sincerely believed she had drifted into her affair with Steve Kemp almost inadvertently. It was like an explosion of sewage from a buried pipe. A similar sewer pipe, she believed, ran beneath the neatly tended lawns of almost every marriage in America.

She hadn't wanted to come to Maine and had been appalled when Vic had sprung the idea on her. In spite of vacations there (and the vacations themselves might have reinforced the idea), she had thought of the state as a woodsy wasteland, a place where the snow drifted twenty feet high in the winters and people were virtually cut off. The thought of taking their baby into such an environment terrified her. She had pictured – to herself and aloud to Vic – sudden snowstorms blowing up, stranding him in Portland and her in Castle Rock. She thought and spoke of Tad swallowing pills in such a situation, or burning himself on the stove, or God knew what. And maybe part of her resistance had been a stubborn refusal to give up the excitement and hurry of New York.

Well, face it – the worst hadn't been any of those things. The worst had been a nagging conviction that Ad Worx would fail and they would have to go crawling back with their tails between their legs. That hadn't happened, because Vic and Roger had worked their butts off. But that had also meant that she was left with a growing-up child and too much time on her hands.

She could count her life's close friends on the fingers of one hand. She was confident that the ones she made would be her friends forever, come hell or high water, but she had never made friends quickly or easily. She had toyed with the idea of getting her Maine certification – Maine and New York were reciprocal; it was mostly a matter of filling out some forms. Then she could go see the Superintendent of Schools and get her name put on the sub list for Castle Rock High. It was a ridiculous notion, and she shelved it after running some figures on her pocket calculator. Gasoline and sitters' fees would eat up most of the twenty-eight bucks a day she might have made.

I've become the fabled Great American Housewife, she had thought dismally one day last winter, watching sleet spick and spack down against the porch storm windows.

Sitting home, feeding Tab his franks and beans and his toasted cheese sandwiches and Campbell's Soup for lunch, getting my slice of life from Lisa on *As the World Turns* and from Mike on *The Young and the Restless*. Every now and then we jive it up with a *Wheel of Fortune* session. She could go over and see Joanie Welsh, who had a little girl about Tad's age, but Joanie always made her uneasy. She was three years older than Donna and ten pounds heavier. The extra ten pounds did not seem to bother her. She said her husband liked her that way. Joanie was contented with things as they were in Castle Rock.

A little at a time, the shit had started to back up in the pipe. She started to sharpshoot at Vic about little things, sublimating the big things because they were hard to define and even harder to articulate. Things like loss and fear and getting older. Things like being lonely and then getting terrified of being lonely. Things like hearing a song on the radio that you remembered from high school and bursting into tears for no reason. Feeling jealous of Vic because his life was a daily struggle to build something, he was a knight-errant with a family crest embossed on his shield, and her life was back here, getting Tad through the day, jollying him when he was cranky, listening to his raps, fixing his meals and snacks. It was a life lived in the trenches. Too much of it was waiting and listening.

And all along she had thought that things would begin to smooth out when Tad was older; the discovery that it wasn't true brought on a kind of low-level horror. This past year he had been out of the house three mornings a week, at Jack and Jill Nursery School; this summer it had been five afternoons a week at playcamp. When he was gone the house seemed shockingly empty. Doorways leaned and gaped with no Tad to fill them; the staircase yawned with no Tad halfway up, sitting there in his pajama bottoms before his nap, owlishly looking at one of his picture books.

Doors were mouths, stairways throats. Empty rooms became traps.

So she washed floors that didn't need to be washed. She

watched the soaps. She thought about Steve Kemp, with whom she'd had a little flirtation since he had rolled into town the previous fall with Virginia license plates on his van and had set up a small stripping and refinishing business. She had caught herself sitting in front of the TV with no idea what was going on because she had been thinking about the way his deep tan contrasted with his tennis whites, or the way his ass pumped when he moved fast. And finally she had done something. And today —

She felt her stomach knot up and she ran for the bathroom, her hands plastered to her mouth, her eyes wide and starey. She made it, barely, and tossed up everything. She looked at the mess she had made, and with a groan she did it again.

When her stomach felt better (but her legs were all atremble again, something lost, something gained), she looked at herself in the bathroom mirror. Her face was thrown into hard and unflattering relief by the fluorescent bar. Her skin was too white, her eyes red-rimmed. Her hair was plastered to her skull in an unflattering helmet. She saw what she was going to look like when she was old, and the most terrifying thing of all was that right now, if Steve Kemp was here, she thought she would let him make love to her if he would only hold her and kiss her and say that she didn't have to be afraid, that time was a myth and death was a dream, that everything was okay.

A sound came out of her, a screaming sob that could surely not have been born in her chest. It was the sound of a madwoman.

She lowered her head and cried.

Charity Camber sat on the double bed she shared with her husband, Joe, and looked down at something she held in her hands. She had just come back from the store, the same one Donna Trenton patronized. Now her hands and feet and cheeks felt numb and cold, as if she had been out with Joe on the snowmobile for too long. But tomorrow as the first of

July; the snowmobile was put neatly away in the back shed
with its tarp snugged down.

It can't be. There's been some mistake.

But there was no mistake. She had checked half a dozen
times, and there was no mistake.

After all, it has to happen to somebody, *doesn't it?*

Yes, of course. To *somebody.* But to *her?*

She could hear Joe pounding on something in his garage, a
high, belling sound that beat its way into the hot afternoon
like a hammer shaping thin metal. There was a pause, and
then, faintly: 'Shit!'

The hammer struck once more and there was a longer
pause. Then her husband hollered: *'Brett!'*

She always cringed a little when he raised his voice that
way and yelled for their boy. Brett loved his father very
much, but Charity had never been sure just how Joe felt
about his son. That was a dreadful thing to be thinking, but
it was true. Once, about two years ago, she had had a
horrible nightmare, one she didn't think she would ever
forget. She dreamed that her husband drove a pitchfork
directly into Brett's chest. The tines went right through him
and poked out the back of Brett's T-shirt, holding it out the
way tent poles hold a tent up in the air. *Little sucker didn't
come when I hollered him down,* her dream husband said,
and she had awakened with a jerk beside her real husband,
who had been sleeping the sleep of beer beside her in his
boxer shorts. The moonlight had been falling through the
window and onto the bed where she now sat, moonlight in a
cold and uncaring flood of light, and she had understood
just how afraid a person could be, how fear was a monster
with yellow teeth, set afoot by an angry God to eat the
unwary and the unfit. Joe had used his hands on her a few
times in the course of their marriage, and she had learned.
She wasn't a genius, maybe, but her mother hadn't raised
any *fools.* Now she did what Joe told her and rarely argued.
She guessed Brett was that way too. But she feared for the
boy sometimes.

She went to the window in time to see Brett run across the

yard and into the barn. Cujo trailed at Brett's heels, looking hot and dispirited.

Faintly: 'Hold this for me, Brett.'

More faintly: 'Sure, Daddy.'

The hammering started again, that merciless icepick sound: *Whing! Whing! Whing!* She imagined Brett holding something against something – a coldchisel against a frozen bearing, maybe, or a square spike against a lockbolt. Her husband a Pall Mall jittering in the corner of his thin mouth, his T-shirt sleeves rolled up, swinging a five-pound pony-hammer. And if he was drunk . . . if his aim was a little off . . .

In her mind she could hear Brett's agonized howl as the hammer mashed his hand to a red, splintered pulp, and she crossed her arms over her bosom against the vision.

She looked at the thing in her hand again and wondered if there was a way she could use it. More than anything in the world, she wanted to go to Connecticut to see her sister Holly. It had been six years now, in the summer of 1974 – she remembered well enough, because it had been a bad summer for her except for that one pleasant weekend. 'Seventy-four had been the year Brett's night problems had begun – restlessness, bad dreams, and, more and more frequently, incidents of sleepwalking. It was also the year Joe began drinking heavily. Brett's uneasy nights and his somnambulism had eventually gone away. Joe's drinking had not.

Brett had been four then; he was ten now and didn't even remember his Aunt Holly, who had been married for six years. She had a little boy, named after her husband, and a little girl. Charity had never seen either child, her own niece and nephew, except for the Kodachromes Holly occasionally sent in the mail.

She had gotten scared of asking Joe. He was tired of hearing her talk about it, and if she asked him again he might hit her. It had been almost sixteen months since she'd last asked him if maybe they couldn't take a little vacation down Connecticut way. Not much of a one for traveling was Mrs.

Camber's son Joe. He liked it just fine in Castle Rock. Once a year he and that old tosspot Gary Pervier and some of their cronies would go up north to Moosehead to shoot deer. Last November he had wanted to take Brett. She had put her foot down and it had *stayed* down, in spite of Joe's sullen mutterings and Brett's wounded eyes. She was not going to have the boy out with that bunch of men for two weeks, listening to a lot of vulgar talk and jokes about sex and seeing what animals men could turn into when they got to drinking nonstop over a period of days and weeks. All of them with loaded guns, walking in the woods. Loaded guns, loaded men, somebody always got hurt sooner or later, fluorescent-orange hats and vests or not. It wasn't going to be Brett. Not her son.

The hammer struck the steel steadily, rhythmically. It stopped. She relaxed a little. Then it started again.

She supposed that sooner or later Brett would go with them, and that would be the end of him for her. He would join their club, and ever after she would be little more than a kitchen drudge that kept the clubhouse neat. Yes, that day would come, and she knew it, and she grieved for it. But at least she had been able to stave it off for another year.

And this year? Would she be able to keep him home with her this November? Maybe not. Either way, it would be better – not all right but at least better – if she could take Brett down to Connecticut first. Take him down there and show him how some . . .

. . . some . . .

Oh, say it, if only to yourself.

(how some decent people lived)

If Joe would let them go alone . . . but there was no sense thinking of that. Joe could go places alone or with his friends, but she couldn't, not even with Brett in tow. That was one of their marriage's ground rules. Yet she couldn't help thinking about how much better it would be without him – without him sitting in Holly's kitchen, swilling beer, looking Holly's Jim up and down with those insolent brown eyes. It would be better without him being impatient to be gone until Holly and Jim were also impatient for them to be gone . . .

She and Brett.

Just the two of them.

They could go on the bus.

She thought: Last November, he wanted to take Brett hunting with him.

She thought: Could a trade be worked out?

Cold came to her, filling the hollows of her bones with spun glass. Would she actually *agree* to such a trade? He could take Brett to Moosehead with him in the fall if Joe in his turn would agree to let them go to Stratford on the bus –?

There was money enough – now there was – but money alone wouldn't do it. He'd take the money and that would be the last she would see of it. Unless she played her cards just right. Just . . . right.

Her mind began to move faster. The pounding outside stopped. She saw Brett leave the barn, trotting, and was dimly grateful. Some premonitory part of her was convinced that if the boy ever came to serious harm, it would be in that dark place with the sawdust spread over the old grease on the plank floor.

There was a way. There *must* be a way.

If she was willing to gamble.

In her fingers she held a lottery ticket. She turned it over and over in her hand as she stood at the window, thinking.

When Steve Kemp got back to his shop, he was in a kind of furious ecstasy. His shop was on the western outskirts of Castle Rock, on Route 11. He had rented it from a farmer who had holdings in both Castle Rock and in neighboring Bridgton. The farmer was not just a nurd; he was a Super Nurd.

The shop was dominated by Steve's stripping vat, a corrugated iron pot that looked big enough to boil an entire congregation of missionaries at one time. Sitting around it like small satellites around a large planet was his work: bureaus, dressers, china cupboards, bookcases, tables. The air was aromatic with varnish, stripping compound, linseed oil.

He had a fresh change of clothes in a battered TWA flightbag; he had planned to change after making love to the fancy cunt. Now he hurled the bag across the shop. It bounced off the far wall and landed on top of a dresser. He walked across to it and batted it aside. He drop-kicked it as it came down, and it hit the ceiling before falling on its side like a dead woodchuck. Then he simply stood, breathing hard, inhaling the heavy smells, staring vacantly at three chairs he had promised to cane by the end of the week. His thumbs were jammed into his belt. His fingers were curled into fists. His lower lip was pooched out. He looked like a kid sulking after a bawling-out.

'Cheap-*shit*!' he breathed, and went after the flightbag. He made as if to kick it again, then changed his mind and picked it up. He went through the shed and into the three-room house that adjoined the shop. If anything, it was hotter in the house. Crazy July heat. It got in your head. The kitchen was full of dirty dishes. Flies buzzed around a green plastic Hefty bag filled with Beefaroni and tuna-fish cans. The living room was dominated by a big old Zenith black-and-white TV he had rescued from the Naples dump. A big spayed brindle cat, name of Bernie Carbo, slept on top of it like a dead thing.

The bedroom was where he worked on his writing. The bed itself was a rollaway, not made, the sheets stiff with come. No matter how much he was getting (and over the last two weeks that had been zero), he masturbated a great deal. Masturbation, he believed, was a sign of creativity. Across from the bed was his desk. A big old-fashioned Underwood sat on top of it. Manuscripts were stacked to both sides. More manuscripts, some in boxes, some secured with rubber bands, were piled up in one corner. He wrote a lot and he moved around a lot and his main luggage was his work – mostly poems, a few stories, a surreal play in which the characters spoke a grand total of nine words, and a novel he had attacked badly from six different angles. It had been five years since he had lived in one place long enough to get completely unpacked.

Last December, while shaving one day, he had discovered the first threads of gray in his beard. The discovery had thrown him into a savage depression, and he had stayed depressed for weeks. He hadn't touched a razor between then and now, as if it was the act of shaving that had somehow caused the gray to show up. He was thirty-eight. He refused to entertain the thought of being that old, but sometimes it crept up on his blind side and surprised him. To be that old – less than seven hundred days shy of forty – terrified him. He had really believed that forty was for other people.

That bitch, he thought over and over again. That *bitch*.

He had left dozens of women since he had first gotten laid by a vague, pretty, softly helpless French substitute when he was a high school junior, but he himself had only been dropped two or three times. He was good at seeing the drop coming and opting out of the relationship first. It was a protective device, like bombing the queen of spades on someone else in a game of Hearts. You had to do it while you could still cover the bitch, or you got screwed. You covered yourself. The way you didn't think about your age. He had known Donna was cooling it, but she had struck him as a woman who could be manipulated with no great difficulty, at least for a while, by a combination of psychological and sexual factors. By fear, if you wanted to be crude. That it hadn't worked that way left him feeling hurt and furious, as if he had been whipped raw.

He got out of his clothes, tossed his wallet and change onto his desk, went into the bathroom, showered. When he came out he felt a little better. He dressed again, pulling jeans and a faded chambray shirt from the flightbag. He picked his change up, put it in a front pocket, and paused, looking speculatively at his Lord Buxton. Some of the business cards had fallen out. They were always doing that, because there were so many of them.

Steve Kemp had a packrat sort of wallet. One of the items he almost always picked up and tucked away were business cards. They made nice bookmarks, and the space on the blank flip side was just right for jotting an address, simple directions, or a phone number. He would sometimes take two or three if he happened to be in a plumbing shop or if an insurance salesman stopped by. Steve would unfailingly ask the nine-to-fiver for his card with a big shiteating grin.

When he and Donna were going at it hot and heavy, he had happened to notice one of her husband's business cards lying on top of the TV. Donna had been taking a shower or something. He had taken the business card. No big reason. Just the packrat thing.

Now he opened his wallet and thumbed through the cards, cards from Prudential agents in Virginia, realtors in Colorado, a dozen businesses in between. For a moment he thought he had lost Handsome Hubby's card, but it had just slipped down between a couple of dollar bills. He fished it out and looked at it. White card, blue lettering done in modish lower case, Mr. Businessman Triumphant. Quiet but impressive. Nothing flashy.

roger breakstone ad worx victor trenton
1633 congress street
telex: ADWORX portland, maine 04001 tel (207) 799–8600

Steve pulled a sheet of paper from a ream of cheap mimeo stuff and cleared a place in front of him. He looked briefly at his typewriter. No. Each machine's typescript was as individual as a fingerprint. It was his crooked lower-case 'a' that hung the blighter, Inspector. The jury was only out long enough to have tea.

This would not be a police matter, nohow, no way, but caution came without even thinking. Cheap paper, available at any office supply store, no typewriter.

He took a Pilot Razor Point from the coffee can on the corner of the desk and printed in large block letters:

> HELLO, VIC.
> NICE WIFE YOU'VE GOT THERE.
> I ENJOYED FUCKING THE SHIT OUT OF HER.

He paused, tapping the pen against his teeth. He was starting to feel good again. On top. Of course, she was a good-looking woman, and he supposed there was always the possibility that Trenton might discount what he had written so far. Talk was cheap, and you could mail someone a letter for less than the price of a coffee. But there was something . . . always something. What might it be?

He smiled suddenly; when he smiled that way his entire face lit up, and it was easy to see why he had never had much trouble with women since the evening with the vague, pretty French sub.

He wrote:

> WHAT'S THAT MOLE JUST ABOVE HER
> PUBIC HAIR LOOK LIKE TO YOU?
> TO ME IT LOOKS LIKE A QUESTION MARK.
> DO _YOU_ HAVE ANY QUESTIONS?

That was enough; a meal is as good as a feast, his mother had always said. He found an envelope and put the message inside. After a pause, he slipped the business card in, and addressed the envelope, also in block letters, to Vic's office. After a moment's thought, he decided to show the poor slob a little mercy and added PERSONAL below the address.

He propped the letter on the windowsill and leaned back in his chair, feeling totally good again. He would be able to write tonight, he felt sure of it.

Outside, a truck with out-of-state plates pulled into his driveway. A pickup with a great big Hoosier cabinet in the back. Someone had picked up a bargain at a barn sale. Lucky them.

Steve strolled out. He would be glad to take their money and their Hoosier cabinet, but he really doubted if he would have time to do the work. Once that letter was mailed, a change of air might be in order. But not too big a change, at least not for a while. He felt he owed it to himself to stay in the area long enough to make at least one more visit to Little Miss Highpockets . . . when it could be ascertained that Handsome Hubby was definitely not around, of course. Steve had played tennis with the guy and he was no ball of fire – thin, heavy glasses, spaghetti backhand – but you never knew when a Handsome Hubby was going to go off his gourd and do something antisocial. A good many Handsome Hubbies kept guns around the house. So he would want to check out the scene carefully before popping in. He would allow himself the one single visit and then close this show entirely. He would maybe go to Ohio for a while. Or Pennsylvania. Or Taos, New Mexico. But like a practical joker who had stuffed a load into someone's cigarette, he wanted to stick around (at a prudent distance, of course) and watch it blow up.

The driver of the pickup and his wife were peering into the shop to see if he was there. Steve strolled out, hands in the pockets of his jeans, smiling. The woman smiled back immediately. 'Hi, folks, can I help you?' he asked, and thought that he would mail the letters as soon as he could get rid of them.

That evening, as the sun went down red and round and hot in the west, Vic Trenton, his shirt tied around his waist by the arms, was looking into the engine compartment of his wife's Pinto. Donna was standing beside him, looking young and fresh in a pair of white shorts and a red-checked sleeveless blouse. Her feet were bare. Tad, dressed only in his bathing suit, was driving his trike madly up and down the driveway, playing some sort of mind game that apparently had Ponch and John from *CHiPS* pitted against Darth Vader.

'Drink your iced tea before it melts,' Donna told Vic.

'Uh-huh.' The glass was on the side of the engine compartment. Vic had a couple of swallows, put it back without looking, and it tumbled off – into his wife's hand.

'Hey,' he said. 'Nice catch.'

She smiled. 'I just know you when your mind's somewhere else, that's all. Look. Didn't spill a drop.'

They smiled into each other's eyes for a moment – a *good* moment, Vic thought. Maybe it was just his imagination, or wishful thinking, but lately it seemed there were more of the good small moments. Less of the sharp words. Fewer silences which were cold, or – maybe this was worse – just indifferent. He didn't know what the cause was, but he was grateful.

'Strictly Triple-A farm club,' he said. 'You got a ways to go before you make the bigs, kid.'

'So what's wrong with my car, coach?'

He had the air cleaner off; it was sitting in the driveway. 'Never saw a Frisbee like that before,' Tad had said matter-of-factly a few moments ago, swerving his trike around it. Vic leaned back in and poked aimlessly at the carburetor with the head of his screwdriver.

'It's in the carb. I think the needle valve's sticking.'

'That's bad?'

'Not too bad,' he said, 'but it can stop you cold if it decides to stick shut. The needle valve controls the flow of gas into the carb, and without gas you don't go. It's like a national law, babe.'

'Daddy, will you push me on the swing?'

'Yeah, in a minute.'

'Good! I'll be in the back!'

Tad started round the house toward the swing-and-gym set Vic had built last summer, while lubricating himself well with gin and tonics, working from a set of plans, doing it after supper on week nights and on weekends with the voices of the Boston Red Sox announcers blaring from the transistor radio beside him. Tad, then three, sat solemnly on the cellar bulkhead or on the back steps, chin cupped in his hands, fetching things sometimes, mostly watching silently. Last summer. A good summer, not as beastly hot as this one. It had seemed then that Donna had finally adjusted and was seeing that Maine, Castle Rock, Ad Worx – those things could be good for all of them.

Then the mystifying bad patch, the worst of it being that nagging, almost psychic feeling that things were even more wrong than he wanted to think about. Things in the house began to seem subtly out of place, as if unfamiliar hands had been moving them around. He had gotten the crazy idea – *was* it crazy? – that Donna was changing the sheets too often. They were always clean, and one night that old fairy-tale question had popped into his mind, echoing unpleasantly: *Who's been sleeping in my bed?*

Now things had loosened up, it seemed. If not for the crazy Razberry Zingers business and the rotten trip hanging over his head, he would feel that this could be a pretty good summer too. It might even turn out that way. You won, sometimes. Not all hopes were vain. He believed that, although his belief had never been seriously tested.

'Tad!' Donna yelled, bringing the boy to a screeching halt. 'Put your trike in the garage.'

'Mom-*mee*!'

'Now, please, monsieur.'

'Monsewer,' Tad said, and laughed into his hands. 'You didn't put your car away, Mom.'

'Daddy is working on my car.'

'Yeah, but –'

'Mind your mom, Tadder,' Vic said, picking up the air cleaner. 'I'll be around shortly.'

Tad mounted his trike and drove it into the garage, accompanying himself with a loud, ululating ambulance wail.

'Why are you putting it back on?' Donna asked. 'Aren't you going to fix it?'

'It's a precision job,' Vic said. 'I don't have the tools. Even if I did, I'd probably make it worse instead of better.'

'Damn,' she said morosely, and kicked a tire. 'These things never happen until after the warranty runs out, do they?' The Pinto had just over 20,000 miles on it, and was still six months from being theirs, free and clear.

'That's like a national law too,' Vic said. He put the air cleaner back on its post and tightened the butterfly nut.

'I guess I can run it over to South Paris while Tad's in his daycamp. I'll have to get a loaner, though, with you being gone. Will it get me to South Paris, Vic?'

'Sure. But you don't have to do that. Take it out to Joe Camber's place. That's only seven miles, and he does good work. Remember when that wheel bearing went on the Jag? He took it out with a chainfall made out of old lengths of telephone pole and charged ten bucks. Man, if I'd gone to that place in Portland, they would have mounted my checkbook like a moosehead.'

'That guy made me nervous,' Donna said. 'Aside from the fact that he was about two and a half sheets to the wind, I mean.'

'How did he make you nervous?'

'Busy eyes.'

Vic laughed. 'Honey, with you, there's a lot to be busy about.'

'Thank you,' she said, 'A woman doesn't necessarily mind being *looked* at. It's being mentally undressed that makes you nervous.' She paused, strangely, he thought, looking away at the grim red light in the west. Then she looked back at him. 'Some men give you the feeling that there's a little movie called *The Rape of the Sabine Women* going on in their heads all the time and you just got the . . . the starring role.'

He had that curious, unpleasant feeling that she was talking about several things at once – again. But he didn't want to get into that tonight, not when he was finally crawling out from under a shitheap of a month.

'Babe, he's probably completely harmless. He's got a wife, a kid –'

'Yes, probably he is.' But she crossed her arms over her breasts and cupped her elbows in her palms, a characteristic gesture of nervousness with her.

'Look,' he said. 'I'll run your Pinto up there this Saturday and leave it if I have to, okay? More likely he'll be able to get right to it. I'll have a couple of beers with him and pat his dog. You remember that Saint Bernard?'

Donna grinned. 'I even remember his name. He practically knocked Tad over licking him. You remember?'

Vic nodded. 'The rest of the afternoon Tad goes around after him saying "*Cooojo . . . heere, Cooojo.*"'

They laughed together.

'I feel so damn stupid sometimes,' Donna said. 'If I could use a standard shift, I could just run the Jag while you're gone.'

'You're just as well off. The Jag's eccentric. You gotta talk to it.' He slammed the hood of the Pinto back down.

'*Ooooh, you DUMMY!*' she moaned. 'Your iced tea glass was in there!'

And he looked so comically surprised that she went off into gales of laughter. After a minute he joined her. Finally it got so bad that they had to hang on to each other like a couple of drunks. Tad came back around the house to see what was going on, his eyes round. At last, convinced that they were mostly all right in spite of the nutty way they were acting, he joined them. This was about the same time that Steve Kemp mailed his letter less than two miles away.

Later, as dusk settled down and the heat slacked off a little and the first fireflies started to stitch seams in the air across the back yard, Vic pushed his son on the swing.

'Higher, Daddy! Higher!'

'If you go any higher, you're gonna loop the loop, kid.'

'Gimme under, then, Dad! Gimme under!'

Vic gave Tad a huge push, propelling the swing toward a sky where the first stars were just beginning to appear, and ran all the way under the swing. Tad screamed joyfully, his head tilted back, his hair blowing.

'That was *good*, Daddy! Gimme under again!'

Vic gave his son under again, from the front this time, and Tad went soaring into the still, hot night. Aunt Evvie Chalmers lived close by, and Tad's shouts of terrified glee were the last sounds she heard as she died; her heart gave out, one of its paper-thin walls breaching suddenly (and almost painlessly) as she sat in her kitchen chair, a cup of coffee by one hand and a straight-eight Herbert Tareyton by the other; she leaned back and her vision darkened and somewhere she heard a child crying, and for a moment it seemed that the cries were joyful, but as she went out, suddenly propelled as if by a hard but not unkind push from behind, it seemed to her that the child was screaming in fear, in agony; then she was gone, and her niece Abby would find her the following day, her coffee as cold as she was, her cigarette a perfect and delicate tube of ash, her lower plate protruding from her wrinkled mouth like a slot filled with teeth.

Just before Tad's bedtime, he and Vic sat on the back stoop. Vic had beer. Tad had milk.

'Daddy?'

'What?'

'I wish you didn't have to go away next week.'

'I'll be back.'

'Yeah, but —'

Tad was looking down, struggling with tears. Vic put a hand on his neck.

'But what, big guy?'

'Who's gonna say the words that keep the monster out of the closet? Mommy doesn't know them! Only you know them!'

Now the tears spilled over and ran down Tad's face.

'Is that all?' Vic asked.

The Monster Words (Vic had originally dubbed them the Monster Catechism, but Tad had trouble with that word, so it had been shortened) had come about in late spring, when Tad began to be afflicted by bad dreams and night fears. There was something in his closet, he said; sometimes at night his closet door would swing open and he would see it in there, something with yellow eyes that wanted to eat him up. Donna had thought it might have been some fallout with Maurice Sendak's book *Where the Wild Things Are.* Vic had wondered aloud to Roger (but not to Donna) if maybe Tad had picked up a garbled account of the mass murders that had taken place in Castle Rock and had decided that the murderer — who had become a kind of town bogeyman — was alive and well in his closet. Roger said he supposed it was possible; with kids, *anything* was possible.

And Donna herself had begun to get a little spooked after a couple of weeks of this; she told Vic one morning in a kind of laughing, nervous way that things in Tad's closet sometimes appeared moved around. Well, Tad did it, Vic had responded. You don't understand, Donna said. He doesn't go back there any more, Vic . . . never. He's scared to. And she had added that sometimes it seemed to her that the closet actually smelled bad after Tad's bouts of nightmare, followed by waking fear. Like an animal had been caged up in there. Disturbed, Vic had gone into the closet and sniffed. In his mind was a half-formed idea that perhaps Tad was sleepwalking; perhaps going into his closet and urinating in there as a part of some odd dream cycle. He had smelled nothing but mothballs. The closet, finished wall on one side and bare lathing on the other, stretched back some eight feet. It was as narrow as a Pullman car. There was no bogeyman back in there, and Vic most certainly did not come out in Narnia. He got a few cobwebs in his hair. That was all.

Donna had suggested first what she called 'good-dream thoughts' to combat Tad's night fears, then prayer. Tad responded to the former by saying that the thing in his closet stole his good-dream thoughts; he responded to the latter by saying that since God didn't believe in monsters, prayers were useless. Her temper had snapped – perhaps partly because she had been spooked by Tad's closet herself. Once, while hanging some of Tad's shirts in there, the door had swung quietly shut behind her and she'd had a bad forty seconds fumbling her way back to the door and getting out. She had smelled something in there that time – something hot and close and violent. A matted smell. It reminded her a little of Steve Kemp's sweat after they finished making love. The upshot was her curt suggestion that since there *were* no such things as monsters, Tad should put the whole thing out of his mind, hug his Teddy, and go to sleep.

Vic either saw more deeply or remembered more clearly about the closet door that turned into an unhinged idiot mouth in the dark of night, a place where strange things sometimes rustled, a place where hanging clothes sometimes turned into hanging men. He remembered vaguely about the shadows the streetlight could throw on the wall in the endless four hours that follow the turn of the day, and the creaking sounds that might have been the house settling or that might – just *might* – be something creeping up.

His solution had been the Monster Catechism, or just the Monster Words if you were four and not into semantics. Either way, it was nothing more (nor less) than a primitive incantation to keep evil at bay. Vic had invented it one day on his lunch hour, and to Donna's mixed relief and chagrin, it worked when her own efforts to use psychology, Parent Effectiveness Training, and, finally, blunt discipline had failed. Vic spoke it over Tad's bed every night like a benediction as Tad lay there naked under a single sheet in the sweltering dark.

'Do you think that's going to do him any good in the long run?' Donna asked. Her voice held both amusement and irritation. This had been in mid-May, when the tensions between them had been running high.

'Admen don't care about the long run,' Vic had answered. 'They care about fast, fast, fast relief. And I'm good at my job.'

'Yeah, nobody to say the Monster Words, that's the matter, that's a *lot* the matter,' Tad answered now, wiping the tears off his cheeks in disgust and embarrassment.

'Well, listen,' Vic said. 'They're written down. That's how I can say them the same every night. I'll print them on a piece of paper and tack them to your wall. And Mommy can read them to you every night I'm gone.'

'Yeah? Will you?'

'Sure. Said I would.'

'You won't forget?'

'No way, man. I'll do it tonight.'

Tad put his arms around his father, and Vic hugged him tight.

That night, after Tad slept, Vic went quietly into the boy's room and tacked a sheet of paper to the wall with a pushpin. He put it right next to Tad's Mighty Marvel Calender, where the kid couldn't miss it. Printed in large, clear letters on this sheet of paper was:

THE MONSTER WORDS

For Tad

Monsters, stay out of this room!
You have no business here.
No monsters under Tad's bed!
You can't fit under there.
No monsters hiding in Tad's closet!
It's too small in there.
No monsters outside of Tad's window!
You can't hold on out there.
No vampires, no werewolves, no things that bite.
You have no business here.
Nothing will touch Tad, or hurt Tad, all this night.
You have no business here.

Vic looked at this for a long time and reminded himself to tell Donna at least twice more before he left to read it to the kid every night. To impress on her how important the Monster Words were to Tad.

On his way out, he saw the closet door was open. Just a crack. He closed the door firmly and left his son's room.

Sometime much later that evening, the door swung open again. Heat lightning flickered sporadically, tattooing crazy shadows in there.

But Tad did not wake.

The next day, at quarter past seven in the morning, Steve Kemp's van backed out onto Route 11. Steve made miles, heading for Route 302. There he would turn left and drive southeast, crossing the state to Portland. He intended to flop at the Portland YMCA for a while.

On the van's dashboard was a neat pile of addressed mail — not printed in block letters this time but typed on his own machine. The typewriter was now in the back of the van, along with the rest of his stuff. It had taken him only an hour and a half to pack in his Castle Rock operation, including Bernie Carbo, who was now snoozing in his box by the rear doors. He and Bernie traveled light.

The typing job on the envelopes was a professional one. Sixteen years of creative writing had turned him into an excellent typist, if nothing else. He pulled over to the same box from which he had posted the anonymous note to Vic Trenton the night before and dropped the letters in. It would not have bothered him in the least to run out owing rent on the shop and the house if he had intended to leave the state, but since he was only going as far as Portland, it seemed prudent to do everything legally. This time he could afford not to cut corners; there was better than six hundred dollars in cash tucked into the small bolthole behind the van's glove compartment.

In addition to a check covering the rent he owed, he was returning deposits to several people who had made them on bigger jobs. Accompanying each check was a polite note saying he was very sorry to have caused any inconvenience, but his mother had been taken suddenly and seriously ill (every red-blooded American was a sucker for a mom-story). Those for whom he had contracted to do work could pick up their furniture at the shop — the key was on the ledge above the door, just to the right, and would they kindly return the key to the same place after they had made their pickup. Thank you, thank you, blahdeblah, bullshit-bullshit. There would be some inconvenience, but no real hassle.

Steve dropped the letters into the mailbox. There was that satisfied feeling of having his ass well covered. He drove away toward Portland, singing along with the Grateful Dead, who were delivering 'Sugaree.' He pushed the van up to fifty-five, hoping traffic would stay light so he could get to Portland early enough to grab a court at Tennis of Maine. All in all, it looked like a good day. If Mr. Businessman hadn't received his little letter bomb yet, he surely would today. Nifty, Steve thought, and burst out laughing.

At half past seven, as Steve Kemp was thinking Tennis and Vic Trenton was reminding himself to call Joe Camber about his wife's balky Pinto, Charity Camber was fixing her son's breakfast. Joe had left for Lewiston half an hour ago, hoping to find a '72 Camaro windshield at one of the city's automobile junkyards or used-parts outfits. This jibed well with Charity's plans, which she had made slowly and carefully.

She put Brett's plate of scrambled eggs and bacon in front of him and then sat down next to the boy. Brett glanced up from the book he was reading in mild surprise. After fixing his breakfast, his mother usually started on her round of morning chores. If you spoke to her too much before she got herself around a second cup of coffee, she was apt to show you the rough side of her tongue.

'Can I talk to you a minute, Brett?'

Mild surprise turned to something like amazement. Looking at her, he saw something utterly foreign to his mother's taciturn nature. She was nervous. He closed his book and said, 'Sure, Mom.'

'Would you like –' She cleared her throat and began again. 'How would you like to go down to Stratford, Connecticut, and see your Aunt Holly and your Uncle Jim? And your cousins?'

Brett grinned. He had only been out of Maine twice in his life, most recently with his father on a trip to Portsmouth, New Hampshire. They had gone to a used-car auction where Joe had picked up a '58 Ford with a hemi engine. 'Sure!' he said. 'When?'

'I was thinking of Monday,' she said. 'After the weekend of the Fourth. We'd be gone a week. Could you do that?'

'I *guess*! Jeez, I thought Dad had a lot of work lined up for next week. He must have –'

'I haven't mentioned this to your father yet.'

Brett's grin fell apart. He picked up a piece of bacon and began to eat it. 'Well, I know he promised Richie Simms he'd pull the motor on his International Harvester. And Mr. Miller from the school was gonna bring over his Ford because the tranny's shot. And –'

'I thought just the two of us would go,' Charity said. 'On the Greyhound from Portland.'

Brett looked doubtful. Outside the back-porch screen, Cujo padded slowly up the steps and collapsed onto the boards in the shade with a grunt. He looked in at THE BOY and THE WOMAN with weary, red-rimmed eyes. He was feeling very bad now, very bad indeed.

'Jeez, Mom, I don't know –'

'Don't say jeez. It's just the same as swearing.'

'Sorry.'

'Would you *like* to go? If your father said it was all right?'

'Yeah, really! Do you really think we could?'

'Maybe.' She was looking out through the window over the sink thoughtfully.

'How far is it to Stratford, Mom?'

'About three hundred and fifty miles, I guess.'

'Jee – I mean, boy, that's a long way. Is it –'

'Brett.'

He looked at her attentively. That curious intense quality was back in her voice and on her face. That nervousness.

'What, Mom?'

'Can you think of anything your father needs out in the shop? Any one thing he's been looking to get?'

The light dawned in Brett's eyes a little. 'Well, he always needs adjustable wrenches . . . and he's been wanting a new set of ball-and-sockets . . . and he could use a new welder's helmet since the old one got a crack in the faceplate –'

'No, I mean anything big. Expensive.'

Brett thought awhile, then smiled. 'Well, what he'd really like to have is a new Jörgen chainfall, I guess. Rip that old motor out of Richie Simms's International just as slick as sh – well, slick.' He blushed and hurried on. 'But you couldn't get him nothing like that, Mom. That's really dear.'

Dear. Joe's word for expensive. She hated it.

'How much?'

'Well, the one in the catalogue says seventeen hundred dollars, but Dad could probably get it from Mr. Belasco at Portland Machine for wholesale. Dad says Mr. Belasco's scared of him.'

'Do you think there's something smart about that?' she asked sharply.

Brett sat back in his chair, a little frightened by her fierceness. He couldn't remember his mother ever acting quite like this. Even Cujo, out on the porch, pricked his ears a little.

'Well? Do you?'

'No, Mom,' he said, but Charity knew in a despairing way that he was lying. If you could scare somebody into giving you wholesale, you were trading a right smart. She had heard the admiration in Brett's voice, even if the boy himself had not. *Wants to be just like him. Thinks his daddy is just standing tall when he scares someone. Oh my God.*

'There's nothing smart about being able to scare people,'

Charity said. 'All it takes is a big voice and a mean disposition. There's no smart to it.' She lowered her voice and flapped a hand at him. 'Go on and eat your eggs. I'm not going to shout at you. I guess it's the heat.'

He ate, but quietly and carefully, looking at her now and then. There were hidden mines around this morning.

'What would wholesale be, I wonder? Thirteen hundred dollars? A thousand?'

'I don't know, Mamma.'

'Would this Belasco deliver? On a big order like that?'

'Ayuh, I guess he would. If we had that kind of money.'

Her hand went to the pocket of her housedress. The lottery ticket was there. The green number on her ticket, 76, and the red number, 434, matched the numbers drawn by the State Lottery Commission two weeks before. She had checked it dozens of times, unable to believe it. She had invested fifty cents that week, as she had done every week since the lottery began in 1975, and this time she had won five thousand dollars. She hadn't cashed the ticket in yet, but neither had she let it out of her sight or her reach since she found out.

'We do have that kind of money,' she said. Brett goggled at her.

At quarter past ten, Vic slipped out of his Ad Worx office and went around to Bentley's for his morning coffee, unable to face the bitch's brew that was available at the office. He had spent the morning writing ads for Decoster Egg Farms. It was hard going. He had hated eggs since his boyhood, when his mother grimly forced one down his throat four days a week. The best he had been able to come up with so far was EGGS SAY LOVE . . . SEAMLESSLY. Not very good. Seamlessly had given him the idea of a trick photo which would show an egg with a zipper running around it's middle. It was a good image, but where did it lead? Noplace that he had been able to discover. Ought to ask the Tadder, he thought, as the waitress brought him coffee and a blueberry muffin. Tad liked eggs.

It wasn't really the egg ad that was bringing him down, of course. It has having to take off for twelve days. Well, it had to be. Roger had convinced him of that. They would have to get in there and pitch like hell.

Good old garrulous Roger, whom Vic loved almost like a brother. Roger would have been more than glad to cruise down here to Bentley's with him, to have a coffee with him, and to talk his ear off. But this one time, Vic needed to be alone. To think. The two of them would be spending most of two weeks together starting Monday, sweating it out, and that was quite enough, even for soul brothers.

His mind turned toward the Red Razberry Zingers fiasco again, and he let it, knowing that sometimes a no-pressure, almost idle review of a bad situation could — for him, at least — result in some new insight, a fresh angle.

What had happened was bad enough, and Zingers had been withdrawn from the market. Bad enough, but not terrible. It wasn't like that canned mushroom thing; no one had gotten sick or died, and even consumers realized that a company could take a pratfall now and then. Look at that McDonald's glass giveaway a couple-three years ago. The paint on the glasses had been found to contain an unacceptably high lead content. The glasses had been withdrawn quickly, consigned to that promotional limbo inhabited by creatures such as Speedy Alka-Seltzer and Vic's own personal favorite, Big Dick Chewing Gum.

The glasses had been bad for the McDonald's Corporation, but no one had accused Ronald McDonald of trying to poison his pre-teen constituency. And no one had actually accused the Sharp Cereal Professor either, although comedians from Bob Hope to Steve Martin had taken potshots at him, and Johnny Carson had run off an entire monologue — couched in careful double entendre — about the Red Razberry Zingers affair one evening during his opening spot on *The Tonight Show*. Needless to say, the Sharp

Cereal Professor ads had been jerked from the tube. Also needless to say, the character actor who played the Professor was wild at the way events had turned on him.

I could imagine a worse situation, Roger had said after the first shock waves had subsided a bit and the thrice-daily long-distance calls between Portland and Cleveland were no longer flying.

What? Vic had asked.

Well, Roger had answered, straight-faced, *we could be working on the Bon Vivant Vichysoisse account.*

'More coffee, sir?'

Vic glanced up at the waitress. He started to say no, then nodded. 'Half a cup, please,' he said.

She poured it and left. Vic stirred it randomly, not drinking it.

There had been a mercifully brief health scare before a number of doctors spoke up on TV and in the papers, all of them saying the coloration was harmless. There had been something like it once before; the stews on a commercial airline had been struck down with weird orange skin discolorations which finally proved to be nothing more serious than a rub-off of the orange dye on the life jackets they demonstrated for their passengers before takeoff. Years before that, the food dye in a certain brand of frankfurters had produced an internal effect similar to that of Red Razberry Zingers.

Old man Sharp's lawyers had lodged a multimillion-dollar damage suit against the dye manufacturer, a case that would probably drag on for three years and then be settled out of court. No matter; the suit provided a forum from which to make the public aware that the fault – the *totally temporary* fault, the *completely harmless* fault – had not been that of the Sharp Company.

Nonetheless, Sharp stock had tumbled sharply on the Big Board. It had since made up less than half the original drop. The cereals themselves had shown a sudden dip in sales but had since made up most of the ground that had been lost after Zingers showed its treacherous red face. Sharp's

All-Grain Blend, in fact, was doing better than ever before.

So there was nothing wrong here, right?

Wrong. So wrong.

The Sharp Cereal Professor was what was wrong. The poor guy would never be able to make a comeback. After the scare come the laughs, and the Professor, with his sober mien and his schoolroom surroundings, had been literally laughed to death.

George Carlin, in his nightclub routine: 'Yeah, it's a crazy world. Crazy world.' Carlin bends his head over his mike for a moment, meditating, and then looks up again. 'The Reagan guys are doing their campaign shit on TV, right? Russians are getting ahead of us in the arms race. The Russians are turning out missiles by the thousands, right? So Jimmy gets on TV to do one of *his* spots, and he says, "My fellow Americans, the day the Russians get ahead of us in the arms race will be the day the youth of America shits red."'

Big laugh from the audience.

'So Ronnie gets on the phone to Jimmy, and he says, "Mr. President, what did Amy have for breakfast?"'

A gigantic laugh from the audience. Carlin pauses. The *real* punchline is then delivered in a low, insinuating tone:

'Nooope . . . nothing wrong here.'

The audience roars its approval, applauds wildly. Carlin shakes his head sadly. 'Red shit, man. Wow. Dig on it awhile.'

That was the problem. George Carlin was the problem. Bob Hope was the problem. Johnny Carson was the problem. Steve Martin was the problem. Every barbershop wit in America was the problem.

And then, consider this: Sharp stock had gone down nine and had only rebounded four and a quarter. The shareholders were going to be hollering for somebody's head. Let's see . . . whose do we give them? Who had the bright idea of the Sharp Cereal Professor in the first place? How about those guys as the most eligible? Never mind the fact that the Professor had been on for four years before the Zingers debacle. Never mind the fact that when the Sharp

Cereal Professor (and his cohorts the Cookie Sharpshooter and George and Gracie) had come on the scene, Sharp stock had been three and a quarter points lower than it was now.

Never mind all that. Mind this instead: Just the *fact*, just the *public announcement* in the trades that Ad Worx had lost the Sharp account – just that would probably cause shares to bob up another point and a half to two points. And when a new ad campaign actually began, investors would take it as a sign that the old woes were finally behind the company, and the stock might creep up another point.

Of course, Vic thought, stirring Sweet 'n Low into his coffee, that was only theory. And even if the theory turned out to be true, both he and Roger believed that a short-run gain for Sharp would be more than offset if a new ad campaign, hastily thrown together by people who didn't know the Sharp Company as he and Roger did, or the competitive cereal market in general, didn't do the job.

And suddenly that new slant, that fresh angle, popped into his mind. It came unbidden and unexpected. His coffee cup paused halfway to his mouth and his eyes widened. In his mind he saw two men – perhaps him and Roger, perhaps old man Sharp and his ageing kid – filling in a grave. Their spades were flying. A lantern flickered fitfully in the windy night. Rain was drizzling down. These corporate sextons threw an occasional furtive glance behind them. It was a burial by night, a covert act performed in the darkness. They were burying the Sharp Cereal Professor in secret, *and that was wrong*.

'Wrong,' he muttered aloud.

Sure it was. Because if they buried him in the dead of night, he could never say what he had to say: that he was sorry.

He took his Pentel pen from his inner coat pocket, took a napkin from the holder, and wrote swiftly across it:

The Sharp Cereal Professor needs to apologize.

He looked at it. The letters were getting larger, fuzzing as the ink sank into the napkin. Below that first sentence he added:

Decent burial.
And below that:
DAYLIGHT burial.
He still wasn't sure what it meant; it was more metaphor than sense, but that was how his best ideas came to him. And there was something there. He felt sure of it.

Cujo lay on the floor of the garage, in semi-gloom. It was hot in here but it was even worse outside . . . and the daylight outside was too bright. It never had been before; in fact, he had never even really noticed the quality of the light before. But he was noticing now. Cujo's head hurt. His muscles hurt. The bright light made his eyes hurt. He was hot. And his muzzle still ached where he had been scratched.

Ached and festered.

THE MAN was gone somewhere. Not long after he left, THE BOY and THE WOMAN had gone somewhere, leaving him alone. THE BOY had put a big dish of food out for Cujo, and Cujo had eaten a little bit. The food made him feel worse instead of better, and he left the rest of it alone.

Now there was the growl of a truck turning into the driveway. Cujo got up and went to the barn door, knowing already it was a stranger. He knew the sound of both THE MAN's truck and the family car. He stood in the doorway, head poking out into the bright glare that hurt his eyes. The truck backed up the driveway and then stopped. Two men got down from the cab and came around to the back. One of them ran up the truck's sliding back door. The rattling, banging noise hurt Cujo's ears. He whined and retreated back into the comforting gloom.

The truck was from Portland Machine. Three hours ago, Charity Camber and her still-dazzled son had gone into Portland Machine's main office on Brighton Avenue and she had written a personal check for a new Jörgen chainfall — wholesale had turned out to be exactly $1,241.71, tax included. Before going to Portland Machine she had gone into the State Liquor Store on Congress Street to fill out a lottery claim form. Brett, forbidden absolutely to come inside with her, stood on the sidewalk with his hands in his pockets.

The clerk told Charity she would get a Lottery Commission check in the mail. How long? Two weeks at the very outside. It would come minus a deduction of roughly eight hundred dollars for taxes. This sum was based on her declaration of Joe's yearly income.

The deduction for taxes before the fact did not anger Charity at all. Up until the moment when the clerk had checked her number against his sheet, she had been holding her breath, still unable to believe this had really happened to her. Then the clerk had nodded, congratulated her. None of that mattered. What mattered was that now she could breathe again, and the ticket was no longer her responsibility. It had returned to the bowels of the Lottery Commission. Her Check Would Be in the Mail — wonderful, mystical, talismanic phrase.

And still she felt a small pang as she watched the dog-eared ticket, limp with her own nervous perspiration, clipped to the form she had filled out and then stored away. Lady Luck had singled her out. For the first time in her life, maybe for the only time, that heavy muslin drape of the everyday had been twitched a little, showing her a bright and shining world beyond. She was a practical woman, and in her heart she knew that she hated her husband more than a little, and feared him more than a little, but that they would grow old together, and he would die, leaving her with his debts and — this she would not admit for sure even in her secret heart, but now she feared it! — perhaps with his spoilt son.

If her name had been plucked from the big drum in the twice-yearly Super Drawing, if she had won ten times the five thousand dollars she had won, she might have entertained notions of pushing aside that dull muslin curtain, taking her son by the hand, and leading them both

out into whatever was beyond Town Road No. 3 and
Camber's Garage, Foreign Cars Our Specialty, and Castle
Rock. She might have taken Brett to Connecticut with the
express purpose of asking her sister how much a small
apartment in Stratford would cost.

But it had only been a twitch of the curtain. That was all.
She had seen Lady Luck for a bare, brief moment, as
wonderful, puzzling, and inexplicable as a bright fairy
dancing under mushrooms in the dewy light of dawn . . .
seen once, never again. So she felt a pang when the ticket
disappeared from her view, even though it had robbed her
sleep. She understood that she would buy a lottery ticket a
week for the rest of her life and never win more than two
dollars all at once.

Never mind. You don't count teeth in a gifthorse. Not if
you were smart.

They went out to Portland Machine and she had written
the check, reminding herself to stop at the bank on their way
home and transfer enough money from savings to checking
so that the check wouldn't bounce. She and Joe had a little
over four thousand dollars in their savings account after
fifteen years. Just about enough to cover three quarters of
their outstanding debts, if you excluded the mortgage on the
farm. She had no right to exclude that, of course, but she
always did. She could not bring herself to think about the
mortgage except payment by payment. But they would dent
the savings all they wanted to now, and then deposit the
Lottery Commission check in that account when it came. All
they would be losing was two weeks' interest.

The man from Portland Machine, Lewis Belasco, said he
would have the chainfall machine delivered that very
afternoon, and he was as good as his word.

Joe Magruder and Ronnie DuBay got the chainfall on the
truck's pneumatic Step-Loader, and it whooshed gently
down to the dirt driveway on a sigh of air.

'Pretty big order for ole Joe Camber,' Ronnie said.

Magruder nodded. 'Put it in the barn, his wife said. That's his garage. Better get a good hold, Ronnie. This is a heavy whore.'

Joe Magruder got his hold, Ronnie got his, and, puffing and grunting, the two of them half walked it, half carried it into the barn.

'Let's set it down a minute,' Ronnie managed. 'I can't see where the hell I'm goin. Let's get used to the dark before we go ass over cowcatcher.'

They set the chainfall down with a thump. After the bright afternoon glare outside, Joe was mostly blinded. He could only make out the vague shapes of things – a car up on jacks, a workbench, a sense of beams going up to a loft.

'This thing ought –' Ronnie began, and then stopped abruptly.

Coming out of the darkness from beyond the front end of the jacked-up car was a low, guttural growling. Ronnie felt the sweat he had worked up suddenly turn clammy. The hairs on the back of his neck stirred.

'Holy crow, you hear that?' Magruder whispered. Ronnie could see Joe now. Joe's eyes were big and scared-looking.

'I hear it.'

It was a sound as low as a powerful outboard engine idling. Ronnie knew it took a big dog to make a sound like that. And when a big dog did, it more often than not meant business. He hadn't seen a BEWARE OF DOG sign when they drove up, but sometimes these bumpkins from the boonies didn't bother with one. He knew one thing. He hoped to God that the dog making that sound was chained up.

'Joe? You ever been out here before?'

'Once. It's a Saint Bernard. Big as a fucking house. He didn't do that before.' Joe gulped. Ronnie heard something in his throat click. 'Oh, God. Lookit there, Ronnie.'

Ronnie's eyes had come partway to adjusting, and his half-sight lent what he was seeing a spectral, almost supernatural cast. He knew you never showed a mean dog your fear – they could smell it coming off you – but he began to shudder helplessly anyway. He couldn't help it.

The dog was a monster. It was standing deep in the barn, beyond the jacked-up car. It was a Saint Bernard for sure; there was no mistaking the heavy coat, tawny even in the shadows, the breadth of shoulder. Its head was down. Its eyes glared at them with steady, sunken animosity.

It wasn't on a chain.

'Back up slow,' Joe said. 'Don't run, for Christ's sake.'

They began to back up, and as they did, the dog began to walk slowly forward. It was a stiff walk; not really a walk at all, Ronnie thought. It was a *stalk*. That dog wasn't fucking around. Its engine was running and it was ready to go. Its head remained low. That growl never changed pitch. It took a step forward for every step they took back.

For Joe Magruder the worst moment came when they backed into the bright sunlight again. It dazzled him, blinded him. He could no longer see the dog. If it came for him now –

Reaching behind him, he felt the side of the truck. That was enough to break his nerve. He bolted for the cab.

On the other side, Ronnie DuBay did the same. He reached the passenger door and fumbled at the latch for an endless moment. He clawed at it. He could still hear that low growling, so much like an idling Evinrude 80 hp motor. The door wouldn't open. He waited for the dog to pull a chunk of his ass off. At last his thumb found the button, the door opened, and he scrambled into the cab, panting.

He looked in the rearview mirror bolted outside his window and saw the dog standing in the open barn door, motionless. He looked over at Joe, who was sitting behind the wheel and grinning at him sheepishly. Ronnie offered his own shaky grin in return.

'Just a dog,' Ronnie said.

'Yeah. Bark's worse'n his bite.'

'Right. Let's go back in there and screw around with that chainfall some more.'

'Fuck you,' Joe said.

'And the horse you rode in on.'

They laughed together. Ronnie passed him a smoke.

'What do you say we get going?'

'I'm your guy,' Joe said, and started the truck.

Halfway back to Portland, Ronnie said, almost to himself: 'That dog's going bad.'

Joe was driving with his elbow cocked out the window. He glanced over at Ronnie. 'I was scared, and I don't mind saying so. One of those little dogs gives me shit in a situation like that, with nobody home, I'd just as soon kick it in the balls, you know? I mean, if people don't chain up a dog that bites, they deserve what they get, you know? *That* thing . . . did you see it? I bet that motherhumper went two hundred pounds.'

'Maybe I ought to give Joe Camber a call,' Ronnie said. 'Tell him what happened. Might save him gettin his arm chewed off. What do you think?'

'What's Joe Camber done for you lately?' Joe Magruder asked with a grin.

Ronnie nodded thoughtfully. 'He don't blow me like you do, that's true.'

'Last blowjob I had was from your wife. Wasn't half bad, either.'

'Get bent, you fairy.'

They laughed together. Nobody called Joe Camber. When they got back to Portland Machine, it was near knocking-off time. Screwing-around time. They took fifteen minutes writing the trip up. Belasco came out back and asked them if Camber had been there to take delivery. Ronnie DuBay said sure. Belasco, who was a prick of the highest order, went away. Joe Magruder told Ronnie to have a nice weekend and a happy fucking Fourth. Ronnie said he planned to get in the bag and stay that way until Sunday night. They clocked out.

Neither of them thought about Cujo again until they read about him in the paper.

Vic spent most of that afternoon before the long weekend going over the details of the trip with Roger. Roger was so careful about details that he was almost paranoid. He had made the plane and hotel reservations through an agency. Their flight to Boston would leave Portland Jetport at 7:10 A.M. Monday. Vic said he would pick Roger up in the Jag at 5:30. He thought that was unnecessarily early, but he knew Roger and Roger's little tics. They talked generally about the trip, consciously avoiding specifics. Vic kept his coffee-break ideas to himself and the napkin stowed safely away in his sport-jacket pocket. Roger would be more receptive when they were away.

Vic thought about leaving early and decided to go back and check the afternoon mail first. Lisa, their secretary, had already left for the day, getting a jump on the holiday weekend. Hell, you couldn't get a secretary to stay until the stroke of five any more, holiday weekend or not. As far as Vic was concerned, it was just another sign of the continuing decay of Western Civ. Probably at this very moment Lisa, who was beautiful, just twenty-one, and almost totally breastless, was entering the Interstate flow of traffic, bound south to Old Orchard or the Hamptons, dressed in tight jeans and a nothing halter. Get down, disco Lisa. Vic thought, and grinned a little.

There was a single unopened letter on his desk blotter.

He picked it up curiously, noting first the word PERSONAL printed below the address, and second the fact that his address had been printed in solid caps.

He held it, turning it over in his hands, feeling a vague thread of disquiet slip into what was a general mood of tired well-being. Far back in his mind, hardly even acknowledged, was a sudden urge to rip the letter into halves, fourths, eighths, and then toss the pieces into the wastebasket.

Instead, he tore it open and pulled out a single sheet of paper.

More block letters.

The simple message – six sentences – hit him like a

straight shot just below the heart. He did not so much sit in his chair as collapse into it. A little grunt escaped him, the sound of a man who has suddenly lost all his wind. His mind roared with nothing but white noise for a length of time he didn't — couldn't — understand or comprehend. If Roger had come in just then, he likely would have thought Vic was having a heart attack. In a way, he was. His face was paper-white. His mouth hung open. Bluish half-moons had appeared under his eyes.

He read the message again.

And then again.

At first his eyes were drawn to the first interrogative:

WHAT'S THAT MOLE JUST ABOVE HER
PUBIC HAIR LOOK LIKE TO YOU?

It's a mistake, he thought confusedly. *No one knows about that but me . . . well, her mother. And her father.* Then, hurt, he felt the first splinters of jealousy: *Even her bikini covers that . . . her* little *bikini.*

He ran a hand through his hair. He put the letter down and ran both hands through his hair. That punched, gasping feeling was still there in his chest. The feeling that his heart was pumping air instead of blood. He felt fright and pain and confusion. But of the three, the dominant feeling, the overriding emotion, was terrible fright.

The letter glared up at him and shouted:

I ENJOYED FUCKING THE SHIT OUT OF HER.

Now it was this line his eyes fixed upon, not wanting to leave. He could hear the drone of a plane in the sky outside, leaving the Jetport, heading up, heading out, making for points unknown, and he thought, I ENJOYED FUCKING THE

SHIT OUT OF HER. *Crude, that's crude.* Yes sir and yes ma'am, yes indeedy. It was the hack of a blunt knife. FUCKING THE SHIT OUT OF HER, what an image that made. Nothing fancy about it. It was like getting a splash in the eyes from a squirtgun loaded up with battery acid.

He tried hard to think coherently and
(I ENJOYED)
just couldn't
(FUCKING THE SHIT OUT OF HER)
do it.

Now his eyes went to the last line and that was the one he read over and over again, as if trying to cram the sense of it somehow into his brain. That huge feeling of fright kept getting in the way.

DO *YOU* HAVE ANY QUESTIONS?

Yes. All of a sudden he had all kinds of questions. The only thing was, he didn't seem to want answers to any of them.

A new thought crossed his mind. What if Roger hadn't gone home? Often he poked his head into Vic's office before leaving if there was a light on. He might be even more likely to do so tonight, with the trip pending. The thought made Vic feel panicky, and an absurd memory surfaced: all those times he had spent masturbating in the bathroom as a teenager, unable to help himself but terribly afraid everyone must know exactly what he was up to in there. If Roger came in, he would see something was wrong. He didn't want that. He got up and went to the window, which looked down six stories to the parking lot which served the building. Roger's bright-yellow Honda Civic was gone from its space. He had gone home.

Pulled out of himself, Vic listened. The offices of Ad Worx were totally silent. There was the resonating quiet that seems the sole property of business quarters after hours. There was not even the sound of old Mr. Steigmeyer, the custodian, rattling around. He would have to sign out in the lobby. He would have to —

Now there *was* a sound. At first he didn't know what it was. It came to him in a moment. It was whimpering. The sound of an animal with a smashed foot. Still looking out the window, he saw the cars left in the parking lot double, then treble, through a film of tears.

Why couldn't he get mad? Why did he have to be so fucking *scared*?

An absurd, antique word came to mind. *Jilted*, he thought. *I've been jilted.*

The whimpering sounds kept coming. He tried to lock his throat, and it did no good. He lowered his head and gripped the convector grille that ran below the window at waist height. Gripped it until his fingers hurt, until the metal creaked and protested.

How long had it been since he had cried? He had cried the night Tad was born, but that had been relief. He had cried when his dad died after fighting grimly for his life for three days after a massive heart attack struck him, and those tears, shed at seventeen, had been like these, burning, not wanting to come; it was more like bleeding than crying. But at seventeen it was easier to cry, easier to bleed. When you were seventeen you still expected to have to do your share of both.

He stopped whimpering. He thought it was done. And then a low cry came out of him, a harsh, wavering sound, and he thought: *Was that me? God, was it me that made that sound?*

The tears began to slide down his cheeks. There was another harsh sound, then another. He gripped the convector grille and cried.

Forty minutes later he was sitting in Deering Oaks Park. He had called home and told Donna he would be late. She started to ask why, and why he sounded so strange. He told her he would be home before dark. He told her to go ahead and feed Tad. Then he hung up before she could say anything else.

Now he was sitting in the park.

The tears had burned off most of the fear. What was left was an ugly slag of anger. That was the next level in this geological column of knowledge. But anger wasn't the right word. He was enraged. He was infuriated. It was as if he had been stung by something. A part of him had recognized that it would be dangerous for him to go home now . . . dangerous for all three of them.

It would be so pleasurable to hide the wreckage by making more; it would (let's face it) be mindlessly pleasurable to punch her cheating face in.

He was sitting beside the duckpond. On the other side, a spirited Frisbee game was going on. He noticed that all four of the girls playing — and two of the boys — were on roller skates. Roller skates were big this summer. He saw a young girl in a tube top pushing a cart of pretzels, peanuts, and canned soft drinks. Her face was soft and fresh and innocent. One of the guys playing Frisbee flipped her the disk; she caught it deftly and flipped it back. In the sixties, Vic thought, she would have been in a commune, diligently picking bugs off tomato plants. Now she was probably a member in good standing of the Small Business Administration.

He and Roger used to come down here to eat their lunches sometimes. That had been in the first year. Then Roger noticed that, although the pond looked lovely, there was a faint but definite odor of putridity hanging around it . . . and the small house on the rock in the center of the pond was whitewashed not with paint but with gullshit. A few weeks later, Vic had noted a decaying rat floating amid the condoms and gum wrappers at the edge of the pond. He didn't think they had been back since then.

The Frisbee, a bright red, floated across the sky.

The image that had provoked his anger kept recurring. He couldn't keep it away. It was as crude as his anonymous correspondent's choice of words had been, but he couldn't ditch it. He saw them screwing in his and Donna's bedroom. Screwing in their bed. What he saw in this mind-movie was every bit as explicit as one of those grainy X-rated pictures you see at the State Theater on Congress Street. She was groaning, sheened lightly with perspiration, beautiful. Every muscle pulled taut. Her eyes had that hungry look they got when the sex was good, their color darker. He knew the expression, he knew the posture, he knew the sounds. He had thought – *thought* – he was the only one who did. Not even her mother and father would know about that.

Then he would think of the man's penis – his cock – going up inside her. *In the saddle*; that phrase came and clanged in his mind idiotically, refusing to die away. He saw them screwing to a Gene Autry soundtrack: *I'm back in the saddle again, out where a friend is a friend. . . .*

It made him feel creepy. It made him feel outraged. It made him feel *infuriated*.

The Frisbee soared and came down. Vic followed its course.

He had suspected something, yes. But suspecting was not like knowing; he knew that now, if nothing else. He could write an essay on the difference between suspecting and knowing. What made it doubly cruel was the fact that he had really begun to believe that the suspicions were groundless. And even if they weren't, what you didn't know couldn't hurt you. Wasn't that right? If a man is crossing a darkened room with a deep, open hole in the middle of it, and if he passes within inches of it, he doesn't need to know he almost fell in. There is no need for fear. Not if the lights are off.

Well, he hadn't fallen in. He had been *pushed*. The question was, What was he going to do about it? The angry part of him, hurt, bruised, and bellowing, was not in the slightest inclined to be 'adult', to acknowledge that there were slips on one or both sides in a great many marriages. Fuck the Penthouse *Forum*, or *Variations*, or whatever they're calling it these days, that's my *wife* we're talking about, she was screwing someone

(out where a friend is a friend)
when my back was turned, when Tad was out of the
house —

The images began to unreel again, crumpled sheets,
straining bodies, soft sounds. Ugly phrases, terrible terms
kept crowding up like a bunch of freaks looking at an
accident: *nooky, hair pie, put the boots to her, shot my load,
I-don't-fuck-for-fortune-and-I-don't-fuck-for-fame-but-
the-way-I-fuck-ya-mamma-is-a-goddam-shame, my turtle
in your mud, bank for the gang, stoop for the troops —*

Inside my wife! he thought, agonized, hands clenching.
Inside my wife!

But the angry, hurt part acknowledged — grudgingly —
that he couldn't go home and beat the hell out of Donna.
He could, however, take Tad and go. Never mind the
explanations. Let her try and stop him, if she had cheek
enough to do it. He didn't think she would. Take Tad, go to
a motel, get a lawyer. Cut the cord cleanly, and don't look
back.

But if he just grabbed Tad and took him to a motel,
wouldn't the boy be frightened? Wouldn't he want an
explanation? He was only four, but that was old enough to
know when something was badly, frighteningly wrong.
Then there was the matter of the trip — Boston, New York,
Cleveland. Vic didn't give a goddam about the trip, not
now; old man Sharp and his kid could take a flying jump at
the moon for all he cared. But he wasn't in it alone. He had a
partner. The partner had a wife and two kids. Even now,
hurting as badly as he was, Vic recognized his responsibility
to at least go through the motions of trying to save the
account — which was tantamount to trying to save Ad Worx
itself.

And although he didn't want to ask it, there was another
question: Exactly why did he want to take Tad and go,
without even hearing her side of the story? Because her
sleeping around was wrecking Tad's morals? He didn't
think so. It was because his mind had immediately seized
upon the fact that the way to hurt her most surely and most

deeply (as deeply as he hurt right now) was through Tad. But
did he want to turn his son into the emotional equivalent of a
crowbar, or a sledgehammer? He thought not.

Other questions.

The note. Think about the note for a minute. Not just
what it said, not just those six lines of battery-acid filth;
think about the *fact* of the note. Someone had just killed the
goose that had been – pardon the pun – laying the golden
eggs. Why had Donna's lover sent that note?

Because the goose was no longer laying, of course. And
the shadow man who had sent the note was mad as hell.

Had Donna dumped the guy?

He tried to see it any other way and couldn't. Stripped of
its sudden, shocking force, wasn't I ENJOYED FUCKING THE
SHIT OUT OF HER the classic dog-in-the-manger ploy? If you
can't have it any more, piss on it so no one else will want
it either. Illogical, but ah so satisfying. The new, easier
atmosphere at home fit into that reading, as well. The almost
palpable sense of relief Donna radiated. She had turned the
shadow man out, and the shadow man had hit back at her
husband with the anonymous note.

Last question: Did it make any difference?

He took the note out of his jacket pocket again and turned
it over and over in his hands, not unfolding it. He watched
the red Frisbee float across the sky and wondered what the
hell he was going to do.

'What the Christ is that?' Joe Camber asked.

Each word came out spaced, almost inflectionless. He
stood in the doorway, looking at his wife. Charity was
setting his place. She and Brett had already eaten. Joe had
come in with a truckful of odds and ends, had begun to drive
into the garage, and had seen what was waiting for him.

'It's a chainfall,' she said. She had sent Brett over to play
with his buddy Dave Bergeron for the evening. She didn't
want him around if this went badly. 'Brett said you wanted
one. A Jörgen chainfall, he said.'

Joe crossed the room. He was a thin man with a scrawny-strong physique, a big blade nose, and a quiet, agile way of walking. Now his green felt hat was tipped back on his head to show his receding hairline. There was a smudge of grease on his forehead. There was beer on his breath. His blue eyes were small and hard. He was a man who didn't like surprises.

'You talk to me, Charity,' he said.

'Sit down. Your supper will get cold.'

His arm shot out like a piston. Hard fingers bit into her arm. 'What the fuck are you up to? Talk to me, I said.'

'Don't curse at me, Joe Camber.' He was hurting her badly, but she wouldn't give him the satisfaction of seeing it in her face or in her eyes. He was like a beast in many ways, and although this had excited her when she was young, it excited her no longer. She had recognized over the course of their years together that she could sometimes gain the upper hand just by seeming brave. Not always, but sometimes.

'You tell me what the fuck you been up to, Charity!'

'Sit down and eat,' she said quietly, 'and I will.'

He sat down and she brought his plate. There was a sirloin steak on it.

'Since when can we afford to eat like the Rockefellers?' he asked. 'You got some pretty tall explaining to do, I'd say.'

She brought his coffee and a split baked potato. 'Can't you use the chainfall?'

'Never said I couldn't use it. But I damn well can't afford it.' He began to eat, his eyes never leaving her. He wouldn't hit her now, she knew. This was her chance, while he was still relatively sober. If he was going to hit her, it would be after he came back from Gary Pervier's, sloshing with vodka and filled with wounded male pride.

Charity sat down across from him and said, 'I won the lottery.'

His jaws halted and then began moving again. He forked steak into his mouth. 'Sure,' he said. 'And tomorrow ole Cujo out there's gonna shit a mess of gold buttons.' He pointed his fork at the dog, who was pacing restlessly up and down the porch. Brett didn't like to take him over to the Bergerons' because they had rabbits in a hutch and they drove Cujo wild.

Charity reached into her apron pocket, took out her copy of the prize claim form that the agent had filled out, and handed it across the table to Joe.

Camber flattened the paper out with one blunt-fingered hand and stared it up and down. His eyes centred on the figure. 'Five –' He began, and then shut his mouth with a snap.

Charity watched him, saying nothing. He didn't smile. He didn't come around the table and kiss her. For a man with his turn of mind, she thought bitterly, good fortune only meant that something was lying in wait.

He looked up at last. 'You won five thousand dollars?'

'Less taxes, ayuh.'

'How long you been playing the lottery?'

'I buy a fifty-center every week . . . and you don't dare dun me about it, either, Joe Camber, with all the beer you buy.'

'Watch your mouth, Charity,' he said. His eyes were unblinking, brilliant blue. 'Just watch your mouth, or it might swell up on you all at once.' He began to eat his steak again, and behind the set mask of her face, she relaxed a little. She had thrust the chair in the tiger's face for the first time, and it hadn't bitten her. At least not yet. 'This money. When do we get it?'

'The check will come in two weeks or a little less. I bought the chainfall out of the money that's in our savings account. That claim form is just as good as gold. That's what the agent said.'

'You went out and bought that thing?'

'I asked Brett what he thought you'd want most. It's a present.'

'Thanks.' He went on eating.

'I got you a present,' she said. 'Now you give me one, Joe. Okay?'

He went on eating and he went on looking at her. He didn't say anything. His eyes were totally expressionless. He was eating with his hat on, still pushed back on his head.

She spoke to him slowly, deliberately, knowing it would be a mistake to rush. 'I want to go away for a week. With Brett. To see Holly and Jim down in Connecticut.'

'No,' he said, and went on eating.

'We could go on the bus. We'd stay with them. It would be cheap. There would be plenty of money left over. That found money. It wouldn't cost a third of what that chainfall cost. I called the bus station and asked them about the round-trip fare.'

'No. I need Brett here to help me.'

She clutched her hands together in a hard, twisting fury under the table, but made her face remain calm and smooth. 'You get along without him in the school year.'

'I said no, Charity,' he said, and she saw with galling, bitter certainty that he was enjoying this. He saw how much she wanted this. How she had planned for it. He was enjoying her pain.

She got up and went to the sink, not because she had anything to do there, but because she needed time to get herself under control. The evening star peeped in at her, high and remote. She ran water. The porcelain was a discolored yellowish color. Like Joe, their water was hard.

Maybe disappointed, feeling that she had given up too easily, Camber elaborated. 'The boy's got to learn some responsibility. Won't hurt him to help me this summer instead of running off to Davy Bergeron's house every day and night.'

She turned off the water. 'I sent him over there.'

'*You* did? Why?'

'Because I thought it might go like this,' she said, turning back to him. 'But I told him you'd say yes, what with the money and the chainfall.'

'If you knew better, you sinned against the boy,' Joe said. 'Next time I guess you'll think before you throw your tongue in gear.' He smiled at her through a mouthfull of food and reached for the bread.

'You could come with us, if you wanted.'

'Sure. I'll just tell Richie Simms to forget getting in his first cutting this summer. Besides, why do I want to go down and see them two? From what I've seen of them and what you tell of them, I got to think they're a couple of first-class snots. Only reason you like them is because you'd like to be a snot like them.' His voice was gradually rising. He began to spray food. When he got like this he frightened her and she gave in. Most times. She would not do that tonight. 'Mostly you'd like the boy to be a snot like them. That's what I think. You'd like to turn him against me, I guess. Am I wrong?'

'Why don't you ever call him by his name?'

'You want to just shut the craphouse door now, Charity,' he said, looking at her hard. A flush had crept up his cheeks and across his forehead. 'Mind me, now.'

'No,' she said. 'That's not the end.'

He dropped his fork, astounded. '*What*? What did you say?'

She walked towards him, allowing herself the luxury of total anger for the first time in her marriage. But it was all inside, burning and sloshing like acid. She could feel it eating. She daren't shout. To shout would be the end for sure. She kept her voice low.

'Yes, you'd think that about my sister and her husband. Sure you would. Look at you, sitting there and eating with your dirty hands and your hat still on. You don't want him down there seeing how other people live. Just the same way I don't want him seeing how you and your friends live when you're off to yourselves. That's why I wouldn't let him go on that hunting trip with you last November.'

She paused and he only sat there, a half-eaten slice of Wonder Bread in one hand, steak juice on his chin. She thought that the only thing keeping him from springing at her was his total amazement that she should be saying these things at all.

'So I'll trade with you,' she said. 'I've got you that chainfall and I'm willing to hand over the rest of the money to you – lots wouldn't – but if you're going to be so ungrateful, I'll go you one more. You let him go down with me to Connecticut, and I'll let him go up to Moosehead with you come deerhunting season.' She felt cold and prickly all over, as if she had just offered to strike a bargain with the devil.

'I ought to strap you,' he said wonderingly. He spoke to her as if she were a child who had misunderstood some very simple case of cause and effect. 'I'll take him hunting with me if I want, when I want. Don't you know that? He's my *son*. God's sake. *If* I want, *when* I want.' He smiled a little, pleased with the sound it made. 'Now – you got that?'

She locked her eyes with his. 'No,' she said. 'You won't.'

He got up in a hurry then. His chair fell over.

'I'll put a stop to it,' she said. She wanted to step back from him, but that would end it too. One false move, one sign of giving, and he would be on her.

He was unbuckling his belt. 'I'm going to strap you, Charity,' he said regretfully.

'I'll put a stop to it any way I can. I'll go up to the school and report him truant. Go to Sheriff Bannerman and report him kidnapped. But most of all . . . I'll see to it that Brett doesn't want to go.'

He pulled his belt from the loops of his pants and held it with the buckle end penduluming back and forth by the floor.

'The only way you'll get him up there with the rest of those drunks and animals before he's fifteen is if I let him go,' she said. 'You sling your belt on me if you want, Joe Camber. Nothing is going to change that.'

'Is that so?'

'I'm standing here and telling you it is.'

But suddenly he didn't seem to be in the room with her any more. His eyes had gone far away, musing. She had seen him do this other times. Something had just crossed his mind, a new fact to be laboriously added into the equation. She prayed that whatever it was would be on her side of the equals sign. She had never gone so much against him before, and she was scared.

Camber suddenly smiled. 'Regular little spitfire, ain't you?'

She said nothing.

He began to slip his belt back into the loops of his pants again. He was still smiling, his eyes still far away. 'You suppose you can screw like one of those spitfires? Like one of those little Mexican spitfires?'

She still said nothing, wary.

'If I say you and him can go, what about then? You suppose we could shoot for the moon?'

'What do you mean?'

'It means okay,' he said. 'You and him.'

He crossed the room in his quick, agile way, and it made her cold to think of how quick he could have crossed it a minute before, how quick he could have had his belt on her. And who would there have been to stop him? What a man did with − or to − his wife, that was their own affair. She could have done nothing, said nothing. Because of Brett. Because of her pride.

He put his hand on her shoulder. He dropped it to one of her breasts. He squeezed it. 'Come on,' he said. 'I'm horny.'

'Brett −'

'He won't be in until nine. Come on. Told you, you can go. You can at least say thanks, can't you?'

A kind of cosmic absurdity rose to her lips and had passed through them before she could stop it: 'Take off your hat.'

He sailed it heedlessly across the kitchen. He was smiling. His teeth were quite yellow. The two top ones in front were dentures. 'If we had the money now, we could screw on a bedful of greenbacks,' he said. 'I saw that in a movie once.'

He took her upstairs and she kept expecting him to turn vicious, but he didn't. His lovemaking was as it usually was, quick and hard, but he was not vicious. He did not hurt her intentionally, and tonight, for perhaps the tenth or eleventh time since they had been married, she had a climax. She let herself go to him, eyes closed, feeling the shelf of his chin dig into the top of her head. She stifled the cry that rose to her lips. It would have made him suspicious if she had cried out.

She was not sure he really knew that what always happened at the end for men sometimes happened for women too.

Not long after (and still an hour before Brett came home from the Bergerons) he left her, not telling her where he was going. She surmised it was down to Gary Pervier's, where the drinking would start. She lay in bed and wondered if what she had done and what she had promised could ever be worth it. Tears tried to come and she drove them back. She lay hot-eyed and straight in bed, and just before Brett came in, his arrival announced by Cujo's barks and the slam of the back-door screen, the moon rose in all its silvery, detached glory. *Moon doesn't care*, Charity thought, but the thought brought her no comfort.

'What is it?' Donna asked.

Her voice was dull, almost defeated. The two of them were sitting in the living room. Vic had not gotten home until nearly Tad's bedtime, and that was now half an hour past. He was sleeping in his room upstairs, the Monster Words tacked up by his bed, the closet door firmly shut.

Vic got up and crossed to the window, which now looked out only on darkness. *She knows*, he thought glumly. *Not the fine tuning, maybe, but she's getting a pretty clear picture.* All the way home he had tried to decide if he should confront her with it, lance the boil, try living with the laudable pus . . . or if he should just deep-six it. After leaving Deering Oaks he had torn the letter up, and on his way home up 302 he had fed the scraps out the window. *Litterbug Trenton*, he thought. And now the choice had been taken out of his hands. He could see her pale reflection in the dark glass, her face a white circle in yellow lamplight.

He turned toward her, having absolutely no idea what he was going to say.

He knows, Donna was thinking.

It was not a new thought, not by now, because the last

three hours had been the longest three of her whole life. She had heard the knowledge in his voice when he called to say he would be home late. At first there had been panic – the raw, fluttering panic of a bird trapped in a garage. The thought had been in italics followed by comic-book exclamation points: *He knows! He knows! He KNOWS!!* She had gotten Tad his supper in a fog of fear, trying to see what might logically happen next, but she was unable. I'll wash the dishes next, she thought. Then dry them. Then put them away. Then read Tad some stories. Then I'll just sail off the edge of the world.

Panic had been superseded by guilt. Terror had followed the guilt. Then a kind of fatalistic apathy had settled in as certain emotional circuits quietly shut themselves down. The apathy was even tinged by a certain relief. The secret was out. She wondered if Steve had done it, or if Vic had guessed on his own. She rather thought it had been Steve, but it didn't really matter. There was also relief that Tad was in bed, safely asleep. But she wondered what sort of morning he would wake up to. And that thought brought her full circle to her original panicky fear again. She felt sick, lost.

He turned toward her from the window and said, 'I got a letter today. An unsigned letter.'

He couldn't finish. He crossed the room again, restlessly, and she found herself thinking what a handsome man he was, and that it was too bad he was going gray so early. It looked good on some young men, but on Vic it was just going to make him look prematurely old and –

– and what was she thinking about his *hair* for? It wasn't his *hair* she had to worry about, was it?

Very softly, still hearing the shake in her voice, she said everything that was salient, spitting it out like some horrible medicine too bitter to swallow. 'Steve Kemp. The man who refinished your desk in the den. Five times. Never in our bed, Vic. Never.'

Vic put out his hand for the pack of Winstons on the endtable by the sofa and knocked it onto the floor. He picked it up, got one out, and lit it. His hands were shaking badly. They weren't looking at each other. *That's bad,* Donna thought. *We should be looking at each other.* But she couldn't be the one to start. She was scared and ashamed. He was only scared.

'Why?'

'Does it matter?'

'It matters to me. It means a lot. Unless you want to cut loose. If you do, I guess it doesn't matter. I'm mad as hell, Donna. I'm trying not to let that . . . that part get on top, because if we never talk straight again, we have to do it now. Do you want to cut loose?'

'Look at me, Vic.'

With a great effort, he did. Maybe he was as mad as he said he was, but she could see only species of miserable fright. Suddenly, like the thud of a boxing glove on her mouth, she saw how close to the edge of everything he was. The agency was tottering, that was bad enough, and now, on top of that, like a grisly dessert following a putrid main course, his marriage was tottering too. She felt a rush of warmth for him, for this man she had sometimes hated and had, for the last three hours, at least, feared. A kind of epiphany filled her. Most of all, she hoped he would always think he had been as mad as hell, and not . . . not the way his face said he felt.

'I don't want to cut loose,' she said. 'I love you. These last few weeks I think I've just found that out again.'

He looked relieved for a moment. He went back to the window, then returned to the couch. He dropped down there and looked at her.

'Why, then?'

The epiphany was lost in low-key, exasperated anger. *Why,* it was a man's question. Its origin lay far down in whatever the concept of masculinity was in an intelligent late-twentieth-century Western man. *I have to know why you did it.* As if she were a car with a stuck needle valve that had caused the machine to start hitching and sputtering or a robot that had gotten its servotapes scrambled so that it was serving meatloaf in the morning and scrambled eggs for dinner. What drove women crazy, she thought suddenly, wasn't really sexism at all, maybe. It was this mad, masculine quest for efficiency.

'I don't know if I can explain. I'm afraid it will sound stupid and petty and trivial.'

'Try. Was it . . .' He cleared his throat, seemed to mentally spit on his hands (that cursed *efficiency* thing again) and then fairly wrenched the thing out. 'Haven't I been satisfying you? Was that it?'

'No,' she said.

'Then what?' he said helplessly. 'For Christ's sake, *what?*' *Okay . . . you asked for it.*

'Fear,' she said. 'Mostly, I think it was fear.'

'Fear?'

'When Tad went to school, there was nothing to keep me from being afraid. Tad was like . . what do they call it? . . . white noise. The sound the TV makes when it isn't tuned to a station that comes in.'

'He wasn't in real school,' Vic said quickly, and she knew he was getting ready to be angry, getting ready to accuse her of trying to lay it off on Tad, and once he was angry things would come out between them that shouldn't be spoken, at least not yet. There were things, being the woman she was, that she would have to rise to. The situation would escalate. Something that was now very fragile was being tossed from his hands to hers and back again. It could easily be dropped.

'That was part of it,' she said. 'He wasn't in real school. I still had him most of the time, and the time when he was gone . . . there was a contrast . . .' She looked at him. 'The quiet seemed very loud by comparison. That was when I started to get scared. Kindergarten next year, I'd think. Half a day every day instead of half a day three times a week. The year after that, all day five days a week. And there would still be all those hours to fill up. And I just got scared.'

'So you thought you'd fill up a little of that time by fucking someone?' he asked bitterly.

That stung her, but she continued on grimly, tracing it out

as best she could, not raising her voice. He had asked. She
would tell him.

'I didn't want to be on the Library Committee and I didn't
want to be on the Hospital Committee and run the bake
sales or be in charge of getting the starter change or making
sure that not everybody is making the same Hamburger
Helper casserole for the Saturday-night supper. I didn't
want to see those same depressing faces over and over again
and listen to the same gossipy stories about who is doing
what in this town. I didn't want to sharpen my claws on
anyone else's reputation.'

The words were gushing out of her now. She couldn't
have stopped them if she wanted to.

'I didn't want to sell Tupperware and I didn't want to sell
Amway and I didn't want to give Stanley parties and I don't
need to join Weight Watchers. You —'

She paused for the tiniest second, grasping it, feeling the
weight of the idea.

'You don't know about emptiness, Vic. Don't think you
do. You're a man, and men *grapple*. Men grapple, and
women dust. You dust the empty rooms and you listen to the
wind blowing outside sometimes. Only sometimes it seems
like the wind's inside, you know? So you put on a record,
Bob Seger or J. J. Cale or someone, and you can *still* hear the
wind, and thoughts come to you, ideas, nothing good, but
they come. So you clean both toilets and you do the sink and
one day you're down in one of the antique shops looking at
little pottery knickknacks, and you think about how your
mother had a shelf of knickknacks like that, and your *aunts*
all had shelves of them, and your *grandmother* had them as
well.'

He was looking at her closely, and his expression was so
honestly perplexed that she felt a wave of her own despair.

'It's *feelings*, I'm talking about, not facts!'

'Yes, but why —'

'I'm *telling* you why! I'm telling you that I got so I was
spending enough time in front of the mirror to see how my
face was changing, how no one was ever going to mistake

me for a teenager again or ask to see my driver's license when I ordered a drink in a bar. I started to be afraid because I grew up after all. Tad's going to preschool and that means he's going to go to *school*, then *high school* —'

'Are you saying you took a lover because you felt *old*?' He was looking at her, surprised, and she loved him for that, because she supposed that *was* a part of it; Steve Kemp had found her attractive and of course that was flattering, that was what had made the flirtation fun in the first place. But it was in no way the greatest part of it.

She took his hands and spoke earnestly into his face, thinking — *knowing* — that she might never speak so earnestly (or honestly) to any man again. 'It's more. It's knowing you can't wait any longer to be a grownup, or wait any longer to make your peace with what you have. It's knowing that your choices are being narrowed almost daily. For a woman — no, for *me* — that's a brutal thing to have to face. Wife, that's fine. But you're gone at work, even when you're home you're gone at work so much. Mother, that's fine, too. But there's a little less of it every year, because every year the world gets another little slice of him.

'Men . . . they know what they are. They have an image of what they are. They never live up to the ideal, and it breaks them, and maybe that's why so many men die unhappy and before their time, but they *know* what being a grownup is supposed to mean. They have some kind of handle on thirty, forty, fifty. They don't hear that wind, or if they do, they find a lance and tilt at it, thinking it must be a windmill or some fucking thing that needs knocking down.

'And what a woman does — what *I* did — was to run from becoming. I got scared of the way the house sounded when Tad was gone. Once, do you know — this is crazy — I was in his room, changing the sheets, and I got thinking about these girlfriends I had in high school. Wondering what happened to them, where they went. I was almost in a daze. And Tad's closet door swung open and . . . I screamed and ran out of the room. I don't know why . . . except I guess I do. I thought for just a second there that Joan Brady would come out of Tad's closet, and her head would be gone and there would be blood all over her clothes and she would say, "I died in a car crash when I was nineteen coming back from Sammy's Pizza and I don't give a damn."'

'Christ, Donna,' Vic said.

'I got scared, that's all. I got scared when I'd start looking at knickknacks or thinking about taking a pottery course or yoga or something like that. And the only place to run from the future is into the past. So . . . . so I started flirting with him.'

She looked down and then suddenly buried her face in her hands. Her words were muffled but still understandable.

'It was fun. It was like being in college again. It was like a dream. A stupid dream. It was like he was white noise. He blotted out that wind sound. The flirting part was fun. The sex . . . it was no good. I had orgasms, but it was no good. I can't explain why not, except that I still loved you through all of it, and understood that I was running away. . . .' She looked up at him again, crying now. 'He's running too. He's made a career of it. He's a poet . . . at least that's what he calls himself. I couldn't make head or tail of the things he showed me. He's a roadrunner, dreaming he's still in college and protesting the war in Vietnam. That's why it was him, I guess. And now I think you know everything I can tell you. An ugly little tale, but mine own.'

'I'd like to beat him up,' Vic said. 'If I could make his nose bleed, I guess that would make me feel better.'

She smiled wanly. 'He's gone. Tad and I went for a Dairy Queen after we finished supper and you still weren't home. There's a FOR RENT sign in the window of his shop. I told you he was a roadrunner.'

'There was no poetry in that note,' Vic said. He looked at her briefly, then down again. She touched his face and he winced back a little. That hurt more than anything else, hurt more than she would have believed. The guilt and fear came again, in a glassy, crushing wave. But she wasn't crying any more. She thought there would be no more tears for a very long time. The wound and the attendant shock trauma were too great.

'Vic,' she said. 'I'm sorry. You're hurt and I'm sorry.'

'When did you break it off?'

She told him about the day she had come back and found him there, omitting the fear she'd had that Steve might actually rape her.

'Then the note was his way of getting back at you.'

She brushed hair away from her forehead and nodded. Her face was pale and wan. There were purplish patches of skin under her eyes. 'I guess so.'

'Let's go upstairs, he said. 'It's late. We're both tired.'

'Will you make love to me?'

He shook his head slowly. 'Not tonight.'

'All right.'

They went to the stairs together. At the foot of them, Donna asked, 'So what comes next, Vic?'

He shook his head. 'I just don't know.'

'Do I write "I promise never to do it again" five hundred times on the blackboard and miss recess? Do we get a divorce? Do we never mention it again? What?' She didn't *feel* hysterical, only tired, but her voice was rising in a way she didn't like and hadn't intended. The shame was the worst, the shame of being found out and seeing how it had punched his face in. And she hated him as well as herself for making her feel so badly ashamed, because she didn't believe she was responsible for the factors leading up to the final decision – if there really had been a decision.

'We ought to be able to get it together,' he said, but she did not mistake him; he wasn't talking to her. 'This thing –' He looked at her pleadingly. 'He was the only one, wasn't he?'

It was the one unforgivable question, the one he had no right to ask. She left him, almost ran up the stairs, before everything could spill out, the stupid recriminations and accusations that would not solve anything but only muddy up whatever poor honesty they had been able to manage.

There was little sleep for either of them that night. And the fact that he had forgotten to call Joe Camber and ask him if he could work on his wife's ailing Pinto Runabout was the furthest thing from Vic's mind.

As for Joe Camber himself, he was sitting with Gary Pervier in one of the decaying lawn chairs which dotted Gary's run-to-riot side yard. They were drinking vodka martinis out of McDonald's glasses under the stars. Lightning bugs flickered across the dark, and the masses of honeysuckle clinging to Gary's fence filled the hot night with its cloying, heavy scent.

Cujo would ordinarily have been chasing after the fireflies, sometimes barking, and tickling both men no end. But tonight he only lay between them with his nose on his paws. They thought he was sleeping, but he wasn't. He simply lay there, feeling the aches that filled his bones and buzzed back and forth in his head. It had gotten hard for him to think what came next in his simple dog's life; something had gotten in the way of ordinary instinct. When he slept, he had dreams of uncommon, unpleasant vividity. In one of these he had savaged THE BOY, had ripped his throat open and then pulled his guts out of his body in steaming bundles. He had awakened from this dream twitching and whining.

He was continually thirsty, but he had already begun to shy away from his water dish some of the time, and when he did drink, the water tasted like steel shavings. The water made his teeth ache. The water sent bolts of pain through his eyes. And now he lay on the grass, not caring about the lightning bugs or anything else. The voices of THE MEN were unimportant rumbles coming from somewhere above him. They meant little to him compared to his own growing misery.

'Boston!' Gary Pervier said, and cackled. '*Boston*! What the hell are you going to do in Boston, and what makes you think I could afford to tag along? I don't think I got enough to go down to the Norge until I get my check cashed.'

'Fuck you, you're rolling in it,' Joe replied. He was getting pretty drunk. 'You might have to dig into what's in your mattress a little, that's all.'

'Nothing in there but bedbugs,' Gary said, and cackled again. 'Place is crawlin with em, and I don't give a shit. You ready for another blast?'

Joe held out his glass. Gary had the makings right beside his chair. He mixed in the dark with the practiced, steady, and heavy hand of the chronic drinker.

'Boston!' He said again, handing Joe his drink. He said slyly, 'Kickin up your heels a little, Joey, I guess.' Gary was the only man in Castle Rock – perhaps in the world – who could have gotten away with calling him Joey. 'Kicking up some whoopee, I guess. Never known you to go further than Portsmouth before.'

'I been to Boston once or twice,' Joe said. 'You better look out, Pervert, or I'll sic my dog on you.'

'You couldn't sic that dog on a yellin nigger with a straight razor in each hand,' Gary said. He reached down and ruffled Cujo's fur briefly. 'What's your wife say about it?'

'She don't know we're goin. She don't have to know.'

'Oh, yeah?'

'She's takin the boy down to Connecticut to see her sister 'n' that freak she's married to. They're gonna be gone a week. She won some money in the lottery. Might as well tell you that right out. They use all the names on the radio, anyway. It's all in the prize form she had to sign.'

'Won some money in the lottery, did she?'

'Five thousand dollars.'

Gary whistled. Cujo flicked his ears uncomfortably at the sound.

Joe told Gary what Charity had told him at supper, leaving out the argument and making it appear a straight trade that had been his idea: The boy could go down to Connecticut for a week with her, and up to Moosehead for a week with him in the fall.

'And you're gonna go down to Boston and spend some of that dividend yourself, you dirty dog,' Gary said. He clapped Joe on the shoulder and laughed. 'Oh, you're a one, all right.'

'Why shouldn't I? You know when the last time was I had a day off? I don't. Can't remember. I ain't got much on this week. I'd planned to take most of a day and a half pulling the motor on Richie's International, doing a valve job and all, but with that chainfall it won't take four hours. I'll get him to bring it in tomorrow and I can do it tomorrow afternoon. I got a transmission job, but that's just a teacher. From the grammar school. I can put that back. A few other things the same way. I'll just call em up and tell em I'm having a little holiday.'

'What you gonna do down in Beantown?'

'Well, maybe see the Dead Sox play a couple at Fenway. Go down there to Washington Street —'

'The combat zone! Hot damn, I knew it!' Gary snorted laughter and slapped his leg. 'See some of those dirty shows and try to catch the clap!'

'Wouldn't be much fun alone.'

'Well, I guess I could tag along with you if you was willin to put some of that money my way until I get my check cashed.'

'I'd do that,' Joe said. Gary was a drunkard, but he took a debt seriously.

'I ain't been with a woman for about four years, I guess,' Gary said reminiscently. 'Lost most of the old sperm factory over there in France. What's left, sometimes it works, sometimes it don't. Might be fun to find out if I still got any ram left in my ramrod.'

'Ayuh,' Joe said. He was slurring now, and his ears were buzzing. 'And don't forget the baseball. You know when the last time was I went to Fenway?'

'No.'

'Nine-teen-six-ty-eight,' Joe said, leaning forward and tapping out each syllable on Gary's arm for emphasis. He spilled most of his new drink in the process. 'Before my kid was born. They played the Tigers and lost six to four, those suckers. Norm Cash hit a homer in the top of the eighth.'

'When you thinking of going?'

'Monday afternoon around three, I thought. The wife and the boy will want to go out that morning, I guess. I'll take them in to the Greyhound station in Portland. That gives me the rest of the morning and half the afternoon to catch up whatever I have to catch up.'

'You takin the car or the truck?'

'Car.'

Gary's eyes went soft and dreamy in the dark. 'Booze, baseball, and broads,' he said. He sat up straighter. 'I don't give a shit if I do.'

'You want to go?'

'Ayuh.'

Joe let out a little whoop and they both got laughing. Neither noticed that Cujo's head had come off his paws at the sound and that he was growling very softly.

Monday morning dawned in shades of pearl and dark gray; the fog was so thick that Brett Camber couldn't see the oak in the side yard from his window, and that oak wasn't but thirty yards away.

The house still slept around him, but there was no more sleep left in him. He was going on a trip, and every part of his being vibrated with the news. Just he and his mother. It would be a good trip, he felt that, and deep down inside, beyond any conscious thought, he was glad his father wasn't coming. He would be free to be himself; he would not have to try to live up to some mysterious ideal of masculinity that he knew his father had achieved but which he himself couldn't yet even begin to comprehend. He felt good – incredibly good and incredibly alive. He felt sorry for anyone in the world who was not going on a trip this fine, foggy morning, which would be another scorcher as soon as the fog burned off. He planned to sit in a window seat of the bus and watch every mile of the journey from the Greyhound terminal on Spring Street all the way to Stratford. It had been a long time before he had been able to get to sleep last night and here it was, not yet five o'clock . . . but if he stayed in bed any longer, he would explode, or something.

Moving as quietly as he could, he put on jeans and his Castle Rock Cougars T-shirt, a pair of white athletic socks, and his Keds. He went downstairs and fixed himself a bowl of Cocoa Bears. He tried to eat quietly but was sure that the crunch of the cereal that he heard in his head must be audible all over the house. Upstairs he heard his dad grunt and turn over in the double bed he and his mom shared. The springs rasped. Brett's jaws froze. After a moment's debate he took his second bowl of Cocoa Bears out on the back porch, being careful not to let the screen door slam.

The summer smells of everything were greatly clarified in the heavy fog, and the air was already warm. In the east, just above the faint fuzz that marked a belt of pines at the end of the east pasture, he could see the sun. It was as small and silver-bright as the full moon when it has risen well up in the sky. Even now the humidity was a dense thing, heavy and quiet. The fog would be gone by eight or nine, but the humidity would remain.

But for now what Brett saw was a white, secret world, and he was filled with the secret joys of it: the husky smell of hay that would be ready for its first cutting in a week, of manure, of his mother's roses. He could even faintly make out the aroma of Gary Pervier's triumphant honeysuckle which was slowly burying the fence which marked the edge of his property – burying it in a drift of cloying, grasping vines.

He put his cereal bowl aside and walked toward where he knew the barn to be. Halfway across the dooryard he looked over his shoulder and saw that the house had receded to nothing but a misty outline. A few steps farther and it was swallowed. He was alone in the white with only the tiny silver sun looking down on him. He could smell dust, damp, honeysuckle, roses.

And then the growling began.

His heart leaped into his throat and he fell back a step, all his muscles tensing into bundles of wire. His first panicky thought, like a child who has suddenly tumbled into a fairy tale, was *wolf*, and he looked around wildly. There was nothing to see but white.

Cujo came out of the fog.

Brett began to make a whining noise in his throat. The dog he had grown up with, the dog who had pulled a yelling, gleeful five-year-old Brett patiently around and around the dooryard on his Flexible Flyer, buckled into a harness Joe had made in the shop, the dog who had been waiting calmly by the mailbox every afternoon during school for the bus, come shine or shower . . . that dog bore only the slightest resemblance to the muddy, matted apparition slowly materializing from the morning mist. The Saint Bernard's big, sad eyes were now reddish and stupid and lowering: more pig's eyes than dog's eyes. His coat was plated with brownish-green-mud, as if he had been rolling around in the boggy place at the bottom of the meadow. His muzzle was wrinkled back in a terrible mock grin that froze Brett with horror. Brett felt his heart slugging away in his throat.

Thick white foam dripped slowly from between Cujo's teeth.

'Cujo?' Brett whispered. 'Cuje?'

Cujo looked at THE BOY, not recognizing him any more, not his looks, not the shadings of his clothes (he could not precisely see colors, at least as human beings understand them), not his scent. What he saw was a monster on two legs. Cujo was sick, and all things appeared monstrous to him now. His head clanged dully with murder. He wanted to bite and rip and tear. Part of him saw a cloudy image of him springing at THE BOY, bringing him down, parting flesh with bone, drinking blood as it still pulsed, driven by a dying heart.

Then the monstrous figure spoke, and Cujo recognized the voice. It was THE BOY, THE BOY, and THE BOY had never done him any harm. Once he had loved THE BOY and would have died for him, had that been called for. There was enough of that feeling left to hold the image of murder at bay until it grew as murky as the fog around them. It broke up and rejoined the buzzing, clamorous river of his sickness.

'Cujo? What's wrong, boy?'

The last of the dog that had been before the bat scratched its nose turned away, and the sick and dangerous dog, subverted for the last time, was forced to turn with it. Cujo stumbled away and moved deeper into the fog. Foam splattered from his muzzle onto the dirt. He broke into a lumbering run, hoping to outrun the sickness, but it ran with him, buzzing and yammering, making him ache with hatred and murder. He began to roll over and over in the high timothy grass, snapping at it, his eyes rolling.

The world was a crazy sea of smells. He would track each to its source and dismember it.

Cujo began to growl again. He found his feet. He slipped deeper into the fog that was even now beginning to thin, a big dog who weighed just under two hundred pounds.

Brett stood in the dooryard for more than fifteen minutes after Cujo had melted back into the fog, not knowing what to do. Cujo had been sick. He might have eaten a poison bait or something. Brett knew about rabies, and if he had ever seen a woodchuck or a fox or a porcupine exhibiting the same symptons, he would have guessed rabies. But it never crossed his mind that his dog could have that awful disease of the brain and the nervous system. A poison bait, that seemed the most likely.

He should tell his father. His father could call the vet. Or maybe Dad could do something himself, like that time two years ago, when he had pulled the porcupine needles out of Cujo's muzzle with his pliers, working each quill first up, then down, then out, being careful not to break them off because they would fester in there. Yes, he would have to tell Dad. Dad would do something, like that time Cuje got into it with Mr. Porky Pine.

But what about the trip?

He didn't need to be told that his mother had won them the trip through some desperate stratagem, or luck, or a combination of the two. Like most children, he could sense the vibrations between his parents, and he knew the way the emotional currents ran from one day to the next the way a veteran guide knows the twists and turns of an upcountry river. It had been a near thing, and even though his dad had agreed, Brett sensed that this agreement had been grudging and unpleasant. The trip was not on for sure until he had dropped them off and driven away. If he told Dad Cujo was sick, might he not seize on that as an excuse to keep them home?

He stood motionless in the dooryard. He was, for the first time in his life, in a total mental and emotional quandary. After a little while he began to hunt for Cujo behind the barn. He called him in a low voice. His parents were still sleeping, and he knew how sound carried in the morning fog. He didn't find Cujo anywhere . . . which was just as well for him.

The alarm burred Vic awake at quarter to five. He got up, shut it off, and blundered down to the bathroom, mentally cursing Roger Breakstone, who could never get to the Portland Jetport twenty minutes before check-in like any normal air traveler. Not Roger. Roger was a contingency man. There might always be a flat tire or a roadblock or a wash out or an earthquake. Aliens from outer space might decide to touch down on runway 22.

He showered, shaved, gobbled vitamins, and went back to the bedroom to dress. The big double bed was empty and he sighed a little. The weekend he and Donna had just passed hadn't been very pleasant . . . in fact, he could honestly say he never wanted to go through such a weekend again in his life. They had kept their normal, pleasant faces on – for Tad – but Vic had felt like a participant at a masquerade ball. He didn't like to be aware of the muscles in his face at work when he smiled.

They had slept in the same bed together, but for the first time the king-sized double seemed too small to Vic. They slept each on one side, the space between them a crisply sheeted no-man's-land. He had lain awake both Friday and Saturday nights, morbidly aware of each shift in Donna's weight as she moved, the sound of her nightdress against her body. He found himself wondering if she was awake, too, on her side of the emptiness that lay between them.

Last night, Sunday night, they had tried to do something about that empty space in the middle of the bed. The sex part had been moderately successful, if a little tentative (at least neither of them had cried when it was over; for some reason he had been morbidly sure that one of them would do that). But Vic was not sure you could call what they had done making love.

He dressed in his summerweight gray suit – as gray as the early light outside – and picked up his two suitcases. One of them was much heavier than the other. That one contained most of the Sharp Cereals file. Roger had all the graphic layouts.

Donna was making waffles in the kitchen. The teapot was on, just beginning to huff and puff. She was wearing his old blue flannel robe. Her face was puffy, as if instead of resting her, sleep had punched her unconscious.

'Will the planes fly when it's like that?' she asked.

'It's going to burn off. You can see the sun already.' He pointed at it and then kissed her lightly on the nape of the neck. 'You shouldn't have gotten up.'

'No problem.' She lifted the waffle iron's lid and deftly turned a waffle out on a plate. She handed it to him. 'I wish you weren't going away.' Her voice was low. 'Not now. After last night.'

'It wasn't that bad, was it?'

'Not like before,' Donna said. A bitter, almost secret smile touched her lips and was gone. She beat the waffle mixture with a wire whisk and then poured a ladleful into the waffle iron and dropped its heavy lid. *Sssss.* She poured boiling water over a couple of Red Rose bags and took the

cups – one said VIC, the other DONNA – over to the table.
'Eat your waffle. There's strawberry preserves, if you want
them.'

He got the preserves and sat down. He spread some oleo
across the top of the waffle and watched it melt into the little
squares, just as he had when he was a child. The preserves
were Smucker's. He liked Smucker's preserves. He spread
the waffle liberally with them. It looked great. But he
wasn't hungry.

'Will you get laid in Boston or New York?' she asked,
turning her back on him. 'Even it out? Tit for tat?'

He jumped a little – perhaps even flushed. He was glad
her back was turned because he felt that at that precise
moment there was more of him on his face than he wanted
her to see. Not that he was angry; the thought of giving the
bellman a ten instead of the usual buck and then asking the
fellow a few questions had certainly crossed his mind. He
knew that Roger had done it on occasion.

'I'm going to be too busy for anything like that.'

'What does the ad say? There's Always Room for Jell-O.'

'Are you trying to make me mad, Donna? Or
what?'

'No. Go on and eat. You got to feed the machine.'

She sat down with a waffle of her own. No oleo for her. A
dash of Vermont Maid Syrup, that was all. How well we
know each other, he thought.

'What time are you picking Roger up?' she asked him.

'After some hot negotiations, we've settled on six.'

She smiled again, but this time the smile was warm and
fond. 'He really took that early-bird business to heart at
some point, didn't he?'

'Yeah. I'm surprised he hasn't called yet to make sure I'm
up.'

The phone rang.

They looked at each other across the table, and after
a silent considering pause they both burst out laughing. It
was a rare moment, certainly more rare than the careful
lovemaking in the dark the night before. He saw how fine

her eyes were, how lucent. They were as gray as the morning mist outside.

'Get it quick before it wakes the Tadder up,' she said.

He did. It was Roger. He assured Roger that he was up, dressed, and in a fighting frame of mind. He would pick Roger up on the dot of six. He hung up wondering if he would end up telling Roger about Donna and Steve Kemp. Probably not. Not because Roger's advice would be bad; it wouldn't be. But, even though Roger would promise not to tell Althea, he most certainly would. And he had a suspicion that Althea would find it difficult to resist sharing out such a juicy bit of bridge-table gossip. Such careful consideration of the question made him feel depressed all over again. It was as if, by trying to work out the problem between them, he and Donna were burying their own body by moonlight.

'Good old Roger,' he said, sitting down again. He tried on a smile but it felt wrong. The moment of spontaneity was gone.

'Will you be able to get all of your stuff and all of Roger's into the Jag?'

'Sure,' he said. 'We'll have to. Althea needs their car, and you've got – oh, *shit*, I completely forgot to call Joe Camber about your Pinto.'

'You had a few other things on your mind,' she said. There was faint irony in her voice. 'That's all right. I'm not going to send Tad to the playground today. He has the sniffles. I may keep him home the rest of the summer, if that suits you. I get into trouble when he's gone.'

There were tears choking her voice, squeezing it and blurring it, and he didn't know what to say or how to respond. He watched helplessly as she found a Kleenex, blew her nose, wiped her eyes.

'Whatever,' he said, shaken. 'Whatever seems best.' He rushed on: 'Just give Camber a call. He's always there, and I don't think it would take him twenty minutes to fix it. Even if he has to put in another carb –'

'Will you think about it while you're gone?' she asked.

'About what we're going to do? The two of us?'

'Yes,' he said.

'Good. I will too. Another waffle?'

'No, thanks.' The whole conversation was turning surreal. Suddenly he wanted to be out and gone. Suddenly the trip felt very necessary and very attractive. The idea of getting away from the whole mess. Putting miles between him and it. He felt a sudden jab of anticipation. In his mind he could see the Delta jet cutting through the unraveling fog and into the blue.

'Can I have a waffle?'

They both looked around, startled. It was Tad, standing in the hallway in his yellow footy pajamas, his stuffed coyote grasped by one ear, his red blanket wrapped around his shoulders. He looked like a small, sleepy Indian.

'I guess I could rustle one up,' Donna said, surprised. Tad was not a notably early riser.

'Was it the phone, Tad?' Vic asked.

Tad shook his head. 'I made myself wake up early so I could say good-bye to you, Daddy. Do you really have to go?'

'It's just for a while.'

'It's too long,' Tad said blackly. 'I put a circle around the day you're coming home on my calendar. Mom showed me which one. I'm going to mark off every day, and she said she'd tell me the Monster Words every night.'

'Well, that's okay, isn't it?'

'Will you call?'

'Every other night,' Vic said.

'Every night,' Tad insisted. He crawled up into Vic's lap and set his coyote next to Vic's plate. Tad began to crunch up a piece of toast. 'Every *night*, Daddy.'

'I can't every night,' Vic said, thinking of the backbreaking schedule Roger had laid out on Friday, before the letter had come.

'Why not?'

'Because —'

'Because your Uncle Roger is a hard taskmaster,' Donna

said, putting Tad's waffle on the table. 'Come on over here
and eat. Bring your coyote. Daddy will call us tomorrow
night from Boston and tell us everything that happened to
him.'

Tad took his place at the end of the table. He had a large
plastic placemat that said TAD. 'Will you bring me a toy?'

'Maybe. If you're good. And maybe I'll call tonight so
you'll know I got to Boston in one piece.'

'Good deal.' Vic watched, fascinated, as Tad poured a
small ocean of syrup over his waffle. 'What kind of
toy?'

'We'll see,' Vic said. He watched Tad eat his waffle. It
suddenly occurred to him that Tad liked eggs. Scrambled,
friend, poached, or hard-boiled, Tad gobbled them up.
'Tad?'

'What, Daddy?'

'If you wanted people to buy eggs, what would you tell
them?'

Tad considered. 'I'd tell em eggs taste good,' he said.

Vic met his wife's eyes again, and they had a second
moment like the one that had occurred when the phone
rang. This time they laughed telepathically.

Their good-byes were light. Only Tad, with his imperfect
grasp of how short the future really was, cried.

'You'll think about it?' Donna asked him again as he
climbed into the Jag.

'Yes.'

But driving into Bridgton to get Roger, what he thought
about were those two moments of near-perfect communication. Two in one morning, not bad. All it took was eight or
nine years together, roughly a quarter of all the years so far
spent on the face of the earth. He got thinking about how
ridiculous the whole concept of human communication
was – what monstrous, absurd overkill was necessary to
achieve even a little. When you'd invested the time and made
it good, you had to be careful. Yes, he'd think about it. It had
been good between them, and although some of the
channels were now closed, filled with God knew how much

muck (and some of that muck might still be squirming), plenty of the others seemed open and in reasonably good working order.

There had to be some careful thought – but perhaps not too much at once. Things had a way of magnifying themselves.

He turned the radio up and began to think about the poor old Sharp Cereal Professor.

Joe Camber pulled up in front of the Greyhound terminal in Portland at ten minutes to eight. The fog had burned off and the digital clock atop the Casco Bank and Trust read 73 degrees already.

He drove with his hat planted squarely on his head, ready to be angry at anyone who pulled out or cut in front of him. He hated to drive in the city. When he and Gary got to Boston he intended to park the car and leave it until they were ready to come home. They could take the subways if they could puzzle them out, walk if they couldn't.

Charity was dressed in her best pants suit – it was a quiet green – and a white cotton blouse with a ruffle at the neck. She was wearing earrings, and this had filled Brett with a mild sense of amazement. He couldn't remember his mother wearing earrings at all, except to church.

Brett had caught her alone when she went upstairs to dress after getting Dad his breakfast oatmeal. Joe had been mostly silent, grunting answers to questions in monosyllables, then shutting off conversation entirely by tuning the radio to WCSH for the ball scores. They were both afraid that the silence might presage a ruinous outburst and a sudden change of mind on their trip.

Charity had the slacks of her pants suit on and was slipping into her blouse. Brett noted she was wearing a peach-colored bra, and that had also amazed him. He hadn't known his mother had underclothes in any color other than white.

'Ma,' he said urgently.

She turned to him – it seemed almost that she was turning *on* him. 'Did he say something to you?'

'No . . . no. It's Cujo.'

'Cujo? What about Cujo?'

'He's sick.'

'What do you mean, sick?'

Brett told her about having his second bowl of Cocoa Bears out on the back steps, about walking into the fog, and how Cujo had suddenly appeared, his eyes red and wild, his muzzle dripping foam.

'And he wasn't walking right,' Brett finished. 'He was kind of, you know, staggering. I think I better tell Daddy.'

'*No*,' his mother said fiercely, and grasped him by the shoulders hard enough to hurt. 'You do no such a thing!'

He looked at her, surprised and frightened. She relaxed her grip a little and spoke more quietly.

'He just scared you, coming out of the fog like that. There's probably nothing wrong with him at all. Right?'

Brett groped for the right words to make her understand how terrible Cujo had looked, and how for a moment he had thought the dog was going to turn on him. He couldn't find the words. Maybe he didn't want to find them.

'If there is something wrong,' Charity continued, 'it's probably just some little thing. He might have gotten a dose of skunk –'

'I didn't smell any sk –'

'– or he might have been running a woodchuck or a rabbit. Might even have jumped a moose down there in that bog. Or he might have eaten some nettles.

'I guess he could have,' Brett said doubtfully.

'Your father would just jump on something like that,' she said. 'I can hear him now. "Sick, is he? Well, he's your dog, Brett. You see to him. I got too much work to do to be messing around with your mutt."'

Brett nodded unhappily. It was his own thought exactly, magnified by the brooding way his father had been eating breakfast while the sports blared around the kitchen.

'If you just leave him, he'll come mooching around your dad, and your dad will take care of him,' Charity said. 'He loves Cujo almost as much as you do, although he'd never say it. If he sees something's wrong, he'll fetch him over to the vet's in South Paris.'

'Yeah, I guess he would.' His mother's words rang true to him, but he was still unhappy about it.

She bent and kissed his cheek. 'I'll tell you! We can call your father tonight, if you want. How would that be? And when you talk to him, you just say, sort of casually, "You feeding my dog, Daddy?" And then you'll know.'

'Yeah,' Brett said. He smiled gratefully at his mother, and she smiled back, relieved, the trouble averted. But, perversely, it had given them something else to worry about during the seemingly interminable period before Joe backed the car up to the porch steps and silently began to load their four pieces of luggage into the wagon (into one of them Charity had surreptitiously placed all six of her snapshot albums). This new worry was that Cujo would lurch into the yard before they could drive away and stick Joe Camber with the problem.

But Cujo hadn't shown up.

Now Joe lowered the tailgate of the Country Squire, handed Brett the two small bags, and took the two large ones for himself.

'Woman, you got so much luggage I wonder if you ain't leavin on one of those Reno divorce cruises instead of going down to Connecticut.'

Charity and Brett smiled uneasily. It sounded like an attempt at humor, but with Joe Camber you were never really sure.

'That would be a day,' she said.

'I guess I'd just have to chase you down and drag you back with my new chainfall,' he said, unsmiling. His green hat was cocked squarely on the back of his head. 'Boy, you gonna take care of your mom?'

Brett nodded.

'Yeah, you better.' He measured the boy. 'You're getting

pretty damn big. Probably you ain't got a kiss to give your old man.'

'I guess I do, Daddy,' Brett said. He hugged his father tight and kissed his stubbly cheek, smelling sour sweat and a phantom of last night's vodka. He was surprised and overwhelmed by his love for his father, a feeling that sometimes still came, always when it was least expected (but less and less often over the last two or three years, something his mother did not know and would not have believed if told). It was a love that had nothing to do with Joe Camber's day-to-day behavior toward him or his mother; it was a brute, biological thing that he would never be free of, a phenomenon with many illusory referents of the sort which haunt for a lifetime: the smell of cigarette smoke, the look of a double-edged razor reflected in a mirror, pants hung over a chair, certain curse words.

His father hugged him back and then turned to Charity. He put a finger under her chin and turned her face up a little. From the loading bays behind the squat brick building they heard a bus warming up. Its engine was a low and guttural diesel rumble. 'Have a good time,' he said.

Her eyes filled with tears and she wiped them away quickly. The gesture was nearly one of anger. 'Okay,' she said.

Abruptly the tight, closed, noncommittal expression descended over his face. It came down like the clap of a knight's visor. He was the perfect country man again. 'Let's get these cases in, boy! Feels like there's lead in this one . . . Jesus-please-us!'

He stayed with them until all four bags had been checked, looking closely at each tag, oblivious of the baggage handler's condescending expression of amusement. He watched the handler trundle the bags out on a dolly and load them into the guts of the bus. Then he turned to Brett again.

'Come on out on the sidewalk with me,' he said.

Charity watched them go. She sat down on one of the hard benches, opened her purse, took out a handkerchief, and began fretting at it. It would just be like him to wish her a good time and then try to talk the boy into going back to the home place with him.

On the sidewalk, Joe said: 'Lemme give you two pieces of advice, boy. You probably won't take neither of them, boys seldom do, but I guess that never stopped a father giving em. First piece of advice is this: That fella you're going to see, that Jim, he's nothing but a piece of shit. One of the reasons I'm letting you go on this jaunt is that you're ten now, and ten's old enough to tell the difference between a turd and a tearose. You watch him and you'll see. He don't do nothing but sit in an office and push papers. People like him is half the trouble with this world, because their brains have got unplugged from their hands.' Thin, hectic color had risen in Joe's cheeks. 'He's a piece of shit. You watch him and see if you don't agree.'

'All right,' Brett said. His voice was low but composed.

Joe Camber smiled a little. 'The second piece of advice is to keep your hand on your pocketbook.'

'I haven't got any mon –'

Camber held out a rumpled five-dollar bill. 'Yeah, you got this. Don't spend it all in one place. The fool and his money soon parted.'

'All right. Thank you!'

'So long,' Camber said. He didn't ask for another kiss.

'Good-bye, Daddy.' Brett stood on the sidewalk and watched his father climb into the car and drive away. He never saw his father alive again.

At quarter past eight that morning, Gary Pervier staggered out of his house in his pee-stained underwear shorts and urinated into the honeysuckle. In a perverse sort of way he hoped that someday his piss would become so rancid with booze that it would blight the honeysuckle. That day hadn't come yet.

'*Arrrouggh, my head!*' he screamed, holding it with his free hand as he watered the honeysuckle which had buried his fence. His eyes were threaded with bright snaps of scarlet. His heart clattered and roared like an old water pump that was drawing more air than water just lately. A terrible stomach cramp seized him as he finished voiding himself – they had been getting more common lately – and as he doubled up a large and foul-smelling flatulence purred out from between his skinny shanks.

He turned to go back in, and that was when he heard the growling begin. It was a low, powerful sound coming from just beyond the point where his overgrown side yard merged with the hayfield beyond it.

He turned toward the sound quickly, his headache forgotten, the clatter and roar of his heart forgotten, the cramp forgotten. It had been a long time since he'd had a flashback to his war in France, but he had one now, Suddenly his mind was screaming, *Germans! Germans! Squad down!*

But it wasn't the Germans. When the grass parted it was Cujo who appeared.

'Hey, boy, what are you growling f –' Gary said, and then faltered.

It had been twenty years since he had seen a rabid dog, but you didn't forget the look. He had been in an Amoco station east of Machias, headed back from a camping trip down Eastport way. He had been driving the old Indian motorcycle he'd had for a while in the mid-fifties. A panting, slat-sided yellow dog had drifted by outside that Amoco station like a ghost. Its sides had been moving in and out in rapid, shallow springs of respiration. Foam was dripping from its mouth in a steady watery stream. It's eyes were rolling wildly. Its hindquarters were caked with shit. It had been reeling rather than walking, as if some unkind soul had opened its jaws an hour before and filled it full of cheap whiskey.

'Hot damn, there he is,' the pump jockey said. He had dropped the adjustable wrench he was holding and had rushed into the cluttered, dingy little office which adjoined the station's garage bay. He had come out with a .30-.30 clutched in his greasy, big-knuckled hands. He went out onto the tarmac, dropped to one knee, and started shooting. His first shot had been low, shearing away one of the dog's back legs in a cloud of blood. That yellow dog never even moved, Gary remembered as he stared at Cujo now. Just looked around blankly as if he didn't have the slightest idea what was happening to it. The pump jockey's second try had cut the dog almost in half. Guts hit the station's one pump in a black and red splash. A moment later three more guys had pulled in, three of Washington County's finest crammed shoulder to shoulder in the cab of a 1940 Dodge pickup. They were all armed. They piled out and pumped another eight or nine rounds into the dead dog. An hour after that, as the pump jockey was finishing up putting a new headlamp on the front of Gary's Indian cycle, the County Dog Officer arrived in a Studebaker with no door on the passenger side. She donned long rubber gloves and cut off what was left of the yellow dog's head to send to State Health and Welfare.

Cujo looked a hell of a lot spryer than that long-ago yellow dog, but the other symptoms were exactly the same. *Not too far gone,* he thought. *More dangerous. Holy Jesus, got to get my gun –*

He started to back away. 'Hi, Cujo . . . nice dog, nice boy, nice doggy –' Cujo stood at the edge of the lawn, his great head lowered, his eyes reddish and filmy, growling.

'Nice boy –'

To Cujo, the words coming from THE MAN meant nothing. They were meaningless sounds, like the wind. What mattered was the *smell* coming from THE MAN. It was hot, rank, and pungent. It was the smell of fear. It was maddening and unbearable. He suddenly understood THE MAN had made him sick. He lunged forward, the growl in his chest mounting into a heavy roar of rage.

Gary saw the dog coming for him. He turned and ran. One bite, one scratch, could mean death. He ran for the porch and the safety of the house beyond the porch. But there had been too many drinks, too many long winter days by the stove, and too many long summer nights in the lawn chair. He could hear Cujo closing in behind him, and then there was the terrible split second when he could hear nothing and understood that Cujo had leaped.

As he reached the first splintery step of his porch, two hundred pounds of Saint Bernard hit him like a locomotive, knocking him flat and driving the wind from him. The dog went for the back of his neck. Gary tried to scramble up. The dog was over him, the thick fur of its underbelly nearly suffocating him, and it knocked him back down easily. Gary screamed.

Cujo bit him high on the shoulder, his powerful jaws closing and crunching through the bare skin, pulling tendons like wires. He continued to growl. Blood flew. Gary felt it running warmly down his skinny upper arm. He turned over and battered at the dog with his fists. It gave back a little and Gary was able to scramble up three more steps on his feet and hands. Then Cujo came again.

Gary kicked at the dog. Cujo feinted the other way and then came boring in, snapping and growling. Foam flew from his jaws, and Gary could smell his breath. It smelled rotten – rank and yellow. Gary balled his right fist and swung in a roundhouse, connecting with the bony shelf of Cujo's lower jaw. It was mostly luck. The jolt of the impact ran all the way up to his shoulder, which was on fire from the deep bite.

Cujo backed off again.

Gary looked at the dog, his thin, hairless chest moving rapidly up and down. His face was ashy gray. The laceration on his shoulder welled blood that splattered on the peeling porch steps. 'Come for me, you sonofawhore,' he said. 'Come on, come on, I don't give a shit.' He screamed, '*You hear me? I don't give a shit!*'

But Cujo backed off another pace.

The words still had no meaning, but the smell of fear had left THE MAN. Cujo was no longer sure if he wanted to attack or not. He hurt, he hurt so miserably, and the world was a crazyquilt of sense and impression –

Gary got shakily to his feet. He backed up the last two steps of the porch. He backed across the porch's width and felt behind him for the handle of the screen door. His shoulder felt as if raw gasoline had been poured under the skin. His mind raved at him, *Rabies! I got the rabies!*

Never mind. One thing at a time. His shotgun was in the hall closet. Thank Christ Charity and Brett Camber were gone from up on the hill. That was God's mercy at work.

He found the screen door's handle and pulled the door open. He kept his eyes locked on Cujo's until he had backed in and pulled the screen door shut behind him. Then a great relief swept through him. His legs went rubbery. For a moment the world swam away, and he pulled himself back by sticking his tongue out and biting down on it. This was no time to swoon like a girl. He could do that after the dog was dead, if he wanted. Christ, but it had been close out there; he had thought he was going to punch out for sure.

He turned and headed down the darkened hallway to the closet, and that was when Cujo smashed through the lower half of the screen door, muzzle wrinkled back from his teeth in a kind of sneer, a dry volley of barking sounds coming from his chest.

Gary screamed again and whirled just in time to catch Cujo in both arms as the dog leaped again, driving him back down the hall, bouncing from side to side and trying to keep his feet. For a moment they almost seemed to waltz. Then Gary, who was fifty pounds lighter, went down. He was dimly aware of Cujo's muzzle burrowing in under his chin, was dimly aware that Cujo's nose was almost sickeningly hot and dry. He tried getting his hands up and was thinking that he would have to go for Cujo's eyes with his thumbs when Cujo seized his throat and tore it open. Gary screamed and the dog savaged him again. Gary felt warm blood sheet across his face and thought, *Dear God, that's mine!* His hands beat weakly and ineffectually at Cujo's upper body, doing no damage. At last they fell away.

Faintly, sick and cloying, he smelled honeysuckle.

'What do you see out there?'

Brett turned a little toward the sound of his mother's voice. Not all the way – he did not want to lose sight of the steadily unrolling view even for a little while. The bus had been on the road for almost an hour. They had crossed the Million Dollar Bridge into South Portland (Brett had stared with fascinated, wondering eyes at the two scum-caked, rustbucket freighters in the harbor), joined the Turnpike going south, and were now approaching the New Hampshire border.

'Everything,' Brett said. 'What do you see, Mom?'

She thought: *Your reflection in the glass – very faint. That's what I see.*

Instead she answered, 'Why, the world, I guess. I see the world unrolling in front of us.'

'Mom? I wish we could ride all the way to California on this bus. See everything there is in the geography books at school.'

She laughed and ruffled his hair. 'You'd get damn tired of scenery, Brett.'

'No. No, I wouldn't.'

And he probably wouldn't, she thought. Suddenly she felt both sad and old. When she had called Holly Saturday morning to ask her if they could come, Holly had been delighted, and her delight had made Charity feel young. It was strange that her own son's delight, his almost palpable euphoria, would make her feel old. Nevertheless . . .

What exactly is there going to be for him? she asked herself, studying his ghostlike face, which was superimposed over the moving scenery like a camera trick. He was bright, brighter than she was and much brighter than Joe.

He ought to go to college, but she knew that when he got to high school Joe would press him to sign up for the shop and automotive maintenance courses so he could be more help around the place. Ten years ago he wouldn't have been able to get away with it, the guidance counselors wouldn't have *allowed* a bright boy like Brett to opt for all manual trades course, but in these days of phase electives and do your own thing, she was terribly afraid it might happen.

It made her afraid. Once she had been able to tell herself that school was far away, so very far away – high school, *real* school. Grammar school was nothing but play to a boy who slipped through his lessons as easily as Brett did. But in high school the business of irrevocable choices began. Doors slipped shut with a faint locking click that was only heard clearly in the dreams of later years.

She gripped her elbows and shivered, not even kidding herself that it was because the Hound's air conditioning was turned up too high.

For Brett, high school was now just four years away.

She shivered again and suddenly found herself wishing viciously that she had never won the money, or that she had lost the ticket. They had only been away from Joe for an hour, but it was the first time she had really been separated from him since they had married in late 1966. She hadn't realized that perspective would be so sudden, so dizzying, and so bitter. Picture this: Woman and boy are let free from brooding castle keep . . . but there's a catch. Stapled to their backs are large hooks, and slipped over the ends of the hooks are heavy-duty invisible rubber bands. And before you can get too far, presto-whizzo! You're snapped back inside for another fourteen years!

She made a little croaking sound in her throat.

'Did you say something, Mom?'

'No. Just clearing my throat.'

She shivered a third time, and this time her arms broke out in gooseflesh. She had recalled a line of poetry from one of her own high school English classes (she had wanted to take the college courses, but her father had been furious at the idea – did she think they were *rich*? – and her mother had laughed the idea to death gently and pityingly). It was from a poem by Dylan Thomas, and she couldn't remember the whole thing, but it had been something about moving through dooms of love.

That line had seemed funny and perplexing to her then, but she thought she understood it now. What else did you call that heavy-duty invisible rubber hand, if not love? Was she going to kid herself and say that she did not, even now, in some way love the man she had married? That she stayed with him only out of duty, or for the sake of the child (*that* was a bitter laugh; if she ever left him it would be for the sake of the child)? That he had never pleasured her in bed? That he could not, sometimes at the most unexpected moments (like the one back at the bus station), be tender?

And yet . . . and yet . . .

Brett was looking out the window, enrapt. Without turning from the view, he said, 'You think Cujo's all right, Mom?'

'I'm sure he's fine,' she said absently.

For the first time she found herself thinking about divorce in a concrete way – what she could do to support herself and her son, how they would get along in such an unthinkable (*almost* unthinkable) situation. If she and Brett didn't come home from this trip, would he come after them, as he had vaguely threatened back in Portland? Would he decide to let Charity go to the bad but try to get Brett back by fair means . . . or foul?

She began to tick the various possibilities over in her mind, weighing them, suddenly thinking that maybe a little perspective wasn't such a bad thing after all. Painful, maybe. Maybe useful, too.

The Greyhound slipped across the state line into New Hampshire and rolled on south.

The Delta 727 rose steeply, buttonhooked over Castle Rock – Vic always looked for his house near Castle Lake and 117, always fruitlessly — and then headed back toward the coast. It was a twenty-minute run to Logan Airport.

Donna was down there, some eighteen thousand feet below. And the Tadder. He felt a sudden depression mixed with a black premonition that it wasn't going to work, that they were crazy to even think it might. When your house blew down, you had to build a new house. You couldn't put the old one back together again with Elmer's Glue.

The stewardess came by. He and Roger were riding in first class ('Might as well enjoy it while we can, buddy,' Roger had said last Wednesday when he made the reservations; 'not everyone can go to the poorfarm in such impeccable style'), and there were only four or five other passengers, most of them reading the morning paper — as was Roger.

'Can I get you anything?' she asked Roger with that professional twinkly smile that seemed to say she had been overjoyed to get up this morning at five thirty to make the upsy-downsy run from Bangor to Portland to Boston to New York to Atlanta.

Roger shook his head absently, and she turned that unearthly smile on Vic. 'Anything for you, sir? Sweet roll? Orange juice?'

'Could you rustle up a screwdriver?' Vic asked, and Roger's head came out of his paper with a snap.

The stew's smile didn't falter; a request for a drink before nine in the morning was no news to her. 'I can rustle one up,' she said, 'but you'll have to hustle to get it all down. It's really only a hop to Boston.'

'I'll hustle,' Vic promised solemnly, and she passed on her way back up to the galley, resplendent in her powder-blue slacks uniform and her smile.

'What's with you?' Roger asked.

'What do you mean, what's with me?'

'You know what I mean. I never even saw you drink a beer before noon before. Usually not before five.'

'I'm launching the boat,' Vic said.

'What boat?'

'The R.M.S. *Titanic*,' Vic said.

Roger frowned. 'That's sort of poor taste, don't you think?'

He did, as a matter of fact. Roger deserved something better, but this morning, with the depression still on him like a foul-smelling blanket, he just couldn't think of anything better. He managed a rather bleak smile instead. But Roger went on frowning at him.

'Look,' Vic said, 'I've got an idea on this Zingers thing. It's going to be a bitch convincing old man Sharp and the kid, but it might work.'

Roger looked relieved. It was the way it had always worked with them; Vic was the raw idea man, Roger the shaper and implementer. They had always worked as a team when it came to translating the ideas into media, and in the matter of presentation.

'What is it?'

'Give me a little while,' Vic said. 'Until tonight, maybe. Then we'll run it up the flagpole –'

'– and see who drops their pants,' Roger finished with a grin. He shook his paper open to the financial page again. 'Okay. As long as I get it by tonight. Sharp stock went up another eighth last week. Were you aware of that?'

'Dandy,' Vic murmured, and looked out the window again. No fog now; the day was as clear as a bell. The beaches at Kennebunk and Ogunquit and York formed a panoramic picture postcard – cobalt blue sea, khaki sand, and then the Maine landscape of low hills, open fields, and thick bands of fir stretching west and out of sight. Beautiful. And it made his depression even worse.

If I have to cry, I'm damn well going into the crapper to do it, he thought grimly. Six sentences on a sheet of cheap paper had done this to him. It was a goddam fragile world, as fragile as one of those Easter eggs that were all pretty colors on the outside but hollow on the inside. Only last week he had been thinking of just taking Tad and moving out. Now he wondered if Tad and Donna would still be there when he and Roger got back. Was it possible that Donna might just take the kid and decamp, maybe to her mother's place in the Poconos?

Sure it was possible. She might decide that ten days apart wasn't enough, not for him, not for her. Maybe a six months' separation would be better. And she had Tad now. Possession was nine points of the law, wasn't it?

And maybe, a crawling, insinuating voice inside spoke up, *maybe she knows where Kemp is. Maybe she'll decide to go to him. Try it with him for a while. They can search for their happy pasts together.* Now *there's* a nice crazy Monday-morning thought, he told himself uneasily.

But the thought wouldn't go away. Almost, but not quite.

He managed to finish every drop of his screwdriver before the plane touched down at Logan. It gave him acid indigestion that he knew would last all morning long – like the thought of Donna and Steve Kemp together, it would come creeping back even if he gobbled a whole roll of Tums – but the depression lifted a little and so maybe it was worth it.

Maybe.

Joe Camber looked at the patch of garage floor below his big vise clamp with something like wonder. He pushed his green felt hat back on his forehead, stared at what was there awhile longer, then put his fingers between his teeth and whistled piercingly.

'*Cujo! Hey, boy! Come, Cujo!*'

He whistled again and then leaned over, hands on his knees. The dog would come, he had no doubt of that. Cujo never went far. But how was he going to handle this?

The dog had shat on the garage floor. He had never known Cujo to do such a thing, not even as a pup. He had piddled around a few times, as puppies will, and he had torn the bejesus out of a chair cushion or two, but there had never been anything like this. He wondered briefly if maybe some other dog had done it, and then dismissed the thought. Cujo was the biggest dog in Castle Rock, so far as he knew. Big dogs ate big, and big dogs crapped big. No poodle or beagle or Heinz Fifty-seven Varieties had done this mess. Joe wondered if the dog could have sensed that Charity and Brett were going away for a spell. If so, maybe this was his way of showing just how that idea set with him. Joe had heard of such things.

He had taken the dog in payment for a job he had done in 1975. The customer had been a one-eyed fellow named Ray Crowell from up Fryeburg way. This Crowell spent most of his time working in the woods, although it was acknowledged that he had a fine touch with dogs – he was good at breeding them and good at training them. He could have made a decent living doing what New England country people sometimes called 'dog farming', but his temper was not good, and he drove many customers away with his sullenness.

'I need a new engine in my truck,' Crowell had told Joe that spring.

'Ayuh,' Joe had said.

'I got the motor, but I can't pay you nothing. I'm tapped out.'

They had been standing just inside Joe's garage, chewing on stems of grass. Brett, then five, had been goofing around in the dooryard while Charity hung out clothes.

'Well, that's too bad, Ray,' Joe said, 'but I don't work for free. This ain't no charitable organization.'

'Mrs. Beasley just had herself a litter,' Ray said. Mrs. Beasley was a prime bitch Saint Bernard. 'Purebreds. You do the work and I'll give you the pick of the litter. What do you say? You'd be coming out ahead, but I can't cut no pulp if I don't have a truck to haul it in.'

'Don't need a dog,' Joe said. 'Especially a big one like that. Goddam Saint Bernards ain't nothing but eatin machines.'

'*You* don't need a dog,' Ray said, casting an eye out at Brett, who was now just sitting on the grass and watching his mother, 'but your boy might appreciate one.'

Joe opened his mouth and then closed it again. He and Charity didn't use any protection, but there had been no more kids since Brett, and Brett himself had been a long while coming. Sometimes, looking at him, a vague question would form itself in Joe's head: Was the boy lonely? Perhaps he was. And perhaps Ray Crowell was right. Brett's birthday was coming up. He could give him the pup then.

'I'll think about it,' he said.

'Well, don't think too long,' Ray said, bridling. 'I can go see Vin Callahan over in North Conway. He's just as handy as you are, Camber. Handier, maybe.'

'Maybe,' Joe said, unperturbed. Ray Crowell's temper did not scare him in the least.

Later that week, the manager of the Shop 'n Save drove his Thunderbird up to Joe's to get the transmission looked at. It was a minor problem, but the manager, whose name was Donovan, fussed around the car like a worried mother while Joe drained the transmission fluid well, refilled it, and tightened the bands. The car was a piece of work, all right, a 1960 T-Bird in cherry condition. And as he finished the job, listening to Donovan talk about how his wife wanted him to sell the car, Joe had had an idea.

'I'm thinking about getting my boy a dog,' he told this Donovan as he let the T-Bird down off the jacks.

'Oh, yes?' Donovan asked politely.

'Ayuh. Saint Bernard. It's just a pup now, but it's gonna eat big when it grows. Now I was just thinking that we might make a little deal, you and me. If you was to guarantee me a discount on that dry dog food, Gaines Meal, Ralston-Purina, whatever you sell, I'd guarantee you to work on your Bird here every once in a while. No labor charges.'

Donovan had been delighted and the two of them had shaken on it. Joe had called Ray Crowell and said he'd decided to take the pup if Crowell was still agreeable. Crowell was, and when his son's birthday rolled around that year, Joe had astounded both Brett and Charity by putting the squirming, wriggling puppy into the boy's arms.

'Thank you, Daddy, thank you, thank you!' Brett had cried, hugging his father and covering his cheeks with kisses.

'Sure,' Joe said. 'But you take care of him, Brett. He's your dog, not mine. I guess if he does any piddling or crapping around, I'll take him out in back of the barn and shoot him for a stranger.'

'I will, Daddy . . . I promise!'

He had kept his promise, pretty much, and on the few occasions he forgot, either Charity or Joe himself had cleaned up after the dog with no comment. And Joe had discovered it was impossible to stand aloof from Cujo; as he grew (and he grew damned fast, developing into exactly the sort of eating machine Joe had foreseen), he simply took his place in the Camber family. He was one of your bona fide good dogs.

He had house-trained quickly and completely . . . and now this. Joe turned around, hands stuffed in his pockets, frowning. No sign of Cuje anywhere.

He stepped outside and whistled again. Damn dog was maybe down in the creek, cooling off. Joe wouldn't blame him. It felt like eighty-five in the shade already. But the dog would come back soon, and when he did, Joe would rub his nose in that mess. He would be sorry to do it if Cujo had made it because he was missing his people, but you couldn't let a dog get away with —

A new thought came. Joe slapped the flat of his hand against his forehead. Who was going to feed Cujo while he and Gary were gone?

He supposed he could fill up that old pig trough behind the barn with Gaines Meal — they had just about a long ton of the stuff stored downstairs in the cellar — but it would get soggy if it rained. And if he left it in the house or the barn, Cujo might just decide to up and crap on the floor again. Also, when it came to food, Cujo was a big cheerful glutton. He would eat half the first day, half the second day, and then walk around hungry until Joe came back.

'Shit,' he muttered.

The dog wasn't coming. Knew Joe would have found his mess and ashamed of it, probably. Cujo was a bright dog, as dogs went, and knowing (or guessing) such a thing was by no means out of his mental reach.

Joe got a shovel and cleaned up the mess. He spilled a capful of the industrial cleaner he kept handy on the spot, mopped it, and rinsed it off with a bucket of water from the faucet at the back of the garage.

That done, he got out the small spiral notebook in which he kept his work schedule and looked it over. Richie's International Harvester was taken care of – that chainfall surely did take the ouch out of pulling a motor. He had pushed the transmission job back with no trouble; the teacher had been every bit as easygoing as Joe had expected. He had another half a dozen jobs lined up, all of them minor.

He went into the house (he had never bothered to have a phone installed in his garage; they charged you dear for that extra line, he had told Charity) and began to call people and tell them he would be out of town for a few days on business. He would get to most of them before they got around to taking their problems somewhere else. And if one or two couldn't wait to get their new fanbelt or radiator hose, piss on em.

The calls made, he went back out to the barn. The last item before he was free was an oil change and a ring job. The owner had promised to come by and pick up his car by noon. Joe got to work, thinking how quiet the home place seemed with Charity and Brett gone . . . and with Cujo gone. Usually the big Saint Bernard would lie in the patch of shade by the big sliding garage door, panting, watching Joe as he worked. Sometimes Joe would talk to him, and Cujo always looked as if he was listening carefully.

Been deserted, he thought semi-resentfully. Been deserted by all three. He glanced at the spot where Cujo had messed and shook his head again in a puzzled sort of disgust. The question of what he was going to do about feeding the dog recurred to him and he came up empty again. Well, later on he would give the old Pervert a call. Maybe he would be able to think of someone – some kid – who would be willing to come up and give Cujo his chow for a couple-three days.

He nodded his head and turned the radio on to WOXO in Norway, turning it up loud. He didn't really hear it unless the news or the ball scores were on, but it was company. Especially with everyone gone. He got to work. And when the phone in the house rang a dozen or so times, he never heard it.

Tad Trenton was in his room at midmorning, playing with his trucks. He had accumulated better than thirty of them in his four years on the earth, an extensive collection which ranged from the seventy-nine-cent plastic jobs that his dad sometimes bought him at the Bridgton Pharmacy where he always got *Time* magazine on Wednesday evenings (you had to play carefully with the seventy-nine-cent trucks because they were MADE IN TAIWAN and had a tendency to fall apart) to the flagship of his line, a great yellow Tonka bulldozer that came up to his knees when he was standing.

He had various 'men' to stick into the cabs of his trucks. Some of them were round-headed guys scrounged from his PlaySkool toys. Others were soldiers. Not a few were what he called 'Star Wars Guys'. These included Luke, Han Solo, the Imperial Creep (aka Darth Vader), a Bespin Warrior, and Tad's absolute favorite, Greedo. Greedo always got to drive the Tonka dozer.

Sometimes he played *Dukes of Hazzard* with his trucks, sometimes *B. J. and the Bear*, sometimes Cops and Moonshiners (his dad and mom had taken him to see *White Lightning* and *White Line Fever* on a double bill at the Norway Drive-In and Tad had been *very* impressed), sometimes a game he had made up himself. That one was called Ten-Truck Wipe-Out.

But the game he played most often – and the one he was playing now – had no name. It consisted of digging the trucks and the 'men' out of his two playchests and lining the trucks up one by one in diagonal parallels, the men inside, as if they were all slant-parked on a street that only Tad could see. Then he would run them to the other side of the room one by one, very slowly, and line them up on that side bumper-to-bumper. Sometimes he would repeat this cycle ten or fifteen times, for an hour or more, without tiring.

Both Vic and Donna had been struck by this game. It was a little disturbing to watch Tad set up this constantly repeating, almost ritualistic pattern. They had both asked him on occasion what the attraction was, but Tad did not have the vocabulary to explain. *Dukes of Hazzard*, Cops and Moonshiners, and Ten-Truck Wipe-Out were simple crash-and-bash games. The no-name game was quiet, peaceful, tranquil, ordered. If his vocabulary *had* been big enough, he might have told his parents it was his way of saying Om and thereby opening the doors to contemplation and reflection.

Now as he played it, he was thinking something was wrong.

His eyes went automatically – unconsciously – to the door of his closet, but the problem wasn't there. The door was firmly latched, and since the Monster Words, it never came open. No, the something wrong was something else.

He didn't know exactly what it was, and wasn't sure he even wanted to know. But, like Brett Camber, he was already adept at reading the currents of the parental river upon which he floated. Just lately he had gotten the feeling that there were black eddies, sandbars, maybe deadfalls hidden just below the surface. There could be rapids. A waterfall. Anything.

Things weren't right between his mother and father.

It was in the way they looked at each other. The way they talked to each other. It was on their faces and behind their faces. In their thoughts.

He finished changing a slant-parked row of trucks on one side of the room to bumper-to-bumper traffic on the other side and got up and went to the window. His knees hurt a little because he had been playing the no-name game for quite a while. Down below in the back yard his mother was hanging out clothes. Half an hour earlier she had tried to call the man who could fix the Pinto, but the man wasn't home. She waited a long time for someone to say hello and then slammed the phone down, mad. And his mom hardly ever got mad at little things like that.

As he watched, she finished hanging the last two sheets. She looked at them . . . and her shoulders kind of sagged. She went to stand by the apple tree beyond the double clothesline, and Tad knew from her posture – her legs spread, her head down, her shoulders in slight motion – that she was crying. He watched her for a little while and then crept back to his trucks. There was a hollow place in the pit of his stomach. He missed his father already, missed him badly, but this was worse.

He ran the trucks slowly back across the room, one by one, returning them to their slant-parked row. He paused once when the screen door slammed. He thought she would call to him, but she didn't. There was the sound of her steps crossing the kitchen, then the creak of her special chair in the living room as she sat down. But the TV didn't go on. He thought of her just sitting down there, just . . . *sitting* . . . and dismissed the thought, quickly from his mind.

He finished the row of trucks. There was Greedo, his best, sitting in the cab of the dozer, looking blankly out of his round black eyes at the door of Tad's closet. His eyes were wide, as if he had seen something there, something so scary it had shocked his eyes wide, something really gooshy, something *horrible*, something that was coming –

Tad glanced nervously at the closet door. It was firmly latched.

Still, he was tired of the game. He put the trucks back in his playchest, clanking them loudly on purpose so she would know he was getting ready to come down and watch *Gunsmoke* on Channel 8. He started for the door and then paused, looking at the Monster Words, fascinated.

> *Monsters, stay out of this room!*
> *You have no business here.*

He knew them by heart. He liked to look at them, read them by rote, look at his daddy's printing.

Nothing will touch Tad, or hurt Tad, all this night.
You have no business here.

On a sudden, powerful impulse, he pulled out the pushpin that held the paper to the wall. He took the Monster Words carefully — almost reverently — down. He folded the sheet of paper up and put it carefully into the back pocket of his jeans. Then, feeling better than he had all day, he ran down the stairs to watch Marshal Dillon and Festus.

That last fellow had come and picked up his car at ten minutes of twelve. He had paid cash, which Joe had tucked away into his old greasy wallet, reminding himself to go down to the Norway Savings and pick up another five hundred before he and Gary took off.

Thinking of taking off made him remember Cujo, and the problem of who was going to feed him. He got into his Ford wagon and drove down to Gary Pervier's at the foot of the hill. He parked in Gary's driveway. He started up the porch steps, and the hail that had been rising in his throat died there. He went back down and bent over the steps.

There was blood there.

Joe touched it with his fingers. It was tacky but not completely dry. He stood up again, a little worried but not yet unduly so. Gary might have been drunk and stumbled with a glass in his hand. He wasn't really worried until he saw the way the rusty bottom panel of the screen door was crashed in.

'Gary?'

There was no answer. He found himself wondering if someone with a grudge had maybe come hunting ole Gary. Or maybe some tourist had come asking directions and Gary had picked the wrong day to tell someone he could take a flying fuck at the moon.

He climbed the steps. There were more splatters of blood on the boards of the porch.

'Gary?' he called again, and suddenly wished for the weight of his shotgun cradled over his right arm. But if someone had punched Gary out, bloodied his nose, or maybe popped out a few of the old Pervert's remaining teeth, that person was gone now, because the only car in the yard other than Joe's rusty Ford LTD wagon was Gary's white '66 Chrysler hardtop. And you just didn't walk out to Town Road No. 3. Gary Pervier's was seven miles from town, two miles off the Maple Sugar Road that led back to Route 117.

More likely he just cut himself, Joe thought. But Christ, I hope it was just his hand he cut and not his throat.

Joe opened the screen door. It squealed on its hinges. 'Gary?'

Still no answer. There was a sickish-sweet smell in here that he didn't like, but at first he thought it was the honeysuckle. The stairs to the second floor went up on his left. Straight ahead was the hall to the kitchen, the living room doorway opening off the hall about halfway down on the right.

There was something on the hall floor, but it was too dark for Joe to make it out. Looked like an endtable that had been knocked over, or something like that . . . but so far as Joe knew, there wasn't now and never had been any furniture in Gary's front hall. He leaned his lawn chairs in here when it rained, but there hadn't been any rain for two weeks. Besides, the chairs had been out by Gary's Chrysler in their accustomed places. By the honeysuckle.

Only that smell wasn't honeysuckle. It was blood. A whole lot of blood. And that was no tipped-over endtable.

Joe hurried down to the shape, his heart hammering in his ears. He knelt by it, and a sound like a squeak escaped his throat. Suddenly the air in the hall seemed too hot and close. It seemed to be strangling him. He turned away from Gary, one hand cupped over his mouth. Someone had murdered Gary. Someone had —

He forced himself to look back. Gary lay in a pool of his own blood. His eyes glared sightlessly up at the hallway ceiling. His throat had been opened. Not just opened, dear God, it looked as if it had been *chewed* open.

This time there was no struggle with his gorge. This time he simply let everything come up in a series of hopeless choking sounds. Crazily, the back of his mind had turned to Charity with childish resentment. Charity had gotten *her* trip, but he wasn't going to get his. He wasn't going to get his because some crazy bastard had done a Jack the Ripper act on poor old Gary Pervier and –

– and he had to call the police. Never mind all the rest of it. Never mind the way the ole Pervert's eyes were glaring up at the ceiling in the shadows, the way the sheared-copper smell of his blood mingled with the sickish-sweet aroma of the honeysuckle.

He got to his feet and staggered down toward the kitchen. He was moaning deep in his throat but was hardly aware of it. The phone was on the wall in the kitchen. He had to call the State Police, Sheriff Bannerman, someone –

He stopped in the doorway. His eyes widened until they actually seemed to be bulging from his head. There was a pile of dog droppings in the doorway of the kitchen . . . and he knew from the size of the pile whose dog had been here.

'Cujo,' he whispered. 'Oh my God, Cujo's gone rabid!'

He thought he heard a sound behind him and he whirled around, hair freezing up from the back of his neck. The hallway was empty except for Gary, Gary who had said the other night that Joe couldn't sic Cujo on a yelling nigger, Gary with his throat laid open all the way to the knob of his backbone.

There was no sense in taking chances. He bolted back down the hallway, skidding momentarily in Gary's blood, leaving an elongated footmark behind him. He moaned again, but when he had shut the heavy inner door he felt a little better.

He went back to the kitchen, shying his way around Gary's body, and looked in, ready to pull the kitchen-hallway door shut quickly if Cujo was in there. Again he wished distractedly for the comforting weight of his shotgun over his arm.

The kitchen was empty. Nothing moved except the curtains, stirring in a sluggish breeze which whispered through the open windows. There was a smell of dead vodka bottles. It was sour, but better than that . . . that other smell. Sunlight lay on the faded hilly linoleum in orderly patterns. The phone, its once-white plastic case now dulled with the grease of many bachelor meals and cracked in some long-ago drunken stumble, hung on the wall as always.

Joe went in and closed the door firmly behind him. He crossed to the two open windows and saw nothing in the tangle of the back yard except the rusting corpses of the two cars that had predated Gary's Chrysler. He closed the windows anyway.

He went to the telephone, pouring sweat in the explosively hot kitchen. The book was hanging beside the phone on a hank of hayrope. Gary had made the hole through the book where the hayrope was threaded with Joe's drillpunch about a year ago, drunk as a lord and proclaiming that he didn't give a shit.

Joe picked the book up and then dropped it. The book thudded against the wall. His hands felt too heavy. His mouth was slimy with the taste of vomit. He got hold of the book again and opened it with a jerk that nearly tore off the cover. He could have dialed O, or 555-1212, but in his shock he never thought of it.

The sound of his rapid, shallow breathing, his racing heart, and the riffle of the thin phonebook pages masked a faint noise from behind him: the low creak of the cellar door as Cujo nosed it open.

He had gone down cellar after killing Gary Pervier. The light in the kitchen had been too bright, too dazzling. It sent white-hot shards of agony into his decomposing brain. The cellar door had been ajar and he had padded jerkily down the stairs into the blessedly cool dark. He had fallen asleep next to Gary's old Army footlocker, and the breeze from the open windows had swung the cellar door most of the way closed. The breeze had not been quite strong enough to latch the door.

The moans, the sound of Joe retching, the thumpings and slammings as Joe ran down the hall to close the front door — these things had awakened him to his pain again. His pain and his dull, ceaseless fury. Now he stood behind Joe in the dark doorway. His head was lowered. His eyes were nearly scarlet. His thick, tawny fur was matted with gore and drying mud. Foam drizzled from his mouth in a lather, and his teeth showed constantly because his tongue was beginning to swell.

Joe had found the Castle Rock section of the book. He got the C's and ran a shaking finger down to CASTLE ROCK MUNICIPAL SERVICES in a boxed-off section halfway down one column. There was the number for the sheriff's office. He reached up a finger to begin dialing, and that was when Cujo began to growl deep in his chest.

All the nerves seemed to run out of Joe Camber's body. The telephone book slithered from his fingers and thudded against the wall again. He turned slowly toward that growling sound. He saw Cujo standing in the cellar doorway.

'Nice doggy,' he whispered huskily, and spit ran down his chin.

He made helpless water in his pants, and the sharp, ammoniac reek of it struck Cujo's nose like a keen slap. He sprang. Joe lurched to one side on legs that felt like stilts and the dog struck the wall hard enough to punch through the wallpaper and knock out plaster dust in a white, gritty puff. Now the dog wasn't growling; a series of heavy, grinding sounds escaped him, sounds more savage than any barks.

Joe backed toward the rear door. His feet tangled in one of the kitchen chairs. He pinwheeled his arms madly for balance, and might have gotten it back, but before that could happen Cujo bore down on him, a bloodstreaked killing machine with strings of foam flying backward from his jaws. There was a green, swampy stench about him.

'*Oh m'God lay off'n me!*' Joe Camber shrieked.

He remembered Gary. He covered his throat with one hand and tried to grapple with Cujo with the other. Cujo backed off momentarily, snapping, his muzzle wrinkled back in a great humorless grin that showed teeth like a row of slightly yellowed fence spikes. Then he came again.

And this time he came for Joe Camber's balls.

'Hey kiddo, you want to come grocery shopping with me? And have lunch at Mario's?'

Tad got up. 'Yeah! Good!'

'Come on, then.'

She had her bag over her shoulder and she was wearing jeans and a faded blue shirt. Tad thought she was looking very pretty. He was relieved to see there were no sign of her tears, because when she cried, *he* cried. He knew it was a baby thing to do, but he couldn't help it.

He was halfway to the car and she was slipping behind the wheel when he remembered that her Pinto was all screwed up.

'Mommy?'

'What? Get in.'

But he hung back a little, afraid. 'What if the car goes kerflooey?'

'Ker —?' She was looking at him, puzzled, and then he saw by her exasperated expression that she had forgotten all about the car being screwed up. He had reminded her, and now she was unhappy again. Was it the Pinto's fault, or was it his? He didn't know, but the guilty feeling inside said it was his. Then her face smoothed out and she gave him a crooked little smile that he knew well enough to feel it was his special smile, the one she saved just for him. He felt better.

'We're just going into town, Tadder. If Mom's ole blue Pinto packs it in, we'll just have to blow two bucks on Castle Rock's one and only taxi getting back home. Right?'

'Oh, Okay.' He got in and managed to pull the door shut.

She watched him closely, ready to move at an instant, and Tad supposed she was thinking about last Christmas, when he had shut the door on his foot and had to wear an Ace bandage for about a month. But he had been just a baby then, and now he was four years old. Now he was a big boy. He knew that was true because his dad had told him. He smiled at his mother to show her the door had been no problem, and she smiled back.

'Did it latch tight?'

'Tight,' Tad agreed, so she opened it and slammed it again, because moms didn't believe you unless you told them something bad, like you spilled the bag of sugar reaching for the peanut butter or broke a window while trying to throw a rock all the way over the garage roof.

'Hook your belt,' she said, getting in herself again. 'When that needle valve or whatever it is messes up, the car jerks a lot.'

A little apprehensively, Tad buckled his seat belt and harness. He sure hoped they weren't going to have an accident, like in Ten-Truck Wipe Out. Even more than that, he hoped Mom wouldn't cry.

'Flaps down?' she asked, adjusting invisible goggles.

'Flaps down,' he agreed, grinning. It was just a game they played.

'Runway clear?'

'Clear.'

'Then here we go.' She keyed the ignition and backed down the driveway. A moment later they were headed for town.

After about a mile they both relaxed. Up to that point Donna had been sitting bolt upright behind the wheel and Tad had been doing the same in the passenger bucket. But the Pinto ran so smoothly that it might have popped off the assembly line only yesterday.

They went to the Agway Market and Donna bought forty dollars' worth of groceries, enough to keep them the ten days that Vic would be gone. Tad insisted on a fresh box of Twinkles, and would have added Cocoa Bears if Donna had let him. They got shipments of the Sharp cereals regularly, but they were currently out. It was a busy trip, but she still had time for bitter reflection as she waited in the checkout lane (Tad sat in the cart's child seat, swinging his legs nonchalantly) on how much three lousy bags of groceries went for these days. It wasn't just depressing; it was scary. That thought led her to the frightening possibility — *probability*, her mind whispered — that Vic and Roger might actually lose the Sharp account and, as a result of that, the agency itself. What price groceries then?

She watched a fat woman with a lumpy behind packed into avocado-colored slacks pull a food-stamp booklet out of her purse, saw the checkout girl roll her eyes at the girl running the next register, and felt sharp rat-teeth of panic gnawing at her belly. It couldn't come to that, could it? *Could it?* No, of course not. Of course not. They would go back to New York first, they would —

She didn't like the way her thoughts were speeding up, and she pushed the whole mess resolutely away before it could grow to avalanche size and bury her in another deep depression. Nex time she wouldn't have to buy coffee, and that would knock three bucks off the bill.

She trundled Tad and the groceries out to the Pinto and put the bags into the hatchback and Tad into the passenger bucket, standing there and listening to make sure the door latched, wanting to close the door herself but understanding it was something he felt he had to do. It was a big-boy thing. She had almost had a heart attack last December when Tad shut his foot in the door. How he had *screamed*! She had nearly fainted . . . and then Vic had been there, charging out of the house in his bathrobe, splashing out fans of driveway slush with his bare feet. And she had let him take over and be competent, which she hardly ever was in emergencies; she usually just turned to mush. He had checked to make sure the foot wasn't broken, then had changed quickly and driven them to the emergency room at the Bridgton hospital.

Groceries stowed, likewise Tad, she got behind the wheel

and started the Pinto. *Now* it'll fuck up, she thought, but the Pinto took them docilely up the street to Mario's, which purveyed delicious pizza stuffed with enough calories to put a spare tire on a lumberjack. She did a passable job of parallel parking, ending up only eighteen inches or so from the curb, and took Tad in, feeling better than she had all day. Maybe Vic had been wrong; maybe it had been bad gas or dirt in the fuel line and it had finally worked its way out of the car's system. She hadn't looked forward to going out to Joe Camber's Garage. It was too far out in the boonies (what Vic always referred to with high good humor as East Galoshes Corners – but of course he could afford high good humor, he was a *man*), and she had been a little scared of Camber the one time she had met him. He was the quintessential back-country Yankee, grunting instead of talking, sullen-faced. And the dog . . . what was his name? Something that sounded Spanish. Cujo, that was it. The same name William Wolfe of the SLA had taken, although Donna found it impossible to believe that Joe Camber had named his Saint Bernard after a radical robber of banks and kidnapper of rich young heiresses. She doubted if Joe Camber had ever heard of the Symbionese Liberation Army. The dog had seemed friendly enough, but it had made her nervous to see Tad patting that monster – the way it made her nervous to stand and watch him close the car door himself. Cujo looked big enough to swallow the likes of Tad in two bites.

She ordered Tad a hot pastrami sandwich because he didn't care much for pizza – kid sure didn't get that from *my* side of the family, she thought – and a pepperoni and onion pizza with double cheese for herself. They ate at one of the tables overlooking the road. My breath will be fit to knock over a horse, she thought. and then realised it didn't matter. She had managed to alienate both her husband and the guy who came to visit in the course of the last six weeks or so.

That brought depression cruising her way again, and once again she forced it back . . . but her arms were getting a little tired.

They were almost home and Springsteen was on the radio when the Pinto started doing it again.

At first there was a small jerk. That was followed by a bigger one. She began to pump the accelerator gently; sometimes that helped.

'Mommy?' Tad asked, alarmed.

'It's all right, Tad,' she said, but it wasn't. The Pinto began to jerk hard, throwing them both against their seatbelts with enough force to lock the harness clasps. The engine chopped and roared. A bag fell over in the hatchback compartment, spilling cans and bottles. She heard something break.

'*You goddamned shitting thing!*' she cried in an exasperated fury. She could see their house just below the brow of the hill, mockingly close, but she didn't think the Pinto was going to get them there.

Frightened as much by her shout as by the car's spasms, Tad began to cry, adding to her confusion and upset and anger.

'*Shut up!*' she yelled at him. '*Oh Christ, just shut up, Tad!*'

He began to cry harder, and his hand went to the bulge in his back pocket, where the Monster Words, folded up to packet size, were stowed away. Touching them made him feel a little bit better. Not much, but a little.

Donna decided she was going to have to pull over and stop; there was nothing else for it. She began to steer toward the shoulder, using the last of her forward motion to get there. They could use Tad's wagon to pull the groceries up to the house and then decide what to do about the Pinto. Maybe –

Just as the Pinto's offside wheels crunched over the sandy gravel at the edge of the road, the engine backfired twice and then the jerks smoothed out as they had done on previous occasions. A moment later she was scooting up to the driveway of the house and turning in. She drove uphill, shifted to park, pulled the emergency brake, turned off the motor, leaned over the wheel, and cried.

'Mommy?' Tad said miserably. *Don't cry no more*, he

tried to add, but he had no voice and he could only mouth the words soundlessly, as if struck dumb by laryngitis. He looked at her only, wanting to comfort, not knowing just how it was done. Comforting her was his daddy's job, not his, and suddenly he hated his father for being somewhere else. The depth of his emotion both shocked and frightened him, and for no reason at all he suddenly saw his closet door coming open and spilling out a darkness that stank of something low and bitter.

At last she looked up, her face puffy. She found a handkerchief in her purse and wiped her eyes. 'I'm sorry, honey. I wasn't really shouting at you. I was shouting at this . . . this *thing*.' She struck the steering wheel with her hand, hard. 'Ow!' She put the edge of her hand in her mouth and then laughed a little. It wasn't a happy laugh.

'Guess it's still kerflooey,' Tad said glumly.

'I guess it is,' she agreed, almost unbearably lonesome for Vic. 'Well, let's get the things in. We got the supplies anyway, Cisco.'

'Right, Pancho,' he said. 'I'll get my wagon.'

He brought his Redball Flyer down and Donna loaded the three bags into it, after repacking the bag that had fallen over. It had been a ketchup bottle that had shattered. You'd figure it, wouldn't you? Half a bottle of Heinz had puddled out on the powder-blue pile carpeting of the hatchback. It looked as if someone had committed hara-kiri back there. She supposed she could sop up the worst of it with a sponge, but the stain would still show. Even if she used a rug shampoo she was afraid it would show.

She tugged the wagon up to the kitchen door at the side of the house while Tad pushed. She lugged the groceries in and was debating whether to put them away or clean up the ketchup before it could set when the phone rang. Tad was off for it like a sprinter at the sound of a gun. He had gotten very good at answering the phone.

'Yes, who is it please?'

He listened, grinned, then held out the phone to her.

Figures, she thought. Someone who'll want to talk for two

hours about nothing. To Tad she said, 'Do you know who it is, hon?'

'Sure,' he said. 'It's Dad.'

Her heart began to beat more rapidly. She took the phone from Tad and said, 'Hello? Vic?'

'Hi, Donna.' It was his voice all right, but so reserved . . . so *careful*. It gave her a deep sinking feeling that she didn't need on top of everything else.

'Are you all right?' she asked.

'Sure.'

'I just thought you'd call later. If at all.

'Well, we went right over to Image-Eye. They did all the Sharp Cereal Professor spots, and what do you think? They can't find the frigging kinescopes. Roger's ripping his hair out by the roots.'

'Yes,' she said, nodding. 'He hates to be off schedule, doesn't he?'

'That's an understatement.' He sighed deeply. 'So I just thought, while they were looking . . .'

He trailed off vaguely, and her feelings of depression – her feelings of *sinking* – feelings that were so unpleasant and yet so childishly passive, turned to a more active sense of fear. Vic *never* trailed off like that, not even if he was being distracted by stuff going on at his end of the wire. She thought of the way he had looked on Thursday night, so ragged and close to the edge.

'Vic, *are* you all right?' She could hear the alarm in her voice and knew he must hear it too; even Tad looked up from the coloring book with which he had sprawled out on the hall floor, his eyes bright, a tight little frown on his small forehead.

'Yeah,' he said. 'I just started to say that I thought I'd call now, while they're rummaging around. Won't have a chance later tonight, I guess. How's Tad?'

'Tad's fine.'

She smiled at Tad and then tipped him a wink. Tad smiled back, the lines on his forehead smoothed out, and he went back to his coloring. *He sounds tired and I'm not going to lay all that shit about the car on him*, she thought, and then found herself going right ahead and doing it anyway.

She heard the familiar whine of self-pity creeping into her voice and struggled to keep it out. Why was she even telling him all of this, for heaven's sake? He sounded like he was falling apart, and she was prattling on about her Pinto's carburetor and a spilled bottle of ketchup.

'Yeah, it sounds like the needle valve, okay,' Vic said. He actually sounded a little better now. A little less down. Maybe because it was a problem which mattered so little in the greater perspective of things which they had now been forced to deal with. 'Couldn't Joe Camber get you in today?'

'I tried him but he wasn't home.'

'He probably was, though,' Vic said. 'There's no phone in his garage. Usually his wife or his kid runs his messages out to him. Probably they were out someplace.'

'Well, he still might be gone –'

'Sure,' Vic said. 'But I really doubt it, babe. If a human being could actually put down roots, Joe Camber's the guy that would do it.'

'Should I just take a chance and drive out there?' Donna asked doubtfully. She was thinking of the empty miles along 117 and the Maple Sugar Road . . . and all that was *before* you got to Camber's road, which was so far out it didn't even have a name. And if that needle valve chose a stretch of that desolation in which to pack up for good, it would just make another hassle.

'No, I guess you better not,' Vic said. 'He's probably there . . . unless you really need him. In which case he'd be gone. Catch-22.' He sounded depressed.

'Then what should I do?'

'Call the Ford dealership and tell them you want a tow.'

'But –'

'No, you have to. If you try to drive twenty-two miles over to South Paris, it'll pack up on you for sure. And if you explain the situation in advance, they might be able to get you a loaner. Barring that, they'll lease you a car.'

'Lease . . . Vic, isn't that expensive?'

'Yeah,' he said.

She thought again that it was wrong of her to be dumping all this on him. He was probably thinking that she wasn't capable of anything . . . except maybe screwing the local furniture refinisher. She was fine at that. Hot salt tears, partly anger, partly self-pity, stung her eyes again. 'I'll take care of it,' she said, striving desperately to keep her voice normal, light. Her elbow was propped on the wall and one hand was over her eyes. 'Not to worry.'

'Well, I – oh, shit, there's Roger. He's dust up to his neck, but they got the kinescopes. Put Tad on for a second, would you?'

Frantic questions backed up in her throat. Was it all right? Did he think it could be all right? Could they get back to go and start again? Too late. No time. She had spent the time gabbing about the car. Dumb broad, stupid quiff.

'Sure,' she said. 'He'll say good-bye for both of us. And . . . Vic?'

'What?' He sounded impatient now, pressed for time.

'I love you,' she said, and then before he could reply, she added: 'Here's Tad.' She gave the phone to Tad quickly, almost conking him on the head with it, and went through the house to the front porch, stumbling over a hassock and sending it spinning, seeing everything through a prism of tears.

She stood on the porch looking out at 117, clutching her elbows, struggling to get herself under control – control, dammit, *control* – and it was amazing, wasn't it, how bad you could hurt when there was nothing physically wrong.

Behind her she could hear the soft murmur of Tad's voice, telling Vic they had eaten at Mario's, that Mommy had her favorite Fat Pizza and the Pinto had been okay until they were almost home. Then he was telling Vic that he loved him. Then there was the soft sound of the phone being hung up. Contact broken.

Control.

At last she felt as if she had some. She went back into the kitchen and began putting away the groceries.

Charity Camber stepped down from the Greyhound bus at quarter past three that afternoon. Brett was right at her heels. She was clutching the strap of her purse spasmodically. She was suddenly, irrationally afraid that she would not recognize Holly. Her sister's face, held in her mind like a photograph all these years (The Younger Sister Who Had Married Well), had gone suddenly and mysteriously out of her mind, leaving only a fogged blank where the picture should have been.

'You see her?' Brett asked as they alighted. He looked around at the Stratford bus depot with bright interest and no more. There was certainly no fear in his face.

'Give me a chance to look around!' Charity said sharply. 'Probably she's in the coffee shop or –'

'Charity?'

She turned and there was Holly. The picture held in her memory came flooding back, but it was now a transparency overlying the real face of the woman standing by the Space Invaders game. Charity's first thought was that Holly was wearing *glasses* – how funny! Her second, shocked, was that Holly had wrinkles – not many, but there could be no question about what they were. Her third thought was not precisely a thought at all. It was an image, as clear, true, and heartbreaking as a sepia-toned photograph: Holly leaping into old man Seltzer's cowpond in her underpants, pigtails standing up against the sky, thumb and forefinger of left hand pinching her nostrils closed for comic effect. *No glasses then*, Charity thought, and pain came to her then, and it squeezed her heart.

Standing at Holly's sides, looking shyly at her and Brett, were a boy of about five and a girl who was perhaps two and a half. The little girl's bulgy pants spoke of diapers beneath. Her stroller stood off to one side.

'Hi, Holly,' Charity said, and her voice was so thin she could hardly hear it.

The wrinkles were small. They turned upward, the way their mother had always said the good ones did. Her dress was dark blue, moderately expensive. The pendant she wore

was either a very good piece of costume jewelry or a very
small emerald.

There was a moment then. Some space of time. In it,
Charity felt her heart fill with a joy so fierce and complete
that she knew there could never be any real question about
what this trip had or had not cost her. For now she was *free*,
her son was free. This was her sister and those children were
her kin, not pictures but real.

Laughing and crying a little, the two women stepped
toward each other, hesitantly at first, then quickly. They
embraced. Brett stood where he was. The little girl, maybe
scared, went to her mother and wrapped a hand firmly
around the hem of her dress, perhaps to keep her mother and
this strange lady from flying off together.

The little boy stared at Brett, then advanced. He was
wearing Tuffskin jeans and a T-shirt with the words HERE
COMES TROUBLE printed on it.

'You're my cousin Brett,' the kid said.

'Yeah.'

'My name's Jim. Just like my dad.'

'Yeah.'

'You're from Maine,' Jim said. Behind him, Charity and
Holly were talking rapidly, interrupting each other and
laughing at their hurry to tell everything right here in this
grimy bus station south of Milford and north of Bridgeport.

'Yeah, I'm from Maine,' Brett said.

'You're ten.'

'Right.'

'I'm five.'

'Oh yeah?'

'Yeah. But I can beat you up, *Ka-whud!*' He hit Brett in
the belly, doubling him up.

Brett uttered a large and surprised 'Oof!' Both women
gasped.

'*Jimmy!*' Holly cried in a kind of resigned horror.

Brett straightened up slowly and saw his mother watching
him, her face in a kind of suspension.

'Yeah, you can beat me up anytime,' Brett said, and smiled.

And it was all right. He saw from his mother's face that it was all right, and he was glad.

By three thirty Donna had decided to leave Tad with a baby-sitter and try taking the Pinto up to Camber's. She had tried the number again and there had still been no response, but she had reasoned that even if Camber wasn't in his garage, he would be back soon, maybe even by the time she arrived there . . . always assuming she *did* arrive there. Vic told her last week that Camber would probably have some old junker to loan her if it looked like her Pinto was going to be an overnight job. That had really been the deciding factor. But she thought that taking Tad would be wrong. If the Pinto seized up on that back road and she had to take a hike, well, okay. But Tad shouldn't have to do it.

Tad, however, had other ideas.

Shortly after talking to his dad, he had gone up to his room and had stretched out on his bed with a stack of Little Golden Books. Fifteen minutes later he had dozed off, and a dream had come to him, a dream which seemed utterly ordinary but which had a strange, nearly terrifying power. In his dream he saw a big boy throwing a friction-taped baseball up and trying to hit it. He missed twice, three times, four. On the fifth swing he hit the ball . . . and the bat, which had also been taped, shattered at the handle. The boy held the handle for a moment (black tape flapped from it), then bent and picked up the fat of the bat. He looked at it for a moment, shook his head disgustedly, and tossed it into the high grass at the side of the driveway. Then he turned, and Tad saw with a sudden shock that was half dread, half delight, that the boy was himself at ten or eleven. Yes, it was him. He was sure of it.

Then the boy was gone, and there was a grayness. In it he could hear two sounds: creaking swing chains . . . and the faint quacking of ducks. With these sounds and the grayness came a sudden scary feeling that he could not breathe, he was suffocating. *And a man was walking out of the mist . . . a man who wore a black shiny raincoat and held a stop sign on a stick in one hand. He grinned, and his eyes were shiny silver coins. He raised one hand to point at Tad, and he saw with horror it wasn't a hand at all, it was* bones, *and the face inside the shiny vinyl hood of the raincoat wasn't a face at all. It was a skull. It was —*

He jerked awake, his body bathed in sweat that was only in part due to the room's almost explosive heat. He sat up, propped on his elbows, breathing in harsh gasps.

Snick.

The closet door was swinging open. And as it swung open he saw something inside, only for a second and then he was flying for the door which gave on the hall as fast as he could. He saw it only for a second, long enough to tell it wasn't the man in the shiny black raincoat, Frank Dodd, the man who had killed the ladies. Not him. Something else. Something with red eyes like bloody sunsets.

But he could not speak of these things to his mother. So he concentrated on Debbie, the sitter, instead.

He didn't *want* to be left with Debbie, Debbie was mean to him, she always played the record player loud, et cetera, et cetera. When none of this had much effect on his mother, Tad suggested ominously that Debbie might shoot him. When Donna made the mistake of giggling helplessly at the thought of fifteen-year-old myopic Debbie Gehringer shooting anyone, Tad burst into miserable tears and ran into the living room. He needed to tell her that Debbie Gehringer might not be strong enough to keep the monster in his closet — that if dark fell and his mother was not back, it might come out. It might be the man in the black raincoat, or it might be the beast.

Donna followed him, sorry for her laughter, wondering how she could have been so insensitive. The boy's father was gone, and that was upsetting enough. He didn't want to lose sight of his mother for even an hour. And —

And isn't it possible he senses some of what's gone on

between Vic and me? Perhaps even heard . . .?

No, she didn't think that. She *couldn't* think that. It was just the upset in his routine.

The door to the living room was shut. She reached for the knob, hesitated, then knocked softly instead. There was no answer. She knocked again and when there was still no answer, she went in quietly. Tad was lying face down on the couch with one of the back cushions pulled firmly down over his head. It was behavior reserved only for major upsets.

'Tad?'

No answer.

'I'm sorry I laughed.'

His face looked out at her from beneath one edge of the puffy, dove-gray sofa cushion. There were fresh tears on his face. 'Please can't I come?' he asked. 'Don't make me stay here with Debbie, Mom.' Great histrionics, she thought. Great histrionics and blatant coercion. She recognized it (or felt she did) and at the same time found it impossible to be tough . . . partly because her own tears were threatening again. Lately it seemed that there was always a cloudburst just over the horizon.

'Honey, you know the way the Pinto was when we came back from town. It could break down in the middle of East Galoshes Corners and we'd have to walk to a house and use the telephone, maybe a long way –'

'So? I'm a good walker!'

'I know, but you might get scared.'

Thinking of the thing in the closet, Tad suddenly cried out with all his force, '*I will not get scared!*' His hand had gone automatically to the bulge in his hip pocket of his jeans, where the Monster Words were stowed away.

'Don't raise your voice that way, please. It sounds ugly.'

He lowered his voice. 'I won't get scared. I just want to go with you.'

She looked at him helplessly, knowing that she really ought to call Debby Gehringer, feeling that she was being shamelessly manipulated by her four-year-old son. And if she gave in it would be for all the wrong reasons. She thought helplessly, *It's like a chain reaction that doesn't stop anyplace and it's gumming up works I didn't even know existed. O God I wish I was in Tahiti.*

She opened her mouth to tell him, quite firmly and once and for all, that she was going to call Debbie and they could make popcorn together if he was good and that he would have to go to bed right after supper if he was bad and that was the *end* of it. Instead, what came out was, 'All right, you can come. But our Pinto might not make it, and if it doesn't we'll have to walk to a house and have the Town Taxi come and pick us up. And if we *do* have to walk, I don't want to have to listen to you crabbing at me, Tad Trenton.'

'No, I won't —'

'Let me finish. I don't want you crabbing at me or asking me to carry you, because I won't do it. Do we have an understanding?'

'Yeah! Yeah, sure!' Tad hopped off the sofa, all grief forgotten. 'Are we going now?'

'Yes, I guess so. Or . . . I know what. Why don't I make us a snack first? A snack and we'll put some milk in the Thermos bottles, too.'

'In case we have to camp out all *night*?' Tad looked suddenly doubtful again.

'No, honey.' She smiled and gave him a little hug. 'But I still haven't been able to get Mr. Camber on the telephone. Your daddy says it's probably just because he doesn't have a phone in his garage so he doesn't know I'm calling. And his wife and his little boy might be someplace, so —'

'He should have a phone in his garage,' Tad said. 'That's *dumb*.'

'Just don't you tell him that,' Donna said quickly, and Tad shook his head that he wouldn't. 'Anyway, if nobody's there, I thought you and I could have a little snack in the car or maybe on his steps and wait for him.'

Ted clapped his hands. 'Great! Great! Can I take my Snoopy lunchbox?'

'Sure,' Donna said, giving in completely.

She found a box of Keebler figbars and a couple of Slim
Jims (Donna thought they were hideous things, but they
were Tad's all-time favorite snack). She wrapped some
green olives and cucumber slices in foil. She filled Tad's
Thermos with milk and half-filled Vic's big Thermos, the
one he took on camping trips.

For some reason, looking at the food made her uneasy.

She looked at the phone and thought about trying Joe
Camber's number again. Then she decided there was no
sense in it, since they would be going out there either way.
Then she thought of asking Tad again if he wouldn't rather
she called Debbie Gehringer, and then wondered what was
wrong with her — Tad had made himself perfectly clear on
that point.

It was just that suddenly she didn't feel good. Not good at
all. It was nothing she could put her finger on. She looked
around the kitchen as if expecting the source of her unease to
announce itself. It didn't.

'We going, Mom?'

'Yes,' she said absently. There was a noteminder on the
wall by the fridge, and on this she scrawled: *Tad & I have
gone out to J. Camber's garage w/Pinto. Back soon.*

'Ready, Tad?'

'Sure.' He grinned. 'Who's the note for, Mom?'

'Oh, Joanie might drop by with those raspberries,' she
said vaguely. 'Or maybe Alison MacKenzie. She was going
to show me some Amway and Avon stuff.'

'Oh.'

Donna ruffled his hair and they went out together. The
heat hit them like a hammer wrapped in pillows. Buggardly
car probably won't even start, she thought.

But it did.

It was 3:45 P.M.

They drove southeast along Route 117 toward the Maple
Sugar Road, which was about five miles out of town. The
Pinto behaved in exemplary fashion, and if it hadn't been for

the bout of snaps and jerks coming home from the shopping trip, Donna would have wondered what she had bothered making such a fuss about. But there *had* been that bout of the shakes, and so she drove sitting bolt upright again, going no faster than forty, pulling as far to the right as she could when a car came up behind her. And there was a lot of traffic on the road. The summer influx of tourists and vacationers had begun. The Pinto had no air conditioning, so they rode with both windows open.

A Continental with New York plates towing a gigantic trailer with two mopeds on the back swung around them on blind curve, the driver bleating his horn. The driver's wife, a fat woman wearing mirror sunglasses, looked at Donna and Tad with imperious contempt.

'Get stuffed!' Donna yelled, and popped her middle finger up at the fat lady. The fat lady turned away quickly. Tad was looking at his mother just a little nervously, and Donna smiled at him. 'No hassle, big guy. We're going good. Just out-of-state fools.'

'Oh,' Tad said cautiously.

Listen to me, she thought. *The big Yankee. Vic would be proud.*

She had to grin to herself, because everyone in Maine understood that if you moved here from another place, you would be an out-of-stater until you were sent to your grave. And on your tombstone they would write something like HARRY JONES, CASTLE CORNERS, MAINE (*Originally from Omaha, Nebraska*).

Most of the tourists were headed toward 302, where they would turn east to Naples or west toward Bridgton, Fryeburg, and North Conway, New Hampshire, with its alpine slides, cut-rate amusement parks, and tax-free restaurants. Donna and Tad were not going up to the 302 junction.

Although their home overlooked downtown Castle Rock and its picturebook Town Common, woods had closed in on both sides of the road before they were five miles from their own front door. These woods drew back occasionally – a little – to show a lot with with a house or a trailer on it, and as they went farther out, the houses were more often of the type that her father had called 'shanty Irish'. The sun still shone brightly down and there was a good four hours of daylight left, but the emptiness made her feel uneasy again. It was not so bad here, on 117, but once they left the main road –

Their turnoff was marked with a sign saying MAPLE SUGAR ROAD in faded, almost unreadable letters. It had been splintered considerably by kids banging away with .22s and birdshot. This road was two-lane blacktop, bumpy and frost-heaved. It wound past two or three nice houses, two or three not-so-nice houses, and one old and shabby RoadKing trailer sitting on a crumbling concrete foundation. There was a yardful of weeds in front of the trailer. Donna could see cheap-looking plastic toys in the weeds. A sign nailed askew to a tree at the head of the driveway read FREE KITTEN'S. A potbellied kid of maybe two stood in the driveway, his sopping Pamper hanging below his tiny penis. His mouth hung open and he was picking his nose with one finger and his navel with another. Looking at him, Donna felt a helpless chill of gooseflesh.

Stop it! For Christ's sake, what's wrong with you?

The woods closed in around them again. An old '68 Ford Fairlane with a lot of rusty-red primer paint on the hood and around the headlights passed them going the other way. A young kid with a lot of hair was slouched nonchalantly behind the wheel. He wasn't wearing a shirt. The Fairlane was doing maybe eighty. Donna winced. It was the only traffic they saw.

The Maple Sugar Road climbed steadily, and when they passed the occasional field or large garden they were afforded a stunning view of western Maine toward Bridgton and Freyburg. Long Lake glittered in the farthest distance like the sapphire pendant of a fabulously rich woman.

They were climbing another long slope up one of these eroded hills (as advertised, the sides of the road were now lined with dusty, heat-drooping maples) when the Pinto began to buck and jolt again. Donna's breath clogged in her throat and she thought, *Oh come on, oh come on, come on, you cruddy little car, come* on!

Tad shifted uneasily in the passenger bucket and held onto his Snoopy lunchbox a little tighter.

She began to tap the accelerator lightly, her mind repeating the same words over and over like an inarticulate prayer: come *on,* come *on,* come *on.*

'Mommy? Is it –'

'Hush, Tad.'

The jerking grew worse. She pressed the gas pedal harder in frustration – and the Pinto squirted ahead, the engine smoothing out once more.

'Yay!' Tad said, so suddenly and loudly that she jumped 'We're not there yet, Tadder.'

A mile farther along they came to an intersection marked with another wooden sign, this one reading TOWN ROAD NO. 3. Donna turned in, feeling triumphant. As well as she remembered, Camber's place was less than a mile and a half from here. If the Pinto gave up the ghost now, she and Tad could ankle it.

They passed a ramshackle house with a station wagon and a big old rusty white car in the driveway. In her rearview mirror, Donna noticed that the honeysuckle had really gone crazy on the side of the house that would catch most of the sun. A field opened up on their left after they passed the house, and the Pinto began to climb a long, steep hill.

Halfway up, the little car began to labor again. This time it was jerking harder than it ever had before.

'Will it get up, Mommy?'

'Yes,' she said grimly.

The Pinto's speedometer needle dropped from forty to thirty. She dropped the transmission selector lever from drive into the lower range, thinking vaguely that it might help compression or something. Instead, the Pinto began to buck worse than ever. A fusillade of backfires roared through the exhaust pipe, making Tad cry out. Now they were down to fast running speed, but she could see the

Camber house and the red barn that served as his garage.

Flooring the accelerator had helped before. She tried again, and for a moment the engine smoothed out. The speedometer needle crept up from fifteen to twenty. Then it began to shake and shudder once more. Donna tried flooring the gas yet again, but this time, instead of smoothing out, the engine began to fail. The AMP idiot light on the dashboard began to flicker dully, signaling the fact that the Pinto was now on the edge of a stall.

But it didn't matter because the Pinto was now laboring past the Camber mailbox. They were here. There was a package hung over the mailbox lid, and she saw the return address clearly as they passed it: J. C. Whitney & Co.

The information went directly to the back of her mind without stopping. Her immediate attention was focused on getting the car into the driveway. *Let it stall then,* she thought. *He'll have to fix it before he can get in or out.*

The driveway was a little beyond the house. If it had been an uphill driveway all the way, as the Trentons' own was, the Pinto would not have made it. But after a small initial rise, the Cambers' driveway ran either dead level or slightly downhill toward the big converted barn.

Donna shifted into neutral and let what was left of the Pinto's forward motion carry them toward the big barn doors, which stood half open on their tracks. As soon as her foot left the accelerator pedal to tap the brake and stop them, the motor began to hitch again ... but feebly this time. The AMP light pulsed like a slow heartbeat, then brightened. The Pinto stalled.

Tad looked at Donna.

She grinned at him. 'Tad, ole buddy,' she said, 'we have arrived.'

'Yeah,' he said. 'But is anybody home?'

There was a dark green pickup truck parked beside the barn. That was Camber's truck, all right, not someone else's waiting to be fixed. She remembered it from last time. But the lights were off inside. She craned her neck to the left and saw they were off in the house too. And there had been a package hung over the mailbox lid.

The return address on the package had been J. C. Whitney & Co. She knew what that was; her brother had gotten their catalogue in the mail when he was a teenager. They sold auto parts, accessories, customizing equipment. A package for Joe Camber from J. C. Whitney was the most natural thing in the world. But if he was here, he surely would have gotten his mail by now.

Nobody home, she thought dispiritedly, and felt a weary sort of anger at Vic. *He's always home, sure he is, the guy would put down roots in his garage if he could, sure he would, except when I need him.*

'Well, let's go see, anyhow,' she said, opening her door.

'I can't get my seatbelt unhooked,' Tad said, scratching futilely at the buckle release.

'Okay, don't have a hemorrhage, Tad. I'll come around and let you out.'

She got out, slammed her door, and took two steps toward the front of the car, intending to cross in front of the hood to the passenger side and let Tad out of his harness. It would give Camber a chance to come out and see who his company was, if he was here. She somehow didn't relish poking her head in on him unannounced. It was probably foolish, but since that ugly and frightening scene with Steve Kemp in her kitchen, she had become more aware of what it was to be an unprotected woman than she had since she was sixteen and her mother and father had let her begin dating.

The quiet struck her at once. It was hot and so quiet that it was somehow unnerving. There were sounds, of course, but even after several years in Castle Rock, the most she could say about her ears was that they had slowly adapted from 'city ears' to 'town ears'. They were by no means 'country ears' . . . and this was the real country.

She heard birdsong, and the harsher music of a crow somewhere in the long field which stretched down the flank of the hill they had just climbed. There was the sigh of a light breeze, and the oaks that lined the driveway made moving patterns of shadow around her feet. But she could not hear a single car engine, not even the faraway burp of a tractor or a baling machine. City ears and town ears are most closely attuned to man-made sounds; those that nature makes tend to fall outside the tightly drawn net of selective perception. A total lack of such sounds makes for unease.

I'd hear him if he was working in the barn, Donna thought. But the only sounds that registered were her own crunching footfalls on the crushed gravel of the driveway and a low humming sound, barely audible – with no real conscious thought at all, her mind placed it as the hum of a power transformer on one of the poles back by the road.

She reached the front of the hood and started to cross in front of the Pinto, and that was when she heard a new sound. A low, thick growling.

She stopped, her head coming up at once, trying to pinpoint the source of that sound. For a moment she couldn't and she was suddenly terrified, not by the sound itself but by its seeming directionlessness. It was nowhere. It was everywhere. And then some internal radar – survival equipment, perhaps – turned on all the way, and she understood that the growling was coming from inside the garage.

'Mommy?' Tad poked his head out his open window as far as the seatbelt harness would allow. 'I can't get this damn old –'

'*Shhhh!*'

(growling)

She took a tentative step backward, her right hand resting lightly on the Pinto's low hood, her nerves on tripwires as thin as filaments, not panicked but in a state of heightened alertness, thinking: *It didn't growl before.*

Cujo came out of Joe Camber's garage. Donna stared at him, feeling her breath come to a painless and yet complete stop in her throat. It was the same dog. It was Cujo. But –

But oh my

(oh my God)

The dog's eyes settled on hers. They were red and rheumy. They were leaking some viscous substance. The dog seemed to be weeping gummy tears. His tawny coat was caked and matted with mud and —

Blood, is that

(it is it's blood Christ Christ)

She couldn't seem to move. No breath. Dead low tide in her lungs. She had heard about being paralyzed with fear but had never realized it could happen with such totality. There was no contact between her brain and her legs. That twisted gray filament running down the core of her spine had shut off the signals. Her hands were stupid blocks of flesh south of her wrists with no feeling in them. Her urine went. She was unaware of it save for some vague sensation of distant warmth.

And the dog seemed to know. His terrible, thoughtless eyes never left Donna Trenton's wide blue ones. He paced forward slowly, almost languidly. Now he was standing on the barnboards at the mouth of the garage. Now he was on the crushed gravel twenty-five feet away. He never stopped growling. It was a low, purring sound, soothing in its menace. Foam dropped from Cujo's snout. And she couldn't move, not at all.

Then Tad saw the dog, recognized the blood which streaked its fur, and shrieked — a high piercing sound that made Cujo shift his eyes. And that was what seemed to free her.

She turned in a great shambling drunk's pivot, slamming her lower leg against the Pinto's fender and sending a steely bolt of pain up to her hip. She ran back around the hood of the car. Cujo's growl rose to a shattering roar of rage and he charged at her. Her feet almost skidded out from under her in the loose gravel, and she was only able to recover by slamming her arm down on the Pinto's hood. She hit her crazybone and uttered a thin shriek of pain.

The car door was shut. She had shut it herself, automatically, after getting out. The chromed button below the handle suddenly seemed dazzlingly bright, winking arrows of sun into her eyes. *I'll never be able to get that door open and get in and get it shut,* she thought, and the choking realization that she might be about to die rose up in her. *Not enough time. No way.*

She raked the door open. She could hear her breath sobbing in and out of her throat. Tad screamed again, a shrill, breaking sound.

She sat down, almost falling into the driver's seat. She got a glimpse of Cujo coming at her, hindquarters tensing down for the leap that would bring all two hundred pounds of him right into her lap.

She yanked the Pinto's door shut with both hands, reaching over the steering wheel with her right arm, honking the horn with her shoulder. She was just in time. A split second after the door slammed closed there was a heavy, solid thud, as if someone had swung a chunk of stovewood against the side of the car. The dog's barking roars of rage were cut off cleanly, and there was silence.

Knocked himself out, she thought hysterically. *Thank God, thank God for that —*

And a moment later Cujo's foam-covered, twisted face popped up outside her window, only inches away, like a horror-movie monster that has decided to give the audience the ultimate thrill by coming right out of the screen. She could see his huge, heavy teeth. And again there was that swooning, terrible feeling that the dog was looking at *her*, not at a woman who just happened to be trapped in her car with her little boy, but at *Donna Trenton*, as if he had just been hanging around, waiting for her to show up.

Cujo began to bark again, the sound incredibly loud even through the Saf-T-Glas. And suddenly it occurred to her that if she had not automatically rolled her window up as she brought the Pinto to a stop (something her father had insisted on: stop the car, roll up the windows, set the brake, take the keys, lock the car), she would now be minus her throat. Her blood would be on the wheel, the dash, the windshield. That one action, so automatic she could not even really remember performing it.

She screamed.

The dog's terrible face dropped from view.

She remembered Tad and looked around. When she saw him, a new fear invaded her, drilling like a hot needle. He had not fainted, but he was not really conscious, either. He had fallen back against the seat, his eyes dazed and blank. His face was white. His lips had gone bluish at the corners.

'Tad!' She snapped her fingers under his nose, and he blinked sluggishly at the dry sound. 'Tad!'

'Mommy,' he said thickly. 'How did the monster in my closet get out? Is it a dream? Is it my nap?'

'It's going to be all right,' she said, chilled by what he had said about his closet nonetheless. 'It's —'

She saw the dog's tail and the top of its broad back over the hood of the Pinto. It was going around to Tad's side of the car —

And Tad's window wasn't shut.

She jackknifed across Tad's lap, moving with such a hard muscular spasm that she cracked her fingers on the window crank. She turned it as fast as she could, panting, feeling Tad squirming beneath her.

It was three quarters of the way up when Cujo leaped at the window. His muzzle shot in through the closing gap and was forced upward toward the ceiling by the closing window. The sound of his snarling barks filled the small car. Tad shrieked again and wrapped his arms around his head, his forearms crossed over his eyes. He tried to dig his face into Donna's belly, reducing her leverage on the window crank in his blind efforts to get away.

'Momma! Momma! Momma! *Make it stop! Make it go away!*'

Something warm was running across the backs of her hands. She saw with mouting horror that it was mixed slime and blood running from the dog's mouth. Using everything that she had, she managed to force the window crank through another quarter turn .. and then Cujo pulled back. She caught just a glimpse of the Saint Bernard's features, twisted and crazy, a mad caricature of a friendly Saint Bernard's face. Then it dropped back to all fours and she could only see its back.

Now the crank turned easily. She shut the window, then wiped the backs of her hands on her jeans, uttering small cries of revulsion.

(oh Christ oh Mary Mother of God)

Tad had gone back to that dazed state of semiconsciousness again. This time when she snapped her fingers in front of his face there was no reaction.

He's going to have some complexes out of this, oh God yes. Oh sweet Tad, if only I'd left you with Debbie.

She took him by the shoulders and began to shake him gently back and forth.

'Is it my nap?' he asked again.

'No,' she said. He moaned – a low, painful sound that tore at her heart. 'No, but it's all right.. Tad? It's okay. That dog can't get in. The windows are shut now. It can't come in. It can't get us.'

That got through and Tad's eyes cleared a little. 'Then let's go home, Mommy. I don't want to be here.'

'Yes. Yes, we'll –

Like a great tawny projectile, Cujo leaped onto the hood of the Pinto and charged at the windshield, barking. Tad uttered another scream, his eyes bulging, his small hands digging at his cheeks, leaving angry red welts there.

'It can't get us!' Donna shouted at him. 'Do you hear me? It can't get in, Tad!'

Cujo struck the windshield with a muffled thud, bounced back, and scrabbled for purchase on the hood. He left a series of new scratches on the paint. Then he came again.

'*I want to go home!*' Tad screamed.

'Hug me tight, Tadder, and don't worry.'

How insane that sounded . . . but what else was there to say?

Tad buried his face against her breasts just as Cujo struck the windshield again. Foam smeared against the glass as he tried to bite his way through. Those muddled, bleary eyes stared into Donna's. I'm going to pull you to pieces, they said. You and the boy both. Just as soon as I find a way to get into this tin can, I'll eat you alive; I'll be swallowing pieces of you while you're still screaming.

Rabid, she thought. *That dog is rabid.*

With steadily mounting fear, she looked past the dog on the hood and at Joe Camber's parked truck. Had the dog bitten him?

She found the horn buttons and pressed them. The Pinto's horn blared and the dog skittered back, again almost losing its balance. 'Don't like that much, do you?' she shrieked triumphantly at it. 'Hurts your ears, doesn't it?' She jammed the horn down again.

Cujo leaped off the hood.

'Mommy, *pleeease* let's go home.'

She turned the key in the ignition. The motor cranked and cranked and cranked . . . but the Pinto did not start. At last she turned the key off again.

'Honey, we can't go just yet. The car —'

'Yes! Yes! Now! *Right now!*'

Her head began to thud. Big, whacking pains that were in perfect sync with her heartbeat.

'Tad. Listen to me. The car doesn't want to start. It's that needle valve thing. We've got to wait until the engine cools off. It'll go then, I think. We can leave.'

All we have to do is get back out of the driveway and get pointed down the hill. Then it won't matter even if it does stall, because we can coast. If I don't chicken out and hit the brake, I should be able to make it most of the way back to the Maple Sugar Road even with the engine shut down . . . or . . .

She thought of the house at the bottom of the hill, the one with the honeysuckle running wild all over the east side. There were people there. She had seen cars.

People!

She began to use the horn again. Three short blasts, three long blasts, three shorts, over and over, the only Morse she remembered from her two years in the Girl Scouts. They would hear. Even if they didn't understand the message, they would come up to see who was raising hell at Joe Camber's — and why.

Where was the dog? She couldn't see him any more. But it didn't matter. The dog couldn't get in and help would be here shortly.

'Everything's going to be fine,' she told Tad. 'Wait and see.'

A dirty brick building in Cambridge housed the offices of Image-Eye Studios. The business offices were on the fourth floor, a suite of two studios were on the fifth, and a poorly air-conditioned screening room only big enough to hold sixteen seats in rows of four was on the sixth and top floor.

On that early Monday evening Vic Trenton and Roger Breakstone sat in the third row of the screening room, jackets off, ties pulled down. They had watched the kinescopes of the Sharp Cereal Professor commercials five times each. There were exactly twenty of them. Of the twenty, three were the infamous Red Razberry Zingers spots.

The last reel of six spots had finished half an hour ago, and the projectionist had called good night and gone to his evening job, which was running films at the Orson Welles Cinema. Fifteen minutes later Rob Martin, the president of Image-Eye, had bade them a glum good night, adding that his door would be open to them all day tomorrow and Wednesday, if they needed him. He avoided what was in all three of their minds: The door'll be open if you think of something worth talking about.

Rob had every right to look glum. He was a Vietnam vet who had lost a leg in the Tet offensive. He had opened I-E Studios in late 1970 with his disability money and a lot of help from his in-laws. The studio had gasped and struggled along since then, mostly catching crumbs from that well-stocked media table at which the larger Boston studios banqueted. Vic and Roger had been taken with him because he reminded them of themselves, in a way — struggling to

make a go of it, to get up to that fabled corner and turn it.
And, of course, Boston was good because it was an easier
commute than New York.

In the last sixteen months, Image-Eye had taken off. Rob
had been able to use the fact that his studio was doing the
Sharp spots to land other business, and for the first time
things had looked solid. In May, just before the cereal had
hit the fan, he sent Vic and Roger a postcard showing a
Boston T-bus going away. On the back were four lovely
ladies, bent over to show their fannies, which were encased
in designer jeans. Written on the back of the card, tabloid
style, was this meassage: IMAGE-EYE LANDS CONTRACT TO
DO BUTTS FOR BOSTON BUSES; BILLS BIG BUCKS. Funny then.
Not such a hoot now. Since the Zingers fiasco, two clients
(including Cannes-Look Jeans) had canceled their arrangements with I-E, and if Ad Worx lost the Sharp account, Rob
would lose other accounts in addition to Sharp. It had left
him feeling angry and scared . . . emotions Vic understood
perfectly.

They had been sitting and smoking in silence for almost
five minutes when Roger said in a low voice, 'It just makes
me want to puke, Vic. I see that guy sitting on his desk and
looking out at me like butter wouldn't melt in his mouth,
taking a big bite of that cereal with the runny dye in it and
saying, "Nope, nothing wrong here," and I get sick to my
stomach. Physically sick to my stomach. I'm glad the
projectionist had to go. If I watched them one more time, I'd
have to do it with an airsick bag in my lap.'

He stubbed out his cigarette in the ashtray set into the arm
of his chair. He *did* look ill; his face had a yellowish sheen
that Vic didn't like at all. Call it shellshock, combat fatigue,
whatever you wanted, but what you meant was scared
shitless, backed into a rathole. It was looking into the dark
and seeing something that was going to eat you up.

'I kept telling myself,' Roger said, reaching for another
cigarette, 'that I'd see something. You know? *Something*. I
couldn't believe it was as bad as it seemed. But the
cumulative effect of those spots . . . it's like watching Jimmy

Carter saying, "I'll never lie to you".' He took a drag from the new cigarette, grimaced, and stuffed it into the ashtray. 'No wonder George Carlin and Steve Martin and fucking *Saturday Night Live* had a field day. That guy just looks so *sanctimonious* to me now . . .' His voice had developed a sudden watery tremble. He shut his mouth with a snap.

'I've got an idea,' Vic said quietly.

'Yeah, you said something on the plane.' Roger looked at him, but without much hope. 'If you got one, let's hear it.'

'I think the Sharp Cereal Professor has to make one more spot,' Vic said. 'I think we have to convince old man Sharp of that. Not the kid. The old man.'

'What's the old prof gonna sell this time?' Roger asked, twisting open another button on his shirt. 'Rat poison or Agent Orange?'

'Come on, Roger. No one got poisoned.'

'Might as well have,' Roger said, and laughed shrilly. 'Sometimes I wonder if you understand what advertising really is. It's holding a wolf by the tail. Well, we lost our grip on this particular wolf and he's just about to come back on us and eat us whole.'

'Roger –'

'This is the country where it's front-page news when some consumer group weighed the McDonald's Quarter Pounder and found out it weighed a little shy of a quarter pound. Some obscure California magazine publishes a report that a rear-end collision can cause a gas-tank explosion in Pintos, and the Ford Motor Company shakes in its shoes –'

'Don't get on that,' Vic said, laughing a little. 'My wife's got a Pinto. I got problems enough.'

'All I'm saying is that getting the Sharp Cereal Professor to do another spot seems about as shrewd to me as having Richard Nixon do an encore State of the Union address. He's *compromised*, Vic, he's totally blown!' He paused, looking at Vic. Vic looked back at him gravely. 'What do you want him to say?'

'That he's sorry.'

Roger blinked at him glassily for a moment. Then he

threw back his head and cackled. 'That he's sorry. *Sorry?* Oh, dear, that's wonderful. Was that your great idea?

'Hold on, Rog. You're not even giving me a chance. That's not like you.'

'No,' Roger said. 'I guess it's not. Tell me what you mean. But I can't believe you're –'

'Serious? I'm serious, all right. You took the courses. What's the basis of all successful advertising? Why bother to advertise at all?'

'The basis of all successful advertising is that people want to believe. That people sell themselves.

'Yeah. When the Maytag Repairman says he's the loneliest guy in town, people want to believe that there really is such a guy someplace, not doing anything but listening to the radio and maybe jacking off once in a while. People want to believe that their Maytags will *never* need repairs. When Joe DiMaggio comes on and says Mr. Coffee saves coffee, saves money, people want to believe *that*. If –'

'But isn't that why we've got our asses in a crack? They wanted to believe the Sharp Cereal Professor and he let them down. Just like they wanted to believe in Nixon, and *he* –'

'Nixon, Nixon, Nixon!' Vic said, surprised by his own angry vehemence. 'You're getting blinded by that particular comparison, I've heard you make it two hundred times since this thing blew, and it *doesn't fit!*'

Roger was looking at him, stunned.

'Nixon was a crook, he knew he was a crook, and he said he wasn't a crook. The Sharp Cereal Professor said there was nothing wrong with Red Razberry Zingers and there *was* something wrong, but he didn't know it.' Vic leaned forward and pushed his finger gently against Roger's arm, emphasizing. 'There was no breach of faith. He has to say that, Rog. He has to get up in front of the American people and tell them there was no breach of faith. What there was, there was a mistake made by a company which manufactures food dye. The mistake was *not* made by the Sharp Company. He has to say that. And most important of all, he has to say he's sorry that mistake happened and that, although no one was *hurt,* he's sorry people were frightened.'

Roger nodded, then shrugged. 'Yes, I see the thrust of it. But neither the old man or the kid will go for it, Vic. They want to bury the b –'

'Yes, yes, *yes!*' Vic cried, actually making Roger flinch. He jumped to his feet and began to walk jerkily up and down the screening room's short aisle. 'Sure they do, and they're right, he's dead and he has to be buried, the Sharp Cereal Professor has to be buried, Zingers has *already* been buried. But the thing we've got to make them see is that it can't be a *midnight* burial. That's the exact point! Their impulse is to go at this thing like a Mafia button man . . . or a scared relative burying a cholera victim.'

He leaned over Roger, so close that their noses were almost touching.

'Our job is to make them understand that the Cereal Professor will never rest easy unless he's interred in broad daylight. And I'd like to make the whole country mourners at his burial.'

'You're cr –' Roger began   . . then closed his mouth with a snap.

At long last Vic saw that scared, vague expression go out of his partner's eyes. A sudden sharpening happened in Roger's face, and the scared expression was replaced by a slightly mad one. Roger began to grin. Vic was so relieved to see that grin that he forgot about Donna and what had happened with her for the first time since he had gotten Kemp's note. The job took over completely, and it was only later that he would wonder, slightly dumbfounded, how long it had been since he had felt that pure, trippy, wonderful feeling of being fully involved with something he was good at.

'On the surface, we just want him to repeat the things Sharp has been saying since it happened,' Vic went on. 'But when the Cereal Professor *himself* says them –'

'It comes full circle,' Roger murmured. He lit another cigarette.

'Sure, right. We can maybe pitch it to the old man as the final scene in the Red Razberry Zingers farce. Coming clean. Getting it behind us –'

'Taking the bitter medicine. Sure, that'd appeal to the old goat. Public penance . . . scourging himself with whips . . .'

'And instead of going out like a dignified guy that took a pratfall in a mudpuddle, everyone laughing at him, he goes out like Douglas MacArthur, saying old soldiers never die, they just fade away. That's the surface of the thing. But underneath, we're looking for a *tone* . . . a *feeling*. . . .' He was crossing the border into Roger's country now. If he could only delineate the shape of what he meant, the idea that had come to him over coffee at Bentley's, Roger would take it from there.

'MacArthur,' Roger said softly. 'But that's it, isn't it? The tone is farewell. The feeling is regret. Give people the feeling that he's been unjustly treated, but it's too late now. And –' He looked at Vic, almost startled.

'What?'

'Prime time,' Roger said.

'Huh?'

'The spots. We run em in prime time. These ads are for the parents, not the kids. Right?'

'Yeah, yeah.'

'If we ever get the damned things made.'

Vic grinned. 'We'll get them made.' And using one of Roger's terms for good ad copy: 'It's a tank, Roger. We'll drive it right to fuck over them if we have to. As long as we can get something concrete down before we go to Cleveland. . . .'

They sat and talked it over in the tiny screening room for another hour, and when they left to go back to the hotel, both of them sweaty and exhausted, it was full dark.

'Can we go home now, Mommy?' Tad asked apathetically.

'Pretty soon, honey.'

She looked at the key in the ignition switch. Three other

keys on the ring: house key, garage key, and the key that opened the Pinto's hatchback. There was a piece of leather attached to the ring with a mushroom branded on it. She had bought the keyring in Swanson's, a Bridgton department store, back in April. Back in April when she had been so disillusioned and scared, never knowing what real fear was, real fear was trying to crank your kid's window shut while a rabid dog drooled on the backs of your hands.

She reached out. She touched the leather tab. She pulled her hand back again.

The truth was this: She was afraid to try.

It was quarter past seven. The day was still bright, although the Pinto's shadow trailed out long, almost to the garage door. Although she did not know it, her husband and his partner were still watching kinescopes of the Sharp Cereal Professor at Image-Eye in Cambridge. She didn't know why no one had answered the SOS she had been beeping out. In a book, someone would have come. It was the heroine's reward for having thought up such a clever idea. But no one had come.

Surely the sound had carried down to the ramshackle house at the foot of the hill. Maybe they were drunk down there. Or maybe the owners of the two cars in the driveway (*dooryard,* her mind corrected automatically, *up here they call it a dooryard*) had both gone off somewhere in a third car. She wished she could see that house from here, but it was out of sight beyond the descending flank of the hill.

Finally she had given the SOS up. She was afraid that if she kept tooting the horn it would drain the Pinto's battery, which had been in since they got the car. She still believed the Pinto would start when the engine was cool enough. It always had before.

But you're afraid to try, because if it doesn't start   what then?

She was reaching for the ignition again when the dog stumbled back into view. It had been lying out of sight in front of the Pinto. Now it moved slowly toward the barn, it's head down and its tail drooping. It was staggering and weaving like a drunk near the bitter end of a long toot. Without looking back, Cujo slipped into the shadows of the building and disappeared.

She drew her hand away from the key again.

'Mommy? Aren't we going?'

'Let me think, hon,' she said.

She looked to her left, out the driver's side window. Eight running steps would take her to the back door of the Camber house. In high school she had been the star of her high school's girls' track team, and she still jogged regularly. She could beat the dog to the door and inside, she was sure of that. There would be a telephone. One call to Sheriff Bannerman's office and this horror would end. On the other hand, if she tried cranking the engine again, it might not start . . . but it would bring the dog on the run. She knew hardly anything about rabies, but she seemed to remember reading at some time or other that rabid animals were almost supernaturally sensitive to sounds. Loud noises could drive them into a frenzy.

'Mommy?'

'Shhh, Tad. Shhh!'

Eight running steps. Dig it.

Even if Cujo was lurking and watching inside the garage just out of sight, she felt sure — she *knew* — she could win a footrace to the back door. The telephone, yes. And . . . a man like Joe Camber surely kept a gun. Maybe a whole rack of them. What pleasure it would give her to blow that fucking dog's head to so much oatmeal and strawberry jam!

Eight running steps.

Sure. Dig on it awhile.

And what if that door giving on the porch was locked?

Worth the risk?

Her heart thudded heavily in her breast as she weighed the chances. If she had been alone, that would have been one thing. But suppose the door was locked? She could beat the dog to the door, but not to the door and then back to the car. Not if it came running, not if it charged her as it had done before. And what would Tad do? What if Tad saw his mother being savaged by a two-hundred-pound mad dog, being ripped and bitten, being pulled open –

No. They were safe here.

Try the engine again!

She reached for the ignition, and part of her mind clamored that it would be safer to wait longer, until the engine was perfectly cool –

Perfectly cool? They had been here three hours or more already.

She grasped the key and turned it.

The engine cranked briefly once, twice, three times – and then caught with a roar.

'Oh, thank God!' she cried.

'Mommy?' Tad asked shrilly. 'Are we going? Are we going?'

'We're going,' she said grimly, and threw the transmission into reverse. Cujo lunged out of the barn . . . and then just stood there, watching. *'Fuck you dog!'* she yelled at it triumphantly.

She touched the gas pedal. The Pinto rolled back perhaps two feet – and stalled.

'*No!*' she screamed as the red idiot lights came on again. Cujo had taken another two steps when the engine cut out, but now he only stood there silent, his head down. *Watching me*, the thought occurred again. His shadow trailed out behind him, as clear as a silhouette cut out of black crepe paper.

Donna fumbled for the ignition switch and turned it from ON to START. The motor began to turn over again, but this time it didn't catch. She could hear a harsh panting sound in her own ears and didn't realize for several seconds that she was making the sound herself – in some vauge way she had the idea that it must be the dog. She ground the starter, grimacing horribly, swearing at it, oblivious of Tad, using words she had hardly known she knew. And all the time Cujo stood there, trailing his shadow from his heels like some surreal funeral drape, watching.

At last he lay down in the driveway, as if deciding there

was no chance for them to escape. She hated it more than she had when it had tried to force its way in through Tad's window.

'*Mommy . . . Mommy . . . Mommy!*'

From far away. Unimportant. What was important now was this goddamned sonofabitching little car. It was going to start. She was going to *make* it start by *pure . . . force . . . of will*!

She had no idea how long, in real time, she sat hunched over the wheel with her hair hanging in her eyes, futilely grinding the starter. What at last broke through to her was not Tad's cries – they had trailed off to whimpers – but the sound of the engine. It would crank briskly for five seconds, then lag off, then crank briskly for another five, then lag off again. A longer lag each time, it seemed.

She was killing the battery.

She stopped.

She came out of it a little at a time, like a woman coming out of a faint. She remembered a bout of gastroenteritis she'd had in college – everything inside her had either come up by the elevator or dropped down the chute – and near the end of it she had grayed out in one of the dorm toilet stalls. Coming back had been like this, as if you were the same but some invisible painter was adding color to the world, bringing it first up to full and then to overfull. Colors shrieked at you. Everything looked plastic and phony, like a display in a department store window – SWING INTO SPRING, perhaps, or READY FOR THE FIRST KICKOFF.

Tad was cringing away from her, his eyes squeezed shut, the thumb of one hand in his mouth. The other hand was pressed against his hip pocket, where the Monster Words were. His respiration was shallow and rapid.

'Tad,' she said. 'Honey, don't worry.'

'Mommy, are you all right?' His voice was little more than a husky whisper.

'Yeah. So are you. At least we're safe. This old car will go. Just wait and see.'

'I thought you were mad at me.'

She took him in her arms and hugged him tight. She could smell sweat in his hair and the lingering undertone of Johnson's No More Tears shampoo. She thought of that bottle sitting safely and sanely on the second shelf of the medicine cabinet in the upstairs bathroom. If only she could touch it! But all that was here was that faint, dying perfume.

'No, honey, not at you,' she said. 'Never at you.'

Tad hugged her back. 'He can't get us in here, can he?'

'No.'

'He can't . . . he can't eat his way in, can he?'

'No.'

'I hate him,' Tad said reflectively. 'I wish he'd die.'

'Yes. Me too.'

She looked out the window and saw that the sun was getting ready to go down. A superstitious dread settled into her at the thought. She remembered the childhood games of hide-and-seek that had always ended when the shadows joined each other and grew into purple lagoons, that mystic call drifting through the suburban streets of her childhood, talismanic and distant, the high voice of a child announcing suppers that were ready, doors ready to be shut against the night:

'Alleee-alleee-infree! Alleee-alleee-infree!'

The dog was watching her. It was crazy, but she could no longer doubt it. Its mad, senseless eyes were fixed unhesitatingly on hers.

No, you're imagining it. It's only a dog, and a sick dog at that. Things are bad enough without you seeing something in that dog's eyes that can't be there.

She told herself that. A few minutes later she told herself that Cujo's eyes were like the eyes of some portraits which seem to follow you wherever you move in the room where they are hung.

But the dog was looking at her. And . . . and there was something familiar about it.

No, she told herself, and tried to dismiss the thought, but it was too late.

*You've seen him before, haven't you? The morning after
Tad had the first of his bad dreams, the morning that the
blankets and sheets were back on the chair, his Teddy on top
of them, and for a moment when you opened the closet door
you only saw a slumped shape with red eyes, something in
Tad's closet ready to spring, it was him, it was Cujo, Tad
was right all along, only the monster wasn't in his closet . . .
it was out here. It was*
(stop it)
out here just waiting to
(! YOU STOP IT DONNA!)

She stared at the dog and imagined she could hear its
thoughts. Simple thoughts. The same simple pattern,
repeated over and over in spite of the whirling boil of its
sickness and delirium.

Kill THE WOMAN. *Kill* THE BOY. *Kill* THE WOMAN. *Kill* –

Stop it, she commanded herself roughly. *It doesn't think
and it's not some goddamned bogeyman out of a child's
closet. It's a sick dog and that's all it is. Next you'll believe
the dog is God's punishment for committing –*

Cujo suddenly got up – almost as if she had called
him – and disappeared into the barn again.

(almost as if I called it)

She uttered a shaky, semi-hysterical laugh.

Tad looked up. 'Mommy?'

'Nothing, hon.'

She looked at the dark maw of the garage-barn, then at
the back door of the house. *Locked? Unlocked? Locked?
Unlocked?* She thought of a coin rising in the air, flipping
over and over. She thought of whirling the chamber drum of
a pistol, five holes empty, one full. *Locked? Unlocked*

The sun went down, and what was left of the day was a
white line painted on the western horizon. It looked no
thicker than the white stripe painted down the center of the
highway. That would be gone soon enough. Crickets sang in
the high grass to the right of the driveway, making a

mindlessly cheerful *rickety-rickety* sound.

Cujo was still in the barn. Sleeping? she wondered. Eating?

That made her remember that she had packed them some food. She crawled between the two front buckets and got the Snoopy lunchbox and her own brown bag. Her Thermos had rolled all the way to the back, probably when the car had started to buck and jerk coming up the road. She had to stretch, her blouse coming untucked, before she could hook it with her fingers. Tad, who had been in a half doze, stirred awake. His voice was immediately filled with a sharp fright that made her hate the damned dog even more.

'Mommy? *Mommy?* What are you –'

'Just getting the food,' she soothed him. 'And my Thermos – see?'

'Okay.' He settled back into his seat and put his thumb in his mouth again.

She shook the big Thermos gently beside her ear, listening for the grating sound of broken glass. She only heard milk swishing around inside. That was something, anyhow.

'Tad? You want to eat?'

'I want to take a nap,' he said around his thumb, not opening his eyes.

'You gotta feed the machine, chum,' she said.

He didn't even smile. 'Not hungry. Sleepy.'

She looked at him, troubled, and decided it would be wrong to force the issue any further. Sleep was Tad's natural weapon – maybe his only one – and it was already half an hour past his regular bedtime. Of course, if they had been home, he would have had a glass of milk and a couple of cookies before brushing his teeth . . . and a story, one of his Mercer Mayer books, maybe . . . and . . .

She felt the hot sting of tears and tried to push all those thoughts away. She opened her Thermos with shaky hands and poured herself half a cup of milk. She set it on the dashboard and took one of the figbars. After one bite she realized she was absolutely ravenous. She ate three more figbars, drank some milk, popped four or five of the green olives, then drained her cup. She burped gently . . . and then looked more sharply at the barn.

There was a darker shadow in front of it now. Except it wasn't just a shadow. It was the dog. It was Cujo.

He's standing watch over us.

No, she didn't believe that. Nor did she believe she had seen a vision of Cujo in a pile of blankets stacked in her son's closet. She didn't . . . except . . . except part of her did. But that part wasn't in her mind.

She glanced up into the rearview mirror at where the road was. It was too dark now to see it, but she knew it was there, just as she knew that nobody was going to go by. When they had come out that other time with Vic's Jag, all three of them *(the dog was nice then*, her brain muttered, *the Tadder patted him and laughed, remember?)*, laughing it up and having a great old time, Vic had told her that until five years ago the Castle Rock Dump had been out at the end of Town Road No. 3. Then the new waste treatment plant had gone into operation on the other side of town, and now, a quarter of a mile beyond the Camber place, the road simply ended at a place where a heavy chain was strung across it. The sign which hung from the chain read NO TRESPASSING DUMP CLOSED. Beyond Cambers', there was just no place to go.

Donna wondered if maybe some people in search of a really private place to go parking might not ride by, but she couldn't imagine that even the horniest of local kids would want to neck at the old town dump. At any rate, no one had passed yet.

The white line on the western horizon had faded to a bare afterglow now . . . and she was afraid that even that was mostly wishful thinking. There was no moon.

Incredibly, she felt drowsy herself. Maybe sleep was her natural weapon, too. And what else was there to do? The dog was still out there (at least she thought it was; the darkness had gotten just deep enough to make it hard to tell if that was a real shape or just a shadow). The battery had to rest. Then she could try again. So why not sleep?

The package on his mailbox. That package from J. C. Whitney.

She sat up a little straighter, a puzzled frown creasing her brow. She turned her head, but from here the front corner of the house blocked her view of the mailbox. But she had seen the package, hung from the front of the box. Why had she thought of that? Did it have some significance?

She was still holding the Tupperware dish with the olives and slices of cucumbers inside, each wrapped neatly in Saran Wrap. Instead of eating anything else, she carefully put the white plastic cover on the Tupperware dish and stowed it back in Tad's lunchbox. She did not let herself think much about why she was being so careful of the food. She settled back in the bucket seat and found the lever that tipped it back. She meant to think about the package hooked over the mailbox – there was something there, she was almost sure of it – but soon her mind had slipped away to another idea, one that took on the bright tones of reality as she began to doze off.

The Cambers had gone to visit relatives. The relatives were in some town that was two, maybe three hours' drive away. Kennebunk, maybe. Or Hollis. Or Augusta. It was a family reunion.

Her beginning-to-dream mind saw a gathering of fifty people or more on a green lawn of TV-commercial size and beauty. There was a fieldstone barbecue pit with a shimmer of heat over it. At a long trestle table there were at least four dozen people, passing platters of corn on the cob and dishes of home-baked beans – pea beans, soldier beans, red kidney beans. There were plates of barbecued franks (Donna's stomach made a low goinging sound at this vision). On the table was a homely checked tablecloth. All this was being presided over by a lovely old woman with pure white hair that had been rolled into a bun at the nape of her neck. Fully inserted into the capsule of her dream now, Donna saw with no surprise at all that this woman was her mother.

The Cambers were there, but they weren't really the Cambers at all. Joe Camber looked like Vic in a clean Sears work coverall, and Mrs. Camber was wearing Donna's green watered-silk dress. Their boy looked the way Tad was going to look when he was in the fifth grade . . .

'Mommy?'

The picture wavered, started to break up. She tried to hold on to it because it was peaceful and lovely: the archetype of a family life she had never had, the type she and Vic would never have with their one planned child and their carefully programmed lives. With sudden rising sadness, she wondered why she had never thought of things in that light before.

'Mommy?'

The picture wavered again and began to darken. That voice from outside, piercing the vision the way a needle may pierce the shell of an egg. Never mind. The Cambers were at their family reunion and they would pull in later, around ten, happy and full of barbecue. Everything would be all right. The Joe Camber with Vic's face would take care of everything. Everything would be all right again. There were some things that God never allowed. It would –

'*Mommy!*'

She came out of the doze, sitting up, surprised to find herself behind the wheel of the Pinto instead of at home in bed . . . but only for a second. Already the lovely, surreal image of the relatives gathered around the trestle picnic table were beginning to dissolve, and in fifteen minutes she would not even remember that she had dreamed.

'Huh? What?'

Suddenly, shockingly, the phone inside the Cambers' house began to ring. The dog rose to its feet, moving shadows that resolved themselves into its large and ungainly form.

'Mommy, I have to go to the bathroom.'

Cujo began to roar at the sound of the telephone. He was not barking; he was *roaring*. Suddenly he charged at the house. He struck the back door hard enough to shake it in its frame.

No, she thought sickly, *oh no, stop, please, stop –*

'Mommy, I have to —'

The dog was snarling, biting at the wood of the door. She could hear the sick splintering sounds its teeth made.

' — go weewee.'

The phone rang six times. Eight times. Ten. Then it stopped.

She realized she had been holding her breath. She let it out through her teeth in a low, hot sigh.

Cujo stood at the door, his back paws on the ground, his forepaws on the top step. He continued to growl low in his chest — a hateful, nightmarish sound. At last he turned and looked at the Pinto for a time — Donna could see the dried foam caked on his muzzle and chest — then he padded back into the shadows and grew indistinct. It was impossible to tell exactly where he went. In the garage, maybe. Or maybe down the side of the barn.

Tad was tugging desperately at the sleeve of her shirt.

'Mommy, I have to go *bad*!'

She looked at him helplessly.

Brett Camber put the phone down slowly. 'No one answered. He's not home, I guess.'

Charity nodded, not terribly surprised. She was glad that Jim had suggested they make the call from his office, which was downstairs and off the 'family room'. The family room was soundproofed. There were shelves of board games in there, a Panasonic large-screen TV with a video recorder and an Atari video-games setup attached to it. And standing in one corner was a lovely old Wurlitzer jukebox that really worked.

'Down at Gary's, I guess,' Brett added disconsolately.

'Yes, I imagine he's with Gary,' she agreed, which wasn't exactly the same as saying they were together at Gary's house. She had seen the faraway look that had come into Joe's eyes when she had finally struck the deal with him, the deal that had gotten her and her son down here. She hoped Brett wouldn't think of calling directory assistance for Gary

Pervier's number, because she doubted if there would be any answer there either. She suspected that there were two old dogs out somewhere tonight howling at the moon.

'Do you think Cuje is okay, Mom?'

'Why, I don't think your father would go off and leave him if he wasn't,' she said, and that was true – she didn't believe he would. 'Why don't we leave it for tonight and you call him in the morning? You ought to be getting to bed anyway. It's past ten. You've had a big day.'

'I'm not tired.'

'Well, it's not good to go too long on nervous excitement. I put your toothbrush out, and your Aunt Holly put out a washcloth and a towel for you. Do you remember which bedroom –?'

'Yeah, sure. You going to bed, Mom?'

'Soon. I'm going to sit up with Holly for a while. We've got a lot of history to catch up on, she and I.'

Shyly, Brett said, 'She looks like you. Y'know that?'

Charity looked at him, surprised. 'Does she? Yes, I suppose she does. A little.'

'And that little kid, Jimmy. He's got a real right hook. Pow!' Brett burst out laughing.

'Did he hurt your stomach?'

'Heck, no.' Brett was looking around Jim's study carefully, noting the Underwood typewriter on the desk, the Rolodex, the neat open file of folders with the names on the tabs in alphabetical order. There was a careful, measuring look in his eyes that she couldn't understand or evaluate. He seemed to come back from far away. 'Nah, he didn't hurt me. He's just a little kid.' He cocked his head at her. 'My cousin, right?'

'Right.'

'Blood relation.' He seemed to muse over it.

'Brett, do you like your Uncle Jim and Aunt Holly?'

'I like her. I can't tell about him yet. That jukebox. That's really neat. But ...' He shook his head in a kind of impatience.

'What about it, Brett?'

'He takes so much *pride* in it!' Brett said. 'It was the first thing he showed me, like a kid with a toy, isn't this neat, you know —'

'Well, he's only had it for a little while,' Charity said. An unformed dread had begun to swirl around inside of her, connected somehow with Joe — what had he told Brett when he took him out on the sidewalk? 'Anyone's partial to something new. Holly wrote me when they finally got it, said Jim had wanted one of those things since he was a young man. People . . . honey, different people buy different things to . . . to show themselves that they're successful, I suppose. There's no accounting for it. But usually it's something they couldn't have when they were poor.'

'Was Uncle Jim poor?'

'I really don't know,' she said. 'But they're not poor now.'

'All I meant was that he didn't have anything to *do* with it. You get what I mean?' He looked at her closely. 'He bought it with money and hired some people to fix it and hired some *more* people to bring it here, and he says it's his, but he didn't . . . you know, he didn't . . . aw, I don't know.'

'He didn't make it with his own hands?' Although her fear was greater now, more coalesced, her voice was gentle.

'Yeah! That's right! He bought it with money, but he didn't really have nothing to do —'

'*Anything* —'

'Okay, yeah, *anything* to do with it, but now he's, like, takin credit for it —'

'He said a jukebox is a delicate, complicated machine —'

'Dad could have gotten it running,' Brett said flatly, and Charity thought she heard a door bang shut suddenly, closing with a loud, toneless, frightening bang. It wasn't in the house. It was in her heart. 'Dad would have tinkered it up and it would have been *his*.'

'Brett,' she said (and her voice sounded weak and justifying to her own ears), 'not everybody is good at tinkering and fixing like your father is.'

'I know that,' he said, still looking around the office. 'Yeah. But Uncle Jim shouldn't take credit for it just because he had the money. See? It's him taking the credit that I don't li – that bothers me.'

She was suddenly furious with him. She wanted to take him by the shoulders and shake him back and forth; to raise her voice until it was loud enough to shout the truth into his brain. That money did not come by accident; that it almost always resulted from some sustained act of will, and that will was the core of character. She would tell him that while his father was perfecting his skills as a tinkerer and swilling down Black Label with the rest of the boys in the back of Emerson's Sunoco, sitting in piles of dead bald tires and telling frenchman jokes, Jim Brooks had been in law school, knocking his brains out to make grades, because when you made the grades you got the diploma, and the diploma was your ticket, you got to ride the merry-go-round. Getting on didn't mean you'd catch the brass ring, no, but it guaranteed you the chance to at least *try.*

'You go on up now and get ready for bed,' she said quietly. 'What you think of your Uncle Jim is between you and you. But . . . give him a chance, Brett. Don't just judge him on that.' They had gone through into the family room now, and she jerked a thumb at the jukebox.

'No, I won't,' he said.

She followed him up into the kitchen, where Holly was making cocoa for the four of them. Jim Junior and Gretchen had gone to bed long before.

'You get your man?' Holly asked.

'No, he's probably down chewing the fat with that friend of his,' Charity said. 'We'll try tomorrow.'

'Want some cocoa, Brett?' Holly asked.

'Yes, please.'

Charity watched him sit down at the table. She saw him put his elbow on it and then take it off again quickly, remembering that it was impolite. Her heart was so full of love and hope and fear that it seemed to stagger in her chest.

Time, she thought. *Time and perspective. Give him that. If you force him, you'll lose him for sure.*

But how much time was there? Only a week, and then he would be back under Joe's influence. And even as she sat down next to her son and thanked Holly for her cup of hot cocoa, her thoughts had turned speculatively to the idea of divorce again.

In her dream, Vic had come.

He simply walked down the driveway to the Pinto and opened her door. He was dressed in his best suit, the three-piece charcoal-gray one (when he put it on she always teased him that he looked like Jerry Ford with hair). *Come on, you two,* he said, and that quirky little grin was on his face. *Time to go home before the vampires come out.*

She tried to warn him, to tell him the dog was rabid, but no words came. And suddenly Cujo was advancing out of the dark, his head down, a steady low growl rumbling in his chest. *Watch out!* she tried to cry. *His bite is death!* But no sound came out.

But just before Cujo launched himself at Vic, he turned and pointed his finger at the dog. Cujo's fur went dead white instantly. His red, rheumy eyes dropped back into his head like marbles into a cup. His muzzle fell off and shattered against the crushed gravel of the driveway like black glass. A moment later all that was left in front of the garage was a blowing fur coat.

Don't you worry, Vic said in a dream. *Don't you worry about that old dog, it's nothing but a fur coat. Did you get the mail yet? Never mind the dog, the mail's coming. The mail's the important thing. Right? The mail —*

His voice was disappearing down a long tunnel, growing echoey and faint. And suddenly it was not a dream of Vic's voice but a memory of a dream — she was awake and her cheeks were wet with tears. She had cried in her sleep. She looked at her watch and could just make out the time: quarter past one. She looked over at Tad and saw he was sleeping soundly, his thumb hooked into his mouth.

Never mind the dog, the mail's coming. The mail's the important thing.

And suddenly the significance of the package hung over the mailbox door came to her, hit her like an arrow fired up from her subconscious mind, an idea she had not quite been able to get hold of before. Perhaps because it was so big, so simple, so elementary-my-dear-Watson. Yesterday was Monday and the mail had come. The J. C. Whitney package for Joe Camber was ample proof of that.

Today was Tuesday and the mail would come again.

Tears of relief began to roll down her not-yet-dry cheeks. She actually had to restrain herself from shaking Tad awake and telling him it was going to be all right, that by two o'clock this afternoon at the lastest – and more probably by ten or eleven in the morning, if the mail delivery out here was as prompt as it was most other places in town – this nightmare would end.

The mailman would come even if he had no mail for the Cambers, that was the beauty of it. It would be his job to see if the flag was up, signifying outgoing mail. He would have to come up here, to his last stop on Town Road No. 3, to check that out, and today he was going to be greeted by a woman who was semi-hysterical with relief.

She eyed Tad's lunchbox and thought of the food inside. She thought of herself carefully saving some of it aside, in case . . . well, in case. Now it didn't matter so much, although Tad was likely to be hungry in the morning. She ate the rest of the cucumber slices. Tad didn't care for cucumbers much anyway. It would be an odd breakfast for him, she thought, smiling. Figbars, olives, and a Slim Jim or two.

Munching the last two or three cucumber slices, she realized it was the coincidences that had scared her the most. That series of coincidences, utterly random but mimicking a kind of sentient fate, had been what seemed to make the dog so horribly purposeful, so . . . so out to get her personally. Vic being gone for ten days, that was coincidence number one. Vic calling early today, that was coincidence number two. If he hadn't got them then, he would have tried later, kept trying, and begun to wonder where they were. The fact that all three of the Cambers were gone, at least for overnight, the way it looked now. That was number three. Mother, son, and father. All gone. But they had left their dog. Oh yes. They had —

A sudden horrible thought occurred to her, freezing her jaws on the last bite of cucumber. She tried to thrust it away, but it came back. It wouldn't go away because it had its own gargoyle-like logic.

What if they were all dead in the barn?

The image rose behind her eyes in an instant. It had the unhealthy vividness of those waking visions which sometimes come in the morning's small hours. The three bodies tumbled about like badly made toys on the floor in there, the sawdust around them stained red, their dusty eyes staring up into the blackness where barnswallows cooed and fluttered, their clothing ripped and chewed, parts of them —

Oh that's crazy, that's —

Maybe he had gotten the boy first. The other two are in the kitchen, or maybe upstairs having a quickie, they hear screams, they rush out —

(stop it won't you stop it)

— they rush out but the boy is already dead, the dog has torn his throat out, and while they're still stunned by the death of their son, the Saint Bernard comes lurching out of the shadows, old and terrible engine of destruction, yes, the old monster comes from the shadows, rabid and snarling. He goes for the woman first and the man tries to save her —

(no, he would have gotten his gun or brained it with a wrench or something and where's the car? There was a car here before they all went off on a family trip — do you hear me FAMILY TRIP — took the car left the truck)

Then why had no one come to feed the dog?

That was the logic of the thing, part of what frightened her. Why hadn't anyone come to feed the dog? Because if you were going to be away for a day or for a couple of days, you made an arrangement with somebody. They fed your dog for you, and then when they were gone, you fed their cat for them, or their fish, or their parakeet, or whatever. So where —

And the dog kept going back into the barn.

Was it eating in there?

That's the answer, her mind told her, relieved. *He didn't have anyone to feed the dog, so he poured it a tray of food. Gaines Meal, or something.*

But then she stuck upon what Joe Camber himself had stuck upon earlier on that long, long day. A big dog would gobble it all at once and then go hungry. Surely it would be better to get a friend to feed the dog if you were going to be gone. On the other hand, maybe they had been held up. Maybe there really had been a family reunion, and Camber had gotten drunk and passed out. Maybe this, maybe that, maybe anything.

Is the dog eating in the barn?

(what *is it* eating in there? Gaines Meal? or people?)

She spat the last of the cucumber into her cupped hand and felt her stomach roll, wanting to send up what she had already eaten. She set her will upon keeping it down, and because she could be very determined when she wanted to, she did keep it down. They had left the dog some food and had gone off in the car. You didn't have to be Sherlock Holmes to deduce that. The rest of it was nothing but a bad case of the willies.

But that image of death kept trying to creep back in. The dominant image was the bloody sawdust, sawdust which had gone the dark color of natural-casing franks.

Stop. Think about the mail, if you have to think about anything. Think about tomorrow. Think about being safe.

There was a soft, scuffling, scratching noise on her side of the car.

She didn't want to look but was helpless to stop herself. Her head began to turn as if forced by invisible yet powerful hands. She could hear the low creak of the tendons in her neck. Cujo was there, looking in at her. His face was less than six inches from her own. Only the Saf-T-Glas of the driver's side window separated them. Those red, bleary eyes stared into hers. The dog's muzzle looked as if it had been badly lathered with shaving cream that had been left to dry.

Cujo was grinning at her.

She felt a scream building in her chest, coming up in her throat like iron, because she could feel the dog thinking at her, telling her *I'm going to get you, babe. I'm going to get you, kiddo. Think about the mailman all you want to. I'll kill him too if I have to, the way I killed all three of the Cambers, the way I'm going to kill you and your son. You might as well get used to the idea. You might as well —*

The scream, coming up her throat. It was a live thing struggling to get out, and everything was coming on her at once: Tad having to pee, she had unrolled his window four inches and held him up so he could do it out the window, watching all the time for the dog, and for a long time he hadn't been able to go and her arms had begun to ache; then the dream, then the images of death, and now this —

The dog was grinning in at her; he was grinning in at her, Cujo was his name, and his bite was death.

The scream had to come

(but Tad's)

or she would go mad.

(sleeping)

She locked her jaws against the scream the way she had locked her throat against the urge to vomit a few moments ago. She struggled with it, she fought it. And at last her heart began to slow down and she knew she had it licked.

She smiled at the dog and raised both of her middle fingers from closed fists. She held them against the glass, which was now slightly fogged on the outside with Cujo's breath. 'Go get fucked,' she whispered.

After what seemed an endless time, the dog put its forepaws down and went back into the barn. Her mind turned down the same dark track again

(what's it eating in there?)

and then she slammed a door shut somewhere in her mind.

But there would be no more sleep, not for a long time, and

it was so long until dawn. She sat upright behind the wheel, trembling, telling herself over and over again that it was ridiculous, really ridiculous, to feel that the dog was some kind of a hideous revenant which had escaped from Tad's closet, or that it knew more about the situation than she did.

Vic jerked awake in total darkness, rapid breath as dry as salt in his throat. His heart was triphammering in his chest, and he was totally disoriented – so disoriented that for a moment he thought he was falling, and reached out to clutch the bed.

He closed his eyes for a moment, forcibly holding himself together, making himself coalesce.

(you are in)

He opened his eyes and saw a window, a bedstand, a lamp.

(the Ritz-Carlton Hotel in Boston Massachusetts)

He relaxed. That reference point given, everything came together with a reassuring *click*, making him wonder how he could have been so lost and totally apart, even momentarily. It was being in a strange place, he supposed. That, and the nightmare.

Nightmare! Jesus, it had been a beaut. He couldn't remember having such a bad one since the falling dreams that had plagued him off and on during early puberty. He reached for the Travel-Ette clock on the nightstand, gripped it in both hands, and brought it close to his face. It was twenty minutes of two. Roger was snoring lightly in the other bed, and now that his eyes had adjusted to the dark he could see him, sleeping flat on his back. He had kicked the sheet over the end of the bed. He was wearing an absurd pair of pajamas covered with small yellow college pennants.

Vic swung his legs out of bed, went quietly into the bathroom, and closed the door. Roger's cigarettes were on the washstand and he helped himself to one. He needed it. He sat on the toilet and smoked, tapping ashes into the sink.

An anxiety dream, Donna would have said, and God

knew he had enough to be anxious about. Yet he had gone to bed around ten thirty in better spirits than he had been in for the last week. After arriving back at the hotel, he and Roger had spent half an hour in the Ritz-Carlton's bar, kicking the apology idea around, and then, from the bowels of the huge old wallet he hauled around, Roger produced the home number of Yancey Harrington. Harrington was the actor who played the Sharp Cereal Professor.

'Might as well see if he'll do it before we go any further,' Roger said. He had picked up the phone and dialed Harrington, who lived in Westport, Connecticut. Vic hadn't known just what to expect. If pressed for his best guess, he would have said that probably Harrington would have to be stroked a little – he had been just miserable over the Zingers affair and what he considered it had done to his image.

Both of them had been in for a happy surprise. Harrington had agreed instantly. He recognized the realities of the situation and knew the Professor was pretty well finished ('Poor old guy's a gone goose,' Harrington had said glumly). But he thought the final ad might be just the thing to get the company over the affair. Put it back on the rails, so to speak.

'Bullshit,' Roger said, grinning, after he had hung up. 'He just likes the idea of one final curtain call. Not many actors in advertising get a chance like that. He'd buy his own plane ticket to Boston if we asked him to.'

So Vic had gone to bed happy and had fallen asleep almost instantly. Then, the dream. He was standing in front of Tad's closet door in the dream and telling Tad that there was nothing in there, nothing at all. *I'll show you once and for all*, he told Tad. He opened the closet door and saw that Tad's clothes and toys were gone. There was a forest growing in Tad's closet – old pines and spruces, ancient hardwoods. The closet floor was covered with fragrant needles and leafy mulch. He had scraped at it, wanting to see if the floor of painted boards was beneath. It wasn't; his foot scraped up rich black forest earth instead.

He stepped into the closet and the door closed behind him. That was all right. There was enough light to see by. He found a trail and began to hike along it. All at once he realized there was a pack on his back and a canteen slung over one shoulder. He could hear the mysterious sound of the wind, soughing through the firs, and faint birdsong. Seven years ago, long before Ad Worx, they had all gone hiking on part of the Appalachian Trail during one of their vacations, and that land had looked a good deal like the geography of his dream. They had done it only that once, sticking to the seacoast after that. Vic, Donna, and Roger had had a wonderful time, but Althea Breakstone loathed hiking and had come down with a good, itchy case of poison oak on top of that.

The first part of the dream had been rather pleasant. The thought that all this had been right inside Tad's closet was, in its own strange way, wonderful. Then he had come into a clearing and he had seen . . . but it was already beginning to tatter, the way dreams do when they are exposed to waking thought.

The other side of the clearing had been a sheer gray wall rising maybe a thousand feet into the sky. About twenty feet up there was a cave — no, not really deep enough to be a cave. It was more of a niche, just a depression in the rock that happened to have a flat floor. Donna and Tad were cowering inside. Cowering from some sort of monster that was trying to reach up, trying to reach up and then reach in. Get them. Eat them.

It had been like that scene in the original *King Kong* after the great ape has shaken Fay Wray's would-be rescuers from the log and is trying to get the lone survivor. But the guy has gotten into a hole, and Kong isn't quite able to get him.

The monster in his dream hadn't been a giant ape, though. It had been a . . . what? Dragon? No, nothing like that. Not a dragon, not a dinosaur, not a troll. He couldn't get it. Whatever it was, it couldn't quite get in and get Donna and Tad, so it was merely waiting outside their bolthole, like a cat waiting with dreadful patience for a mouse.

He began to run, but no matter how fast he went, he never got any closer to the other side of the clearing. He could hear

Donna screaming for help, but when he called back his words seemed to die two feet out of his mouth. It was Tad who had finally spotted him.

'*They don't work!*' Tad had screamed in a hopeless, despairing voice that had hollowed out Vic's guts with fear. '*Daddy, the Monster Words don't work! Oh, Daddy, they don't work, they never worked! You lied, Daddy! You lied!*'

He ran on, but it was as if he were on a treadmill. And he had looked at the base of that high gray wall and had seen a heaped drift of old bones and grinning skulls, some of them furred with green moss.

That was when he woke up.

What had the monster been, anyway?

He just couldn't remember. Already the dream seemed like a scene observed through the wrong end of a telescope. He dropped the cigarette into the john, flushed it, and ran water into the sink as well to swirl the ashes down the drain.

He urinated, shut off the light, and went back to bed. As he lay down he glanced at the telephone and felt a sudden irrational urge to call home. Irrational? That was putting it mildly. It was ten minutes of two in the morning. He would not only wake her up, he would probably scare the living hell out of her in the bargain. You didn't interpret dreams literally; everyone knew that. When both your marriage and your business seemed in danger of running off the rails at the same time, it wasn't really surprising that your mind pulled a few unsettling head games, was it?

Still, just to hear her voice and know she's okay —

He turned away from the telephone, punched up the pillow, and resolutely shut his eyes.

Call her in the morning, if that'll make you feel better. Call her right after breakfast.

That eased his mind, and very shortly he drifted off to sleep again. This time he did not dream — or if he did, these dreams never imprinted themselves on his conscious mind. And when the wake-up call came on Tuesday, he had forgotten all about the dream of the beast in the clearing. He had only the vaguest recollection of having gotten up in the night at all. Vic did not call home that day.

Charity Camber awoke that Tuesday morning on the dot of five and went through her own brief period of disorientation – yellow wallpaper instead of wood walls, colorful green print curtains instead of white chintz, a narrow single bed instead of the double that had begun to sag in the middle.

Then she saw where she was – Stratford, Connecticut – and felt a burst of pleased anticipation. She would have the whole day to talk to her sister, to hash over old times, to find out what she had been doing the last few years. And Holly had talked about going into Bridgeport to do some shopping.

She had awakened an hour and a half before her usual time, probably two hours or more before things began to stir in this household. But a person never slept well in a strange bed until the third night – that had been one of her mother's sayings, and it was a true one.

The silence began to give up its little sounds as she lay awake and listening, looking at the thin five-o'clock light that fell between the half-drawn curtains . . . dawn's early light, always so white and clear and fine. She heard the creak of a single board. A bluejay having its morning tantrum. The day's first commuter train, bound for Westport, Greenwich, and New York City.

The board creaked again.

And again.

It wasn't just the house settling. It was footsteps.

Charity sat up in bed, the blanket and sheet pooling around the waist of her sensible pink nightgown. Now the steps were going slowly downstairs. It was a light tread: bare feet or sock feet. It was Brett. When you lived with people, you got to know the sound of their walk. It was one of those mysterious things that just happen over a course of years, like the shape of a leaf sinking into a rock.

She pushed the covers back, got up, and went to the door. Her room opened on the upstairs hall, and she just saw the top of Brett's head disappearing, his cowlick sticking up for a moment and then gone.

She went after him.

When Charity reached the top of the stairs, Brett was just disappearing down the hallway that ran the width of the house, from the front door to the kitchen. She opened her mouth to call him ... and then shut it again. She was intimidated by the sleeping house that wasn't her house.

Something about the way he had been walking ... the set of his body ... but it had been years since —

She descended the stairs quickly and quietly in her bare feet. She followed Brett into the kitchen. He was dressed only in light blue pajama bottoms, their white cotton drawstring hanging down to below the neat fork of his crotch. Although it was barely midsummer he was already very brown — he was naturally dark, like his father, and tanned easily.

Standing in the doorway she saw him in profile, that same fine, clear morning light pouring over his body as he hunted along the line of cupboards above the stove and the counter and the sink. Her heart was full of wonder and fear. *He's beautiful,* she thought. *Everything that's beautiful, or ever was, in us, is in him.* It was a moment she never forgot — she saw her son clad only in his pajama bottoms and for a moment dimly comprehended the mystery of his boyhood, so soon to be left behind. Her mother's eyes loved the slim curves of his muscles, the line of his buttocks, the clean soles of his feet. He seemed ... utterly perfect.

She saw it clearly because Brett wasn't awake. As a child there had been episodes of sleepwalking; about two dozen of them in all, between the ages of four and eight. She had finally gotten worried enough — scared enough — to consult with Dr. Gresham (without Joe's knowledge). She wasn't afraid that Brett was losing his mind — anyone who was around him could see he was bright and normal — but she was afraid that he might hurt himself while he was in that strange state. Dr. Gresham had told her that was very unlikely, and that most of the funny ideas people had about somnambulism came from cheap, badly researched movies.

'We only know a little about sleepwalking,' he had told her, 'but we do know that it is more common in children than it is in adults. There's a constantly growing, constantly maturing interaction between the mind and body, Mrs. Camber, and a lot of people who have done research in this field believe that sleepwalking may be a sympton of a temporary and not terribly significant imbalance between the two.'

'Like growing pains?' she had asked doubtfully.

'Very much like that,' Gresham had said with a grin. He drew a bell curve on his office pad, suggesting that Brett's somnambulism would reach a peak, hold for a while, then begin to taper off. Eventually it would disappear.

She had gone away a little reassured by the doctor's conviction that Brett would not go sleepwalking out a window or down the middle of a highway, but without being much enlightened. A week later she had brought Brett in. He had been just a month or two past his sixth birthday then. Gresham had given him a complete physical and had pronounced him normal in every way. And indeed, Gresham had appeared to be right. The last of what Charity thought of as his 'nighwalks' had occurred more than two years ago.

The last, that was, until now.

Brett opened the cupboards one by one, closing each neatly before going on to the next, disclosing Holly's casserole dishes, the extra elements to her Jenn-Aire range, her dishtowels neatly folded, her coffee-and-tea creamer, her as-yet-incomplete set of Depression glassware. His eyes were wide and blank, and she felt a cool certainty that he was seeing the contents of other cabinets, in another place.

She felt the old, helpless terror that she had almost completely forgotten as parents do the alarms and the excursions of their children's early years: the teething, the vaccination that brought the frighteningly high fever as a little extra added attraction, the croup, the ear infection, the hand or leg that suddenly began to spray irrational blood. *What's he thinking?* she wondered. *Where is he? And why now, after two quiet years?* Was it being in a strange place? He hadn't seemed duly upset . . . at least, not until now.

He opened the last cupboard and took down a pink gravy boat. He put it on the counter. He picked up empty air and mimed pouring something into the gravy boat. Her arms suddenly broke out in gooseflesh as she realized where he was and what this dumbshow was all about. It was a routine he went through each day at home. He was feeding Cujo.

She took an involuntary step toward him and then stopped. She didn't believe those wives' tales about what might happen if you woke a sleepwalker – that the soul would be forever shut out of the body, that madness might result, or sudden death – and she hadn't needed Dr. Gresham to reassure her on that score. She had gotten a book on special loan from the Portland City Library . . . but she hadn't really needed that, either. Her own good common sense told her what happened when you woke up a sleepwalker was that they woke up – no more and no less than just that. There might be tears, even mild hysteria, but that sort of reaction would be provoked by simple disorientation.

Still, she had never wakened Brett during one of his nightwalks, and she didn't dare to do so now. Good common sense was one thing. Her unreasoning fear was another, and she was suddenly very afraid, and unable to think why. What could be so dreadful in Brett's acted-out dream of feeding his dog? It was perfectly natural, as worried as he had been about Cujo.

He was bent over now, holding the gravy boat out, the drawstring of his pajama trousers making a right-angled white line to the horizontal plane of the red and black linoleum floor. His face went though a slow-motion pantomime of sorrow. He spoke then, muttering the words as sleepers so often do, gutturally, rapidly, almost unintelligibly. And with no emotion in the words themselves, that was all inside, held in the cocoon of whatever dream had been vivid enough to make him nightwalk again, after two quiet years. There was nothing inherently melodramatic about the words, spoken all of a rush in a quick sleeping sigh, but Charity's hand went to her throat anyway. The flesh there was cold, cold.

'Cujo's not hungry no more,' Brett said, the words riding out on that sigh. He stood up again, now holding the gravy boat cradled to his chest. 'Not no more, not no more.'

He stood immobile for a short time by the counter, and Charity did likewise by the kitchen door. A single tear had slipped down his face. He put the gravy boat on the counter and headed for the door. His eyes were open but they slipped indifferently and unseeingly over his mother. He stopped, looking back.

'Look in the weeds,' he said to someone who was not there.

Then be began to walk toward her again. She stood aside, her hand still pressed against her throat. He passed her quickly and noiselessly on his bare feet and was gone up the hall toward the stairs.

She turned to follow him and remembered the gravy boat. It stood by itself on the bare, ready-for-the-day counter like the focal point in a weird painting. She picked it up and it slipped through her fingers – she hadn't realized that her fingers were slick with sweat. She juggled it briefly, imagining the crash in the still, sleeping hours. Then she had it cradled safely in both hands. She put it back on the shelf and closed the cupboard door and could only stand there for a moment, listening to the heavy thud of her heart, feeling her strangeness in this kitchen. She was an intruder in this kitchen. Then she followed her son.

She got to the doorway of his room just in time to see him climb into bed. He pulled the sheet up and rolled over on his left side, his usual sleeping position. Although she knew it was over now, Charity stood there yet awhile longer.

Somebody down the hall coughed, reminding her again that this was someone else's house. She felt a strong wave of homesickness; for a few moments it was as if her stomach were full of some numbing gas, the kind of stuff dentists use. In this fine still morning light, her thoughts of divorce seemed as immature and without regard for the realities as the thoughts of a child. It was easy for her to think of such things here. It wasn't her house, not her place.

Why had his pantomime of feeding Cujo, and those rapid, sighing words, frightened her so much? *Cujo's not hungry no more, not no more.*

She went back to her own room and lay there in bed as the sun came up and brightened the room. At breakfast, Brett seemed no different than ever. He did not mention Cujo, and he had apparently forgotten about calling home, at least for the time being. After some interior debate, Charity decided to let the matter rest there.

It was hot.

Donna uncranked her window a little farther – about a quarter of the way, as far as she dared – and then leaned across Tad's lap to unroll his too. That was when she noticed the creased yellow sheet on paper in his lap.

'What's that, Tad?'

He looked up at her. There were smudged brown circles under his eyes. 'The Monster Words,' he said.

'Can I see?'

He held them tightly for a moment and then let her take the paper. There was a watchful, almost proprietary expression on his face, and she felt an instant's jealousy. It was brief but very strong. So far she had managed to keep him alive and unhurt, but it was Vic's hocus-pocus he cared about. Then the feeling dissipated into bewilderment, sadness, and self-disgust. It was she who had put him in this situation in the first place. If she hadn't given in to him about the baby-sitter . . .

'I put them in my pocket yesterday,' he said, 'before we went shopping. Mommy, is the monster going to eat us?'

'It's not a monster, Tad, it's just a *dog*, and no, it isn't

going to eat us!' She spoke more sharply than she had
intended. 'I told you, when the mailman comes, we can go
home.' *And I told him the car would start in just a little
while, and I told him someone would come, that the
Cambers would be home soon –*

But what was the use of thinking that?

'May I have my Monster Words back?' he asked.

For a moment she felt a totally insane urge to tear the
sweat-stained, creased sheet of yellow legal paper to bits and
toss them out of her window, so much fluttering confetti.
Then she handed the paper back to Tad and ran both hands
through her hair, ashamed and scared. What was happening
to her, for Christ's sake? A sadistic thought like that. Why
would she want to make it worse for him? Was it Vic?
Herself? What?

It was so hot – too hot to think. Sweat was streaming
down her face and she could see it trickling down Tad's
cheeks as well. His hair was plastered against his skull in
unlovely chunks, and it looked two shades darker than its
usual medium-blond. *He needs his hair washed*, she thought
randomly, and that made her think of the bottle of
Johnson's No More Tears again, sitting safely and sanely on
the bathroom shelf, waiting for someone to take it down and
pour a capful or two into one cupped palm.

(don't lose control of yourself)

No, of course not. She had no *reason* to lose control of
herself. Everything was going to be all right, wasn't it? Of
course it was. The dog wasn't even in sight, hadn't been for
more than an hour. And the mailman. It was almost ten
o'clock now. The mailman would be along soon, and then
it wouldn't matter that it was so hot in the car. 'The
greenhouse effect', they called it. She had seen that on an
SPCA handout somewhere, explaining why you shouldn't
shut your dog up in your car for any length of time when it
was hot like this. The greenhouse effect. The pamphlet had
said that the temperature in a car that was parked in the sun
could go as high as 140 degrees Fahrenheit if the windows
were rolled up, so it was cruel and dangerous to lock up a pet

while you did your shopping or went to see a movie. Donna uttered a short, cracked-sounding chuckle. The shoe certainly was on the other foot here, wasn't it? It was the dog that had the people locked up.

Well, the mailman was coming. The mailman was coming and that would end it. It wouldn't matter that they had only a quarter of a Thermos of milk left, or that early this morning she had to go to the bathroom and she had used Tad's smaller Thermos – or had tried to – and it had overflowed and now the Pinto smelled of urine, an unpleasant smell that only seemed to grow stronger with the heat. She had capped the Thermos and thrown it out the window. She had heard it shatter as it hit the gravel. Then she had cried.

But none of it mattered. It was humiliating and demeaning to have to try and pee into a Thermos bottle, sure it was, but it didn't matter because the mailman was coming – even now he would be loading his small blue-and-white truck at the ivy-covered brick post office on Carbine Street . . . or maybe he had already begun his route, working his way out Route 117 toward the Maple Sugar Road. Soon it would end. She would take Tad home, and they would go upstairs. They would strip and shower together, but before she got into the tub with him and under the shower, she would take the bottle of shampoo from the shelf and put the cap neatly on the edge of the sink, and she would wash first Tad's hair and then her own.

Tad was reading the yellow paper again, his lips moving soundlessly. Not real reading, not the way he would be reading in a couple of years (*if we get out of this*, her traitorous mind insisted on adding senselessly but instantly), but the kind that came from rote memorization. The way driving schools prepared functional illiterates for the written part of the driver's exam. She had read that somewhere too, or maybe seen it on a TV news story, and wasn't it amazing, the amount of crud the human mind was capable of storing up? And wasn't it amazing how easily it all came spewing out when there was nothing else to engage it? Like a subconscious garbage disposal running in reverse.

That made her think of something that had happened in her parents' house, back when it had still been her house too. Less than two hours before one of her mother's Famous Cocktail Parties (that was how Donna's father always referred to them, with a satirical tone that automatically conferred the capital letters – the same satirical tone that could sometimes drive Samantha into a frenzy), the disposal in the kitchen sink had somehow backed up into the bar sink, and when her mother turned the gadget on again in an effort to get rid of everything, green goo had exploded all over the ceiling. Donna had been about fourteen at the time, and she remembered that her mother's utter, hysterical rage had both frighened and sickened her. She had been sickened because her mother was throwing a tantrum in front of the people who loved and needed her most over the opinion of a group of casual acquaintances who were coming over to drink free booze and munch up a lot of free canapés. She had been frightened because she could see no *logic* in her mother's tantrum . . . and because of the expression she had seen in her father's eyes. It had been a kind of resigned disgust. That had been the first time she had really believed – believed in her gut – that she was going to grow up and become a woman, a woman with at least a fighting chance to be a *better* woman than her own mother, who could get into such a frightening state over what was really such a little thing. . . .

She closed her eyes and tried to dismiss the whole train of thought, uneasy at the vivid emotions that memory called up. SPCA, greenhouse effect, garbage disposals, what next? How I Lost My Virginity? Six Well-Loved Vacations? The *mailman*, that was the thing to think about, the goddam *mailman*.

'Mommy, maybe the car will start now.'

'Honey, I'm scared to try it because the battery is so low.'

'But we're just *sitting* here,' he said, sounding petulant and tired and cross. 'What does it matter if the battery's low or not if we're just *sitting* here? Try it!'

'Don't you go giving me orders, kiddo, or I'll whack your ass for you!'

He cringed away from her hoarse, angry voice and she cursed herself again. He was scratchy . . . so, who could blame him? Besides, he was right. That was what had really made her angry. But Tad didn't understand, the real reason she didn't want to try the engine again was because she was afraid it would bring the dog. She was afraid it would bring Cujo, and more than anything else she didn't want that.

Grimly, she turned the key in the ignition. The Pinto's engine cranked very slowly now, with a draggy, protesting sound. It coughed twice but did not fire. She turned the key off and tapped the horn. It gave a foggy, low honk that probably didn't carry fifty yards, let alone to that house at the bottom of the hill.

'There,' she said briskly and cruelly. 'Are you happy? Good.'

Tad began to cry. He began the way she always remembered it beginning when he was a baby: his mouth drawing into a trembling bow, the tears spilling down his cheeks even before the first sobs came. She pulled him to her then, saying she was sorry, saying she didn't mean to be mean, it was just that she was upset too, telling him that it would be over as soon as the mailman got there, that she would take him home and wash his hair. And thought: *A fighting chance to be a better woman than your mother. Sure. Sure, kid. You're just like her. That's just the kind of thing she would have said in a situation like this. When you're feeling bad, what you do is spread the misery, share the wealth. Well, like mother like daughter, right? And maybe when Tad grows up, he'll feel the same way about you as you feel about —*

'Why is it so hot, Mommy?' Tad asked dully.

'The greenhouse effect,' she answered, without even thinking about it. She wasn't up to this, and she knew it now. If this was, in any sense, a final examination on motherhood — or on adulthood itself — then she was flagging the test. How long had they been stuck in this driveway? Fifteen hours at the very most. And she was cracking up, falling apart.

'Can I have a Dr Pepper when we get home, Mommy?' The Monster Words, sweaty and wrinkled, lay limply on his lap.

'All you can drink,' she said, and hugged him tight. But the feel of his body was frighteningly wooden. I shouldn't have shouted at him, she thought distractedly. If only I hadn't shouted.

But she would do better, she promised herself. Because the mailman would be along soon.

'I think the muh – I think the doggy's going to eat us,' Tad said.

She started to reply and then didn't. Cujo still wasn't around. The sound of the Pinto's engine turning over hadn't brought him. Maybe he was asleep. Maybe he had had a convulsion and died. That would be wonderful ... especially if it had been a *slow* convulsion. A painful one. She looked at the back door again. It was so temptingly near. It was locked. She was sure of that now. When people went away, they locked up. It would be foolhardy to try for the door, especially with the mailman due so soon. Play it as though it were real, Vic sometimes said. She would have to, because it *was* real. Better to assume the dog was still alive, and lying just inside those half-open garage doors. Lying in the shade.

The thought of shade made her mouth water.

It was almost eleven o'clock then. It was about forty-five minutes later when she spotted something in the grass beyond the edge of Tad's side of the car. Another fifteen minutes of examination convinced her that it was an old baseball bat with a friction-taped handle, half obscured by witch grass and timothy.

A few minutes after that, just before noon, Cujo stumbled out of the barn, blinking his red, rheumy eyes stupidly in the hot sun.

When they come to take you down,
When they bring that wagon 'round,
When they come to call on you
And drag your poor body down . . .

Jerry Garcia's voice, easy but somehow weary, came
floating down the hall, magnified and distorted by someone's transistor radio until it sounded as if the vocal were
floating down a long steel tube. Closer by, someone was
moaning. That morning, when he went down to the smelly
industrial bathroom to shave and shower, there had been a
puddle of vomit in one of the urinals and a large quantity of
dried blood in one of the washbasins.

'*Shake it, shake it, Sugaree,*' Jerry Garcia sang, '*just don't
tell 'em you know me.*'

Steve Kemp stood at the window of his room on the fifth
floor of the Portland YMCA, looking down at Spring Street,
feeling bad and not knowing why. His head was bad. He
kept thinking about Donna Trenton and how he had fucked
her over – fucked her over and then hung around. Hung
around for what? What the fuck had happened?

He wished he were in Idaho. Idaho had been much on his
mind lately. So why didn't he stop honking his donk and just
go? He didn't know. He didn't like not knowing. He didn't
like all these questions screwing up his head. Questions were
counterproductive to a state of serenity, and serenity was
necessary to the development of the artist. He had looked at
himself this morning in one of the toothpaste-spotted
mirrors and had thought he looked old. Really old. When he
came back to his room he had seen a cockroach zigzagging
busily across the floor. The omens were bad.

She didn't give me the brush because I'm old, he thought.
*I'm not old. She did it because her itch was scratched,
because she's a bitch, and because I gave her a spoonful of
her own medicine. How did Handsome Hubby like his little
love note, Donna? Did Handsome Hubby dig it?*

Did hubby *get* his little love note?

Steve crushed his cigarette out in the jar top that served

the room as an ashtray. That was really the central question, wasn't it? With that one answered, the answers to the other questions would drop into place. The hateful hold she had gotten over him by telling him to get lost before he was ready to end the affair (she had *humiliated* him, goddammit), for one thing – for one very *big* thing.

Suddenly he knew what to do, and his heart began to thud heavily with anticipation. He put a hand into his pocket and jingled the change there. He went out. It was just past noon, and in Castle Rock, the mailman for whom Donna hoped had begun that part of his rounds which covered the Maple Sugar Road and Town Road No. 3.

Vic, Roger, and Rob Martin spent Tuesday morning at Image-Eye and then went out for beers and burgers. A few burgers and a great many beers later, Vic suddenly realized that he was drunker than he had ever been at a business luncheon in his life. Usually he had a single cocktail or a glass of white wine; he had seen too many good New York admen drown themselves slowly in those dark places just off Madison Avenue, talking to their friends about campaigns they would never mount ... or, if they became drunk enough, to the barmen in those places about novels which they would assuredly never write.

It was a strange occasion, half victory celebration, half wake. Rob had greeted their idea of a final Sharp Cereal Professor ad with tempered enthusiasm, saying that he could knock it a mile ... always assuming he was given the chance. That was the wake half. Without the approval of old man Sharp and his fabled kid, the greatest spot in the world would do them no good. They would all be out on their asses.

Under the circumstances, Vic supposed it was all right to get loaded.

Now, as the main rush of the restaurant's lunchtime clientele came in, the three of them sat in their shirtsleeves at a corner booth, the remains of their burgers on waxed paper, beer bottles scattered around the table, the ashtray overflowing. Vic was reminded of the day he and Roger had sat in the Yellow Sub back in Portland, discussing this little safari. Back when everything that had been wrong had been wrong with the business. Incredibly, he felt a wave of nostalgia for that day and wondered what Tad and Donna were doing. *Got to call them tonight*, he thought. *If I can stay sober enough to remember, that is.*

'So what now?' Rob asked. 'You hangin out in Boston or going on to New York? I can get you guys tickets to the Boston-Kansas City series, if you want them. Might cheer you up to watch George Brett knock a few holes in the left-field wall.'

Vic looked at Roger, who shrugged and said, 'On to New York, I guess. Thanks are in order, Rob, but I don't think either of us are in the mood for baseball.'

'There's nothing more we can do here,' Vic agreed. 'We had a lot of time scheduled on this trip for brainstorming, but I guess we're all agreed to go with the final spot idea.'

'There's still plenty of rough edges,' Rob said. 'Don't get too proud.'

'We can mill off the rough edges,' Roger said. 'One day with the marketing people ought to do it, I think. You agree, Vic?'

'It might take two,' Vic said. 'Still, there's no reason why we can't tie things up a lot earlier than we'd expected.'

'Then what?'

Vic grinned bleakly. 'Then we call old man Sharp and make an appointment to see him. I imagine we'll end up going straight on to Cleveland from New York. The Magical Mystery Tour.'

'See Cleveland and die,' Roger said gloomily, and poured the remainder of his beer into his glass. 'I just can't wait to see that old fart.'

'Don't forget the young fart,' Vic said, grinning a little.

'How could I forget that little prick?' Roger replied. 'Gentlemen, I propose another round.'

Rob looked at his watch. 'I really ought to –'

'One last round,' Roger insisted. 'Auld Lang Syne, if you want.'

Rob shrugged. 'Okay. But I still got a business to run, don't forget that. Although without Sharp Cereals, there's going to be space for a lot of long lunches.' He raised his glass in the air and waggled it until a waiter saw him and nodded back.

'Tell me what you really think,' Vic said to Rob. 'No bullshit. You think it's a bust?'

Rob looked at him, seemed about to speak, then shook his head.

Roger said, 'No, go ahead. We all set out to sea in the same pea-green boat. Or Red Razberry Zingers carton, or whatever. You think it's no go, don't you?'

'I don't think there's a chance in hell,' Rob said. 'You'll work up a good presentation – you always do. You'll get your background work done in New York, and I have a feeling that everything the market-research boys can tell you on such short notice is all going to be in your favor. And Yancey Harrington. . . . I think he'll emote his fucking heart out. His big deathbed scene. He'll be so good he'll make Bette Davis in *Dark Victory* look like Ali MacGraw in *Love Story*.'

'Oh, but it's not like that at all –' Roger began.

Rob shrugged. 'Yeah, maybe that's a little unfair. Okay. Call it his curtain call, then. Whatever you want to call it, I've been in this business long enough to believe that there wouldn't be a dry eye in the house after that commercial was shown over a three- or four-week period. It would knock *everybody* on their asses. But –'

The beers came. The waiter said to Rob, 'Mr. Johnson asked me to tell you that he has several parties of three waiting, Mr. Martin.'

'Well, you run back and tell Mr. Johnson that the boys are on their last round and to keep his undies dry. Okay, Rocky?'

The waiter smiled, emptied the ashtray, and nodded.

He left. Rob turned back to Vic and Roger. 'So what's the bottom line? You're bright boys. You don't need a one-legged cameraman with a snootful of beer to tell you where the bear shat in the buckwheat.'

'Sharp just won't apologize,' Vic said. 'That's what you think, isn't it?' Rob saluted him with his bottle of beer. 'Go to the head of the class.'

'It's not an apology,' Roger said plaintively. 'It's a fucking *explanation*.'

'You see it that way,' Rob answered, 'but will he? Ask yourself that. I've met that old geezer a couple of times. He'd see it in terms of the captain deserting the sinking ship ahead of the women and children, giving up the Alamo, every stereotype you can think of. No, I'll tell you what I think is going to happen, my friends.' He raised his glass and drank slowly. 'I think a valuable and all too short relationship is going to come to an end very soon now. Old man Sharp is going to listen to your proposal, he's going to shake his head, he's going to usher you out. Permanently. And the next PR firm will be chosen by his son, who will make his pick based on which one he believes will give him the freest rein to indulge his crackpot ideas.'

'Maybe,' Roger said. 'But maybe he'll —'

'Maybe doesn't matter *shit* one way or the other,' Vic said vehemently. 'The only difference between a good advertising man and a good snake-oil salesman is that a good advertising man does the best job he can with the materials at hand . . . without stepping outside the bounds of honesty. That's what this commercial is about. If he turns it down, he's turning down the best we can do. And that's the end. Toot-finny.' He snuffed his cigarette and almost knocked over Roger's half-full bottle of beer. His hands were shaking.

Rob nodded. 'I'll drink to that.' He raised his glass. 'A toast, gentlemen.'

Vic and Roger raised their own glasses.

Rob thought for a moment and then said: 'May things turn out all right, even against the odds.'

'Amen,' Roger said.

They clinked their glasses together and drank. As he downed the rest of his beer, Vic found himself thinking about Donna and Tad again.

George Meara, the mailman, lifted one leg clad in blue-gray Post Office issue and farted. Just lately he farted a great deal. He was mildly worried about it. It didn't seem to matter what he had been eating. Last night he and the wife had had creamed cod on toast and he had farted. This morning, Kellog's Product 19 with a banana cut up in it – and he had farted. This noon, down at the Mellow Tiger in town, two cheeseburgers with mayonnaise . . . ditto farts.

He had looked up the symptom in *The Home Medical Encyclopedia*, an invaluable tome in twelve volumes which his wife had gotten a volume at a time by saving her checkout slips from the Shop 'n Save in South Paris. What George Meara had discovered under the EXCESSIVE FLATULENCE heading had not been particularly encouraging. It could be a symptom of gastric upset. It could mean he had a nice little ulcer incubating in there. It could be a bowel problem. It could even mean the big C. If it kept up he supposed he would go and see old Dr. Quentin. Dr. Quentin would tell him he was farting a lot because he was getting older and that was it.

Aunt Evvie Chalmers's death that late spring had hit George hard – harder than he ever would have believed – and just lately he didn't like to think about getting older. He preferred to think about the Golden Years of Retirement, years that he and Cathy would spend together. No more getting up at six thirty. No more heaving around sacks of mail and listening to that asshole Michael Fournier, who was the Castle Rock postmaster. No more freezing his balls off in the winter and going crazy with all the summer people who wanted delivery to their camps and cottages when the warm weather came. Instead, there would be a Winnebago for 'Scenic Trips Through New England.' There would be

'Puttering in the Garden.' There would be 'All Sorts of New Hobbies'. Most of all, there would be 'Rest and Relaxation'. And somehow, the thought of farting his way through his late sixties and early seventies like a defective rocket just didn't jibe with his fond picture of the Golden Years of Retirement.

He turned the small blue-and-white mail truck onto Town Road No. 3, wincing as the glare of sunlight shifted briefly across the windshield. The summer had turned out every bit as hot as Aunt Evvie had prophesied – all of that, and then some. He could hear crickets singing sleepily in the high summer grass and had a brief vision out of the Golden Years of Retirement, a scene entitled 'George Relaxes in the Back Yard Hammock'.

He stopped at the Millikens' and pushed a Zayre's advertising circular and a CMP power bill into the box. This was the day all the power bills went out, but he hoped the CMP folks wouldn't hold their breath until the Millikens' check came in. The Millikens were poor white trash, like that Gary Pervier just up the road. It was nothing but a scandal to see what was happening to Pervier, a man who had once won a DSC. And old Joe Camber wasn't a hell of a lot better. They were going to the dogs, the both of them.

John Milliken was out in the side yard, repairing what looked like a harrow. George gave him a wave, and Milliken flicked one finger curtly in return before going back to his work.

Here's one for you, you welfare chiseler, George Meara thought. He lifted his leg and blew his trombone. It was a hell of a thing, this farting. You had to be pretty damn careful when you were out in company.

He drove on up the road to Gary Pervier's, produced another Zayre's circular, another power bill, and added a VFW newsletter. He tucked them into the box and then turned around in Gary's driveway, because he didn't have to drive all the way up to Camber's place today. Joe had called the post office yesterday morning around ten and had asked them to hold his mail for a few days. Mike Fournier, the big talker who was in charge of things at the Castle Rock P.O., had routinely filled out a HOLD MAIL UNTIL NOTIFIED card and flipped it over to George's station.

Fournier told Joe Camber he had called just about fifteen minutes too late to stop the Monday delivery of mail, if that had been his intention.

'Don't matter,' Joe had said. 'I guess I'll be around to get today's.'

When George put Gary Pervier's mail into his box, he noticed that Gary's Monday delivery – a *Popular Mechanix* and a charity begging letter from the Rural Scholarship Fund – had not been removed. Now, turning around, he noticed that Gary's big old Chrysler was in the dooryard and Joe Camber's rusting-around-the-edges station wagon was parked right behind it.

'Gone off together,' he muttered aloud. 'Two fools off hooting somewhere.'

He lifted his leg and farted again.

George's conclusion was that the two of them were probably off drinking and whoring, wheeling around in Joe Camber's pickup truck. It didn't occur to him to wonder why they would have taken Joe's truck when there were two much more comfortable vehicles near at hand, and he didn't notice the blood on the porch steps or the fact that there was a large hole in the lower panel of Gary's screen door.

'Two fools off hooting,' he repeated. 'At least Joe Camber remembered to cancel his mail.'

He drove off the way he had come, back towards Castle Rock, lifting his leg every now and then to blow his trombone.

Steve Kemp drove out to the Dairy Queen by the Westbrook Shopping Mall for a couple of cheeseburgers and a Dilly Bar. He sat in his van, eating and looking out at Brighton Avenue, not really seeing the road or tasting the food.

He had called Handsome Hubby's office. He gave his name as Adam Swallow when the secretary asked. Said he was the marketing director for House of Lights, Inc., and would like to talk to Mr. Trenton. He had been dry-mouthed with excitement. And when Trenton got on the old hooter, they could find more interesting things than marketing to talk about. Like the little woman's birthmark, and what it might look like. Like how she had bitten him once when she came, hard enough to draw blood. Like how things were going for the Bitch Goddess since Handsome Hubby discovered she had a little taste for what she was on the other side of the sheets.

But things hadn't turned out that way. The secretary had said, 'I'm sorry, but both Mr. Trenton and Mr. Breakstone are out of the office this week. They'll probably be out most of the next week, as well. If I could help you –?' Her voice had a rising, hopeful inflection. She really did want to help. It was her big chance to land an account while the bosses were taking care of business in Boston or maybe New York – surely no place as exotic as LA, not a little dipshit agency like Ad Worx. So get out there and tapdance until your shoes smoke, kid.

He thanked her and told her he would ring back toward the end of the month. He hung up before she could ask for his number, since the office of the House of Lights, Inc., was in a Congress Street phone booth across from Joe's Smoke Shop.

Now here he was, eating cheeseburgers and wondering what to do next. *As if you didn't know*, an interior voice whispered.

He started the van up and headed for Castle Rock. By the time he finished his lunch (the Dilly Bar was practically running down the stick in the heat), he was in North Windham. He threw his trash on the floor of the van, where it joined a drift of like stuff – plastic drink containers, Big Mac boxes, returnable beer and soda bottles, empty cigarette packs. Littering was an antisocial, anti-environmentalist act, and he didn't do it.

Steve got to the Trenton house at just half past three on that hot, glaring afternoon. Acting with almost subliminal caution, he drove past the house without slowing and parked around the corner on a side street about a quarter of a mile away. He walked back.

The driveway was empty, and he felt a pang of frustrated disappointment. He would not admit to himself – especially now that it looked like she was out – that he had intended to give her a taste of what she had been so eager to have during the spring. Nevertheless, he had driven all the way from Westbrook to Castle Rock with a semi-erection that only now collapsed completely.

She was gone.

No; the *car* was gone. One thing didn't necessarily prove the other, did it?

Steve looked around himself.

What we have here, ladies and gents, is a peaceful suburban street on a summer's day, most of the kiddies in for naps, most of the little wifies either doing likewise or glued to their TVs, checking out Love of Life *or* Search for Tomorrow. *All the Handsome Hubbies are busy earning their way into higher tax brackets and very possibly a bed in the Intensive Care ward at the Eastern Maine Medical Center.* Two little kids were playing hopscotch on a blurred chalk grid; they were wearing bathing suits and sweating heavily. An old balding lady was trundling a wire shopping caddy back from town as if both she and it were made of the finest bone china. She gave the kids playing hopscotch a wide berth.

In short, not much happening. The street was dozing in the heat.

Steve walked up the sloping driveway as if he had every right to be there. First he looked in the tiny one-car garage. He had never known Donna to use it, because the doorway was so narrow. If she put a dent in the car, Handsome Hubby would give her hell – no, excuse me; he would give her *heck*.

The garage was empty. No Pinto, no elderly Jag –

Donna's Handsome Hubby was into what was known as sports car menopause. She hadn't liked him saying that, but Steve had never seen a more obvious case.

Steve left the garage and went up the three steps to the back stoop. Tried the door. Found it unlocked. He went inside without knocking after another casual glance around to make sure no one was in sight.

He closed the door on the silence of the house. Once more his heart was knocking heavily in his chest, seeming to shake his whole ribcage. And once again he was not admitting things. He didn't *have* to admit them. They were there just the same.

'Hi? Anybody home?' His voice was loud, honest, pleasant, inquiring.

'Hi?' He was halfway down the hall now.

Obviously no one home. The house had a silent, hot, waiting feel. An empty house full of furniture was somehow creepy when it wasn't your house. You felt watched.

'Hello? Anybody home?' One last time.

Give her something to remember you by, then. And split.

He went into the living room and stood looking around. His shirtsleeves were rolled up, his forearms lightly slicked with sweat. Now things could be admitted. How he had wanted to kill her when she called him a son of a bitch, her spittle spraying on his face. How he had wanted to kill her for making him feel old and scared and not able to keep on top of the situation any more. The letter had been something, but the letter hadn't been enough.

To his right, knickknacks stood on a series of glass shelves. He turned and gave the bottom shelf a sudden hard kick. It disintegrated. The frame tottered and then fell over, spraying glass, spraying little china figurines of cats and shepherds and all that happy bourgeois horseshit. A pulse throbbed in the center of his forehead. He was grimacing, unaware of the fact. He walked carefully over the unbroken figurines, crushing them into powder. He pulled a family portrait from the wall, looked curiously at the smiling face of Vic Trenton for a moment (Tad was sitting on his lap, and

his arm was around Donna's waist), and then he dropped
the picture to the floor and stamped down hard on the glass.

He looked around, breathing hard, as if he had just run a
race. And suddenly he went after the room as if it were
something alive, something that had hurt him badly and
needed to be punished, as if it were the room that had caused
his pain. He pushed over Vic's La-Z-Boy recliner. He
upended the couch. It stood on end for a moment, rocking
uneasily, and then went down with a crash, breaking the
back of the coffee table which had stood in front of it. He
pulled all the books out of the bookcases, cursing the shitty
taste of the people who had bought them under his breath as
he did it. He picked up the magazine stand and threw it
overhand at the mirror over the mantelpiece, shattering it.
Big pieces of black-backed mirror fell onto the floor like
chunks of a jigsaw puzzle. He was snorting now, like a bull
in heat. His thin cheeks were almost purple with color.

He went into the kitchen by way of the small dining room.
As he walked past the dining-room table Donna's parents
had bought them as a housewarming present, he extended
his arm straight out and swept everything off onto the
floor – the lazy Susan with its complement of spices, the
cut-glass vase Donna had gotten for a dollar and a quarter at
the Emporium Galorium in Bridgton the summer previous,
Vic's graduation beer stein. The ceramic salt and pepper
shakers shattered like bombs. His erection was back now,
raging. Thoughts of caution, of possible discovery, had
departed his mind. He was somewhere inside. He was down
a dark hole.

In the kitchen he yanked the bottom drawer of the stove
out to its stop and threw pots and pans everywhere. They
made a dreadful clatter, but there was no satisfaction in
mere clatter. A rank of cupboards ran around three of the
room's four sides. He pulled them open one after the other.
He grabbed plates by the double handful and threw them on
the floor. Crockery jingled musically. He swept the glasses
out and grunted as they broke. Among them was a set of
eight delicate long-stemmed wine glasses that Donna had

had since she was twelve years old. She had read about 'hope chests' in some magazine or other and had determined to have such a chest of her own. As it turned out, the wine glasses were the only thing she had actually put in hers before losing interest (her original grand intention had been to lay by enough to completely furnish her bridal house or flat), but she had had them for more than half her life, and they were treasured.

The gravy boat went. The big serving platter. The Sears radio/tape player went on the floor with a heavy crunch. Steve Kemp danced on it; he boogied on it. His penis, hard as stone, throbbed inside his pants. The vein in the center of his forehead throbbed in counterpoint. He discovered booze under the small chromium sink in the corner. He yanked out half- and three-quarters-full bottles by the armload and then flung them at the closed door of the kitchen closet one by one, throwing them overhand as hard as he could; the next day his right arm would be so stiff and sore he would barely be able to lift it to shoulder level. Soon the blue closet door was running with Gilbey's gin, Jack Daniel's, J & B whisky, sticky green crème de menthe, the amaretto that had been a Christmas present from Roger and Althea Breakstone. Glass twinkled benignly in the hot afternoon sunlight pouring through the windows over the sink.

Steve tore into the laundry room, where he found boxes of bleach, Spic 'n Span, Downy fabric softener in a large blue plastic bottle, Lestoil, Top Job, and three kinds of powdered detergent. He ran back and forth pouring these cleaning potions everywhere.

He had just emptied the last carton – when he saw the message scrawled on the noteminder in Donna's unmistakable spiky handwriting: *Tad & I have gone out to J. Camber's garage w/Pinto. Back soon.*

That brought him back to the realities of the situation with a bang. He had already been here half an hour at least, maybe longer. The time had passed in a red blur, and it was hard to peg it any more closely than that. How long had she been gone when he came in? Who had the note been left for?

Anybody who might pop in, or someone specific? He had to get out of here . . . but there was one other thing he had to do first.

He erased the message on the noteminder with one swipe of his sleeve and wrote in large block letters:

I LEFT SOMETHING UPSTAIRS FOR YOU, BABY.

He took the stairs two by two and came into their bedroom, which was to the left of the second-floor landing. He felt terribly pressed now, almost positive that the doorbell was going to ring or someone – another happy housewife, most likely – would poke her head in the back door and call (as he had), 'Hi! Anybody home?'

But, perversely, that added the final spice of excitement to this mad happening. He unbuckled his belt, jerked his fly down, and let his jeans drop down around his knees. He wasn't wearing underpants; he rarely did. His cock stood out stiffly from a mass of reddish-gold pubic hair. It didn't take long; he was too excited. Two or three quick jerks through his closed fist and orgasm came, immediate and savage. He spat semen onto the bedspread in a convulsion.

He yanked his jeans back up, raked the zipper closed (almost catching the head of his penis in the zipper's small gold teeth – *that* would have been a laugh, all right), and ran for the door, buckling his belt again. He would meet someone as he was going out. Yes. He felt positive of it, as if it were preordained. Some happy housewife who would take one look at his flushed face, his bulging eyes, his tented jeans, and scream her head off.

He tried to prepare himself for it as he opened the back door and went out. In retrospect it seemed that he had made enough noise to wake the dead . . . those pans! Why had he thrown those fucking pans around? What had he been thinking of? Everyone in the neighborhood must have heard.

But there was no one in the yard or in the driveway. The peace of the afternoon was undisturbed. Across the street, a lawn sprinkler twirled unconcernedly. A kid went by on roller skates. Straight ahead was a high hedge which separated the Trentons' house lot from the next one over. Looking to the left from the back stoop was a view of the town nestled at the bottom of the hill. Steve could see the intersection of Route 117 and High Street quite clearly, the Town Common nestled in one of the angles made by the crossing of the two roads. He stood there on the stoop, trying to get his shit back together. His breath slowed a little at a time back into a more normal inhale-exhale pattern. He found a pleasant afternoon face and put it on. All this happened in the length of time it took for the traffic light on the corner to cycle from red to amber to green and back to red again.

What if she pulls into the driveway right now?

That got him going again. He'd left his calling card; he didn't need any hassle from her on top of it. There was no way she could do a thing anyway, unless she called the cops, and he didn't think she'd do that. There were too many things he could tell: The Sex Life of the Great American Happy Housewife in Its Natural Habitat. It had been a crazy scene, though. Best to put miles between himself and Castle Rock. Maybe later he would give her a call. Ask her how she had liked his work. That might be sort of fun.

He walked down the driveway, turned left, and went back to his van. He wasn't stopped. Nobody took any undue notice of him. A kid on roller skates zipped past him and shouted 'Hi!' Steve hi'd him right back.

He got in the van and started it up. He drove up 117 to 302 and followed that road to its intersection with Interstate 95 in Portland. He took an Interstate time-and-toll ticket and rolled south. He had begun having uneasy thoughts about what he had done – the red rage of destruction he had gone into when he saw that no one was home. Had the retribution been too heavy for the offense? So she didn't want to make it with him any more, so what? He had trashed most of the goddamn house. Did that, maybe, say something unpleasant about where his head was at?

He began to work on these questions a little at a time, the way most people do, running an objective set of facts through a bath of various chemicals which, when taken together, make up the complex human perceptual mechanism known as subjectivity. Like a schoolchild who works carefully first with the pencil, then with the eraser, then with the pencil again, he tore down what had happened and then carefully rebuilt it — redrew it in his mind — until both the facts and his perception of the facts jibed in a way he could live with.

When he reached Route 495, he turned west toward New York and the country that sprawled beyond, all the way to the silent reaches of Idaho, the place that Papa Hemingway had gone to when he was old and mortally hurt. He felt the familiar lift in his feelings that came with cutting old ties and moving on — that magical thing that Huck had called 'lighting out for the territory.' At such times he felt almost newborn, felt strongly that he was in possession of the greatest freedom of all, the freedom to recreate himself. He would have been unable to understand the significance if someone had pointed out the fact that, whether in Maine or in Idaho, he would still be apt to throw his racket down in angry frustration if he lost a game of tennis; that he would refuse to shake the hand of his opponent over the net, as he always had when he lost. He only shook over the net when he won.

He stopped for the night in a small town called Twickenham. His sleep was easy. He had convinced himself that trashing the Trentons' house had not been an act of half-mad jealous pique but a piece of revolutionary anarchy — offing a couple of fat middle-class pigs, the sort who made it easy for the fascist overlords to remain in power by blindly paying their taxes and their telephone bills. It had been an act of courage and of clean, justified fury. It was his way of saying 'power to the people', an idea he tried to incorporate in all his poems.

Still, he mused, as he turned toward sleep in the narrow motel bed, he wondered what Donna had thought of it when she and the kid got home. That sent him to sleep with a slight smile on his lips.

By three thirty that Tuesday afternoon, Donna had given up on the mailman.

She sat with one arm lightly around Tad, who was in a dazed half sleep, his lips cruelly puffed from the heat, his face hectic and flushed. There was a tiny bit of milk left, and soon she would give it to him. During the last three and a half hours — since what would have been lunchtime at home — the sun had been monstrous and unremitting. Even with her window and Tad's window open a quarter of the way, the temperature inside must have reached 100 degrees, maybe more. It was the way your car got when you left it in the sun, that was all. Except, under normal circumstances, what you did when your car got like that was you unrolled all the windows, pulled the knobs that opened the air-ducts, and got rolling. *Let's get rolling* — what a sweet sound those words had!

She licked her lips.

For short periods she had unrolled the windows all the way, creating a mild draft, but she was afraid to leave them that way. She might doze off. The heat scared her — it scared her for herself and even more for Tad, what it might be taking out of him — but it didn't scare her as badly as the face of that dog, slavering foam and staring at her with its sullen red eyes.

The last time she had unrolled the windows all the way was when Cujo had disappeared into the shadows of the barn-garage. But now Cujo was back.

He sat in the lengthening shadow of the big barn, his head lowered, staring at the blue Pinto. The ground between his front paws was muddy from his slaver. Every now and then he would growl and snap at empty air, as if he might be hallucinating.

How long? How long before he dies?

She was a rational woman. She did not believe in monsters

from closets; she believed in things she could see and touch. There was nothing supernatural about the slobbering wreck of a Saint Bernard sitting in the shade of a barn; he was merely a sick animal that had been bitten by a rabid fox or skunk or something. He wasn't out to get her personally. He wasn't the Reverend Dimmesdale or Moby Dog. He was not four-footed Fate.

But . . . she had just about decided to make a run for the back door of the enclosed Camber porch when Cujo had come rolling and staggering out of the darkness of the barn.

Tad. Tad was the thing. She had to get him out of this. No more fucking around. He wasn't answering very coherently any more. He seemed to be in touch only with the peaks of reality. The glazed way his eyes rolled toward her when she spoke to him, like the eyes of a fighter who has been struck and struck and struck, a fighter who has lost his coherence along with his mouthguard and is waiting only for the final flurry of punches to drop him insensible to the canvas — those things terrified her and roused all her motherhood. Tad was the thing. If she had been alone, she would have gone for that door long ago. It was Tad who had held her back, because her mind kept circling back to the thought of the dog pulling her down, and of Tad in the car alone.

Still, until Cujo had returned fifteen minutes ago, she had been preparing herself to go for the door. She played it over and over in her mind like a home movie, did it until it seemed to one part of her mind as if it had already happened. She would shake Tad fully awake, slap him awake if she had to. Tell him he was not to leave the car and follow her — *under no circumstances, no matter what happens.* She would run from the car to the porch door. Try the knob. If it was unlocked, well and fine. But she was prepared for the very real possibility that it was locked. She had taken off her shirt and now sat behind the wheel in her white cotton bra, the shirt in her lap. When she went, she would go with the shirt wrapped around her hand. Far from perfect protection, but better than none at all. She would smash in the pane of glass nearest the doorknob, reach through, and let herself onto the little back porch. And if the inner door was locked, she would cope with that too. Somehow.

But Cujo had come back out, and that took away her edge.

Never mind. He'll go back in. He has before.

But will he? her mind chattered. *It's all too perfect, isn't it? The Cambers are gone, and they remembered to shut off their mail like good citizens; Vic is gone, and the chances are slim that he'll call before tomorrow night, because we just can't afford long distance every night. And if he does call, he'll call early. When he doesn't get any answer he'll assume we went out to catch some chow at Mario's or maybe a couple of ice creams at the Tastee Freeze. And he won't call later because he'll think we're asleep. He'll call tomorrow instead. Considerate Vic. Yes, it's all just too perfect. Wasn't there a dog in the front of the boat in that story about the boatman on the River Charon? The boatman's dog. Just call me Cujo. All out for the Valley of Death.*

Go in, she silently willed the dog. *Go back in the barn, damn you.*

Cujo didn't move.

She licked her lips, which felt almost as puffy as Tad's looked.

She brushed his hair off his forehead and said softly, 'How you going, Tadder?'

'Shhh,' Tad muttered distractedly. 'The ducks . . .'

She gave him a shake. 'Tad? Honey? You okay? Talk to me!'

His eyes opened a little at a time. He looked around, a small boy who was puzzled and hot and dreadfully tired. 'Mommy? Can't we go home? I'm so *hot* . . .'

'We'll go home,' she soothed.

'When, Mom? *When?*' He began to cry helplessly.

Oh Tad, save your moisture, she thought. *You may need it.* Crazy thing to have to be thinking. But the entire situation was ridiculous to the point of lunacy, wasn't it? The idea of a small boy dying of dehydration

(stop it he is NOT dying)

less than seven miles from the nearest good-sized town was crazy.

But the situation is what it is, she reminded herself roughly. And don't you think anything else, sister. It's like a war on a miniaturized scale, so everything that looked small before looks big now. The smallest puff of air through the quarter-open windows was a zephyr. The distance to the back porch was half a mile across no-man's-land. And if you want to believe the dog is Fate, or the Ghost of Sins Remembered, or even the reincarnation of Elvis Presley, then believe it. In this curiously scaled-down situation – this life-or-death situation – even having to go to the bathroom became a skirmish.

We're going to get out of it. No dog is going to do this to my son.

'When, Mommy?' He looked up at her, his eyes wet, his face as pale as cheese.

'Soon,' she said grimly. 'Very soon.' She brushed his hair back and held him against her. She looked out Tad's window and again her eyes fixed on that thing lying in the high grass, that old friction-taped baseball bat.

I'd like to bash your head in with it.

Inside the house, the phone began to ring.

She jerked her head around, suddenly wild with hope.

'Is it for us, Mommy? Is the phone for us?'

She didn't answer him. She didn't know who it was for. But if they were lucky – and their luck was due to change soon, wasn't it? – it would be from someone with cause to be suspicious that no one was answering the phone at the Cambers'. Someone who would come out and check around.

Cujo's head had come up. His head cocked to one side, and for a moment he bore an insane resemblance to Nipper, the RCA dog with his ear to the gramophone horn. He got shakily to his feet and started toward the house and the sound of the ringing telephone.

'Maybe the doggy's going to answer the telephone,' Tad said. 'Maybe –'

With a speed and agility that was terrifying, the big dog changed direction and came at the car. The awkward stagger was gone now, as if it had been nothing but a sly act all along. It was roaring and bellowing rather than barking. Its red eyes burned. It struck the car with a hard, dull crunch and rebounded – with stunned eyes, Donna saw that the side of her door was actually bowed in a bit. *It must be dead,* she thought hysterically, *bashed its sick brains in spinal fusion deep concussion must have – must have MUST HAVE –*

Cujo got back up. His muzzle was bloody. His eyes seemed wandering, vacuous again. Inside the house the phone rang on and on. The dog made as if to walk away, suddenly snapped viciously at its own flank as if stung, whirled, and sprang at Donna's window. It struck right in front of Donna's face with another tremendous dull thud. Blood sprayed across the glass, and a long silver crack appeared. Tad shrieked and clapped his hands to his face, pulling his cheeks down, harrowing them with his fingernails.

The dog leaped again. Ropes of foam runnered back from his bleeding muzzle. She could see his teeth, heavy as old yellow ivory. His claws clicked on the glass. A cut between his eyes was streaming blood. His eyes were fixed on hers; dumb, dull eyes, but not without – she would have sworn it – not without some knowledge. Some malign knowledge.

'*Get out of here!*' she screamed at it.

Cujo threw himself against the side of the car below her window again. And again. And again. Now her door was badly dented inward. Each time the dog's two-hundred-pound bulk struck the Pinto, it rocked on its springs. Each time she heard that heavy, toneless thud, she felt sure it must have killed itself, at least knocked itself unconscious. And each time it trotted back toward the house, whirled and charged the car again. Cujo's face was a mask of blood and matted fur from which his eyes, once a kind, mild brown, peered with stupid fury.

She looked at Tad and saw that he had gone into a shock

reaction, curling himself up into a tight, fetal ball in his bucket seat, his hands laced together at the nape of his neck, his chest hitching.

Maybe that's best. Maybe —

Inside the house the phone stopped ringing. Cujo, in the act of whirling around for another charge, paused. He cocked his head again in that curious, evocative gesture. Donna held her breath. The silence seemed very big. Cujo sat down, raised his horribly mangled nose toward the sky, and howled once — such a dark and lonesome sound and she shivered, no longer hot but as cold as a crypt. In that instant she knew — she did not feel or just think — she *knew* that the dog was something more than just a dog.

The moment passed. Cujo got to his feet, very slowly and wearily, and walked around to the front of the Pinto. She supposed he had lain down there — she could no longer see his tail. Nevertheless she held herself tensed for a few moments longer, mentally ready in case the dog should spring up onto the hood as it had done before. It hadn't. There was nothing but silence.

She gathered Tad into her arms and began to croon to him.

When Brett had at last given up and come out of the telephone booth, Charity took his hand and led him into Caldor's coffee shop. They had come to Caldor's to look at matching tablecloths and curtains.

Holly was waiting for them, sipping the last of an ice-cream soda. 'Nothing wrong, is there?' she asked.

'Nothing too serious,' Charity said, and ruffled his hair. 'He's worried about his dog. Aren't you, Brett?'

Brett shrugged — nodded miserably.

'You go on ahead, if you want,' Charity said to her. 'We'll catch up.'

'All right. I'll be downstairs.'

Holly finished her soda and said, 'I bet your pooch is just fine, Brett.'

Brett smiled at her as best he could but didn't reply. They

watched Holly walk away, smart in her dark burgundy dress and cork-soled sandals, smart in a way Charity knew she would never be able to duplicate. Maybe once, but not now. Holly had left her two with a sitter, and they had come into Bridgeport around noon. Holly had bought them a nice lunch – paying with a Diners Club card – and since then they had been shopping. But Brett had been quiet and withdrawn, worrying about Cujo. Charity didn't feel much like shopping herself; it was hot, and she was still a little unnerved by Brett's sleepwalking that morning. Finally she had suggested that he try calling home from one of the booths around the corner from the snack bar . . . but the results had been precisely those of which she had been afraid.

The waitress came. Charity ordered coffee, milk, and two Danish pastries.

'Brett,' she said, 'when I told your father I wanted us to go on this trip, he was against it –'

'Yeah, I figured that.'

'– and then he changed his mind. He changed it all at once. I think that maybe . . . maybe he saw it as a chance for a little vacation of his own. Sometimes men like to go off by themselves, you know, and do things –'

'Like hunting?'

(and whoring and drinking and God alone knows what else or why)

'Yes, like that.'

'And movies,' Brett said. Their snacks came, and he began munching his Danish.

(yes the X-rated kind on Washington Street they call it the Combat Zone)

'Could be. Anyway, your father might have taken a couple of days to go to Boston –'

'Oh, I don't think so,' Brett said earnestly. 'He had a lot of work. A *lot* of work. He told me so.'

'There might not have been as much as he thought,' she said, hoping that the cynicism she felt hadn't rubbed through into her voice. 'Anyway, that's what I think he did, and that's why he didn't answer the phone yesterday or today. Drink your milk, Brett. It builds up your bones.'

He drank half his milk and grew an old man's mustache. He set the glass down. 'Maybe he did. He could have got Gary to go with him, maybe. He likes Gary a lot.'

'Yes, maybe he did get Gary to go with him,' Charity said. She spoke as if this idea had never occurred to her, but in fact she had called Gary's house this morning while Brett had been out in the back yard, playing with Jim Junior. There had been no answer. She hadn't a doubt in the world that they were together, wherever they were. 'You haven't eaten much of that Danish.'

He picked it up, took a token bite, and put it down again. 'Mom, I think Cujo was sick. He looked sick when I saw him yesterday morning. Honest to God.'

'Brett —'

'He *did*, Mom. You didn't see him. He looked . . . well, gross.'

'If you knew Cujo was all right, would it set your mind at rest?'

Brett nodded.

'Then we'll call Alva Thornton down on the Maple Sugar tonight,' she said. 'Have him go up and check, okay? My guess is your father already called him and asked him to feed Cujo while he's gone.'

'Do you really think so?'

'Yes, I do.' Alva or someone like Alva; not really Joe's friends, because to the best of her knowledge Gary was the only real friend Joe had, but men who would do a favor for a favor in return at some future time.

Brett's expression cleared magically. Once again the grownup had produced the right answer, like a rabbit from a hat. Instead of cheering her, it turned her momentarily glum. What was she going to tell him if she called Alva and he said he hadn't seen Joe since mud season? Well, she would cross that bridge if she came to it, but she continued to believe that Joe wouldn't have just left Cujo to shift for himself. It wasn't like him.

'Want to go and find your aunt now?'

'Sure. Just lemme finish this.'

She watched, half amused and half appalled, as he gobbled the rest of the Danish in three great bites and chased it with the rest of the milk. Then he pushed his chair back.

Charity paid the check and they went out to the down escalator.

'Jeez, this sure is a big store,' Brett said wonderingly. 'It's a big city, isn't it, Mom?'

'New York makes this look like Castle Rock,' she said. 'And don't say jeez, Brett, it's the same as swearing.'

'Okay.' He held the moving railing, looking around. To the right of them was a maze of twittering chirruping parakeets. To the left was the housewares department, with chrome glittering everywhere and a dishwasher that had a front made entirely of glass so you could check out its sudsing action. He looked up at his mother as they got off the escalator. 'You two grew up together, huh?'

'Hope to tell you,' Charity said, smiling.

'She's real nice,' Brett said.

'Well, I'm glad you think so. I was always partial to her myself.'

'How did she get so rich?'

Charity stopped. 'Is that what you think Holly and Jim are? *Rich?*'

'That house they live in didn't come cheap,' he said, and again she could see his father peeking around the corners of his unformed face, Joe Camber with his shapeless green hat tipped far back on his head, his eyes, too wise, shifted off to one side. 'And that jukebox. That was dear, too. She's got a whole wallet of those credit cards and all we've got is the Texaco —'

She rounded on him. 'You think it's smart to go peeking into people's wallets when they've just bought you a nice lunch?'

His face looked hurt and surprised, then it closed up and became smooth. That was a Joe Camber trick too. 'I just noticed. Would have been hard not to, the way she was showing them off —'

'She was *not* showing them off!' Charity said, shocked. She stopped again. They had reached the edge of the drapery department.

'Yeah, she was,' Brett said. 'If they'd been an accordion, she would have been playing "Lady of Spain."'

She was suddenly furious with him – partly because she suspected he might be right.

'She wanted you to see all of them,' Brett said. 'That's what *I* think.'

'I'm not particularly interested in what you think on the subject, Brett Camber.' Her face felt hot. Her hands itched to strike him. A few moments ago, in the cafeteria, she had been loving him . . . just as important, she had felt like his friend. Where had those good feelings gone?

'I just wondered how she got so much dough.'

'That's sort of a crude word to use for it, don't you think?'

He shrugged, openly antagonistic now, provoking her purposely, she suspected. It went back to his perception of what had happened at lunch, but it went further back than that. He was contrasting his own way of life and his father's way of life with another one. Had she thought he would automatically embrace the way that her sister and her husband lived, just because Charity wanted him to embrace it – a life-style that she herself had been denied, either by bad luck, her own stupidity, or both? Had he no right to criticize . . . or analyze?

Yes, she acknowledged that he did, but she hadn't expected that his observation would be so unsettlingly (if intuitively) sophisticated, so accurate, or so depressingly negative.

'I suppose it was Jim who made the money,' she said. 'You know what he does –'

'Yeah, he's a pencil-pusher.'

But this time she refused to be drawn.

'If you want to see it that way. Holly married him when he was in college at the University of Maine in Portland, studying pre-law. While he was in law school in Denver, she worked a lot of crummy jobs to see that he got through. It's often done that way. Wives work so their husbands can go to school and learn some special skill. . . .'

She was searching for Holly with her eyes, and finally thought she saw the top of her younger sister's head several aisles to the left.

'Anyway, when Jim finally got out of school, he and Holly came back east and he went to work in Bridgeport with a big firm of lawyers. He didn't make much money then. They lived in a third-floor apartment with no air conditioning in the summer and not much heat in the winter. But he's worked his way up, and now he's what's called a junior partner. And I suppose he does make a lot of money, by our standards.'

'Maybe she shows her credit cards around because sometimes she still feels poor inside,' Brett said.

She was struck by the almost eerie perceptiveness of that, as well. She ruffled his hair gently, no longer angry at him. 'You did say you liked her.'

'Yeah, I do. There she is, right over there.'

'I see her.'

They went over and joined Holly, who already had an armload of curtains and was now prospecting for table-cloths.

The sun had finally gone down behind the house.

Little by little, the oven that was inside the Trentons' Pinto began to cool off. A more-or-less steady breeze sprang up, and Tad turned his face into it gratefully. He felt better, at least for the time being, than he had all day. In fact, all the rest of the day before now seemed like a terribly bad dream, one he could only partly remember. At times he had gone away; had simply left the car and gone away. He could remember that. He had gone on a horse. He and the horse had ridden down a long field, and there were rabbits playing there, just like in that cartoon his mommy and daddy had taken him to see at the Magic Lantern Theater in Bridgton. There was a pond at the end of the field, and ducks in the pond. The ducks were friendly. Tad played with them. It was better there than with Mommy, because the monster was where Mommy was, the monster that had gotten out of his closet. The monster was not in the place where the ducks were. Tad liked it there, although he knew in a vague way that if he stayed in that place too long, he might forget how to get back to the car.

Then the sun had gone behind the house. There were cool shadows, almost thick enough to have a texture, like velvet. The monster had stopped trying to get them. The mailman hadn't come, but at least now he was able to rest comfortably. The worst thing was being so thirsty. Never in his life had he wanted a drink so much. That was what made the place where the ducks were so nice – it was a wet, green place.

'What did you say, honey?' Mommy's face bending down over him.

'Thirsty,' he said in a frog's croak. 'I'm so thirsty, Mommy.' He remembered that he used to say 'firsty' instead of 'thirsty.' But some of the kids at daycamp had laughed at him and called him a baby, the same way they laughed at Randy Hofnager for saying 'brefkust' when he meant 'breakfast'. So he began to say it right, scolding himself fiercely inside whenever he forgot.

'Yes, I know. Mommy's thirsty too.'

'I bet there's water in that house.'

'Honey, we can't go into the house. Not just yet. The bad dog's in front of the car.'

'Where?' Tad got up on his knees and was surprised at the lightness that ran lazily through his head, like a slow-breaking wave. He put a hand on the dashboard to support himself, and the hand seemed on the end of an arm that was a mile long. 'I don't see him.' Even his voice was distant, echoey.

'Sit back down, Tad. You're . . .'

She was still talking, and he could feel her sitting him back into the seat, but it was all distant. The words were coming to him over a long gray distance; it was foggy between him and her, as it had been foggy this morning . . . or yesterday morning . . . or on whatever morning it had been when his daddy left to go on his trip. But there was a bright place up ahead, so he left his mother to go to it. It was the duck place.

Ducks and a pool and lilypads. Mommy's voice became a faraway drone. Her beautiful face, so large, always there, so calm, so like the moon that sometimes looked in his window when he awoke late at night having to go peepee . . . that face became gray and lost definition. It melted into the gray mist. Her voice became the lazy sound of bees which were far too nice to sting, and lapping water.

Tad played with the ducks.

Donna dozed off, and when she woke up again all the shadows had blended with one another and the last of the light in the Camber driveway was the color of ashes. It was dusk. Somehow it had gotten around to dusk again and they were – unbelievably – still here. The sun sat on the horizon, round and scarlet-orange. It looked to her like a basketball that had been dipped in blood. She moved her tongue around in her mouth. Saliva that had clotted into a thick gum broke apart reluctantly and became more or less ordinary spit again. Her throat felt like a flannel. She thought how wonderful it would be to lie under the garden faucet at home, turn the spigot on full, open her mouth, and just let the icy water cascade in. The image was powerful enough to make her shiver and break out in a skitter of gooseflesh, powerful enough to make her head ache.

Was the dog still in front of the car?

She looked, but of course there was no real way of telling. All she could see for sure was that it wasn't in front of the barn.

She tapped the horn, but it only produced a rusty hoot and nothing changed. He could be anywhere. She ran her finger along the silver crack in her window and wondered what would happen if the dog hit the glass a few more times. Could it break through? She wouldn't have believed so twenty-four hours before, but now she wasn't so sure.

She looked at the door leading to Cambers' porch again. It seemed father away than it had before. That made her think of a concept they had discussed in a college psychology course. *Idée fixe*, the instructor, a prissy little man with a toothbrush mustache, had called it. *If you get on a down escalator that isn't moving, you'll suddenly find it very hard to walk.* That had amused her so much that she had eventually found a down escalator in Bloomingdale's that was marked OUT OF ORDER and had walked down it. She had found to her further amusement that the prissy little associate professor was right – your legs just didn't want to move. That had led her to try and imagine what would happen to your head if the stairs in your house suddenly started to move as you were walking down them. The very idea had made her laugh out loud.

But it wasn't so funny now. As a matter of fact, it wasn't funny at all.

That porch door definitely looked farther away.

The dog's psyching me out.

She tried to reject the thought as soon as it occurred to her, and then stopped trying. Things had become too desperate now to indulge in the luxury of lying to herself. Knowingly or unknowingly, Cujo was psyching her out. Using, perhaps, her own *idée fixe* of how the world was supposed to be. But things had changed. The smooth escalator ride was over. She could not just continue to stand on the still steps with her son and wait for somebody to start the motor again. The fact was, she and Tad were under siege by dog.

Tad was sleeping. If the dog was in the barn, she could make it now.

But if it's still in front of the car? Or under it?

She remembered something her father used to say sometimes when he was watching the pro football games on TV. Her dad almost always got tanked for these occasions, and usually ate a large plate of cold beans left over from Saturday-night supper. As a result, the TV room was uninhabitable for normal earth life by the fourth quarter; even the dog would slink out, an uneasy deserter's grin on its face.

This saying of her father's was reserved for particularly fine tackles and intercepted passes. 'He laid back in the tall bushes

on that one!' her father would cry. It drove her mother crazy
. . . but by the time Donna was a teenager, almost everything
about her father drove her mother crazy.

She now had a vision of Cujo in front of the Pinto, not
sleeping at all but crouched on the gravel with his back legs
coiled under him, his bloodshot eyes fixed intently on the spot
where she would first appear if she left the car on the driver's
side. He was waiting for her, hoping she would be foolish
enough to get out. He was laying back in the tall bushes for her.

She rubbed both hands over her face in a quick and nervous
washing gesture. Overhead, Venus now peeked out of the
darkening blue. The sun had made its exit, leaving a still but
somehow crazed yellow light over the fields. Somewhere a
bird sang, stopped, then sang again.

It came to her that she was nowhere near as anxious to
leave the car and run for the door as she had been that
afternoon. Part of it was having dozed off and then wakened
not knowing exactly where the dog was. Part of it was the
simple fact that the heat was drawing back — the tormenting
heat and what it was doing to Tad had been the biggest thing
goading her to make a move. It was quite comfortable in the
car now, and Tad's half-lidded, half-swooning state had
become a real sleep. He was resting comfortably, at least for
the time being.

But she was afraid those things were secondary to the main
reason she was still here — that, little by little, some
psychological point of readiness had been reached and
passed. She remembered from her childhood diving lessons at
Camp Tapawingo that there came an instant, that first time
on the high board, when you either had to try it or retreat
ignominiously to let the girl behind you have her crack at it.
There came a day during the learning-to-drive experience
when you finally had to leave the empty country roads behind
and try it in the city. There came a time. Always there came a
time. A time to dive, a time to drive, a time to try for the back
door.

Sooner or later the dog would show itself. The situation
was bad, granted, but not yet desperate. The right time came

around in cycles — that was not anything she had been taught
in a psychology class; it was something she knew instinctive-
ly. If you chickened down from the high board on Monday,
there was no law that said you couldn't go right back again on
Tuesday. You could —

Reluctantly, her mind told her that was a deadly-false bit of
reasoning.

She was not as strong tonight as she had been last night. She
would be even weaker and more dehydrated tomorrow
morning. And that was not the worst of it. She had been
sitting almost all the time for — how long? — it didn't seem
possible, but it was now some twenty-eight hours. What if she
was too stiff to do it? What if she got halfway to the porch
only to be doubled up and then dropped flopping to the
ground by charley horses in the big muscles of her thighs?

In matters of life and death, her mind told her implacably,
*the right time only comes around once — once and then it's
gone.*

Her breathing and heart rate had speeded up. Her body
was aware she was going to make the try before her mind was.
Then she was wrapping her shirt more firmly about her right
hand, her left hand was settling on the doorhandle, and she
knew. There had been no conscious decision she was aware
of; suddenly she was simply going. She was going now, while
Tad slept deeply and there was no danger he would bolt out
after her.

She pulled the doorhandle up, her hand sweat-slick. She
was holding her breath, listening for any change in the world.

The bird sang again. That was all.

*If he's bashed the door too far out of shape it won't even
open*, she thought. That would be a kind of bitter relief. She
could sit back then, rethink her options, see if there was
anything she had left out of her calculations . . . and get a little
thirstier . . . a little weaker . . . a little slower. . . .

She brought pressure to bear against the door, slugging her
left shoulder against it, gradually settling more and more of
her weight upon it. Her right hand was sweating inside the
cotton shirt. Her fist was so tightly clenched that the fingers

ached. Dimly, she could feel the crescents of her nails biting into her palm. Over and over in her mind's eye she saw herself punching through the glass beside the knob of the porch door, heard the tinkle of the shards striking the boards inside, saw herself reaching for the handle . . .

But the car door wasn't opening. She shoved as hard as she could, straining, the cords in her neck standing out. But it wasn't opening. It —

Then it did open, all of a sudden. It swung wide with a terrible clunking sound, almost spilling her out on all fours. She grabbed for the doorhandle, missed, and grabbed again. She held the handle, and suddenly a panicky certainty stole into her mind. It was as cold and numbing as a doctor's verdict of inoperable cancer. She had gotten the door open, but it wouldn't close again. The dog was going to leap in and kill them both. Tad would have perhaps one confused moment of waking, one last merciful instant in which to believe it was a dream, before Cujo's teeth ripped his throat open.

Her breath rattled in and out, quick and quick. It felt like hot straw. It seemed that she could see each and every piece of gravel in the driveway, but it was hard to think. Her thoughts tumbled wildly. Scenes out of her past zipped through the foreground of her mind like a film of a parade which had been speeded up until the marching bands and horseback riders and baton twirlers seemed to be fleeing the scene of some weird crime.

The garbage disposal regurgitating a nasty green mess all over the kitchen ceiling, backing up through the bar sink.

Falling off the back porch when she was five and breaking her wrist.

Looking down at herself during period 2 — algebra — one day when she was a high school freshman and seeing to her utter shame and horror that there were spots of blood on her light blue linen skirt, she had started her period, how was she ever going to get up from her seat when the bell rang without everybody seeing, without everyone knowing that Donna-Rose was having her period?

The first boy she had ever kissed with her mouth open. Dwight Sampson.

Holding Tad in her arms, newborn, then the nurse taking him away; she wanted to tell the nurse not to do that — *Give him back, I'm not done with him*, those were the words that had come to mind — but she was too weak to talk and then the horrible, squelching, gutty sound of the afterbirth coming out of her; she remembered thinking *I'm puking up his life-support systems*, and then she had passed out.

Her father, crying at her wedding and then getting drunk at the reception.

Faces. Voices. Rooms. Scenes. Books. The terror of this moment, thinking *I AM GOING TO DIE* —

With a tremendous effort, she got herself under some kind of control. She got the Pinto's doorhandle in both hands and gave it a tremendous yank. The door flew shut. There was that clunk again as the hinge Cujo had knocked out of true protested. There was a hefty bang when the door slammed closed that made Tad jump and then mutter a bit in his sleep.

Donna leaned back in the seat, shaking helplessly all over, and cried silently. Hot tears slipped out from under her lids and ran back on a slant toward her ears. She had never in her life been so afraid of anything, not even in her room at night when she was little and it had seemed to her that there were spiders everywhere. She couldn't go now, she assured herself. It was unthinkable. She was totally done up. Her nerves were shot. Better to wait, wait for a better chance. . . .

But she didn't dare let that *idée* become *fixe*.

There wasn't going to be a better chance than this one. Tad was out of it, and the dog was out of it too. It had to be true; all logic declared it to be true. That first loud clunk, then another one when she pulled the door to, and the slam of the door actually shutting again. It would have brought him on the run if he had been in front of the car. He might be in the barn, but she believed he would have heard the noise in there, as well. He had almost surely gone wandering off somewhere. There was never going to be a better chance than right now, and if she was too scared to do it for herself, she musn't be too scared to do it for Tad.

All suitably noble. But what finally persuaded her was a vision of letting herself into the Cambers' darkened house, the reassuring feel of the telephone in her hand. She could hear herself talking to one of Sheriff Bannerman's deputies, quite calmly and rationally, and then putting the phone down. Then going into the kitchen for a cold glass of water.

She opened the door again, prepared for the clunking sound this time but still wincing when it came. She cursed the dog in her heart, hoping it was already lying someplace dead of a convulsion, and fly-blown.

She swung her legs out, wincing at the stiffness and the pain. She put her tennis shoes on the gravel. And little by little she stood up under the darkling sky.

The bird sang somewhere nearby: it sang three notes and was still.

Cujo heard the door open again, as instinct had told him it would. The first time it opened he had almost come around from the front of the car where he had been lying in a semi-stupor. He had almost come around to get THE WOMAN who had caused this dreadful pain in his head and in his body. He had almost come around, but that instinct had commanded him to lie still instead. THE WOMAN was only trying to draw him out, the instinct counseled, and this had proved to be true.

As the sickness had tightened down on him, sinking into his nervous system like a ravenous grassfire, all dove-gray smoke and low rose-colored flame, as it continued to go about its work of destroying his established patterns of thought and behaviour, it had somehow deepened his cunning. He was sure to get THE WOMAN and THE BOY. They had caused his pain – both the agony in his body and the terrible hurt in his head which had come from leaping against the car again and again.

Twice today he had forgotten about THE WOMAN and THE

BOY, leaving the barn by the dog bolthole that Joe Camber had cut in the door of the back room where he kept his accounts. He had gone down to the marsh at the back of the Camber property, both times passing quite close to the overgrown entrance to the limestone cave where the bats roosted. There was water in the marsh and he was horribly thirsty, but the actual sight of the water had driven him into a frenzy both times. He wanted to drink the water; kill the water; bathe in the water; piss and shit in the water; cover it over with dirt; savage it; make it bleed. Both times this terrible confusion of feelings had driven him away, whining and trembling. THE WOMAN and THE BOY had made all this happen. And he would leave them no more. No human who had ever lived would have found a dog more faithful or more set in his purpose. He would wait until he could get at them. If necessary he would wait until the world ended. He would wait. He would stand a watch.

It was THE WOMAN most of all. The way she looked at him, as if to say, *Yes, yes, I did it, I made you sick, I made you hurt, I devised this agony just for you and it will be with you always now.*

Oh kill her, kill her!

A sound came. It was a soft sound, but it did not escape Cujo; his ears were preternaturally attuned to all sounds now. The entire spectrum of the aural world was his. He heard the chimes of heaven and the hoarse screams which uprose from hell. In his madness he heard the real and the unreal.

It was the soft sound of small stones slipping and grinding against each other.

Cujo screwed his hindquarters down against the ground and waited for her. Urine, warm and painful, ran out of him unheeded. He waited for THE WOMAN to show herself. When she did, he would kill her.

In the downstairs wreckage of the Trenton house, the telephone began to ring.

It burred six times, eight times, ten. Then it was silent. Shortly after, the Trentons' copy of the Castle Rock *Call* thumped against the front door and Billy Freeman pedaled on up the street on his Raleigh with his canvas sack over his shoulder, whistling.

In Tad's room, the closet door stood open, and an unspeakable dry smell, lionlike and savage, hung in the air.

In Boston, an operator asked Vic Trenton if he would like her to keep trying. 'No, that's okay, operator,' he said, and hung up.

Roger had found the Red Sox playing Kansas City on Channel 38 and was sitting on the sofa in his skivvies with a room-service sandwich and a glass of milk, watching the warm-ups.

'Of all your habits,' Vic said, 'most of which range from the actively offensive to the mildly disgusting, I think that eating in your underpants is probably the worst.'

'Listen to this guy,' Roger said mildly to the empty room at large. 'He's thirty-two years old and he still calls underwear shorts underpants.'

'What's wrong with that?'

'Nothing . . . if you're still one of the Owl Tent at summer camp.'

'I'm going to cut your throat tonight, Rog,' Vic said, smiling happily. 'You'll wake up strangling in your own blood. You'll be sorry, but it will be . . . *too late!*' He picked up half of Roger's hot pastrami sandwich and wounded it grievously.

'That's pretty fucking unsanitary,' Roger said, brushing crumbs from his bare, hairy chest. 'Donna wasn't home, huh?'

'Uh-uh. She and Tad probably went down to the Tastee Freeze to catch a couple of burgers or something. I wish to God I was there instead of Boston.'

'Oh, just think,' Roger said, grinning maliciously, 'we'll be in the Apple tomorrow night. Having cocktails under the clock at the Biltmore . . .'

'Fuck the Biltmore and fuck the clock,' Vic said. 'Anyone who spends a week away from Maine on business in Boston and New York – and during the summertime – has got to be crazy.'

'Yeah, I'll buy that,' Roger said. On the TV screen, Bob Stanley popped a good curve over the outside corner to start the game. 'It is rawtha shitteh.'

'That's a pretty good sandwich, Roger,' Vic said, smiling winningly at his partner.

Roger grabbed up the plate and held it to his chest. 'Call down for your own, you damn mooch.'

'What's the number?'

'Six-eight-one, I think. It's on the dial there.'

'Don't you want some beer with that?' Vic asked, going to the phone again.

Roger shook his head. 'I had too much at lunch. My head's bad, my stomach's bad, and by tomorrow morning I'll probably have the Hershey-squirts. I'm rapidly discovering the truth, goodbuddy. I'm no kid any more.'

Vic called down for a hot pastrami on rye and two bottles of Tuborg. When he hung up and looked back at Roger, Roger was sitting with his eyes fixed on the TV. His sandwich plate was balanced on his considerable belly and he was crying. At first Vic thought he hadn't seen right; it was some sort of optical illusion. But no, those were tears. The color TV reflected off them in prisms of light.

For a moment Vic stood there, unable to decide if he should go over to Roger or go over the other side of the room and pick up the newspaper, pretending he hadn't seen. Then Roger looked over at him, his face working and utterly naked, as defenseless and as vulnerable as Tad's face when he fell off the swing and scraped his knees or took a tumble on the sidewalk.

'What am I going to do, Vic?' he asked hoarsely.

'Rog, what are you talk –'

'You know what I'm talking about,' he said. The crowd at

Fenway cheered as Boston turned a double play to end the top of the first.

'Take it easy, Roger. You —'

'This is going to fall through and we both know it,' Roger said. 'It smells as bad as a carton of eggs that's been sitting all week in the sun. This is some nice little game we're playing. We've got Rob Martin on our side. We've got that refugee from the Home for Old Actors on our side. Undoubtedly we'll have Summers Marketing & Research on our side, since they bill us. How wonderful. We've got everybody on our side but the people who matter.'

'Nothing's decided, Rog. Not yet.'

'Althea doesn't really understand how much is at stake,' Roger said. 'My fault; okay, so I'm a chicken, cluck-cluck. But she loves it in Bridgton, Vic. She *loves* it there. And the girls, they've got their school friends . . . and the lake in the summer . . . they don't know what the fuck's coming down *at all*.'

'Yeah, it's scary. I'm not trying to talk you out of that, Rog.'

'Does Donna know how bad it is?'

'I think she just thought it was an awfully good joke on us at first. But she's getting the drift of it now.'

'But she never took to Maine the way the rest of us did.'

'Not at first, maybe. I think she'd raise her hands in horror at the idea of taking Tad back to New York now.'

'What am I going to do?' Roger asked again. 'I'm no kid any more. You're thirty-two, but Vic, I'm going to be forty-one next month. What am I supposed to do? Start taking my résumé around? Is J. Walter Thompson going to welcome me in with open arms? "Hi, Rog-baby, I've been holding your old spot for you. You start at thirty-five-five." Is that what he's going to say?'

Vic only shook his head, but a part of him was a little irritated with Roger.

'I used to be just mad. Well, I'm still mad, but now I'm more scared than anything else. I lie in bed at night and try to imagine how it's going to be — after. *What* it's going to be. I can't imagine it. You look at me and you say to yourself, "Roger's dramatizing." You –'

'I never thought any such thing,' Vic said, hoping he didn't sound guilty.

'I won't say you're lying,' Roger said, 'but I've been working with you long enough to have a pretty good idea of how you think. Better than you might know. Anyway, I wouldn't blame you for the thought – but there's a big difference between thirty-two and forty-one, Vic. They kick a lot of the guts out of you in between thirty-two and forty-one.'

'Look, I still think we've got a fighting chance with this proposal –'

'What I'd like to do is bring about two dozen boxes of Red Razberry Zingers along with us to Cleveland,' Roger said, 'and then get them to bend over after they tie the can to our tails. I'd have a place for all that cereal, you know it?'

Vic clapped Roger on the shoulder. 'Yeah, I get you.'

'What *are* you going to do if they pull the account?' Roger asked.

Vic had thought about that. He had been around it from every possible angle. It would have been fair to say that he had gotten to the problem quite a while before Roger had been able to make himself approach it.

'If they pull out, I'm going to work harder than I ever have in my life,' Vic said. 'Thirty hours a day, if I have to. If I have to rope in sixty small New England accounts to make up for what Sharp billed, then I'll do it.'

'We'll kill ourselves for nothing.'

'Maybe,' Vic said. 'But we'll go down with all guns firing. Right?'

'I figure,' Roger said unsteadily, 'that if Althea goes to work, we can hold on to the house for about a year. That ought to be just about enough time to sell it, the way interest rates are.'

Suddenly Vic felt it trembling right behind his lips: the whole shitty black mess that Donna had managed to get herself into because of her need to keep pretending that she was still nineteen-going-on-twenty. He felt a certain dull anger at Roger, Roger who had been happily and unquestioningly married for fifteen years, Roger who had pretty, unassuming Althea to warm his bed (if Althea Breakstone had so much as contemplated infidelity, Vic would have been surprised), Roger who had absolutely no idea of how many things could go wrong at once.

'Listen,' he said. 'Thursday I got a note in the late mail –'

There was a sharp rap on the door.

'That'll be room service,' Roger said. He picked up his shirt and wiped his face with it . . . and with the tears gone, it was suddenly unthinkable to Vic that he should tell Roger. Maybe because Roger was right after all, and the one big difference was the nine years lying between thirty-two and forty-one.

Vic went to the door and got his beers and his sandwich. He didn't finish what he had been about to say when the room-service waiter knocked, and Roger didn't ask him. He was back in the ballgame and his own problems.

Vic sat down to eat his sandwich, not entirely surprised to find that most of his appetite was gone. His eyes fell on the telephone, and, still munching, he tried home again. He let it ring a dozen times before hanging up. He was frowning slightly. It was five past eight, five minutes past Tad's usual bedtime. Perhaps Donna had met someone, or maybe they had gotten feeling dragged down by the empty house and gone visiting. After all, there was no law that said the Tadder had to be in bed on the stroke of eight, especially when it stayed light so late and it was so damned hot. Sure, that was likely. They had maybe gone down to the Common to goof around until it got cool enough to make sleep possible. Right.

(or maybe she's with Kemp)

That was crazy. She had said it was over and he believed it. He really did believe it. Donna didn't lie.

(and she doesn't play around, either, right, champ?)

He tried to dismiss it, but it was no good. The rat was loose and it was going to be busy gnawing at him for some time now. What would she have done with Tad if she had suddenly taken it into her head to go off with Kemp? Were the three of them maybe in some motel right now, some motel between Castle Rock and Baltimore? Don't be a chump, Trenton. They might –

The band concert, that was it, of course. There was a concert at the Common bandstand every Tuesday night. Some Tuesdays the high school band played, sometimes a chamber music group, sometimes a local ragtime group that called themselves the Ragged Edge. That's where they were, of course – enjoying the cool and listening to the Ragged Edge belt their way through John Hurt's 'Candy Man' or maybe 'Beulah Land'.

(unless she's with Kemp)

He drained his beer and started on another.

Donna just stood outside the car for thirty seconds, moving her feet slightly on the gravel to get the pins and needles out of her legs. She watched the front of the garage, still feeling that if Cujo came, he would come from that way – maybe out of the mouth of the barn, maybe from around one of the sides, or perhaps from behind the farm truck, which looked rather canine itself by starlight – a big dusty black mongrel that was fast asleep.

She stood there, not quite ready to commit herself to it yet. The night breathed at her, small fragrances that reminded her of how it had been to be small, and to smell these fragrances in all their intensity almost as a matter of routine. Clover and hay from the house at the bottom of the hill, the sweet smell of honeysuckle.

And she heard something: music. It was very faint, almost not there, but her ears, almost eerily attuned to the night now, picked it up. *Someone's radio*, she thought at first, and then realized with a dawning wonder that it was the band concert on the Common. That was Dixieland jazz she was hearing. She could even identify the tune; it was 'Shuffle Off to Buffalo.' *Seven miles*, she thought. *I never would have believed it – how still the night must be! How calm!*

She felt very alive.

Her heart was a small, powerful machine flexing in her chest. Her blood was up. Her eyes seemed to move effortlessly and perfectly in their bed of moisture. Her kidneys were heavy but not unpleasantly so. This was it; this was for keeps. The thought that it was her *life* she was putting on the line, her very own *real life*, had a heavy, silent fascination, like a great weight which has reached the outermost degree of its angle of repose. She swung the car door shut – *clunk*.

She waited, scenting the air like an animal. There was nothing. The maw of Joe Camber's barn-garage was dark and silent. The chrome of the Pinto's front bumper twinkled dimly. Faintly, the Dixieland music played on, fast and brassy and cheerful. She bent down, expecting her knees to pop, but they didn't. She picked up a handful of the loose gravel. One by one she began to toss the stones over the Pinto's hood at the place she couldn't see.

The first small stone landed in front of Cujo's nose, clicked off more stones, and then lay still. Cujo twitched a little. His tongue hung out. He seemed to be grinning. The second stone struck beyond him. The third struck his shoulder. He didn't move. THE WOMAN was still trying to draw him out.

Donna stood by the car, frowning. She had heard the first stone click off the gravel, also the second. But the third . . . it was as if it had never come down. There had been no minor click. What did that mean?

Suddenly she didn't want to run for the porch door until she could see that there was nothing lurking in front of the car. Then, yes. Okay. But . . . just to make sure.

She took one step. Two. Three.

Cujo got ready. His eyes glowed in the darkness.

Four steps from the door of the car. Her heart was a drum in her chest.

Now Cujo could see THE WOMAN's hip and thigh. In a moment she would see him. Good. He wanted her to see him.

Five steps from the door.

Donna turned her head. Her neck creaked like the spring on an old screen door. She felt a premonition, a sense of low sureness. She turned her head, looking for Cujo. Cujo was there. He had been there all the time, crouched low, hiding from her, waiting for her, laying back in the tall bushes.

Their eyes locked for a moment – Donna's wide blue ones, Cujo's muddy red ones. For a moment she was looking out of his eyes, seeing herself, seeing THE WOMAN – was he seeing himself through hers?

Then he sprang at her.

There was no paralysis this time. She threw herself backward, fumbling behind her for the doorhandle. He was snarling and grinning, and the drool ran out between his teeth in thick strings. He landed where she had been and skidded stiff-legged in the gravel, giving her a precious extra second.

Her thumb found the door button below the handle and depressed it. She pulled. The door was stuck. The door wouldn't open. Cujo leaped at her.

It was as if someone had slung a medicine ball right into the soft, vulnerable flesh of her breasts. She could feel them push out toward her ribs – it *hurt* – and then she had the dog by the throat, her fingers sinking into its heavy, rough fur, trying to hold it away from her. She could hear the quickening sob of her respiration. Starlight ran across Cujo's mad eyes in dull semicircles. His teeth were snapping only inches from her face and she could smell a dead world on his breath, terminal sickness, senseless murder. She thought crazily of the drain backing up just before her mother's party, spurting green goo all over the ceiling.

Somehow, using all her strength, she was able to fling him away when his back feet left the ground in another lunge at her throat. She beat helplessly behind her for the door button. She found it, but before she could even push it in, Cujo came again. She kicked out at him, and the sole of her sandal struck his muzzle, already badly lacerated in his earlier kamikaze charges at the door. The dog sprawled back on his haunches, howling out his pain and his fury.

She found the button set in the doorhandle again, knowing perfectly well that it was her last chance, Tad's last chance. She pushed it in and pulled with all her might as the dog came again, some creature from hell that would come and come and come until she was dead or it was. It was the wrong angle for her arm; her muscles were working at cross-purposes, and she felt an agonizing flare of pain in her back above her right shoulderblade as something sprained. But the door opened. She had just time to fall back into the bucket seat, and then the dog was on her again.

Tad woke up. He saw his mother being driven back toward the Pinto's center console; there was something in his mother's lap, some terrible, hairy thing with red eyes and he knew what it was, oh yes, it was the thing from his closet, the thing that had promised to come a little closer and a little closer until it finally arrived *right by your bed, Tad*, and yes, here it was, all right, here it was. The Monster Words had failed; the monster was here, now, and it was murdering his mommy. He began to scream, his hands clapped over his eyes.

Its snapping jaws were inches from the bare flesh of her midriff. She held it off as best she could, only faintly aware of her son's screams behind her. Cujo's eyes were locked on her. Incredibly, his tail was wagging. His back legs worked at the gravel, trying to get a footing solid enough to allow him to jump right in, but the gravel kept splurting out from under his driving rear paws.

He lunged forward, her hands slipped, and suddenly he was *biting* her, biting her bare stomach just below the white cotton cups of her bra, digging for her entrails –

Donna uttered a low, feral cry of pain and shoved with both hands as hard as she could. Now she was sitting up again, blood trickling down to the waistband of her pants. She held Cujo with her left hand. Her right hand groped for the Pinto's doorhandle and found it. She began to slam the door against the dog. Each time she swept it forward into Cujo's ribs, there was a heavy *whopping* sound, like a heavy rug beater striking a carpet hung over a clothesline. Each time the door hit him, Cujo would grunt, snorting his warm, foggy breath over her.

He drew back a little to spring. She timed it and brought the door toward her again, using all of her failing strength. This time the door closed on his neck and head, and she heard a crunching sound. Cujo howled his pain and she thought, *He must draw back now, he must, he MUST,* but Cujo drove forward instead and his jaws closed on her lower thigh, just above her knee, and with one quick ripping motion he pulled a chunk out of her. Donna shrieked.

She slammed the door on Cujo's head again and again, her screams melting into Tad's, melting into a gray shockworld as Cujo worked on her leg, turning it into something else, something that was red and muddy and churned up. The dog's head was plastered with thick, sticky blood, as black as insect blood in the chancey starlight. Little by little he was forcing his way in again; her strength was on the ebb now.

She pulled the door to one final time, her head thrown back, her mouth drawn open in a quivering circle, her face a livid, moving blur in the darkness. It really was the last time; there was just no more left.

But suddenly Cujo had had enough.

He drew back, whining, staggered away, and suddenly fell over on the gravel, trembling, legs scratching weakly at nothing. He began to dig at his wounded head with his right forepaw.

Donna slammed the door shut and lay back, sobbing weakly.

'Mommy – Mommy – Mommy –'

'Tad . . . okay . . .'

'*Mommy!*'

' . . . Okay . . .'

Hands: his on her, fluttering and birdlike; hers on Tad's face, touching, trying to reassure, then falling back.

'Mommy . . . home . . . please . . . Daddy and home . . . Daddy and home . . .'

'Sure, Tad we will . . . we will, honest to God, I'll get you there . . . we will . . .'

No sense in the words. It was all right. She could feel herself fading back, fading into that gray shockworld, those mists in herself which she had never suspected until now. Tad's words took on a deep chaining sound, words in an echo chamber. But it was all right. It was –

No. *It wasn't all right.*

Because the dog had bitten her –

– and the dog was rabid.

Holly told her sister not to be foolish, to just dial her call direct, but Charity insisted on calling the operator and having it billed to her home number. Taking handouts, even a little thing like an after-six long-distance call, wasn't her way.

The operator got her directory assistance for Maine and Charity asked for Alva Thornton's number in Castle Rock. A few moments later, Alva's phone was ringing.

'Hello, Thornton's Egg Farms.

'Hi, Bessie?'

'Ayuh, 'tis.'

'This is Charity Camber. I'm calling from Connecticut. Is Alva right around handy?'

Brett sat on the sofa, pretending to read a book.

'Gee, Charity, he ain't. He's got his bowling league t'night. They're all over to the Pondicherry Lanes in Bridgton. Somethin wrong?'

Charity had carefully and consciously decided what she was going to say. The situation was a bit delicate. Like almost every other married woman in Castle Rock (and that was not to necessarily let out the single ones), Bessie loved to talk, and if she found out that Joe Camber had gone shooting off somewhere without his wife's knowledge as soon as Charity and Brett had left to visit her sister in Connecticut . . . why, that would be something to talk about on the party line, wouldn't it?

'No, except that Brett and I got a little worried about the dog.'

'Your Saint Bernard?'

'Ayuh, Cujo. Brett and I are down here visiting my sister while Joe's in Portsmouth on business.' This was a barefaced lie, but a safe one; Joe did occasionally go to Portsmouth to buy parts (there was no sales tax) and to the car auctions. 'I just wanted to make sure he got someone to feed the dog. You know how men are.'

'Well, Joe was over here yesterday or the day before, I think,' Bessie said doubtfully. Actually, it had been the previous Thursday. Bessie Thornton was not a terribly bright woman (her great-aunt, the late Evvie Chalmers, had been fond of screaming to anyone who would listen that Bessie 'wouldn't never pass none of those IQ tests, but she's goodhearted'), her life on Alva's chicken farm was a hard one, and she lived most fully during her 'stories' – *As the World Turns, The Doctors,* and *All My Children* (she had tried *The Young and the Restless* but considered it 'too racy by half'). She tended to be fuzzy on those parts of the real world that did not bear on feeding and watering the chickens, adjusting their piped-in music, candling and sorting eggs, washing floors and clothes, doing dishes, selling eggs, tending the garden. And in the winter, of course, she could have told a questioner the exact date of the next meeting of the Castle Rock SnoDevils, the snowmobile club she and Alva belonged to.

Joe had come over on that day with a tractor tire he had repaired for Alva. Joe had done the job free of charge since the Cambers got all their eggs from the Thorntons at half price. Alva also harrowed Joe's small patch of garden each April, and so Joe was glad to patch the tire. It was the way country people got along.

Charity knew perfectly well that Joe had gone over to the Thorntons' with the repaired tire the previous Thursday. She also knew that Bessie was apt to get her days mixed up. All of which left her in a pretty dilemma. She could ask Bessie if Joe had had a tractor tire with him when he came up 'yesterday or the day before,' and if Bessie said why yes, now that you mention it, he did, that would mean that Joe hadn't been up to see Alva since last Thursday, which would mean that Joe hadn't asked Alva to feed Cujo, which would *also* mean that Alva wouldn't have any information about Cujo's health and well-being.

Or she could just leave well enough alone and ease Brett's mind. They could enjoy the rest of their visit without thoughts of home intruding constantly. And . . . well, she was a little jealous of Cujo right about now. Tell the truth and shame the devil. Cujo was distracting Brett's attention from what could be the most important trip he ever took. She wanted the boy to see a whole new life, a whole new set of *possibilities*, so that when the time came, a few years from now, for him to decide which doors he wanted to step through and which ones he would allow to swing closed, he could make those decisions with a bit of perspective. Perhaps she had been wrong to believe she could steer him, but let him at least have enough experience to make up his mind for himself.

Was it fair to let his worries about the damned dog stand in the way of that?

'Charity? You there? I said I thought –'

'Ayuh, I heard you, Bessie. He probably did ask Alva to feed him, then.'

'Well, I'll ask him when he gets home, Charity. And I'll let you know, too.'

'You do that. Thanks ever so much, Bessie.'

'Don't even mention it.'

'Fine. Good-bye.' And Charity hung up, realizing that Bessie had forgotten to ask for Jim and Holly's phone number. Which was fine. She turned toward Brett, composing her face. She would say nothing that was a lie. She would lie to her son.

'Bessie said your dad was over to see Alva Sunday night,' Charity said. 'Must have asked him to take care of Cujo then.'

'Oh.' Brett was looking at her in a speculative way that made her a little uneasy. 'But you didn't talk to Alva himself.'

'No, he was out bowling. But Bessie said she'd let us know if —'

She doesn't have our number down here.' Was Brett's tone now faintly accusatory? Or was that her own conscience talking?

'Well, I'll call her back in the morning, then,' Charity said, hoping to close the conversation and applying some salve to her conscience at the same time.

'Daddy took a tractor tire over last week,' Brett said thoughtfully. 'Maybe Mrs. Thornton got mixed up on which day Daddy was there.'

'I think Bessie Thornton can keep her days straighter in her head than that,' Charity said, not thinking so at all. 'Besides, she didn't mention anything to me about a tractor tire.'

'Yeah, but you didn't ask her.'

'Go ahead and call her back, then!' Charity flashed at him. A sudden helpless fury swept her, the same ugly feeling that had come when Brett had offered his wickedly exact observation about Holly and her deck of credit cards. When he had done that his father's intonation, even his father's pattern of speech, had crept into his voice, and it had seemed to her, then and now, that the only thing this trip was doing was to show her once and for all who Brett really belonged to – lock, stock, and barrel.

'Mom –'

'No, go ahead, call her back, the number's right here on the scratchpad. Just tell the operator to charge it to our phone so it won't go on Holly's bill. Ask Bessie all your questions. I only did the best I could.'

There, she thought with sad and bitter amusement. *Just five minutes ago I wasn't going to lie to him.*

That afternoon her anger had sparked anger in him. Tonight he only said quietly, 'Naw, that's okay.'

'If you want, we'll call somebody else and have them go up and check,' Charity said. She was already sorry for her outburst.

'Who would we call?' Brett asked.

'Well, what about one of the Milliken brothers?'

Brett only looked at her.

'Maybe that's not such a good idea,' Charity agreed. Late last winter, Joe Camber and John Milliken had had a bitter argument over the charge on some repair work Joe had done on the Milliken brothers' old Chevy Bel Air. Since then, the Cambers and the Millikens hadn't been talking much. The last time Charity had gone to play Beano down at the Grange, she had tried to pass a friendly word with Kim Milliken, Freddy's daughter, but Kim wouldn't say a word to her; just walked away with her head up as if she hadn't been acting the slut with half the boys in Castle Rock High School.

It occurred to her now how really isolated they were, up at the end of Town Road No.3. It made her feel lonely and a little chilled. She could think of no one she could reasonably ask to go up to their place with a flashlight and hunt up Cujo and make sure he was okay.

'Never mind,' Brett said listlessly. 'Probably stupid, anyway. He probably just ate some burdocks or something.'

'Listen,' Charity said, putting an arm around him. 'One

thing you aren't is stupid, Brett. I'll call Alva himself in the morning and ask him to go up. I'll do it as soon as we get up. Okay?'

'Would you, Mom?'

'Yes.'

'That'd be great. I'm sorry to bug you about it, but I can't seem to get it off my mind.

Jim popped his head in. 'I got out the Scrabble board. Anyone want to play?'

'I will,' Brett said, getting up, 'if you show me how.'

'What about you, Charity?'

Charity smiled. 'Not just now, I guess. I'll be in for some of the popcorn.'

Brett went out with his uncle. She sat on the sofa and looked at the telephone and thought of Brett night-walking, feeding a phantom dog phantom dogfood in her sister's modern kitchen.

Cujo's not hungry no more, not no more.

Her arms suddenly tightened, and she shivered. We're going to take care of this business tomorrow morning, she promised herself. One way or the other. Either that or go back and take care of it ourselves. That's a promise, Brett.

Vic tried home again at ten o'clock. There was no answer. He tried again at eleven o'clock and there was still no answer, although he let the phone ring two dozen times. At ten he was beginning to get scared. At eleven he was good and scared – of what, he was not precisely sure.

Roger was sleeping. Vic dialed the number in the dark, listened to it ring in the dark, hung up in the dark. He felt alone, childlike, lost. He didn't know what to do or what to think. Over and over his mind played a simple litany: *She's gone off with Kemp, gone off with Kemp, gone off with Kemp.*

All reason and logic was against it. He played over everything he and Donna had said to each other – he played it over again and again, listening to the words and to the nuances of tone in his mind. She and Kemp had had a falling out. She had told him to go peddle his papers somewhere else. And that had prompted Kemp's vengeful little *billet doux*. It did not seem the rosy scenery into which two mad lovers might decide to elope.

A falling out doesn't preclude a later rapprochement, his mind retorted with a kind of grave and implacable calm.

But what about Tad? She wouldn't have taken Tad with her, would she? From her description, Kemp sounded like some sort of wildman, and although Donna hadn't said so, Vic had gotten the feeling that something damned violent had almost happened on the day she told him to fuck off.

People in love do strange things.

That strange and jealous part of his mind — he hadn't even been aware of that part in him until that afternoon in Deering Oaks — had an answer for everything, and in the dark it didn't seem to matter that most of the answers were irrational.

He was doing a slow dance back and forth between two sharpened points: Kemp on one (DO YOU HAVE ANY QUESTIONS?); a vision of the telephone ringing on and on in their empty Castle Rock house on the other. She could have had an accident. She and Tad could be in hospital. Someone could have broken in. They could be lying murdered in their bedrooms. Of course if she'd had an accident, someone official would have been in touch — the office as well as Donna knew in which Boston hotel he and Roger were staying — but in the dark that thought, which should have been a comfort since no one *had* been in touch, only inclined his thoughts more toward murder.

Robbery and murder, his mind whispered as he lay awake in the dark. Then it danced slowly across to the other sharpened point and took up its original litany: *Gone off with Kemp.*

In between these points, his mind saw a more reasonable explanation, one that made him feel helplessly angry. Perhaps she and Tad had decided to spend the night with someone and had simply forgotten to call and tell him. Now it was too late to just start calling around and asking people without alarming them. He supposed he could call the sheriff's office and ask them to send someone up and check. But wouldn't that be overreacting?

No, his mind said.

Yes, his mind said, *definitely*.

She and Tad are both dead with knives stuck in their throats, his mind said. *You read about it in the papers all the time. It even happened in Castle Rock just before we came to town. That crazy cop. That Frank Dodd.*

Gone off with Kemp, his mind said.

At midnight he tried again, and this time the constant ringing of the phone with no one to pick it up froze him into a deadly certainty of trouble. Kemp, robbers, murderers, something. Trouble. Trouble at home.

He dropped the phone back into its cradle and turned on the bed lamp. 'Roger,' he said. 'Wake up.'

'Huh. Wuh. Hzzzzzz. . . .' Roger had his arm over his eyes, trying to block out the light. He was in his pajamas with the little yellow college pennants.

'Roger. Roger!'

Roger opened his eyes, blinked, looked at the Travel-Ette clock.

'Hey, Vic, it's the middle of the night.'

'Roger . . .' He swallowed and something clicked in his throat. 'Roger, it's midnight and Tad and Donna still aren't home. I'm scared.'

Roger sat up and brought the clock close to his face to verify what Vic had said. It was now four past the hour.

'Well, they probably got freaked out staying there by themselves, Vic. Sometimes Althea takes the girls and goes over to Sally Petrie's when I'm gone. She gets nervous when the wind blows off the lake at night, she says.'

'She would have called.' With the light on, with Roger sitting up and talking to him, the idea that Donna might have just run off with Steve Kemp seemed absurd – he couldn't believe he had even indulged it. Forget logic. She had told him it was over, and he had believed her. He believed her now.

'Called?' Roger said. He was still having trouble tracking things.

'She knows I call home almost every night when I'm away. She would have called the hotel and left a message if she was going to be gone overnight. Wouldn't Althea?'

Roger nodded. 'Yeah. She would.'

'She'd call and leave a message so you wouldn't worry. Like I'm worrying now.'

'Yeah. But she might have just forgotten, Vic.' Still, Roger's brown eyes were troubled.

'Sure,' Vic said. 'On the other hand, maybe something's happened.'

'She carries ID, doesn't she? If she and Tad were in an accident, God forbid, the cops would try home first and then the office. The answering service would –'

'I wasn't thinking about an accident,' Vic said. 'I was thinking about . . .' His voice began to tremble. 'I was thinking about her and Tadder being there alone, and . . . shit, I don't know . . . I just got scared, that's all.'

'Call the sheriff's office,' Roger said promptly.

'Yeah, but –'

'Yeah, but nothing. You aren't going to scare Donna, that's for sure. She's not there. But what the hell, set your mind at rest. It doesn't have to be sirens and flashing lights. Just ask if they can send a cop by to check and make sure that everything looks normal. There must be a thousand places she could be. Hell, maybe she just tied into a really good Tupperware party.'

'Donna hates Tupperware parties.'

'So maybe the girls got playing penny-ante poker and lost track of the time and Tad's asleep in someone's spare room.'

Vic remembered her telling him how she had steered clear of any deep involvement with 'the girls' – *I don't want to be one of those faces you see at the bake sales*, she had said. But he didn't want to tell Roger that; it was too close to the subject of Kemp.

'Yeah, maybe something like that,' Vic said.

'Have you got an extra key to the place tucked away somewhere?'

'There's one on a hook under the eave of the front porch.'

'Tell the cops. Someone can go in and have a good look around . . . unless you've got pot or coke or something you'd just as soon they didn't stumble over.'

'Nothing like that.'

'Then do it,' Roger said earnestly. 'She'll probably call here while they're out checking and you'll feel like a fool, but sometimes it's *good* to feel like a fool. You know what I mean?'

'Yeah,' Vic said, grinning a little. 'Yeah, I do.'

He picked the telephone up again, hesitated, then tried home again first. No answer. Some of the comfort he had gotten from Roger evaporated. He got directory assistance for Maine and jotted down the number of the Castle County Sheriff's Department. It was now nearly fifteen minutes past twelve on Wednesday morning.

Donna Trenton was sitting with her hands resting lightly on the steering wheel of the Pinto. Tad had finally fallen asleep again, but his sleep was not restful; he twisted, turned, sometimes moaned. She was afraid he was reliving in his dreams what had happened earlier.

She felt his forehead; he muttered something and pulled away from her touch. His eyelids fluttered and then slipped closed again. He felt feverish – almost surely a result of the constant tension and fear. She felt feverish herself, and she was in severe pain. Her belly hurt, but those wounds were superficial, little more than scratches. She had been lucky there. Cujo had damaged her left leg more. The wounds there (the *bites*, her mind insisted, as if relishing the horror of it) were deep and ugly. They had bled a lot before clotting, and she hadn't tried to apply a bandage right away, although there was a first-aid kit in the Pinto's glovebox. Vaguely she supposed she had hoped that the flowing blood would wash the wound clean . . . did that really happen, or was it just an old wives' tale? She didn't know. There was so much she didn't know, so goddam much.

By the time the lacerated punctures had finally clotted, her thigh and the driver's bucket seat were both tacky with her blood. She needed three gauze pads from the first-aid kit to cover the wound. They were the last three in the kit. *Have to replace those*, she thought, and that brought on a short, hysterical fit of the giggles.

In the faint light, the flesh just above her knee had looked like dark plowed earth. There was a steady throbbing ache there that had not changed since the dog bit her. She had dry-swallowed a couple of aspirin from the kit, but they didn't make a dent in the pain. Her head ached badly too, as if a bundle of wires were slowly being twisted tighter and tighter inside each temple.

Flexing the leg brought the quality of the pain up from a throbbing ache to a sharp, glassy beat. She had no idea if she could even walk on the leg now, let alone run for the porch door. And did it really matter? The dog was sitting on the gravel between her car door and the door which gave on the porch, its hideously mangled head drooping . . . but with its eyes fixed unfailingly on the car. On *her*.

Somehow she didn't think Cujo was going to move again, at least not tonight. Tomorrow the sun might drive him into the barn, if it was as hot as it had been yesterday.

'It wants me,' she whispered through her blistered lips. It was true. Somehow it was true. For reasons decreed by Fate, or for its own unknowable ones, the dog wanted her.

When it had fallen on the gravel, she had been sure it was dying. No living thing could have taken the pounding she had given it with the door. Even its thick fur hadn't been able to cushion the blows. One of the Saint Bernard's ears appeared to be dangling by no more than a string of flesh.

But it had regained its feet, little by little. She hadn't been able to believe her eyes . . . hadn't *wanted* to believe her eyes.

'No!' she had shrieked, totally out of control. 'No, *lie*

down, you're supposed to be dead, lie down, lie down and die, you shit dog!'

'Mommy, don't,' Tad had murmured, holding his head. 'It hurts . . . it hurts me . . .'

Since then, nothing in the situation had changed. Time had resumed its former slow crawl. She had put her watch to her ear several times to make sure it was still ticking, because the hands never seemed to change position.

Twenty past twelve.

What do we know about rabies, class?

Precious little. Some hazy fragments that had probably come from Sunday-supplement articles. A pamphlet leafed through idly back in New York when she had taken the family cat, Dinah, for her distemper shot at the vet's. Excuse me, distemper and *rabies* shots.

Rabies, a disease of the central nervous system, the good old CNS. Causes slow destruction of same – but how? She was blank on that, and probably the doctors were, too. Otherwise the disease wouldn't be considered so damned dangerous. Of course, she thought hopefully, I don't even know for sure that the dog *is* rabid. The only rabid dog I've ever seen was the one Gregory Peck shot with a rifle in *To Kill a Mockingbird*. Except of course that dog wasn't *really* rabid, it was just pretend, it was probably some mangy mutt they'd gotten from the local pound and they put Gillette Foamy all over him. . . .

She pulled her mind back to the point. Better to make what Vic called a worst-case analysis, at least for now. Besides, in her heart she was sure the dog was rabid – what else would make it behave as it had? The dog was as mad as a hatter.

And it had bitten her. Badly. What did that mean?

People could get rabies, she knew, and it was a horrible way to die. Maybe the worst. There was a vaccine for it, and a series of injections was the prescribed method of treatment. The injections were quite painful, although probably not as painful as going the way the dog out there was going. But . . .

She seemed to remember reading that there were only two instances where people had lived through an advanced case of rabies — a case, that is, that had not been diagnosed until the carriers had begun exhibiting symptoms. One of the survivors was a boy who had recovered entirely. The other had been an animal researcher who had suffered permanent brain damage. The good old CNS had just fallen apart.

The longer the disease went untreated, the less chance there was. She rubbed her forehead and her hand skidded across a film of cold sweat.

How long was too long? Hours? Days? Weeks? A month, maybe? She didn't know.

Suddenly the car seemed to be shrinking. It was the size of a Honda, then the size of those strange little three-wheelers they used to give disabled people in England, then the size of an enclosed motorcycle sidecar, finally the size of a coffin. A double coffin for her and Tad. They had to get out, get out, get *out* —

Her hand was fumbling for the doorhandle before she got hold of herself again. Her heart was racing, accelerating the thudding in her head. *Please*, she thought. *It's bad enough without claustrophobia, so please . . . please . . . please.*

Her thirst was back again, raging.

She looked out and Cujo stared implacably back at her, his body seemingly split in two by the silver crack running through the window.

Help us, someone, she thought. *Please, please, help us.*

Roscoe Fisher was parked back in the shadows of Jerry's Citgo when the call came in. He was ostensibly watching for speeders, but in actual fact he was cooping. At twelve thirty on a Wednesday morning, Route 117 was totally dead. He had a little alarm clock inside his skull, and he trusted it to wake him up around one, when the Norway Drive-In let out. Then there might be some action.

'Unit three, come in, unit three. Over.'

Roscoe snapped awake, spilling cold coffee in a Styrofoam cup down into his crotch.

'Oh *shitfire*,' Roscoe said dolefully. 'Now that's nice, isn't it? Kee-rist!'

'Unit three, you copy? Over?'

He grabbed the mike and pushed the button on the side. 'I copy, base.' He would have liked to have added that he hoped it was good because he was sitting with his balls in a puddle of cold coffee, but you never knew who was monitoring police calls on his or her trusty Bearcat scanner . . . even at twelve thirty in the morning.

'Want you to take a run up to Eighty-three Larch Street,' Billy said. 'Residence of Mr. and Mrs. Victor Trenton. Check the place out. Over.'

'What am I checking for, base? Over.'

'Trenton's in Boston and no one's answering his calls. He thinks someone should be home. Over.'

Well, that's wonderful, isn't it? Roscoe Fisher thought sourly. For this I got a four-buck cleaning bill, and if I do have to stop a speeder, the guy's going to think I got so excited at the prospect of a collar that I pissed myself.

'Ten-four and time out,' Roscoe said, starting his cruiser. 'Over.'

'I make it twelve thirty-four A.M.,' Billy said. 'There's a key hanging on a nail under the front porch eave, unit three. Mr. Trenton would like you to go right on inside and look around if the premises appear deserted. Over.'

'Roger, base. Over and out.'

'Out.'

Roscoe popped on his headlights and cruised down Castle Rock's deserted Main Street, past the Common and the bandstand with its conical green roof. He went up the hill and turned right on Larch Street near the top. The Trentons' was the second house from the corner, and he saw that in the daytime they would have a nice view of the town below. He pulled the Sheriff's Department Fury III up to the curb and got out, closing the door quietly. The street was dark, fast asleep.

He paused for a moment, pulling the wet cloth of his uniform trousers away from his crotch (grimacing as he did it), and then went up the driveway. The driveway was empty, and so was the small one-car garage at the end of it. He saw a Big Wheels trike parked inside. It was just like the one his own son had.

He closed the garage door and went around to the front porch. He saw that this week's copy of the *Call* was leaning against the porch door. Roscoe picked it up and tried the door. It was unlocked. He went onto the porch, feeling like an intruder. He tossed the paper on the porch glider and pushed the bell beside the inner door. Chimes went off in the house, but no one came. He rang twice more over a space of about three minutes, allowing for the time it would take the lady to wake up, put on a robe, and come downstairs . . . if the lady was there.

When there was still no answer, he tried the door. It was locked.

Husband's away and she's probably staying over with friends, he thought — but the fact that she hadn't notified her husband also struck Roscoe Fisher as mildly strange.

He felt under the peaked eave, and his fingers knocked off the key Vic had hung up there not long after the Trentons had moved in. He took it down and unlocked the front door — if he had tried the kitchen door as Steve Kemp had that afternoon, he could have walked right in. Like most people in Castle Rock, Donna was slipshod about buttoning up when she went out.

Roscoe went in. He had his flashlight, but he preferred not to use it. That would have made him feel even more like an unlawful intruder — a burglar with a large coffee stain on his crotch. He felt for a switchplate and eventually found one with two switches. The top one turned on the porch light, and he turned that one off quickly. The bottom one turned on the living-room light.

He looked around for a long moment, doubting what he was seeing — at first he thought it must be some trick of his eyes, that they had not adjusted to the light or something. But nothing changed, and his heart began to pump quickly.

Musn't touch anything, he thought. *Can't balls this up*.

He had forgotten about the wet coffee splotch on his pants, and he had forgotten about feeling like an intruder. He was scared and excited.

Something had happened here, all right. The living room had been turned topsy-turvy. There was shattered glass from a knickknack shelf all over the floor. The furniture had been overturned, the books had been scattered every whichway. The big mirror over the fireplace was also broken — *seven years' bad luck for somebody*, Roscoe thought, and found himself thinking suddenly and for no reason about Frank Dodd, with whom he had often shared a cruiser. Frank Dodd, the friendly small-town cop who had just happened to also be a psycho who murdered women and little children. Roscoe's arms broke out in gooseflesh suddenly. This was no place to be thinking about Frank.

He went into the kitchen through the dining room, where everything had been swept off the table — he skirted that mess carefully. The kitchen was worse. He felt a fresh chill creep down his spine. Someone had gone absolutely crazy in here. The doors to the bar cabinet stood open, and someone had used the length of the kitchen like a Pitch-Til-U-Win alley at a county fair. Pots were everywhere, and white stuff that looked like snow but had to be soap powder.

Written on the message board in large and hurried block letters was this:

I LEFT SOMETHING UPSTAIRS FOR YOU, BABY.

Suddenly Roscoe Fisher didn't want to go upstairs. More than anything else, he didn't want to go up there. He had helped clean up three of the messes Frank Dodd had left behind him, including the body of Mary Kate Hendrasen, who had been raped and murdered on the Castle Rock bandstand in the Common. He never wanted to see anything like that again . . . and suppose the woman was up there, shot or slashed or strangled? Roscoe had seen plenty of mayhem on the roads and had even got used to it, after a fashion. Two summers ago he and Billy and Sheriff

Bannerman had pulled a man out of a potato-grading machine in pieces, and *that* had been one to tell your grandchildren about. But he had not seen a homicide since the Hendrasen girl, and he did not want to see one now.

He didn't know whether to be relieved or disgusted by what he found on the Trentons' bedspread.

He went back to his car and called in.

When the telephone rang, Vic and Roger were both up, sitting in front of the TV, not talking much, smoking their heads off. *Frankenstein*, the original film, was on. It was twenty minutes after one.

Vic grabbed the phone before it had completed its first ring. 'Hello? Donna? Is that –'

'Is this Mr. Trenton?' A man's voice.

'Yes?'

'This is Sheriff Bannerman, Mr. Trenton. I'm afraid I have some rather upsetting information for you. I'm sor –'

'Are they dead?' Vic asked. Suddenly he felt totally unreal and two-dimensional, no more real than the face of an extra glimpsed in the background of an old movie such as the one he and Roger had been watching. The question came out in a perfectly conversational tone of voice. From the corner of his eye he saw Roger's shadow move as he stood up quickly. It didn't matter. Nothing else did, either. In the space of the few seconds that had passed since he had answered the phone, he had had a chance to get a good look behind his life and had seen it was all stage scenery and false fronts.

'Mr. Trenton, Officer Fisher was dispatched –'

'Dispense with the official bullshit and answer my question. Are they dead?' He turned to Roger. Roger's face was gray and wondering. Behind him, on the TV, a phony windmill turned against a phony sky. 'Rog, got a cigarette?' Roger handed him one.

'Mr. Trenton, are you still there?'

'Yes. Are they dead?'

'We have no idea where your wife and son are as of right

now,' Bannerman said, and Vic suddenly felt all of his guts drop back into place. The world took on a little of its former color. He began to tremble. The unlit cigarette jittered between his lips.

'What's going on? What do you know? You're Bannerman, you said?'

'Castle County Sheriff, that's right. And I'll try to put you in the picture, if you'll give me a minute.'

'Yes, okay.' Now he was afraid; everything seemed to be going too fast.

'Officer Fisher was dispatched to your home at Eighty-three Larch Street as per your request at twelve thirty-four this morning. He ascertained that there was no car in the driveway or in the garage. He rang the front doorbell repeatedly, and when there was no answer, he let himself in using the key over the porch eave. He found that the house had been severely vandalized. Furnishings were overturned, liquor bottles broken, soap powder had been poured over the floor and the built-ins of the kitchen –'

'Jesus, Kemp,' Vic whispered. His whirling mind fixed on the note: DO YOU HAVE ANY QUESTIONS? He remembered thinking that note, regardless of anything else, was a disquieting index into the man's psychology. A vicious act of revenge for being dumped. What had Kemp done now? What had he done besides go through their house like a harpy on the warpath?

'Mr. Trenton?'

'I'm here.'

Bannerman cleared his throat as if he were having some difficulty with the next. 'Officer Fisher proceeded upstairs. The upstairs had not been vandalized, but he found traces of – uh, some whitish fluid, most probably semen, on the bedspread of the master bedroom.' And in an unwitting comic ellipsis, he added, 'The bed did not appear to have been slept in.'

'Where's my wife?' Vic shouted into the phone. 'Where's my boy? Don't you have any idea?'

'Take it easy,' Roger said, and put a hand on Vic's

shoulder. Roger could afford to say take it easy. His wife was home in bed. So were his twin girls. Vic shook the hand off.

'Mr. Trenton, all I can tell you right now is that a team of State Police detectives are on the scene, and my own men are assisting. Neither the master bedroom nor your son's room appear to have been disturbed.'

'Except for the come on our bed, you mean,' Vic said savagely, and Roger flinched as if struck. His mouth dropped open in a gape.

'Yes, well, that.' Bannerman sounded embarrassed. 'But what I mean is that there are no signs of – uh, violence against person or persons. It looks like straight vandalism.'

'Then where are Donna and Tad?' The harshness was now breaking up into bewilderment, and he felt the sting of helpless little-boy tears at the corners of his eyes.

'At this time we have no idea.'

Kemp . . . my God, what if Kemp has them?

For just a moment a confusing flash of the dream he had the previous night recurred: Donna and Tad hiding in their cave, menaced by some terrible beast. Then it was gone.

'If you have any idea of who might be behind this, Mr. Trenton –'

'I'm going out to the airport and rent a car,' Vic said. 'I can be there by five o'clock.'

Patiently, Bannerman said: 'Yes, Mr. Trenton. But if your wife and son's disappearance is somehow connected with this vandalism, time could be a very precious commodity. If you have even the slightest idea of who might bear a grudge against you and your wife, either real or imagined –'

'Kemp,' Vic said in a small, strangled voice. He couldn't hold the tears back now. The tears were going to come. He could feel them running down his face.' Kemp did it, I'm sure it was Kemp. Oh my Christ, what if he's got them?'

'Who is this Kemp?' Bannerman asked. His voice was not embarrassed now; it was sharp and demanding.

He held the phone in his right hand. He put his left hand over his eyes, shutting out Roger, shutting out the hotel room, the sound of the TV, everything. Now he was in blackness, alone with the unsteady sound of his voice and the hot, shifting texture of his tears.

'Steve Kemp,' he said. 'Steven Kemp. He ran a place called the Village Stripper there in town. He's gone now. At least, my wife said he was gone. He and my wife . . . Donna . . . they . . . they had . . . well, they had an affair. Banging each other. It didn't last long. She told him it was over. I found out because he wrote me a note. It was . . . it was a pretty ugly note. He was getting his own back, I guess. I guess he didn't like to get brushed off much. This . . . it sounds like a grander version of that note.'

He rubbed his hand viciously across his eyes, making a galaxy of red shooting stars.

'Maybe he didn't like it that the marriage didn't just blow apart. Or maybe he's just . . . just fucked up. Donna said he got fucked up when he lost a tennis match. Wouldn't shake hands over the net. It's a question . . .' Suddenly his voice was gone and he had to clear his throat before it would come back. There was a band around his chest, tightening and loosening, then tightening again. 'I think it's a question of how far he might go. He could have taken them, Bannerman. He's capable of it, from what I know of him.'

There was a silence at the other end; no, not quite silence. The scratching of a pencil on paper. Roger put his hand on Vic's shoulder again, and this time he let it stay, grateful for the warmth. He felt very cold.

'Mr. Trenton, do you have the note Kemp sent you?'

'No. I tore it up. I'm sorry, but under the circumstances –'

'Was it by any chance printed in block letters?'

'Yes. Yes, it was.'

'Officer Fisher found a note written in block letters on the message board in the kitchen. It said, "I left something upstairs for you, baby."'

Vic grunted a little. The last faint hope that it might have been someone else – a thief, or maybe just kids – blew away. Come on upstairs and see what I left on the bed. It was

Kemp. The line on the noteminder at home would have fit into Kemp's little note.

'The note seems to indicate that your wife wasn't there when he did it,' Bannerman said, but even in his shocked state, Vic heard a false note in the sheriff's voice.

'She could have walked in while he was still there and you know it,' Vic said dully. 'Back from shopping, back from getting the carb adjusted on her car. Anything.'

'What sort of car did Kemp drive? Do you know?'

'I don't think he had a car. He had a van.'

'Color?'

'I don't know.'

'Mr. Trenton, I'm going to suggest you come on up from Boston. I'm going to suggest that if you rent a car, you take it easy. It would be one hell of a note if your people turned up just fine and you got yourself killed on the Interstate coming up here.'

'Yes, all right.' He didn't want to drive anywhere, fast or slow. He wanted to hide. Better still, he wanted to have the last six days over again.

'Another thing, sir.'

'What's that?'

'On your way up here, try to make a mental list of your wife's friends and acquaintances in the area. It's still perfectly possible that she could be spending the night with someone.'

'Sure.'

'The most important thing to remember right now is that there are no signs of violence.'

'The whole downstairs is ripped to hell,' Vic said. 'That sounds pretty fucking violent to me.'

'Yes,' Banner said uncomfortably. 'Well.'

'I'll be there,' Vic said. He hung up.

'Vic, I'm sorry,' Roger said.

Vic couldn't meet his old friend's eyes. *Wearing the horns*, he thought. *Isn't that what the English call it? Now Roger knows I'm wearing the horns.*

'It's all right,' Vic said, starting to dress.

'All this on your mind . . . and you went ahead with the trip?'

'What good would it have done to stay at home?' Vic asked. 'It happened. I . . . I only found out on Thursday. I thought . . . some distance . . . time to think . . . perspective . . . I don't know all the stupid goddam things I thought. Now this.'

'Not your fault,' Roger said earnestly.

'Rog, at this point I don't know what's my fault and what isn't. I'm worried about Donna, and I'm out of my mind about Tad. I just want to get back there. And I'd like to get my hands on that fucker Kemp. I'd . . .' His voice had been rising. It abruptly sank. His shoulders sagged. For a moment he looked drawn and old and almost totally used up. Then he went to the suitcase on the floor and began to hunt for fresh clothes. 'Call Avis at the airport, would you, and get me a car? My wallet's there on the nightstand. They'll want the American Express number.'

'I'll call for both of us. I'm going back with you.'

'No.'

'But —'

'But nothing.' Vic slipped into a dark blue shirt. He had it buttoned halfway up before he saw he had it wrong; one tail hung far below the other. He unbuttoned it and started again. He was in motion now, and being in motion was better, but that feeling of unreality persisted. He kept having thoughts about movie sets, where what looks like Italian marble is really just Con-Tact paper, where all the rooms end just above the camera's sight line and where someone is always lurking in the background with a clapper board. Scene #41, Vic convinces Roger to Keep On Plugging, Take One. He was an actor and this was some crazy absurdist film. But it was undeniably better when the body was in motion.

'Hey, man —'

'Roger, this changes nothing in the situation between Ad Worx and the Sharp Company. I came along after I knew about Donna and this guy Kemp partly because I wanted to keep up a front – I guess no guy wants to advertise when he finds out his wife has been getting it on the side – but mostly because I knew that the people who depend on us have to keep eating no matter who my wife decides to go to bed with.'

'Go easy on yourself, Vic. Stop digging yourself with it.'

'I can't seem to do that,' Vic said. 'Even now I can't seem to do that.'

'And I can't just go on to New York as if nothing's happened!'

'As far as we know, nothing has. The cop kept emphasizing that to me. You *can* go on. You can see it through. Maybe it'll turn out to have been nothing but a charade all along, but . . . people have to *try*, Roger. There's nothing else to do. Besides, there's nothing you can do back in Maine except hang out.'

'Jesus, it feels wrong. It feels all wrong.'

'It's not. I'll call you at the Biltmore as soon as I know something.' Vic zippered his slacks and stepped into his loafers. 'Now go on and call Avis for me. I'll catch a cab out to Logan from downstairs. Here, I'll write my Amex number down for you.'

He did this, and Roger stood silently by as he got his coat and went to the door.

'Vic,' Roger said.

He turned, and Roger embraced him clumsily but with surprising strength. Vic hugged him back, his cheek against Roger's shoulder.

'I'll pray to God everything's okay,' Roger said hoarsely.

'Okay,' Vic said, and went out.

The elevator hummed faintly on the way down – *not really moving at all*, he thought. *It's a sound effect.* Two drunks supporting each other got on at lobby level as he got off. *Extras*, he thought.

He spoke to the doorman – another extra – and after about five minutes a cab rolled up to the blue hotel awning.

The cab driver was black and silent. He had his radio tuned to an FM soul station. The Temptations sang 'Power' endlessly as the cab took him toward Logan Airport through streets that were almost completely deserted. *Helluva good movie set*, he thought. As the Temptations faded out, a jiveass dj came on with the weather forecast. It had been hot yesterday, he reported, but you didn't see *nuthin* yesterday, brothers and sisters. Today was going to be the hottest day of the summer so far, maybe a record-breaker. The big G's weather prognosticator, Altitude Lou McNally, was calling for temperatures of over 100 degrees inland and not much cooler on the coast. A mass of warm, stagnant air had moved up from the south and was being held in place over New England by hands of high pressure. 'So if you gas gonna reach, you gotta head for the beach,' the jiveass dj finished. 'It ain't goan be too pretty if you hangin out in the city. And just to prove the point, here's Michael Jackson. He's goin "Off the Wall".'

The forecast meant little or nothing to Vic, but it would have terrified Donna even more than she already was, had she known.

As she had the day before, Charity awoke just before dawn. She awoke listening, and for a few moments she wasn't even sure what she was listening for. Then she remembered. Boards creaking. Footsteps. She was listening to see if her son was going to go walking again.

But the house was silent.

She got out of bed, went to the door, and looked out into the hall. The hall was empty. After a moment's debate she went down to Brett's room and looked in on him. There was nothing showing under his sheet but a lick of his hair. If he had gone walking, he had done it before she woke up. He was deeply asleep now.

Charity went back to her room and sat on her bed, looking out at the faint white line on the horizon. She was aware that her decision had been made. Somehow, secretly, in the night while she slept. Now, in the first cold light of day, she was able to examine what she had decided, and she felt that she could count the cost.

It occurred to her that she had never unburdened herself to her sister Holly as she had expected she would do. She still might have, if not for the credit cards at lunch yesterday. And then last night she had told Charity how much this, that, and the other had cost – the Buick four-door, the Sony color set, the parquet floor in the hallway. As if, in Holly's mind, each of these things still carried invisible price tags and always would.

Charity still liked her sister. Holly was giving and kindhearted, impulsive, affectionate, warm. But her way of living had forced her to close off some of the heartless truths about the way she and Charity had grown up poor in rural Maine, the truths that had more or less forced Charity into marriage with Joe Camber while luck – really no different from Charity's winning lottery ticket – had allowed Holly to meet Jim and escape the life back home forever.

She was afraid that if she had told Holly that she had been trying to get Joe's permission to come down here for *years*, that this trip had only occurred because of brutal general-ship on her part, and that even so it had almost come down to Joe's strapping her with his leather belt . . . she was afraid that if she told Holly those things, her sister's reaction would be horrified anger rather than anything rational and helpful. Why horrified anger? Perhaps because, deep down in a part of the human soul where Buick station wagons, and Sony color TVs with Trinitron picture tubes, and parquet floors can never quite make their final stilling impact, Holly would recognize that she might have escaped a similar marriage, a similar *life*, by the thinnest of margins.

She hadn't told because Holly had entrenched herself in her upper-middle-class suburban life like a watchful soldier in a foxhole. She hadn't told because horrified anger could not solve her problems. She hadn't told because no one likes to look like a freak in a sideshow, living through the days and weeks and months and years with an unpleasant, uncommunicative, sometimes frightening man. Charity had discovered there were things you didn't want to tell. Shame wasn't the reason. Sometimes it was just better – kinder – to keep up a front.

Mostly she hadn't told because these things were her problems. What happened to Brett was her problem . . . and over the last two days she had come more and more to believe that what he did with his life would depend less on her and Joe in the final reckoning than it would on Brett himself.

There would be no divorce. She would continue to fight her unceasing guerilla war with Joe for the boy's soul . . . for whatever good that would do. In her worry over Brett's wanting to emulate his father, she had perhaps forgotten – or overlooked – the fact that there comes a time when children stand in judgment and their parents – mother as well as father – must stand in the dock. Brett had noticed Holly's ostentatious display of credit cards. Charity could only hope Brett would notice that his father ate with his hat on . . . among other things.

The dawn was brightening. She took her robe from the back of the door and put it on. She wanted a shower but would not take one until the others in the house were stirring. The strangers. That was what they were. Even Holly's face was strange to her now, a face that bore only a faint resemblance to the snapshots in the family albums she had brought with them . . . even Holly herself had looked at those photographs with a faint air of puzzlement.

They would go back to Castle Rock, back to the house at the end of Town Road No. 3, back to Joe. She would pick up the threads of her life, and things would continue. That would be best.

She reminded herself to call Alva just before seven o'clock, when he would be at breakfast.

It was just past 6 A.M. and the day was coming bright when Tad had his convulsion.

He had awakened from an apparently sound sleep around 5:15 and had roused Donna from a low doze, complaining of being hungry and thirsty. As if he had pressed a button deep down inside her, Donna had become aware for the first time that she was hungry too. The thirst she had been aware of – it was more or less constant – but she could not remember actually thinking of food since sometime yesterday morning. Now she was suddenly ravenous.

She soothed Tad as best she could, telling him hollow things that no longer meant anything real to her one way or another – that people would show up soon, the bad dog would be taken away, they would be rescued.

The real thing was the thought of food.

Breakfasts, for instance, take breakfasts: two eggs fried in butter, over easy if you don't mind, waiter. French toast. Big glasses of fresh-squeezed orange juice so cold that moisture beaded the glass. Canadian bacon. Home fries. Bran flakes in cream with a sprinkle of blueberries on top – bloobies, her father had always called them, another one of those comic irrationalities that had irritated her mother out of all proportion.

Her stomach made a loud rumbling sound, and Tad laughed. The sound of his laughter startled her and pleased her with its unexpectedness. It was like finding a rose growing in a rubbish heap, and she smiled back. The smile hurt her lips.

'Heard that, huh?'

'I think you must be hungry too.'

'Well, I wouldn't turn down an Egg McMuffin if someone threw it my way.'

Tad groaned, and that made them both laugh again. In the yard, Cujo had pricked up his ears. He growled at the sound of their laughter. For a moment he made as if to get to his feet, perhaps to charge the car again; then he settled wearily back on his haunches, head drooping.

Donna felt that irrational lift in her spirits that almost always comes with daybreak. Surely it would be over soon; surely they had passed the worst. All the luck had been against them, but sooner or later even the worst luck changes.

Tad seemed almost his old self. Too pale, badly used, terribly tired in spite of his sleep, but still indubitably the Tadder. She hugged him, and he hugged her back. The pain in her belly had subsided somewhat, although the scrapes and gouges there had a puffy, inflamed look. Her leg was worse, but she found she was able to flex it, although it hurt to do so and the bleeding started again. She would have a scar.

The two of them talked for the next forty minutes or so. Donna, hunting for a way to keep Tad alert and to also pass the time for both of them, suggested Twenty Questions. Tad agreed eagerly. He had never been able to get enough of the game; the only problem had always been getting one or the other of his parents to play it with him. They were on their fourth game when the convulsion struck.

Donna had guessed some five questions ago that the subject of the interrogation was Fred Redding, one of Tad's daycamp chums, but had been spinning things out.'

'Does he have red hair?' she asked.

'No, he's . . . he's . . . he's . . .'

Suddenly Tad was struggling to catch his breath. It came and went in gasping, tearing whoops that caused fear to leap up her throat in a sour, coppery-tasting rush.

'Tad? *Tad?*'

Tad gasped. He clawed at his throat, leaving red lines there. His eyes rolled up, showing only the bottoms of the irises and the silvery whites.

'*Tad!*'

She grabbed him, shook him. His Adam's apple went up and down rapidly, like a mechanical bear on a stick. His hands began to flop aimlessly about, and then they rose to his throat again and tore at it. He began to make animal choking sounds.

For a moment Donna entirely forgot where she was. She grabbed for the doorhandle, pulled it up, and shoved the door of the Pinto open, as if this had happened while she was in the supermarket parking lot and there was help close by.

Cujo was on his feet in an instant. He leaped at the car before the door was more than half open, perhaps saving her from being savaged at that instant. He struck the opening door, fell back, and then came again, snarling thickly. Loose excrement poured onto the crushed gravel of the driveway.

Screaming, she yanked the door closed. Cujo leaped at the side of the car again, bashing the dent in a little deeper. He reeled back, then sprang at the window, thudding off it with a dull cracking sound. The silver crack running through the glass suddenly developed half a dozen tributaries. He leaped at it again and the Saf-T-Glas starred inward, still holding together but sagging now. The outside world was suddenly a milky blur.

If he comes again —

Instead, Cujo withdrew, waiting to see what she would do next.

She turned to her son.

Tad's entire body was jerking, as if with epilepsy. His back was bowed. His buttocks came out of the seat, thumped back, rose again, thumped back. His face was taking on a bluish color. The veins in his temples stood out prominently. She had been a candy-striper for three years, her last two in high school and the summer following her freshman year at college, and she knew what was happening here. He had not swallowed his tongue; outside of the more purple mystery novels, that was impossible. But his tongue had slid down his throat and was now blocking his windpipe. He was choking to death in front of her eyes.

She grabbed his chin in her left hand and yanked his mouth open. Panic made her rough, and she heard the tendons in his jaw creak. Her probing fingers found the tip of his tongue incredibly far back, almost to where his wisdom teeth would be if they every grew out. She tried to grip it and couldn't; it was as wet and slippery as a baby eel. She tried to tweeze it between her thumb and forefinger, only faintly aware of the lunatic race of her heart. *I think I'm losing him,* she thought. *Oh my dear God, I think I'm losing my son.*

Now his teeth suddenly clashed down, drawing blood from her probing fingers and from his own cracked and blistered lips. Blood ran down his chin. She was hardly aware of the pain. Tad's feet began to rattle a mad tattoo against the floormat of the Pinto. She groped for the tip of his tongue desperately. She had it . . . and it slipped through her fingers again.

(the dog the goddamned dog it's his fault goddam dog goddam hellhound I'LL KILL YOU I SWEAR TO GOD)

Tad's teeth clamped down on her fingers again, and then she had his tongue again and this time she did not hesitate: she dug her fingernails into its spongy top and underside and pulled it forward like a woman pulling a windowshade down; at the same time she put her other hand under his chin and tipped his head back, creating the maximum airway. Tad began to gasp again – a harsh, rattling sound, like the breathing of an old man with emphysema. Then he began to whoop.

She slapped him. She didn't know what else to do, so she did that.

Tad uttered one final tearing gasp, and then his breathing settled into a rapid pant. She was panting herself. Waves of dizziness rushed over her. She had twisted her bad leg somehow, and there was the warm wetness of fresh bleeding.

'Tad!' She swallowed harshly. 'Tad, can you hear me?'

His head nodded. A little. His eyes remained closed.

'Take it as easy as you can. I want you to relax.'

'. . . want to go home . . . Mommy . . . the monster . . .'

'Shhh, Tadder. Don't talk, and don't think about monsters. Here.' The Monster Words had fallen to the floor. She picked the yellow paper up and put it in his hand. Tad gripped it with panicky tightness. 'Now concentrate on breathing slowly and regularly, Tad. That's the way to get home. Slow and regular breaths.'

Her eyes wandered past him and once again she saw the

splintery bat, its handle wrapped in friction tape, lying in the high weeds at the right side of the driveway.

'Just take it easy, Tadder, can you try to do that?'

Tad nodded a little without opening his eyes.

'Just a little longer, hon. I promise. I promise.'

Outside, the day continued to brighten. Already it was warm. The temperature inside the small car began to climb.

Vic got home at twenty past five. At the time his wife was pulling his son's tongue out of the back of his mouth, he was walking around the living room, putting things slowly and dreamily to rights, while Bannerman, a State Police detective, and a detective from the state Attorney General's office sat on the long sectional sofa drinking instant coffee.

'I've already told you everything I know,' Vic said. 'If she isn't with the people you've contacted already, she's not with anybody.' He had a broom and a dustpan, and he had brought in the box of Hefty bags from the kitchen closet. Now he let a panful of broken glass slide into one of the bags with an atonal jingle. 'Unless it's Kemp.'

There was an uncomfortable silence. Vic couldn't remember ever being as tired as he was now, but he didn't believe he would be able to sleep unless someone gave him a shot. He wasn't thinking very well. Ten minutes after he arrived the telephone had rung and he had sprung at it like an animal, not heeding the A. G.'s man's mild statement that it was probably for him. It hadn't been; it was Roger, wanting to know if Vic had gotten there, and if there was any news.

There *was* some news, but all of it was maddeningly inconclusive. There had been fingerprints all over the house, and a fingerprint team, also from Augusta, had taken a number of sets from the living quarters adjacent to the small stripping shop where Steven Kemp had worked until recently. Before long the matching would be done and they would know conclusively if Kemp had been the one who had turned the downstairs floor upside down. To Vic it was so much redundancy; he knew in his guts that it had been Kemp.

The State Police detective had run a make on Kemp's van. It was a 1971 Ford Econoline, Maine license 641-644. The color was light gray, but they knew from Kemp's landlord — they had routed him out of bed at 4 A.M. — that the van had desert murals painted on the sides: buttes, mesas, sand dunes. There were two bumper stickers on the rear, one which said SPLIT WOOD, NOT ATOMS and one which said RONALD REAGAN SHOT J.R. A very funny guy, Steve Kemp, the murals and the bumper stickers would make the van easier to identify, and unless he had ditched it, he would almost certainly be spotted before the day was out. The MV alert had gone out to all the New England states and to upstate New York. In addition, the FBI in Portland and Boston had been alerted to a possible kidnapping, and they were now running Steve Kemp's name through their files in Washington. They would find three minor busts dating back to the Vietnam war protests, one each for the years 1968–1970.

'There's only one thing about all of this that bothers me,' the A. G.'s man said. His pad was on his knee, but anything Vic could tell he had already told them. The man from Augusta was only doodling. 'If I may be frank, it bothers the shit out of me.'

'What's that?' Vic asked. He picked up the family portrait, looked down at it, and then tilted it so the shattered glass facing tumbled into the Hefty bag with another evil little jingle.

'The car. Where's your wife's car?'

His name was Masen – Masen with an 'e', he had informed Vic as they shook hands. Now he went to the window, slapping his pad absently against his leg. Vic's battered sports car was in the driveway, parked to one side of Bannerman's cruiser. Vic had picked it up at the Portland Jetport and dropped off the Avis car he had driven north from Boston.

'What's that got to do with it?' Vic asked.

Masen shrugged. 'Maybe nothing. Maybe something. Maybe everything. Probably nothing, but I just don't like it. Kemp comes here, right? Grabs your wife and son. Why? He's crazy. That's reason enough. Can't stand to lose. Maybe it's even his twisted idea of a joke.'

These were all things Vic himself had said, repeated back almost verbatim.

'So what does he do? He bundles them into his Ford van with the desert murals on the sides. He's either running with them or he's holed up somewhere. Right?'

'Yes, that's what I'm afraid –'

Masen turned from the window to look at him. 'So where's her car?'

'Well –' Vic tried hard to think. It was hard. He was very tired. 'Maybe –'

'Maybe he had a confederate who drove it away,' Masen said. 'That would probably mean a kidnapping for ransom. If he took them on his own, it was probably just a crazy spur-of-the-moment thing. If it was a kidnapping for money, why take the car at all? To switch over to? Ridiculous. That Pinto's every bit as hot as the van, if a little harder to recognize. And I repeat, if there was no confederate, if he was by himself, who drove the car?'

'Maybe he came back for it,' the State Police detective rumbled. 'Stowed the boy and the missus and came back for the car.'

'That would present some problems without a confederate,' Masen said, 'but I suppose he could do it. Take them someplace close and walk back for Mrs. Trenton's Pinto, or take them someplace far away and thumb a ride back. But why?'

Bannerman spoke for the first time. 'She could have driven it herself.'

Masen swung to look at him, his eyebrows going up.

'If he took the boy with him –' Bannerman looked at Vic and nodded a little. 'I'm sorry, Mr. Trenton, but if Kemp took the boy with him, belted him in, held a gun on him, and told your wife to follow close, and that something might happen to the boy if she tried anything clever, like turning off or flashing her lights –'

Vic nodded, feeling sick at the picture it made.

Masen seemed irritated with Bannerman, perhaps because he hadn't thought of the possibility himself. 'I repeat: to what purpose?'

Bannerman shook his head. Vic himself couldn't think of a single reason why Kemp would want Donna's car.

Masen lit a Pall Mall, coughed, and looked around for an ashtray.

'I'm sorry,' Vic said, again feeling like an actor, someone outside himself, saying lines that had been written for him. 'The two ashtrays in here were broken. I'll get you one from the kitchen.'

Masen walked out with him, took an ashtray, and said, 'Let's go out on the steps, do you mind? It's going to be a bitch of a hot day. I like to enjoy them while they're still civilized during July.'

'Okay,' Vic said listlessly.

He glanced at the thermometer-barometer screwed to the side of the house as they went out . . . a gift from Donna last Christmas. The temperature already stood at 73. The needle of the barometer was planted squarely in the quadrant marked FAIR.

'Let's pursue this a little further,' Masen said. 'It fascinates me. Here's a woman with a son, a woman whose husband is away on a business trip. She needs her car if she's going to get around very well. Even downtown's half a mile away and the walk back is all uphill. So if we assume that Kemp grabbed her here, the car would still be here. Try this, instead. Kemp comes up and trashes the house, but he's still furious. He sees them someplace else in town and grabs them. In that case, the car would still be in that other place. Downtown, maybe. Or in the parking lot at the shopping center.'

'Wouldn't someone have tagged it in the middle of the night?' Vic asked.

'Probably,' Masen said. 'Do you think she herself might have left it somewhere, Mr. Trenton?'

Then Vic remembered. The needle valve.

'You look like something just clicked,' Masen said.

'It didn't click, it clunked. The car isn't here because it's at the Ford dealership in South Paris. She was having carburetor trouble. The needle valve in there kept wanting to jam. We talked about it on the phone Monday afternoon. She was really pissed off and upset about it. I meant to make an appointment for her to get it done by a local guy here in town, but I forgot because . . .'

He trailed off, thinking about the reasons why he had forgotten.

'You forgot to the make the appointment here in town, so she would have taken it to South Paris?'

'Yeah, I guess so.' He couldn't remember exactly what the run of the conversation had been now, except that she had been afraid the car would seize up while she was taking it to be fixed.

Masen glanced at his watch and got up. Vic started to rise with him.

'No, stay put. I just want to make a quick phone call. I'll be back.'

Vic sat where he was. The screen door banged closed behind Masen, a sound that reminded him so much of Tad that he winced and had to grit his teeth against fresh tears. Where were they? The thing about the Pinto not being here had only been momentarily promising after all.

The sun was fully up now, throwing a bright rose light over the houses and the streets below, and across Castle Hill. It touched the swing set where he had pushed Tad times without number . . . all he wanted was to push his son on the swing again with his wife standing beside him. He would push until his hands fell off, if that was what Tad wanted.

Daddy, I wanna loop the loop! I wanna!

The voice in his mind chilled his heart. It was like a ghost voice.

The screen door opened again a moment later. Masen sat

down beside him and lit a fresh cigarette. 'Twin City Ford in South Paris,' he said. 'That was the one, wasn't it?'

'Yeah. We bought the Pinto there.'

'I took a shot and called them. Got lucky; the service manager was already in. Your Pinto's not there, and it hasn't been there. Who's the local guy?'

'Joe Camber,' Vic said. 'She must have taken the car out there after all. She didn't want to because he's way out in the back of beyond and she couldn't get any answer on the phone when she called. I told her he was probably there anyway, just working in the garage. It's this converted barn, and I don't think he's got a phone in there. At least he didn't the last time I was out there.'

'We'll check it out,' Masen said, 'but her car's not there either, Mr. Trenton. Depend on it.'

'Why not?'

'Doesn't make a bit of logical sense,' Masen said. 'I was ninety-five percent sure it wasn't in South Paris, either. Look, everything we said before still holds true. A young woman with a child needs a car. Suppose she took the car over to Twin City Ford and they told her it was going to be a couple of days. How does she get back?'

'Well . . . a loaner . . . or if they wouldn't give her a loaner, I guess they'd rent her one of their lease cars. From the cheap fleet.'

'Right! Beautiful! So where is it?'

Vic looked at the driveway, almost as if expecting it to appear.

'There'd be no more reason for Kemp to abscond with your wife's loaner than there would be for him to abscond with her Pinto,' Masen said. 'That pretty well ruled out the Ford dealership in advance. Now let's say she takes it out to this guy Camber's garage. If he gives her an old junker to run around in while he fixes her Pinto, we're back at square one right away: Where's the junker? So let's say that she takes it up there and Camber says he'll have to keep it awhile but she calls a friend, and the friend comes out to pick her up. With me so far?'

'Yes, sure.'

'So who was the friend? You gave us a list, and we got them all out of bed. Lucky they were all home, it being summer and all. None of them mentioned bringing your people home from anywhere. No one has seen them any later than Monday morning.'

'Well, why don't we stop crapping around?' Vic asked. 'Let's give Camber a call and find out for sure.'

'Let's wait until seven,' Masen said. 'That's only fifteen minutes. Give him a chance to get his face washed and wake up a little. Service managers usually clock in early. This guy's an independent.'

Vic shrugged. This whole thing was a crazy blind alley. Kemp had Donna and Tad. He knew it in his guts, just as he knew it was Kemp who had trashed the house and shot his come on the bed he and Donna shared.

'Of course, it didn't have to be a friend,' Masen said, dreamily watching his cigarette smoke drift off into the morning. 'There are all sorts of possibilities. She gets the car up there, and someone she knows slightly happens to be there, and the guy or gal offers Mrs. Trenton and your son a ride back into town. Or maybe Camber runs them home himself. Or his wife. Is he married?'

'Yes. Nice woman.'

'Could have been him, her, anyone. People are always willing to help a lady in distress.'

'Yeah,' Vic said, and lit a cigarette of his own.

'But none of that matters either, because the question always remains the same: Where's the fucking car? Because the situation's the same. Woman and kid on their own. She has to get groceries, go to the dry cleaner's, go to the post office, dozens of little errands. If the husband was only going to be gone a few days, a week, even, she might try to get along without a car. But ten days or two weeks? Jesus, that's a long haul in a town that's only got one goddam cab. Rental car people are happy to deliver in a situation like that. She could have gotten Hertz or Avis or National to deliver the car here or out to Camber's. So where's the *rental* car? I keep coming back to that. There should have been a vehicle in this yard. Dig?'

'I don't think it's important,' Vic said.

'And probably it's not. We'll find some simple explanation and say *Oy vay, how could we be so stupid?* But it fascinates me strangely . . . it was the needle valve? You're sure of that?'

'Postitive.'

Masen shook his head. 'Why would she need all that rigamarole about loaners or rental cars anyway? That's a fifteen-minute fix for somebody with the tools and the know-how. Drive in, drive out. So where's –'

'– her goddam car?' Vic finished wearily. The world was coming and going in waves now.

'Why don't you go upstairs and lie down?' Masen said. 'You looked wiped out.'

'No, I want to be awake if something happens –'

'And if something does, somebody will be here to wake you up. The FBI's coming with a trace-back system to hook up on your phone. Those people are noisy enough to wake the dead – so don't worry.'

Vic was too tired to feel much more than a dull dread. 'Do you think that trace-back shit is really necessary?'

'Better to have it and not need it than need it and not have it,' Masen said, and pitched his cigarette. 'Get a little rest and you'll be able to cope better, Vic. Go on.'

'All right.'

He went slowly upstairs. The bed had been stripped to the mattress. He had done it himself. He put two pillows on his side, took off his shoes, and lay down. The morning sun shone fiercely in through the window. *I won't sleep*, he thought, *but I'll rest. I'll try to, anyway. Fifteen minutes . . . maybe half an hour . . .*

But by the time the phone woke him up, that day's burning noon had come.

Charity Camber had her morning coffee and then called Alva Thornton in Castle Rock. This time Alva himself answered.

He knew that she had chatted with Bessie the night before.

'Nope,' Alva said. 'I ain't seed hide nor hair of Joe since last Thursday or so, Charity. He brought over a tractor tire he fixed for me. Never said nothing about feeding Cujo, although I'd've been happy to.'

'Alva, could you run up to the house and check on Cujo? Brett saw him Monday morning before we left for my sister's, and he thought he looked sick. And I just don't know who Joe would have gotten to feed him.' After the way of country people, she added: 'No hurry.'

'I'll take a run up and check,' Alva said. 'Let me get those damn cacklers fed and watered and I'm gone.'

'That would be fine, Alva,' Charity said gratefully, and gave him her sister's number. 'Thanks so much.'

They talked a little more, mostly about the weather. The constant heat had Alva worried about his chickens. Then she hung up.

Brett looked up from his cereal when she came into the kitchen. Jim Junior was very carefully making rings on the table with his orange juice glass and talking a mile a minute. He had decided sometime during the last forty-eight hours that Brett Camber was a close relation to Jesus Christ.

'Well?' Brett asked.

'You were right. Dad didn't ask Alva to feed him.' She saw the disappointment and worry on Brett's face and went on: 'But he's going up to check on Cujo this morning, as soon as he's got his chickens tended to. I left the number this time. He said he'd call back one way or the other.'

'Thanks, Mom.'

Jim clattered back from the table as Holly called him to come upstairs and get dressed. 'Wanna come up with me, Brett?'

Brett smiled. 'I'll wait for you, slugger.'

'Okay.' Jim ran out trumpeting, 'Mom! Brett said he'd wait! Brett's gonna wait for me to get dressed!'

A thunder, as of elephants, on the stairs.

'He's a nice kid,' Brett said casually.

'I thought,' Charity said, 'that we might go home a little early. If that's all right with you.'

Brett's face brightened, and in spite of all the decisions she had come to, that brightness made her feel a little sad. 'When?' he asked.

'How does tomorrow sound? She had been intending to suggest Friday.

'Great! But' – he looked at her closely – 'are you done visiting, Mom? I mean, she's your sister.'

Charity thought of the credit cards, and of the Wurlitzer jukebox Holly's husband had been able to afford but did not know how to fix. Those were the things that had impressed Brett, and she supposed they had impressed her as well in some way. Perhaps she had seen them through Brett's eyes a little . . . through Joe's eyes. And enough was enough.

'Yes,' she said. 'I guess I've done my visiting. I'll tell Holly this morning.'

'Okay, Mom.' He looked at her a little shyly. 'I wouldn't mind coming back, you know. I do like them. And he's a neat little kid. Maybe he can come up to Maine sometime.'

'Yes,' she said, surprised and grateful. She didn't think Joe would object to that. 'Yes, maybe that could be arranged.'

'Okay. And tell me what Mr. Thornton said.'

'I will.'

But Alva never called back. As he was feeding his chickens that morning, the motor in his big air conditioner blew, and he was immediately in a life-or-death struggle to save his birds before the day's heat could kill them. Donna Trenton might have called it another stroke of that same Fate she saw reflected in Cujo's muddy, homicidal eyes. By the time the issue of the air conditioner was settled, it was four in the afternoon (Alva Thornton lost sixty-two chickens that day and counted himself off cheaply), and the confrontation which had begun Monday afternoon in the Cambers' sunstruck dooryard was over.

Andy Masen was the Maine Attorney General's *Wunderkind*, and there were those who said that someday – and not too distant a day, either – he would lead the A. G.'s criminal division. Andy Masen's sights were set a good deal higher than that. He hoped to be Attorney General himself in 1984, and in a position to run for Governor by 1987. And after eight years as Governor, who knew?

He came from a large, poor family. He and his three brothers and two sisters had grown up in a ramshackle 'poor white trash' house on the outer Sabbatus Road in the town of Lisbon. His brothers and sisters had been exactly up – or down – to town expectations. Only Andy Masen and his youngest brother, Marty, had managed to finish high school. For a while it had looked as if Roberta might make it, but she had gotten herself knocked up higher than a kite following a dance her senior year. She had left school to marry the boy, who still had pimples at twenty-nine, drank Narragansett straight from the can, and knocked both her and the kid around. Marty had been killed in a car crash over on Route 9 in Durham. He and some of his drunk friends had tried to take the tight curve up Sirois Hill at seventy. The Camaro in which they were riding rolled over twice and burned.

Andy had been the star of the family, but his mother had never liked him. She was a little afraid of him. When talking to friends she would say, 'My Andy's a cold fish,' but he was more than that. He was always tightly controlled, always buttoned up. He knew from the fifth grade on that he was going to somehow get through college and become a lawyer. Lawyers made a lot of money. Lawyers worked with logic. Logic was Andy's God.

He saw each event as a point from which a finite number of possibilities radiated. At the end of each possibility line was another event point. And so on. This point-to-point blueprint of life had served him very well. He made straight A's through grammar school and high school, got a Merit Scholarship, and could have gone to college almost anywhere. He decided on the University of Maine, throwing away his chance at Harvard because he had already decided to start his career in

Augusta, and he didn't want some piney-woodser in gumrubber boots and a lumberman's jacket throwing Harvard in his face.

On this hot July morning, things were right on schedule.

He put Vic Trenton's phone down. There had been no answer at the Camber telephone number. The State Police detective and Bannerman were still here, waiting for instructions like well-trained dogs. He had worked with Townsend, the State Police guy, before, and he was the sort of fellow Andy Masen felt comfortable with. When you said fetch, Townsend fetched. Bannerman was a new one, and Masen didn't care for him. His eyes were a little too bright, and the way he had suddenly come out with the idea that Kemp might have coerced the woman by using the kid . . . well, such ideas, if they were going to come, ought to come from Andy Masen. The three of them sat on the sectional sofa, not talking, just drinking coffee and waiting for the FBI boys to show up with the trace-back equipment.

Andy thought about the case. It might be a tempest in a teapot, but it might well be something more. The husband was convinced it was a kidnapping and attached no importance to the missing car. He was fixated on the idea that Steven Kemp had taken his people.

Andy Masen was not so sure.

Camber wasn't home; no one was home up there. Maybe they had all gone on vacation. That was likely enough; July was the quintessential vacation month, and they had been due to hit someone who was gone. Would he have taken her car in for a repair job if he was going away? Unlikely. Unlikely that the car was there at all. But it had to be checked, and there was one possibility he had neglected to mention to Vic.

Suppose she *had* taken the car up to Camber's Garage? Suppose someone *had* offered her a lift back? Not a friend, not an acquaintance, not Camber or his wife, but a total stranger? Andy could hear Trenton saying, 'Oh, no, my wife would never accept a ride from a stranger.' But, in the vernacular, she had accepted several rides from Steven Kemp, who was almost a stranger. If the hypothetical man was friendly, and if she was anxious to get her son home, she might have accepted. And maybe the nice, smiling man was some kind of a freak. They had had just such a freak here in Castle Rock before, Frank Dodd. Maybe the nice, smiling man had left them in the brush with their throats cut and had hied on his merry way. If that was the case, the Pinto would be at Camber's.

Andy did not think this line of reasoning *likely*, but it was *possible*. He would have sent a man up to the Cambers' anyway — it was routine — but he liked to understand why he was doing each thing he was doing. He thought that, for all practical purposes, he could dismiss Camber's Garage from the structure of logic and order he was building. He supposed she could have gone up there, discovered the Cambers were gone, and *then* had her car conk out on her, but Castle Rock's Town Road No. 3 was hardly Antartica. She and the kid had only to walk to the nearest house and ask to use the phone in that case, but they hadn't done it.

'Mr. Townsend,' he said in his soft voice. 'You and Sheriff Bannerman here ought to take a ride out to this Joe Camber's Garage. Verify three things: no blue Pinto there, license. number 218-864, no Donna and Theodore Trenton there, no Cambers there. Got that?'

'Fine,' Townsend said. 'Do you want —'

'I want only those three things,' Andy said softly. He didn't like the way Bannerman was looking at him, and with a kind of weary contempt. It upset him. 'If any of those three *are* there, call me here. And if I'm not here, I'll leave a number. Understood?'

The telephone rang. Bannerman picked it up, listened, and offered it to Andy Masen. 'For you, hotshot.'

Their eyes locked over the telephone. Masen thought that Bannerman would drop his, but he didn't. After a moment Andy took the phone. The call was from the State Police barracks in Scarborough. Steve Kemp had been picked up. His van had been spotted in the courtyard of a small motel in the Massachusetts town of Twickenham. The woman and the boy were not with him. After receiving the Miranda,

Kemp had given his name and had since been standing on his right to remain silent.

Andy Masen found that extremely ominous news.

'Townsend, you come with me,' he said. 'You can handle the Camber place by yourself, can't you, Sheriff Bannerman?'

'It's my town,' Bannerman said.

Andy Masen lit a cigarette and looked at Bannerman through the shifting smoke. 'Have you got a problem with me, Sheriff?'

Bannerman smiled. 'Nothing I can't handle.'

Christ, I hate these hicks, Masen thought, watching Bannerman leave. *But he's out of the play now, anyway. Thank God for small favors.*

Bannerman got behind the wheel of his cruiser, fired it up, and backed out of the Trenton driveway. It was twenty minutes after seven. He was almost amused at how neatly Masen had shunted him off onto a siding. They were headed toward the heart of the matter; he was headed nowhere. But ole Hank Townsend was going to have to listen to a whole morning's worth of Masen's bullshit, so maybe he had gotten off well at that.

George Bannerman loafed out Route 117 toward the Maple Sugar Road, siren and flashers off. It surely was a pretty day. And he saw no need to hurry.

Donna and Tad Trenton were sleeping.

Their positions were very similar: the awkward sleeping positions of those forced to spend long hours on interstate buses. Their heads lolled against the sockets of their shoulders, Donna's turned to the left, Tad's to the right. Tad's hands lay in his lap like a beached fish. Now and again they would twitch. His breathing was harsh and stertorous. His lips were blistered, his eyelids a purplish color. A line of spittle running from the corner of his mouth to the soft line of his jaw had begun to dry.

Donna was in middle sleep. As exhausted as she was, her cramped position and the pain in her leg and belly and now her fingers (in his seizure Tad had bitten them to the bone) would let her sink no deeper. Her hair clung to her head in sweaty strings. The gauze pads on her left leg had soaked through again, and the flesh around the superficial wounds on her belly had gone an ugly red. Her breathing was also harsh, but not as uneven as Tad's.

Tad Trenton was very close to the end of his endurance. Dehydration was well advanced. He had lost electrolytes, chlorides, and sodium through his perspiration. Nothing had replaced them. His inner defenses were being steadily rolled back, and now he had entered the final critical stage. His life had grown light, not sunken firmly into his flesh and bones but trembling, ready to depart on any puff of wind.

In his feverish dreams his father pushed him on the swing, higher and higher, and he did not see their back yard but the duckpond, and the breeze was cool on his sunburned forehead, his aching eyes, his blistered lips.

Cujo also slept.

He lay on the verge of grass by the porch, his mangled snout on his forepaws. His dreams were confused, lunatic things. It was dusk, and the sky was dark with wheeling, red-eyed bats. He leaped at them again and again, and each time he leaped he brought one down, teeth clamped on a leathery, twitching wing. But the bats kept biting his tender face with their sharp little rat-teeth. That was where the pain came from. That was where all the hurt came from. But he would kill them all. He would —

He woke suddenly, his head lifting from his paws, his head cocking.

A car was coming.

To his hellishly alert ears, the sound of the approaching car was dreadful, insupportable; it was the sound of some great stinging insect coming to fill him with poison.

He lurched to his feet, whining. All his joints seemed filled with crushed glass. He looked at the dead car. Inside, he could see the unmoving outline of THE WOMAN's head. Before, Cujo had been able to look right through the glass and see her, but THE WOMAN had done something to the glass that made it hard to see. It didn't matter what she did to the windows. She couldn't get out. Nor THE BOY, either.

The drone was closer now. The car was coming up the hill, but . . . *was* it a car? Or a giant bee or wasp come to batten on him, to sting him, to make his pain even worse?

Better wait and see.

Cujo slunk under the porch, where he had often spent hot summer days in the past. It was drifted sleep with the decaying autumn leaves of other years, leaves which released a smell he had thought incredibly sweet and pleasant in those same other years. Now the smell seemed immense and cloying, suffocating and well-nigh unbearable. He growled at the smell and began to slobber foam again. If a dog could kill a scent, Cujo would have killed this one.

The drone was very close now. And then a car was turning into the driveway. A car with blue sides and a white roof and lights on the top.

The one thing George Bannerman had been least prepared to see when he turned into Joe Camber's dooryard was the Pinto belonging to the missing woman. He was not a stupid man, and while he would have been impatient with Andy Masen's point-to-point kind of logic (he had dealt with the horror of Frank Dodd and understood that sometimes there *was* no logic), he arrived at his own mostly solid conclusions in much the same way, if on a more subconscious level. And he agreed with Masen's belief that it was highly unlikely the Trenton woman and her son would be here. But the car was here, anyway.

Bannerman grabbed for the mike hung under his dashboard and then decided to check the car first. From this angle, directly behind the Pinto, it was impossible to see if anyone was in there or not. The backs of the bucket seats were a bit too high, and both Tad and Donna had slumped down in their sleep.

Bannerman got out of the cruiser and slammed the door behind him. Before he had gotten two steps, he saw the entire driver's side window was a buckled mass of shatter-shot cracks. His heart began to beat harder, and his hand went to the butt of his .38 Police Special.

Cujo stared out at THE MAN from the blue car with rising hate. It was this MAN who had caused all his pain; he felt sure of it. THE MAN had caused the pain in his joints and the high, rotten singing in his head; it was THE MAN's fault that the drift of old leaves here beneath the porch now smelled putrescent; it was THE MAN's fault that he could not look at water without whining and shrinking away and wanting to kill it in spite of his great thirst.

A growl began somewhere deep in his heavy chest as his legs coiled beneath him. He could smell THE MAN, his oil of sweat and excitement, the heavy meat set against his bones. The growl deepened, then rose to a great and shattering cry of fury. He sprang out from beneath the porch and charged at this awful MAN who had caused his pain.

During that first crucial moment, Bannerman didn't even hear Cujo's low, rising growl. He had approached the Pinto closely enough to see a mass of hair lying against the driver's side window. His first thought was that the woman must have been shot to death, but where was the bullet hole? The glass looked as if it had been bludgeoned, not shot.

Then he saw the head move. Not much – only slightly – but it *had* moved. The woman was alive. He stepped forward . . and that was when Cujo's roar, followed by a volley of snarling barks came. His first thought.

(Rusty?)

was of his Irish setter, but he'd had Rusty put down four years ago, not long after the Frank Dodd thing. And Rusty had never sounded like this, and for a second crucial moment, Bannerman was frozen in his tracks with a terribly, atavistic horror

He turned then, pulling his gun, and caught just a blurred glimpse of a dog – an incredibly big dog – launching itself into the air at him. It struck him chest-high, driving him against the Pinto's hatchback. He grunted. His right hand was driven up and his wrist struck the chrome guttering of the hatchback hard. His gun went flying. It whirled over the top of the car, butt-for-barrel and butt-for-barrel, to land in the high weeds on the other side of the driveway.

The dog was *biting* him, and as Bannerman saw the first flowers of blood open on the front of his light blue shirt, he suddenly understood everything. They'd come here, their car had seized up . . . and the dog had been here. The dog hadn't been in Masen's neat little point-to-point analysis.

Bannerman grappled with it, trying to get his hands under the dog's muzzle and bring it up and out of his belly. There was a sudden deep and numbing pain down there. His shirt was in tatters down there. Blood was pouring over his pants in a freshet. He lurched forward and the dog drove him back with frightening force, drove him back against the Pinto with a thud that rocked the little car on its springs.

He found himself trying to remember if he and his wife had made love last night.

Crazy thing to be thinking. Crazy –

The dog bored in again. Bannerman tried to dodge away but the dog anticipated him, it was *grinning*, at him, and suddenly there was more pain that he had ever felt in his life. It galvanized him. Screaming, he got both hands under the dog's muzzle again and yanked it up. For a moment, staring into those dark, crazed eyes, a swoony kind of horror came over him and he thought: *Hello, Frank. It's you, isn't it? Was hell too hot for you?*

Then Cujo was snapping at his fingers, tearing them, laying them open. Bannerman forgot about Frank Dodd. He forgot about everything but trying to save his life. He tried to get his knee up, between him and the dog, and found he couldn't. When he tried to raise his knee, the pain in his lower belly flared to a sheeting agony.

What's he done to me down there? Oh my God, what's he done? Vicky, Vicky —

Then the driver's side door of the Pinto opened. It was the woman. He had looked at the family portrait Steve Kemp had stepped on and had seen a pretty, neatly coiffed woman, the sort you look at twice on the street, the second look being mildly speculative. You saw a woman like that and you thought that her husband was lucky to have her in the kip.

This woman was a ruin. The dog had been at her as well. Her belly was streaked with dried blood. One leg of her jeans had been chewed away, and there was a sopping bandage just over her knee. But her face was the worst; it was like a hideous baked apple. Her forehead had blistered and peeled. Her lips were cracked and suppurating. Her eyes were sunken in deep purple pouches of flesh.

The dog left Bannerman in a flash and advanced on the woman, stiff-legged and growling. She retreated into the car and slammed the door.

(cruiser now got to call in got to call this in)

He turned and ran back to the cruiser. The dog chased him but he outran it. He slammed the door, grabbed the mike, and called for help, Code 3, officer needs assistance. Help came. The dog was shot. They were all saved.

All of this happened in just three seconds, and only in George Bannerman's mind. As he turned to go back to his police cruiser, his legs gave out and spilled him into the driveway.

(Oh Vicky what's he done to me down there?)

The world was all dazzling sun. It was hard to see. Bannerman scrambled, clawed at the gravel, and finally made it to his knees. He looked down at himself and saw a thick gray rope of intestine hanging out of his tattered shirt. His pants were soaked with blood to both knees.

Enough. The dog had done enough to him down there.

Hold your guts in, Bannerman. If you're stepping out, you're stepping out. But not until you get to that fucking mike and call this in. Hold your guts in and get on your big flat feet —

(the kid jesus her kid is her kid in there?)

That made him think of his own daughter, Katrina, who would be going into the seventh grade this year. She was getting breasts now. Becoming quite the little lady. Piano lessons. Wanted a horse. There had been a day when, if she had crossed from the school to the library alone, Dodd would have had her instead of Mary Kate Hendrasen. When —

(move your ass)

Bannerman got to his feet. Everything was sunshine and brightness and all his insides seemed to want to slip out of the hole the dog had torn in him. The car. The police radio. Behind him, the dog was distracted; he was throwing himself crazily against the Pinto's buckled driver's side door again and again, barking and snarling.

Bannerman staggered toward the cruiser. His face was as white as pie dough. His lips were blue gray. It was the biggest dog he had ever seen, and it had gutted him. *Gutted* him, for Christ's sake, and why was everything so hot and bright?

His intestines were slipping through his fingers.

He reached the car door. He could hear the radio under the dash, crackling out its message. *Should have called in first. That's procedure. You never argue with procedure, but if I'd believed that, I never would have called Smith in the Dodd case. Vicky, Katrina, I'm sorry —*

The boy. He had to get help for the boy.

He almost fell and grabbed the edge of the door for support.

And then he heard the dog coming for him and he began to scream again. He tried to hurry. If he could only get the door shut . . . oh, God, if only he could close the door before the dog got to him again . . . *oh, God* . . .

(oh GOD)

Tad was screaming again, screaming and clawing at his face, whipping his head from side to side as Cujo thudded against the door, making it rock.

'Tad, don't! Don't . . .honey, please don't!'

'*Want Daddy . . . want Daddy . . . want Daddy . . .*'

Suddenly it stopped.

Holding Tad against her breasts, Donna turned her head in time to see Cujo strike the man as he tried to swing into his car. The force of it knocked his hand loose from the door.

After that she couldn't watch. She wished she could block her ears somehow as well, from the sounds of Cujo finishing with whoever it had been.

He hid, she thought hysterically. *He heard the car coming and he* hid.

The porch door. Now was the time to go for the porch door while Cujo was . . . was occupied.

She put her hand on the doorhandle, yanked it, and shoved. Nothing happened. The door wouldn't open. Cujo had finally buckled the frame enough to seal it shut.

'Tad,' she whispered feverishly. 'Tad, change places with me, *quick.* Tad? *Tad?*'

Tad was shivering all over. His eyes had rolled up again.

'Ducks,' he said gutturally. 'Go see the ducks. Monster Words. Daddy. Ah . . . ahh. . . *ahhhhhhh –*'

He was convulsing again. His arms flopped bonelessly. She began to shake him, crying his name over and over again, trying to keep his mouth open, trying to keep the airway open. There was a monstrous buzzing in her head and she began to be afraid that she was going to faint. This was hell, they were in hell. The morning sun streamed into the car, creating the greenhouse effect, dry and remorseless.

At last Tad quieted. His eyes had closed again. His breathing was very rapid and shallow. When she put her fingers on his wrist she found a runaway pulse, weak, thready, and irregular.

She looked outside. Cujo had hold of the man's arm and was shaking it in the way a puppy will shake a rag toy. Every now and then he would pounce on the limp body. The blood . . . there was so much blood.

As if aware he was being observed, Cujo looked up, his muzzle dripping. He looked at her with an expression (could a dog *have* an expression? she wondered madly) that seemed to convey both sternness and pity . . . and again Donna had the feeling that they had come to know each other intimately, and that there could be no stopping or resting for either of them until they had explored this terrible relationship to some ultimate conclusion.

It pounced on the man in the blood-spattered blue shirt and the khaki pants again. The dead man's head lolled on his neck. She looked away, her empty stomach sour with hot acid. Her torn leg ached and throbbed. She had torn the wound there open yet again.

Tad . . . how was he now?

He's terrible, her mind answered inexorably. *So what are you going to do? You're his mother, what are you going to do?*

What *could* she do? Would it help Tad if she went out there and got herself killed?

The policeman. Someone had sent the policeman up here. And when he didn't come back —

'Please,' she croaked. 'Soon, please.'

It was eight o'clock now, and outside it was still relatively cool — 77 degrees. By noon, the recorded temperature at the Portland Jetport would be 102, a new record for that date.

Townsend and Andy Masen arrived at the State Police barracks in Scarborough at 8:30 A.M. Masen let Townsend run with the ball. This was his bailiwick, not Masen's, and there was not a thing wrong with Andy's ears.

The duty officer told them that Steven Kemp was on his way back to Maine. There had been no problem about that, but Kemp still wasn't talking. His van had been given a thorough going-over by Massachusetts lab technicians and forensic experts. Nothing had turned up which might indicate a woman and a boy had been held in the back, but they had found a nice little pharmacy in the van's wheel well — marijuana, some cocaine in an Anacin bottle, three amyl nitrate poppers, and two speedy combinations of the type known as Black Beauties. It gave them a handy hook to hang Mr. Kemp on for the time being.

'That Pinto,' Andy said to Townsend, bringing them each a cup of coffee. 'Where's that fucking Pinto of hers?'

Townsend shook his head.

'Has Bannerman called anything in?'

'Nope.'

'Well, give him a shout. Tell him I want him down here when they bring Kemp in. It's his jurisiction, and I guess he's got to be the questioning officer. Technically, at least.'

Townsend came back five minutes later looking puzzled. 'I can't get him, Mr. Masen. Their dispatcher's tried him and says he must not be in his car.'

'Christ, he's probably having coffee down at the Cozy Corner. Well, fuck him. He's out of it.' Andy Masen lit a fresh Pall Mall, coughed, and then grinned at Townsend. 'Think we can handle this Kemp without him?'

Townsend smiled back. 'Oh, I think we can manage.'

Masen nodded. 'This thing is starting to look bad, Mr. Townsend. Very bad.'

'It's not good.'

'I'm beginning to wonder if this Kemp didn't bury them in the ditch beside some farm road between Castle Rock and Twickenham.' Masen smiled again. 'But we'll crack him, Mr. Townsend. I've cracked tough nuts before this.'

'Yessir,' Townsend said respectfully. He believed Masen had.

'We'll crack him if we have to sit him in this office and sweat him for two days.'

Townsend slipped out every fifteen minutes or so, trying to make contact with George Bannerman. He knew Bannerman only slightly, but he held a higher opinion of him than Masen did, and he thought Bannerman deserved to be warned that Andy Masen was on the prod for him. When he still hadn't reached Bannerman by ten o'clock, he began to feel worried. He also began to wonder if he should mention Bannerman's continued silence to Masen, or if he should hold his peace.

Roger Breakstone arrived in New York at 8:49 A.M. on the Eastern shuttle, cabbed into the city, and checked into the Biltmore a little before 9:30.

'The reservation was for two?' the desk clerk asked.

'My partner has been called home on an emergency.'

'What a pity,' the desk clerk said indifferently, and gave Roger a card to fill out. While he did so, the desk clerk talked to the cashier about the Yankee tickets he had gotten for the following weekend.

Roger lay down in his room, trying to nap, but in spite of his poor rest the night before, no sleep would come. Donna screwing some other man, Vic holding on to all of that – trying to, anyway – in addition to this stinking mess over a red, sugary kiddies' cereal. Now Donna and Tad had disappeared. Vic had disappeared. Everything had somehow gone up in smoke this last week. Neatest trick you ever saw, presto chango, everything's a big pile of shit. His head ached. The ache came in big, greasy, thumping waves.

At last he got up, not wanting to be alone with his bad head and his bad thoughts any longer. He thought he might as well go on over to Summers Marketing & Research on 47th and Park the spread some gloom around there – after all, what else did Ad Worx pay them for?

He stopped in the lobby for aspirin and walked over. The walk did nothing for his head, but it did give him a chance to renew his hate/hate relationship with New York.

Not back here, he thought. *I'll go to work throwing cartons of Pepsi on a truck before I bring Althea and the girls back here.*

Summers was on the fourteenth floor of a big, stupid-looking, energy-inefficient skyscraper. The receptionist smiled and nodded when Roger identified himself. 'Mr. Hewitt has just stepped out for a few minutes. Is Mr. Trenton with you?'

'No, he was called home.'

'Well, I have something for you. It just came in this morning.'

She handed Roger a telegram in a yellow envelope. It was

addressed to V. TRENTON/R. BREAKSTONE/AD WORX/CARE OF
IMAGE-EYE STUDIOS. Rob had forwarded it to Summers
Marketing late yesterday.

Roger tore it open and saw at once that it was from old man
Sharp, and that it was fairly long.

Walking papers, here we come, he thought, and read the
telegram.

The telephone woke Vic up at a few minutes before twelve;
otherwise he might have slept most of the afternoon away as
well. His sleep had been heavy and soggy, and he woke with a
terrible feeling of disorientation. The dream had come again.
Donna and Tad in a rocky niche, barely beyond the reach of
some terrible, mythical beast. The room actually seemed to
whirl around him as he reached for the telephone.

Donna and Tad, he thought. *They're safe.*

'Hello?'

'Vic, it's Roger.'

'Roger?' He sat up. His shirt was plastered to his body.
Half his mind was still asleep and grappling with that dream.
The light was too strong. The heat . . . it had been relatively
cool when he went to sleep. Now the bedroom was an oven.
How late was it? How late had they let him sleep? The house
was so *silent.*

'Roger, what time is it?'

'Time?' Roger paused. 'Why, just about twelve o'clock.
What –'

'Twelve? Oh, Christ. . . . Roger, I've been asleep.'

'What's happened, Vic? Are they back?'

'They weren't when I went to sleep. That bastard Masen
promised –'

'Who's Masen?'

'He's in charge of the investigation. Roger, I have to go. I
have to find out –'

'Hold on, man. I'm calling from Summers. I've got to tell
you. There was a telegram from Sharp in Cleveland. We're
keeping the account.'

'What? What? It was all going too fast for him. Donna . . . the account . . . Roger, sounding almost absurdly cheerful.

'There was a telegram here when I came in. The old man and his kid sent it to Image-Eye and Rob forwarded it here. You want me to read it?'

'Give me the gist.'

'Old man Sharp and the kid apparently came to the same conclusion using different chains of logic. The old man sees the Zingers thing as a replay of the Alamo – we're the good guys standing on the battlements, standing by to repel the boarders. All got to stick together, all for one and one for all.'

'Yeah, I knew he had that in him,' Vic said, rubbing the back of his neck. 'He's a loyal old bastard. That's why he came with us when we left New York.'

'The kid would still like to get rid of us, but he doesn't think this is the right time. He thinks it would be interpreted as a sign of weakness and even possible culpability. Can you *believe* it?'

'I could believe anything coming from that paranoid little twerp.'

'They want us to fly to Cleveland and sign a new two-year contract. It's not a five-year deal, and when it's up the kid's almost sure to be in charge and we'll undoubtedly be invited to take a long walk off a short dock, but two years . . . it's enough time, Vic! In two years we'll be on top of it! We can tell them –'

'Roger, I've got to –'

'– to take their lousy pound cake and pound it up their asses! They also want to discuss the new campaign, and I think they'll go for the Cereal Professor's swan song, too.'

'That's great, Roger, but I've got to find out what the Christ has been happening with Donna and Tad.'

'Yeah. Yeah. I guess it was a lousy time to call, but I couldn't keep it to myself, man. I would have busted like a balloon.'

'There's no bad time for good news,' Vic said. All the same, he felt a stab of jealousy, as painful as a silver sharpened bone, at the happy relief in Roger's voice, and a bitter disappointment that he couldn't share in Roger's feelings. But maybe it was a good omen.

'Vic, call me when you hear, okay?'

'I will, Rog. Thanks for the call.'

He hung up, slipped into his loafers, and went downstairs. The kitchen was still a mess — it made his stomach do a slow and giddy rollover just to look at it. But there was a note from Masen on the table, pegged down with a salt shaker.

Mr. Trenton,

Steve Kemp has been picked up in a western Massachusetts town, Twickenham. Your wife and son are not, repeat, are not, with him. I did not wake you with this news because Kemp is standing on his right to remain silent. Barring any complication, he will be brought directly to the Scarborough S.P. barracks for charging on vandalism and possession of illegal drugs. We estimate him here by 11:30 A.M. If anything breaks, I'll call you soonest.

Andy Masen

'*Fuck* his right to remain silent,' Vic growled. He went into the living room, got the number of the Scarborough State Police barracks, and made the call.

'Mr. Kemp is here,' the duty officer told him. 'He got here about fifteen minutes ago. Mr. Masen is with him now. Kemp's called a lawyer. I don't think Mr. Masen can come to the —'

'You never mind what he can or can't do,' Vic said. 'You tell him it's Donna Trenton's husband and I want him to shag his ass over to the phone and talk to me.'

A few moments later, Masen came on the line.

'Mr. Trenton, I appreciate your concern, but this brief time before Kemp's lawyer gets here can be very valuable.'

'What's he told you?'

Masen hesitated and then said, 'He's admitted to the

vandalism. I think he finally realized this thing was a lot heavier than a little nose candy stashed in the wheel well of his van. He admitted the vandalism to the Massachusetts officers who brought him over here. But he claims that nobody was home when he did it, and that he left it undisturbed.'

'You don't believe that shit, do you?'

Masen said carefully, 'He's quite convincing. I couldn't say that I believe anything right now. If I could just ask him a few more questions —'

'Nothing came of Camber's Garage?'

'No. I sent Sheriff Bannerman up there with instructions to call in immediately if Mrs Trenton had been there or if her car was there. And since he didn't call back in —'

'That's hardly definitive, is it?' Vic asked sharply.

'Mr. Trenton, I really must go. If we hear any —'

Vic slammed the telephone down and stood breathing rapidly in the hot silence of the living room. Then he went slowly to the stairs and mounted them. He stood in the upstairs hall for a moment and then went into his son's room. Tad's trucks were lined up neatly against the wall, slant-parking style. Looking at them hurt his heart. Tad's yellow slicker was hung on the brass hook by his bed, and his coloring books were piled neatly on his desk. His closet door was open. Vic shut it absently and, barely thinking about what he was doing, put Tad's chair in front of it.

He sat on Tad's bed, hands dangling between his legs, and looked out into the hot, bright day.

Dead ends. Nothing but dead ends, and where *were* they?

(dead ends)

Now there was an ominous phrase if ever one had been coined. *Dead ends*. As a boy Tad's age he had been fascinated with dead-end roads, his mother had told him once. He wondered if that sort of thing was inherited, if Tad was interested in dead-end roads. He wondered if Tad was still alive.

And it suddenly occurred to him that Town Road No. 3, where Joe Camber's Garage stood, was a dead-end road.

He suddenly looked around and saw that the wall over the

head of Tad's bed was bare. The Monster Words were gone. Now why had he taken those? Or had Kemp taken them for some weird reason of his own? But if Kemp had been in here, why hadn't he trashed Tad's room as he had those downstairs?

(dead ends and Monster Words)

Had she taken the Pinto up to Camber's? He remembered the conversation they'd had about the balky needle valve only vaguely. She was a little scared of Joe Camber, hadn't she said that?

No. Not Camber. Camber only wanted to mentally undress her. No, it was the *dog* she was a little scared of. What was his name?

They had joked about it. Tad. Tad calling the dog.

And again he heard Tad's phantom, ghostly voice, so hopeless and lost in this too-empty, suddenly creepy room: *Cujo . . . heere, Cujo . . . Coooojo . . .*

And then something happened which Vic never spoke of to anyone in the rest of his life. Instead of hearing Tad's voice in his mind he was *actually* hearing it, high and lonely and terrified, a going-away voice *that was coming from inside the closet*.

A cry escaped Vic's throat and he pushed himself up on Tad's bed, his eyes widening. The closet door was swinging open, pushing the chair in front of it, and his son was crying '*Coooooooooo –*'

And then he realized it wasn't Tad's voice; it was his own tired, overwrought mind making Tad's voice from the thin scraping sound of the chair legs on the painted plank floor. That was all it was and –

– and there were eyes in the closet, he saw eyes, red and sunken and terrible –

A little scream escaped his throat. The chair tipped over for no earthly reason. And he saw Tad's teddybear inside the closet, perched on a stack of sheets and blankets. It was the bear's glass eyes he had seen. No more.

Heart thumping heavily in his throat, Vic got up and went to the closet. He could smell something in there, something heavy and unpleasant. Perhaps it was only mothballs — that smell was certainly part of it — but it smelled . . . savage.

Don't be ridiculous. It's just a closet. Not a cave. Not a monster lair.

He looked at Tad's bear. Tad's bear looked back at him, unblinking. Behind the bear, behind the hanging clothes, all was darkness. Anything could be back there. *Anything.* But, of course, nothing was.

You gave me a scare, bear, he said.

Monsters, stay out of this room, the bear said. Its eyes sparkled. They were dead glass, but they sparkled.

The door's out of true, that's all, Vic said. He was sweating; huge salty drops ran slowly down his face like tears.

You have no business here, the bear replied.

What's the matter with me? Vic asked the bear. *Am I going crazy? Is this what going crazy is like?*

To which Tad's bear replied: *Monsters, leave Tad alone.*

He closed the closet door and watched, as wide-eyed as a child, as the latch lifted and popped free of its notch. The door began to swing open again.

I didn't see that. I won't believe I saw that.

He slammed the door and put the chair against it again. Then he took a large stack of Tad's picturebooks and put them on the chair's seat to weight it down. This time the door stayed closed. Vic stood there looking at the closed door, thinking about dead-end roads. Not much traffic on dead-end roads. All monsters should live under bridges or in closets or at the ends of dead-end roads. It should be a national law.

He was very uneasy now.

He left Tad's room, went downstairs, and sat on the back steps. He lit a cigarette with a hand that shook slightly and looked at the gunmetal sky, feeling the sense of unease grow. Something had happened in Tad's room. He wasn't sure what it had been, but it had been something. Yeah. Something.

Monsters and dogs and closets and garages and dead-end roads.

Do we add these up, teacher? Subtract them? Divide? Fractionate?

He threw his cigarette away.

He did believe it was Kemp, didn't he? Kemp had been responsible for everything. Kemp had wrecked the house. Kemp had damn near wrecked his marriage. Kemp had gone upstairs and shot his semen onto the bed Vic and his wife had slept in for the last three years. Kemp had torn a great big hole in the mostly comfortable fabric of Vic Trenton's life.

Kemp. Kemp. All Steve Kemp's fault. Let's blame the Cold War and the hostage situation in Iran and the depletion of the ozone layer on Kemp.

Stupid. Because not everything was Kemp's fault, now, was it? The Zinger's business, for instance; Kemp had had nothing to do with *that*. And Kemp could hardly be blamed for the bad needle valve on Donna's Pinto.

He looked at his old Jag. He was going to go somewhere in it. He couldn't stay here; he would go crazy if he stayed here. He should get in the car and beat it down to Scarborough. Grab hold of Kemp and shake him until it came out, until he told what he had done with Donna and Tad. Except by then his lawyer would have arrived, and, incredible as it seemed, the lawyer might even have sprung him.

Spring. It was a spring that held the needle valve in place. If the spring was bad, the valve could freeze and choke off the flow of gasoline to the carb.

Vic went down to the Jag and got in, wincing at the hot leather seat. Get rolling quick. Get some cool in here.

Get rolling where?

Camber's Garage, his mind answered immediately.

But that was stupid, wasn't it? Masen had sent Sheriff Bannerman up there with instructions to report immediately if anything was wrong and the cop hadn't reported back so that meant —

(that the monster got him)

Well, it wouldn't hurt to go up there, would it? And it was something to do.

He started the Jag up and headed down the hill toward

Route 117, still not entirely sure if he was going to turn left toward 1-95 and Scarborough or right toward Town Road No. 3.

He paused at the stop sign until someone in back gave him the horn. Then, abruptly, he turned right. It wouldn't hurt to take a quick run up to Joe Camber's. He could be there in fifteen minutes. He checked his watch and saw that it was twenty past twelve.

The time had come, and Donna knew it.

The time might also have gone, but she would have to live with that — and perhaps die with it. No one was going to come. There was going to be no knight on a silver steed riding up Town Road No. 3 — Travis McGee was apparently otherwise engaged.

Tad was dying.

She made herself repeat it aloud in a husky, choked whisper: 'Tad's dying.'

She had not been able to create any breeze through the car this morning. Her window would no longer go down, and Tad's window let in nothing but more heat. The one time she had tried to unroll it more than a quarter of the way, Cujo had left his place in the shade of the garage and had come around to Tad's side as fast as he could, growling eagerly.

The sweat had now stopped rolling down Tad's face and neck. There was no more sweat left. His skin was dry and hot. His tongue, swelled and dead-looking, protruded over his bottom lip. His breathing had grown so faint that she could barely hear it. Twice she had had to put her head against his chest to make sure that he still breathed at all.

Her condition was bad. The car was a blast furnace. The metalwork was now too hot to touch, and so was the plastic wheel. Her leg was a steady, throbbing ache, and she no longer doubted that the dog's bite had infected her with something. Perhaps it was too early for rabies — she prayed to God it was — but the bites were red and inflamed.

Cujo was not in much better shape. The big dog seemed to

have shrunk inside his matted and blood-streaked coat. His eyes were hazy and nearly vacant, the eyes of an old man stricken with cataracts. Like some old engine of destruction, now gradually beating itself to death but still terribly dangerous, he kept his watch. He was no longer foaming; his muzzle was a dried and lacerated horror. It looked like a gouged chunk of igneous rock that had been coughed out of the hotbed of an old volcano.

The old monster, she thought incoherently, *keeps his watch still.*

Had this terrible vigil been only a matter of hours, or had it been her whole life? Surely everything that had gone before had been a dream, little more than a short wait in the wings? The mother who had seemed to be disgusted and repulsed by all those around her, the well-meaning but ineffectual father, the schools, the friends, the dates and dances – they were all a dream to her now, as youth must seem to the old. Nothing mattered, nothing *was* but this silent and sunstruck dooryard where death had been dealt and yet more death waited in the cards, as sure as aces and eights. The old monster kept his watch still, and her son was slipping, slipping, slipping away.

The baseball bat. That was all that remained to her now.

The baseball bat and maybe, if she could get there, something in the dead man's police car. Something like a shotgun.

She began to lift Tad into the back, grunting and puffing, fighting the waves of dizziness that made her sight gray over. Finally he was in the hatchback, as silent and still as a sack of grain.

She looked out of his window, saw the baseball bat lying in the high grass, and opened the door.

In the dark mouth of the garage, Cujo stood up and began to advance slowly, head lowered, down the crushed gravel toward her.

It was twelve thirty when Donna Trenton stepped out of her Pinto for the last time.

Vic turned off the Maple Sugar Road and onto Town Road
No. 3 just as his wife was going for Brett Camber's old
Hillerich & Bradsby in the weeds. He was driving fast, intent
on getting up to Camber's so he could turn around and go to
Scarborough, some fifty miles away. Perversely, as soon as he
had made his decision to come out here first, his mind began
dolefully telling him that he was on a wild goosechase. On the
whole, he had never felt so impotent in his life.

He was moving the Jag along at better than sixty, so intent
on the road that he was past Gary Pervier's before he realized
that Joe Camber's station wagon had been parked there. He
slammed on the Jag's brakes, burning twenty feet of rubber.
The Jag's nose dipped toward the road. The cop might have
gone up to Camber's and found nobody home because
Camber was down here.

He glanced in the rearview mirror, saw the road was
empty, and backed up quickly. He wheeled the Jag into
Pervier's driveway and got out.

His feelings were remarkably like those of Joe Camber
himself when, two days before, Joe had discovered the
splatters of blood (only now these were dried and
maroon-colored) and the smashed bottom panel of the screen
door. A foul, metallic taste flooded Vic's mouth. This was all
a part of it. Somehow it was all a part of Tad's and Donna's
disappearance.

He let himself in and the smell hit him at once – be bloated,
green smell of corruption. It had been a hot two days. There
was something halfway down the hall that looked like a
knocked-over endtable, except that Vic was mortally sure
that it wasn't an endtable. Because of the smell. He went
down to the thing in the hall and it wasn't an endtable. It was a
man. The man appeared to have had his throat cut with an
extremely dull blade.

Vic stepped back. A dry gagging sound came from
his throat. The telephone. He had to call someone about
this.

He started for the kitchen and then stopped. Suddenly
everything came together in his mind. There was an instant of

crushing revelation; it was like two half pictures coming
together to make a three-dimensional whole.

The dog. The dog had done this.

The Pinto was at Joe Camber's. The Pinto had been there
all along. The Pinto and —

'Oh my God, Donna —'

Vic turned and ran for the door and his car.

Donna almost went sprawling; that was how bad her legs
were. She caught herself and grabbed for the baseball bat, not
daring to look around for Cujo until she had it tightly in her
hands, afraid she might lose her balance again. If she had had
time to look a little further — just a little — she would have
seen George Bannerman's service pistol laying in the grass.
But she did not.

She turned unsteadily and Cujo was running at her.

She thrust the heavy end of the baseball bat at the Saint
Bernard, and her heart sank at the unsteady way the thing
wiggled in her hand — the handle was badly splintered, then.
The Saint Bernard shied away, growling. Her breasts rose
and fell rapidly in the white cotton bra. The cups were blood
streaked; she had wiped her hands on them after clearing
Tad's mouth.

They stood staring at each other, measuring each other, in
the still summer sunlight. The only sounds were her low rapid
breathing, the sound of Cujo growling deep in his chest, and
the bright squawk of a sparrow somewhere near. Their
shadows were short, shapeless things at their feet.

Cujo began to move to his left. Donna moved right. They
circled. She held the bat at the point where she believed the
split in the wood to be the deepest, her palms tight on the
rough texture of the Black Cat friction tape the handle had
been wrapped with.

Cujo tensed down.

'Come on, then!' she screamed at him, and Cujo leaped.

She swung the bat like Micky Mantle going after a high
fastball. She missed Cujo's head but the bat struck him in the

ribs. There was a heavy, dull thump and a snapping sound from somewhere inside Cujo. The dog uttered a sound like a scream and went sprawling in the gravel. She felt the bat give sickeningly under the friction tape – but for the moment it still held.

Donna cried out in a high, breaking voice and brought the bat down on Cujo's hindquarters. Something else broke. She heard it. The dog bellowed and tried to scramble away but she was on it again, swinging, pounding, screaming. Her head was high wine and deep iron. The world danced. She was the harpies, the Weird Sisters, she was all vengeance – not for herself, but for what had been done to her boy. The splintered handle of the bat bulged and pumped like a racing heart beneath her hands and beneath its binding of friction tape.

The bat was bloody now. Cujo was still trying to get away, but his movements had slowed. He ducked one blow – the head of the bat skittered through the gravel – but the next one struck him midway on his back, driving him to his rear legs.

She thought he was done; she even backed off a step or two, her breath screaming in and out of her lungs like some hot liquid. Then he uttered a deep snarl of rage and leaped at her again . . . but as Cujo went rolling in the gravel, the old bat finally split in two. The fat part flew away and struck the right front hubcap of the Pinto with a musical *bong*! She was left with a splintered eighteen-inch wand in her hand.

Cujo was getting to his feet again . . . *dragging* himself to his feet. Blood poured down his sides. His eyes flickered like lights on a defective pinball machine.

And still it seemed to her that he was grinning.

'Come on, then!' she shrieked.

For the last time the dying ruin that had been Brett Camber's good dog Cujo leaped at THE WOMAN that had caused all his misery. Donna lunged forward with the remains of the baseball bat, and a long, sharp hickory splinter plunged deep into Cujo's right eye and then into his brain. There was a small and unimportant popping sound – the sound a grape might make when squeezed suddenly between the fingers. Cujo's forward motion carried him into her and knocked her sprawling. His teeth now snapped and snarled bare inches from her neck. She put her arm up as Cujo crawled farther on top of her. His eye was now oozing down the side of his face. His breath was hideous. She tried to push his muzzle up, and his jaws clamped on her forearm.

'Stop!' she screamed 'Oh stop, won't you ever stop? Please! Please! Please!'

Blood was flowing down onto her face in a sticky drizzle – her blood, the dog's blood. The pain in her arm was a sheeting flare that seemed to fill the whole world . . . and little by little he was forcing it down. The splintered handle of the bat wavered and jiggled grotesquely, seeming to grow from his head where his eye had been.

He went for her neck.

Donna felt his teeth there and with a final wavering cry she pistoned her arms out and pushed him aside. Cujo thudded heavily to the ground.

His rear legs scratched at the gravel. They slowed . . . slowed . . . stopped. His remaining eye glared up at the hot summer sky. His tail lay across her shins, as heavy as a Turkish rug runner. He pulled in a breath and let it out. He took another. He made a thick snorting sound, and suddenly a rill of blood ran from his mouth. Then he died.

Donna Trenton howled her triumph. She got halfway to her feet, fell down, and managed to get up again. She took two shuffling steps and stumbled over the dog's body, scoring her knees with scrapes. She crawled to where the heavy end of the baseball bat lay, its far end streaked with gore. She picked it up and gained her feet again by holding on to the hood of the Pinto. She tottered back to where Cujo lay. She began to pound him with the baseball bat. Each downward swing ended with a heavy meat thud. Black strips of friction tape danced and flew in the hot air. Splinters gouged into the soft pads of her palms, and blood ran down her wrists and forearms. She was still screaming, but her voice had broken with that first howl of triumph and all that came out now was a series of growling croaks; she sounded as Cujo himself had near the end. The bat rose and fell. She bludgeoned the dead dog. Behind her, Vic's Jag turned into the Camber's driveway.

He didn't know what he had expected, but it hadn't been this. He had been afraid, but the sight of his wife – could that *really* be Donna? – standing over the twisted and smashed thing in the driveway, striking it again and again with something that looked like a caveman's club . . . that turned his fear to a bright, silvery panic that almost precluded thought. For one infinite moment, which he would never admit to himself later, he felt an impulse to throw the Jag in reverse and drive away . . . to drive forever. What was going on in this still and sunny dooryard was monstrous.

Instead, he turned off the engine and leaped out. 'Donna! *Donna!*'

She appeared not to hear him or to even realize that he was there. Her cheeks and forehead were savagely welted with sunburn. The left leg of her slacks was shredded and soaked with blood. And her belly looked . . . it looked *gored*.

The baseball bat rose and fell, rose and fell. She made harsh cawing sounds. Blood flew up from the dog's limp carcass.

'*Donna!*'

He got hold of the baseball bat on the backswing and wrenched it out of her hands. He threw it away and grabbed her naked shoulder. She turned to face him, her eyes blank and hazed, her hair straggling, witchlike, any way. She stared at him . . . shook her head . . . and stepped away.

'Donna, honey, my Jesus,' he said softly.

It was Vic, but Vic couldn't be here. It was a mirage. It was the dog's sickening disease at work in her, making her hallucinate. She stepped away . . . rubbed her eyes . . . and he was still there. She stretched out one trembling hand, and the mirage folded strong brown hands over it. That was good. Her hands hurt dreadfully.

'Vuh?' she croaked in a whisper. 'Vuh –Vuh – Vic?'

'Yes, honey. It's me. Where's Tad?'

The mirage was real. It was really him. She wanted to cry, but no tears came. Her eyes only moved in their sockets like overheated ball bearings.

'Vic? Vic?'

He put an arm around her. 'Where's *Tad*, Donna?'

'Car. Car. Sick. Hospital.' She could now barely whisper, and even that was failing her. Soon she would be able to do no more than mouth words. But it didn't matter, did It? Vic was here. She and Tad were saved.

He left her and went to the car. She stood where he had left her, looking fixedly down at the dog's battered body. At the end, it hadn't been so bad, had it? When there was nothing left but survival, when you were right down to the strings and nap and ticking of yourself, you survived or you died and that seemed perfectly all right. The blood didn't seem so bad now, nor the brains that were leaking out of Cujo's cloven head. Nothing seemed so bad now. Vic was here and they were saved.

'Oh my *God*,' Vic said, his voice rising thinly in the stillness.

She looked over and saw him taking something out of the back of her Pinto. A sack of something. Potatoes? Oranges? What? Had she been shopping before all this happened? Yes, but she had taken the groceries into the house. She and Tad had taken them in. They used his wagon. So what –

Tad! she tried to say, and ran to him.

Vic carried Tad into the thin shade at the side of the house and laid him down. Tad's face was very white. His hair lay like straw on his fragile skull. His hands lay on the grass, seemingly without enough weight to crush the stems beneath their backs.

Vic put his head on Tad's chest. He looked up at Donna. His face was white but calm enough.

'How long has he been dead, Donna?'

Dead? she tried to scream at him. Her mouth moved like the mouth of a figure on a TV set the volume control of which has been turned all the way down. *He's not dead, he wasn't dead when I put him in the hatchback, what are you telling me, he's dead? What are you telling me, you bastard!*

She tried to say those things in her voiceless voice. Had Tad's life slid away at the same time the dog's life had slid away? It was impossible. No God, no fate, could be so monstrously cruel.

She ran at her husband and shoved him. Vic, expecting anything but that, fell over on his butt. She crouched over Tad. She put his hands above his head. She opened his mouth, pinched his nostrils shut, and breathed her voiceless breath into her son's lungs.

In the driveway, the somnolent summer flies had found the corpse of Cujo and that of Sheriff Bannerman, husband to Victoria, father to Katrina. They had no preference between the dog and the man. They were democratic flies. The sun blared triumphantly down. It was ten minutes of one now, and the fields shimmered and danced with silent summer. The sky was faded blue denim. Aunt Evvie's prediction had come true.

She breathed for her son. She breathed. She breathed. Her son was not dead; she had not gone through this hell for her son to be dead, and it simply would not be.

It would not be.

She breathed. She breathed. She breathed for her son.

She was still doing it when the ambulance pulled into the driveway twenty minutes later. She would not let Vic near the boy. When he came near, she bared her teeth and growled soundlessly at him.

Stunned with grief nearly to the point of distraction, deeply sure at the final bedrock level of his consciousness that none of this could be happening, he broke into Camber's house by way of the porch door at which Donna had stared so long and hard. The inner door beyond it had not been locked. He used the telephone.

When he came outside again, Donna was still administering mouth-to-mouth resuscitation to their dead son. He started toward her and then swerved away. He went to the Pinto instead and opened the hatchback again. Heat roared out at him like an invisible lion. Had they existed in there Monday afternoon and all day Tuesday and until noon of today? It was impossible to believe they had.

Underneath the hatchback's floor, where the spare tire was, he found an old blanket. He shook it out and put it over Bannerman's mutilated body. He sat down on the grass then, and stared out at Town Road No. 3 and the dusty pines beyond. His mind floated serenely away.

The ambulance driver and the two orderlies loaded Bannerman's body into the Castle Rock Rescue Unit. They approached Donna. Donna bared her teeth at them. Her parched lips formed the words *He's alive! Alive!* When one of the orderlies tried to pull her gently to her feet and lead her away, she bit him. Later this orderly would need to go to hospital himself for anti-rabies treatment. The other orderly came to help. She fought them.

They stood away warily. Vic still sat on the lawn, his chin propped in his hands, looking across the road.

The Rescue Unit driver brought a syringe. There was a struggle. The syringe was broken. Tad lay on the grass, still dead. His patch of shade was a little bigger now.

Two more police cars arrived. Roscoe Fisher was in one of them. When the ambulance driver told him that George Bannerman was dead, Roscoe began to cry. Two other policemen advanced on Donna. There was another struggle, short and furious, and Donna Trenton was finally pulled away from her son by four sweating, straining men. She nearly broke free again and Roscoe Fisher, still crying, joined them. She screamed soundlessly, whipping her head from side to side. Another syringe was produced, and she was injected successfully this time.

A stretcher came down from the ambulance, and the orderlies wheeled it over to where Tad lay on the grass. Tad, still dead, was put on it. A sheet was pulled up over his head. At the sight of this, Donna redoubled her struggles. She freed one hand and began to flail about wildly with it. Then, suddenly, she was free.

'Donna,' Vic said. He got to his feet. 'Honey, it's over. Honey, please. Let go, let go.'

She did not go for the stretcher that her son lay on. She went for the baseball bat. She picked it up and began to bludgeon the dog again. The flies rose in a shiny green-black cloud. The sound of the ball bat making contact was heavy and terrible, a butcher-shop sound. Cujo's body jumped a little each time she struck it.

The cops began to move forward.

'No,' one of the orderlies said quietly, and a few moments later Donna simply collapsed. Brett Camber's bat rolled away from her relaxing hand.

The ambulance left five minutes or so later, siren howling. Vic had been offered a shot – 'to calm your nerves, Mr. Trenton' – and although he felt utterly tranquilized already, he had accepted the shot to be polite. He picked up the cellophane the orderly had stripped from the syrette and examined the word UPJOHN printed on it carefully. 'We ran an advertising campaign for these guys once,' he told the orderly.

'That so?' the orderly asked cautiously. He was a fairly young man and he felt that he might throw up sometime soon. He had never seen such a mess in his life.

One of the police cars was standing by to take Vic to Northern Cumberland Hospital in Bridgton.

'Can you wait a minute?' he asked.

The two cops nodded. They were also staring at Vic Trenton in a very cautious way, as if whatever he had might be catching.

He opened both doors of the Pinto. He had to tug long and hard at Donna's; the dog had dented it in a way he wouldn't have believed. Her purse was in there. Her shirt. The shirt had a jagged tear in it, as if maybe the dog had taken a chomp out of it. There was some empty Slim Jim wrappers on the dashboard and Tad's Thermos bottle, smelling of sour milk. Tad's Snoopy lunchbox. His heart gave a heavy, horrid wrench at the sight of that, and he wouldn't allow himself to think of what that meant in terms of the future – if there was any future after this terrible hot day. He found one of Tad's sneakers.

Tadder, he thought. *Oh Tadder.*

The strength went out of his legs and he sat down heavily on the passenger seat, looking between his legs at the strip of chrome at the bottom of the doorframe. Why? Why had something like this been allowed to happen? How could so many events have conspired together?

His head was suddenly throbbing violently. His nose closed with tears and his sinuses began to pound. He snorted the tears back and passed a hand over his face. It occurred to him that, counting Tad, Cujo had been responsible for the deaths of at least three people, more than that if the Cambers were discovered to be among his victims. Did the cop he had covered with the blanket have a wife and children? Probably.

If I'd gotten here even an hour earlier. If I hadn't gone to sleep –

His mind cried: *I was so sure it was Kemp! So sure!*

If I'd gotten here just fifteen minutes earlier, would that have been enough? If I hadn't talked to Roger so long, would Tad be alive now? When did he die? Did it really happen at all? And how am I supposed to deal with it for the rest of my life without going mad? What's going to happen to Donna?

Another police car pulled up. One of the cops got out of it and conferred with one of the cops waiting for Vic. The latter stepped forward and said quietly. 'I think we ought to go, Mr. Trenton. Quentin here says there are reporters on

the way. You don't want to talk to any reporters just
now.'

'No,' Vic agreed, and started to get up. As he did, he saw a
bit of yellow at the very bottom of his field of vision. A bit of
paper poking out from under Tad's seat. He pulled it out
and saw it was the Monster Words he had written to ease
Tad's mind at bedtime. The sheet was crumpled and ripped
in two places and badly stained with sweat; along the deep
creases it was nearly transparent.

Monsters, stay out of this room!
You have no business here.
No monsters under Tad's bed!
You can't fit under there.
No monsters hiding in Tad's closet!
It's too small in there.
No monsters outside of Tad's window!
You can't hold on out there.
No vampires, no werewolves, no things that bite.
You have no business here.
Nothing will touch Tad, or hurt Tad, all this ni —

He could read no more. He crumpled the sheet of paper
up and threw it at the dead dog's body. The paper was a
sentimental lie, it's sentiments as inconstant as the color in
that stupid runny-dyed cereal. It was all a lie. The world was
full of monsters, and they were all allowed to bite the
innocent and the unwary.

He let himself be led to the police car. They drove him
away, as George Bannerman and Tad Trenton and Donna
Trenton had been driven away before him. After a while, a
veterinarian came in a panel truck. She looked at the dead
dog, then donned long rubber gloves and brought out a
circular bone saw. The cops, realizing what she was going to
do, turned away.

The vet cut off the Saint Bernard's head and put it in a
large white plastic garbage bag. Later that day it was

forwarded to the State Commissioner of Animals, where the brain would be tested for rabies.

So Cujo was gone, too.

It was quarter to four that afternoon when Holly called Charity to the telephone. Holly looked mildly worried. 'It sounds like somebody official,' she said. About an hour earlier, Brett had given in to Jim Junior's endless supplications and had accompanied his young cousin down to the playground at the Stratford Community Center.

Since then the house had been silent except for the women's voices as they talked over old times -- the *good* old times, Charity amended slightly. The time Daddy had fallen off the haytruck and gone into a great big cowflop in Back Field (but no mention of the times he had beaten them until they couldn't sit down in payment for some real or imagined transgression); the time they had snuck into the old Met Theater in Lisbon Falls to see Elvis in *Love Me Tender* (but not the time Momma had had her credit cut off at the Red & White and had backed out of the grocery in tears, leaving a full basket of provisions behind and everybody watching); how Red Timmins from up the road was always trying to kiss Holly on their walk back from school (but not how Red had lost an arm when his tractor turned turtle on him in August of 1962). The two of them had discovered it was all right to open the closets . . . as long as you didn't poke too far back in them. Because things might still be lurking there, ready to bite.

Twice, Charity had opened her mouth to tell Holly that she and Brett would be going home tomorrow, and both times she had closed it again, trying to think of a way she could say it without leading Holly to believe they didn't like it here.

Now the problem was momentarily forgotten as she sat at the telephone table, a fresh cup of tea beside her. She felt a little anxious -- nobody likes to get a telephone call while they're on vacation from someone who sounds official.

'Hello?' she said.

Holly watched her sister's face go white, listened as her sister said, 'What? *What*? No ... no! There must be some mistake. I tell you, there must –'

She fell silent, listening to the telephone. Some dreadful news was being passed down the wire from Maine, Holly thought. She could see it in the gradually tightening mask of her sister's face, although she could hear nothing from the phone itself except a series of meaningless squawks.

Bad news from Maine. To her it was an old story. It was all right for her and Charity to sit in the sunny morning kitchen, drinking tea and eating orange sections and talking about sneaking into the Met Theater. It was all right, but it didn't change the fact that every day she could remember of her childhood had brought a little piece of bad news with it, each piece a part of her early life's jigsaw, the whole picture so terrible that she would not really have minded if she had never seen her older sister again. Torn cotton underpants that the other girls at school made fun of. Picking potatoes until her back ached and if you stood up suddenly the blood rushed out of your head so fast you felt like you were going to faint. Red Timmins – how carefully she and Charity had avoided mentioning Red's arm, so badly crushed it had to be amputated, but when Holly heard she had been glad, so *glad*. Because she remembered Red throwing a green apple at her one day, hitting her in the face, making her nose bleed, making her cry. She remembered Red giving her Indian rubs and laughing. She remembered an occasional nourishing dinner of Shedd's Peanut Butter and Cheerios when things were particularly bad. She remembered the way the outhouse stank in high summer, that smell was *shit*, and in case you should wonder, that wasn't a good smell.

Bad news from Maine. And somehow, for some crazed reason she knew they would never discuss even if they both lived to be a hundred and spent the last twenty old-maid years together, Charity had elected to stick with that life. Her looks were almost entirely gone. There were wrinkles around her eyes. Her breasts sagged; even in her bra they sagged. There were only six years between them, but an observer might well have thought it was more like sixteen. And worst of all, she seemed totally unconcerned about dooming her lovely, intelligent boy to a similar life . . . unless he got smart, unless he wised up. For the tourists, Holly thought with an angry bitterness that all the good years had not changed, it was Vacationland. But if you came from the puckies, it was day after day of bad news. Then one day you looked in the mirror and the face looking back at you was Charity Camber's face. And now there was more dreadful news from Maine, that home of all dreadful news. Charity was hanging up the telephone. She sat staring at it, her hot tea steaming beside her.

'Joe's dead,' she announced suddenly.

Holly sucked in breath. Her teeth felt cold. *Why did you come?* she felt like shrieking. *I knew you'd bring it all with you, and sure enough, you did.*

'Oh, honey,' she said, 'are you sure?'

'That was a man from Augusta. Name of Masen. From the Attorney General's office, Law Enforcement Division.'

'Was it . . . was it a car accident?

Charity looked directly at her then, and Holly was both shocked and terrified to see that her sister did not look like someone who has just received dreadful news; she looked like someone who has just received *good* news. The lines in her face had smoothed out. Her eyes were blank . . . but was it shock behind that blankness or the dreamy awakening of possibility?

If she had seen Charity Camber's face when she had checked the numbers on her winning lottery ticket, she might have known.

'Charity?'

'It was the dog,' Charity said. 'It was Cujo.'

'The dog?' At first she was bewildered, unable to see any possible connection between the death of Charity's husband and the Camber family dog. Then she realized. The implications came in terms of Red Timmins's horribly mangled left arm, and she said, in a higher, shriller tone, 'The *dog?*'

Before Charity could reply – if she had meant to – there were cheery voices in the back yard: Jim Junior's high, piping one and then Brett's, lower and amused, answering. And now Charity's face changed. It became stricken. It was a face that Holly remembered and hated well, an expression that made all faces the same – an expression she had felt often enough on her own face in those old days.

'The boy,' Charity said. 'Brett. Holly . . . how am I going to tell Brett his father is dead?'

Holly had no answer for her. She could only stare helplessly at her sister and wish neither of them had come.

RABID DOG KILLS 4 IN BIZARRE THREE-DAY REIGN OF TERROR, the headline on that evening's edition of the Portland *Evening Express* blared. The subhead read: *Lone Survivor at Northern Cumberland Hospital in Guarded Condition.* The headline on the following day's *Press-Herald* read: FATHER TELLS OF WIFE'S DOOMED STRUGGLE TO SAVE SON. That evening the story had been relegated to the bottom of page one: MRS. TRENTON RESPONDING TO RABIES TREATMENT, DOCTOR SAYS. And in a sidebar: DOG HAD NO SHOTS: LOCAL VET. Three days after it had ended, the story was inside, on page four: STATE HEALTH AGENCY BLAMES RABID FOX OR RACCOON FOR DOG'S CASTLE ROCK RAMPAGE. A final story that week carried the news that Victor Trenton had no intention of suing the surviving members of the Camber family, who were said to be in 'deep shock'. This intelligence was scant, but provided a pretext upon which the entire tale could be rehashed. A week later, the front page of the Sunday paper carried a feature story on what had happened. A week after that, a national tabloid offered a fervid synopsis of what had happened, headed: TRAGIC BATTLE IN MAINE AS MOM BATTLES KILLER SAINT BERNARD. And that was really the end of the coverage.

There was a rabies scare in central Maine that fall. An expert attributed it to 'rumor and the horrifying but isolated incident in Castle Rock.'

Donna Trenton was in the hospital for nearly four weeks. She finished her cycle of treatments for the rabid dog bites with a good deal of pain but no serious problems, but because of the potential seriousness of the disease – and because of her deep mental depression – she was closely watched.

In late August, Vic drove her home.

They spent a quiet, showery day around the house. That evening as they sat in front of the television, not really watching it, Donna asked him about Ad Worx.

'Everything's fine there,' he said. 'Roger got the last Cereal Professor commercial on the rails single-handed . . . with Rob Martin's help, of course. Now we're involved in a major new campaign for the whole Sharp line.' Half a lie; Roger was involved. Vic went in three, sometimes four days a week, and either pushed his pencil around or looked at his typewriter. 'But the Sharp people are being very careful to make sure that none of what we're doing will go beyond the two-year period we signed for. Roger was right. They're going to dump us. But by then it won't matter if they do.'

'Good,' she said. She had bright periods now, periods when she seemed very much like her old self, but she was still listless most of the time. She had lost twenty pounds and looked scrawny. Her complexion was not very good. Her nails were ragged.

She looked at the TV for a while and then turned to him. She was crying.

'Donna,' he said. 'Oh babe.' He put his arms around her and held her. She was soft but unyielding to his arms. Through the softness he could feel the angles of her bones in too many places.

'Can we live here?' she managed in an unsteady voice. 'Vic, can we live here?'

'I don't know,' he said. 'I think we ought to give it a damned good shot.'

'Maybe I should ask if you can go on living with me. If you said no, I'd understand. I'd understand perfectly.'

'I don't want anything else but to live with you. I knew that all along, I think. Maybe there was an hour – right after I got

Kemp's note — when I didn't know. But that was the only time. Donna, I love you. I always have.

Now she put her arms around him and hugged him tight. Soft summer rain struck the windows and made gray and black shadow patterns on the floor.

'I couldn't save him,' she said. 'That's what keeps coming back on me. I can't get rid of it. I go over it again . . . and again . . . and again. If I'd run for the porch sooner . . . or gotten the baseball bat . . .' She swallowed. 'And when I finally did get up the guts to go out there, it was just . . . over. He was dead.'

He could have reminded her that she'd had Tad's welfare in mind above her own all the time. That the reason she hadn't gone for the door was because of what would have happened to Tad if the dog had gotten to her before she could get inside. He could have told her that the siege had probably weakened the dog as much as it had Donna herself, and if she had tried Cujo with the baseball bat earlier on, the outcome might have been terribly different; as it was, the dog had almost killed her in the end. But he understood that these points had been brought to her attention again and again, by himself and by others, and that not all the logic in the world could blunt the pain of coming upon that mute pile of coloring books, or seeing the swing, empty and motionless at the bottom of its arc, in the back yard. Logic could not blunt her terrible sense of personal failure. Only time could do those things, and time would do an imperfect job.

He said, 'I couldn't save him either.'

'You —'

'I was so sure it was Kemp. If I'd gone up there earlier, if I hadn't fallen asleep, even if I hadn't talked to Roger on the phone.'

'No,' she said gently. 'Don't.'

'I have to. I guess you do too. We'll just have to get along. That's what people do, you know? They just get along. And try to help each other.'

'I keep feeling him . . . sensing him . . . around every corner.'

'Yeah. Me too.'

He and Roger had taken all of Tad's toys to the Salvation Army two Saturdays ago. When it was done, they had come back here and had a few beers in front of the ballgame, not talking much. And when Roger went home, Vic went upstairs and sat on the bed in Tad's room and wept until it seemed the weeping would pull all his insides apart. He wept and wanted to die but he hadn't died and the next day he had gone back to work.

'Make us some coffee,' he said, and slapped her lightly on the rump. 'I'll light a fire. Chilly in here.'

'All right.' She got up. 'Vic?'

'What?'

Her throat worked. 'I love you too.'

'Thanks,' he said. 'I think I needed that.'

She smiled wanly and went to make the coffee. And they got through the evening, although Tad was still dead. They got through the next day as well. And the next. It was not much better at the end of August, nor in September, but by the time the leaves had turned and began to fall, it was a little better. A little.

She was wired with tension and trying not to show it.

When Brett came back from the barn, knocked the snow from his boots, and let himself in the kitchen door, she was sitting at the kitchen table, drinking a cup of tea. For a moment he only looked at her. He had lost some weight and had grown taller in the last six months. The total effect was to make him look gangling, where he had always before seemed compact and yet lithe. His grades during the first quarter hadn't been so good, and he had been in trouble twice – scuffles in the schoolyard both times, probably over what had happened this last summer. But his second-quarter marks had been a lot better.

'Mom? Momma? Is it –'

'Alva brought him over,' she said. She set the teacup on the saucer carefully, and it did not chatter. 'No law says you have to keep him.'

'Has he had his shots?' Brett asked, and her heart broke a little that this should be his first question.

'As a matter of fact, he has,' she said. 'Alva tried to slip that over on me, but I made him show me the vet's bill. Nine dollars, it was. Distemper and rabies. Also, there's a tube of cream for ticks and ear mites. If you don't want him, Alva will give me my nine dollars back.'

Money had become important to them. For a little bit she hadn't been sure if they would be able to keep the place, or even if they should try to keep it. She had talked it over with Brett, being level with him. There had been a small life insurance policy. Mr. Shouper at the Casco Bank in Bridgton had explained to her that if the money was put in a special trust account, it plus the lottery money would make nearly all the outstanding mortgage payments over the next five years. She had landed a decent job in the packing and billing department of Castle Rock's one real industry, Trace Optical. The sale of Joe's equipment – including the new chainfall – had brought them in an additional three thousand dollars. It was *possible* for them to keep the place, she had explained to Brett, but it was apt to be a hard scrabble. The alternative was an apartment in town. Brett had slept on it, and it had turned out that what he wanted was what she wanted – to keep the home place. And so they had stayed.

'What's his name?' Brett asked.

'Doesn't have a name. He's just weaned.'

'Is he a breed?'

'Yes,' she said, and then laughed. 'He's a Heinz. Fifty-seven Varieties.'

He smiled back, and the smile was strained. But Charity reckoned it better than no smile at all.

'Could he come in? It's started to snow again.'

'He can come in if you put down papers. And if he piddles around, you clean it up.'

'All right.' He opened the door to go out.

'What do you want to call him, Brett?'

'I don't know,' Brett said. There was a long, long pause. 'I don't know yet. I'll have to think on it.

She had an impression that he was crying, and restrained an impulse to go to him. Besides, his back was to her and she couldn't really tell. He was getting to be a big boy, and as much as it pained her to know it, she understood that big boys often don't want their mothers to know they're crying.

He went outside and brought the dog back in, carrying it cradled in his arms. It remained unnamed until the following spring, when for no reason either of them could exactly pinpoint, they began to call it Willie. It was a small, lively, short-haired dog, mostly terrier. Somehow it just looked like a Willie. The name stuck.

Much later, that spring, Charity got a small pay raise. She began to put away ten dollars a week. Toward's Brett's college.

Shortly before those mortal events in the Camber dooryard, Cujo's remains were cremated. The ashes went out with the trash and were disposed of at the Augusta waste-treatment plant. It would perhaps not be amiss to point out that he had always tried to be a good dog. He had tried to do all the things his MAN and his WOMAN, and most of all his BOY, had asked or expected of him. He would have died for them, if that had been required. He had never wanted to kill anybody. He had been struck by something, possibly destiny, or fate, or only a degenerative nerve disease called rabies. Free will was not a factor.

The small cave into which Cujo had chased the rabbit was never discovered. Eventually, for whatever vague reasons small creatures may have, the bats moved on. The rabbit was unable to get out and it starved to death in slow, soundless misery. Its bones, so far as I know, still remain there with the bones of those small animals unlucky enough to have tumbled into that place before it.

I'm tellin you so you'll know,
I'm tellin you so you'll know,
I'm tellin you so you'll know,
Ole Blue's gone where the good dogs go.

—FOLK SONG

September 1977–
March 1981